God's Intervention

A Second Chance for Humankind

Kenneth B. Little
Helen Davies

God's Intervention
Copyright © 2022 by Kenneth B. Little and Helen Davies

All rights reserved. No part of this publication may be reproduced, distributed, or transmitted in any form or by any means, including photocopying, recording, or other electronic or mechanical methods, without the prior written permission of the author, except in the case of brief quotations embodied in critical reviews and certain other non-commercial uses permitted by copyright law.

Tellwell Talent
www.tellwell.ca

ISBN
978-0-2288-6395-3 (Paperback)
978-0-2288-6396-0 (eBook)

TABLE OF CONTENTS

Prologue v
Chapter 1   First Contact 1
Chapter 2   Understanding the Message 19
Chapter 3   The U.S. Team 32
Chapter 4   Thou Shalt Not Kill 49
Chapter 5   Weapons of Mass Destruction 66
Chapter 6   Financial and Economic Response 75
Chapter 7   Calming the Public 95
Chapter 8   Global Initiatives 113
Chapter 9   Show Time 138
Chapter 10   Day One 156
Chapter 11   Death By the Hand of God 185
Chapter 12   State of the Union Address 205
Chapter 13   Financial Markets 218
Chapter 14   The Cork Out of the Bottle 225
Chapter 15   Nuclear Disarmament Conference 231
Chapter 16   Biological and Chemical Weapons Conference 239
Chapter 17   Cyberwarfare Conference 246
Chapter 18   Glorification of War and Killing Conference 252
Chapter 19   Military Repatriation Begins / Denver Meetings 264
Chapter 20   Water Czar 274
Chapter 21   Climate Change Czar 287
Chapter 22   High-Speed Electric Train 300
Chapter 23   Colonization of Space 310
Chapter 24   USE Private Sector Meetings 320
Chapter 25   Conventional Weapons Disarmament 332
Chapter 26   Personal Guns and Personal Changes 347

Chapter 27 U.S. Economic Projects...359
Chapter 28 A Family Meeting... 370
Chapter 29 A New Russian President 384
Chapter 30 United Space Exchange... 397
Chapter 31 Global Institutions.. 407
Chapter 32 Global Space Colonization.. 422
Chapter 33 Climate Change Conference... 436
Chapter 34 Women's Changing Roles 449
Chapter 35 World Religious Forum 467
Chapter 36 The Church of Humanity... 488
Chapter 37 Worthiness in the Eyes of God..................................... 498
Chapter 38 Sarah's Manifesto 515
Chapter 39 Sarah Returns 523
Chapter 40 Unity Festival 535
Epilogue..555

Prologue

I am Sarah. I am of God. I was sent by God to intervene on Earth to save humankind from itself.

God is the universal, intelligent, ever-growing life force. God was present when the universe burst into existence, and will survive when it destroys itself. God sparked evolution, and reaps expanded life force when creatures die—life force that is then recycled into ongoing evolution.

All creatures grow life force during physical existence, but only those with spiritual wisdom can significantly expand it. Humans are such creatures; Through acts of compassion, they can grow the life force exponentially.

Sadly, the reverse is also true. Humans live in a world where spiritual evolution has not kept pace with technological evolution, making annihilation an ever-increasing threat. Violence, cruelty, and indifference are robbing the Earth of the life force and threatening the very existence of humankind. And that is why God has chosen to intervene.

I am an emissary of God. I am not an angel. I am not a prophet. I am a composition of 40 million women's souls, and the life force within me is strong enough to bend space and time to ensure God's message is heard by all.

Because women generate more life force than men through their maternal natures, I am made of only women's souls—a counterbalance to the male energy that has dominated power structures in government, religion and business throughout human history.

I am made of 40 million women's souls because that number reflects every type of life, death, language, culture, and faith on Earth, giving me the ability to understand and empathize with every living being.

For humankind to realize its full potential, it must become one with its own kind. God's intervention will stop you from killing each other so that you may become unified, both spiritually and ideologically. Where there is division, there will be cohesion; Where there is mistrust, there will be understanding.

I am Sarah, and I am here to stage God's intervention.

Chapter 1

First Contact

It was 9:02 p.m. on a Friday evening in late April, and American President Samuel Cummings sat alone in the Oval Office. He was tired. He had been watching the progress of the North Koreans with horror as they launched their first military satellite into space, and as usual, he was brooding about the state of the world, the events that had led up to this moment, and the jeopardy that his country was currently facing.

Cummings was awaiting the arrival of his Chief of Staff, Bradley Northrup. It was customary for them to meet on Friday evenings for a weekly 'round-up', a discussion of the past week's events, so they could plan for the upcoming week. Northrup was running a little late, and President Cummings did his best not to be annoyed. However, he was getting hungry, and he wished he was in the White House living quarters, having dinner with the First Lady, his wife, Lorena.

He stared at his briefing notes, scanning them for the latest policy to do with North Korea, and then rubbed his eyes with fatigue. When he focused again on the paper he held in his hands, he was surprised to note the glaring whiteness of it. It suddenly seemed much brighter than normal, and the words appeared to swim nonsensically on the page. He blinked a couple of times, wondering if his eyes were playing tricks on him, and made a mental note to book an appointment with his optometrist. Then he shook the paper and tried once more to focus on the typed text, but it was no use; The letters started moving again, appearing disturbingly three-dimensional, almost as if they were going to jump off the page. He frowned, thinking, *I'm tired . . . where is that damn Northrup?*

Then suddenly, an unearthly light, so bright he had to shut his eyes, filled the room. *It's finally happened,* he thought in shock. *The Russians have nuked us.* But there was no explosion, and when he opened them, he was clearly still alive. He was also beyond startled to see a woman standing in front of his desk.

Immediately on alert, and with as much bravado as he could muster, he stuttered, "What in the hell are you *doing* here . . . ?" He punched a button on his desk and yelped, "Security!" as loudly as he could, expecting his personal bodyguard, Don Taylor, to rush into the room and usher this intruder out posthaste . . . but Don didn't come.

Instead, the woman continued to stand in front of him as bright as a satellite in space. Glowing, it seemed.

"You must leave immediately!" he shouted at her, but she appeared unperturbed by his anxiety and did not move. "Now!" he yelled again, this time with more fervor as he pointed toward the door.

When she did not react, he slowly glanced around the room and noted an unnatural stillness. The usual electronic sounds that were part and parcel of day-to-day life—like lights buzzing and clocks ticking—were absent. It was like he was in a vacuum of some sort. He started to realize that he was alone with this woman and that no one was going to save him.

Don't panic, he told himself, and he calmed down a little. He glanced quickly at her and had the uncomfortable sensation that she was flitting around the room. He looked away, at the door behind her, still hoping Taylor would bust through and usher her out, but nothing happened.

Finally, he managed to muster the words, "Where did you come from . . . ?" and then his tongue tied itself into a knot, and further speech failed him as he felt the full power of her presence.

This was no ordinary woman. She seemed to suck the oxygen from the room, leaving him light-headed, and oddly light-hearted as well. As he felt himself being somehow drawn to her, he could hear his heart beating as if in anticipation of something delightful, though his rational mind told him it was probably just due to surprise and shock. He fought to hide his odd mix of feelings from her by reminding himself that she was an intruder. *The truth of the matter,* he told himself sternly, *is that this woman breached White House security in order to threaten me in the Oval Office.*

Steeling himself, Cummings gazed at the woman before him with all the focus he could muster. Not only did he hope to intimidate her, but he also wanted to later be able to describe her to the police. However, despite the fact that he was a highly observant and intelligent man, as he tried to note her features for later reference, he found that beyond describing her as beautiful—*heavenly*, even—he could not clearly make out the contours of her face. At first, he'd taken her to be Caucasian, but when he blinked, he realized that she actually looked vaguely Asian. He'd thought her blond, but a millisecond later, she'd taken on red-coloured hair . . . the short, flat nose that had a moment ago been long, aquiline, and vaguely Middle Eastern was now smattered with freckles . . . and then it seemed quite pointed with narrow nostrils *and . . .*

He shook his head in confusion. All he could do was keep blinking. Focusing on her face felt like chasing water in a creek. Later, when he tried to describe what she looked like to his wife, all he could come up with was that she appeared to be a collage of women's faces, all different ages and nationalities—as if this woman was *many* women.

What is going on here? he wondered as he searched for a salient point in her face, something that would give a clue to her identity and intentions . . . but the more he tried to focus, the more she changed. This lady's face shimmered in an unearthly way, though it consistently remained female. *Perhaps it's a hologram? Those damn Russians are capable of beaming something over here. And they're probably in league with the North Koreans. Maybe it's some type of spy-bot . . .*

But even as he thought this, he knew that wasn't the case because along with the unknowable face, the woman in front of him projected such a peaceful presence that he felt his shoulders slumping the way they did after a good sauna or a hot bath. For a second, he wondered if she was some sort of new holographic technology that also delivered nerve gas, and if perhaps he was dying, but then he decided that wasn't possible. The feeling he was experiencing was not unpleasant—and he was sure nerve gas *was*. No, this couldn't be nerve gas. It was too enjoyable, like being massaged from the inside out. In fact, it was so relaxing that he felt a need to lean on his desk for support, and so he did.

He glanced down at his hands on the desktop, his white knuckles ensuring he would remain upright for the moment, and then back up at her. Her ever-shifting eyes locked onto his. *Are they blue? Green? Brown?* he wondered—and instantly, he was transfixed. They were bottomless pools of . . . well, *hope*. And as angry as he was at this person's unwelcome intrusion into his lair—the Oval Office, the seat of power for the United States of America—he was also mesmerized by the overwhelming sense of *rightness* she projected. It felt like whatever wrong he carried in his heart and mind was being put to rights, and with sudden insight, he understood that just being near her was relieving him of some long-held emotional burdens he was not even aware he was carrying. In fact, something about the woman in front of him was *energizing* him, making him feel stronger and more confident than he had in years, though she still hadn't even uttered a word. He was awed, and without conscious thought, his resolve to be angry and defensive drifted away like steamy breath in winter.

And then she spoke, though he could swear her lips did not move. Her eyes, however, projected deep feeling into his heart, and he had to look away as she said, "Mr. President, I am of God. You may call me Sarah of God."

Cummings couldn't immediately absorb her words. He just simply could not take them in. His body was vibrating for reasons he could not explain, and his brain had not yet got past the mystery of her presence. Bible stories from his youth flitted through his mind as she stood before him, memories of Grade 4 and the poorly produced Christmas pageant of his childhood when he'd played Joseph to Clair McCoy's Mary. A smile flitted over his face as he recalled how both of them had sniggered and cracked jokes about detergent when David Clarke, the angel, said, "Do not be afraid, for behold . . . I bring you Tide . . . and Joy . . . which will cleanse all people."

It didn't seem that funny now.

Is she an angel? he wondered. He imagined wings on her back, glanced at her shoulders and was not fully certain that he did not see them there. And then he suddenly realized he was gaping and his well-cultivated manners and hard-won statesmanship kicked in.

With some effort, he closed his mouth, cleared his throat, and said rather shakily, "I'm pleased to meet you, Sarah. Can you tell me how you got in?"

She smiled—at least he thought it was a smile. Technically, it was more of a glow or some sort of energy shift that made the atmosphere around him ripple in subtle, almost unseeable ways. It caused a light flutter in his own heart as sweet and exciting as jam bubbling over. He fought an unwelcome urge to giggle, rightly thinking that giggling like a little girl would be somewhat unseemly under the circumstances.

She spoke again, and this time, he noticed how eerily melodic her 'voice' was, like millions of tiny, harmonic bells rung by fairies—or angels. "It is not hard to 'get in' to *any* place when you are everywhere at once, as I am. I am of God. I told you this. Do you doubt it?"

Cummings suddenly realized that despite a Harvard education in economics and a life spent with his feet firmly planted in facts and figures, he absolutely did *not* doubt her. He also realized that a strange feeling of lightness had displaced all residual fear lurking in his heart.

"No," he said.

He pulled his gaze away from the pools of starlight that were Sarah's eyes and studied her ever-shifting face. This time, he examined it with intent as it moved from the darkness of black skin, to the tan of brown, to the whiteness that contrasted so suddenly with all of that. He noted freckles, wide nostrils, hooked noses, blemishes, harelips, scarring . . . a myriad of ever-changing shapes, sizes, and expressions.

"You are a woman," he said flatly, though that was perhaps self-explanatory. "God's daughter?" he guessed, though he was thinking, *that's impossible.*

"Yes and no, Samuel," she tinkled, again with the golden glow. "I am the life force of 40 million women who once lived on Earth, whose energy—souls, if you like—have been handpicked by God to represent every race, culture and time. All of the women whose energy resides within me created and fed the life force that is God through generating an abundance of goodness during their earthly journeys. I am God's daughter only in the sense that every one of us is a child of God. Instead, think of me as pure feminine energy, a composite of souls who lived exemplary lives. Through the women I am composed of, I have seen every part of the Earth, belonged to every religion, and experienced every kind of death as well."

He had trouble focusing on her words. They seemed to come from far away and yet from all around him as well. Once more, a ripple of golden energy passed through the Oval Office and everything in it—and once more, Cummings felt an urge to giggle with joy. *Is this how angels laugh*, he wondered, *by sending out radiance? Is she happy?*

"Yes, Samuel, I am expressing joy," Sarah said, clearly reading his thoughts, "but I am not an angel. I am *much* more than that. I will explain . . . but until then, rest assured that you will meet with Mr. Northrup as planned, as well as some other key members of your cabinet—but not until you and I have discussed some very important matters. Until we are done, I have suspended time as you know it."

Cummings feigned a calmness he didn't feel as he tried once more to stare into her ever-shifting eyes. *Did I hear her right? Did she say she has suspended time?* He glanced at the Oval Office's grandfather clock beside his secretary's door and saw that despite him having noted Sarah's presence almost ten minutes previous (according to his internal sense of time), the minute hand was frozen at 9:02, which was when he'd noted Northrop's tardiness. Briefly, he wondered if he had perhaps had a seizure and was in a coma, but then he gazed at the whitened knuckles of his hands as he grasped the desk in front of him and decided that he was as conscious as he'd ever been.

Sarah looked at him, and in a voice that was somehow oddly redolent of the smell of winter pine, she said, "President Cummings . . . Samuel . . . You must listen, and listen well. This is the most important meeting of your life, and we have much to discuss. We must talk deeply so that you can thoroughly absorb what I have to say. Do you understand?"

Cummings gulped, and Sarah noted his barely suppressed panic. Trying to ease his mind, she said, "As I've mentioned, this meeting is occurring outside of normal space and time. Please feel confident that nothing you do to run this great country will be compromised by my presence, no matter how long we talk. Okay?"

He nodded.

"May I go on?" she asked politely. "Are you ready to listen to me, Samuel Cummings?"

There was nothing to do but nod once more, and so he did.

"Samuel," she said, "there is going to be a great shift on this planet as ordained by God. It will affect every single person on Earth."

Her words got his attention, though a small section of his mind still wondered if he was addressing a crazy person . . . or possibly going crazy himself. Nevertheless, he decided to listen to what she had to say, so he responded, "Please continue," in as calm a voice as he could muster.

"Thank you, Samuel," she said. "Please know that as I speak to you, I am also speaking simultaneously to the leaders of every other country in the world, as well as key cabinet members, including several of *your* key cabinet members. They must be prepared to govern in your stead if you cannot lead this great country any longer, for any reason."

Despite himself, Cumming bristled at her words. *What?* he thought. He wondered once again if she was sent by the Russians.

As before, she knew his thoughts, though he hadn't spoken aloud. "I was not sent by the Russians, Samuel. I already told you, I was sent by God. I am here to deliver a message. Do you doubt me, Samuel? Will you hear the rest of my message?"

The question seemed somewhat loaded, so he didn't answer. Instead, he gripped his desk tighter, noting how his knuckles became even whiter, and nodded his assent, though he wanted to shout at her to get out of his office.

An airiness that was at once soothing and unnerving prevailed in the room, and Sarah's words floated on it as she said, "What I am going to say may impact your tenure in office—in fact, if you don't listen well, it may cut short your very *life,* which is why I am simultaneously speaking to the key Democratic cabinet members most likely to succeed you if you cease to exist, as well as your Republican senate head."

Cummings couldn't help himself. "Pardon me?" he asked in disbelief.

Sarah ignored his clear offense to her words. "I am speaking specifically of Vice President, Angelica Lopez; Majority Senate Leader, Hana Shriver; Chief of Staff, Bradley Northrup; Defence Secretary, Gordon Blackstone; and Secretary of the Treasury, Norman Feldman," Sarah replied. "They may be required to step in and run key facets of your government if you are unable to do so."

"What are you talking about?" he asked.

"Your life may be in danger if you don't heed my words today," Sarah replied calmly.

Cummings mulled this thought for a moment, and though he had almost been ready to accept her as a heavenly being, doubt crept in. "Why not the house speaker? Or the president pro tempore of the senate? Or the secretary of state?" asked Cummings, testing her authority. These positions were all higher than the secretary of treasury in the line of presidential succession, and he wanted to know if she understood that.

"They don't need to be involved in the emergency procedures you will be enacting in the next twenty-four hours," Sarah told him. "Nor do I need to involve your attorney general just yet. The five people I specified are the ones who will really make a difference in what happens next. The world is about to change dramatically, Samuel—and you and your team will need to work quickly and efficiently to convey what is about to happen to the citizens of your country if you are to survive this change."

He looked at her with as much composure as he could muster and managed to utter, a bit more weakly than he had hoped to, "I'm listening."

"Good," Sarah replied, a flutter of golden energy carrying the word from her like a song on a breeze. He noted a hint of expression that he took to be a smile on her eerily shifting face as she conveyed wordlessly to him, "Starting today, you—and they—will need to stand ready to do what is required to change the nature of the human race. Together, we are going to right many things that are wrong and work toward ensuring the survival of humanity as is the will of the intelligence that is God."

She gazed toward him with her shifting, alluring eyes. That face was making him dizzy, and he felt some vertigo acting up. He steeled himself against it, forced himself to stand firm, and then met her gaze as best he could. By luck, he locked his eyes onto her pupils and realized with some relief that they were the one thing about her that remained stable. While Sarah's irises changed rapidly in a dizzying dance of colours, her pupils remained a deep velvety blue with white entrancing stars in the middle. *I would like to dive into them*, he thought. *They are galaxies unto themselves.*

"Do I have your undivided attention, Samuel?" Sarah asked him gently. "Shall I tell you what is going to happen?"

He nodded.

"Then I will begin at the beginning," she said.

At that, it felt as if the lights dimmed in the room, and when she spoke, her words seemed darker and more forceful than they had before, drifting toward him on waves of rippling energy that he could feel as currents in the air.

"God is the life force of the universe," Sarah announced in a powerful, resonating voice. "This life force, like dark matter and dark energy, is undetectable by human technology. Just as the physical universe is dominated by powerful forces—like the nuclear fusion within stars and the crushing force of gravity—the life force that is God is also extremely powerful, but it has the advantage of being intelligent and capable of boundless love."

Cummings looked at her balefully. He had not expected a lecture on physics, or metaphysics for that matter. He just wanted to know why she was here and what she wanted from him. Impatiently, he inadvertently moved his hand in a circular motion to indicate that she should carry on and perhaps speed things up, a movement he tended to use frequently when meeting with his cabinet members.

She paused at his gesture, and the golden tinkle of energy that had permeated the room earlier returned, seemingly indicating amusement. Cummings felt his hungry, rumbling tummy clench slightly when it did, as it made him feel as if a feather was tickling his ribs.

"President Cummings," Sarah said gently. "It would seem you have the attention of a schoolboy just before summer vacation. Does it not trouble you to know that the message I bring may affect your lifespan on this Earth?"

He started at her words, and then looked at his upraised, offending hand as if it didn't belong to him, realizing that what he'd just done was rude. Lowering it back to grip the desk with his other hand, he said, "My apologies, Sarah, please go on."

"Samuel," she said gently. "everyone needs to know where they come from before they understand where they are going, don't you think?"

Embarrassed by his own rudeness still, he cleared his throat uncomfortably. "Understood," he said.

"Then I will continue," she breathed, a slight smell of fresh winter snow accompanying her words.

He nodded his understanding.

And she said, "Samuel, did you know that every living creature in the universe receives life force from God at inception?"

He furrowed his brow. "Not really," he said.

"And so you probably don't understand what happens next, do you?"

He shook his head 'no' again.

And she said, "Then I will tell you. Upon death, those who successfully navigate their earthly journeys return to God, carrying a slightly strengthened life force with them . . . like little bees returning to the hive," she tinkled goldenly.

"Okay . . ." he ventured, a little perplexed.

"Complex creatures, such as humans, require more life force to survive because they operate at a higher level than other creatures," Sarah told him.

Cummings nodded. This was in line with some of his own beliefs, though he didn't understand where she was going with it. He remained silent.

And she continued, "But this is a wonderful investment for God, because complex creatures can generate great amounts of life force during their earthly journeys. Do you understand?" she asked.

He nodded, and he felt the golden energy of her approval.

Then she asked, "Do you know what one of the most life-affirming wonders of human beings is, Samuel?" The words were delivered with an emanation of gentleness that Cummings could only take to be a sigh.

"There are many good things about humans," he ventured, thinking of his wife, Lorena, and what a kind and loving person she is.

"Ah," tinkled Sarah, "you have been wondering what I'm getting at, and yet you've answered your own question."

"I have?" asked Cummings.

"Yes, by thinking of your wife. It is wonderful how humans develop strong family attachments, how they love and nurture their offspring and mates, and how they care for their elderly. It is even more wonderful how some have the capacity to care for complete strangers in this way. The ability to show compassion, and to share love, is the wonder that I speak of."

"Well, I can't argue with that," said Cummings as he remembered what a great and caring mother Lorena is to their children.

"All humans carry the seed of God's life force inside, Samuel," Sarah clarified. "It is a gift, and you are meant to nurture it. It begins growing in childhood when little ones learn such simple things as how to share with siblings and friends, and it gains strength as people mature and grow past the imminent needs of their own egos. In simpler terms, once a person realizes the universe doesn't revolve around him or her, they become more selfless. That is when they learn that it is better to give than to receive."

"I think we call that 'growing up' here on Earth," Samuel said dryly.

He still didn't *completely* buy her 'I'm from God' act, and his tone indicated he was holding back trust. She didn't acknowledge this reticence, though. Instead, his words were rewarded with a burst of golden energy, which he took to be laughter, as if he'd just told the greatest joke.

"Yes!" Sarah exclaimed mirthfully. "Humans 'grow up', as you say, to have a greater capacity than any other creature to expand the life force within them. Do you know why?"

Cummings shook his head. "No, but I think you're going to tell me," he said.

"Yes, you are correct," Sarah tinkled, her words a whisper of golden light. "It's because most have at least *some* control over their environment—meaning they don't have to struggle for survival in the same way the animal kingdom does. This gives them the luxury of being able to spend more time nurturing and loving other people, including those beyond their immediate family . . . and this is what God wants from all of us. This is what grows the life force."

This was not earth-shattering news to Samuel; Life force, karma, good will . . . Sarah could call it whatever she wanted, but in the end, it was only another version of The Golden Rule: Do unto others as you would have them do unto you.

Somewhat condescendingly he said, "All the major religions of the world have this at their core, Sarah. All religions teach their practitioners that if you dedicate your life to helping others, you will be rewarded."

In response, again she created a golden energy that permeated the room—and his heart—as she said, "Yes, and the reward is that your life force will flourish and grow, and your spirit will join God and share the wonders of the universe forever. But, my dear Samuel, things are not working properly here on Earth. The system, so to speak, is broken . . . and that is why God has sent me."

"What do you mean?" asked Cummings, intrigued despite his efforts not to be.

Though he was no longer frightened of Sarah, he was still entertaining thoughts of his bodyguard bursting through the doors to evict this intruder so he could get home to dinner.

"Oh, Samuel," said Sarah. "You know the answer. All you have to do is look around at the unfortunate state of the world. Humans have developed technologically in wondrous ways . . . but they have neglected their own spiritual growth, at their own peril. And it is affecting God—and the generation of precious life force. Things cannot go on in this way."

"And what way, exactly, is that?" asked Cummings, though North Korea immediately sprang to mind again. It was certainly not a country that encouraged spiritual growth; Instead, government-enforced socialism was compulsory.

He knew now that Sarah could read his innermost thoughts, but he still twitched a little when she said conversationally, "Yes, North Korea is a good example, yet look at your *own* country, Samuel. Acknowledgement of God in any form is outlawed in schools, but corporate sponsorship is *not*. Does that seem right to you?"

He had to admit that it didn't, but he'd been too afraid to open that can of worms, from a legislative and governance point of view. You never knew who would be offended if you allowed acknowledgement of a higher power in schools. Even if you tried to paint it as 'general' thanks and gratitude, someone was bound to be pissed off about it. *The atheists will start picketing,* he thought morosely. *And if not them, then someone else.*

Sarah's golden tinkle permeated his dire thoughts. "Yes, there is always a group who bands together to object to what other groups admire or adopt as truth, isn't there? Humans find strength in numbers, just like wolves and lions do, and so they band together in tribes. Tribes are a way to secure and protect territory and resources—but as they grow, so does competition between them. This competition has led to *so much* warfare. Warfare, and . . ."

Cummings noted a sense of disappointment waft through the room. "Death?" he guessed.

"Yes, death and so *many* unmentionable atrocities. Have you ever noticed that people commit heinous acts in groups that they would *never* dream of committing as individuals?" she asked sadly.

Cummings cleared his throat. He was all too aware of what types of atrocities people were capable of; It was a hazard of his job to not only know such things but to also be the ultimate responsibility for them. He frowned as Sarah emitted a slightly foggy breeze, reminiscent of the decay of fall leaves.

And then, almost as if talking to herself, she asked him, "Have you ever wondered, Samuel, why human tribes are usually led by dominant males?"

He wondered for a moment if she was criticizing him. After all, here he was, a middle-aged white male in charge of a country who had never yet had a woman president. He inexplicably felt guilty.

She tinkled at him then, sending that intangible golden light forward and letting him know his thoughts were clear to her. "You've done nothing wrong, Samuel," she assured him. "I don't criticize you. I am simply telling you that having a strong male in the seat of power has always been the most effective governance structure for tribes under threat of attack. But while such a tribal structure was effective thousands of years ago when men fought one another with spears, today's proliferation of nuclear, biological, and cyberweapons has created much higher stakes. People must find a way to govern themselves so their tribal heritage doesn't destroy the human race. Do you agree with me, Samuel?" There was true sorrow in her voice as she asked him this question.

Cummings thought immediately of the crisis he was now facing with North Korea's increasing technological prowess, and wondered—as he'd been doing for several weeks now—about the soullessness of a leader who would starve his own people but spend millions of dollars on a military satellite. He nodded with regret.

In that uncanny way of hers, she clearly read his thoughts once again and responded wordlessly, "What you are facing with the so-called 'Hermit Kingdom' is certainly one example of this . . . and yes, the man that leads that country is broken. But so *much* of this world is broken, don't you think?"

Again, all he could do was nod and try not to display the melancholy emotions that were tugging at his heart. The North Korean leader was a bastard, it was true . . . but occasionally, Samuel thought it might only be in terms of degree. His *own* job sometimes required him to make ruthless decisions in the name of his country, and it wasn't easy to be the man who sometimes instructed others to act in violent ways. It made him feel like the proverbial 'see no evil, hear no evil, speak no evil' monkey, and despite attempts to justify his actions to himself, he intuitively felt he might be doing wrong on a deep level.

"Yes, such things are challenging," Sarah breathed, conveying compassion with her fluttery, golden presence.

Cummings felt himself flinch again as she read his thoughts in this way. It wasn't rational—and above all things, Samuel Cummings was a rational man.

An economist by trade, numbers were what Samuel Cummings understood. He'd started his career as an economic consultant in Hartford, Connecticut. He had invested his money wisely, and ultimately, founded his own successful investment company, Cummings and Co. Success built upon success, and in short order, he married his hometown sweetheart, Lorena. They had two children—Laura, now a dentist, and Geordie, a successful artist. By the age of fifty-five, Cummings had everything a man could ask for in life: health, wealth, wisdom, and all the love he thought he would ever need.

He was about to retire . . . and then, the unthinkable happened. His son's partner, Flores, made a bad investment that bankrupted both him and Geordie. Instead of seeking Samuel's advice about how to turn things around, Flores felt so terrible about it that he took his own life, leaving Geordie distraught and almost suicidal himself in his bereavement.

It was an 'aha' moment for Samuel. He had loved his son's husband almost as much as he loved his own children, and he had not truly understood, until Flores died, how economic management was not as easy for some as it was for him. From that moment on, he made it his mission to help others to reach their financial goals.

He sold his company and began teaching a common sense approach to managing money, through low-key seminars held in local community halls. Quickly, he became a sought-after speaker and lecturer, receiving accolades for making investing easy for his working-class clients.

He won many grateful friends in the process, friends who jokingly told him he should be running the city. He surprised himself by agreeing with them, and he soon stepped into municipal politics, handily winning his first council election.

Then, after seven years in municipal politics (the last four as mayor), he ran at the state level and surprised himself by winning a senate seat. He never expected to take his political career further than that... but now, at sixty-eight, he was still somewhat amazed to find himself halfway through his first term as the president of the United States, taking the reins after two successive Democratic governments before him.

But the astonishment he felt at becoming the leader of the great nation of America was nothing compared to what he felt as he gazed at the being in front of him who was telling him that God was unhappy with the trajectory of human life on Earth.

She seemed to expect him to say something, and so he obliged, forcing his wheels to churn and to wrap his head around what she was telling him. He managed to say, "Sarah, you say that most human battles arise from deep-rooted tribal tendencies. It seems to me that larger wars are about religious differences, or they occur between nations with different political ideologies. Aren't we fighting over more important issues than who gets to eat the leftover mastodon meat?"

He felt the golden flitter of energy again and recognized it as her version of laughing. He was suddenly worried that he'd said something stupid.

"Ah, yes, Samuel... but mastodon meat, like water and arable land, is a type of resource—food. Tribes fight over territory and resources, and they always have. And when you look at the many conflicts in this world over the years, you will see that offensive actions taken to accumulate resources are always led by the same old dominant males of yesteryear. Not much has changed since time began, though the stakes are much higher now."

He couldn't argue. He was an old dominant male himself, and it was his job to place his tribe—the citizens of the United States—on a pedestal to ensure they had access to a vast array of resources, sometimes at the expense of the countries that *held* those resources... oil-producing countries, for example. He couldn't lie; This made him feel conflicted.

"Yes," said Sarah, once again accurately reading his thoughts, "it *is* conflicting to be in the position of power that you are in. It is within the tenets of your presidential role to do what is best for your citizens... but as a being who carries the spark of God within, it is also your mission to think about what is best for the *whole* human race."

Cummings was silent at her words. He had not given a lot of thought to this larger, more spiritual picture of how the Earth could ideally be, but her words made sense to him, hitting him in his heart in an unexpected way.

Feeling suddenly deflated and a little unsure of himself, he asked, "And you are saying that you are here to fix this?"

Again, that flitter of golden energy encompassed his soul, making his heart beat fast and his stomach flutter with good feelings, joyous feelings which had the effect of immediately energizing him and buoying his spirits.

"Yes!" she tinkled through the ether, tickling his stomach again with her joy. "I am here to stage an intervention of sorts . . ." Then, more mildly, she asked, "Samuel, do you know what an intervention is?"

He nodded. He'd once helped stage an intervention with an alcoholic brother-in-law, Mitch, a decade ago.

"I see you do," she tinkled knowingly, and Samuel was amazed when she unexpectedly projected into the room a vision of Mitch, now clean, sober, and working as an insurance salesman in Salt Lake City, Utah.

Mitch looked so real that Samuel could have reached out to touch him. "Oh my God," he gasped. "How did you do that?"

His amazement amused her. He felt the golden tinkle of her laughter again, and his stomach fluttered. Then she fixed her endless blue pupils on him, and the stars in the middle focused directly on his eyes.

A deep calm settled over him as she said, "I have been sent by God to intervene in the way the human race has been conducting its affairs before it's too late to change things. Until now, God has generally avoided directly intervening in humanity's path because free will is an important part of the human experience . . . but free will is a *gift*, Samuel, and we are meant to use it to feed the life force that is God. Too many of us squander it instead. This is a shame, don't you think?"

Cummings nodded his agreement, his eyes never leaving hers. Every day, as he negotiated 'rights' for energy, timber, fish, water, and oil, he struggled with the concept. It seemed that all the world felt entitled to get their share of *something* . . . and when the 'free will' of the country he represented was questioned, he was the man who made decisions about who would suffer America's wrath. Such decisions haunted him, and he often secretly thought, *the riches of this Earth are not mine to take or give away.* He wondered if God thought less of him for doing so.

Reading his thoughts once again, Sarah asked softly, "Do you know why you have such thoughts, Samuel? It is because, along with free will, God also plants in humans a seed. If you cultivate this seed, it grows into the path that takes you home to be with God for eternity. It is not enough to simply believe in God, or harbour good intentions toward others, Samuel. Humans are here on Earth to generate positive life force through good works and displays of love. By doing so, you build your pathway home."

"Like *Jack and the Beanstalk*?" asked Cummings, instantly wishing he could claw back this infantile response—but Sarah found it funny. He felt the ripple of her laughter touch his soul again.

"Exactly," she responded lightly. "For some, growing that beanstalk is a peaceful and personal calling. I speak of those who place the needs of others above their own desires, do good works and seek no recognition for it. Others, however, feel a need to display—or worse, *impose*—their version of the 'goodness of God' on others. This is the antithesis of what God envisages for us, as it's self-serving and driven by ego."

She paused then, as if considering her words, and Cummings felt a shadow of sorrow suddenly fill the room, a lifting of the lightness her presence had created.

When she found her voiceless words again, she breathed softly into his mind, "Periodically, God—or Allah, or Jehovah, or the Great Spirit, or whatever you choose to call the life force that feeds us all—sends spiritual leaders to guide us. Most are men, but some are women, such as the ancient prophet Miriam, sister of Moses, or more recently, Mother Teresa of Calcutta, who taught by example that divine love does not see flaws in others. People found the nubs of their *own* souls in her presence."

"She was sainted," Cummings said. "In 2003."

"An earthly award that means nothing if people refuse to follow her example," Sarah said. "My point is that such spiritual engines come here quite frequently to guide us in our spiritual growth, yet they are quickly forgotten, if they are noticed at all. Instead, people prefer to believe that God is not among us, and they allow their free will to have free rein . . .

but those who think God has abandoned us are so very wrong. It is we who have abandoned *God*. It is *so* unfortunate."

Samuel suddenly remembered the cotton wool he used to glue onto crudely drawn sheep in Sunday school as part of a lesson about being a 'lamb of God.' He chuckled. "When I was a kid, I thought that if we toed the line, we'd be nurtured like pet sheep by a guy with a beard who lived behind a cloud . . . but I guess the flip side of that idea is that we have a way of wandering off."

"That is one way of putting it," agreed Sarah, "though I think the situation is a little more dire than that."

At that, the golden glow surrounding Sarah gave way once more to something darker. To Cummings, it felt as if the air got thick like jelly, and that he was suspended in it. All the hair on his arms, as well as on the back of his neck, stood up. Luckily, he was still leaning on his desk because his knees buckled, and it stopped him from falling like a sack of potatoes. It felt like being in a hurricane without the wind, though Cummings felt excited instead of afraid.

"Samuel," Sarah intoned, sounding something like a baritone saxophone, robust and dark.

"Yes? Yes, what?" Cummings asked excitedly. He knew he was about to hear something wonderful, and he found himself eagerly anticipating whatever it was she was going to say.

A rush of energy emanated from her as strings of light that were jarring in their intensity. She raised her arms and the deep, velvet blueness of her pupils became more intense. He saw the stars inside them grow, hypnotic in their brilliance. It was as if there was a universe inside those eyes that was pulling him in. He had to fight not to rush toward her; He had to stop himself from crying out.

"God," she projected to him in waves, "is the life force behind all universes. It matters not the 'how' of this; God is the *'why.'* God is powerful, intelligent, and capable of boundless love. I am God's emissary. I am Sarah of God."

Chapter 2

Understanding the Message

Cummings thought he heard a distant crack of thunder as Sarah's words rolled around in his head. Somewhere in the back of his mind, he wondered if he'd brought an umbrella to work, but then the thought drifted away, along with all other thoughts, as if his mind had been vacuumed. He could focus only on Sarah; He could listen only to her.

As he stood in shock, a strange whining sound filled the air, and Cummings thought he smelled something burning. His head began to hurt, as if a migraine was coming on. He wanted to grab his ears, to protect himself somehow, but he knew that if he let go of the desk, he would fall to his knees and maybe take out a few teeth in the process. With great effort, he remained standing, trying to prepare himself for what would come. He wasn't going to like it much; Of this, he was certain.

He was not wrong. Without warning, Sarah unleashed an onslaught of images—projecting them into his mind like a fast-motion movie—and Cummings almost vomited. He saw scenes rife with the horror of war, torture, abuse, rape, killing, disfigurement, and more abuse, and the scenes were flitting through his mind's eye like a movie at warp speed. Sarah never slowed them down long enough for him to have to focus intently on this orgy of hatred; She spared him that. But she 'ran the tape' anyway, despite his silent protestations. It probably took only a few seconds for it to be over, but it felt like a lifetime for Samuel. He was left weeping.

"Stop," he whispered. "Please stop."

"Yes, you have seen enough," she said. "As have I. As has *God*."

Humbly, Samuel straightened up. "I truly *have* seen enough," he agreed, his voice raspy with emotion.

"Samuel, do you know what God wants from us?" she asked softly, and the golden jingle of her ethereal tone back, at least for the moment.

"To be better," he replied, with no doubt in his heart.

"Yes," agreed Sarah. "To be better. God wants us to nurture and love one another, not to fight over the scraps on the table. Only in this way, though cultivating the goodness of God that resides in our souls, do we create our path—or 'beanstalk' as you so humorously put it—to take us home." Then she asked, "Samuel, if you were a betting man, would you bet on you or on your wife as being the one most likely to return to God?"

He was speechless for a moment. "What do you mean?" he finally asked. "Aren't our chances more or less the same? Don't we all have a chance to return?" he asked, a little alarmed.

"Well, *yes*," Sarah said, "we all have a *chance* to return. But, as you know, the pull of the ego when given free will is too much for some souls. Those who succumb to this pull, putting their faith in the ways of man instead of God, often display hatred, intolerance, and greed, stifling not only the growth of the life force within them, but often that of those around them as well. Such people are a drain on the overall life force of God. Upon their earthly death, they will not find their healthy beanstalk—as you so charmingly put it—to take them home. And their life force, whatever is left of it, is redistributed."

"I don't understand," said Cummings.

"You are a man of numbers," Sarah said, injecting an unexpected lightness back into their conversation. "Suffice it to say, there are some among you on Earth who will 'blow the bank', the amount of life force God injected them with, during their earthly journey. So it is, and so it has always been. Perhaps think of such people as the ones who treat their time here as a spiritual trip to Vegas. Such men and women squander their boundless gifts selfishly, and then when it's time to buy a ticket home, they are penniless because their life force is gone."

"And so they can't return?" ventured Cummings.

"Exactly," said Sarah, and he thought he felt her sigh.

"What about our souls?" he asked. "I thought we all had souls?"

"Yes, we have souls," she intoned, and Cummings felt the familiar flutter of positive energy course through him, indicating that she was pleased by his question. "But our souls can be heavy or light. The heavier the soul, the harder it is to climb the proverbial beanstalk—indeed, if we even bothered to cultivate one. The tried and true saying of 'you reap what you sow' applies here, Samuel. The more positive life force you generate while you are on the earthly plane, the lighter your soul. Light souls can easily ascend and carry their life force home, feeding us all in doing so. Dark and troubled souls, with little life force to buoy them, will sink."

"To hell?" asked the president, thinking of the stress, anger and darkness that seemed to plague the culture of the nation he governed, worried for the people he represented.

Sarah's pupils flashed brightly, the stars inside them eclipsing the blue for a millisecond. There was a jingle in the air, a golden, metallic sound, and a rush of energy that felt like being tickled. He knew, now, that this was her version of laughter.

"Hell?" she asked, smiling—or so it seemed. "Oh no, not fire and brimstone as generally imagined," she said. "There is no eternal damnation. However, if a person continually places his or her own needs above those of others, their life force dwindles during their earthly journey, and at death, they cease to exist. If that happens, whatever meagre life force remains within them is then redistributed to the lowest life-forms in the universe."

"I find that difficult to imagine," remarked Cummings, as he tried to reconcile her words to the visions of hell of his youth. Then, a little more morosely, he said, "Nor do I understand how somebody in my position, who had to make difficult decisions on a daily basis on behalf of my 'tribe,' as you call it, can live up to God's expectations on a daily basis."

"Your job does indeed present significant distractions . . . but you also have unique opportunities," Sarah responded.

"To do what?" asked Cummings. "I am certainly not capable of healing the world."

"Of course not," tinkled Sarah, "that's God's job, which is why he sent me here to intervene. But you are more than qualified to work with me on this intervention! You believe in generating goodness, which is why some of the decisions you make as president trouble you so much, and you have *never* believed people who cultivate darkness should simply be able to just ask for forgiveness and then carry on with their wicked ways. Isn't that why you broke with your Christian roots? Because you thought perpetual sinners should not be able to get away with their crimes?"

He was starting to hate it when she looked into his mind in this way—but yes, she had correctly read his core beliefs, which were fueled by the knowledge that the man who had swindled Flores out of his and Geordie's savings was living in the Cayman Islands, presumably quite happily.

"It is planted in people—in *you*—that you are to cultivate joy for the good of the whole. And as the president of America, you have the opportunity to inspire and motivate millions, as well as to deliver assistance to people in need on a massive scale. Don't sell yourself short, Samuel. Follow your *heart*."

It was a challenge, and he knew it.

She breathed softly into the atmosphere, "And now, I must ask you once again . . . if you were a betting man, would you bet on you or on your wife as being the one most likely to return to God?"

As before, he was puzzled by the question. "I . . . I don't *know*," he confessed. "I have tried to be a good man, and there is no question that my wife Lorena is a wonderful, caring woman. She is an amazing partner and did the lion's share of raising our children while I pursued my own goals," he said, sincerity etched into his face.

There was a light rush of golden wind into the room, and almost before Sarah spoke, Samuel knew what she was going to say.

"Women," she told him in her melodic, tinkling voice, "become mothers. As mothers, they cultivate a higher affinity for love and sharing than most men ever do. As a result, women collectively contribute more to the life force, bringing beautiful, motherly energy home to God. So what is the answer to my question, Samuel?"

He understood she was teasing, but answered anyway. "I only hope I meet Lorena there," he said ruefully. "She *is* more giving than I am. She has always put me and the kids first, and without her, none of us would have been able to grow into the people we have become."

"Yes," agreed Sarah. "But, just to be clear, *all* human beings have enormous untapped potential to grow their life force. Women are just more open to it."

"Is that why you are composed only of women's energy?" asked Cummings, already certain of the answer.

"Yes," Sarah whispered, the scent of roses accompanying the answer.

Cummings couldn't help it. He quipped, "Well, how about that! I finally get to meet the ultimate woman!"

Immediately, Sarah's radiant laughter encircled and passed through him in a wave. Reading his joke correctly, with her golden, energetic tinkle, she communicated, "Yes, but I'm not Marilyn Monroe—though she is part of me. She created a great deal of positive life force while she was alive, giving hope to the many thousands of servicemen in Korea and spreading joy with her skill as a comedienne, and so she has ascended to her rightful place in the spectrum of God."

With that, to Samuel's great delight, Sarah flashed the familiar face of the beautiful screen and stage icon onto her own face, and let it remain for a few seconds, making Cummings gasp with glee.

"Thank you!" he exclaimed in wonder.

"You're welcome," Sarah communicated to him in her wordless way, and Cumming again caught a whiff of rose-scented air as Sarah's energy passed through him. Then she added, "If I was you, though, I would have asked for Mother Mary."

The president was immediately ashamed, knowing as he did that Sarah was an agent of God . . . until with a golden tinkle, Sarah said, "I was only joking, Samuel. Laughter is an important part of the life force, as long as it is well-intentioned and shared."

"Thank . . . *God*," he said.

"I will," said Sarah. "And now, I will explain my mission to you. Please listen, Samuel."

Cummings nodded, and as had happened before, Sarah's voice deepened, and the atmosphere in the room became somehow thicker.

"As I've mentioned," Sarah said, "God has decided to intervene in the course humanity has set for itself. God sees imminent destruction in the future of mankind and has decided this cannot happen. As a united group, humans have enormous untapped potential to generate positive life force. Divided as you are, you are detracting from it. If you destroy yourselves as a group, which you appear intent on doing, a life force deficit will occur. Do you understand, Samuel?"

Cummings smiled slightly. "If we were penny stocks invested well, we'd generate small but steady returns. But if pennies are thrown in the gutter, zilch is returned."

"Yes," Sarah agreed. "Spoken like a man of numbers. I'm here to protect God's investment." Then she caught his eyes with her vivid, starlit pupils, ensuring that he was paying attention, and added, "As I noted earlier, the souls of women are generally more developed than those of men due to the selflessness they display when rearing children. We need to inject more of this way of being into the fabric of humanity if we are to save this fragile world."

Cummings nodded and remained quiet.

"Only female souls have been selected for this intervention," she continued, "as God believes it will more effectively counteract the dominant male energy that has created unchecked aggression on Earth. God would not be making a major intervention if not for the proliferation of weapons of mass destruction. Too many countries and terrorist groups have the ability to trigger a global cataclysm. Life on Earth, and its contribution to the life force that is God, cannot be subjected to that risk."

"Sarah," Cummings asked, "do you have the power of God?"

Sarah's trademark golden tinkle flittered about the room and directly through Cummings' heart, as if he was being tickled on the inside. Her energy was so delightful; Despite himself, he laughed.

"Do I amuse you?" asked Sarah, her words flitting through his mind like a ripple of sand. She didn't seem annoyed, just curious.

"No," he answered honestly. "Not your words or your message, at least. But the energy you project has a physical effect on me, and it makes me want to . . . well, laugh and be *silly* . . . Please don't take it as disrespect."

"On the contrary," whispered Sarah, "to create joy in another is the greatest gift one can give. If I give it to you, then I am pleased. *You're welcome* . . ." she intoned, again with her trademark golden tinkle of energy.

Cummings realized she was teasing and laughed. "Thank you," he said. "The feeling it gives me is like that Christmas Eve feeling I used to get as a kid, when I knew I would *finally* be able to unwrap all my presents soon." He sighed as he tried to recapture what that felt like. "My stomach would just be in knots thinking about those presents . . . but I've lost the ability to feel that way now. I guess it happens when you get older."

"You can regain it, Samuel. You *must*," Sarah breathed, and Cummings knew without a doubt that she was right. "Humanity has lost the capacity to feel joy," she said, "and I am here to help you find it again. But first, we must stop you from self-destructing. To answer your previous question, I do not have *all* the power of God, but I have more than sufficient power to deliver God's message to all the leaders of the world, and to help them communicate it to every human being on Earth. But only God can impose the intervention on the human race. My role is to communicate God's plans to you and your fellow humans, and to help you prepare for change."

"So what do you want from *me*?" asked Cummings.

"Samuel," she said, her words rippling in the ether like will-o'-wisps at play, "I want your faith and your cooperation. What I say to you now will keep you alive if you listen to me. When our meeting ends, God is going to change this world, and it is imperative that you and your team spread God's message to your people. There will be a twenty-four-hour grace period for you, beginning the minute I reactivate time as you know it. During this period, you must spread the word. Once the twenty-four-hour grace period is over, those who do not heed it will do so at their own peril."

At Cummings' shocked expression, Sarah asked, "It's quite simple, Samuel. Are you familiar with the Ten Commandments?"

"Of course," he replied, his Sunday school training kicking in as he automatically began listing them. "There will be no Gods before me, no images, don't take God's name in vain, honour your parents and . . ."

"Thou shalt not *kill!*" interrupted Sarah harshly, her words like an unexpected thunderbolt to the guts. The dark blue of her pupils sank into an inky black as she spoke, making the stars in her eyes jump dangerously toward him. He flinched.

There was a hiss in the atmosphere, like cats facing off. When it dissipated, Sarah spoke again. The baritone quality was back in her tone, rippling through his sternum so deeply that he felt his lungs resonating with the sound. He could almost picture a staff in her hands, and the sky opening to reveal a choir of angels behind her as she said, "From this moment forward, it will be impossible for any human being to intentionally kill another. Anyone who attempts to kill another person will immediately drop dead, and any weapon used in the attempt will be rendered inoperable."

She fixed her gaze more firmly on him, and he was cowed by its intensity. "Further," she continued, "any person responsible for *enabling* killings has only twenty-four hours to notify those under their command to cease killing, or they will also immediately drop dead. As commander-in-chief of the U.S. military, please understand that your life is in grave danger unless you get all of your troops to stand down in the next twenty-four hours, reprieve all people on death row, and stop unwarranted killing of all kinds. Do you understand me?"

Cummings said nothing. He simply gawked, his jaw hanging open like a man who had lost his bearings—which is exactly what he had become.

Sarah paid him no mind. She added, "Please understand that, until you get the word out, thousands of your citizens will die every day. The odds are that most of them will be people who have not significantly contributed to growing the shared life force from which we spring, but there are others you may need to consider who don't deserve to die. There are children who fight, for example. They cannot easily control their emotions and sometimes strike one another with the sincere intention that their rival should die. God's edict about killing does not have exceptions. You must warn your people immediately so that they, in turn, can impart this knowledge to their children and teach them how to live with this new reality. Do you understand, Samuel?"

All the colour drained from President Cummings' face, and he trembled as he exclaimed, "Sarah, you can't mean that! Many people who are otherwise good and productive citizens may be unnecessarily punished for simple lapses in character. What about some poor schmuck who gets cut off in traffic and tries to punch out a fellow commuter? When people are raging, they think they want to kill someone else, but mostly they are just out of control."

"Intent followed by attempted *action* is the key, Samuel. Yelling doesn't normally kill people—but when yelling out your intention to kill someone is followed by trying to force them to crash their vehicle and die, then yes, the aggressor in this scenario will die. It's the *premature termination* of another's life that detracts from the life force, not negative intention alone. And right now, humanity is walking a slippery slope because your love of killing has created a deficit in the life force. God has sent me here to guide you into behaviour that will bring this deficit back into balance.

A weakening of the life force affects *all* of us, Samuel. It detracts from the whole."

Cummings was trying in vain to process what her words would look like when translated to 'boots on the ground.' "But Sarah," he said in a somewhat pained voice, "how will countries protect their borders if we don't have an ultimate threat of retaliation in our back pockets? How will we fight crime? How will we prevent the collapse of global financial markets?"

"Ah yes, like the good leader you are, you have touched on the top issues that must be dealt with right away," Sarah responded.

Cummings was almost certain she sent a calming energy out with her words. He felt his rage dissipate and his knees buckle, and he found himself inexplicably yearning for a piece of the caramel apple pie his mother used to make.

Then there was another burst of the golden, tinkling energy he was becoming familiar with as she said, "With regard to retaliating against aggressors, given what I've told you, you should see that it's somewhat self-evident that this will not be a threat. Any man who shoots to kill will die, whether a citizen of your nation or an invader, so protecting borders from hostile invasion is a bit of a non-issue, don't you think? And if you are talking about protecting borders from so-called illegal immigration . . . well, that's the least of your worries when you're facing imminent death if you don't call back your dogs!"

A tape began playing in Cummings' head. His forces in Afghanistan had a direct presidential order to 'dispose' of certain targeted detainees. His prison at Guantánamo Bay in Cuba had received the same edict. Suddenly, Cummings felt dirty.

Sarah focused her fearsome, starlit eyes on him again. "Quick action in the next twenty-four hours is essential if you, and the men and women who report to you, are to live. But mark my words . . . Killing *will* stop, either by your command, or by God's power. God won't play favourites, and those who aren't aware of this edict and attempt to kill another will most certainly die."

"I see that," Cummings said as the implications sank in. "But what happens after that? How do I govern without ultimate power? It's never been done in all the years of . . . well . . . *tribalism*, I guess. What happens after that?"

"Nothing short of a new world order," Sarah breathed.

For a moment, Cummings' heart was uplifted as if he'd just heard a robin's song after a long, hard winter.

Then she tinkled in her golden way, "I will remain here for 365 days—a full year—to help you and your leadership colleagues around the world establish a new governance that doesn't hold death as a final trump card. You may look at me as a mediator, or a facilitator of sorts. My role will be to ensure effective communication with and between all of you—in real time, in all places, and in all languages. My goal is that everybody on the planet comes through this intervention with a new sense of purpose, hope for the future, and a renewed understanding of God."

"How will you do this?" asked Cummings, unable to fully understand the scope of what she was proposing.

"I will be active across all media channels," Sarah responded lightly, giving Cummings a sense that she thought he should know this already, "and I will organize and moderate global conferences among world leaders in government, religion, business, education, and environmental preservation."

"I see," said Cummings, absorbing her words as he pondered her seemingly unlimited power. "I guess the technological implications of such mass communication are nothing to you . . . but can't you give me—can't you give the *world*—more time? This is going to be a very difficult transition."

"No," said Sarah. "You've had thousands of years to learn what you all so gaily call 'the Golden Rule,' and it *still* hasn't sunk in. Many human beings have lost their ability to feel compassion and empathy for others. They kill freely, and it has led us to the terrible deficit in life force that we face today."

Suddenly, Cummings felt great sadness emanating from Sarah. The best way he could describe it later to Lorena was that it was as if winter seeped into the room and froze the windows shut. It was suddenly so cold that he was afraid to take a breath in case he flash froze his lungs.

He actually shivered as she said, "Most creatures that engage in physical aggression stop fighting once dominance is established, but human beings do not. In fact, human beings are one of few creatures on Earth who intentionally kill members of their own species, in large numbers at that. No, my friend . . . weapons of mass destruction and human aggression are not a good mix."

Cummings exhaled slowly. "So answer me this, Sarah," he said. "If God is so concerned about us all running around killing one another, and if—as you've said—God is particularly concerned about weapons of mass destruction, why not just render them all ineffective? Surely that's within God's power!"

"Ah, what a good question," Sarah said, almost purring with pleasure, a jasmine smell filling the room as the rotation of her faces speeded up with what Cummings took to be approval. "The answer is this, Samuel . . . why do good parents make their children—who've had a wonderful time destroying the living room while at play—work together to clean it up, despite their protests and the manner in which they blame one another for the mess?"

"I understand," he said thoughtfully, head bowed, "though I still think there will be many lives unnecessarily—and unfairly—lost once this edict takes effect." Then he looked up at her, wary, and questioned, "I'm almost afraid to ask, but are there other significant changes God wants to make? You've made it clear that he wants morality restored. Killing others is only one unsavory aspect of human behaviour. What about bullying? What about torture? Rape? Incest? If we're discussing how far we've devolved from God, then these are also considerations. Am I right?"

The golden ripple returned, and Cummings could tell Sarah was pleased by the question. But he was still in such shock that it had a milder effect on his insides this time. He unconsciously brushed at his stomach as if trying to dislodge an overly large moth.

"You are correct, Samuel," she emanated gently, and once again, he thought he smelled roses as the words echoed in his skull. "The other changes God plans to make are designed to reduce male dominance in world affairs, both social and political. The 40 million female souls within me had significant input into this part of the plan."

"How so?" asked Cummings.

"The supreme intelligence that is God has decided to modify human reproductive processes to curb the preponderance of unplanned pregnancies and premature marriages. God's plan will also greatly reduce child pornography, human trafficking, and sexual slavery. These are problems we can all do without ... don't you think so, Samuel?"

Cummings couldn't argue. He had a manila envelope on his desk relating to an FBI effort to crack a global child porn network. He had been putting off reading the dossier because it enraged him to the point of murder to know what was going on.

Reading his mind again, Sarah said, "You need to curb such emotions, Samuel, lest they lead to wrong action."

Samuel shook his head to clear it. "I wish you wouldn't do that," he said, referring to her unsettling way of reading his thoughts.

She acknowledged his displeasure with her trademark golden tinkle. Then she inserted a hush into her tone that he knew indicated she wanted his undivided attention.

"Samuel," she said, "surely you have noted that puberty, in both boys and girls, is occurring at ever younger ages across the world. The food people eat, the water they drink—these things are tainted. The pure food God provided through the life force that courses over this planet has been bastardized so badly that sexual maturation has been affected ... and when that is combined with unchecked media promoting sexuality at every turn, it is truly unfair to the young. Children should be allowed to be children. Don't you agree?"

He did, but until this moment, he'd felt there was nothing that could be done about it. To him, the media, particularly social media, was the proverbial Pandora's Box. There was no going back now that it was open, and the best that could be hoped for was that hard-won control could be pushed through legislatively. He was well-intentioned in this regard, but not all of his cabinet agreed with his efforts, citing freedom of the press legislation as precedent. He perked up now, hoping Sarah had a more robust solution.

"Over the next ten years," she said, the baritone intonation creeping back into her expression, "God will change human physiology so that puberty will be delayed until age eighteen for both sexes, and sexuality will completely stop at age forty."

He couldn't help himself. Cummings actually gasped at this. "What?" he asked.

The golden tinkle came again, as she told him, "God delights in the human joke that man has two brains, but only enough blood to allow one to operate at a time. With this new plan for sexuality, the difficulties of this physiological flaw will be eliminated. Humans will be more mature when they begin their sex lives, and their sexual activity will end before they become vain enough to try to seduce age-inappropriate partners. With the sex drive removed after the age of forty, marriages are far more likely to evolve into true partnerships. Such loving friendships will generate more life force for God."

"Wow," said Cummings. "I mean . . . just . . . *wow*." He could see, without being told, what a huge cultural shift this would create.

"The delay in puberty will be phased in over ten years to avoid disrupting the lives of innocents who have already begun the process," Sarah continued. "This means that boys and girls who are now under the age of ten will be the first group to have their sexual maturity delayed. Furthermore," she added, "from this day forward, no woman can become impregnated unless she *wants* to have a child. This will eliminate the social tensions caused by family planning and abortion."

Cummings was conflicted at this news. He lived in a country where reproductive rights and corralling them was a national pastime and a subject of heated debate, both political and social. He couldn't imagine a presidency where this charged topic disappeared virtually overnight . . . yet, Sarah was telling him it *would*.

Clearly reading his thoughts again, Sarah projected her golden tinkle into his heart, and her version of laughter was stronger this time as she lightly tickled him with this thought: "Think of it, Samuel . . . in your country, it means Evangelicals will finally be able to vote for democrats!"

Samuel Cummings could only shake his head as he wondered about how different life would be in a world with no war, no killing . . . and a sex drive that shut off after twenty years.

Chapter 3

The U.S. Team

When Sarah finished speaking, it felt for a moment as if a lamp had switched off. There was a dearth of energy in the atmosphere, and if Cummings had not been staring right at her, he'd have sworn she'd left the room. However, she was still in front of him, still glowing unnaturally, and still as unknowable and unearthly as she had been before. What was missing, however, was the buzzing of power she'd projected from the minute she'd entered his office. It was as if she'd stopped to breathe, or perhaps to take direction from some celestial source.

Afraid to interrupt her, he just watched her and waited. She soon broke the silence with a flicker of her golden light, and the sweet sensation of a warm, rushing breeze.

"Samuel," she communicated to him. "How are you feeling? What do you think of the news that I bring? I know you think an impossible task lies before us, but please have faith."

Cummings swallowed hard. All he could think of was being the ten-year-old catcher for his baseball team, the Greenville Cubs, and accidentally letting Ronnie Braithwaite slide home. It was the winning run for the Rosentown Panthers, their rivals, and it was a huge lesson in what it felt like to let others down.

"How could you have missed that!?" his friend Pete Lubben yelled in frustration on that long-ago summer day. "It was an easy out!"

The rest of the team seemed to collectively sigh with disappointment as the Panthers went crazy with jubilation, hopping up and down and throwing their gloves in the air. That was the lowest he had ever felt in his full ten years of life on Earth . . . and now he was responsible for much more than the outcome of a simple game—now he was responsible for the lives and well-being of millions of people. *I'm sitting on a hotseat no mortal man should have to sit on,* he thought.

The idea made him morose. The rational, androgen-fueled mind that had guided him so far through his sixty-eight years on Earth was protesting Sarah's presence, telling him that this was too much, too soon and that there was no way that he could ever warn and guide his people in the short amount of time that had been allotted for him to do so. *What if I fail?* he wondered. That long-ago baseball game, and the lesson he had learned that day about the responsibility of having people depend on you, remained close to him all these years later. *But this time, if I let down the team, it will mean certain death for some . . . maybe even me.*

As was her way, Sarah responded to him as if he'd spoken aloud. "You did not fail that day, Samuel," she whispered as though through the rustle of a hayfield at dawn. "You just didn't react quickly enough. You were a little boy who was still second-guessing himself. You no longer are."

Her voiceless words softened the little wedge that was forming in his heart. He smelled the scent of roses again as she spoke. Her words were soothing, like dew on parched soil.

"Samuel, you are a good man, and you are a good leader. Your staff admires you. Your people trust you. Within the rigid framework of the governmental hierarchy in which you operate, you have built as much fairness as is possible. You *do* understand that your integrity is not in question, do you not?"

He wanted to tell her yes, but couldn't utter the word. Pride prevented him because, no matter what she said, he carried an innate sense that he should somehow be better at creating harmony in his government, his country, and in the world. Instead, cities burned on his home soil as long-held conflicts erupted, his citizens hurting and killing one another at the slightest provocation. Overseas, oil ruled the day *still* . . . and fighting for it never ceased. It was as if anger, hatred, evil, and darkness had seeded themselves across the nation and the world, like the dandelions in his lawn, creating a lack of morality, *a lack of . . .*

"A lack of positive life force?" interjected Sarah. The golden glow was back, the tinkle of her inaudible laughter reaching into his soul to lift his heavy thoughts.

"Yes," he agreed.

"Samuel," she said, "you are a proud man. It's such a flaw in your gender. Do you understand how it weighs you down?" she asked.

"Weighs me down?" he questioned. He hadn't really thought about it before, though he supposed it was true. He ventured an answer. "Is it because I feel responsible for what my nation has become?" he guessed hesitantly.

"Precisely," she said, "and that feeling is simply your ego talking. You most certainly have a significant role to play in God's plans for this Earth, but you are no more responsible for another's action than any other human. However, you are in a position of leadership, and so you must be a guide."

This made him wonder how good of a 'guide' he could possibly be. Guiltily, he thought again of Guantánamo Bay. He knew there were men there who would never leave, though he'd promised in his election speeches to close the place down. And he had indeed shut down *part* of it—but he hadn't been completely truthful about the fact that this incarceration facility for terrorists would never completely close.

Sarah easily read his thoughts and emitted what Cummings could only interpret as a sigh. The energy that flowed through him reminded him of whirls of dry leaves on a fall day, windily moving in circles as if alive.

"Samuel," she said, "you're flawed, as are all human beings. But you are well-intentioned, are you not?"

Her words made him feel strangely exposed. "Are you making fun of me, Sarah?" he asked, looking down at his hands, which were still firmly fixed on the edge of his desk, his knuckles white as they gripped it. Gingerly, he released them, stood tall, and watched as the whitened skin became rosy again.

"Of course not," Sarah tinkled lightly. "I am pointing out the truth, and the truth is that your powers are finite. There is, however, strength in numbers," she continued, "and this is where the souls of women have so much to teach. Women are better cooperators, don't you think? Men can learn *so* much about cooperation from them."

"I'm not sure I know what you mean," he replied a little stiffly. "I am currently running a nation with the help and expertise of some remarkable colleagues and staff members. If that isn't cooperation, then what is?"

Sarah tinkled at him again. "Oh, Samuel," she said, and he got the distinct feeling that she thought his response was somewhat infantile. "Most of your gender is only able to cooperate within the confines of specific rules. If you didn't have such rules, your warrior selves would seek to do battle. This is the root of so much angst. People hate rules, yet they still require them. Someday, you may evolve past that—but only if we repair the erosion of the life force balance."

He felt a little attacked. "I am doing a difficult job to the best of my ability, Sarah," he said defensively.

"So you are," she responded pleasantly, "but you, like most men, don't like playing 'second fiddle,' to use that delightful term. Think about this: What if you were not the top dog in this administration? What if you were in Angelica Lopez's position, for example, and she in yours. Could you sit comfortably in a lesser seat and freely offer advice? Or would you sometimes hold back and think that perhaps the president should figure things out by himself or herself?"

Cummings didn't have a good reply for that.

"*True* cooperation is about giving your energy freely for the good of the whole," said Sarah. "You have defiled the intent in the minute you think 'what's in it for me?' Do you understand?"

Cummings nodded, though his feathers were ruffled by how close to home she had hit and how well she understood him. The oldest of three children, he'd grown up being the boss, and he had to admit that he had a taste for it. His happy childhood had been marred only by constant fighting with his younger brother, the middle child, Bryan. Bryan had not appreciated being ruled over by his older brother, and many fistfights had ensued as the two of them childishly fought for supremacy. As time went on, however, things cooled. By their early twenties, Bryan had become much more easygoing than his older brother—an outcome, Cummings supposed, of the dynamics of their relationship. Now Bryan was a psychology professor at the University of Hawaii . . . *living the good life and surfing every day,* Cummings thought resentfully.

He was a little embarrassed when Sarah, obviously reading his feelings, sent a tinkle of golden laughter rippling around the room.

"You see how strong your competitive spirit is?" she asked. "You're the president of the United States of America, yet you are worried still that your brother's life is better than yours."

Cummings' face immediately fell in shame, causing Sarah to remark comfortingly, "It's human nature to 'compare and despair,' as they say . . . but the need to be 'the best' is particularly strong in men. Until a *true* spirit of cooperation—one that doesn't need rules to bound it—reins on this Earth, humans have a long way to go."

"Do you really think such a thing is possible?" Samuel asked. In his experience, the world was a place where the 'top dog' ruled.

Sarah tinkled again. "Samuel," she emoted gently, lightly touching him inside his rib cage, just below his heart, with her special, soothing energy. "All things are possible with God."

At that, Cummings thought of how mercilessly he'd made Bryan bend to his will when they were children. It was always Samuel's favourite television shows that they watched; It was always salt and vinegar chips (Samuel's favourite) instead of barbeque. And then, he thought suddenly of his little sister, Samantha, the youngest.

"Yes, Sam and Sam," joked Sarah, probing his thoughts again. "You loved her deeply."

Cummings cleared his throat roughly. He had indeed loved her deeply. When Sam died of a particularly virulent strain of leukemia when she was not quite thirteen years old, losing her had broken his heart in ways he hadn't known were possible. He was eighteen and in his first year of college—with Bryan, at sixteen, hot on his tail—when she got sick. During the painful year that followed, leading up to her death, he remembered wishing more than once that it was Bryan who was sick and not his beloved sister, Sam. *She* had never cared what flavour of chip they shared.

"And this is why God doesn't give us more than a smidgeon of his power," said Sarah, to Samuel's chagrin. "Humans have only the tiniest drop of it in their souls. If you had more than that, not only would your brother be dead, but so would your vice president, who challenges your decisions daily; the taxi driver who was late in picking you up today; your wife when she refuses to allow you to eat too much salt, and . . ."

"Stop!" Cummings said, putting up his hand in a 'halt' gesture. "I know my failings only too well. But here's the flip side of what you say: If I had God's power, Sam would still be alive, dammit!"

"And Bryan would be dead," said Sarah softly, with a white, fluttering energy that was both uncomfortable and strangely pleasant, "but by *your* will, not God's."

Cummings considered this for a moment. He could feel Sarah's unearthly energy focused on him as he pondered the power of giving or taking away life.

Finally he said, "I know what you're doing. You're trying to make me understand that killing is personal, even when it's done as an order from the office of the president of the United States."

"Am I?" asked Sarah mildly, followed with, "What was it about your sister that made you so faithful to her, Samuel?"

Samuel didn't hesitate in his reply. "She was *good*," he said, clearing his throat of the lump that arose every time he remembered her. "She was good, and she knew how to bring Bryan and I together. She was a mediator. She hated to fight. She . . . she . . ."

"She embodied the spirit of cooperation?" Sarah finished for him.

"Yes," he admitted. "I didn't have to coerce her into seeing things my way as I did with Bryan. She knew how to *listen*."

"She knew how to *listen*, or she knew how to *cooperate*?" Sarah prompted.

Cummings suddenly remembered how he'd once gladly gone to see *Beauty and the Beast* with her, though he'd wanted to see *Spiderman*. He'd even bought the popcorn.

"She knew how to get her way without fighting about things," he admitted, "if that's what you call cooperation." His eyes misted up as he added, "I miss her still. She was such a great kid, just a good-hearted person, and so smart . . ."

"She was your teacher, perhaps?" whispered Sarah, her words reverberating in his heart like an echo.

Still attached to the title of 'oldest brother and leader,' he didn't want to admit this, though he managed to sputter roughly, "I learned a great deal from my little sister."

He couldn't deny it. Sam had always been the one to bring calm to the childhood storms and to settle standoffs between him and his brother (admittedly, usually by finking to their parents)—and he'd loved her for it.

"Samuel... do you understand that *true* cooperation, such as displayed by your sister, is a matter of spirit?" Sarah conveyed wordlessly with her golden energy. "You cannot teach it, you cannot force it, and you cannot grow it through a matter of will. It must be cultivated on the level of soul. It involves trust... something most people find hard to give. Do you trust me, Samuel?"

There was no going back, Cummings knew. And so he gave the truest answer he could. "I want to," he said.

Her golden ripple of laughter coursed through the room and through Samuel as well. "I appreciate your honesty," she said, "and so, that is where we will start."

He looked at her, and once more, caught the stars in her deep blue pupils. He felt like he might have to hold on to them for dear life. "I'm ready," he said.

"Samuel," Sarah breathed, and he noticed a rose scent perfuming the air once more. "As you know, I have suspended time while we get to know one another. We will remain suspended in time in this way for what will seem to you like hours. If I was calculating time in the manner that most humans do, I would estimate that we will spend the next three hours as you know them in consultation with your team, and another four hours discussing the edict and coordinating communications efforts with other world leaders. Do you understand?"

Cummings nodded. "Yes," he said. "If what you say is true, you are speaking to my staff members, the ones you have selected, right now—just as you are speaking to me. You are also speaking to other leaders around the globe and presumably, their staff members as well."

"Yes," said Sarah.

Cummings continued. "You expect us to band together to notify the world that an edict from God has taken effect. The rule is 'those who would kill, will be killed.'"

"I couldn't have said it better," purred Sarah in a voiceless wave of energy that immediately made Cummings think of early summer days and freshly mowed grass. Then she said, "I will transport your staff here momentarily. Perhaps this act will allay any doubts you may still have about whether I am truly God's emissary. Perhaps then you will not doubt that the words I say are true."

Cummings swallowed hard and wondered, *does she really plan to teleport them? How is that possible?*

Again, there was a golden energy shift in the atmosphere around him and heavenly laughter that was both wonderous and baffling.

"Yes," Sarah assured him, "I plan to energetically bring them here, or 'teleport' them as you refer to it. Do you have any questions before your team joins you?"

He did. "Sarah," he said, "the five people you selected to join me in this effort are all of my political party, except for the senate leader. Is there room to negotiate on this? Can I select someone with the same political stripes?"

"Oh Samuel," Sarah breathed, a flutter of doves' wings in the ether. "Partisan politics should be shoved to the side when it comes to the fate of the world, don't you think?"

Cummings immediately felt chastised.

She added, "You and *all* world leaders must work together, despite political disparity of all kinds, or the world will fall fast and hard. It's almost too late already—and so it is time for us to start."

With that, there was a brilliant flash of light and a waver in the surrounding atmosphere. Instantly, Vice President Angelica Lopez; Senate Majority Leader, Hana Shriver; Chief of Staff, Bradley Northrup; Secretary of Defence, Gordon Blackstone; and Secretary of the Treasury, Norman Feldman appeared in the Oval Office, understandably disoriented and wearing expressions of awe and shock on their faces.

Northrup blinked, looked around the room, and caught the president's eye. His expression clearly asked, *what the hell?*, but he didn't utter a word. Cummings nodded subtly at him, intending to convey, *yes, this is happening* . . . to which Northrup blinked assent in return.

And then, Sarah spoke in that baritone voice once more, and all eyes immediately became fixed on her. "Please be seated, everybody," she said.

Her starry pupils flashed, and the group hastily seated themselves on the two couches that were positioned perpendicular to the president's desk, facing one another. Cummings sat down at his desk, with Sarah just to the left of him, though she remained in front of his desk, facing the group.

When everyone was settled, she said in her 'tinkling tone,' as Cummings was starting to think of it, "You all know why we are here, and you all know we have a lot of work to do."

"I'll say," said Angelica Lopez, the vice president. "Do you really think we can achieve this? It's mass communication at a level that has not been attempted before."

Sarah just looked at her, smiled, and said, "As I'm sure you've heard before: with God, all things are possible."

She then returned her focus to the rest of the group and wordlessly asked, "Who knows what 9:00 p.m. Eastern Standard Time is in Greenwich Mean Time?"

Defence Secretary Gordon Blackstone volunteered, "It's 2:00 a.m. on the following day—they're five hours ahead."

"Exactly," Sarah tinkled.

Cummings wondered how many primary school teachers were embedded in the multitude of female life force she was composed of.

He didn't have to wonder long; He could have sworn she winked at him as she said, "Samuel, you are so full of *questions*. Multitudes of teachers are within me, of course. Teachers have to display much more love and patience than the average human. Almost all teachers find their way back to God, bringing with them marvelous amounts of life force."

"That doesn't surprise me," Cummings said. "You'd have to be a saint to keep control of thirty plus children at a time." He chuckled. "Especially right before summer vacation."

He was surprised when none of the others in the room reacted to his joke; Instead, they remained looking at Sarah with serious faces, awaiting her words and instructions.

"Does it surprise you that I can suspend time within the suspension of time?" Sarah asked him, her golden tinkle rippling through his sternum as his eyes widened in awe.

Then there was a subtle shift of energy and Cummings heard Northrup clear his throat, clearly unaware of the conversation he had just privately had with Sarah. He wondered if she had the ability to have 'side conversations' with everybody in the room, and decided that she did.

Addressing the group once more, Sarah continued, "I make the distinction about Greenwich Mean Time because this is the standard we will be following when we inform the world of what is about to happen. Do you understand?"

There were nods all around.

"That's good," she said lightly, her words a flutter of energy. She continued, "As I've told you, just as I'm meeting with you right now, I'm meeting with other leaders. When we're done here, we'll meet as a 'committee of the whole,' as you like to say, to strategize how to spread this message across the world as quickly as possible." Then she quipped, "God sends apologies to European and African leaders, who are in their pajamas," which caused a ripple of laughter around the room.

"When we are done, I will return you to the 'where' and 'when' you were in time before I removed you from it. It was 9:00 p.m. Eastern Standard Time," she reminded them, and then her golden tinkle breezed through the room as she briefly directed her attention to President Cummings. "Samuel, she said, "I know you think it was 9:02, but your clock is fast."

Cummings acknowledged this with a nod and a wry grin.

Norman Feldman, the secretary of the treasury, put up his hand to speak.

"Yes, Norman?" Sarah acknowledged him.

"I'm guessing that the 2:00 a.m. GMT time was chosen to allow the maximum time for communication plans to be developed and implemented before the financial markets open on Monday morning?" he asked.

"You guessed correctly," said Sarah. "God doesn't want chaos to rein in this world; He just wants evil and hatred to return to their natural places in the shadows. Right now, the spread of darkness is proliferating to the point where it is overtaking the generation of positive life force. The first thing God will do to remedy this, as I've told you, is to make all killing *stop*."

Hana Shriver, the senate leader, put up her hand next. "There's something I don't understand," she said. "If killing is generating negative life force in the world, and God intends to simply wipe out all would-be killers whenever they act on a murderous intention, then how does killing *them* contribute to God's life force?"

Cummings saw Northrup nod in approval at Shriver's question. He could tell his chief of staff had been wondering the same thing.

"Ah, that is a very good question, Hana," Sarah breathed, causing Cummings to feel as if his head was suddenly surrounded by hummingbirds in spring.

This particular way of communicating seemed to be a new emotion for Sarah, a sort of whirring. He wondered what it represented, and assumed it meant factual thinking. He shook his head, clearing it as Sarah answered Shriver's question.

"God wants first and foremost to prevent mass annihilation of human beings by weapons of mass destruction," Sarah said. "This is why I am working with world leaders as a first step in ceasing senseless killing. But to answer your question, Hana, if God takes a life, he is retrieving a life force before it becomes depleted by the action of killing another. You could say he is protecting his assets by collecting on them before they are invested badly."

She looked around the room, gauging the reactions of the assembled group and added, "The human race has tremendous potential to grow the life force. It will grow within every person if people can learn to be at one with their species. Humans also have great long range potential, but only if they can also learn to be at one with the *Earth*. Symbiotic relationships between planets and their inhabitants have thrived on billions of planets within older solar systems, throughout the universes. Humans need to grow in this direction."

Vice President Lopez cut in then. "So, it is my understanding that God's intent is to do what is best for humanity as a whole," she said, "but is God also focused upon individual human beings?"

"Of course," responded Sarah with a tinkle. "And that is why he doesn't want any single person prematurely and needlessly killed. Each individual's life force is meant to grow throughout their lives and feed the supreme intelligence that is God. It is unfortunate that would-be killers have to die because, like everyone else, they carry life force and have the potential to generate more."

"I see," said Lopez, "but clearly people who are firmly focused upon loving and helping other people are less likely to become potential killers."

"Yes," agreed Sarah.

"Tell me though," said Lopez, "in the case of innocents such as children, or mentally incapacitated adults—will they also die if they attempt a killing?"

"Yes," Sarah replied, "unfortunately, they will. But they will be reincarnated as new human beings."

"What about compassionate killing?" Lopez persisted. "In some states, we allow assisted suicide. Would the physician who administers the medication immediately die at God's hand?"

There were murmurs all around, and Cummings could see the restlessness of his staff as they adjusted to what Sarah was telling them. He felt the whirr of hummingbirds in his ribs again as she prepared to answer the question.

"Ms. Vice President . . . Angelica," Sarah said, "all I can tell you is that intent applies here. If the intent in such a situation is to ease the suffering of a dying person, and the act is conducted by a licensed practitioner, then the doctor will not die. Compassion *feeds* the life force. However, if there is joy in the taking of this life, or a motive of greed from those who would benefit from the person's death, then anyone enacting such a thing will die. God absorbs all that is good and will note a lack of goodness and act in kind."

At that, silence dominated the room. The group looked at one another uncertainly.

Finally, President Cummings spoke, "It's a lot to take in, Sarah," he said, "and planning will extend beyond communicating this message. People everywhere are going to be overwhelmed by news of this intervention, and I'm pretty sure there will be some highly emotional reactions. It's a good thing that the ban on killing will take immediate effect," he said with a sigh.

Suddenly, he felt very old, thinking of the panic that could ensue if the announcements were mishandled. He wondered if he was up to this task.

"I understand your fear, Samuel," Sarah breathed to him, and he instinctively knew they were in a 'side conversation' once more, and that she was speaking only to him. "I know you will do your job well. This is a positive intervention for the human race, and you and I will make that clear in our communications. It is a chance for hope and salvation, and people will soon come to understand that."

Cummings thought perhaps she was being overly optimistic, but her words offered encouragement, which he appreciated.

"You are uniquely qualified to lead your country—and the *world*—through this," she assured him with a whisper of golden joy that lightened his heart.

And then, as if dialing into a radio station, she tuned the rest of the group back in, leaving her private conversation with him behind.

"Our first step is to ensure that all of you don't drop dead once the twenty-four-hour grace period is up," she said firmly to them in her unique, 'you must listen,' baritone resonance. "We will need to immediately inform your military institutions and law enforcement agencies what is going to happen. This will not only protect the lives of service personnel, but your own lives as well—especially yours, Mr. President," she said, addressing Cummings. "After all, you are the ultimate in the chain of command. If even one military man or woman kills someone after the twenty-four-hour grace period is up, it could mean your own death."

The weight of that quickly sunk in, creasing the brows of the assembled team. "Understood," said Gordon Blackstone, the defence secretary. "The military has a well-established chain of command, and I think we can manage to get that message out to our troops quickly, at least on home soil. It may be more difficult to communicate with our overseas personnel, but I'm fairly confident we will be able to reach all but the most remotely stationed." Then he looked at Cummings, his commanding officer, and added, "That is, with your permission, Sir."

"Of course!" Cummings quickly agreed.

Blackstone then addressed Sarah again, saying, "Quite frankly, I'm surprised you didn't invite the attorney general to this meeting. As the country's top cop, shouldn't he be the one to get the message out to police departments and law enforcement agencies?"

Sarah emitted a golden tinkle of energy as she replied, "I think this responsibility is better suited to you, Gordon. While the attorney general is indeed the chief law enforcement officer of the federal government, the Tenth Amendment restricts his powers. The bottom line is, he can't give a direct order and expect it to be obeyed, but as head of the military, *you* can."

"Through the threat of martial law?" asked Blackstone.

"I suppose so," agreed Sarah. "Martial law—without the threat of death, of course—as an ultimate outcome for not obeying orders. Do you think this can be communicated to the forces you command?"

"God, I hope so," replied Blackstone, clearly worried. "All I can do is tell them what we are facing and what the consequences are, and hope they don't let personal emotions override what their chief commanding officer tells them. But I wouldn't blame them for thinking the whole thing is strange at best—and a hoax at worst. It sounds unbelievable."

President Cummings noted Blackstone's distress, and seeking to relieve him of it, said, "Gordon, there will be media blasts on all platforms to get the word out. Communication around the world will support Sarah's story. I would think any rational human who checks multiple streams on their phone, or programs on their TV, will become convinced that the message is true." Then he looked into Sarah's galaxy-filled pupils, hoping against hope that she would feature herself in their media blast. "Sarah," he asked, "will you appear on-screen? Will you co-announce this with me? One look at *you* should convince people of the truth."

"Unless people think it's CGI," said Vice President Lopez dryly. "Special effects can bring *dinosaurs* to life . . . what if people think that's what brought *Sarah* to life?"

Cummings was immediately worried. "You're right, Angelica," he said.

"People have a tendency to believe what they want to believe," remarked Norman Feldman. "Remember the pandemic of 2020? Some people thought the virus was a hoax." He looked morose, and it was clear he was fearing the worst.

Sarah sent an energetic, tinkling burst of energy through the room which had the effect of raising people's spirits. "People do, indeed, believe what they want to believe," she said, "and they may simply carry on their proverbial 'merry ways.' However, most people's 'merry way' is not one where they kill others, so much of your fear about citizens dropping dead unnecessarily is unwarranted. We all feel anger, we all feel despair . . . but we don't all wake up with the intent to kill others in our hearts. Only those who *do* need to immediately be concerned."

The relief in the room was palpable.

Cummings spoke. "Well then," he said, "we have to immediately rescind standing orders for our military and law enforcement personnel, and issue new ones that prevent the use of lethal force, or else our troops will unnecessarily die in the line of duty," he said, looking at Northrup. "We better get on it."

He was feeling quite guilty that he and his team were being given the twenty-four-hour grace period, thinking to himself, *why is my life worth more than theirs?*

"Just to confirm," said Blackstone to Sarah, "you are saying that if any service person attempts to commit an act that is lethal to another person, even in self-defence, they will die immediately, is that correct? And the weapon that was used in the attempt will be rendered useless as well?"

Sarah's flutter of assent wafted through the room like a wave of ions. "Yes," said Sarah.

"Understood," said Blackstone. "Thank you."

Norman Feldman raised his hand to speak, and all eyes turned to him. He said, "There will be huge financial and economic impacts associated with de-weaponizing the world. Closing financial markets for one week will be necessary to allow investors, companies, and financial institutions enough time to assimilate the impact this will have on debt and equity values."

As soon as the words were out of the treasury secretary's mouth, President Cummings immediately grasped the impact. "We'll have to develop and announce plans to deal with job losses right away," he said, "as well as instill a feeling that the economic future can actually be brighter than the course we have been following."

"You're right," agreed Northrup. "People are going to wonder about these changes. There will be enormous confusion and anxiety, especially when you inform them that their reproductive lives are going to . . . well . . . change. I can't help thinking that's going to affect people in a negative way."

"Possibly," responded Sarah, again with the hummingbird energy. "But let's take 'baby steps,' as people like to say. We will not inform the general public about the changes to their sexual and reproductive lives immediately. First, we announce the non-killing edict and allow people to adjust."

Cummings pulled at his chin, wishing he had a beard to play with. "The minute we're out of the time suspension Sarah has placed us in, we will step into a world with no military power. It will be extremely difficult for the countries that rely heavily on military might to govern," he said, almost as if talking to himself.

"It will," agreed Sarah, and Cummings was sure that a type of joy was emanating from her because the rose scent presented itself again. "But think, Samuel, of the happiness of those poor souls in North Korea when they understand that they are finally free!"

"I *am* thinking of that," he said cautiously, "but I am also thinking of those who don't have access to global media. I'm pretty sure the North Korean government won't run a message from God on their government-controlled media networks. What about the many thousands of interred people in that country, slaves of the state, who no doubt want to murder their captors? What if they don't hear this message?"

He could feel his heart beating in his chest in outrage, and Sarah immediately calmed him with a rush of warm, rose-scented air.

"Do you think the supreme intelligence of God hasn't thought of that?" she asked him, and Cummings got the sense that she was amused. "They will hear the message, Samuel, as will the rest of the world. And they will be free to choose their path, just like all others. Many of those people you speak of, in North Korea and in other nations where atrocities occur, have generated positive life force under the worst of conditions—and they will *not* be abandoned by God."

She didn't need to specifically say to him that she could hijack media channels at will. Instead, an image of a dank, stark room, with cinderblock walls and ragged, pink curtains ran through his mind. On one wall was a large portrait of Korea's 'supreme leader,' and in one corner was an old black and white television. Around a low, three-legged table squatted a gaunt, black-haired woman with her three children. They were eating noodles in watery broth, their haunted eyes fixed on the TV as images of drill-stepping Korean soldiers filled the screen. Despair was written into their eyes, along with infinite boredom. And then, as if the channel had suddenly changed, an Asian woman with a shimmering face suddenly appeared in that dismal television box. More interestingly, she was in *colour*. The despairing, eating woman in front of the television dropped her chopsticks, and her mouth hung open as a glimmer of hope entered her eyes . . . and then Sarah took the vision out of Samuel's mind.

"You see?" she questioned him, and once more, he understood that only he in the room had been treated to this communication from her.

"I see," he said.

Then she addressed the rest of the group who were waiting expectantly for more information. "Government leaders such as yourself are facing an immediate challenge in the next twenty-four hours," she said, "but as time goes on—and the true nature of God becomes clearer—religious leaders will face a significant one as well. There will be an opportunity for cooperation between church and state that is unprecedented in modern times," she said.

"I never thought of that," said Vice President Lopez thoughtfully. "There will be much debate and shifting of doctrines. It will shake the foundations of most religious institutions."

"Yes," said Sarah in her voiceless, energetic flutter, "but this intervention will provide a strong incentive for the great religions to move closer together and simplify their doctrines. This can only benefit mankind, don't you think?" Her golden tinkle permeated the room as the question hung in the air.

"Perhaps it will result in a new religion," said Hana Shriver, furrowing her brow.

"Yes," responded Sarah. "A new religion where people understand that more unites than divides you all."

"A unified religion would sure improve things on this planet," said Vice President Lopez thoughtfully, adding with a wry grin, "And with fewer male hormones on the loose, perhaps women will have more opportunity to take leadership roles."

"All of this is possible," said Sarah in her voiceless, joyous way. "Once we have effectively stopped senseless killing on this Earth, political leaders such as yourselves will be able to work with religious and business leaders to reshape the world into something better than it's ever been. The world will be brighter and better in the future," she assured the group.

Cummings hoped she was right. Out of habit, he looked down at his watch, which still said 9:02. He noted a slight grin on Northrup's face as he did so, which he ignored.

Opening his laptop, he said, "Then we better get planning."

Chapter 4

Thou Shalt Not Kill

Cummings immediately began thinking about how to develop an announcement, something concise and clear that would lay out the salient points of Sarah's message to the American people in a way that would make them understand what was going to happen. His hope was that he could create something that would generate instant public response, and that killing on the streets of America would immediately cease.

Because Cummings' background was in the private sector, and he did not have military experience like Gordon Blackstone—or Bradley Northrup, who had commanded troops in Afghanistan—he rightly felt Blackstone should be the primary lead on notifying the military chain of command about what was going to happen.

"Blackstone," he said, "Can you work on a strategy to inform our military and law enforcement personnel about what to expect? I think Vice President Lopez and I can handle the civilian end."

"Yes, Sir," Northrup responded, nodding assent to his commander-in-chief.

As he opened the laptop on the desk in front of him, eager to take action, Sarah, in her energetic, fluttering way, hovered near Cummings' shoulder and stayed his hand.

"Mr. President," she said voicelessly, her energy soothing but sharp, like cool mint in melted chocolate. "You must think *strategically*. While it is important to communicate to your general population what is going to happen and what the risks are, it is more important for you to protect *yourself* at the moment. You are, after all, the highest authority in the land—and if anyone should die due to an order you have given, your life may very well be over. Your first task, Samuel, should be to rescind any outstanding authorizations to kill that have your signature on them."

Blackstone, listening in, immediately volunteered his services. "I can help you with that, Sir," he said, popping open a computer that was resting on his lap. Its screen quickly sprang to life, and in short order, it revealed a green homepage that awaited the entry of classified codes. The defence secretary said, "I have the database right here, Sir. I just have to enter the appropriate coding. Do I have your permission to do that?"

Cummings was impressed by Blackstone's eagerness. Blackstone looked at Cummings shrewdly as he awaited command, his military bearing impressive to all in the room. What the defence secretary was asking Cummings was if it was okay to use a series of coded passwords known only to Cummings and himself. These codes allowed access to top secret information about some of the more unsavory government activities that were an unfortunate, but necessary, part of running a great nation. In the database were such things as an imminent drone strike against an ISIS leader in Syria, which Cummings had approved only twenty-four hours before; an approval for waterboarding two Guantánamo Bay detainees—again, ISIS members; and a covert military strike planned in an effort to kill the newly appointed Islamic State leader who was believed to be hiding in Pakistan.

Cummings nodded assent, knowing how serious the information in the file was. But not for the first time that day, he suddenly felt ashamed. *No one likes to think of themselves as a killer, but what else am I when I give orders that mean others will either live or die?* he wondered dourly.

The secretary of defence nodded back and then typed in the appropriate codes. A series of blip noises emanated from the computer as it allowed him access, and then the database sprang to life, revealing the list of atrocities hidden within.

As it populated the page, Sarah fluttered over Blackstone's shoulder, apparently reading what was on the screen—and then a certain darkness flitted over her being, and Cummings felt an energetic shift that could only be interpreted as disapproval. He involuntarily shivered. It felt like fingers of ice in his abdomen.

Then Sarah whispered in her airy, voiceless way, "Oh Samuel . . . these are very dangerous things for you to be approving. You must immediately retract all of these orders if you want to live! Why would anyone want such blood on their hands, Samuel? Is this who you thought you would become?"

Cummings cleared his throat uncomfortably. It was a question he really didn't want to examine. He'd entered politics because he wanted to help others. Knowing how much relief, hope and joy he'd brought to those he'd shared his money management skills with—average working joes who just wanted to provide for their families—his initial thought had been that if he ran for public office, he could apply his knack for financial management on a broader scale, for the good of *all*. His motives had been sound; He'd truly felt he had the knowledge, skills, and abilities to make the country better, stronger, and a shining example to the world . . . and it had been a rude awakening to discover that leadership often involved making decisions that were right on one level but very wrong on another. When he discovered that the financial aspect of governance was a much smaller part of the job than he'd first expected, he also discovered that being president was, in some ways, way out of his comfort zone. He'd never admitted this to anyone . . . but he knew that Sarah knew.

As his sins lay exposed on the spreadsheet in front of Blackstone, Cummings suddenly remembered how his old Sunday school teacher, Mrs. Pineo, had hammered the Ten Commandments into him and his classmates every Sunday morning, right before they sang "This Little Light of Mine." *Good old number six, 'thou shalt not kill,'* he recalled. Clearly the lesson hadn't stuck.

"Mr. President, I suggest you retract these orders at your earliest convenience," Blackstone told him, clearly worried. "It would be a shame to lose you on a technicality."

"Or *you*," the president shot back. "Unless I'm wrong, every person who has a part in the string of orders that culminates in killing, right down to the person who does the actual killing, gets zapped. That means you too, Blackstone."

"And me," said Angelica Lopez.

"And possibly *me*," said Northrup.

"Yes, depending on the circumstances, I guess it could mean any, or all, of us," sighed Cummings as he looked at his team.

Sarah's presence shifted then, sending waves of energetic purpose around the room. "This *does* seem like a fine time for accounting for the things you have done," she said as she glanced at the group and noted the somber faces. "However, it's actually a time for *action*!" Suddenly, there was a sharp crack, like static electricity in the air, as she said earnestly, "You need to move on this *immediately*—all of you!"

"I'll say," muttered Vice President Lopez, nodding hasty agreement. "We have a lot to do and not much time to do it!" Then the vice president sat up a little straighter, and said with determination, "I think we need to send out a nationwide alert over all cell phone providers in the same way that we broadcast Amber Alerts. But first, we will need to establish a website and create a video announcement that can be broadcast on demand. Then we can distribute the link in the alert message and drive people to the site."

"Good thinking," said Cummings, envious of his vice president's ability to think on her feet.

She's better at taking concrete action than I am, he thought. He was a little ashamed of the jealousy he felt at that, an insecurity that was caused by the fact that both of them knew the only reason *she* wasn't president was because she'd agreed to step down as his main competitor and become his running mate—and the only reason they'd struck this deal was because she was a woman. No woman had yet managed to make it into the presidential office in the United States of America, though there had been one woman vice president before Angelica. The idea of a woman president seemed to polarize people. It made Cummings feel cheap to know this.

As if reading his thoughts, Sarah took that moment to lock her starry pupils onto his. "There will be time for such analysis and remorse later, Samuel," she said.

He knew that once again she had removed him from the pack and singled him out for special solace. He replied, "Will there? I have my doubts . . . " Then he broke off, shaking his head with disbelief.

Here he was, in the top position of power in the country, and it had turned him into a sitting duck. An hour ago, nothing could touch him, but now he was one of the most vulnerable men on the planet. He thought of Lorena, his loving and loyal wife, waiting for him in the White House living quarters, probably in her pajamas with a glass of wine and takeout from their favourite Chinese restaurant. He wondered if he'd ever thanked her for her boundless patience, or properly appreciated her wisdom. He wondered if he'd ever get the chance to.

Once more, Sarah read his thoughts as Cummings knew she would. "Samuel," she said, "you can't second-guess yourself or wonder about your choices anymore. The only way is *forward*."

Though he felt conflicted, and his heart beat uncomfortably quickly at what he was being called to do, Cummings nodded his agreement.

"This is your destiny, Samuel," Sarah breathed, calming him with her trademark rose scent . . . and then suddenly, the two of them were back in communication with the rest of the team.

Before Cummings could even get his bearings, he heard Vice President Lopez ask Defence Secretary Blackstone, "Gordon, does that spreadsheet you're looking at include naval assets located in hot zones where the vessel's commander and crew are authorized to respond with deadly force if they believe they are under attack?"

In true military form, Blackstone automatically replied, "That is classified information."

Lopez just looked at him coolly, one well-groomed eyebrow arched in disbelief. "You're kidding, right?" she asked. "Not only am I the vice president of the United States, and your *colleague* . . . but given what is happening here, you're going to be a protectionist with your information?"

Sarah's golden energy immediately filled the room, making it impossible for hostility to rein. "We're off to a bad start, people," she emitted to the assembled group. "This is not the way to find solutions, only to create more problems." Then, focusing her attention on Blackstone, she noted the death-grip he had on the computer and how he was protectively shielding the screen from Angelica with his body. "Gordon," she said kindly, "what is the point of withholding information? Given what I have discussed privately with each and every one of you, you must certainly be aware by now that I know the answer to every question I ask. That includes anything to do with your weapon systems and military deployments. Do you understand me?"

Blackstone looked a little embarrassed. He was a trained military man, and his instinct to protect the sensitive military information he was in charge of was strong.

Sarah was having none of it, though. "Gordon," she breathed gently, reminding Cummings of a cool breeze over a lake on a hot day, "You *do* understand that there can no longer be any classified information with regard to military strategy, don't you? No military weapons will ever be successfully used again."

Blackstone shifted uncomfortably in his seat. "Yes, I suppose I do," he admitted grudgingly, and then, clearly fighting years of conditioning, he reluctantly adjusted his body so the assembled group could look at the screen he had been holding close to his body in an effort to hide it. Then he looked at Lopez and replied, "The answer is affirmative, Vice President Lopez. The U.S. navy does indeed have navel assets in hot zones where the crew is authorized to protect themselves, by whatever means, in several locations."

"Thank you, Secretary Blackstone," said the vice president. "I appreciate your disclosure. I am only asking because I sincerely want to work with Sarah, here," she glanced at Sarah, "and the rest of you to save lives. We're *all* in danger, especially your service personnel—not to mention any of us in the chain of command who've authorized the option to kill."

Blackstone nodded his understanding, though he still looked somewhat unhappy about having to share information in this way. Picking up on his discomfort, Sarah breathed soothingly to him. "I understand you are overwhelmed, Gordon. These are unprecedented times, which is why God is taking unprecedented action. But humanity's survival depends on its ability to *create* life force—not destroy it. You must shift your thinking so that you truly understand this."

Cummings saw the Adam's apple on Blackstone's throat bob as the man fought to suppress his urge to be secretive. He admired him for it; He, too, was having trouble wrapping his head around this new path they were all going to be walking, and he could imagine what the head of his military was thinking. He was inspired to console the man.

"Thank you, Mr. Secretary," he said to Blackstone by way of encouragement. "I appreciate your service as the top military official in the United States, and your commitment to duty. I also appreciate your ability to change direction. You are a strong and noble man, Gordon. And I mean that."

Blackstone seemed mollified by the president's kind words, and when Cummings glanced over at Sarah, he could have sworn that 40 million women were smiling at him. The rose scent crossed his nose again, and he couldn't help himself from smiling in return. Then the moment was gone and a touch of darkness clouded the air.

Sarah breathed out, like a gust of wind preceding a storm and uttered, in what Cummings could only describe as a tone of formal command, "The United States of America—indeed, all countries with naval assets in so-called 'unfriendly' territory—should not only move their ships out of harm's way but should immediately belay all authorization for defensive military action."

Cummings saw Blackstone flinch. He knew that despite Blackstone's best efforts to accept this 'new normal,' the man was struggling. Sarah's command went against the lifetime of training and experience. Blackstone was a career military man who had sweated his way to the top of the food chain and demonstrated exemplary service while doing so. Unmarried, the military was his life and his wife, and he was loyal to it to a fault. But now, he was being called upon to do the unexpected, and Cummings could see what it was costing him. To his credit, though, Blackstone nodded reluctant understanding and assent.

Correctly reading his discomfort, Sarah assured him, "As I've told you, Gordon, you do not need to fear for national security. No country or terrorist group can launch an attack on any of your vessels. If they do, the weapons they deploy will instantly be destroyed and everybody involved in the decision to fire them will drop dead."

Vice President Lopez smiled at this. "Sarah," she said, "I think this intervention is a long time coming and I, for one, am pleased at what you—I mean, what *God*—is doing." This earned her a small frown from Blackstone, but she ignored it and continued. "I have a question, though. Does automatic protection extend to non-aggressive, potential targets of an attack—innocent bystanders? I'm thinking in particular of civilian planes that get hit as unintended targets during the course of military attack. It happens sometimes."

"You are a quick study, Vice President Lopez," said Sarah. "And I know that you are speaking of the four airliners recently destroyed by the U.S., Russia, North Korea, and Iran." Lopez nodded, and Sarah said, "Yes, Angelica, of course protection is extended to the innocent. No one can die at another's hand, and so no group can shoot down civilian airliners, whether accidentally or by design."

"Thank God," muttered Hana Shriver, who had been following the conversation with interest. "It nearly broke my heart when I heard about the Iranian wedding party that died during . . . uh . . . that, um, recent military strike." She stumbled over her words, fighting to choose them carefully, and then glanced surreptitiously at Cummings before quickly looking away. She ended with, "A whole family . . . just gone—parents, grandparents, uncles, aunts, and cousins . . . just *gone*."

Cummings understood that she had been about to say 'our' military strike instead of 'that' military strike. It upset him a little to know she was referring to recent U.S. military action—authorized by him—that resulted in an Iranian civilian aircraft being shot down outside of Tehran. Suddenly, he remembered that she was married to a naturalized Iranian, and that her husband had family in that beleaguered country. *I never thought to ask her if she had relatives on that plane,* he thought, ashamed. *What if she lost someone?* A dirty feeling crept over him as he wondered if the Iranian plane had been shot down on purpose as a means of intimidation. The military had covert standing orders from him to intimidate as *well* as to engage—and intimidation sometimes took the form of 'accidents' that could never be proven.

He tried to catch Blackstone's eye, looking for answers, but the man did not meet his gaze. *All's fair in love and war,* he told himself by way of comfort. But it didn't make him feel any better. He hoped he'd have the opportunity to talk to senate head Shriver once the immediate emergency was over—and to offer condolences if he found out she had indeed lost someone she loved on that plane.

Just then, Northrup spoke up. "Sarah, I know we've been over this, but it doesn't hurt to reiterate. I'm sure you understand that this is a lot for us to swallow at the moment, so please bear with me. You—or God, I should say—expect us to lay down our arms because, according to what you've said, nobody will ever be able to *purposely* kill anyone else ever again. I know we've been over it, I know we've agreed to it, but I would be remiss if I didn't express my feeling that this suggestion is irresponsible at the least and dangerous at the most."

"Oh, Bradley," said Sarah, wafting her words over toward him in a gust of fresh air that Samuel could only describe as cloaked in the scent of spring. "The leaders of *every* country think the same thing. But you need to let go of this—*now*—and accept that what I say is the truth . . ."

Suddenly, Cummings cut in, fear rather than common sense propelling him to speak. "Yes, but what if you are *wrong*?" he asked, the words popping out of him like a cork from a bottle. "Sarah, this is terrifying on every level. We have a duty to our citizens to protect them!"

Sarah sent calming energy out to touch his heart. "*Trust*, Samuel, *trust*," she entreated. "You know in your heart that it is imperative that you believe."

At Cummings' blank look, she took a firmer stance. "Samuel, you must act *now*! You have twenty-four hours to relieve yourself of the duty of 'chief architect' of industrial killing in America. The same goes for the rest of the 200-plus government leaders around the world, all of whom I am concurrently speaking with. Rescind those orders, or you will die whenever a killing is attempted. I can't be more clear than that, can I?"

It was apparent from the expressions around the room that the assembled group thought she *could* be more clear—and if an immortal being composed of 40 million souls could sigh, Sarah did then. Each person in the group reacted differently to the energetic expression of her thoughts. Cummings felt her sigh of exasperation as a whirlwind of frosty air, which caused his nostrils to contract as frigidness crept up them like tiny, icy fingers.

"Listen to me," Sarah said, scanning the room and the questioning faces in front of her. "There are twelve executions scheduled around the world on Monday. One is for a state execution in Texas. If that execution is not aborted, the governor will die because he was a death 'enabler'— he failed to grant an appeal; The judge and jury who ordered the death penalty will *not* die, because their decisions were made five years ago, and they do not have the power to rescind their orders; The person performing the execution will most certainly die; And the equipment used for administering the lethal injection will melt and be rendered unusable.

The person who was to be executed will *not* die. Does this example make things more clear?"

Sarah looked around the room at each and every one of them, focusing her midnight, starlit pupils on the assembled group one by one. Cummings noted the stunned expressions of his colleagues—as well as the way the breeze emanating from Sarah intensified.

Then the baritone expression was back, and the vibration in the air became serious and dark once more as Sarah said, "Anybody who attempts to kill someone from here onward will *die*!" Looking at Blackstone, she added grimly, "You must immediately contact law enforcement agencies across the nation to ensure that none of the men and women who police your towns and cities make the fatal mistake of pulling a trigger when they respond to a crime. Do you understand?"

Blackstone nodded, still uncertain that what she was proposing was a good idea, but clearly in awe of this unearthly being who was telling them all such unbelievable things.

Then, as if to comfort them, Sarah returned to the golden tinkle style of communicating and added, a bit more softly, "They will be mystified when you tell them not to shoot when a suspect pulls out a gun and threatens them. But once the bad guys start dropping dead in front of them, they will feel a lot more comfortable. After the first one, they will know you haven't lost your marbles."

Vice President Lopez snickered softly. "That will be truly amazing, Sarah," she said. "Tell me, will it apply to bad cops too? Like the one who kneeled on that guy's neck in Minneapolis? The one who killed George Floyd?"

"Of course," said Sarah.

"Good," said Lopez with a little more satisfaction than Cummings would have expected from her, making him wonder for the first time about what racism challenges his vice president had experienced as a Latina—a female *and* a minority—in a country where white males traditionally held all the trump cards.

"So, we are clear?" asked Sarah. "Do I need to reiterate?" No one responded, so she said, "Vice President Lopez, please let me know when you have managed to get your proposed website in place. We will need your website and your alert system as soon as possible to post information about the deaths of would-be killers."

Angelica Lopez nodded.

"Good," said Sarah. "This is how it will roll out. Starting at 2:00 a.m. GMT, I will report all deaths that occur within U.S. territory due to attempted killings, whether American or non-American, to Angelica's communications team for posting. My reports will include the nature of the attempted killing; the weapon or weapons used, if any; the identity of the perpetrator; the identities of the enablers, if any; and the name of the target or targets. Angelica, the information will have to be reported in real time, twenty-four seven, and you must assemble staff to do this. It is important to relay this information to the public daily to reinforce the reality of what is happening, and to save lives."

"Got it," said the vice president as she hunched over her computer and started typing madly. "I'm getting staff on it right now . . . though I guess my emails won't go through until we return to normal time, am I right?" she asked.

"Yes," said Sarah, "but it doesn't hurt to have them cued up. It will just make the process of spreading the word that much faster once the clock starts ticking."

"That's what I thought," said Angelica, returning to her typing.

Sarah then turned to Gordon Blackstone. "Secretary Blackstone," she said, "you will need to think about how to handle your ground forces in hostile zones. Do you want to leave unarmed military personnel in foreign countries where they could be subject to isolation and abuse? While it is true they cannot be murdered, they *can* be captured and tortured. You will need to consider what purposes your troops are serving overseas."

"Sarah, this is something we will need to deal with on a case by case basis," said Blackstone thoughtfully. "Some of our personnel are helping countries rebuild after war or natural disasters. In general, U.S. aid is welcome, and many of these places are in dire need of it. If I recall all the troops with no discretion, I may do more harm than good."

Cummings ventured, "These efforts may need to be transferred to the Department of State since they will no longer be military in nature."

"Possibly," replied Blackstone. "But that's a little further down the line. For the next twenty-four hours, I just have to ensure that those who might be endangered when the no-killing edict takes effect are able to get out of harm's way. I could see a lot of hand-to-hand combat taking place as people try to capture each other on the ground because, as Sarah pointed out, torture is not off the table."

Sarah looked at Cummings, and he felt the full weight of her starlit eyes as she said, almost joyously, "You and Gordon will also need to consider withdrawing U.S. troops and military assets you have posted in *allied* countries. Perhaps some of those troops would like to come home to be with their families. Once God's edict takes effect, their overseas presence won't be necessary because would-be attackers are doomed to die in the attempt."

"Yes," agreed Blackstone. "There seems little point in having overseas military postings now, particularly in allied countries."

Sarah then turned to Cummings once more. "Samuel," she said, "you do understand that all the weaponry the U.S. has abroad will soon be rendered useless, don't you? I would suggest you start planning how you will repatriate and recycle military hardware. If you don't bring it home and keep it out of prying hands, innocent locals could die trying to fire weapons or detonate bombs . . . which would, of course, end your *own* life. The same is true of military equipment in the United States. It will no longer serve a purpose, so it should be appropriately disposed of."

President Cummings reacted strongly to where this line of reasoning was leading. "Sarah, I can't order our troops to surrender their weapons any more than I can throw out the Second Amendment and take away the guns of American citizens!"

At his words, he noticed Angelica Lopez look up from her screen and cock an eyebrow as if to say, 'Yes you can, you're the president,' but he ignored her. Instead, defending his outburst, he said to Sarah, "Not all guns are for killing *people*. There are many people who have guns to hunt for food or sport. There are farmers who keep them for putting down animals or shooting rabbits and gophers when they become pests in the field . . ."

Even as he heard himself speak, he knew that the examples he was giving were the exception rather than the rule. Most people had guns for self-protection, a means to dispatch intruders who tried to enter their homes. But he stood by his words, finishing with, ". . . and a threatened homeowner can still protect his home by shooting an intruder *without* the intent to kill. According to what you've said, intent followed by *action* is the key. If the intent is to put someone out of commission by shooting him or her in the leg, then the gun is still a valid weapon!"

"As you will, Samuel," responded Sarah. "That is your choice. Just be sure you strictly enforce all safe storage laws so that when an innocent child gets hold of a gun and attempts to shoot somebody, it will only be the enabling parent and the child who drop dead, and not you."

Cummings' indignant, flushed face immediately blanched as he pondered the idea that refusing to take steps to round up weapons in his country might make him guilty—an enabler—in the eyes of God, which could very well end his life.

Secretary Blackstone asked, "What about the manufacturers and vendors of the weapons? Will they drop dead if one of their weapons is used in an attempted killing?"

"No," said Sarah, causing startled looks around the room. "Let me explain why," she continued. "First, any person responsible for manufacturing or selling weapons meant for killing humans is under the same twenty-four-hour reprieve as you are. But second, and more importantly, as of this instant, there is no such thing as a weapon that can be manufactured or sold on the premise that it can be used to kill anybody."

"Bravo!" exclaimed Hana Shriver. She was positively beaming, and again, Cummings had to wonder if she'd seen more than her share of tragedy through her husband's side of the family.

"Thank you," said Sarah graciously, and Cummings could smell the rose scent once again, "but I am simply the messenger. The supreme intelligence that is God is the architect of this intervention."

"Most gun manufacturers and defence industry companies will likely go out of business within months," said Shriver, with no small degree of wonder in her voice.

"I would expect so," Sarah replied. "However, I would still advise you to gather up and destroy as many weapons as you can. As you so astutely pointed out, Samuel," she said, eyeing the president, "weapons can still be used to maim. Some humans have decidedly cruel natures and may engage in this behaviour once they understand that killing others is no longer an option."

Cummings gulped and nodded. Unfortunately, she was right.

Sarah then fixed her gaze on the secretary of defence. A large man with a statuesque military bearing, Blackstone seemed to shrink under that intense gaze.

She said, "Secretary Blackstone, when it comes to military planes, submarines and ships, you have flexibility to decide whether they need to be destroyed or not. It goes without saying that they must be completely disarmed, but you may be able to repurpose some of them. They could be used as tools in the areas of border security, crime fighting, environmental efforts . . . or even for civilian use."

"I suppose so," said Blackstone. He was clearly not used to thinking in this manner, having been a warrior all of his life, and there was no doubt that Sarah understood this.

Cummings recognized a measure of empathy for Blackstone emanating from her as, on a breath of summer-scented air, she said to his secretary of defence, "Think about the possibilities! Aircraft carriers could make wonderful floating hospitals for use in natural disaster areas, and helicopters could be used to assist in life-saving efforts. Submarines and military surveillance equipment could be repurposed to be used in the fight against climate change and its impact on the Earth. There is so much potential, don't you think?"

Blackstone nodded grudgingly, and Sarah said soothingly, "Don't be so glum, Gordon. This intervention may feel personal, and will indeed change the nature of your career path, but it won't put you out of a job. There is still a purpose for the military. Order will need to be maintained, emergencies will need to be dealt with. But the killing will *stop*."

Cummings thought he saw a slight shift in Blackstone's rigid shoulders, though he didn't speak; He just looked down at the computer on his lap and typed in a few words. When he was done, he looked at Cummings and said, "I have drafted several messages to our top commanders around the world and am prepared to send them over secured military channels at your say-so, Sir." Then he looked at Sarah and said, almost shyly, "Or at yours, Ma'am." Cummings knew this was as close as the man could get, for the moment, to indicating his belief in this incredible being who was guiding them in how to change the world.

"Thank you, Gordon," Sarah breathed in her voiceless way, dandelion fluff in a breeze. "However, let's hold off until we've finished our discussion. We still have a lot to of work to do." Then she turned the full force of her gaze upon Cummings and said, "I understand the United States has been a leader in the cry to abolish the use of land mines, but I also know you still use mines to block shipping channels upon occasion. Is that true?"

Cummings looked to Blackstone for help and he nodded. "Affirmative," he said.

"You will have to ensure that all such weapons are removed if you want to avoid accidents—which would, of course, lead to the untimely deaths of both you and those you command who have knowledge of them but fail to remove them," Sarah said to Blackstone.

"Or me," said Cummings. "The buck stops with me."

Sarah turned her gaze back onto Cummings. "Yes," she said, "it does."

Cummings gulped, feeling like a dead man walking. How would they ever accomplish all she was asking?

He focused on her starry eyes, which seemed to be delving into his soul, and said, "Sarah, it will take time to physically repatriate military personnel and equipment from around the world, not to mention to disarm weapons—especially weapons like mines. Accidents will almost surely happen during the process. How can I protect my people and myself as these things play out?"

"Samuel," said Sarah gently but firmly, an edge of cold ocean permeating the warm energy she rippled around the room, "your best and only defence is to be 100% open and clear in your communications. Tell the world where the mines are. Make sure every soldier and sailor under your command knows that they are not to respond to perceived threats with deadly force. If you and your people do everything reasonably possible to prevent untimely deaths, God will protect you."

Cummings was relieved by her words, but still trepidatious. By the looks of his colleagues, they were too. Sarah sensed this, and Cummings felt comforting energy emanate from her as she injected lightness into the heavy thoughts of the assembled group.

"Life will go on," she assured them, "and it will be *better*. Think of the possibilities for helping others once the prospect of intentionally killing another person is removed from the table!"

"Such as?" ventured Norman Feldman, who had been sitting silently, absorbing the ramifications this great change would have on the financial health of America.

"The United States has an opportunity to demonstrate great leadership," said Sarah. "You will be able to lead the way in helping other countries, and even terrorist groups, in disabling roadside bombs and other booby traps. Many countries have great skill in creating the devices but little equipment suitable for removing them."

"Do you actually think terrorist groups will care if we dismantle roadside bombs?" asked Angelica Lopez archly. "There may be *some* terrorists who want to remain alive by not killing people—but we are talking about suicide bombers here! How will the new world order change their perspective? They don't care if they die!"

It was a fair question, and Sarah addressed it with aplomb. "Remember, Angelica," she said, "most suicide bombers have been brainwashed, or otherwise cajoled into the act. Many are mere children who've been convinced by loved ones, sometimes family members, that they are dying for a greater good. Most often, they don't have a clear understanding of what they are doing, let alone *why*. They have been manipulated by those who seek power . . . and just as the chain of command in your own military will be held responsible for an order to kill, right up to Samuel here," she said, turning her starlit gaze onto Cummings, "so will it occur in the chain of command of terrorist groups. Make no mistake, those at the top don't want to die. Like cowards throughout time, they want *others* to make such sacrifices for them."

Cummings cringed inwardly at her words. Though he knew they weren't intended as a personal barb, the more he thought about the dawning of this new age that Sarah was describing, the more his mind wandered over the life—and lies—he had been living. He'd thought himself honourable when he'd approved the orders to 'incapacitate' terrorist leaders, all the time knowing that it meant bombing towns and cities where the innocent abided along with the guilty. It was a slippery slope, and he often found himself flinching at news footage revealing casualties of American strikes, particularly when they portrayed women and children weeping. *What kind of hypocrite am I?* he wondered in disgust. *I can't even look at the carnage I cause!*

Sarah didn't respond to his self-recrimination with anything more than a whiff of roses. Instead, she was eager to keep the discussion going by addressing the white elephant in the room. Looking firmly at each person with her shifting, unearthly eyes and a crackle of electricity, she said powerfully, "It goes without saying that we need to deal with weapons of mass destruction," she said.

The group immediately sat up and paid attention.

Chapter 5

Weapons of Mass Destruction

"The existence of nuclear weapons, particularly nuclear bombs, is an affront to both nature and God," said Sarah, her breath hissing in the air around the group like a deflating tire.

Cummings saw immense depth in her eyes as she spoke, and he was both cowed and awed by their fierceness.

"The proliferation of nuclear weapons is the main reason God is intervening at this time," she said firmly. "Nuclear weapons must be decommissioned around the globe. They are a huge threat to the life force. Merely having one detonate at the time of launch would create destruction at a level God finds unacceptable. And nuclear fuel enrichment facilities will have to be shut down and decommissioned as well."

The assembled group nodded in agreement, though it was Shriver who vocalized her relief.

"My father's mother—my grandmother—lived through Hiroshima, and she lost all of her family," she said firmly. "It's about time the world woke up and got rid of nuclear weapons, for once and for all!"

As before, Cummings was surprised to find out this personal detail offered by Hana Shriver. He shifted his gaze to the woman and studied her, suddenly recognizing the hazel eyes and dark hair as having a faint Asian cast to them. Then he looked around the room, and it occurred to him that he had never really gotten to know *any* of these people well—the people he worked so closely with every day. *We're virtually strangers,* he thought with some dismay, *strangers who hold an uncertain future in their hands.*

Sarah sent a wave of compassion toward Shriver, and Cummings saw it as an almost indiscernible ripple in the air. Then she met and held Blackstone's eyes and said, "The other weapons that must be demobilized are chemical and biological weapons."

Cummings saw Blackstone open his mouth, as if preparing to say, 'What chemical weapons?'

Sarah simply continued with, "All countries typically deny they have such weapons, but they will have to destroy them anyway."

This made Blackstone shut his mouth right away. If the situation had not been so dire, Cummings would have laughed at Blackstone's aborted attempt at denial.

And then Sarah said, "And last but not least, the world is becoming infested with cyberweaponry. The same rules apply. Any system designed to kill people, directly or indirectly, will fail to operate—and every person involved in building, releasing, or *authorizing* the release of such weaponry, will die. Further, should hostile malware created to knock out crucial technological operations of other countries cause situations that cost lives—for example, a deadly riot when a country's monetary fund is hacked—the creators of such malware will die."

There were worried looks around the room at that. Norman Feldman anxiously thought about some stocks he was considering buying in an upstart 'software' company that was producing blocking technology to deflect external vote tampering. An option to use it to spy on the Chinese had been put forward as a military initiative, and while both he and Gordon Blackstone knew about this offer, he wasn't sure if Cummings did yet. He glanced at Samuel but could not tell from his expression what the man was thinking. Then and there, he decided to turn down the offer.

Hana Shriver broke the silence that had befallen the room. "Sarah," she said, "getting back to the discussion about terrorists . . . from a public safety standpoint, what happens when someone driving a vehicle decides to purposely crash into a crowd and kill as many people as possible? Or perhaps a more extreme example would be the events of 9/11."

"Excellent question, Hana," said Sarah, her trademark golden tinkle back in place. "In such cases, God will intervene and force the individual in charge of the vehicle to proceed safely to the nearest practical stopping point and then the plane, train, or truck will be shut down and the would-be killer will confess his intentions and die. These events should be widely publicized to help the general public have faith that God is here to protect them."

Shriver continued her line of questioning. "Also, we've already discussed compassionate killings," she said, "but what will God do in cases of attempted suicide?"

Cummings watched as Sarah's many faces shifted to express an overall impression of compassion, and he inhaled deeply as a gentle, pine-scented breeze flowed through the room, ruffling his hair.

"Ah, yes . . . suicide," Sarah said. "Suicide is complicated. Attempts most often occur when a person is in despair. If these attempts *fail*, however, and the despair lifts, would-be victims of suicides often go on to live healthy, productive lives. Not only that but, having suffered themselves, many gravitate toward jobs or situations where they can help others overcome their *own* despair, generating a great deal of positive life force for God. God will therefore prevent suicide, and before a person can damage themselves, God will cause him or her to seek help."

"That's good," said Hana Shriver.

And once again, Cummings had cause to wonder about her. Her hand trembled slightly as she spoke; This was obviously a topic that was close to her heart.

She began twisting one corner of her shirt tightly as she added, "It is my hope that some of the military budget no longer needed for overseas offensives will be redirected toward mental health in this country."

"There are *many* positive things that will come from these changes," said Sarah. "And that may be one of them." She looked at Cummings then, possibly for some sort of confirmation, but his thoughts were miles away.

"Sarah," he said, his mind churning, "you and God are creating a world where governments can no longer use lethal force to protect borders or prevent crime. I recognize that the bad guys won't be able to use lethal force either, but human nature being what it is, people are going to form groups, gangs, mobs and tribes, and they are going to fight each other with sticks and rocks if they have to. Is God going to monitor all the squabbles? If a combatant picks up a tire iron or a broken bottle and starts swinging it out of control, or with malicious intent, will God intervene? How can my administration prevent anarchy?"

Another cool ripple of air wafted through the room as Sarah said, "It is still the duty of your administration to protect against border incursions and crime. But while law enforcement personnel and the military are no longer able to shoot to *kill*, peacekeepers can still use crowd dispersal equipment, like tear gas, rubber bullets, water cannons, tasers, and even clubs to hit people on their arms or legs if unchecked violence erupts. But when somebody—on either side of a skirmish—attacks with the intent to kill, that person will die. Killing is killing, whether the act is premeditated or committed in a froth of rage."

Cummings nodded tersely. It seemed such a fine line to navigate in such an angry world.

Once more reading his thoughts, Sarah said kindly, "Take heart, Samuel. It will soon be clear to everybody that hatred, intolerance, and greed are not acceptable to God—and as we report the number of people who die each day because they tried to take another's life, you can expect the level of rage in the world to drop very quickly."

"Along with an exponential increase in religious belief," said Angelica Lopez, as she fingered a tiny, silver cross that hung on a delicate chain around her neck.

"Yes," agreed Sarah. "As the true nature of God becomes better understood, the religions of the world will grow closer together, which will further reduce tensions around the globe."

"Hallelujah!" said Lopez enthusiastically.

Then she crossed herself, which made Cummings realize that she was probably Catholic, given her Hispanic background. He'd never really considered the religions of his cabinet members, and he wondered how they were reconciling their belief systems, whatever they were, with the message Sarah was bringing. Certainly, her words were a departure from everything he'd been taught in the Anglican church of his parents.

"It's sure going to cause a huge shift in thinking," he remarked, exhaling slowly as he thought of the ramifications.

"Yes," agreed Sarah. "I expect there will be great turmoil within religious institutions as they come to grips with God's simple message . . . not to mention when they realize that women are the dominant gender in the life force that is God."

President Cummings reflected upon Sarah's words for a moment and then said, "That turmoil will be all through society . . . and it's going to be a pretty horrific adjustment in the short term. How will countries that rely on military might, like Russia and North Korea, survive? Russia's economy is comparable to that of Texas. It's about the same size and pretty much based on oil and gas, which, as we know, has a questionable long-term outlook. And North Korea has lots of military bluster but almost no economy at all. I can see full-scale revolution in these places if standards of living drop any lower. I wouldn't want to be the one trying to maintain control of one of *those* governments."

"Yes, countries with little economic power will face many challenges," agreed Sarah, "but make no mistake, your country will face challenges too. Losing your military superpower status will result in a massive decline in U.S. influence around the globe. And since you have such a protectionist economy, don't expect other countries to want to do you favours."

"It's true we have a protectionist economy," cut in Feldman defensively, "but it has created jobs and kept money in our coffers. What's wrong with that?"

Cummings nodded his agreement. He had been working with the secretary of the treasury on economic strategies to boost the U.S. economy for the past two years, and he was satisfied with how Norman Feldman was performing. So when Sarah's golden tinkle permeated the room, Cummings wondered why she was laughing.

He soon found out.

"Yes," she said, "you have indeed improved some aspects of your economy, but at what cost? The United States is not exactly a favourite trading partner with those who have to pay high prices for the privilege. Can you truly tell me that you don't rely on your identity as a military powerhouse to broker deals? What happens when you no longer have any muscle? You may want to think about the rights of other nations to demand fair compensation. How much do your people love coffee? Or sugar?"

Cummings was taken aback at the thought. A lack of military might could certainly change the economic landscape, and protectionist economics might become a straw to break the camel's back.

"This country without coffee is *not* an option," said Vice President Lopez. "We have a lot of rethinking to do."

"You do," said Sarah. "And think about this as well: The United States defines its national identity by the Second Amendment... and the minute you leave this time suspension, the right to bear arms will mean *nothing*."

Cummings had a vision of Clint Eastwood as *Dirty Harry*, saying, "Go ahead, make my day," while pointing his .44 Magnum at the bad guy holding the waitress hostage in *Sudden Impact*. This was what many Americans, and all members of the National Rifle Association, liked to think they were—heroes who were rough around the edges but always on the moral high ground.

Reading his thoughts again, Sarah said, "Long guns and shotguns will probably still be manufactured, Samuel, even if most gun manufacturers and defence companies go belly-up. I imagine a remnant of the NRA will be around for a while too. Americans will want to keep their handguns... and, as long as they don't shoot to kill, they can."

"Do you think people will ever give up their guns voluntarily?" asked Hana Shriver. "And if so, how long do you think it will take?"

"One or two generations," Sarah said, "but before that happens, your country—and the rest of the world—will need to make a cultural shift from one that glorifies guns, weapons, and violence to one that values a life centred on peaceful living and the acquisition of joy. Acquiring joy can only be accomplished by serving and loving others. So many people struggle with this. But it is simply the golden rule. There is no mystery to treating others as you would be treated yourself."

Cummings rubbed his nonexistent beard again. He was just as guilty as anyone else of enjoying countless movies featuring well-muscled men fighting the odds to singularly take down tanks, assassins, enemy agents, and the like.

"Hollywood's not going to like that," he said, partly in jest.

"No," agreed Sarah. "People in the entertainment industry have made billions of dollars promoting violence, whether by glorifying successful military missions or celebrating the killing of undesirable individuals."

"Books, blogs, movies, and songs celebrating war and killing should be strictly controlled—or even better, destroyed," said Shriver vehemently, and once more, Cummings was left to wonder if she had experienced something tied to war that he was unaware of.

Sarah emanated compassion as she looked at Hana Shriver. "Hana, you are so right," she said, the scent of roses wafting once more in her energetic breeze. "So long as such items remain available to influence people, innocents—particularly children—are vulnerable to their messages of hatred, revenge, and death. Political leaders will need to address this issue globally."

"Are we talking censorship?" asked Bradley Northrup, clearly worried.

"Not censorship of the *truth*," Sarah reassured him.

"What do you mean by that?" asked Cummings. "If you're talking about making books about war unavailable, that's censorship, plain and simple."

"But I'm not," said Sarah. "I'm talking about limiting fictional entertainment that glorifies violence. History, such as books about World War II, is a reminder of how far humans have come—but *fictional* violence glorifies the hunt and desensitizes people to the true horror of war."

"What about video games?" asked Shriver, an edge to her voice and hard glitter in her eyes. "Sometimes, I wonder at the games my son plays online. He balks when we try to limit his time with them, but it gives me a sick feeling to know he's pretending to kill others, even if it's not real."

"And so it should," said Sarah solemnly, "because you are human, and you feel God's touch in your heart."

Then she caught the eyes of each person in the room one by one, and Cummings could feel a hint of winter in her tone.

"Such games are an insidious threat," she said fiercely. "They encourage young people to directly engage in virtual killing, which is in opposition to the idea of a non-killing culture."

Shriver nodded sagely, clearly in agreement. Northrup didn't look so convinced.

Sarah's tone deepened to the baritone vibration again as she said, "Such games must be destroyed immediately. Any world leader who fails to take this step will be considered an enabler and will die if one of their citizens is inspired to attempt to kill somebody due to the influence of such a game."

President Cummings was shocked. "Now, wait a minute," he protested, "how can an act of aggression be linked directly to the use of a video game? Not every kid who plays video games grows up twisted!"

Sarah sighed softly, sending another hair-ruffling breeze around the room. "God has the capacity to make this link," she said, "just as God knows who the attempted killer is when two people fight. Only one of them will drop dead."

"Direct justice by the hand of God is going to be very difficult for people to understand and accept," noted Cummings in awe and uncertainty.

"Who better to put your faith in, Samuel?" Sarah asked gently.

"I can see why you didn't need the attorney general here," said Gordon Blackstone. "If God is judge and jury when it comes to killings, and dead bodies are proof of guilt, then judicial systems all over the world will change dramatically, and the AG will be out of a job."

"Don't be so dire," said Angelica Lopez dryly. "We'll still be locking up rapists, drug dealers, and child molesters. The courts aren't going away any time soon." Then she looked at Sarah and said, "Unless there's something you haven't told us?"

"No, Angelica," Sarah said, "though in a few generations, when the cultural shift is complete, God expects the types of crimes you have mentioned to diminish as an offshoot of this intervention."

Blackstone stifled a nervous laugh as he said, "There will be no need for homicide investigators, lengthy trials, jail terms, or capital punishment for killers!"

"And there will no longer be any reason for the public to question whether the administration of justice was tainted," added Shriver with a small smile.

"No," said Sarah. "Justice will be quick and lethal if anyone tries to kill another."

"You know what?" asked Lopez. "It's something of a relief. I don't know about the rest of you, but this whole thing makes me feel safer. It feels *right*."

Lopez and Shriver exchanged a glance, and Cummings saw Shriver nod. He suddenly understood that these two women were friends, and that both of them welcomed the news that Sarah brought in a way he and his male colleagues did not.

"Ladies," said Sarah gently, in a rush of warm air, to the vice president and the senate head, "do you have anything you wish to add?"

Lopez spoke up. "Only that I am 100% on board, Sarah. Killing is wrong, and teaching children that it's *not* wrong is even worse."

She suddenly thought of her eleven-year-old twin daughters, Audrey and Arianna, in bed right now, hopefully asleep. Her husband, Andrew, would have read a chapter of Tolkien's *The Lord of the Rings* to them as a final treat before lights-out. The girls were big *Hobbit* fans and desperately wanted to see the classic movie trilogy, but she and Andrew decided to introduce them to the books first. Nighttimes had been lovely as they explored Frodo's big adventure . . . but once the fighting and wars started, Angelica was surprised to find out how strongly she wanted to stop reading the book. The violence left her anxious, though she tried not to show that to her girls. Now she wished she had. She hoped they were dreaming of hobbits, and not war.

"You're not wrong," Sarah said to the vice president, reading her thoughts and sending a soft ripple of air toward her. "War, even fictional war, is hard to digest. Your human heart wants lightness, kindness. And so does God."

Angelica smiled. "Thank you," she said, feeling validated.

Then Sarah asked, "Gentlemen? Do you have anything to add to this part of the discussion before we move on?"

Norman Feldman spoke up. "Sarah, I have some questions about the financial and economic implications of the intervention."

The golden tinkle of energy returned as Sarah said, "Yes, I thought you might, Norman. Let's move on to that topic, shall we?"

Feldman smiled, and Cummings could see he was relieved.

Chapter 6

Financial and Economic Response

Sarah got right down to business. "Norman," she said, "as you suggested earlier, a one-week global shutdown of all financial markets will be required so the world can 'reset,' if you will."

"That's a tall order," replied Feldman. "We're going to need to maintain domestic banking networks."

"And to restrict withdrawals to normal levels. We don't need panic withdrawals, or the system will collapse," Cummings added, still a little overwhelmed at the short turnaround time they had to compile the information the public would need to know.

"Maybe we need to create a fact sheet, a 'do and don't' sort of thing that we can post on the website Angelica is going to put together," suggested Feldman. "I could work on that."

"You'd better work fast," said Lopez. "When Sarah removes the time suspension, we'll have only twenty-four hours to let people know what's happening, or we're going to all be dead. We're going to have to hit the ground running."

"I'm working as fast as I can," said Feldman with a baleful glare. Then he began hammering away at his computer keys.

Cummings saw one of his eyes twitch. The man was clearly stressed.

In her calming, transcendent way, Sarah stepped into the fray. "Now, now," she breathed, instantly quelling the anxiety in the room. "An orderly transition to this new world requires that we work harmoniously. Surely we can agree to set personal differences aside? The well-being of the millions of souls who live in America is at stake."

A man of action, Feldman nodded tersely in agreement but kept typing.

Lopez politely said, "Of course, Sarah."

"Wonderful," Sarah said, her words like a rustle of wind through grass. "We need to work together to make sure things unfold as God means for them to. We all want the same thing, am I right? Peace, order, and understanding."

There were uncomfortable glances around the room, but in the end, there was a communal nod which indicated to them all that they were on the same page.

"How do you see the public briefing unfolding, Sarah?" asked Cummings. "What is your advice?"

"Well," Sarah said, sending a rose-scented breeze out with her words. "You will need to call a press conference within the first hour to announce the no-killing edict. Then you and all other heads of state will speak concurrently to your respective people, Samuel. You will tell them God's will. You will tell them what to expect."

"As God's emissary, shouldn't you be communicating it yourself?" asked Cummings.

"No," said Sarah, "every country needs to hear the message from their leaders first—the heads of their own tribes, as it were. Your words will pave the way for me, and then I will deliver the same message later on social media, around the globe, and in every language on Earth."

"You're going to have your own social media accounts?" asked Hana Shriver in disbelief.

"What better way to reach the masses?" Sarah questioned with a laugh, sending a tickle of joy into Cummings' belly, a sensation he was starting to enjoy. "And not only will I have my own accounts, but I am fully capable of hijacking the accounts of every 'influencer' or celebrity who might currently be using social media to stoke hatred, envy, or other undesirable emotions—and I intend to do so. It is by far the quickest way to spread God's message."

"Well, I think you have more to say than your average Kardashian," noted Angelica Lopez dryly, followed by the question, "What happens next?"

"Next, after Samuel here has spoken to the press," Sarah replied, waving a fluttery, almost iridescent arm toward him, "the head of every central bank will make a joint announcement alongside all the 'Normans' of the world, announcing steps to protect the banking system and international trade, including the news about the one-week market closure."

"Got it," said Feldman. "As soon as we're out of this . . . um . . . time suspension, I will get in touch with Graydon Pierce, the Chair of the Federal Reserve. But I'm a little concerned that when I phone him to tell him what's happening, he won't believe me."

"Not to worry, Norman," reassured Sarah. "I'm speaking concurrently with Mr. Pierce so that he, too, can prepare for this momentous event."

Cummings was quiet, absorbing the magnitude of what they were facing. "Sarah," he finally said, "there are a myriad of problems that might occur with this change, and I think we'll have to announce some solutions if we want our people to remain calm. In particular, I'm worried about the impact these changes will have on the defence industry. Many jobs, not to mention billions of dollars of investments, will be wiped out. I expect governments around the world will need to bail out some folks."

"Yes," Sarah agreed, "the gun industry will lose not only its value, but its allure—yet consider this, Samuel . . . when a hole is made in the sand, water rushes in to fill it, don't you think?"

"I see what you're trying to say, Sarah," Cummings said, "but sand and economies are different things."

"Are they?" asked Sarah, not expecting an answer.

"Other jobs will be created in the long-term, I'm sure . . . but in the short term, a lot of people are going to be upset. It's going to take a while for the country to rebound."

"There will most certainly be aftershocks throughout the financial industry," Feldman agreed, looking up from his computer. "It will probably be like the financial crisis of 2008. Specialized companies will take a hit, but conglomerates will survive—they always do."

"You paint a bleak picture, Norman," said Lopez.

"Sorry," replied Feldman. "The good news is that once we call Blackstone's troops home, this country will have more liquid capital than it's seen for a long, long time."

"That's definitely a positive," said Cummings, who was still trying to sort out his thoughts. "If we use that money wisely, it will definitely motivate people to embrace God's changes more quickly."

"Yes," agreed Lopez. "We will be able to create domestic programs to inspire people and create loyalty."

"Loyalty to the Democrats?" asked Shriver pointedly.

"Not necessarily," said Cummings, trying to smooth what he saw as ruffled feathers. "More so loyalty to the country and to the democratic process."

Shriver wrinkled her nose, clearly not believing him.

Sarah chose that moment to cut in, her gentle, airy words bringing an aura of peace back into the room. "It will not be easy in many parts of the world when these changes take effect," she said. "In countries like Russia and North Korea, where the military is used to suppress people, currencies will crash and people will suffer. You," she looked directly at Cummings, "along with global leaders around the world, must play your part well and lead by example. Do you understand?"

"I do," said Cummings, more firmly than he felt. "You're saying we have to create exemplary domestic policy to keep things on an even-keel in America while these changes take effect."

From her spot on the couch, Lopez—a bit frustrated at the president's failure to see the bigger picture, said, "Samuel, she's also saying we should create global outreach strategies to help the 'have-nots' that will be left hanging when military dictatorships fail."

"Well said," Sarah breathed at the vice president in a warm, satisfied way.

"And I'm going to go out on a limb, here," Lopez added, "by assuming that political and religious differences are not to be a factor in any humanitarian efforts we make . . . am I right, Sarah?"

"Yes," Sarah said.

Cummings saw her starlit pupils expand and contract in what he could only assume was approval of his vice president's words. It was a noble idea, to give aid no matter what the circumstances . . . but Cummings wondered what U.S. aid to Afghanistan would look like. Would Muslim leaders even accept aid from a primarily Christian country? Would they appreciate it, or would they just use it to fund non-lethal, but still horrendous, ways to further their fight with the infidels?

Sarah sensed his thoughts; He could tell by the darkening irises that she turned on him, and the flickering of the stars within them. "Soon the world will know that God is not what they thought," she told him softly. "And when they do, so much hostility and misunderstanding will cease. And kindness will be accepted and returned in kind. It will be a different global stage."

He sighed. "Yes," he said wearily, "but a great deal of religious and social turmoil will kick up first. It will take a while for people to really get their heads around God's true nature."

"It will," agreed Sarah.

"And then, when we announce the biological interventions that will be coming . . . well, I hate to think what will happen. People—especially men—will find it *immensely* threatening. I know I do."

Feldman looked up from his laptop at that moment. "I've done some preliminary calculations about what downsizing our defence industry will mean to this country," he said. "As near as I can tell, it will increase our trade deficit by nearly 50% and cause the stock market to fall by at least 10%. Basically, the financial influence of the U.S. will fall dramatically."

"That sounds kind of extreme, Norman," said Bradly Northrup, who for the greater part of the meeting had been sitting quietly, keeping minutes for the group in the old 'pen and paper' style that he preferred.

"Maybe it *does*," agreed Feldman, "but if I'm right, within ten years, our global debt and equity markets will not represent anywhere *near* what we currently enjoy."

Shriver, who Cummings noted was frowning and looking somewhat perplexed, spoke then. "Our debt could become a real problem," she said. "What if the world moves to a reserve currency other than the American dollar?"

There was something of a smirk on her face when she said the words, which made Cummings instantly suspicious. He wondered, *is she secretly pleased that a Democratic president is going to be blamed when the American economy crumbles, even though it's mostly the fault of the Republicans?* He frowned in consternation. The Republican senate had been blocking Democratic initiatives for more than a decade.

Sarah immediately read his thoughts, and the waft of cold air she projected toward him was not comfortable in any way. He looked around the room and did not see any of his colleagues indicating discomfort, so he understood that, once again, she had singled him out for a side talk.

"Her loyalties lie with what is *fair*," chastised Sarah wordlessly, "and so should yours."

"They do not!" he insisted. "Nearly every good idea my party has gets blocked by her cronies in the senate. They oppose *anything* that improves the standard of living for the normal, working people of this country."

"Oh you are so *dramatic*, Samuel!" Sarah said, amused.

"Am I?" he asked hotly. "The world is facing unprecedented change, but she is still looking at things in an 'us and them' way. How am I to effectively lead when I know I will be blocked at every turn?

"I understand," Sarah whispered, and for the first time since she'd appeared to him, she seemed to breath out colour with her words, a turquoise mist that smelled like carnations and made him instantly calm.

Then the two of them 'returned' to the presence of the others, which was a little jarring to Samuel—sort of like dropping out of one movie and into another—and the calmness dissipated.

Tension returned to his heart and mind the second he heard Norman Feldman say nervously, "Engaging in business bailouts is going to be *extremely* unpopular from a political perspective. How do you feel about that, Samuel?"

Jarred by the question and feeling somewhat on the spot, Cummings was at a loss for words—but only for a moment. Seizing control of the conversation, he shot from the hip. "Norman," he said in as jovial a tone as he could muster, "I feel lower than a snake's belly. How do you *think* I feel?"

The rhetorical question was an unexpected response, and Feldman looked at him in surprise.

"I don't think popularity is the issue here, do you?" Cummings asked, before turning to Sarah and quipping, "Sarah, as long as God is intervening, can we send all the financial people to Mars?"

The comment lightened the mood in the room.

Even Feldman laughed. "If we downsize the military, we might have enough money to do it," he said. "Sign me up!"

Cummings suddenly felt stronger and more in charge than he had for the previous part of the meeting. Motivated, he said, "We're not going to let the challenges before us diminish America's role as a world leader."

"Hear, hear," said Northrup, applauding lightly.

"As Sarah has pointed out," Cummings said, "we will be in an enviable position compared to most other countries. Think about this: We will no longer be spending almost a *trillion* dollars a year on interfering in other people's politics with our military might. I say we should brainstorm, right now, about ways to use that money to rejuvenate our economy. If we announce even one key, positive plan for reenergizing our economy when we announce the edict, it will make a huge difference to people."

At that, he glanced at Sarah to let her know he was trusting and moving ahead as she had asked him to. She flittered lightly, and glowed brightly for a moment, indicating approval. *She is the most beautiful thing I have ever seen,* thought Samuel, infused with fresh joy at the sight.

"Good idea, and with all that money, we might even reduce our government deficit a bit," said Lopez with a sly grin, looking at Feldman out of the corner of her eye.

He frowned slightly; Clearly, he didn't find the comment as funny as she did.

Enthused, Cummings said to the group, "Okay, people. Now let's figure out what we are going to tell the citizens of the United States about this new world. We need to come up with messages about the benefits."

"Let's focus on three or four major initiatives to get our economy, markets and people on the right footing," suggested Feldman.

"Good idea, Norman," said Cummings lightly. He was feeling remarkably motivated and energetic. "I suggest we start with ideas about what to do with disenfranchised troops. If we come up with some good solutions, we can present the sugar with the medicine, so to speak."

"I have some ideas on that," said Defence Secretary Blackstone.

"Gordon, the floor is yours," replied Cummings.

"Thank you," said Blackstone. "The Army Corp of Engineers could be redeployed on infrastructure projects that never quite seem to get to the top of our political agendas. Buttressing our shorelines to help offset the impacts of rising sea levels could also become a specialty."

"Good," said Cummings, "I like where you're going with this. Anything else?"

"Well," said Blackstone, "I like Sarah's suggestion about turning our aircraft carriers into floating hospitals. This will make us a leader in disaster mitigation, and it will also provide long-term employment for medical officers and sailors."

Cummings could see the wheels turning in the minds of the assembled group as the possibilities began surfacing. "I like it," he said to Blackstone. "Go on."

"We could redeploy our radar system experts to upgrade civilian air navigation. Our air force bases could be converted to public airports or cargo plane depots—or they could even become space launch sites."

"Good, good," Cummings said, grinning broadly. "It's high time we reestablished clear leadership in the space race. We could make a mission to Mars a national priority—that is, if Elon Musk doesn't get there first. He's come so close. Maybe he'd partner with us."

"Naval assets could be repurposed to help the Coast Guard," Blackstone continued, "or to support ocean-based research, particularly research to do with climate change."

"I like that idea," cut in Angelica Lopez. "What's the point of saving us all from our own wicked ways if we continue destroying the planet and wind up with no home? Good thinking, Gordon."

Despite the slight element of hostility that generally existed between Lopez and Blackstone, Cummings noticed that her comment seemed to sit well with the man. As much as the rather serious, ominously tense Blackstone could crack a smile, he did.

It looked a little like a fissure in a piece of granite, but Cummings kept that thought to himself, asking only, "What else do you have, Gordon?"

"Disarming our ships and planes, and safely dismantling and destroying missiles, bombs, and weapons of mass destruction, will require considerable expertise—which a large military workforce is well-suited for," he said.

"Yes, indeed," replied Cummings. "We covered some of that with our discussion about land mines but keep going—you're on a roll."

Blackstone nodded. "Steel recycling will be a large financial opportunity for the country, and troops could be redeployed to do that . . ."

Feldman suddenly jumped into the fray, exclaiming, "Great idea! It will generate significant revenue . . ." then he stopped and seemed to think better of it, adding, ". . . although global competition *will* be fierce."

Ignoring the enthusiastic interruption, Blackstone picked up where he'd left off. "Another thought," he said, addressing Cummings, "is that we have large military bases across the country which could be made safe, and then sold. Some of these sites would be attractive for wind or solar power generation."

"Excellent thought!" exclaimed Cummings. "Well done, Gordon! These are great ideas."

Cummings looked over at Northrup. "Are you getting this?" he asked.

"You bet," said Northrup. "I've written it all down."

"Thanks, Bradley," Cummings said. Then he turned back to Blackstone, saying, "Your ideas are great and just what we need for our public announcement. Let's work on a news release and fact sheet, and we'll promise people an action plan within a month. Just the high level points for now, though, to put anxious minds at ease. We can work on the details and timelines later. I really think redeploying troops to work on national infrastructure improvements is a gem of a thought, and it sounds doable."

"Agreed," said Blackstone. "However, even with all the suggestions I've made, there will still be large numbers of personnel left hanging who will have to be integrated into the private sector. We should be generous with offering ongoing benefits and severance to make this as painless as possible for our loyal troops."

"And maybe we should consider giving similar support to the 2 million American civilians who will lose their jobs when the defence industry shuts down," suggested Hana Shriver unexpectedly.

Cummings furrowed his brows at her words, clearly surprised by her sentiments—and truthfully, she was *just* as surprised. She hadn't meant to say that out loud; It was just a thought that somehow managed to jump out of her throat. Normally, she prided herself on her sternness, stoicism, and ability to toe the party line, which certainly wasn't to promote 'handouts'— as some members of her party viewed subsidies—to the unemployed. Shriver had worked hard to cultivate an iron shell. In her job, a thick skin and no-nonsense nature were necessary to prove to the powerful, rich men who dominated her party, and her politics, just how tough she was. Soft sentiments were not to seep out . . . yet, surprisingly, they *had*.

She wondered if Sarah's presence was chipping away at her walls, softening her fight, and bringing out a level of compassion she preferred to keep buried. If so, she would have to double her efforts to keep sentiment at bay. Her well-cultivated, tough exterior had led her to the coveted seat of Senate Majority Leader, and she was not going to lose that hard-won spot by getting a reputation as a weakling.

She glanced at Cummings, who met her eyes, and she could read the unbridled surprise in them.

"That's a great idea, Hana," Cummings told her.

"Thank you," she replied in a somewhat regal tone, trying to communicate that she was not likely to make such a suggestion again.

Cummings smiled, but she maintained a poker face.

Blackstone rubbed his forehead, clearly pondering something. He cleared his throat, and the rest of the group looked at him. "I have to add a note of caution," he said, "before we go too far down the road of downsizing the military. We should talk about how we're going to secure our borders, and protect ourselves from domestic terrorism or other acts of insurgence. Killing may be off the table, but there are other ways to threaten a nation."

"I hear you, Bradley," said Cummings. "You just can't trust those Canadians, can you?" he joked. When laughter at the idea of the friendly nation to the north being aggressive had died down, he followed up with, "And who knows? Maybe Mexico wants Texas back."

"Hey, Texas is my home state," Lopez quickly cut in, "and sometimes, I wish it *was* part of Mexico! They have better mariachi music."

Cummings smiled at her comment. "That is one of my favourite types of music too," he confided, somehow inordinately pleased to find out he had this in common with his vice president. She smiled back, and a little ice he hadn't even known was in his heart shifted. He suddenly realized he'd been more threatened by her than he had ever suspected.

Inadvertently, he stole a glance at Sarah, who was emitting a dusky shade of pink along with the rose scent. He could tell she'd understood the self-revelation he'd just had—and clearly she approved.

Then he shifted his focus back to Blackstone. "We'll still need strong military intelligence capability," his defence secretary continued, "along with the ability to move troops to hot zones quickly—and we'll also need to work on non-lethal crowd suppression methods. I don't think rubber bullets and tasers are going to cut it in the long run."

"Yes," agreed Lopez, who'd clearly been thinking along the same lines. "We'll need to keep *some* ground, air, and sea bases operational. And we'll need our military satellites too."

"But even with these things in place, we still won't be spending *nearly* as much on our military as we have been," Cummings pointed out.

"No," agreed Feldman. "However, if you were having visions of funding a *national* infrastructure plan with former military assets, we're going to have to come up with something less ambitious."

"The idea of a national plan for upgrading infrastructure has been tossed around for years, but it's never been put into action," Cummings said.

"Because the military traditionally gets the lion's share of funding," remarked Lopez.

"Yes," agreed Cummings.

"We could create an incentive program for state governments," said Feldman. "If we offer to pay 50% for airports, bridges, and roads, I bet they'll bite."

"Good thinking, Norman," Cummings told the treasury secretary. Then he looked over at Hana Shriver. She was sitting, tight-lipped, an island unto herself, the lone Republican in the room. "Hana," said the president, "as the senate majority leader, you have some say in these things. I, for one, think it would be a shame for such great ideas to be . . . well . . . shoved under the table."

Shriver gazed coolly at him and said nothing, so Cummings tried again. "It's about time we faced a challenge big enough to put aside bipartisan politics and unite our country. I promise you, whatever efforts this group makes will be recorded as a shared victory. Are you with me?"

She deliberately paused before speaking, thinking hard about how to phrase her answer. Finally, she said, "I guess that depends on what projects we are speaking of and the feasibility of them."

Cummings could see the tension in her body as she spoke. It seemed as if she was fighting some unknowable war inside herself.

Somewhat exasperated at her reluctance to get on board, he said, "Come on, Hana. The situation we are in right now is unlike anything that's ever happened to the Earth before! This is a chance to address some serious problems in this country. Will you work with us on these initiatives, as a partner?"

The look she gave him was one of mistrust, and he was immediately reminded of how he'd felt earlier, when wondering if she was glad his party—and not *hers*—would be stuck with whatever economic crisis God's intervention caused.

And then suddenly, there was a whoosh of air that was almost supersonic in nature, and Cummings instantly forgot his resentment. Panicked, he wondered, *did Sarah implode? Are we under attack?* Impulsively, he ducked and shut his eyes, awaiting the feeling of shrapnel raining down on him—but nothing happened.

When he raised his head again, he felt quite disoriented . . . and he had reason to be. He was no longer in the Oval Office, sitting at his desk. Instead, he was in a peaceful setting that he took to be a park. He was sitting on a bench in front of a large pond, his desk nowhere to be seen. He looked out at the pond. It was exceedingly beautiful, with pink, blooming waterlilies on top, and ducks paddling to and fro between them.

"What the hell?" he muttered.

He looked at his hands; They appeared normal, and the wedding ring Lorena had lovingly put on his finger forty years ago was still in place. He looked to his left side to see a young couple with a baby carriage strolling past, laughing as they held hands and cooed at the little bundle of joy they were pushing. He looked to his right and saw a man walking a small fluffy dog. The dog was proudly carrying a tiny, orange ball, which looked comical and made him smile. He looked down at his feet. He was wearing his favourite runners, something he would do on a Saturday when he was taking time for himself by going for a long walk. The sight of his comfortable shoes made him feel instantly at peace—though he had no idea where he was, or why he was there.

"Samuel?" he heard a woman ask. There was confusion and perhaps a little fear in her voice.

He looked up and saw Hana Shriver, her black hair messy, her stern 'lady suit' somewhat askew, and incongruous, fuzzy bunny slippers on her feet. He had never seen her look vulnerable before, but she did now. She looked like someone who wants nothing more than to be cuddling on the sofa with a good book and a cup of tea.

"Hello, Hana," he said, and not really sure what else to say, he added, "Won't you sit down?"

She walked over and sat down on the bench, a respectable foot or so away from him. She wrapped her arms around herself as if she was cold, though it was a balmy day in this mysterious park. Cummings noted a bag of peanuts on the seat between them. He could not think how it got there; He hadn't noticed it before. He picked it up and offered her one. She took it.

"Thanks," she said as she removed the shell and ate the nuts inside.

He noted that she carefully put the shell in her pocket, not wanting to litter this amazing place they had found themselves in. He followed suit, and the two of them sat in silence, eating peanuts, waiting . . .

Inevitably, a bright, golden light began streaming from the sky, casting its reflection into the crystal clear pond in front of them. Then there was a flash that reminded Cummings of a magic trick he'd seen in a theatre once, and suddenly, Sarah stood, glowing, in front of them.

"Hello," she said, the rose scent drifting toward the two of them as it floated from where she hovered over two ducks, who were innocently floating on the pond. "What do you think of my version of a place where two warring tribal leaders can create peace?" she asked.

Cummings and Shriver looked at each other in surprise, and then back at Sara.

"Warring?" asked Cummings. "I don't think it's *that* bad."

"Isn't it?" asked Sarah. "You are products of a political system that encourages discord instead of cooperation. All that narrative may be disguised as 'checks and balances,' but everyone knows the truth. It's a game where each tries to block the other's moves. In the end, no one wins."

Guiltily, Shriver decided to take the bull by the horns. "You're talking about my unwillingness to accept the olive branch Samuel offered me," she said.

"Yes," agreed Sarah, "and also Samuel's inability to trust *you*."

Shriver looked at Cummings, assessing him with interest. It's not that she expected him to feel any differently—after all, they were of opposite political stripes—but it was still unsettling to hear it.

"I've brought you here to speed up the so-called 'checks and balances,'" said Sarah. "You will work things out here so we can move ahead in peace and harmony. It will save so much time, don't you think?"

They knew it would be pointless to object, and so both of them nodded. Cummings couldn't help but admire Sarah's creativity; This setting, and the way he was dressed, created in him a sense of possibility. He wondered if it did the same for Hana Shriver.

"Let's start with the two biggest issues that have traditionally divided your political parties—abortion and guns," began Sarah. "Since God has made both of these issues disappear, you are going to have to find new things to fight about."

She seemed to find her own words funny, and she sent out the golden tinkle to vibrate in their innards. As usual, Cummings felt a shudder of joy course through him, but immediately after that, he felt sheepish. She was right. He and Hana were hanging onto old emotions in a new situation. Things had changed, and they would have to change as well.

As if reading his mind, Sarah emitted to the two of them, "You two need to find common ground, and then teach your people how to find the same place. Do you understand?"

They both nodded. Cummings noticed that Shriver had relaxed a little and was no longer folded into herself as she had been.

Sarah continued. "Let's start with immigration. In this country, you're *all* immigrants, except for the Indigenous people. Can you two agree on that?"

Again, both of them nodded. Cummings own lineage was Irish on his father's side and Hungarian on his mother's. He wondered about Shriver's; All he knew was that her grandmother was Japanese. Then he wondered if she was related, perhaps by marriage, to the Shriver family associated with the Kennedys. He decided against it. She was far too staunch a Republican to have Democrats in her closet.

Looking at each of them, her starry pupils shining bright, Sarah then asked, "Can you agree that immigration is important to the future of the United States?"

Samuel nodded a strong affirmation, but Hana was a bit hesitant in agreeing. "There is a difference in my mind between immigrants and refugees," she said cautiously.

"Ah, yes," Sarah responded, "your party is concerned about the financial burden of refugees. But Hana, God has ended war and killing. People will no longer need to seek refuge from war zones."

"Okay," said Hana cautiously, "Given that, I could back down on my stance on immigration."

Sarah then asked, "What about income inequality? Do you both agree that pay equity should be the standard, no matter what gender or race a person is?"

Hana was hesitant in her response. "My party is enormously resistant to upsetting the applecart of white male privilege," she said, "so from a party solidarity standpoint, I'd have to say 'no.' However, on a personal level, I would very much like to see equal pay for work of equal value across our nation—so yes, I guess I could support that."

Cummings looked at her intently, regarding the serious demeanor and guarded look on her face. He suddenly had a sense of how hard she'd probably had to fight to attain the senior position of senate majority leader, and he felt a grudging respect for her that he'd never allowed himself to feel before.

He said, "I feel the same way you do, Hana."

"It might grease Republican palms if we prorate pay equity based on regional differences in the cost of living," Hana said cautiously. "That way, we might be able to get buy-in."

"That's a detail that can be worked out later," Sarah said with an energetic flutter. "I just want you two to think in general terms for the moment, okay?"

"Okay," they both said.

Then Sarah asked, "My next question is, what do you two think of a minimum wage high enough for people to live on?"

"You know I'm for it," said Cummings with no hesitation, but the question made Hana squirm in her seat. As with pay equity, *personally*, she thought it was a good idea; However, Republican donors had a history of lobbying against it.

There was a warm rush of lilac-scented air. Cummings saw the surface of the pond ripple at this delightful intrusion of a breeze, though one of the ducks quacked in alarm.

Finally, after a few moments of thinking about it, Hana said, "I could agree to it."

"Good!" said Sarah, flashing brightly with delight, her many visages moving quickly across the screen of her face, leaving the impression of a broad smile.

Finally, Sarah lobbed the hardest question of all at them, a political hot potato that had been bandied back and forth between Republicans and Democrats for almost a century.

"Samuel and Hana," she asked in the baritone voice Cummings knew meant she wanted their undivided attention, "can the two of you *ever* agree on a plan for universal health care? It's a travesty that America has the highest quality of health care in the world, but that only the wealthy can *afford* it."

"We also have the highest drug costs and over-consumption of medicine," added Cummings sourly. "We've been brainwashed into believing pills solve *everything,* from erectile dysfunction to hair loss."

Hana cautiously responded. "I agree with the idea of universal access to health care, as long as we don't destroy the private health insurance business. The COVID pandemic in the early 2020s taught this country a big lesson. I couldn't believe that frontline workers were paid so little that when they became ill themselves, they couldn't afford medical care. However, powerful companies and lobby groups will fight hard and dirty to protect the status quo."

"Hana, what if we jointly commissioned a task force of medical professionals and other experts, with no ties to the health care system and no political affiliations, to develop recommendations on the matter?" Cummings asked, trying to be conciliatory. "Do you think your party could support that?"

"Career-wise, it would be foolish for me to get behind that," she said with a sigh, "but maybe it's something I could convince *some* of my Republican colleagues to wrap their heads around."

Sarah's golden laughter floated out on a breeze toward them. "You are both so *resolute!*" she said airily, her words tinkling in the breeze. "You act as if you will be hung from the nearest tree if you back down on anything! Relax . . . God will see that your heads remain attached to your bodies. Now is a time to set examples, to support God's goal of a human race that is at one with itself. If you work together to unite the citizens of *your* country, other nations will look to your shining example. Step forward in trust and unity!"

Cummings looked at Shriver. She looked back at him. He saw a flicker of something in her eyes that seemed to be willingness.

"I'm good if you are," he said.

"Okay," she agreed. "We will work together on the things we've discussed here. I will support your initiatives to my Republican colleagues, as long as I personally agree that they are for the good of the country."

Cummings smiled . . . and then the same supersonic rush they had experienced before took over their consciousnesses, and they immediately found themselves back in the Oval Office with the rest of the group, who seemed unaware that they had ever left.

"You know," said Lopez, "if we're discussing infrastructure projects, I would say that fresh, clean water would be at the top of my list as a priority. Upgrading old piping could be a financially shared initiative. Think of those poor people in Flint, Michigan who got lead poisoning! Our cities need help with their plumbing."

"I agree," said Shriver firmly, causing several sets of eyes to turn to her in sudden surprise. "The scale of the problem is so large that federal incentives are the only way to repair old pipes on such a scale. Also, we have a chronic water shortage in the Southwest that will continue to get worse with climate change, and perhaps we could allocate some funds to solving that crisis before it gets worse."

"Do you think we can convince the wet states to service the dry ones?" asked Lopez thoughtfully. "They seem pretty protective of their water."

"We'll have to find ways to make water sharing attractive," said Cummings. Then, looking at Northrup, who was scribbling furiously, he asked, "Could you put that on the list, Bradley?" At Northrup's affirmative nod, he said, "Great!" Then he gazed around the room and asked, "Any other ideas?"

"Electric trains!" Lopez exclaimed.

Cummings suddenly remembered that before running for office, she'd been an award-winning environmental engineer—which explained why she was so excited about the idea of upgrading the rail system. "We are *decades* behind Europe and Asia with high-speed rail transportation," she said. "Japan and Europe put us to shame with their technology. Our existing systems are archaic."

"A high-speed train network would require long-term federal government support," said Feldman, with a covert glance at Shriver, who met his gaze evenly.

Addressing his unasked question, she replied, "In light of this unusual situation we are in, I am not going to stand in the way of any well-intentioned suggestions based on my *political* leanings. However, you can expect me to provide a sober second thought. Because I will."

Her words caused an almost imperceptible, shared sigh of relief in the room.

"Okay then," said Feldman. "Even if this is a bipartisan effort, it would take *decades* to build something like that," sniffed Feldman.

"It only took three years to build the First Transcontinental Railroad between Iowa and California," Lopez sniffed back.

"Different technology," argued Feldman. "Spikes, rails, horses, and cheap labor from China."

Lopez looked miffed.

Then Feldman looked down at his computer and added, "Did you know that bringing home our troops will reduce greenhouse gas emissions by nearly 10%, while an electric train system won't contribute as much to offsetting climate change for at least fifteen years?"

"That doesn't mean it's a bad idea," said Lopez, bristling at his lack of enthusiasm.

Cummings cut the argument-in-progress off. "I like the idea," he interjected, "but only if we draft legislation ensuring that incoming governments don't axe the project when our time at the helm is done. I'd hate to see such a major project get cancelled mid-stream by an incoming government putting their 'stamp' on things."

"Here's something to consider for generating funds," said Blackstone, who'd been sitting silently, mulling things over for the past twenty minutes. "Our military has a lot of valuable bandwidth tied up for intelligence purposes. If we're going to downsize the military, much of it could be freed up so 5G technology can be delivered on a competitive basis across the country. Money from that could be funneled into these big projects we're discussing."

"I *love* it, Gordon," said Cummings. "An extensive 5G network would make it easier for people to work from home, which ties in nicely to some environmental initiatives I hope we can work toward."

"I would really like to see this country recommit to environmental protection," said Lopez.

"What about electric vehicles?" asked Northrup. "Shouldn't we infuse that industry?"

"It depends how widely they are adopted," said Feldman cautiously.

Lopez was having none of that. "We should support our electric car manufacturers," said Lopez . "It's the way of the future . . . though we'll need renewable energy to support widespread adoption of electric vehicles. Perhaps we could use some of the money to invest in solar and wind power. California and Texas have demonstrated they are a viable energy production method."

"Yes," Feldman said, "but fracking technology has flooded the market with natural gas, and its price is so low that green electricity can't compete."

"Fracking is a threat to fresh water!" exclaimed Lopez, her eyes flashing. "It should be stopped."

"I agree," said Shriver. "It's going to take us down a road of wrong technology."

Lopez smiled gratefully at her for her support.

"Agreed, fracking is not sustainable," Cummings said. "But we're not going to convince the oil and gas companies of that, at least not right away."

It was an uncomfortable truth, and an impasse.

Silence reigned until Sarah broke it, saying in her soft, breezy way, "Samuel . . . it is your time to lead. What kind of country—what kind of world—do you want?"

Cummings immediately thought of his eleven-year-old granddaughter, Jessica, and six-year-old grandson, Jayson, children to his dentist daughter Laura and her partner, Leon. He wanted a cleaner environment and a more sustainable economy for *them*; However, he needed to apply the brakes while the world transitioned under the edict from God.

He sighed. "While I intend to grow the sustainable energy industry and work toward an economy that doesn't rely on oil and gas, right now, I think we should focus on initiatives that don't pose a threat to other industries. Upgrading infrastructure and building electric railways wins the day for me. We should use those as the anchor for our announcement."

"I agree," said Hana Shriver.

"So, we should sidestep anything to do with the oil and gas industry? No subsidies for creating fuel efficiencies?" asked Feldman.

"Yes, for now we should steer clear of it," Cummings said. "Let's just worry about getting God's message out, and announcing positive initiatives that the majority of people would welcome. We want to create optimism about the future, and we don't want to overwhelm people."

"Will you mention anything about reinvigorating the space program?" asked Blackstone. "You mentioned it earlier."

"Perhaps we could put that idea out to other world leaders as a *shared* goal," suggested Cummings. "It might provide a focal point for bringing the world together."

"It could be a multinational public-private endeavor!" said Shriver, showing excitement for the first time.

"It will likely cost more than a trillion dollars," Feldman warned.

"But isn't it worth it to foster a new, cooperative world?" Lopez shot at him.

"I have some very talented people who could contribute greatly to an enhanced space program," Blackstone said.

"The Russians and the Chinese do too, Gordon," said Cummings, "though we'd have to be scrub the military demeanor out of them." Then he chuckled as he added, "And we already have some passengers for the Mars Express! Don't forget, we're planning to send Norman and all the other finance people to Mars!"

Chapter 7

Calming the Public

When the laughter at Cummings' comment had died down, the business of drafting an announcement commenced.

"Who wants to take charge of writing this thing?" asked Lopez, looking at Cummings expectantly.

"I get the hint, Angelica," Cummings said, reading the anticipation on his vice-president's face and glancing around the room at his anxious colleagues. "Of course I'll do it—with input from all of you . . . and you as well, of course, Sarah," he said to the radiant being who was shimmering in front of his desk in her unearthly way.

"Samuel," Sarah said, "there is no need. I have taken the liberty of creating your announcement for you. It's already on your computer."

"It is?" asked Cummings in disbelief. He looked down at the open laptop on his desk and was pleasantly surprised to see speaking notes, fully created, open for his review. "How did you do that?" he gasped.

There was no answer from Sarah, except for her trademark golden tinkle.

Lopez, however, took the opportunity to arch one eyebrow in a 'Do you really have to ask?' manner and remarked, "She's of *God*, Samuel. She can pretty much do *anything*."

Briefly, Cummings wondered how Lopez could be so accepting of Sarah and her ways; He still had a hard time fully comprehending Sarah's magic. He supposed it had to do with Lopez's faith; The Catholic tradition was full of miracles. To Lopez, this was probably just one more.

He looked at the speech Sarah had written for him, quickly scanning a few lines. It was exactly what he would have written—better, even.

Impressed, he said, "This is amazing. Thank you, Sarah." Then he smiled and added, "Did you know how much I didn't want to draft this announcement in front of my colleagues? I'm a terrible typist. I still use the 'hunt and peck' style. I didn't want them to know." At his words, he caught a couple of knowing glances and smirks around the room; Clearly, they already knew. He laughed. "Quit making fun of me," he chastened lightly.

"Luckily for you, today, I am your assistant," said Sarah, emitting a gentle mist that reminded Cummings of what it felt like to step out of a shower into a steamy bathroom.

Suddenly, the magnitude of her powers struck him with an emotional force he did not expect. "No," he said with all the sincerity he could muster. "Today, I am *your* assistant."

Sarah emitted the rose scent at this, clearly a show of both pleasure and solidarity. Samuel felt flustered, but in a good way. He didn't have time to enjoy the moment, however.

Lopez was tapping her well-manicured fingernails, looking at him impatiently "Well?" she asked. "Aren't you going to read it to us?"

"Yes, of course," replied Cummings. "Take it easy, Angelica!" Then he cleared his throat and began.

My fellow Americans:

I stand before you today with a message I never, in all my life, expected to be communicating. What I am about to say to you will challenge the fabric of your belief systems and change how you view both life and death. All I can say is that if you don't believe my words, change channels. You will soon learn that what I say is concurrently being said by every government leader around the globe.

Thirty minutes ago, I was visited by a being sent directly from God, an emissary if you will. This being, called Sarah, was sent here to intervene in the state of the world, particularly with regard to killing and warfare.

Sarah's first job was to meet with heads of state around the world and some of their key cabinet members. In these meetings, she told us that God is unhappy with the state of the world and is imposing an edict upon humanity that will dramatically affect life on Earth as we know it. She also told us what is behind God's intention and what will happen next. Then she asked all heads of state around this planet to gather together to deliver this message to their citizens in a coordinated manner, which I am doing now.

The message is this: <u>From this moment forward, any person who attempts to kill another person, or any person responsible for enabling or ordering such an attempt, will immediately drop dead, and the weapon of choice will be destroyed.</u>

I cannot stress strongly enough: the edict that no person can kill another person is effective <u>immediately</u>. In a world where human beings seem intent on finding new and better ways to kill one another, we are being forced to <u>stop.</u>

I will break it down for you so that you can clearly understand what I am saying here:

- *Any person who willfully attempts to kill another person, using any weapon from a kitchen knife to a garden mallet, will die, and their weapon of choice will self-destruct.*
- *Any person who <u>enables</u> a person to kill another person will also immediately die—so, if you are the type to leave your firearms where your children can get them, I suggest you put them away.*
- *Further, any weapons created specifically to kill humans, such as multi-round firearms, rocket launchers, tanks, explosive devices, and so on, as of this moment are no longer functional.*
- *Single shot firearms will continue to be functional and available—for example, rifles such as used by farmers or hunters—but if they are used in an attempt to kill another human being, the shooter will die, and the rifle will become inoperable.*

No person, including me, is exempt from this edict. If, for example, I were to order a military strike on behalf of our great nation, the minute it was attempted, I would drop dead.

God is particularly concerned about permanently disabling weapons of mass destruction, such as nuclear and chemical weapons. The proliferation of them is primarily what has prompted God to intervene in our affairs. Such weapons can literally kill millions of people at a time, which detracts from our purpose, which is to bring 'life force,' or good energy, home to God.

Without getting too much into theology, let me take a moment to elaborate. According to Sarah, humans are on this Earth at God's discretion with a mission to create positive life force to take home to God upon their passing. Those who do so, flourish and return to God. Those who do not, do not. You can think of it as being sent to Earth to gather treasure in the form of good will, kindness, and charitable action—anything that springs from following the classic Golden Rule.

Sadly, most of us have lost sight of this simple idea of being kind to others, and instead have devolved into pettiness, jealousy, greed, hatred, and intolerance. God has stepped in to give us a chance to rise again. By taking lethal force off the table, God is forcing us to tap into our higher selves and work together for a better world.

I imagine many of you are wondering about security for our country, cities, and towns. This is an understandable concern. Let me assure you that border security and the law will continue to be as strictly enforced as always. Our enforcement officials can still use whatever means necessary to subdue those who break the law, so be warned. Guns can still injure. Tasers can stun. Rubber bullets hurt more than a person would think. This is not a time to engage in civil disobedience; It is a time for us to band together in unity under God.

There are many things we will need to iron out, particularly from an economic perspective, as we move forward. The military-industrial complex has traditionally been the economic backbone of our country, and its importance will be diminished by the inability to use lethal force. My administration is working overtime to fill in the significant gap its demise will leave. I will present a State of the Union address as soon as possible to lay out some of the plans this government is creating for transitioning America into the new and better future promised by God. Bipartisan efforts like the U.S. has never seen before will be key to our success, and for the first time in history, both the reds and the blues will be working as one for the good of all.

I understand the words I'm saying will leave you with many questions. Most of the answers you need can be found by going to the American government website and typing 'Sarah Said' into the search bar. Along with regularly updated information on our 'frequently asked questions' page, you will be able to use an online chat function to interact with government representatives.

Let me close by saying that these are unprecedented times, but ultimately, these changes are for the betterment of the whole human race. Above all, I would ask that you remain calm and face the future with optimism.

Fellow Americans, I wish you well as we step into this bright new world together.

When Cummings finished, he looked at the group and asked, "What do you think?"

"That was *great*!" said Angelica Lopez enthusiastically, beaming at Sarah as she spoke. "It laid out all the salient points. It was clear, concise, and to the point. Bravo."

"I didn't write it—God did," Sarah said humbly.

Her words were a warm, scented breeze that made Cummings think of the shoestring licorice of his childhood. He'd liked the red kind best, while Bryan had liked the black. Of course, this difference had provided an opportunity to fight whenever their father took them to a movie theatre and told them they had to share a package. If they were lucky, before their dad got mad at the bickering and marched them home with no movie, his sister Sam would turn the tide by asking if they could have Smarties instead. It was always the right compromise. *Bryan and I were like the U.S. and Russia,* mused Cummings, *while Sam was like Canada.* Then, he thought again of Sarah's question to him: *"What kind of country—what kind of world—do you want?"* . . . and he suddenly realized that she'd asked something much deeper than he'd first thought. She'd actually been asking him what kind of man he wanted to *be*.

He looked at Sarah, brow furrowed, as he pondered for the umpteenth time the position he was in as leader of the American people, with their divided natures and deep hostilities. He was afraid to tell them the things that he must—especially the part about the reproductive changes. Sarah flickered brightly at him for a second, something he took to be reassurance.

Then he steeled himself, took a deep breath, and asked her, "Sarah, when do I mention the biological changes that are coming?"

"Ah, yes," breathed Sarah with a ruffle of spring-scented air. "I know that idea troubles you greatly, Samuel."

"Yes," he agreed. "It does."

"Based on your *own* reaction to the news, Samuel, I have decided that this part of God's message is something that needs to be announced by *me*," she said with a gentle glow. "People have a tendency to want to 'shoot the messenger,' and I am most definitely more capable of quelling the emotions of fear, shock, and anger that may arise from this announcement than you are."

Cummings nodded his agreement. He had no doubt that people would react poorly to having their sexual activities curtailed. Sexuality, and the flaunting of it, was practically a rite of passage, and social media was rife with it. People of all shapes and sizes flocked to plastic surgeons and body modification experts to 'fix' themselves, presumably in an effort to have better, or more, sex—at least that was what the pouty-lipped selfies they posted online implied.

Women in particular seemed unhappy with their natural blessings. They often spent thousands of dollars to get their lips filled, their eyelashes glued on, their breasts made larger, their cellulite viciously removed . . . all in an effort to look 'better' than someone else. To Cummings, this preoccupation with unrealistic perfection was not only ridiculous, but sad. It revealed a sham world where people appeared to be beautiful but would not forfeit a single martini to buy a street person a sandwich.

"And so God is stepping in," said Sarah, a whisper of solace into his ear. "He is just as appalled as you."

Just then, Northrup took advantage of a pause in the conversation to stop his furious scribbling—he had filled up eight pages of notes so far during the course of the meeting—and mused out loud, "I imagine we'll need a list of questions and answers for the reporters . . . and we should probably post all this information on the web as soon as possible too."

"Yes, we should," agreed Cummings quickly, rousing himself from his uncomfortable introspection. "It will be a hell of a press scrum, and I expect the reporters to lob some real doozies at me. I need to be prepared." Then he looked at Sarah and—a little embarrassed at his neediness—said, "I wish you would stand there with me, Sarah."

If anyone noticed the pleading in his tone, they didn't let on.

In response, Sarah sent a fluttering energy his way. "For this initial announcement, I think it's best I do not," she said. "My presence would only overshadow the message."

"You're like John the Baptist, Samuel," cut in the Catholic Lopez. "You're going to tell America that an agent of change sent directly from God is coming!"

"I appreciate the reference, Angelica," he said, "but I don't think it's the same thing."

"Have it your way," said Lopez with a shrug.

Cummings felt the weight of the world on his shoulders. He'd never expected that being president of the United States of America would be a walk in the park, but he'd also never expected to be the first and only president in history to have to announce that the freedom and liberty Americans held so dear was, in some ways, being usurped—even if it *was* by God. He was terrified about backlash. The people of his country were, in their own way, quite fierce. It wouldn't matter to them to know this edict was for their own good. They, as he had initially done, might simply react to the idea of being bossed around. There could be full-scale revolt.

As if he'd said the words out loud, Sarah responded. "Yes, there could be," in a soothing, sweet whisper. "But there will be no revolt. You are just the messenger, Samuel. Your people will understand that."

Judging by the lack of reaction the rest of the group had to her words, he understood that she had taken him aside once more, and that she was trying to reassure him and encourage him to put his best foot forward. But despite Sarah's reassurance, he was feeling less and less up to the task before him.

Sarah understood. "Take heart, Samuel," she whispered. "God wants this to happen, and if you walk in good faith, God will support you in your efforts to lead your nation."

Cummings nodded. "This is much harder for me than I could ever have anticipated," he said.

"Of course, Samuel," she said. "Most things worth doing *are*."

And then, with a strange, energetic shift that only Cummings could feel, they were back among the rest of the group.

Northrup, oblivious to their momentary departure, asked, "Sarah, will you write the Q's and A's for Samuel as you did the speech?"

Sarah answered by letting her trademark golden tinkle ripple around the room as she said, "Of course! And rest assured that it is within my power to ensure that the reporters at the press conference ask only the questions God *wants* them to ask." Then she looked at Cummings and said gently, "Have no fear. You will be fully prepared, Samuel."

"And his answers will be absolutely . . . well . . . *divine*?" questioned Lopez, tongue in cheek.

At that, a small guffaw escaped from Hana Shriver's throat. Lopez arched her expressive eyebrows and smirked, pleased to see the usually serious Republican laugh.

Meanwhile, Sarah fixed her deep, starlit pupils on Cummings and said, "Look at your computer, Samuel. The questions and answers are there."

He did as she told him, and there on his computer was a completed page of questions and answers.

"You're much better than my assistant at getting this stuff together," remarked Cummings gruffly, and he thought he saw a flicker of a smile pass across Sarah's shimmering, ever-changing face.

"Let's hear those Q's and A's, then," said Feldman, stifling a yawn.

He was the first to show the effects of the long meeting. Though time was suspended, their physical bodies were feeling its passage in the regular way, and more than one tummy had rumbled in the last ten minutes.

"Okay," Cummings said, "here goes." He began reading.

Questions and Answers:

1. *Who, or what, is Sarah?*

Answer: Sarah is a composite of the souls of 40 million women who joined God upon their deaths. This particular number was chosen at God's discretion and is believed to represent every language, culture, spiritual persuasion, type of life, and type of death.

2. *Why is Sarah made of only women's souls?*

Answer: Women carry stronger life force than men because they are generally more compassionate people; However, the life force of a man who disavows a competitive nature and puts the needs of others above his own can be just as strong.

3. *Is Sarah here to rule the Earth?*

Answer: No, though Sarah will remain on Earth for one year to help us adapt to the new world order that God is imposing.

4. *Can we see Sarah?*

Answer: Yes, Sarah will begin direct communication with people on social media as soon as this press briefing ends. She will explain the true nature of God and will provide more detail about why this intervention is occurring.

5. *If killing is no longer allowed, will people have to surrender their firearms?*

Answer: It is this administration's policy to leave the Second Amendment alone, although we will implement a gun buy-back program and recycle all collected weapons.

6. *What will happen to weapons manufacturers?*

Answer: Because weapons specifically manufactured to kill humans won't work, an orderly but expeditious termination of weapons development will soon be underway.

7. *What will happen to all the unusable military hardware?*

Answer: A large-scale 'reduce, reuse, recycle' plan will see much of this equipment repurposed. We will release details of that plan within a few weeks.

8. *What will happen to the military budget when large sectors of the military are shut down?*

Answer: Military budgets will be redirected to economic programs designed to create employment opportunities for displaced troops and defence industry workers.

9. *What will happen to the troops who will be recalled from overseas?*

Answer: This government is working on plans to retrain and redeploy these loyal men and women in other government services, or in the private sector. We will keep all troops on payroll for twelve months and extend health benefits to those who need it for an additional twelve months.

10. What are the plans for defence industry workers affected by these changes?

Answer: Compensation plans, as well as proposals for replacing defence spending as this country's economic driver, are still being discussed. Preliminary plans will be announced during the presidential State of the Union address.

11. How will you address the economic consequences of demilitarization?

Answer: Central banks will act to calm markets and stimulate the economy, and the federal government will provide funding to accelerate the development of new employment opportunities. I will provide more details in my upcoming State of the Union address.

12. What can we expect from financial markets when this change takes effect?

Answer: Financial markets will close for one week to allow time for the creation of new initiatives to replace defence spending. Central banks will act as needed to maintain stability when the markets reopen.

13. Should I be worried about my investments?

Answer: Some investors may experience losses, and to offset this, the federal government and the central bank will work together to stimulate the economy with new projects and businesses, which will create far greater optimism about the long-term future of our economy than there currently is.

14. What are you doing to stop military and law enforcement personnel from endangering themselves by attempting to use deadly force?

Answer: Defence Secretary Gordon Blackstone has briefed the troops and this country's law enforcement leaders, and they have been instructed on appropriate behaviour.

15. Will deaths that result from God's edict be monitored?

Answer: Yes, Sarah will be reporting the number of people killed every hour, along with relevant statistics that led to each death, including the nature of the attempted killing; the weapon or weapons used, if any; the identity of the perpetrator; the identities of the enablers, if any; and the name of the target or targets.

When Cummings had finished reading the Q's and A's, he looked at Sarah and said, "I think you covered it, Sarah. I like it."

"Sounds good to me too," said Blackstone.

"I like it too," said Lopez, "but . . ."

"But what?" asked Cummings.

"Well," Lopez responded, choosing her words carefully, "I think before we head into the most turbulent week we're ever going to face, we should talk about public backlash." She looked directly at Shriver, and said, "Hana, If we don't present a consistent message—supported by both of our parties—we might wind up in hot water."

"It's true," said Cummings. "People tend to lash out in highly charged situations. We don't want division along red and blue lines—we could wind up with civil war!"

Feldman cut in. "You want to talk about lashing out?" he asked. "Think about what jihadists who've been looking forward to seventy celestial virgins as their heavenly reward for killing infidels are going to do when they find out about the true nature of God!"

Cummings ignored this remark. He wanted to be sure of Shriver's buy-in before going down the rabbit hole of discussing the volatility that was no doubt going to be extreme in the heated Middle East. Though his country might have to step in at some point to help with cultural restructuring efforts, getting his own country's affairs in order was the first priority.

He examined the senate head, trying to read her thoughts. Given the private discussion Sarah had made them have, he was pretty sure she was on his side . . . but it was hard to tell from her expression. She was a tough nut to crack; She had a way of locking down her face and emotions that made her seem as cold as ice. She was frowning now, and all he could hope was that whatever she was thinking would not affect her decisions with regard to what they must now face together.

Then, just when he thought she wasn't going to answer, she caught his eye. "Mr. President," she said, "I agree with . . ."

But before she could finish, Feldman butted in, "The Chinese will be shocked to find out there really *is* a God," he said, "and that it isn't money."

"Not fair," shot back Lopez. "Just because Communism doesn't recognize God doesn't mean Chinese *people* don't. And they're not all rich in China, Norman. There's a lot of poverty, just like anywhere else. Your average Chinese person is just trying to make a living, same as the rest of us."

"Point taken," said Feldman, "but perhaps you'll agree with me when I say that many faiths, yours included," he pointed at the cross around her neck, which she was still unconsciously fingering, "will be rocked by the high regard God has for *women*."

Lopez looked down at the hand that held the symbol of her faith as if surprised to find it acting of its own accord. "Yes," she said thoughtfully. "I *do* agree with you."

"All religions," cut in Northrup, pen poised in mid-air as he spoke, "will be surprised by the simplicity of what God wants from us. It's all about loving, respecting, and helping others."

"It would seem, then," said the opinionated Feldman, "that adherence to dogma is not required, or expected, to get into Heaven—*big* surprise there."

Shriver spoke up then. "Please don't be disrespectful, Norman," she said. "Many people rely on churches, synagogues, or whatever their respective houses of worship as places for community and spiritual expression."

"Yeah, Norman," added Lopez. "Religious worship is not just dogma. The ritual, words, and spirit are real to those who believe."

"It's dogma," muttered Feldman, "and it serves little purpose."

At that, a flutter of cool air from Sarah circulated around the room as she interceded. "Are you so sure, Norman?" she breezed, and Cummings could have sworn he saw the colour lavender permeating the air. "Churches, temples, mosques, and synagogues provide a forum for people to gather, express their love for each other, and affirm their faith in God. It is institutionalized kindness. It feeds the life force."

"So what?" asked Feldman. "I can be a kind person without attending a church just as well as if I attend one. I have no need to jump through hoops to prove that."

"But *are* you?" asked Lopez, clearly incensed by what she took as criticism of her faith.

He shot her a sour look in response.

Sarah eased the moment. "Norman," she said gently. "What may seem a tedious hoop to you is almost always a golden ring to someone else. Don't sneer at others' beliefs. Belief and worship are very personal matters. Belittling others for their belief systems detracts from what God wants, which is simply prevailing kindness among humans."

"So you say," replied Feldman, somewhat snippily.

This made Cummings wonder what was eating his treasury secretary. The man was usually solid as a rock. Then he looked around the room, noted the drawn faces, and realized just how tired his team was.

"Sarah," he said, "we're all overwhelmed and tired, and since I'm pretty confident about what I need to say with regard to the 'do not kill edict,' I wonder if we could move on and touch on some of the biological changes you've mentioned. That news will be equally, if not more, unsettling to the public."

"I'm with you there," said Lopez. "All you've really told us is that there will be a shortening of the period of sexual activity, presumably for both men and women. That will be very upsetting for a lot of people."

Shriver, who'd been watching the exchange between Lopez and Feldman with interest, spoke up, saying thoughtfully, "I can see some benefits, though. I believe Sarah said earlier that each woman will personally be in charge of when, or *if*, she wants to have a child. If that's the case, family planning and abortion will no longer be divisive political and social issues."

"Can you imagine?" asked Lopez enthusiastically. "Finally having control over reproduction will give women a chance to really excel." She laughed at this, adding, "It's been a *long* time coming."

"Don't make light of it," cautioned Cummings. "A decline in male dominance probably won't impact us too much here in America, since women are already mainstays in most social and political spectrums . . . but in less progressive cultures, it will rock some very institutionalized ground. It's likely it will cause complete chaos and social breakdown."

"Why? Because every stone some barbarian male throws at some poor, sexually abused woman, who supposedly brought shame on her family, will bounce off her head and kill him instead? I say *good*," Lopez remarked tersely.

"Maybe the loss of men's power will be offset by knowing for certain that there really *is* a God, and that entrance requirements for Heaven are much simpler than most would have us believe," mused Northrup.

Sarah's golden tinkle emanated around the room at this remark. "Yes, Bradley," Sarah replied, "there will be people who will be mollified to learn this. However, there will always be those who continue to think of women as possessions."

"But at least they won't be able to kill them when they tire of them," said Lopez.

"No, for to do so would be instant death," replied Sarah.

"What about marriage?" asked Shriver, thinking of her husband, Peter. She respected the institution of marriage and was intensely pleased with her own. Her husband's family were steadfast Germans who lived in Leipzig, Saxony, spoke no English, and were proud of it. They made no secret of their disappointment when Peter fell in love with her—an American woman with Japanese heritage. They'd hoped their only son would marry a milk-fed German girl when he finished his nuclear medicine training at Stanford University, but instead he fell in love with the overly serious, studious teacher's assistant in his imaging class. Ultimately, his parents came to accept Hana, but it had been challenging to win them over, to say the least.

"Do you think marriage will endure?" Shriver pressed Sarah. "If women get all the say in reproduction, won't that cause conflict in some families?"

"It may," Sarah replied, "but then perhaps those in conflict should think twice about bringing a child into the world."

"Marriage is a ritual people *won't* give up," said Lopez with confidence. "It means more than just having kids!"

"It does until married people get *divorced*," sniped Feldman, "and then it means they lose a house and all their savings."

Cummings furrowed his brow at the comment, and suddenly recalled that Feldman never arrived at any official functions with a spouse. He wondered at the man's marital status. He was quite certain he was straight, as his son Geordie had once had a discussion about marriage with him and Cummings had never indicated any understanding of Geordie's preferences; Therefore, it stood to reason that he was divorced. And clearly, he was bitter about it.

Lopez, not one to waste time on analyzing people's responses the way Cummings did, didn't cut the man any slack in that regard. Instead, she said hotly with a certain degree of disdain, "It's always about the money with you, isn't it? You can't start a family with the *expectation* that you're going to get divorced!"

Ever the voice of reason, Northrup looked up from his pad of paper to remark, "These days, 'family' is a loaded word. You can't equate family and marriage anymore. They're different things."

"Yes, Bradley," breathed Sarah, emitting her rose scent as she seized on his comment, likely as a way to stop Lopez and Feldman bickering. "Family possibilities are endless." Then she locked her starry eyes onto Cummings' and asked, "Wouldn't you agree, Samuel?"

He was taken aback by the question, but quickly understood why she'd asked it. He thought of how much Geordie had loved Flores, and what wonderful parents they would have been if Flores had not ended his own life in such a tragic way.

He nodded his agreement. "Indeed," he said to Sarah.

"There are just as many ways to get or have a child as there are to raise that child into a good adult," Blackstone cut in all of a sudden, startling everyone. He'd been silent ever since the conversation had veered away from the military, so his input was unexpected. "Adoption, surrogate relationships, cryobanks that sell ova and sperm . . . all sorts of things." As the groups' eyes turned to him, he didn't hesitate in following up with, "You're all probably aware that I'm single . . . but that doesn't mean I don't want a son someday. I've researched the options, and I have a plan, which I choose not to share. However, I will tell you this: Someday, I will have a son, and I will raise him in this new world that Sarah has promised us."

His mouth was firmly set in a serious line, and his deep, dark eyes were unusually bright. Cummings had never supposed the warlike, manly Blackstone to have any interest in children—and now he understood that under that granite exterior, the man had yearnings much deeper than he ever showed. Once again, he was forced to take stock of the fact that he didn't know his team members as well as he probably should.

In response to Blackstone's words, Sarah sent the delightful smell of melted butter—or at least that's what Cummings equated it to—into the room. "That is wonderful news, Gordon," she said softly, "and know that God supports your efforts to become a parent. You will make a human soul very happy when this comes to pass. And you and your child will create much life force for God, which will offset your history as a warrior."

Northrup said to Blackstone, "That's amazing, Gordon. Good for you!" and then as he had earlier done for Cummings' speech, he clapped.

But Lopez, who had been fiddling with her cross again for the last few seconds, only furrowed her brow. "I have a question, Sarah," she said. "Given all these options, what will happen if fewer women choose to give birth? Do you think the population will begin to decline?"

She looked worried, and once again, Cummings thought about Lopez's Catholic roots. There was a strict 'no birth control' component to sexuality as defined by Catholics.

Sarah, clearly sensing the vice president's concern, answered truthfully, "Yes. It may."

"And God would *want* this?" asked Lopez. "I thought God was all about sending treasure hunters out to collect as much life force as possible! Doesn't that mean we should be making *more* kids?"

"It does," Sarah tinkled, and Cummings felt the ripple in his tummy again. "But positive life force is not generated by children who are unplanned, unwanted, unloved, and unhappy. Such people may never heal enough to generate the amount of life force needed to offset what they used just staying *alive*. This is not the answer for God. Only love begets love. That is God's way."

Lopez was silent at this. She thought of how much she loved her twin daughters . . . and how grateful she was for the aunt who took her in and loved *her* when she was only twelve years old. Sarah was right about one thing—her *own* life force had been severely depleted by the time her Auntie Magdalena had adopted her. It had taken nearly eight years of love, therapy, and faith in God for her to overcome the emotional trauma she'd been through at the hands of her narcissistic, coke-addicted parents. It brought tears to her eyes to remember it now.

"The biological changes are going to impact some economic things too," said Feldman. "Sports, for example. Boys won't be scouted in high school for college sports anymore. They won't have testosterone until they're eighteen!"

"That will put a damper on your bookie career, won't it?" sniffed Lopez, quickly bouncing back from her emotional jag to take a shot at Feldman. She was teasing . . . but she also *wasn't*.

"Take it down a notch, Angelica," warned Cummings. "He's not wrong—sports is a huge industry and a national pastime. It's worth discussing."

"*Men's* sports are indeed a national pastime," purred Sarah, and her collage of faces seemed to speed up in their shifting patterns as she spoke, "but women get far less adoration. It is God's hope that the shorter careers of males might level the playing field . . ."

Cummings laughed at her play on words, and then said, "I'm starting to understand just how much this biological transformation might change our cultural landscape. It will be fascinating—if a little unnerving."

"Yes," agreed Sarah with her trademark flutter of energy. "You would be wise to track the long-term psychological and sociological impacts with a study. It will be something that can be referred to in the future, and a way to teach children about how the people of this planet were saved from themselves."

"That's a good idea," agreed Cummings. He looked at Northrup. "Brad, could you look into what's required to set up a government-funded, long-term study?"

Northrup nodded. "Yes," he said, scribbling onto his notepad.

"Don't waste your money," said Feldman darkly. "I can tell you right now what's going to happen. People will get depressed at losing their mojo. All the billions of dollars people have spent trying to preserve youth and sexuality will be for *nothing*. Enter mass depression."

"What about self-esteem?" asked Shriver. "People look after their bodies as a way to feel good about themselves, not just to attract sexual attention."

"Oh, come on," Feldman said. "We want others to admire us so we can have sex with them. Now we can't *have* sex, so what's the point?"

"Are you sorry that a bunch of overpaid plastic surgeons will cry and go broke?" Lopez asked, clearly annoyed and trying to get a reaction from the man.

"Ha!" snorted Feldman, "I never thought of that." Then he looked at Cummings and asked, "So tell me, Samuel, will we bail out the plastic surgeons when we're handing out money to disenfranchised military?"

"Hey," interjected Blackstone, a little riled. "It's not the same!"

"Isn't it?" asked Feldman.

"Now, now, settle down," said Cummings. "I know we're all tired, but let's remain civil, okay? I'm relying on you guys to let cool heads prevail."

"My head's cool," said Shriver.

Cummings noted a tone of something he couldn't quite put his finger on—was it shyness?—in her voice.

Then she said, "You know what I like about this reproductive change? There will be no more innocent children in Thailand catering to fat, white . . ." She stopped speaking then, and Cummings could see her coolness had turned to rage.

His heart went out to her; He felt exactly the same way.

Chapter 8

Global Initiatives

There was an uncomfortable silence after Shriver's comment. All of them knew about child sex tourism; Worse, at least one person in the room thought someone he knew might be participating in it. An extremely wealthy acquaintance of Feldman's spent an awful lot of time visiting Thailand, often without his trophy wife . . . who had been not quite eighteen when they married and was now an 'over the hill' thirty-two—or so Feldman's friend liked to joke.

Many times, the friend had offered Feldman a visit to his private resort, 'when the need struck him,' and it was always offered in a 'wink, wink, nudge, nudge' manner that turned Feldman's stomach. That said, there was nothing in *particular* the man had said or done to make Feldman think he was a pedophile; Moreover, it was a sense that he had something unpleasant clinging to him—guilt, maybe. For that reason, Feldman kept him at a distance; Feldman liked knowing rich people . . . but he had a limit on how well he wanted to know *this* man.

Cummings broke the somewhat uncomfortable silence that had been brought on by Shriver's comment about the appalling sex tourism trade in Thailand. "What's next, Sarah?" he asked in an effort to move on. "As far as I can tell, I'm prepared for the speech I will be giving to the American public."

Sarah's many faces began to speed their cycling, lending a multitude of expressions to her visage that was staggering. It gave Cummings vertigo to look at her, and so he doubled his efforts to focus only on her pupils.

"Samuel," said Sarah, releasing a minty gust of wind into the room. "As you know, I have been speaking concurrently with all other heads of state. It is time for all you global leaders to come together to share ideas. We must begin the discussion on global initiatives."

There were puzzled looks around the room. Everyone had become used to the idea that she had teleported them to meet with one another... but could she—*would* she—get all world leaders together in one room?

The answer was yes. There was a whooshing sound and a rush of air similar to what Cummings had felt when Sarah had removed him and Shriver from the rest of the group so they could iron out their differences privately. Then, before he could even say his own name, he found himself at the United Nations Headquarters in New York City, along with every other world leader, some of whom were—as Sarah had mentioned earlier to his group—in their pajamas.

He looked around, a little disoriented. He was in a big auditorium in which successive chairs encircled a table that held a muddle of electronic gear. Around him, people were cautiously making their way toward their seats. He could hear the British prime minister, Charles Grafton, a generally outspoken individual, complaining about the time and choice of venue.

"Why couldn't we have gone to the UN office in Geneva? It's much closer, and it wouldn't be the middle of the damn night," he griped to the fellow beside him, who Cummings recognized as the First Minister of Scotland, Blair Stewart. Then Grafton yawned and stretched, not embarrassed at all about his striped blue and white pajamas.

As Cummings started trying to figure out where he should sit, he suddenly saw an immense, ominous shadow on the ground in front of him. Reflexively, he looked up to see Sarah hovering angelically over the group, larger and more imposing than he had ever seen her before.

"Please take your seats," she boomed thunderously through the room.

No microphone was needed to get the attention of the assembled group; Her roar whirled around like a hurricane. Those who weren't already sitting, of whom Cummings was one, hastily did so. He took his place as commanded, plopping quickly down into a plush leather chair near an aisle. For a moment, he questioned how everyone—no matter what their native tongue—simultaneously understood Sarah's command, and then he remembered that she could communicate in every language at once. Despite himself, his eyes widened in awe at the thought. He was *almost* used to this magic of hers . . . but not quite.

When everyone was settled, she began. "Hello, world leaders, and welcome," she said in a loud, chiming tone that reminded Cummings of a bell gong.

It was an effective way to start a meeting. Everyone's rapt attention was on her.

"Before I begin speaking of matters of global concern," she said, "I wish to inform you that the reason your team members could not accompany you is simply a matter of logistics. There are over 200 of you physically present in this room right now, all of you heads of state of the diverse nations and people on this complex and interesting planet. However, rest assured that your support teams are exactly where you left them and are tuning in remotely from those places. Feel free to wave at them."

Surprisingly, the majority of world leaders did so, including Cummings. He thought that the way the assembled group responded was a good indication of how well Sarah had done her job on Earth so far.

When everyone's attention turned back to her, Sarah said, "All of you are aware of why I am here. I have met with each of you, and we have discussed the particular nuances, needs, and expectations of your respective peoples."

She paused, and the assembled group murmured and nodded assent.

When silence resumed, she said, "I will waste no time with backstory, then. I will begin imparting to you what God's expectations are for humanity as a whole!"

Inexplicably, the lights in the room flickered—*dramatically,* thought Cummings—and then Sarah said, "There are many changes coming to your world, some as a result of direct intervention from God, such as global demilitarization, and others that are more secondary, such as social shifts that will occur because of the biological changes God is making. Over the next year, as these changes unfold, I will bring both political and religious leaders to the table in a series of conferences to discuss the impacts, real and perceived, of God's edict, and how to address them. God would like the world to move forward united in common goals, shared understanding, and renewed faith. These conferences will set the groundwork for how we will achieve this."

She looked around the room, seemingly catching everyone's eyes at once, and asked, "Global leaders, do I have your assent?"

And nearly every person in the room, including Cummings, replied, "Aye!"

"Good," said Sarah. "I will preside over each of these meetings and do everything I can to bolster solidarity among you all. You will find the topics I would like to discuss on your laps."

Puzzled, Cummings looked down at his lap to see a small booklet there. Intrigued, he picked it up and looked at the front cover. It featured an image that, at first glance, looked like a plain black and white line sketch of a woman's form . . . yet when Cummings tried to focus on it, it started to move around the page, much the same way Sarah's face did when he tried to focus on *its* contours. It felt to Cummings like he was looking at a puzzle, and for a moment, he became distracted by the picture's maneuvers. First, it straightened out and became a line. Then, it wiggled like a serpent around the page. Next, it made itself into the shape of an apple. Finally, the line that was once a woman became a spiral and kept swirling around and around like water in a flushed toilet, making Cummings dizzy.

He shut his eyes in order to stop looking at it. When he opened them, he ignored the line—which was shaped like a woman again—and read the title of the pamphlet. It was called *Intervention 101,* and despite the seriousness of the moment and the meeting, he laughed. *It's like we're a bunch of college students, learning from the master,* he thought.

He could have sworn he heard Sarah say gently in his ear, "You are."

"Please take a look at the table of contents," Sarah boomed energetically through the room.

And so, Samuel and everyone else opened their books. He saw the following index:

Global Conferences: Improving Planet Earth
1. Disarmament (Nuclear Weapons)
2. Disarmament (Biological & Chemical Weapons)
3. Cyber and Space Warfare
4. Disarmament (Conventional Weapons)
5. Disarmament (Personal Guns)

6. Glorification of War and Killing
7. Global Institutions
8. Colonization of Space
9. Role of Women in the Family
10. Role of Women in Business and Government
11. Religion Revisited

Background Information: Earth as a Member of a Universal Community
12. Did God Create the Universe?
13. Is There Intelligent Life on Other Planets?
14. Are We at Risk of Being Invaded by Aliens?

Wow, thought Cummings to himself, *this is great*. He was excited at the topic matter—particularly the discussions about Earth's place in the universe. It was profound to have proof that God existed; It was even more profound to find out that human beings were not alone.

He looked up at Sarah, who still hovered above the group, gazing down at them all with her immense, star-filled pupils, and he smiled. He felt her acknowledgement of his feelings emanating back toward him in waves of joyful energy.

When Sarah was satisfied that each member of the assembled group had each perused the index, she sent a rumble into the room that sounded very much like thunder. It startled Cummings and made him flinch. He noted that the fellow next to him—who he recognized as the prime minister of Sri Lanka—did so as well. They grinned at each other in embarrassment.

Then the moment was gone. "Let us start, shall we?" suggested Sarah.

Cummings remembered how she'd told him there were the souls of many teachers interspersed in the 40 million women's souls within her. *Their influence is strong,* he thought as he sat up like an obedient schoolboy and paid attention.

"All the information we will cover at this meeting is in the booklet," Sarah said, "but we will go over it together to make sure everyone's questions are addressed. First, let's discuss nuclear disarmament."

There was a rustling of pages as the assembled world leaders obediently turned to the first page of the booklet. Cummings opened his and read:

Disarmament (Nuclear Weapons)

God has decreed that the production of nuclear weapons must cease within seven days, or their production facilities will be destroyed by God. God has also decreed that all existing nuclear weapons must be fully disabled within one year, or they will melt in situ.

Within three years, all weapons must be dismantled. Their radioactive components must be placed in safe storage, along with all stockpiles of weapons-grade uranium or plutonium. If this does not occur, God will cause the non-compliant weapons and fuel to melt in situ.

The Conference

The planning conference for nuclear disarmament will be held in Geneva, Switzerland within thirty days, at a time of God's choosing. God has decreed that you ratify these items:

- Those who possess nuclear weapons, or weapons-grade uranium or plutonium, must disclose this fact to their home governments within sixty days.
- All disarmament initiatives will be verified, under Swiss leadership, by third-party inspectors from non-nuclear countries.
- Disarmed countries must agree to ongoing surveillance by the above-mentioned inspection team.
- No person or group will ever again initiate a program to create any nuclear weapon, under threat of death by God's hand.

If God is forced to melt weapons and fuel due to non-compliance, it will cause a nuclear disaster, killing many people. Given the 'do not kill' edict, enablers to such tragedy will immediately drop dead.

When Cummings finished reading this first part of the booklet, he became aware of a soft humming in the room. He immediately looked up toward Sarah, who was still hovering above the assembled group, and saw that, while her amazing, ever-shifting eyes were closed, her mouth was moving at a dizzying speed. He knew instinctively that she was speaking, reading aloud the words in the book—at the same time, in multiple languages—to every person in the room. Almost as soon as he had the thought, he further realized that he could hear her English version quite clearly.

When Sarah had concluded speaking, she asked, "Are there any questions?"

A coffee-coloured hand was raised several rows away from Cummings. An attractive woman wearing a striking turquoise-coloured sari said, in English, "Yes, Madam, I have a question." Cummings recognized her as Aisha Singh, the Indian prime minister.

"Yes, Aisha?" said Sarah.

Singh asked, "Since God will be aware of all disarmament efforts, why do we need a verification process?"

"Ah, good question," replied Sarah. "The verification process, and ongoing monitoring, is God's way of giving confidence to the *public* that dismantling, disposal, and safe storage of nuclear weapons and fuel has occurred," answered Sarah. "As you are already clearly aware, God sees all and doesn't need human-grade proof of *anything*."

Aisha Singh nodded. "Thank you," she said politely.

Sarah looked around the room with her unsettling eyes, which to Cummings looked particularly sharp and probing at the moment. She asked, "Anything else?"

There was not.

"Let's move on, then," said Sarah. "Please, let's discuss biological and chemical weapon disarmament." Along with these words, she sent a wave of rose-scented air into the room, which had the effect of immediately calming the uncomfortable, still somewhat agitated group.

Cummings and the rest of the assembled leaders immediately turned to the next page in the booklet.

Disarmament (Biological & Chemical Weapons)

God has decreed that the production of biological and chemical weapons must cease within seven days, or production facilities will be destroyed by God.

Within one year, all such weapons must be securely stored in central repositories within their country of origin.

Within three years, all such weapons must be safely disposed of, or God will destroy them and kill all persons involved in the decision to keep them.

The Conference

The planning conference for biological and chemical weapon disarmament will be held in Tokyo, Japan, within thirty days, at a time of God's choosing. God has decreed that you ratify these items:

- Those who possess biological or chemical weapons must disclose this fact to their home governments within sixty days.
- All disarmament initiatives will be verified, under Japanese leadership, by third-party inspectors from countries that do not harbour such weapons.
- Disarmed countries must agree to ongoing surveillance by the above-mentioned inspection team.
- No person or group will ever again initiate a program to create any chemical or biological weapons, under threat of death by God's hand.

When Sarah had finished speaking, she once more caught the eyes of all present. "Are there any questions?" she asked.

This time, Cummings saw the president of Mozambique, Joaquim Mabote, raise his hand.

"Yes?" Sarah asked, and the flutter of her presence felt large and imposing to Samuel.

"Ms. Sarah," said the man, in English, "do all countries have to come to the meeting? I am certain we have none of the biological or chemical weapons of which you of speak in Mozambique."

There was an energetic whirlwind of air that blew downward from Sarah's floating presence, and Cummings felt it to be somewhat dark and a little threatening.

"Yes," she said to Mabote in the baritone voice Cummings knew meant she was very serious. "*All* countries must attend. While your government may not officially condone, or even be aware of, the production of such weapons, your country may be home to other groups that are developing such weapons."

Mabote scratched his brow like a puzzled child doing mathematics, and Cummings wondered if perhaps he knew more than he was letting on.

Then he simply said, "Yes . . . yes indeed, Madam." And he sat down.

Sarah said, "Turn to the next page, please."

The assembled world leaders immediately did so.

Cyber and Space Warfare

God has decreed that the production of malware, capable of hacking into computer or electrical control systems and manipulating them in a manner that threatens human life, must immediately cease. If it does not, God will destroy the malware and kill every individual involved in enabling, creating, or executing such digital attacks.

God has also decreed that space-based warfare efforts that could result in the loss of human life, specifically digital or physical interference with satellites essential to navigation and early warning systems, must immediately cease. God can, and will, thwart such planning efforts or attacks and kill all involved in their creation.

The Conference

The planning conference for cyber and space warfare weapons disarmament will be held in Beijing, China, within thirty days, at a time of God's choosing. God has decreed that you ratify these items:

- Those who possess malware that has been designed with the intent to enable killing must disclose this fact to their home governments within sixty days.
- All disarmament initiatives will be verified, under Canadian leadership, by third-party inspectors from countries that do not promote such research and development.
- Disarmed countries must agree to ongoing surveillance by the above-mentioned inspection team.
- No person or group will ever again initiate a program to create any malware weapons, under threat of death by God's hand.

When the last of her words had finished ringing around the room, she asked, as she had before, "Are there any questions?"

There were no responses. Clearly, the message that no one would get away with anything was getting through. Cummings flipped to the next page.

Disarmament (Conventional Weapons)

God has decreed that all conventional weapons used in military warfare are to become useless as tools to kill other human beings. Anybody who tries to use such a weapon to kill another human will die as soon as the attempt is made, as will any person (or persons) who order or otherwise enable an attempted killing. Dismantling the devices and salvaging the metals involved will be prudent, and more importantly, will demonstrate political leadership to the citizens of the world.

The Conference

The planning conference for managing the collection and disposal of conventional weapons will be held in Moscow, Russia, within thirty days, at a time of God's choosing, and a global initiative to collect, dismantle, and recycle such weapons must be created within sixty days.

Cummings knew that everyone in the room was already well informed about this. He and his team had their plans for the U.S.A.'s military disarmament underway, but he suspected the more militarized countries were not as far along as they were. He glanced at the Russian president, Misha Verenich. The man's lips were pursed; He looked seriously displeased—but he said nothing. *He's probably debating the value of arguing with her,* thought Cummings. Cummings was certain that would be a bad idea.

As before, Sarah glanced around the room and asked, "Are there any questions?"

No one had anything to add, though judging by some uncomfortable looks, the leaders of countries where being armed and ready to kill was a rite of passage were wondering how things were going to unfold for them as time went on. Cummings was grimly satisfied that their strangleholds on their people were about to change.

"Let's move on," Sarah suggested.

There was a fluttering of pages. Cummings turned to the next topic in his booklet.

Disarmament (Personal Guns)

God has decreed that all personal weapons are to become useless as tools to kill other human beings. Since the people most likely to die from personal guns are the gun owners and their family members, God sees no reason to impose gun bans at this time. However, citizens should be encouraged to give up their guns as governments demonstrate their resolve to remove guns from border patrol and law enforcement personnel through gun collection and recycling programs.

The Conference

The planning conference for managing the collection and disposal of personal guns will be held in Denver, U.S.A., within three months, at a time of God's choosing.

"I have been over this with all of you already," said Sarah when she had finished reading. "But are there are more questions, please ask them now."

"Yes," said Cummings, putting up his hand. "Are you holding this particular conference in America for a specific reason?"

"You know the answer to that, Samuel," she said in a rush of warm air, and once more, Cummings had the sense that she had lifted him away from the rest of the people.

"Because we have more personal handguns than any other nation?" he asked, knowing he was right.

"Yes," Sarah told him, her golden tinkle permeating his thoughts. "You must now be the ones to show the other nations how to put them away for good."

Cummings nodded and immediately found himself back in the presence of the other world leaders, some of whom were looking less and less happy at the idea that the guns they'd waved for so long were now an avenue to self-harm.

"Shall we proceed?" asked Sarah. She didn't wait for an answer; Instead, she simply began projecting the words of the book into the room in her booming voice.

There was a fluttering of pages as the assembled group hurriedly turned to the next topic.

Glorification of War and Killing

God has decreed that all art forms and computer games that glorify war, or the killing of intelligent beings, be immediately banished. Books and movies glorifying violence must immediately be pulled from the public arena. Electronic games that glorify violence must be uninstalled from personal computers and electronic gaming consoles.

God had decreed that, so long as such things exist, the innocent become corrupted to believe:

a) Deadly weapons are harmless.
b) People recover easily from mortal injuries.
c) There are few consequences for killing.
d) Revenge in kind is an acceptable response to killing.
e) Killing others for sport/pleasure is not only acceptable but is an activity void of emotional response.

Wars and killing are now things of the past, and that is where those acts should remain—in documentary films and historical novels.

The Conference

The planning conference for managing the recall and disposal of entertainment items that glorify killing and war will be hosted by the European Union and will be held in Brussels, Belgium, within three months, at a time of God's choosing. Possible compensation to holders of the rights to such entertainment items should be an agenda topic.

When she'd finished speaking, as before, Sarah's voice boomed around the room, asking, "Are there any questions?"

"Oui," came a woman's voice from just behind Cummings. "Qu'en est-il de l'art historique?" He looked behind him to see the president of France, Delphine Allard, with her hand in the air. A great patron of history and culture, she seemed quite distraught.

"Delphine," Sarah replied, turning her starlit pupils on the woman. "Have no fear for your country's prized art. Classic historical works, such as those depicting famous battles, or the crucifixion of Jesus, will be preserved and categorized in the same way historical novels and documentaries are. The contents of the Louvre, for example, can remain as they are . . . unless they *glorify* killing. The key to God's edict is that any work, whether historical or modern, that tries to show the killing of a human being as pleasurable, desirable, enviable, or attractive, must be recalled from public display and possibly destroyed."

"But how will such a thing be enforced?" asked the Australian prime minister, Ben Morrison in dismay—without putting up his hand, Cummings noted. "There are literally *millions* of Xboxes and whatnot out there. Surely you can't expect us to monitor who turns their games in and who does not!"

"No," agreed Sarah. "But *God* can monitor this. And if any one of those games—or violent books, movies, or other artwork—influences a person to attempt to kill another person, there will be severe consequences. For example, any parent who doesn't remove such games from the home will die if their child tries to kill another person, even if the attempted killing doesn't take place for a decade. Second, if it's within the power of the game's, or artwork's, creator to recall it, or remove it from public view, and they do *not* . . . well, if an attempted killing results from their lack of action, then they will immediately die. God sees all, and God will judge all."

The silence in the room could have been cut with a knife. Cummings was already aware of God's view of violent artwork and games, but it seemed some of the assembled group had not yet had that conversation with Sarah. There were some shocked faces.

"Shall we move on?" asked Sarah, infusing the air with a rose scent—presumably, Cummings thought, to calm the group.

Global Institutions

There are many global institutions that will be affected by the changes God is imposing on humanity. Most of them are economic, such as the World Bank, the International Monetary Fund, and the World Trade Organization.

The most notable non-economic organization on Earth is the United Nations (UN). The UN was formed to protect global peace following

World War II. Over the years, it has also come to oversee many other international organizations, not all of which deal with global issues.

Given God's decision to permanently end war and killing, God has decreed that the UN be reconfigured to focus *only* on global issues affecting the well-being of Earth and the human race, such as disease control and global warming. Further, it is God's will that the UN Security Council be abolished, and that the UN's mandate and governance be revised to reflect this.

The Conference

The planning conference for restructuring global institutions, particularly the UN, will be held at the United Nations Headquarters in New York City within six months, at a time of God's choosing. God expects every world leader to attend the meeting in person and to leave their domestic political agendas at home. **From this day forward, when coming together under the UN umbrella, you will collectively represent the human race and the planet as a *whole*.**

To Cummings, that was welcome news. He was optimistic about the possibilities of a UN that was no longer the 'big daddy' of retribution when member countries stepped out of line, and he was happy when no one overtly expressed dissatisfaction about dismantling the Security Council—though, judging by the looks on a few faces, he was certain some people had reservations.

Sarah didn't address any of these people directly, though, so he could only assume she took them aside as she'd done with him, to ally their concerns personally.

She simply said, "Let's move on, shall we?"

And everyone turned the pages of their booklets.

Cummings was pleased to see that the next topic was one he and his team had already started working on. *Yes, this is great,* he thought.

Colonization of Space

Colonization of the moon and Mars are important for the long-term survival of the human race, and God believes these projects should become global initiatives. Currently, research into commercial space travel and settlement are highly secretive, expensive, and cost-prohibitive for most nations. The combined resources of intellect and money will produce faster results and create a shared goal for humanity that will foster global community.

The Conference

An initial planning conference for space colonization will be held in Houston, U.S.A within six months, at a time of God's choosing. Leaders representing the twenty largest economies in the world should attend this meeting to define the general nature of the global arrangement. Business leaders prominent in the aerospace industry should also attend.

The priority agenda item should be to define an investment and governance structure under which *all* countries and companies can be part of the initiative to colonize space.

When it comes to technologies and resource ownership, competition is a major hurdle. As God's emissary, I am committed to working with all parties to navigate these complex negotiations.

Three months after the initial meeting, an inclusive, global meeting will be held at the United Nations Headquarters in New York to offer other countries a chance to participate.

When Sarah had finished speaking, Cummings noted some muted excitement in the room. The prime minister of Sri Lanka, who had earlier smiled at him in embarrassment when they'd both flinched at Sarah's thunderous voice, caught his eye.

In English he said, "It is a good plan. It is inclusive."

"Yes," Cummings said. "I agree."

"You are the president of the United States, no?" asked the man.

"Yes," said Cummings, sticking out his hand. "Samuel Cummings."

The man shook heartily and said, "Jegan Bandara, Sri Lanka."

"I know who you are," said Cummings. "I've been to your country. It's very beautiful."

"Certainly, you weren't there on business?" the man asked, clearly concerned that he couldn't remember meeting Cummings before.

"No," laughed Cummings. "I was on vacation with my wife. It was always a dream of hers to see where Ceylon tea comes from. She comes from traditional British stock—and she loves her Ceylon tea."

"And did she enjoy the visit?" asked Prime Minister Bandara.

"She most certainly did," said Cummings, picturing Lorena's beloved face.

He suddenly deeply missed her. He knew she was still waiting for him, suspended in time, in their private living quarters in the White House. He knew he would eventually walk into that room, and she would welcome him with a smile. He knew that she was blissfully unaware of all that he was going through at the moment. And, he knew that he would have to ignore her embrace and tell her quickly what he must do, and why. *If I don't do it, I will die,* thought Cummings. And the idea of leaving her alone broke his heart.

Bandara, sensing his sudden shift in mood, asked with concern, "President Cummings, are you quite all right?"

His attention came back to the room. "Yes," he said, feigning a cheery smile. "I'm fine."

At that moment, Sarah indicated that they should move on to the next topic, and so the two men returned to looking at their respective booklets.

Role of Women in the Family

God has decreed that a women's conference on family dynamics be held to determine how women think their role in family structures will change over time, given the biological changes being imposed upon humanity by God.

God further decrees that a long-term study of how family roles evolve in different countries and cultures be implemented, and the findings reported annually.

The Conference

The women's conference on family dynamics will be held in Cairo, Egypt within six months, at a time of God's choosing. Each country should send three family structure experts and three women between the ages of twenty and forty who represent the following:

- Living with a male partner and children.
- Living with a female partner and children.
- Living alone with children.

The panel should represent a cross section of socio-economic, educational, and cultural backgrounds. Agreement in principle about the nature of the long-term studies should be reached. Over time, the following topics should be monitored:

- How losing their sex drive at age forty affects women (physical, psychological, sociological changes).
- How their *male* partner's loss of sex drive at age forty affects women's relationships with their male partner.
- Whether biological changes have a long-term effect on what gender a woman chooses for a *child-rearing partner* (exclusive of sexual preference).
- Whether biological changes affect earning power and division of labour in the home.

When she had finished speaking, Sarah's starlit, sparkling pupils scanned the room, looking for quizzical faces. The German chancellor put up her hand.

"Yes?" asked Sarah.

"Berdine Schmidt, German Chancellor," said Schmidt in heavily accented English. "I want to know if there will be a men's conference as well?"

"Yes," Sarah replied in her ethereal way, a flutter of golden energy coursing through the room, tickling Cummings' stomach as it always did, making him stroke his navel unconsciously. "There will be a men's conference, but not until humanity has started anew. God has decreed that first women must be empowered to stand toe to toe with their male brethren. Only when equality has been achieved will men be able to accurately assess who they are in the world. At the moment, their opinions of themselves tend to be . . . shall we say . . . *inflated*."

Ben Morrison, the Australian prime minister, put up his hand in protest. "I don't think that's true, Sarah," he objected. "There are some powerful women in this world who could kick my ass fair dinkum! You're speaking as if they always get the short end of the stick!"

There was a gentle rush of warm air, salty smelling, like a day at the beach. "Ben," responded Sarah, "you are correct. There are women who have done amazing things in this world, including some fine-spirited Australians, such as 2009 Nobel Prize winner Elizabeth Helen Blackburn—the same woman who was president of the Salk Institute for Biological Studies. However, such women are the exception and not the rule. There is still systemic exclusion of women in many facets of society. Removing a system that no longer relies on hierarchy sustained by classic male aggression will equal the playing field for both genders, as well as all nations and peoples. This is God's plan."

Morrison didn't know what to say to that. Clearly, he disagreed—but Cummings could see in his face that he was not about to start an argument with an emissary of God. He wondered if Sarah would take Morrison aside to address his concerns, as she had done with him. He hoped so. The man looked quite confused.

There were no more questions, and so, like obedient students, the group moved to the next topic.

Role of Women in Business and Government

God has decreed that a women's conference on gender discrimination in the workplace be held for female business and government leaders to determine how women think their role in the workplace will change over time, given the biological changes being imposed upon humanity by God.

God further decrees that a long-term study about women's evolving roles in the workplace be conducted, and the findings reported annually.

The Conference

The conference on women's roles in business and government will be held in Stockholm, Sweden within twelve months, at a time of God's choosing. Over time, the following topics should be monitored:

- How biological changes in men and women have affected the 'glass ceiling' and pay equity.

- Whether biological changes and increased reproductive control have brought new business or political opportunities to women.
- Whether men's role in the workplace has changed following the loss of their sex drive at age forty.

The venue for the conference should be changed each year, and to keep the world focused on the issue, the most senior female politician in the host country should speak at the event.

When Sarah finished speaking, Ben Morrison didn't even raise his hand. He simply exclaimed, "Preposterous!"

Sarah's golden tinkle reverberated throughout the room.

And that's when Cummings spoke. "Prime Minister Morrison," he said evenly, "it's not preposterous. It's, as you say, 'fair dinkum.' We're leveling the playing field and starting over, in a way."

"I beg to differ, Cummings," said Morrison, clearly riled. "It's reverse sexism, and it's putting the boots to men's necks. We have no problem like that in Australia. In 1896, Australia was the second country to give women the right to vote, and the first to let 'em be elected to a national parliament. Our state of South Australia was the first parliament in the world to grant women full suffrage rights!" Then he spat, "We're way ahead of you Yankee fruit loops! You didn't even let women vote until the 1920s—and only the white ones at that. And if you had it your way, you *still* wouldn't let 'em!"

They were heated words, but they were also the truth.

Cummings paused to consider what the man was saying, and then looked at Sarah and said, "Sarah, it seems my country is behind others in this area . . . I'm getting quite an education here."

"You're behind *some* countries . . . but far ahead of others. God's goal, as you say, is to create a new beginning for men and women, a world where gender and skin colour no longer impact status in life. Don't we all want to live in a world where it's actually true that you reap what you sow?"

Cummings was satisfied with this answer, but Morrison was still huffing. "I think you should leave that stuff alone, dammit! It's been going fine, but now the boat's going to get rocked to hell! There's a shipwreck on the horizon, mark my words!"

Cummings wondered if Sarah would be offended by the cursing, but she appeared nonplussed. "True equality will not be achieved without sacrifice, Ben," she said.

And then she moved on, and Cummings and the rest of the group turned the page.

Religion Revisited

God has decreed that a conference of religious leaders be held to allow me, Sarah of God, to explain the true nature of God, and to give religious leaders the opportunity to question me thoroughly. Following this initial meeting, over the following sixty days, I will meet with ten representatives of each faith in a series of meetings. These more detailed discussions will address the beliefs and practices of individual faiths that are <u>not essential</u> for access to Heaven, or that are contrary to God's will.

The role of women in religion is also a topic that needs to be addressed. Upon the realignment of the world's major religions to reflect the true nature of God, a conference of female religious scholars will be held to discuss ways to promote the acceptance of women in leadership roles in faith-based institutions.

The Conferences

1. The conference of religious leaders will be held in Jerusalem, Israel thirty days from now.
2. The conference of female religious scholars will be held in Melbourne, Australia six months from now.

The following topics should be addressed:

- How respective religious leaders decide what to do with their new perspective(s) on God.
- The possibility of religious institutions declining in popularity if they continue to adhere to incorrect doctrine.

When she'd finished speaking, Sarah looked around the room with her flickering, deep, entrancing eyes. Cummings never failed to be transfixed by the depth he found in them.

As before, she asked, "Are there any questions?"

When no one raised their hand, she said, "Before I restart time, and you all get to work notifying the world of these changes, I would like to discuss some bigger questions about God and creation that I am certain many of you would like answers to."

Cummings, for one, was eager to delve into this. He had spent long summer evenings as a child looking up at the stars in the sky, stars that now seemed like pale reflections of Sarah's eyes, wondering . . . *why am I here?* He'd always felt in his heart that he had a purpose, and a connection to God—though he'd never fully believed in the Anglican God of his parents. But he believed in Sarah's God, and he was excited that the many, many questions of his youth were finally going to be answered. It was humbling and exciting at the same time. Eagerly, he turned to the next page as Sarah began speaking.

Question 1: Did God Create the Universe?

The universe you live in burst forth about 14 billion years ago in a process usually referred to as the Big Bang. All the basic ingredients necessary to create matter and energy were present at that time. Space has been expanding ever since.

Rudimentary matter and gases, under the influence of crushing gravity, over time became stars—nuclear furnaces. Planets emerged from the dense disk of gas and dust encircling young stars.

As the earliest stars aged, the nuclear fusion process within them created heavy, complex atoms, like oxygen, carbon, and other elements necessary for life. As their lives ended, these stars exploded, distributing these elements to planets, and planting the seeds of life. When conditions on the planets became right to create complex organic molecules, God provided the life force necessary to create basic life forms. Evolution took over from there—not just on Earth, but throughout this vast universe, on billions of other planets as well.

The intelligent life force that is God has always been part of this mix. God was present when the Big Bang occurred. God exists in every part of the universe, and like entangled electrons, God's component parts are connected through space and time.

"I don't believe it!" said a coffee-coloured man sitting across the room from Cummings, in deeply accented English. "This cannot be true!"

Cummings struggled to recognize him but could not.

Luckily, the man followed his outburst with, "I am Mohamed Ould Sidi, the prime minister of Mauritania."

At Ould Sidi's comment, there was an earth-shattering rumble in the room, much like thunder. Cummings literally jumped out of his seat, terrified. Then he looked up at Sarah, still floating above the group, and he saw her pupils dilating, the stars seemingly descending down from her eyes as if to crush them all. He sat down quickly, his heart racing in unparalleled fear.

"Oh, you don't *believe* it?" asked Sarah of Ould Sidi in a booming voice that rattled the chair upon which Samuel sat.

Ould Sidi, positively terrified, cowered.

Sarah's fearsome eyes flashed, sending lightning bolts around the room as she said, "Perhaps that's because you think theocracy is an effective way to subjugate your people and force them to do your bidding. But I speak directly from God when I say that no matter how much you pretend you've been divinely appointed, God does not run military dictatorships. You will need to rethink the nature of your government, and the human rights abuses you are guilty of, or you will *die*!"

At that, the man sat down heavily. He clearly had not expected to be called out in such a manner. It made Cummings wonder how he could be so foolish as to challenge an emissary of God.

Silence reigned in the room for a few long seconds.

Finally, Sarah infused the room with the scent of jasmine, as if cleansing it, and said, "There are just a few more points I would like to discuss with you before I return you to your home environments to begin the work you have been asked to do."

With that, the assembled group turned to the next topic.

Question 2: Is There Intelligent Life on Other Planets?

The short answer to this question is yes.

Life force from God was the spark that ignited the initial building blocks of life. I'm sure most of you are familiar with the theory of evolution, but here is a primer for those who have ignored it or do not believe it:

- God is the source of life force.
- Primitive organisms receiving life force began reproducing and evolving.
- Complex organisms developed and evolved to pass on life force through genetic information in spores, seeds, or eggs.
- Life forms, particularly human life forms, became capable of intelligent thought and learned to control their external environment.

It took millions of years for human beings to evolve, but the species still retains many animalistic tendencies, despite rapidly growing brain power. Humans are currently at the most damaging, dangerous stage in their evolution. They are advanced in technology but lacking in spirituality. This lack of moral compass, and an animalistic adherence to tribalism, has provided fertile soil for the development of weapons of mass destruction. This is what has prompted God to intervene in the affairs of humanity at this time. God is saving you from *yourselves*.

God's will is that humans evolve spiritually. Those who live to help other people will end up joining God, and they will come to know the secrets of the entire universe. Those who do not will cease to exist.

Humans seem largely unaware of how fragile the Earth is and how much they have damaged it, and *not* just through the proliferation of weapons of mass destruction. The Earth's population has grown to the point that human life is becoming unsustainable. Instead of living in harmony with their environment, humans pillage the Earth's resources to fill insatiable desires for possessions. This cannot go on.

This universe contains intelligent life forms that have evolved over billions of years, and it is God's hope that you will continue your evolutional journey to be on par with them. Such beings are highly spiritually developed, and their connection with God is so strong that they are able to experience 'Heaven on Earth' while still in physical form. They have strengthened their life force, both individually and collectively, by helping, loving, and nurturing members of their species, as well as the flora and fauna on their home planets.

This is God's hope for humanity, and it should be the goal for all humans—to be exemplary stewards of the gifts God has entrusted them with.

When Sarah had finished speaking, she scanned the room in an almost personal way, waiting for questions. The German chancellor put up her hand again.

"Wie machen wir das?" she asked, somewhat excitedly. She was smiling with the possibility of a better world.

"One way you can do that is by developing clothing that regulates the body's temperature so you don't need so much fuel every day," said Sarah. "It is surprising to God that humans have not explored technology such as this."

"Is this what the advanced beings you speak of do?" asked the German chancellor, this time in English.

"The beings I speak of learned to absorb energy directly into their bodies, without killing and eating animals or plants," replied Sarah. "They get 80% of their energy needs directly from their sun, like alligators on Earth have done for millions of years. Alligators can last through an entire winter on their energy reserves, surviving freezing conditions, if they remain in the water."

Cummings was somewhat floored by her words. He hadn't thought about solar energy that way before.

Just then, the Italian president, Lorenzo Rossi, asked in English, "If there are other life forms in our universe, do we need to be afraid?"

"No," said Sarah, "you do not. And that brings me to my last topic before you re-enter a world you may no longer recognize."

Everyone dutifully turned their pages.

Question 3: Are We at Risk of Being Invaded by Aliens?

The Earth is not at risk of alien invasion. Alien species capable of travelling to Earth don't carry weapons, and if they come at all, they will come in peace.

Many human-comparable life forms in this universe—by that I mean free-thinking beings as opposed to instinct-driven beings (animals)—have been able to avoid the type of intervention that has become necessary on Earth because their spiritual evolution outpaced their technological evolution.

Other species have, like humans, evolved to have less focus on spiritual development, and so they have been subject to the same kind of intervention by the hand of God that is now occurring on Earth.

In either case, once a higher state of spiritual evolution is reached, the urge to kill others dissipates. For this reason, alien life forms who have evolved to the point of being technologically capable of reaching Earth are not interested in killing any of God's other children.

When she finished speaking, there was a rustle of paper as the assembled group closed the books in front of them.

"That is the end of our meeting," Sarah concluded. "I want you all to know how pleased God is with your reactions to the plan for humanity's future. Most of you have been quick to line up to get rid of your weapons. Most of you want this type of world for your people—and for the future of Earth."

Cummings noticed nods all around the room—except from the North Korean leader who, as he had done for the whole meeting, sat hunched in a corner, clearly resentful that Sarah had plucked him from his hermit kingdom and forced him to attend.

Cummings examined the man's sullen face. He knew there would be trouble in North Korea. He was worried for a moment about what that might mean for the downtrodden people who lived there, but then he remembered the vision Sarah had given him, showing him how she would spread the word of God's new world to the North Korean people despite resistance from their government, and he was comforted.

Chapter 9

Show Time

When Sarah had finished speaking, the leaders of the world, who had so raptly been listening to her words, were uncertain what to do. Eventually, the French president, Marcel Brassard, started clapping, and the rest of the group joined him. Then the majority of them stood and began to look around in a confused manner, wondering what would happen next. They had been teleported in and would most certainly be teleported out.

All of them knew what was expected of them, though most of them were still quite overwhelmed by the idea.

As they gathered up their belongings, Sarah, with her golden ripple of energy—her 'tinkle'—said to them, by way of farewell, "Leaders of the world, you know what you have to do. Time as you know it has been restarted. I am sending you home. Go forth and address your people. Tell them the word of God."

Then there was the same sudden, supersonic rush of air he'd felt before . . . and suddenly, Cummings found himself back in the Oval Office with his team.

He was just in time to hear Angelica Lopez say excitedly, "This is it, this is it! I've sent all my emails out, and now I'm heading to my office to get my tech team working. I want that website operational within the hour, and fully staffed and functional within three. I've got a team assembled and some contractors at the ready to do the tech work and expand the broadband. I'm working on getting assured twenty-four-hour staffing for the chat service, and the company I contacted said they can set up a couple of 1–800 lines as well, and provide operators. This is going to be a smooth communications machine by tomorrow, and I'll work all night to get it done if I have to!"

"Good stuff, Angelica," Cummings said, shaking his head to clear it as his thoughts caught up with what was going on in the Oval Office, and he left the meeting at the United Nations behind.

Cummings was bone weary, but could feel his adrenaline kicking in. He was up for this. He had to be.

Blackstone stood up, saluted Cummings, and said, "Welcome back from New York, Sir. As we discussed earlier, I'm going to reach out on all high-priority military channels to ensure the troops are ordered to stand down. It could take a while to reach some of our agents who are operating covertly overseas, so I need to get back to my office, same as Lopez. That's where my tools are."

"Can you make sure you get the word out to law enforcement and border security as well?" he said to Blackstone.

"You bet," replied the defence secretary. "That's my next priority, right after I get the military message system going high-speed."

"Sounds good, Gordon," Cummings told the defence secretary. "Just make sure to keep me posted, okay?"

Blackstone nodded.

Then Cummings turned to Northrup. "Bradley," he said, "could you call the press and arrange the emergency news conference? Let them know we have an announcement about national security that we need to make as soon as possible, but remain tight-lipped about what we're announcing, okay? I think it's best no one gets a scoop. We have to make sure we're the one source for information, or all hell could break loose out there."

"Got it, Chief," said Northrup. "I'll get in touch with the usual press scrum and anyone else I can think of as well."

"I can help with that," said Hana Shriver. "I have some researchers on my staff who can provide contact information for the more obscure media channels. And I can also help Angelica. I have some social media experts who can work with her to get the web blasts out quickly and in unison over multiple platforms. We need to send one well-coordinated announcement over social media. That's the only way to nip the conspiracy pages in the bud."

"Thanks, Hana," said Cummings, suddenly feeling a bit useless. "You guys are so on top of things! I feel as if I should offer to help someone."

"You can help me soon," said Feldman. "I'm going to get some information together for the announcement about economic recovery that I'll be giving with Graydon Pierce from the Federal Reserve. I'm going to need you to approve my notes."

"Consider it done," said Cummings. Clearly fatigued, he sat heavily on one of the couches so recently vacated by his team. He added, "I guess my job is to make sure I look better than I feel. I've got to get my ass out in front of the reporters and read the speech Sarah wrote. I need to look like a leader, but I'm afraid I feel like a shitshow."

Feldman laughed. "You'll be fine," he said.

Just then, Lorena walked in. She looked startled to see everyone, and they were just as surprised to see her.

"Hello!" she said. She looked around at the assembled group, who were trying to be respectful toward their First Lady by standing up and waiting to be formally dismissed. She could tell they were eager to leave. "Oh," she said, "clearly I've interrupted something." Then she looked at her husband, her brows furrowed and questioning. "Sam," she said, "what's going on? I thought you'd be back for Chinese food and a movie and . . ."

"Okay, team, get going," said Cummings, waving his hand at his anxious colleagues, giving them leave to sprint like rabbits out of the Oval Office.

"What is going on?" asked Lorena in confusion when the others had left.

Cummings said nothing. He simply stood up and grabbed her in a tight embrace.

"What has happened, Sam?" she asked fearfully. "What's gotten into you?"

"Our world is about to change, Lorena," he mumbled into her neck, inhaling the smell of the rose-scented shampoo that lingered in her shoulder-length hair—and desperately hoping he would be alive to smell it again tomorrow.

She squeezed him back and asked, "Can I help?"

This made Cummings hug her even tighter.

"Yes," said Cummings, and then the corners of his mouth curled up in a small grin as he said, "I have to give a press conference, and I haven't a thing to wear."

She smiled. "You know I can fix that. And you better tell me *everything* while I do, okay?"

He nodded, and the two of them left to get ready.

At precisely 2:30 a.m. GMT, reporters from every major television network in the world gathered to receive news of the edict and to broadcast the message of God's intervention. All world leaders—with the exception of the North Korean leader who had, predictably, refused to cooperate—were prepared with speeches and ready to go.

In the United States of America, First Lady Lorena Cummings had effectively freshened up her husband, ensured he was wearing his 'lucky' tie, shed her pajamas, and donned a businesslike, dark purple skirt-and-jacket suit. Now, she stood proudly at her husband's side in the White House briefing room, her face set, her expression firm, awaiting the press scrum that was about to begin.

When Cummings told his wife earlier that his life might very well be over if God's word was not delivered quickly, efficiently, and with no mistakes, she had taken the news as he'd known she would—with steadfast courage. It was the same courage that had seen her birth two children, pursue a career as a publisher (while working from home and raising the kids), and stand by him firmly during his political rise. Her steadfast nature, and her hand in his, gave him courage.

As soon as Cummings took the podium, lights began flashing in his face from reporters' cameras. He did not waver, and he delivered the speech Sarah had written for him with no deviation from the text in front of him. Then he answered the questions she'd anticipated the press would ask, all the while marveling at how the reporters asked, word for word, the exact questions that were printed in black and white on the paper before him. Ultimately, he was glad Sarah had prepared him so well for this moment because, truth be told, he felt numb at the possibility of his untimely death, and he could never have stickhandled the press under his own steam.

The minute he'd finished speaking, Lorena, correctly reading his dour thoughts, took his hand and pulled him quickly away from the press scrum and back into the safety of the Oval Office.

"Sit down, Samuel," she said when Don Taylor, Cummings' bodyguard, had left the room, and they were alone.

He sat gingerly on one of the couches, while she walked over to his desk and pulled a bottle of scotch whisky and two shot glasses out of the bottom left-hand drawer. She poured them each a finger and took his over to him. He accepted it gratefully. Then she sat down across from him and unconsciously pushed an errant strand of her brunette hair behind her ear as she focused her intense, knowing, grey eyes on him. The compassion she felt for her husband was splashed across her face.

"You won't fail, husband," she said firmly. "Now drink up."

He did as she suggested. He immediately felt some relief.

Lorena then reached for the remote and turned on the Oval Office television. "We need to see what's going on," she said.

"Yes," he agreed. "Now that the world leaders have finished delivering their messages, Sarah is going to deliver hers."

"I'm looking forward to seeing this . . . being," said Lorena, "though I imagine much of the world will sleep through her message."

"Yes, but those who miss it will assuredly get it first thing in the morning. It will be broadcast multiple times," Cummings replied.

Lorena clicked on the remote, and the screen sprang to life.

Fox News Channel was streaming, and the female reporter was saying excitedly, "Today, President Cummings announced that he, and all other heads of state, were simultaneously visited by a being sent from God to intervene in world affairs . . ."

Lorena flicked over to NBC, where a serious-sounding male reporter was saying, "We have heard from the White House today that God is going to intervene in the affairs of humanity. Can it be true? Here's what leaders from all around the world have been saying . . ."

Cummings and his wife sat and watched as the NBC coverage showed snippets of Cummings' announcement of the visitation, followed by the British prime minister's, the Canadian prime minister's . . . the Japanese prime minister's . . . the German chancellor's . . . and then suddenly, at precisely 3:00 a.m. GMT, the television flickered oddly and made an interesting tinkling noise that Cummings recognized right away as Sarah's 'laughing' sound. There was a flash of golden light, so bright it seemed to leap out of the television at them—and then suddenly, there was Sarah, her multitude of faces flickering on the screen one after another in dizzying succession.

Beside him, Lorena gasped in awe and then cried out, "It's really *her*!"

"Yes," Cummings said, clearing his throat. "It is."

"Oh, isn't she *marvelous*!" his wife exclaimed, her eyes wide with delight.

"Yes," said Cummings, though he wasn't nearly as enraptured by her as Lorena clearly was.

Sarah spoke. "Greetings, Planet Earth," she said, with a hint of joviality in her tone that surprised Cummings.

He suddenly realized why. When he had communicated with her 'in person,' she had spoken mind to mind, or energetically; Now, when projecting over the limited, two-dimensional medium of television, she had to articulate her words as a human would in order to be heard over the airwaves.

"She has adopted a voice," he said, more to himself than Lorena.

"What do you mean?" asked Lorena, not understanding why her husband would make such an observation.

He didn't answer, and she didn't ask again. Instead, the two stared at the television as Sarah said, ". . . and so I have intervened in all global communications networks to deliver a message directly from God. Citizens of the world, I am Sarah—Sarah of God."

At that, Lorena gripped Cummings' hand in excitement. He squeezed hers tightly back in return.

"Earlier," Sarah continued, "your respective heads of state announced my existence and provided context for my visit. If you watched the emergency broadcasts from your leaders, then you know that God has deemed it necessary to directly intervene in the affairs of humankind in order to save your species. God has sent me to Earth to help you adapt to the changes that will be made."

"She is *magnificent*!" exclaimed Lorena, her eyes as wide as saucers as she gazed at Sarah on the television.

"Depending on the resolution of your screen," Sarah said, "you may find it difficult to focus on my image. This is not because your television signal is unclear; It's because I am not human, nor am I three-dimensional in the ordinary sense. God created me from the souls of 40 million women.

Their physical features are mixed within me, and they are not static. You could say that I am a coalition of female souls, representing women from every part of the world, every period of time, and every country that has ever existed on Earth. My composition gives me an intimate knowledge of every culture that has ever existed on this planet and allows me to speak every language ever known to humankind."

"This is so *exciting*!" exclaimed Lorena to Samuel. "I can't believe I am part of a world where the presence of God has been manifested for us to see with our own eyes!"

Cummings looked at his wife in surprise. He had never really considered Sarah's visitation in such a way before. Suddenly, he thought of the wise men who'd faithfully followed the star into Bethlehem, knowing Jesus was due to be born and that they were going to see something extraordinary. He got an inkling of what Lorena was experiencing. He wondered, *Why doesn't Sarah affect me in the same way?* He wondered if it was, as Sarah had pointed out, a difference in how men and women experienced life. Where he'd perceived a threat, Lorena had perceived a miracle.

"Do not be afraid. I bring you a message of love and hope," Sarah said at that moment, and the familiarity of her words (*I bring you tidings of great joy,* thought Cummings, thinking of *A Christmas Story*) caused him to instinctively move closer to the television. Feeling her husband's sudden intensity, Lorena put a reassuring hand on his arm and smiled at him, and in her face was a look of such gentleness and care that for a moment he was stunned. It was the face of compassion—and Cummings was suddenly aware that he'd seen that loving, womanly expression flit over Sarah's face about 40 million times.

He leaned over and kissed Lorena's cheek. "You're right, my dear," he said. "We *are* witnessing a miracle."

And then the two of them turned back to the television to watch as Sarah carried God's message to the world.

"As you already know," Sarah said, "I have met separately with the leaders of every country on Earth. They have already spoken to you, the people of the world, about God's intervention. Now I am furthering this message. The world has devolved from its highest potential. God has decided that intervention is necessary to right the course of humanity. God wants people to live in peace and harmony. God wants people to place the needs of others above their own. That is the key to eternal life."

There was a dramatic pause, and Cummings noted the stars in her eyes—which were every bit as impressive on television as they were in real life—getting bigger and more imposing. He wondered if there was a hypnotic component to them; He, for one, could not look away. In fact, he leaned forward, so far toward the television's siren call that Lorena had to pull him back to stop him from toppling over onto his face.

Sarah continued, "People who lead lives filled with hatred, intolerance, and greed will never be with God after death. Their life force will be dismantled and redistributed to the lowest life forms on Earth when they die. They will never join their brothers and sisters who spent their lives developing spiritually by cultivating love and kindness. Instead, they will cease to exist.

"Men, in particular, face the threat of having their individual life forces extinguished. Many men are hampered in their spiritual development because of their unchecked aggressive natures. For the same amount of time that men have predominantly been the leaders of human groups, they have led through violent means, holding out the threat of death as ultimate retribution to enemies. This model is obsolete. It must be replaced by kinder ways. It may have been a realistic way of securing power when humans wielded sticks and rocks, but weapons of mass destruction have made this barbaric thought pattern no longer sustainable.

"I'm sure some of you wonder why I am made up solely of *women's* souls. It is because women's souls are generally more spiritually evolved than men's. Where men rush in swinging swords, women choose compassion before violence. Women's lives and positions in the world are shaped by their tendency toward loving and nurturing, whether it be toward their families—including their male partners—or toward clients, students, or patients in one of the many helping professions in which women prevail. In general, women know how to put others before themselves more effectively than men do, which results in them growing stronger souls.

"God created me from women's souls because this 'maternal instinct,' as it's called, has given women an advantage in their spiritual evolution. God created me to be strong, flexible, compassionate, and wise. I am here to offer support, knowledge, and care. I am here to help you to help yourselves.

"You may wonder why God doesn't just send a mighty wind to blow away all the evil on this planet, and you would be right to think it is well within God's power to do so . . . but God has determined that working together to save yourselves from the mess that you have *created* is the only way humanity will learn that more unites you all than divides you.

"Earlier, your leaders spoke about the nature of God. I will expand on that a little. God is not an old man with a beard behind a cloud. God is not male, female, or beast. Instead, God is an ocean of energy, a river of love, and the fount of all wisdom—and you are the drops. Every drop rains down onto Earth for the purpose of nourishing goodness. That is why you are here—to learn how to love unconditionally as God does. Surely by looking at me, you can see that the God who created you is as much a part of you as you are of God? And surely you can also see that there is no ritual, and nothing worth killing another for, in this scenario? God is, and always has been, bigger than all the minutiae you humans choose to fight about on this planet. God is at once far simpler and far more complex than you can ever imagine."

Beside him, Cummings could feel Lorena stir with emotion. "Oh, Samuel," she said, "this is exactly what I've always thought about God."

He patted her hand in agreement, glad to hear her accept so readily this new version of God that went against her own early religious upbringing, just as it went against his.

Sarah continued, "Over millennia, humans have created countless religious constructs, complete with texts and ceremonies, for the purpose of bringing the faithful closer to God. Each respective faith insists that theirs alone is the one true path to Heaven, and each faith uses this belief to justify killing those who don't agree. Has this created nations of people who know God? I think you all know the answer to that. Certainly, *God* knows the answer. And this is why God has decreed that human beings will no longer be able to kill one another without dropping dead themselves."

At that, Sarah gazed out at her audience, and Cummings thought he had never seen her look more beautiful. Her eyes were glowing and almost appeared three-dimensional in their intensity. He felt he could reach out and touch her, and beside him, it seemed Lorena felt the same way. She was trembling. He put his arm around her and pulled her close. He smelled the rose scent again and wondered if it was indeed his wife's shampoo, or if Sarah had somehow sent the delightful smell out into the ether with her formidable powers. *Maybe it's a little of both,* he decided.

"Know this," Sarah said when she spoke again. "All that is required to join God upon your passing is to live a life where you treat others as you want to be treated. If someone needs your help, offer it freely. Feed the hungry . . . clothe those who are cold . . . comfort the weary . . . help the needy . . . these are things you should already know how to do, yet too many have not learned. How is that so? God has provided boundless riches in this world, enough for all. Yet some would take only for themselves—and others would kill with no remorse to ensure they get what they feel is their due.

"You need to understand that the nature of God is *love*. As children, you learned the 'Golden Rule' at your mother's knee: do unto others as you would have them do unto you. Do not slap your sister because she has your toy. Do not steal your brother's cookie because he locked you out of his bedroom. It sounds so simple . . . but still you humans struggle, don't you? The way to God is simple: treat others as you would yourself if you want the life force within you to grow stronger. If you do this simple thing, you will become part of the life force when you leave this Earth, and you will experience all the wonders of the universe for eternity."

Again there was a pause, and Sarah's eyes flashed.

Beside him, Lorena trembled at her words. "Yes, Sarah, I understand," she whispered under her breath.

Cummings wondered if Sarah was talking to his wife personally, though he could think of no reason why she would. Still, Lorena seemed to be somehow transported.

Sarah resumed speaking. "There is no shortcut to God," she said. "The faithful flock to their churches, mosques, tabernacles, ashrams . . . all institutions that should reflect God's true nature. But when they get there, they are asked to live up to particular ideals—with no exceptions—if they are to be one with the flock. I am here to tell you that such perfectionism is not the way to God, and humanity's religious institutions will need to adapt if they are to play an ongoing role in helping people develop spiritually. If they do not, the flock will move on. My presence is indisputable truth that God is neither an anachronism nor a fantastic fairy tale—and religious institutions will need to change to reflect this truth."

Cummings couldn't imagine what the world's religious leaders were thinking while hearing Sarah's words. To him, it seemed as if what she said was undoing thousands of years of 'bondage by doctrine.' He wondered if Sarah's truth about God would cause someone to make corrections to the Old Testament. He'd never felt comfortable believing in those stories and had always questioned whether they were true.

Then Sarah spoke again. "Dear humans," she said, "you are a fragile race. Most of you are eager both to please others and to please God, but some would please only themselves, and unfortunately, such people have come to dominate your power structures and are leading only through the threat of violence." Then her eyes flashed, and there was a boom of thunder as Sarah cried out in her baritone voice, "No more!"

She paused after those two powerful words, and Cummings felt for a millisecond as if her eyes were directly on him.

Then she said the now familiar words in a slow, almost threatening voice. "As of this moment, no person will be able to kill any other person. Any person who tries to kill somebody will drop dead, and the weapon they wielded will be destroyed. There can no longer be wars. All armies in the world will be demobilized. All weapons of mass destruction will be destroyed. Countries will still be able to protect their borders, and law enforcement agencies will continue to uphold the law, but lethal force will no longer be allowed. God wants you to look at the direction you were headed and understand how futile that path was. And then God wants you to recognize that the only way forward is through the evolution of your minds and souls."

When Sarah finished speaking, she flashed her eyes quickly—and then simply disappeared. The screen on the television went blank, and NBC news came back on, the serious-looking male reporter now slack-jawed and somewhat terrorized.

He recovered quickly, though, and with the aid of a teleprompter managed to sputter, "We've just received notification from the White House via the brand-new Sarah Says platform that orders to recall all overseas troops have been issued. As we report live from Naval Station Pearl

Harbor in Hawaii, I can tell you that there is a sense of disbelief among some of the naval personnel we have interviewed . . ."

"She never said anything about the biological changes," muttered Cummings to himself, a little concerned.

"What?" asked Lorena, "What biological changes?"

But before he could explain, a flash of unearthly, bright, white light, nearly blinded them both, and then Sarah was suddenly in the Oval Office, shimmering before them in all her glory.

Lorena's eyes nearly popped out of her head. "Oh my God!" she shrieked. Then her cheeks flushed and tears began streaming unchecked down her face. "You are so much more amazing in . . . um . . . *person*," she gasped, clearly overwhelmed.

"Lorena Cummings," emitted Sarah with her classic golden tinkle of joy, "I am so happy to see you and tell you that you have lived an exemplary life that pleases God. You have been kind, you have been patient, and you have been loving. Your place with God is assured."

"Oh, thank you, thank you . . ." Lorena said, hastily wiping her eyes as she struggled to gain some composure. "It is *such* a privilege to meet you," she managed to add, breathless with adoration.

Sarah sent a flow of rose-scented air around the room and charged the energy around them all with her glow. "A woman of my own soul," she said, touching her shimmering women's hands to where her 40 million hearts were most likely to reside.

Cummings was a little unnerved at the way she was speaking to his wife—as if Lorena's time on Earth was almost done—but he did not feel comfortable questioning her about it at the moment.

Instead, he asked the question that was bothering him most, "Aren't you going to announce the biological changes?"

He was hoping against hope that perhaps there would be a change in this decision to modify human physiology. On the one hand, he understood that a global emphasis on sexuality had created many social ills in the world; On the other hand, he knew the changes to human sexuality would be perceived by some as a reduction of liberty at the deepest level.

"Yes, Samuel, I am," Sarah said, sending her radiance around the room as a golden light. "I am just allowing a moment for the words I've so recently imparted to 'sink in,' so to speak. The broadcasts have not yet been seen by those who are asleep or otherwise engaged. Once God confirms to me that every comprehending human being on this planet understands what is afoot, I will step forward to tell them about these changes . . . and I will deal with their outrage and wrath as God would have me do."

"*What* changes?" asked Lorena, linking her fingers through her husband's for reassurance.

"God will put an end not only to humans killing other humans, Lorena," said Sarah with an overtone of authority that—while it made Cummings flinch—seemed to draw his wife nearer to her. "God plans to put an end to unplanned pregnancies, abortion, rape, and sexual predation as well."

"That is remarkable," said Lorena in disbelief. "May I ask how?"

"God is changing human physiology and putting boundaries around the sex lives of humans. Humans will not be able to reproduce until the age of eighteen, and they will lose their sex drive after the age of forty—and women will no longer get pregnant unless they want, and plan, to do so."

Lorena's mouth dropped open. "That seems extreme," she said, pulling away a little from Sarah, who she obviously adored, in horror. Then she squeezed Cummings' hand and gazed up at her husband, her eyes full of questions. "Did you know about this?" she asked.

"Yes," he said, a little sadly.

Neither of them were quite ready to give up this part of their shared life. Though they were both in their sixties, they still had desire for each other. It was certainly not rocket-fueled by the hormones of youth, but it was sweet, tender, and loving, a shared bond. They didn't want to lose it.

"Don't worry," said Sarah directly to Lorena, and though Cummings could hear the words, he felt somehow left out of the conversation. "The bond with your husband will remain, as will the feeling of desire. But if you are honest with yourself, Lorena, perhaps you can admit what you feel isn't totally sexual desire—instead, your desire for your husband has been driven by your love for him as a fellow human and a man, as human pair-bonding was meant to be. Sexual desire evolved from your admiration for his presence, kindness, and support . . . am I correct?"

Lorena blushed a little. She was not used to discussing such personal things with others. But while she and Samuel had certainly had many wonderful, intimate moments during the course of their marriage—and had created two children together—she knew Sarah's words to be true, and so she nodded her agreement. She had always considered herself lucky to be with someone she trusted and regarded as a wonderful, intimate friend. So many of her women friends had ended up with cheaters, liars, and narcissists.

"You are a good woman," said Sarah. "You understand what it means to love."

Then, Sarah reached out and gently touched Lorena's cheek, a physical expression neither Cummings nor Lorena had expected. Lorena did not flinch or shrink back; Instead, she seemed to grow taller at Sarah's touch, and for as long as Sarah's hand remained on her cheek, she glowed almost as brightly as Sarah herself.

Cummings was afraid for his wife and was about to protest that perhaps Sarah was hurting her . . . but then suddenly, Sarah was gone again, and the level of brightness in the room returned to that of an April evening, just before 10:00 p.m. Eastern Standard Time, in Washington D.C.

Lorena, still overcome by her meeting with Sarah, turned to Samuel, and hugged him long. "I can't believe it," she said. "I still can't *believe* it."

He hugged her back. "She's real," he said, "and all of the things she says are real as well."

They let go of each other, and Lorena went back to Cummings' desk. She pulled the scotch out again, and this time brought it over to where Cummings was sitting on one of the Oval Office couches, refocusing on the television. She plopped down beside him, opened the bottle, and took a swig. Then she passed it to him, and he did the same.

A segment on how God's intervention was going to affect the markets was just beginning, and Cummings expected to see Feldman's face at any moment—however, as before, Sarah cut into the broadcast, causing the television screen to waver and glow in an unearthly way as her presence filled the screen.

"I am Sarah," she said regally, sending chills down Cummings' spine. "Sarah of God."

He took another swig from the bottle when Lorena passed it to him, and then suddenly, the private Oval Office phone on his desk started ringing. He passed the bottle back to her and got up to answer it.

"Cummings here," he said.

It was his attorney general, Franklin Bishop. "What the hell?" yelped Bishop. "What is going on, Samuel? Is this a joke?"

"Calm down, Frank," said Cummings. "It's no joke."

Cummings' instructions to calm down had no effect.

Franklin Bishop remained agitated, and said tersely, "I thought someone was having the nation on! Then I saw that every channel is carrying the same story. But how come no one called me? Don't you think I should have been in the loop on this?"

Despite himself, Cummings laughed. "I understand your feelings, Frank," he said, "but none of this was my doing. Believe me, I'm just doing as I'm told, same as everyone else."

"So you're saying this godly woman-thing is the real deal?" asked Bishop in shock.

"Yes," Cummings said, "and the edict against killing is just the start. Turn on your TV."

He heard Bishop yell to his wife, "Maisie, turn on the TV again!"

A woman's voice said something that sounded suspiciously like, 'Hold your damn horses, already.'

And then Cummings heard Bishop exclaim, "What in the holy hell!?"

"Yes, that's her . . . and she's announcing biological changes to the human race," Cummings told him matter-of-factly.

There was no answer from the AG; In fact, Cummings was sure he heard Bishop's phone hit the carpet.

He turned back toward the Oval Office television to see Lorena watching raptly as Sarah said, "Your leaders introduced me earlier. You met me earlier. Now I will tell you once again why I'm here. I have been sent to Earth to intervene in human affairs on God's behalf. First, God demands that all killing of humans by other humans stop. Those who saw earlier broadcasts are aware that, as of this moment, no weapons will ever be effective to kill other humans ever again. If you try to kill another person, it will backfire on you. Your intended victim will live, but you will surely die. It doesn't matter if you kill in anger or are motivated by rage, greed, or lust. If you try to kill another human, you will die, and the weapon you attempted the killing with will become ineffective, by God's hand."

Sarah paused in her speech, and on the other end of the line, Cummings could hear Bishop fumbling with his phone.

"Well, I'll be damned," Bishop said to Cummings in shock. "She looks like the real thing. My TV started glowing or something when she came on the screen. Maisie ran for the bathroom to take out her contact lenses. She was certain she was seeing things . . . but I told her, 'Maisie, I see it too,' and now she's crying and wondering if she should call her mother . . ."

"Well, take a deep breath and listen to what she's going to say now," said Cummings. "It gets crazier . . ."

"What could be crazier than this?" asked Bishop.

"Just listen," said Cummings.

Sarah resumed speaking. "God is also making changes to human physiology," she said. "Puberty will be gradually delayed until age eighteen for both men and women, and the human sex drive will terminate at age forty. Also, no woman can become pregnant unless she *wants* to have a child."

"Good God," said Bishop. "Can this Sarah-thing actually do that?"

"She's not doing it, Franklin," said Cummings. "God is."

Bishop, a one-time atheist, had nothing to say.

Sarah continued, "These changes will delay reproduction until would-be parents are mature enough to handle the responsibilities of child rearing. The changes will also eliminate unwanted pregnancies and the need for abortion. Further, they will curb the disturbing trend of sexual predation that is often practiced by powerful, older men."

Bishop yelped, "There's gonna be a lot of anxious guys out there when people hear about the changes God is making! What else can you tell me about what this Sarah plans to do to us?" he asked fearfully.

"I can tell you that political, business, and religious leaders will be coming together in a series of global meetings to help make sure that every person on Earth has a better future ahead of them," Cummings told him. "I can also tell you that Lopez is working on a website I expect she'll have launched within the hour. Blackstone has already taken steps to get the military to stand down, to recall troops, and to notify law enforcement and border security not to try lethal force. Feldman will be presenting an economic recovery program within minutes. Northrup set up the press conference and is stickhandling the press. And Hana Shriver is working with both Lopez and Northrup to get the word out to any obscure, untapped media we might have missed in the first pass."

"Shriver!?" shrieked Bishop. "You mean *she's* on board, but somehow I got left out of this thing? She's Republican, for God's sake! What's she doing on your team?"

"That wouldn't have been my first call either," said Cummings, "but Sarah thought it was good to have a bipartisan unit so we would present an example of unity to all Americans. We're leading by example."

Bishop was clearly flabbergasted. Cummings could hear him clearing his throat on the other end of the line. It seemed he wanted to say something but could not find the words. Cummings grinned wryly. He knew how Bishop felt.

Meanwhile, Sarah kept speaking. "No doubt my presence on Earth has made many of you wonder about the true nature of God, particularly those of you who have scientific, rational minds. The story of God and creation is both simple and indescribably complex. However, science and God intersect at the truth, and there is no need for one to exclude the other. God was present 14 billion years ago at the time of the Big Bang that created this universe. God exists in every part of this universe and is responsible for distributing the life force that fuels every living organism on the billions of planets that support life."

There was a pregnant pause as Sarah left some room in her speech for people to absorb her words. Then she picked up her words again, saying, "Yes, there is intelligent life throughout this universe. There are species on other planets who are so advanced that they can simply manipulate energy to create the things they need for their sustenance. They have this power because they have evolved spiritually to the point where they use such power only for good."

"Well, I'll be," said Bishop, whistling through his teeth in astonishment, right into Cummings' ear.

Sarah continued, "Some of these beings evolved spiritually to be in line with God without need of God's intervention; Other more warlike creatures required the same treatment as humans. God interceded when their ability to self-destruct developed faster than their ability to demonstrate compassion."

"Wow," said Bishop with a long exhalation.

Sarah concluded with, "People of Earth, I will be staying on this planet for one full year to help your species adjust to these changes and to keep your leaders on track as a better, kinder world evolves. Also, I will be here to answer any questions about what is happening."

Then she looked out of the television screen with her deep, starlit pupils, and the forcefield she projected was so heavy that Samuel felt as if gravity was pulling him into the core of the Earth.

"God is providing certainty about humanity's long-term future, and God wants you to move forward together in peace and harmony," she said . . . and then her image flickered off the screen.

On the phone, Bishop sputtered inanely into Cummings' ear. Beside him, Lorena started to cry with joy.

Chapter 10

Day One

In less than twenty-four hours, 80% of the world's population had heard the news of God's intervention, most receiving word via social media, which was buzzing with the message 'thou shalt not kill,' hashtag #shaltnotkill.

Sarah's appearances quickly went viral on all major social media platforms, and her image was displayed on the front pages of major newspapers around the world, under headlines ranging from the stoic New York Times banner: *Sarah of God: Emissary Intervenes in Earth's Affairs,* to the tabloid announcements that carried variations of: *Angel of Death Says, "Shape Up or Else!"*

At the White House, feedback was coming in fast and furious over the website set up by Vice President Lopez. It was clear to Cummings that most people were overjoyed about the idea of an end to war though, as expected, there was a massive outcry against the suggestion that it would be a good idea to surrender personal weapons. *That's classic,* thought Cummings. *Everyone thinks it's a good idea as long as it doesn't cost them anything.*

Lopez forwarded a sample of these 'no, never!' emails to him and—after laying down with Lorena for a short, scotch-fueled nap—Cummings opened them up the minute he got back to his desk in the Oval Office to read such things as:

You'll have to pry my gun out of my cold, dead hands, wrote Rick C. from West Virginia.

This is a hoax, and you're gunna burn in Hell for lying to us, wrote Hayley S. from Alabama.

The Lord giveth and the Lord taketh away. And you're not getting my gun because you're an agent of the devil, wrote Jeremiah L. from Utah.

Cummings sighed as he read the emails. He could only hope these people didn't try to kill anyone with the weapons they insisted on keeping. Sarah had told him to do his best to notify his people, and he had done so. The message was out there. The military was stepping down and stepping out of active, aggressive service. Non-lethal weapons were being dispatched to law enforcement and border security units as fast as they could be procured from manufacturers. The execution in Texas had been canceled. Prisoners at Guantánamo Bay facility were on lockdown, and authorities there had been ordered to refrain from using life-threatening techniques to make them talk. In short, his country had been notified, and Cummings could not think of another thing he could do, at least in the short term, to ensure the safety of his people—or himself.

There was a knock at the door, and Feldman poked his head in. He looked as tired as Cummings felt.

"Did you get any sleep, Norman?" asked Cummings with a big yawn.

"Only about forty minutes, Chief," replied Feldman, yawning back. "I put my head down for a bit to clear it so I could get some reports together without falling asleep at my desk. Graydon Pierce and I agreed to do another update over the Sarah Says site to let investors know how the markets are doing. I have a few projections I could use your help with, if you're feeling up to it."

"Sure, sure," Cummings said, signaling to Feldman that he was welcome to come closer to his desk. "Let me see those reports."

Feldman walked over to Cummings' desk and laid some printouts of the reports he had been working on down in front of the president. "Financial experts are having a field day trying to figure out how the demise of the defence industry is going to affect global markets, not to mention international economies," he told Cummings with a worried frown. "There's been a lot of speculation about which governments won't survive."

"I can imagine," said Cummings as he picked up the sheets Feldman had given him and started examining them.

The two men were silent as Cummings did a quick review.

When he was finished, Cummings looked up at his treasury secretary and said, "Good work, Norman. I couldn't have done better myself. I'll sign off on these." With that, he looped his signature on the papers and handed them back to Feldman.

"Great, thanks," said Feldman as he took the approved papers. "I've got to get going. I told Graydon at the Federal Reserve I'd call him ASAP so we could prep for our announcement."

He turned to go, took a couple of steps toward the door, and then seemed to think better of it. Turning around, he asked Cummings, "Are you okay, Chief? I know you're tired, but you're looking . . . well . . . really *down*. Do you need to talk?"

It was uncharacteristic of the normally self-involved Feldman to reach out in this way, and Cummings was touched by the man's concern.

However, he felt no need to share his thoughts, so he just said, "I'm fine, Norman. Thanks for asking. I'm just getting used to . . . well, the 'new normal,' I guess."

"I understand," said Feldman, "and I don't blame you one bit." With that, he spun on his heel and made his way out of the Oval Office to prepare for the market briefing he was giving with Graydon Pierce.

What Cummings had not been able to say to Feldman was that he and Lorena had lain in bed and reminisced about their shared past for the last two hours. Both were afraid of what they would lose when the edict was fully deployed. If God determined Cummings to be an enabler, he was facing the potential loss of his life, and Lorena had to be prepared for his sudden demise. But even if he was saved from death by God's grace, he—and every other male over the age of forty—was going to essentially become a eunuch. It seemed like punishment on a personal level, and Cummings was both worried and saddened by the idea.

He was certainly not the only one speculating about how the shortening of human sexuality would affect his life, let alone how it would affect the world. Questions coming in over Sarah Says ranged from concerns about the future of marriage, to the viability of the cosmetics industry, to whether or not Viagra would work on men over forty.

Lopez's team of customer service agents were ready with all the answers, as provided by Sarah.

1. ***Effect on marriage:*** Marriage is for more than sexual activity; It is for procreation, long-term partnership, and companionship as well.
2. ***Effect on the cosmetics industry:*** It is doubtful that the cosmetics industry will feel much impact, as people will continue to want to attract others by putting forward the best version of themselves as possible. If that version currently involves the use of cosmetics, then it will likely continue to.
3. ***Using Viagra after age forty:*** Viagra will not work on men over forty, as this artificial stimulant will violate God's edict that men over forty will no longer be able to reproduce or pursue inappropriate sexual activity.

Cummings read the questions and answers, and he found the common threads to be largely predictable. Men were universally upset by *any* changes to the status quo, particularly the idea of enforced erectile dysfunction. He knew intimately that at least part of this reaction stemmed from his gender's need to be in control and to feel powerful. They did not like having an edict forced upon them in any way, shape, or form.

Women, on the other hand, were surprisingly supportive of the idea of delayed puberty. Judging by many of the comments that came in over Sarah Says, there were thousands upon thousands of women who had been initiated into sexual activity at ages and times that were not appropriate for them. They were glad to know this discomfort would not be foisted onto the next generation of women.

Both genders were unhappy about the idea of sexuality ending at age forty. Like him, adults past their prime were wondering what this would do to the nature of their physical expressions of love.

All around the world, people were absorbing the news of God sending a heavenly being to Earth to change the destructive path of humankind, while at the same time praying that things really would be better, as promised.

The World Reacts

Boston, Massachusetts, U.S.A: Beat cop Brody Murphy was looking forward to retiring from the Boston Police Department in two and a half years, at the golden age of sixty-five. He was home with his wife, watching TV before bed, when the news came on about the intervention from God.

"Geez," he said, sipping the last of his nightly beer. Then he called out to his wife, "Fiona! Come on in here! Get a load of this."

Fiona had been in the kitchen, packing lunches for them both. She was a nurse's aide at the local clinic and was at work by 7:00 a.m. every morning, so she'd long made it a habit to be prepared the night before.

"What are you yelling about now, Brody?" she teased from the kitchen. "Is it one of those cute cat videos you like so much again?"

"No, I mean it, come here," insisted her husband of thirty-five years. "You gotta see this, Fi!"

Drying her hands on a dish towel, Fiona wandered nonchalantly into the living room. Brody was always trying to show her things she thought were silly. Though she appreciated that her husband wanted to share whatever it was he was interested in, she really just wanted to get the lunches made and get to bed. The closer she got to sixty years of age, the longer the weeks were beginning to seem.

Her husband was staring at the TV, transfixed. On it was a woman, or a close approximation of one. She looked a little out of focus, and she glowed. Fiona blinked a couple of times to clear her vision.

"What the heck is that?" she asked Brody.

Uncharacteristically, Brody grabbed her hand and pulled her closer to where he sat on the couch, causing her to stumble a bit. "Sit," he commanded.

Surprised at his insistence, she plopped down beside him.

The woman on the television said, "It doesn't matter if you kill in anger, or you are motivated by rage, greed, or lust. If you try to kill another human, you will die, and the weapon you attempted the killing with will become ineffective, by God's hand."

Fiona frowned, trying to make sense of the glowing being on the screen who every few seconds seemed to change faces, and who somehow seemed three-dimensional, though she was firmly encased within the two dimensions of the television screen.

"What is this show?" she asked, aware of her husband's preoccupation with police-themed drama.

"It's not a *show*," said Brody, and his words slurred as if he was in shock. "It's the goddamn *news*."

"The *news*? Where is the anchor who's usually on there?"

Even as she asked the question, Fiona knew that something momentous was happening, and that the news anchor they usually tuned into was probably in a corner gaping at this being on the television, just as she was.

"According to what the president said earlier, this woman here is sent from God," Brody explained to his wife. "She going to change the world, I guess. All killing is gonna stop, and no weapons will work anymore. That's what they're saying."

Fiona looked at Brody cautiously, to see if he was buying this 'news.' It was clear by his expression that he was, which instantly convinced her that what he was saying was true. Brody Murphy was many things, but he was not gullible, nor was he a fool.

Instantly, Fiona put her hand on her husband's knee and said, "Oh Brody, *now* will you consider retiring early?"

Both of them knew what she was talking about. Brody was a good fifty pounds overweight, and his knees were shot. The only reason he'd been able to carry on as a beat cop for the past three years was because he'd been given modified duties—and because he carried a gun.

"Yeah," he said to his wife. "I can't work without a gun, Fiona—not unless they give me a desk job. I'm too old for street fights and chases. The last thing I need before retiring is a massive coronary!"

"You're so right, Brody," said Fiona, pecking his cheek, pleased.

She'd been pressing for the last few years for him to retire early because she was worried about the stress of the job and the health issues she could see creeping up on him, such as a diagnosis of pre-diabetes and metabolic syndrome. As far as she was concerned, this 'intervention,' as the lady on the television called it, was well-timed. She got up and went back to the kitchen, leaving Brody to think about it.

Sitting on the couch, Brody reminisced about his career. Being a cop had made him into a much harder man than the one Fiona had married thirty-five years ago. When they'd first met, he'd been idealistic, always trying to help out other folks, but after he'd been in the job for a while, he become harder by necessity, as a way to protect his inner, gentle nature from the inhumanity he witnessed on a daily basis.

He hadn't paid a great deal of attention to God during his life, but he had always assumed he had the option of repenting at the last minute to get him through the pearly gates. Now it didn't sound like that was going to work anymore. Maybe by leaving the police force and turning to charitable works, he could make up for three decades of thinking of fellow humans as vermin and scum—and for referring to those he'd manhandled harshly over the years as the 'nearly departed.'

The earlier I retire, the more time I will have to get enough brownie points to get into Heaven, he thought as he mulled a future in which, with or without a gun, he would become highly vulnerable.

Just then, a flyer on the coffee table caught his eye. He picked it up and looked at it. St John's Mission was looking for volunteers to help feed the homeless. *That's it,* thought Brody. *I'm going to do that a couple of nights a week from now on.* He made a vow to himself to call the organization first thing in the morning.

Fiona poked her head back into the living room. "Brody," she said, "what did you think about all that stuff about aliens?"

"It don't affect me one way or the other, Fi," he told her. "I'm not much interested in all that gibberish."

Fiona had a far-away look in her eyes. "I am," she said. "I want to see one of them one day."

***

Beijing, Hebei Province, China: Li Na, age twenty, was waiting for her boyfriend at their favourite lunch spot, sitting outside the small building on a bench under a cherry blossom tree. They were going to get noodle bowls and take them to the park where they could watch the ducks swimming. Sometimes, Li Na gave the ducks some of her noodles.

Her boyfriend, twenty-three-year-old Wang Chow, was a little bit late. Somewhat bored as she waited, she decided to check out the newsfeed on China's Tencent social media platform. Immediately, she saw posts about the end of the world, and she read a few messages about an angel that had come to Earth.

"What?" she asked in amazement. In China, open, online religious discussion was uncommon.

Intrigued, when she saw a video link, she clicked on it, not too concerned about it being a virus or scam link given the preponderance of messages discussing the same thing. Suddenly, there it was: On her screen, up popped up an image of a woman—or was it an angel as people were saying?

Li Na's eyes widened in surprise as she looked at the womanly creature called Sarah of God. Sarah was glowing and appeared lifelike, but this did not convince Li Na that she was real. A computer engineering student, she had seen some amazing technology and hoped to be able to create such things herself someday.

She pressed play. The woman on the screen claimed to be a creature composed of 40 million souls speaking with one voice. Li Na squinted at the video and tried to analyze what technology could create such a realistic holographic image. She was amazed at the ability of whoever had programmed it, and she couldn't wait to show this amazing technology to her boyfriend.

Then the woman said that God had not only abolished war, but that no human could ever kill another human again, and Li Na got interested in her words.

"What?" she asked out loud.

She forgot about analyzing the technology and started listening to the message. Her grandmother, a Buddhist, was a pacifist and had tried to instill in her favourite granddaughter the same love of peace that had guided her own, long life. It had worked. Nothing would please Li Na more than an end to war. However, she still wasn't certain that this being was real, and so she navigated on her phone to the official site of the People's Republic of China. On it, she was surprised to find a video message from the Chinese president, Dong Yang. She didn't want to watch yet another speech from China's long-winded leader, so instead she scrolled down the webpage to a list of the major speaking points, and saw these three highlighted:

- *An emissary of God has come to be among us.*
- *War and killing have ended.*
- *God is responsible.*

At first, Li Na was taken aback because the words seemed honest and in keeping with what the angel woman had said. And honesty was not something she'd come to expect from China's government. Officially a communist nation governed by the Marxist philosophy—and touting the 'from each according to his ability, to each according to his needs' philosophy—Li Na had only to look around to see this was in no way applied in China. Despite what the government's official party line was, there was a huge gap between rich and poor, still and always, and the needs of the poor were *never* effectively met. From this, she garnered that China was governed by hypocrites who could not be believed.

But what if God has really stepped in to stop the lies . . . ? The words on the country's official website infused Li Na with a new sense of hope. She doubted that it had come easy for her country's leaders to announce this thing, and most certainly, the rather secretive Chinese government would not have done so if its proverbial arm had not been twisted.

She furrowed her brows in consternation, and pressed the back button on her phone so she could listen to Sarah's message again. She began to get excited about the idea of people being unable to kill one another. She wondered if it might lead to a more free China, and she thought of the brave student known as 'Tank Man' who'd stood in front of China's military might, prepared to be crushed by a tank, in Tiananmen Square in 1989. Her government denied it had happened, but her parents talked about it still. They had seen it. They had been at the protests. They had pictures.

She watched Sarah's message two more times, allowing the words to sink in, and when she finished, Wang Chow arrived, breathless from running.

"Did you see it?" Wang Chow asked Li Na in excitement as he plopped down beside her and took a few long breaths. "Did you see the message from the one called Sarah of God? I am so excited to know there is intelligent life throughout the universe. I knew it in my heart . . . and now I know it is true!"

An aeronautics student at Peking University—which is where the two of them had met—Wang Chow had high hopes of joining the China National Space Administration someday, if for no other reason than to satisfy his curiosity about this very thing. Now, of course, he was more enthused than ever about his choice of vocation. "Can you believe this, Li Na?" he asked. "It is like a dream come true."

"I know!" exclaimed Li Na. "It is amazing. My grandmother has prayed for this her whole life."

At that, Wang Chow put his arm around Li Na and gave her a squeeze. She leaned her head on his shoulder, thinking of a type of freedom China had never known.

"No more tanks," said Li Na, her eyes shining brightly.

"No more tanks," agreed Wang Chow.

Then Wang Chow removed his arm and turned to face her. He took Li Na's shoulders in his hands, turned her toward him, and looked deeply into her eyes as he said, "Li Na, you and I have discussed marriage, and we agreed we should wait until we are in our thirties and both have good careers . . . but perhaps we should think differently about that now. We have only twenty years to enjoy each other's bodies as husband and wife, and to make children. I think we should marry as quickly as possible. What do you think?"

Li Na could see the sense of this. "Yes," she said. "We must tell our parents and arrange it as soon as we can."

"Perhaps we should go back to my place to discuss it?" he asked hopefully.

Li Na smiled, took his hand, and pulled him in toward her for a kiss. In the end, they forgot about getting a noodle bowl, and they went back to his flat to bring the discussion to a whole new level.

***

Idlib, Idlib Governorate, Syria*:* Amira Hassan awoke with a start. Something was wrong; Around her was not only the typical blackness of a bombed out city but also an immense silence, something she had never experienced in her short twelve years on Earth. There were no artillery shells splitting the night with their roars and crashes. There were no gunshots rat-a-tat-tatting as they sought out warm bodies to tear apart.

There were no planes overhead threatening to send her flying from her bed in pieces, the victim of yet another explosion.

She was terrified but did not dare wake her parents.

She lay quietly in her bed, fearful of what the dawn might reveal. Perhaps the city was gone, and she was the only person left alive. And then light crept in through the small window in the concrete walls of her room, and with it came a sound she hadn't heard for weeks . . . birds chirping, followed by dogs cautiously barking at them as if they were as confused as Amira by the sound.

Finally, after uttering a short prayer to Allah that her family was both well and alive—and that her mother and father were in the bedroom down the hall where they usually slept—she heard her parents' cautious voices.

"Abbas," her mother said to her father in Arabic, in a hushed, worried voice. "It is so quiet out there this morning. I am afraid to look out the window to find out why. Can you do it for me?"

Like her daughter, Amira's mother Madiha was afraid to face the possibility that all of their Idlib neighbourhood had been evaporated overnight by some sort of new, torturous, destructive weapon, and that all their neighbours, family and friends had been vaporized.

As his wife had requested he do, Abbas looked out the window, just as Amira walked into their room and gave her mother a great hug. They both watched the man of the family as the expression on his face changed from one of extreme trepidation to one of disbelief, followed by joy.

"Abbas?" asked Madiha. "What is it?"

"*Eaqila* . . . wife, come and see!" he said excitedly, and both Madiha and Amira rushed to the window.

Looking out, they could see that the whole village was out and about in the open square, chatting with one another excitedly—something that had not happened in years.

Then, as their friends and neighbours milled about in the midst of the rubble left by successive bombings, a crescendo of voices began to chant, "*Alhamdulillah*—Allah be praised!"

"The bombing has stopped. The fighting has stopped," said Abbas in disbelief.

"Are you sure?" asked his worried wife. "I have believed for so long that this is not possible."

"I am sure, my wife," said Abbas. "Come, let us see!"

With that, he took his wife's hand, and she took Amira's hand, and the whole family went out into the square to join the joyous celebration that was taking place there.

"What has happened? What has happened?" demanded Abbas of his neighbour Karam Abboud.

"It is a miracle!" cried Karam Abboud, but he gave no answer other than that.

Just then, Karam's twenty-five-year-old son, Rifat Abboud, raised his cell phone above his head and appealed for quiet.

When the excited group around him had quit shouting and laughing at the wonder of clear blue skies devoid of fighter jets, he looked around at them with tears in his eyes and said, his voice cracking with emotion, "Allah has sent a great angel to end all war and killing! She is called Sarah, and she has proclaimed herself to all people of the Earth."

"What?" exclaimed Abbas in disbelief. "What do you say?"

"It is true," insisted Rifat. "I have a Wi-Fi signal from the Hafez Hotel," he insisted, pointing to a small, run-down building that Amira had been warned to stay away from. Then Rifat started to shake his phone. "Damn!" he yelped, and he began to run toward the community generator that her father and some of the other men had scraped enough money together to purchase some months before so that their small, tight-knit community would have a shared power source. "I must plug in my phone!" he yelled back to the group. "It is almost dead!"

Quickly, people began scrambling to their feet to follow him. Rifat primed the generator, prayed quickly to Allah that it had gas, and then pulled the rip cord. The group was in luck; It began to rumble loudly.

"I have a long extension cord that we can plug into the generator!" Amira's father yelled over the generator's roar. "I will get it for you!" With that, he said something into Amira's mother's ear, and then quickly ran back to their home to get the cord.

He was only gone about five minutes, and he returned with an old, orange extension cord in his hands that had seen better days. He plugged it into the generator, and this allowed the whole group to move about thirty feet away from it, which significantly lessened the noise.

Quickly, Rifat plugged his phone into the cable, and it made a pleasant beeping noise that indicated it was charging. Then Rifat made some movements on the screen of it with his finger, and soon a video was called up on the astounding device.

"Look!" exclaimed Rifat, holding up the phone. "See?"

The five people closest to the small screen leaned in to view the video, and the five next closest began to form a line behind them. Amira was lucky enough to be the daughter of the man who had provided the extension cord, and so her mother, putting her hands on Amira's shoulders, placed her smack dab in front of the video and watched it herself over her daughter's head.

Amira's young eyes grew wide as saucers as she watched the godly being on the small screen in front of her.

"Mother," she whispered in awe. "She says the war is over!"

Behind her, her mother started to cry and fell to her knees.

***

Hong Kong, Special Administrative Region of China: Forty-six-year-old Wong Jian was extremely upset when he heard the news about God's intervention. He was in his luxury penthouse apartment, fifty-eight stories in the air, having a well-earned glass of Screaming Eagle Sauvignon Blanc (purchased for a mere $3,500 USD—a steal) and watching the news, after spending the day examining product proposals for his tech company to develop.

The president of China was announcing that a godly being named Sarah had come to Earth to stop war and murder . . . and, from the sounds of it, sex for fun as well.

"Damn!" he exclaimed in Cantonese, his mother tongue. "This must be a pack of lies. It's bullshit!"

He just didn't believe it. He had to do more research. He pulled out his tablet to check out what other information he could find about this preposterous claim, and he was startled to find that the whole internet was full of this odd proclamation. Further, while China kept strict control over what type of digital information could leak through its borders, a video of this 'Sarah' relaying her message from God was playing across all supposedly protected Chinese platforms.

Jian watched the video in fascination. The effects used in creating the 'Sarah' video were startlingly lifelike, and he wondered what super-hacker had not only created such magnificence but managed to get through China's firewalls to get this video played over Weibo, WeChat, Baidu, and Taobao, among other platforms. He was going to hunt that asshole down and hire him!

Then he sat back and pondered what he'd just heard, wondering, *What if it's true that God sent an angel down?* He threw the wine back without even tasting it.

"It's bullshit!" he said again.

Wong Jian was a rising star in the high tech sector. He'd earned his first billion dollars by age thirty-five, and at forty-six, he was well on his way to his second. He spent most of his days in the executive suite of the skyscraper that bore the name of his multinational corporation, overseeing product design and investments.

He was brilliant at what he did, but also ruthless. During his rise in the business world, he had crushed hundreds of competitors—not to mention axed weak performers on his own team. At Wong Jian Enterprises, if you could not work twelve-hour shifts, six days a week, you were off the team. His company motto was 'work long and prosper'—and those who didn't comply were ruthlessly fired, despite the fact that the Chinese work week was supposed to be only forty-four hours.

Apart from the accumulation of money, Jian's only joy in life was a very active late night sex life, generally purchased from the finest brothels Hong Kong had to offer. However, if the videos he'd seen today had even a grain of truth to them, it meant that, at forty-six, this luxury and means of relaxation had been removed—permanently.

"Bullshit," he said, still not believing it. "Bullshit!"

He flicked his remote control until he'd called up his favourite porn channel. He watched the women on the screen as they writhed about in very little clothing. He waited for a physical reaction to it . . . and there was nothing.

He looked down at his pants, puzzled. Normally, there would be a tent of expectation where his zipper was, but there was nothing there. Worse, the zillions of neurons in his imagination should have begun firing the minute Patty Peaches and the Iron Stud began to go at it, but there was nothing, nada, zero desire invoked by the spectacle in front of him.

"What the hell?" he exclaimed out loud.

This *never* happened to him. He prided himself on not needing to use Viagra like many men his age, but now he wished he had some to try. Nevertheless, he was also becoming convinced that perhaps what was said by the Chinese president and Sarah, the godly being who'd appeared on all the social media channels, was actually *true*.

Somewhat chastened, he shut off the porn and replayed Sarah's video, searching for answers. He was frightened at the thought that his sex life was over. What was he supposed to do to relieve stress now? Lift weights? Knit?

He watched Sarah's video again, listening to the message about no killing and no more war. He listened once more to the explanation about the physiological changes being made to the human race. Then he tried to absorb what Sarah was saying about the nature of God, and how the goal of life was to help your fellow man. The formula for getting into Heaven seemed pretty simple—but he hadn't become successful by being Mr. Nice Guy, so he supposed he was on the shit list with God.

Suddenly, he was angry, very angry. He still wasn't completely convinced that Sarah was the real deal or that the video wasn't just a bunch of bullshit . . . but even if it *was* a hoax, he could see some serious decline in productivity if Wong Jian Enterprises' employees bought into this bullshit and used it as an excuse to turn away from their dedication to their jobs and toward the so-called 'God' Sarah claimed to represent.

"This is such *bullshit*!" he cried as he threw his tablet across the room and watched it bounce off the coffee table.

He immediately regretted doing so and picked it up, glad to see there was only a small crack at one corner.

Then he went into the bathroom to take a shower, and as the hot water poured down on his back, he started to feel guilty about his ruthless behaviour during his climb to the top. He'd stepped on a lot of people on the way up, without a second thought. He wondered if it was too late to make up for his misdeeds. He decided he'd better hedge his bets. *Tomorrow*, he told himself, *I'm going to donate a million dollars to Amnesty International*.

***

Syrian Refugee Camp Outside Dresden, Saxony, Germany: Hans Eckstein was frustrated. He had been searching for a particular refugee who he had some business with, and Shakeel Abboud was nowhere to be found.

The two men were not friends; Hans was a guard at the Syrian refugee camp where Shakeel lived, and Shakeel owed him 120 euros. Shakeel had assured him he'd pay him back when he received money from his brother Rifat, who was still in Syria, but so far, there had been not a dime. Hans, at age twenty-eight, was full of testosterone and aggression, and all he could think was, *When I find that little bugger, I will teach him not to fuck with me!* He could just imagine getting his hands around the smaller man's neck, choking him until he turned purple, and then kneeling on his neck until he prayed to whatever God he worshipped for mercy.

Hans had lent Shakeel 70 euros so that the Syrian man could buy supplies for his family, and to ensure he was paid back quickly, Hans had insisted on an interest rate of five euros a day after a three-day grace period. He was more than angry when the man, his wife, and his three children vanished into the bowels of the 1,200 person refugee camp several days later. He was bound and determined to root them out and exact his revenge. He wasn't called the Teutonic Tiger for nothing. If he was crossed, he *got* cross.

As he mulled over just what kind of punishment he would dole out to Shakeel, he spotted a man walking through the throngs of people toward the refugee assistance tent, a man he was pretty sure was friends with Shakeel.

He called to him, "Are you Kaden?"

"Yes, I am Kaden," said the man politely, looking at Hans with no recognition—though the guard uniform and the buffed up, dangerous-looking body of Hans clearly garnered a certain respect.

"I am looking for Shakeel Abboud," said Hans, his voice dark.

The man understood the threat, and his face paled. "I have not seen him for several days," he said, his eyes darting around, looking for escape.

"Are you sure?" asked Hans, narrowing his eyes.

"Yes, by Allah's name, I am sure," swore Kaden.

Hans decided not to make an issue of it at the moment. It was enough to put the fear of God into Kaden; If he was in touch with Shakeel, then at least the message would be passed on.

He said smoothly, but with just a hint of danger, "If you see him, you tell him I'm looking for him."

Kaden nodded in agreement and then hurried off, obviously eager to get away from Hans. Once more, Hans thought about what he would do to Shakeel's scrawny Syrian neck when he found him.

"Verdammt," he cursed in German.

He decided to head to the chow tent that had been set up for the guards and other employees of the camp. As he started walking in that direction, his cell phone rang. It was his girlfriend, Helge.

"Hallo," said Hans.

"Hans!" she exclaimed. "Have you seen the news?"

"Was meinst du—what are you talking about?" asked Hans, somewhat annoyed.

Helge was a nice girl, and he liked her very big breasts, but sometimes she got excited about things that he did not care about in the least. He imagined she was probably just excited about a movie star having a baby or something.

Instead she said, "Chancellor Schmidt is on the news! She is saying God is going to stop war and killing, and a heavenly being has been sent to Earth to kill all the killers. I thought perhaps she was crazy, but it seems all other world leaders are saying the same thing!"

"She *is* crazy," said Hans authoritatively, thinking of all the grimy Syrians—and other disgusting refugees—she'd let into his country. "Let me call you back. I will look into it."

With that, he hung up and immediately did a search online. He found the video of Chancellor Schmidt's address to the nation. He was surprised to find out that what Helge had said was true.

He frowned in consternation. He didn't like this news. Without the threat of lethal force, how could Germany protect itself from all the refugees—lying scum like Shakeel—and keep Germany pure? He thought of his great-grandfather, a proud Nazi who was probably rolling over in his grave right now. He had fought for what he believed in, and Hans had long wanted to honour this hero of his. He had hopes of joining the Patriotic

Europeans Against the Islamisation of the Occident (PEGIDA). He'd been to one of their rallies, and it energized him to march with 20,000 others to protest the increase in Islamic immigration that was threatening the harmonious lives of hardworking Germans like him.

He reached the chow tent, grabbed a sandwich, and sat down to eat. As he finished the last of his midday coffee, he found Sarah's video. His eyes widened as he saw her on the small screen of his phone. Something in her eyes seemed dark and frightening to him, and he wondered if she could see into his soul.

"Anyone who attempts to kill another person will immediately drop dead, and any weapon used in the attempt will be rendered inoperable," said the intense, strange-looking woman-thing on his phone.

He dropped his cell, his hand tingling as if it had been burned.

Just then, he saw him . . . Shakeel sprinted past the tent door, running as if a ferret was biting his heels. Hans sprang to his feet.

"You there! Thief!" he yelped as he gave pursuit.

Shakeel saw him coming and increased his pace, fear firing his limbs. He ran toward a noise, the sound of people yelling, screaming, and cheering, with Hans in pursuit.

"Was ist los? What is going on?" asked Hans to himself.

He slowed his pace. He had no wish to run willy-nilly into the centre of a group of seemingly exultant Syrians. He was not particularly popular with the ones he had been shaking down, and his 'peacekeeping' baton had landed more than once on the knees of some of the men who were no doubt in that group.

He decided to quit chasing Shakeel, and instead, he slowed his pace and approached the celebrating group cautiously. They were singing prayers of joy and chanting, some in Arabic and some in English, "Take us home!"

On the other side of the throng of people, Hans could see his boss, Jurgen. Jurgen caught his eye and made his way toward Hans by delicately skirting around the celebrating group.

"This is out of control," he acknowledged when he arrived. "That angel, or whatever she is, has ended war, and the boys want to get out of this dump. Can't say I blame them. It's a shithole, no matter how nice we try to make it. It's ironic that the chancellor almost destroyed her political career to get them here, and now she's going to have to jump through hoops to get them all home again!"

"Well, we don't want them here anyway," muttered Hans darkly.

"What did you say?" asked Jurgen, shocked. Hans immediately looked guilty, and Jurgen said coldly, "You may feel that way, but I do *not*!" And he stalked off, leaving Hans feeling embarrassed, chastised, and fearing for his job.

At that moment, Shakeel showed up. In his hand was a stack of grubby euros.

"Here are 80 euros," he said, throwing the money on the ground in front of Hans. "The seventy I borrowed and ten more for interest. I have no more money for you, and you will not treat me like a dog. I am a child of Allah, and today, Allah has shown favour to me."

Hans just stared after Shakeel as he walked away with his head held high. Then he stooped and picked up the money, blew on it, and dusted it off. He began to wonder if joining PEGIDA was actually such a good idea after all.

***

Mumbai, Maharashtra, India: Priya Anand and her betrothed, Raj Acharya, were working with Raj's aunt on their upcoming wedding. The two had been betrothed to each other in childhood. After a lifetime of shared activities during which both families frequently came together for social events, they had come to be pleased at the idea of this arranged marriage. They were glad they would be spending a lifetime with one another, and truly in love.

Priya, twenty-three, was a few months away from completing a degree in biology and was hoping to enter medical school when she was done. Talented mathematician Raj, twenty-six, was getting ready to defend his thesis for his doctoral degree, and had a tentative teaching job lined up at the University of Mumbai.

"You two lovebirds go along," said Raj's aunt in Hindi, their native tongue, when they had finished looking at venues and samples of decorations, including a white horse for Raj to ride in on as per Hindu custom. "I can handle this now."

"Thank you, Auntie," said Raj, pecking her cheek.

Raj's talented aunt had ably stepped in to help them that day because the couple's respective parents were busy.

As the two left Raj's aunt's home and leisurely strolled back to the University of Mumbai campus where they both attended classes, they stopped for a cup of tea at a small shop. Priya sat down at an outdoor table, while Raj procured the drinks. As she waited for him to return, she scrolled through the newsfeed on her phone. It was full of notifications about someone, or some*thing*, named Sarah.

She clicked on one of the links, and immediately, the small screen was filled with a womanly image who was glowing in an unearthly way. Priya was so startled, she almost dropped the phone; It looked as if this being was going to float right out of the device, and the light accompanying Sarah was so startlingly bright that Priya had the funny idea that she might get burned.

Priya's eyes widened in disbelief as she listened to the words Sarah spoke . . . no more killing, no more war . . . perhaps an end to the rampant violence that took place every day on the streets of Mumbai? One could only hope.

Raj came back with their cups of tea to find her engrossed in her phone. "What are you looking at, my dear?" he asked. Then he teased, "Surely you are not looking at Bollywood stars again?"

Priya didn't smile at the jibe, which was not like her at all. She had a wonderful sense of humour, which is one of the things Raj loved most about her.

Instead, she said, "There is something strange going on in the world today, Raj. The prime minister has a video announcing that a being has come to Earth on behalf of God . . . and now I am looking at the video of this being, who is called Sarah. She says there will be no more killing or war, and that it is God's will!"

"You're joking," said Raj, putting Priya's tea on the table in front of her.

"No, I'm not joking. The videos look real. It's really the prime minister speaking!"

Raj brought the prime minister's broadcast up on his phone while Priya continued to watch Sarah's video. They sat in silence until both had finished, and then they looked at each other in astonishment.

Priya was first to speak. "What a wonderful wedding present, Raj!" she said with tears in her eyes. "No more war. No more nuclear threat from Pakistan. No killing."

"I can hardly dare to believe it," said Raj with a lump in his throat. "With our upcoming marriage, I have been worrying so much about whether it is fair to bring a child into this world. This seems to be the answer to my prayers. It will remove so many threats and make the future more certain, but best of all, it will make the world a much friendlier place in which to raise a family."

Priya agreed. "Praise be to Brahman," she said.

"God's intervention is a miracle," said Raj, "but humans still have a long way to go, I'm afraid."

"Yes," agreed Priya sadly, thinking of a former schoolmate who, at fifteen, was viciously beaten and raped by a gang of men on a bus, and who later died from her injuries. She looked at Raj with tears in her eyes and asked him, "Do you think the men that attacked Kali would die if they did now what they did then?"

"I don't know," he said softly, taking her hand and looking deeply into the eyes of the woman he was going to marry. "But I do know that God has not abandoned us—and that can only lead to a better future." Then, with his eyes full of all the love he felt in his heart for her, he suggested, "Priya, why don't we make a pact in our wedding vows that we will dedicate our lives to helping others? If we do this, we can join God and become one with the universe as Sarah has promised."

Priya looked at Raj with shining eyes. "I would be happy to do this with you, Raj. I want the same thing."

Raj laughed with joy and then teased his bride-to-be, "Besides, I want to know whether God's name is 'Raj' like my mother told me."

Priya cheered up a little at that, and teased, "Next you will tell me that your aunt arranged for God to send Sarah just as a wedding gift for us."

"I'm sure she did," said Raj.

***

Tehran, Tehran Province, Iran: Mahmoud Jafari, a sixty-five-year-old imam at a mosque in the District 12 area of Tehran was absorbed in his daily ritual of studying the Qur'an, when one of the faithful, Milad

Fouladianpour, who volunteered in the mosque, brought him news of the intervention of Allah.

"You say Allah has sent an angel to Earth?" he asked Milad in disbelief.

"Yes, Imam," the man replied, bowing low to show respect for his revered teacher. "I will show you." He reached under the long, white, traditional Arabic thobe he wore to a belt he had strapped around his waist, and he pulled out a mobile device. "I have downloaded the video," he said to Imam Jafari. "I think you must see it."

The imam put on his reading glasses and watched, first with disbelief, and then with growing interest as the video of Sarah's announcement played. His face paled as he quickly grasped the momentousness of this day. When the video was over, he asked Milad to play it again, and Milad did. Then he asked to be alone.

When Milad left the room, the first thing the imam did was turn to Allah. "Praise be to Allah, the good and holy," he whispered under his breath. "May thy will be done, and may the angel you have sent be truly a messenger from you, the one and only Allah."

When Mahmoud had finished his prayers, he felt calm and centred. Now he tried to process the words that had come from the mouth of this wondrous being, this Sarah.

Since the imam was already a believer, he did not question that Sarah was sent from God—in fact, he took this quite for granted; And when he heard the news about the abolition of war and killing, he clasped his hands to his heart, overjoyed to think that perhaps his country might finally find peace. He was even reluctantly pleased to hear about the limitations being placed on human sexuality. In fact, he hoped this would curb the Islamist extremist practice of marrying child brides to older men—men generally selected by a girl's father for economic or status reasons. While the imam understood the practicalities of this archaic version of Islamic law, it was not something he personally supported.

Other parts of Sarah's message, however, made him scratch his head. *She said there are countless intelligent life-forms on billions of planets in this universe,* he thought. He supposed this could be true, though it was a concept he had shoved aside in favour of adherence to his faith. However, while he loved Allah and Islam with all his heart, he'd also earned a doctoral degree in theology at the University of Tehran forty years before, and there he had familiarized himself with many subjects—including astronomy. He was well aware that there were galaxies upon galaxies in the universe and that, simply by the law of averages, it was unlikely that humans were the only life forms under Allah's watchful, loving eyes.

She said that prayer and attendance at mosque are not particularly important when it comes to getting into Heaven, he remembered. This too was not overly shocking to the imam, though he disagreed—but not because he felt it made Allah angry if people did not attend. Instead, he had learned that attendance kept people focused on Allah, which disinclined them to stray into misdeeds. However, he was sure this message would anger his countrymen who believed in a harsh and angry Allah, and whose focus was on revenge and a Holy War.

Only one part of Sarah's message, however, bothered him somewhat, and that was the implication that Allah did not create the universe—that Allah was simply an observer to the Big Bang and all that followed. At sixty-five years old, he had spent a lifetime devoted to the study and interpretation of the Holy Book, the Qur'an, and he firmly believed that Allah created all that is, was, and ever will be. But while he differed with Sarah on this point, he did appreciate her explanation of how God sent sparks of life force to the planets to ignite the process of life. To him, this made far more sense than the 'creation' story long told to Muslims, Christians, and Jews alike.

And then he thought long and deeply about the idea that there were more women in Heaven than men, and he wondered what implications this revelation would have on the Islamic extremists. *Perhaps,* he mused, *it will create a kinder society if men understand that their unfair actions toward their mothers, wives, and sisters have not gone unseen by Allah.* He hoped it would change women's status in the mosque—and in some cases, simply allow them in the door to worship. He also hoped it would spark a return to the old ways, before the 1979 Islamic Revolution, when women were men's equals, if not their betters.

When the imam was a boy, Tehran, his lifetime home, had been a modern, cosmopolitan city, full of culture. University students with a thirst for knowledge drove around the town in Volkswagen Beetles, sporting mullets and miniskirts, just like their counterparts in the United States . . . except—in the imam's eyes at least—the Persian women were far more beautiful than American ones, with their dark, thick eyelashes and long, glossy, ebony hair.

As a child, he'd looked forward to being a teenager, admiring his older sister's popularity and his older brother's success at school . . . and then, in a heartbeat, the government of Shah Mohammad Reza Pahlavi was replaced by the Islamic Republic under Grand Ayatollah Ruhollah Khomeini—and it was like his country stepped backward in time.

Under the shah, Iranian women had free universal education, careers, and were not restricted by the head-to-toe covering of the chador. They were government ministers, scientists, and judges. They voted. They drove cars. They were free. After the revolution, wearing the chador was enforced by threat of public whipping and prison, and women became nothing but the property of men. Worst of all, men could simply declare, "I divorce you," three times to dissolve their marriages, as the imam's father had done to his mother.

Khomeini was long dead, and things had improved a little for women, but the tentacles of Islamic extremism had taken deep root. The chador was no longer required, but headscarves still were . . . and to this day, women accused of adultery could be executed by stoning.

He desperately hoped Allah would make this right.

***

Rural Area Outside Manizales, Caldas Department, Colombia: Over the last fifteen years, Emilio Lopez had transformed half of his medium sized coffee plantation into an avocado farm. Avocados brought higher prices at market, and for the first time in decades, fifty-six-year-old Emilio was actually getting ahead.

It was hard to make a living in Colombia, especially in Caldas, one of the smaller, less prosperous of the thirty-two departments (and one capital district) that made up the country of Colombia. However, Lopez was a hard worker and a big dreamer, so he cheerfully persevered. He knew dreams could come true. He only had to look at his cousin's daughter for proof. The oldest child of Mateo Lopez, Angelica, was now—praise be to God—the vice president of the United States!

Mateo, who was fifteen years older than Emilio, had fled Colombia three decades ago in fear of the drug cartels, who had been 'disappearing' anybody who got in their way for half a century. He had the good fortune to fall in love with and marry an American woman, which helped him in his quest for citizenship. His wife, a woman whose parents had emigrated from Mexico a decade before, owned a thriving import/export business, and Mateo easily integrated himself into it, helping her to expand it into three successful retail shops in the Houston area.

Two daughters soon followed. The oldest, Angelica, demonstrated a remarkable aptitude for science, and by age fifteen, she was accepted to the University of Houston College of Technology, while the younger one, Rosita, went on to work with her parents.

Surprisingly politically minded, within two years, seventeen-year-old Angelica Lopez was president of the student council, and from all accounts, she was very good at it. Given her natural intelligence and her outgoing personality, this had not been particularly surprising to anyone who knew her . . . but for her to make it all the way to the office of the vice president of the United States? Well, that was a miracle from God!

Whenever Emilio drove his beat up old truck into Manizales, the capital city of Caldas, and stopped for a beer at his favourite watering hole, he touted her success and was roundly applauded for his connection to her. He rarely confessed that he had only met her once, when she was a small girl; Instead, he told his friends that he had high hopes his cousin's daughter could help with problems with the drug cartels, who were extorting money from him and other local farmers.

Government and law enforcement were deeply in the cartel's pockets, so many villages had formed vigilante groups to protect themselves, but the criminals were heavily armed and ruthless. It was a losing battle. Reaching out to his cousin to ask for assistance was a long shot, and Emilio knew it; However, he was frightened that one day soon, he would be identified as one of the vigilantes and become 'disappeared' himself. If anyone would understand this threat, it would be Mateo—surely he could petition Angelica to see if there was anything she could do?

He was walking among his avocado plants, checking the fruit, and thinking about these things, when his foreman, Pablo, came hobbling over, clearly excited by something. Pablo could not walk properly because several years ago, he'd been tortured and his toes were cut off by the cartel when his son, a former cartel member, had run away to escape what he'd come to realize was a terrible, violent future. The group did not believe Pablo when he told them he did not know where his son had gone, and Pablo's feet paid the price. But despite the torture, he never told them that the twenty-one-year-old was cloistered away in a dugout hole in Emilio's barn, hiding until Emilio and Pablo could smuggle him out of the country through the Andes.

"Emilio!" Pablo called excitedly as he approached his friend and employer, holding a small radio in his hand. "Escuchar esto . . . listen to this!"

"What is it, Pablo?" Emilio asked.

"It has finally happened!" exclaimed Pablo, falling to his knees with tears in his eyes. "God has answered our prayers!"

Emilio listened to the tinny words coming out of the small radio, and he was surprised when as he listened, the tiny speaker seemed to take on a life of its own. The tones were becoming robust and realistic, the hiss of the radio fading in kind until it seemed that the woman who spoke was standing in the field with him and Pablo, talking right to them.

". . . as of this moment, no weapons will ever be effective to kill other humans ever again. If you try to kill another person, it will backfire on you. Your intended victim will live, but you will surely die. It doesn't matter if you kill in anger, or you are motivated by rage, greed, or lust . . ."

Emilio's eyes widened in surprise and disbelief. "What is this, Pablo?" he asked. "Is this true?"

Pablo didn't answer. Instead, still on his knees, he began uttering prayers of thanks to the Holy Virgin. In a few minutes, Emilio joined him.

Later, Emilio listened to a replay of the news as he sat in his small house, eating a simple dinner of beans, rice, and chorizo sausage he had made himself when he'd slaughtered two pigs last fall. He smiled with joy as he pondered the abolition of war and killing. The Armadas Revolucionarias de Colombia (FARC) had been disarmed and could no longer kill anybody—a miracle from God Almighty. *It may not get rid of organized crime*, he thought, *but if they are stripped of their intimidating weapons, vigilantes like me can at least look forward to a fair fight.*

The rest of the news Sarah brought did not concern Emilio much. Despite that she spoke of a 14 billion-year-old universe and aliens on other planets, his faith in Jesus would not be altered; In fact, it was now stronger than ever. If what Sarah said about the nature of God was true, then Jesus had created more life force while on Earth than a thousand men—no, a *hundred* thousand men.

Neither was Emilio too concerned about his own place in Heaven. He would keep his head down, continue to lead an honest life, and look out, as always, for those he loved. He had always put the welfare of others before himself as his father taught him. He was confident that eternal life with God was in his future.

As he poured himself a cup of coffee and sliced an avocado, however, he admitted to himself that he would miss having a sexual life. He wondered, *What will I disclose as a sin when I visit Father Rodrigues in the confessional now?*

***

Seattle, Washington, U.S.A.: Professor Emeritus Nathaniel Wayne, one of the world's most renowned experts on comparative religion, had to struggle to control his heart rate and breathing when he first heard Sarah speak. He was overwhelmed, overjoyed, and overexcited—something his doctor would not recommend, since he was on beta-blockers to lower his heart rate. However, after experiencing the extraordinary spectacle of a bona fide being from God commandeering his television station, he felt he could happily die at seventy-two, and suddenly, he didn't give a fig about his doctor's advice. His quest was complete. He finally knew the answer to the age old question, 'What is God?'

Nathaniel had dedicated his professional life to studying the world's major faiths. It was more than an intellectual passion that drove him; He was a spiritual seeker, and he had always wanted to know the true nature of God.

Until today's news had rocked his world, after many years and much study, Nathaniel had reached the conclusion that the faith that most closely mirrored the results of his research was the Hindu faith, which taught that there were four goals for human life—dharma (ethics and duties); artha (work and prosperity); kama (passion and desires); and moksha (liberation from 'samsara,' the cycle of death and rebirth).

Nathaniel was sold on the idea of multiple lives, and over the years, he'd had many lively discussions with colleagues about the topic. In his view, there was no other way to explain little children coming to Earth with the innate capacity to play the piano like Chopin. *That can't be taught,* he thought. Not only that, but there were documented cases of children dragging parents to houses they claimed to have lived in before and unearthing things they had hidden there to prove their claims.

It was not surprising, therefore, that he was not particularly happy with Sarah's insistence that those who squandered their opportunities had their life force redistributed by the hand of God; However, he *was* happy that Sarah was confirming that dharma made a difference. He had always believed that service and kindness were key to entry into Heaven, and so he'd tried to live a life of service, not only as a teacher—his paid profession—but as a volunteer and a philanthropist. He was pretty certain he had fulfilled his mission on Earth in that respect, and that he would be allowed to return to God, carrying life force with him in the way Sarah had described.

He was also pleased at the idea that women were now going to have more choice in matters to do with reproduction, and he hoped this would result in more women in spiritual service. He'd always noted that, while men approached the esoteric questions he asked in his classes as problems to be solved—as if they, themselves, were God—women took such concepts as springboards by which to draw closer to God. The rest of the physiological changes didn't worry him too much; At his age, his libido was long since gone.

A researcher by nature, upon his first moments of hearing Sarah's words, Nathanial had jotted down his predictions of how he expected the top religions of the world to react to her words. He was certain that the leaders of all the great faiths, with the possible exception of Buddhism, would claim that Sarah's revelations confirmed *their* religion to be most in line with her revelations. Then he laughed aloud at the thought that even the Scientologists might claim victory because Sarah had told the world that there were aliens out there who already lived in a tangible version of Heaven.

But what excited him most about Sarah's visitation was that he now had a new project. He planned to launch a new study immediately and produce a paper within a year entitled "The Adaptability of Established Religion to the New Word of God." He would have to select a PhD student who he could redirect toward this project, and he pondered the possibility of bringing on another faculty member as well, in case his ticker gave out and he was prematurely called to serve in Heaven.

Giddy at the prospect of what could become the crowning achievement of his life's work, Nathaniel immediately thought of Dr. Amelia Goddard, a theology expert and friend whose office was just two floors down. He picked up the phone and dialed her number, all the while humming Louis Armstrong's "What a Wonderful World."

Chapter 11

Death By the Hand of God

Junior Richards, a gun-toting republican and devout evangelical, was a member of the largest white supremacist group in Michigan. He listened only to right wing radio, specifically the station featuring DJ GoodnRight, and got most of his opinions from an underground, encrypted website that fed into his belief that scum-sucking, vile democrats were destroying the United States of America.

In Junior's somewhat biased opinion, the worst of the traitors was the governor of his home state, Annie Bergen. He was convinced that socialist bitch wanted to bring his country down, and he was going to make sure it didn't happen.

Junior and his group of like-minded buddies, who called themselves the Cleanup Crew, spent months planning what they were going to do about it. Eventually, details of Annie Bergen's calendar were obtained, provided to Junior by Michigan's one remaining Republican senator, Jacob Williams.

Williams, an easygoing, back-slapping type who had spent his whole career positioning himself as a saviour for the disenfranchised, was happy to help Junior out. However, at the bottom of his decision was not his politics; Instead, it was a personal dislike of Annie Bergen—after all, not only was she a woman (a hysterical, feeble-minded creature, in his eyes), but she was biracial, something that Williams, a racist, couldn't accept.

Williams was ambitious enough to be careful about appearing *too* sympathetic to the causes of the far right, and he made sure that, while he supported their sentiments, he didn't do it overly vocally. For example, he was known for tweeting comments that, while inflammatory, were so nuanced Williams could squiggle out of responsibility for his words if called on them. He was an expert at never quite crossing the line into overt racism . . . but he was a man with a very dark heart.

It had been easy for Williams to get his hands on Annie's schedule. Charming, good-looking, and still on the south side of forty, all he'd had to do was smile coyly at the governor's newly hired, inexperienced assistant, and then convince her that all senators, no matter what their political stripes, were allowed to see the governor's calendar. It was lunch time and the senior assistant was on a break. The flustered young woman had no one to consult with, and she not only wanted to be helpful, but was cowed by his authoritative nature. *Stupid little girl,* thought Williams as he thanked her for the information with a saccharine smile.

Later, when Senator Williams handed Junior a slip of paper with two weeks' worth of Annie Bergen's engagements printed on it, Junior saluted him. "Thank you, Sir!" he snapped, calling on his reservist training to ensure he imparted the appropriate level of respect.

"You go do something *good* with this now, boy," said Senator Williams with a wink and a handshake.

After that, Junior and his buddies only had to pick a day when they were all available . . . and within a week, a full-on march on the state capitol had been planned—timed to intercept the governor on her way to a fundraising event.

When the big day arrived, in full combat fatigues and armed with assault rifles, Junior and his buddies marched down to Lansing, to the capital building. Confident in their right to bear arms and to assemble, Junior mostly ignored the significant police presence along the route that he and the other nineteen Cleanup Crew members had commandeered for their march. They strutted four abreast in five rows between the watchful eyes of the police officers who flanked them, and Junior strode proudly on the end of the second line, scanning for his target like a hunter for a deer.

Just as the twenty-strong group of armed militants approached the historical, castle-like building that housed the state's legislature, Junior saw the governor's limo leaving the place. It was heading directly toward him and his marching comrades, and he knew his big moment had arrived. He had a shot at Annie Bergen—and he took it.

As he pulled the trigger, he did not expect the weapon he was holding to become molten steel in his hands, yet by some trick of nature or God, that's what it did. Immediately, his hands began burning, and he screamed in a high-pitched, ungodly monotone for a total of ten seconds. He had a momentary view of Annie Bergen looking at him in astonishment out the window of her limo as her driver sped quickly away. He died immediately after that. Later, the autopsy would say he died of shock.

Two of his comrades also dropped dead, their weapons clattering to the ground and melting into the asphalt as they fell. One had spent several late nights with Junior discussing where he should be positioned in order to get the best shot at the governor, and had even practiced timing the assassination with him. The other, when Junior expressed reservations about what he was planning to do, convinced him that his name would go down in history as a soldier for the cause, and that shooting the governor was his destiny. Together, their support enabled Junior to attempt the murder, making them as guilty in the eyes of God as Junior.

Simultaneously, at the radio station where Junior got most of his information about the world, the announcer known as DJ GoodnRight died as well. Earlier, when word about the planned march had been covertly supplied to the station by one of Junior's Cleanup Crew cronies, the DJ had congratulated the group on their 'inspirational resolve' and told listeners that, "Within the hearts of these young men marching on the state capitol today, the hand of God is at work to keep America pure." Junior craved approval, and so the announcer's words removed any ambivalence he'd felt, further enabling him to proceed with his plan.

Within minutes of DJ GoodnRight's death, the station manager who'd encouraged the announcer to extoll his racist opinions—and who'd egged his employees on in spreading such questionable ideology—died as well, as did the owner of the station, who specifically hired people who were bigoted and racist ('purists,' in his opinion).

Further, the webmaster and owner of Junior's favourite website died, as did five freelance video producers who'd supplied 'conspiracy theory' content to the site, and whose movies had influenced Junior's decision to try to kill Annie Bergen. The videos featured white supremist themes, including one that denied the Holocaust ever happened. Junior's favourite, the one he watched repeatedly, was an exposé of the Democratic party, claiming that at the top level was a secret pedophile ring. He was convinced that Annie Bergen was a procurer for the ring. He was also convinced that Democrats were seizing power in order to give America over to a 'coloured' army, which was going to rise up to eradicate all whites. The documentary advocated for violence and a race war as the only way to 'Keep America Clean'—the slogan of the website.

In Lansing, Senator Jacob Williams also dropped dead, ostensibly from a heart attack, on his way to a business luncheon at the capitol. At his office, his secretary, Jasmine Hollingsworth, also died. Jasmine was a nice girl, but during the course of her cliché, 'secretary-does-the-boss' affair with the married Williams, as a way to ingratiate herself to her lover, she'd affirmed his racist ideals. First, she began following the same warped social media posts that he did (the author of the 'Nicely Whitely' blog died at the same time as Jasmine); Next, she lied and told Williams she'd seen Annie Bergen in the washroom trying to seduce a twelve-year-old boy. Knowing Bergen to be biracial, she'd added, "You know how those people are," which caused Williams to look into Bergen's heritage. Until then, he'd been unaware that the governor had descended from slaves—not because she'd hidden it, but because he was obtuse. After he found out, he saw her as someone who did not deserve to be in a powerful political position . . . which is why he felt no guilt about supplying Junior with information about her whereabouts.

All in all, fifteen people died due to Junior's attempt to assassinate Annie Bergen—one would-be killer, and fourteen enablers.

The naïve young girl who gave Jacob Williams the information about Senator Bergen's whereabouts did not die. God understood that had she known what the senator was doing, she would have refused him access to the governor's calendar.

***

Globally, 42,673 people died by God's hand on day one, which amazed Cummings. He had done the math and knew that if even 1% of the 7 billion people on Earth died by God's hand, that would equal 70 million deaths. Fortunately, the number was far, far below 1%.

Of those deaths, only 1,702 were Americans, and of that number, only forty-four died as a result of directly attempting to take another person's life, while 1,658 were enablers. Further, of the would-be killers, only three of the dead were military personnel—a miracle, in Cummings' eyes.

Sarah provided the tally of day one deaths to Angelica Lopez as soon as the first twenty-four hours were up, and Lopez's multimedia team dutifully posted it on the Sarah Says website, and then began tweeting and otherwise dispersing the news across America.

As Cummings reviewed the information on the website, he frowned, dismayed at this look into the nature of the citizens to whom he felt responsible. The number of enablers was much larger than he felt comfortable with. An example of the fates of enablers was apparent with the attempted assassination of his close friend, Michigan governor, Annie Bergen. Along with her would-be assassin, fourteen other people died, 'enablers' in God's eyes.

Cummings was glad God's edict had saved Annie's life, though it pained him to know that, had the attempt on her life taken place just one day earlier, she would be in a morgue right now. Instead, her would-be killer lay cold and dead in her place.

Strangely, he felt sorry for this misguided young man and so, completely uncharacteristically, he found himself uttering a little prayer: *God*, he prayed, *wake them up before too many needlessly die.*

There was no answer from God, but for the first time in his life, Cummings was certain that God had actually *heard* his prayer.

Then he began reading the web postings about the deaths.

DAY ONE AMERICAN DEATHS (ABROAD)

Rural area, 367 Miles North of Baghdad, Iraq: (Three Primary Killers / Zero Enablers)

- *Three American soldiers died when they returned fire on an Iraqi ambush.*

[Link to details and enabler information]
[Link to media reports]

When Cummings clicked on the 'details' link, he read:

A U.S. army convoy delivering food and medical supplies to an outpost in Northern Iraq was attacked. The American soldiers were out of radio range when news of God's intervention was announced, and so did not receive the same notification to stand down as the rest of their military brethren did. Upon encountering their attackers, and seeing raised weapons, they immediately returned fire, and did not notice that their assailants were dropping dead without actually discharging their weapons.

Dead:
- Jonathan Billings (twenty-four), Butte, Montana
- Kareem Jackson (thirty-seven), NYC, New York
- Keith Clarkson (thirty-five), Savannah, Georgia

Enablers:
- N/A

Cummings breathed a sigh of relief. Given that he was still alive, apparently God had decided that he and Blackstone had done all they could to inform the military to stand down.

He continued reading.

DAY ONE AMERICAN DEATHS (STATESIDE)

Lansing, Michigan (One Primary Killer / Fourteen Enablers)
- *One man died trying to assassinate the governor of Michigan.*

[Link to details and enabler information]
[Link to media reports]

Cummings already knew the details of his friend's close call, and so he moved on quickly.

Baltimore, Maryland: (Eight Primary Killers / Thirty-Seven enablers)
- *Five young men died trying to knife enemy gang members.*
- *Three police officers died attempting to use lethal force to quell the disturbance.*

[Link to details and enabler information]
[Link to media reports]

Cummings clicked on the link and read:

In a turf dispute, thirty gang members from two local area gangs met to rumble in the warehouse district. Four squad cars and eight police officers attended the scene. After the first several deaths, all attendees at the altercation understood that would-be killers were being instantly felled. All men at the scene put down their weapons.

Dead:
- Officer Richard Jenkins (thirty-seven), Baltimore, Maryland
- Officer Nigel Greenstone (thirty-nine), Baltimore, Maryland
- Officer Rhonda Brennan (thirty-five), Baltimore, Maryland
- Jace Hawkins (twenty-one), Baltimore, Maryland
- Sonny 'Slim' Moseanko (nineteen), Baltimore, Maryland
- Philip Joseph (twenty-three), Arlington, Maryland
- Conner Penner (eighteen), Arlington, Maryland
- Robert Collins (seventeen), Alrington, Maryland

Enablers:
1. Wayne '2Cool2Care4U' Foster (thirty-nine), Los Angeles, California. *(inciting hatred through lyrics)*
2. Grady Penner (forty-five), Charleston, West Virginia. *(father of Philip Penner, supplied handgun)*
3. Tracey Joseph (sixty-two), NYC, New York. *(encouraged aggression, supplied methamphetamine)*
4. Jack Shen (twenty-six), Silicon Valley, California. *(created 'Gang War Turfland' video game)*

Cummings didn't really want to read all the details about the enablers. He knew that whatever created a killer was a long, dark rabbit hole that he didn't want to go down. Nor did he want to read the article about the gang violence, as the idea of it sickened him. He did, however, think a statistical analysis of the information was in order, and so he picked up his phone and immediately called Bradley Northrup.

"President Cummings," answered Northrup, attempting to sound upbeat. "What can I do for you?"

"Hi, Bradley," said Cummings. "I was just checking to see how it was going with the long-term studies you were going to commission."

"They're on the list," said Northrup wearily.

"Thank you," said Cummings, adding more sympathetically, "I know you're tired, but I have to ask you to add one more thing to that list, if you could . . ."

"Let me guess," said Northrup, "you're looking at this infernal website of Angelica's and wondering what the hell makes people become hateful, spiteful trolls . . ." He stopped and sighed heavily.

"You got me," said Cummings. "That's exactly right. It's depressing, isn't it?"

"Yes, Sir, it is," replied Northrup. "But I suspect it's going to make a lot of people think about the impact of their words in the future, don't you?"

"I sure hope so," said Cummings, ". . . and Northrup?" he asked.

"Yes?" said his chief of staff.

"Go get a burger and take a nap. I know you've been working on this as hard as you can. Take a break, okay?"

"Yes, Sir, I will," said Northrup.

As Cummings hung up, he felt gratitude for his dedicated chief of staff. He hoped the man would indeed take his advice and get some rest.

Then he began to read again, this time only reading the high-level information about the actual killer deaths. His curiosity about the roles of the enablers had been satisfied. He knew the nature of their sins as well as he knew the nature of his own.

New York City, New York: (One Primary Killer)
- *One man died trying to kill a bartender.*

A man, angry and drunk, smashed a bottle and tried to slash a bartender's throat over a dispute about his bill, which immediately caused him to drop dead. Patrons assumed he'd had a heart attack and called 911.

New York City, New York: (One Primary Killer)
- *One man died as he attempted to push a woman onto the subway track in front of an approaching train.*

Cummings was interested in the circumstances behind this incident, and so he clicked on the link to the media reports. He read:

The man, Glenn Stefaniak (fifty-six), who was unknown to the intended victim, walked toward her as she was reading a magazine, and then suddenly rushed at her, intending to push her. Instead, he fell onto the tracks himself and was killed. It was later determined that Mr. Stefaniak was mentally ill and had not been taking his medication due to inappropriate advice from a 'healer' who, along with her two partners, had secured power of attorney over his legal and financial matters.

Though the official cause of death was reported as a suicide, the intended target said, "It was like when he came at me, he ran into a great big wall and got electrocuted or something. He just came to a quick stop and froze like a statue. Then he fell on the tracks and the train ran over him."

"Wow," said Cummings. He did not have to read up on the list of enablers to know that, at the very least, the healer was dead, along with her two partners.

He kept reading the media reports.

Atlanta, Georgia: (Three Primary Killers)
- *One man died while trying to strangle a woman.*

A pimp, Alvin Moxley (forty-one), died punishing one of his prostitutes for holding back $50, money she needed for medicine for her two-year-old child.

"At first, he was only trying to scare me," said the shaken victim, "but then he got excited by the idea of killing me, I guess. But as soon as he got into it for real, he just died."

The gagging reflex that choked him was attributed to epilepsy.

- *One man died while trying to kill a child.*

A man died while attempting to kill one of his children as payback to his wife for throwing him out of the family home. While pressing a pillow over his eleven-year-old daughter's face, he suffered an apparent heart attack.

The attending paramedic, Janet Simpson, said, "The survivors are doing well. They attribute the death to God's intervention, and as soon as we pronounced the man dead, they began praising God for ending the bullying they had been living with."

- *One law enforcement official died while firing at a suspect.*

A police officer died while attempting to shoot a hit-and-run driver who was fleeing the scene of a minor accident.

"Like all my troops, he received the news not to use lethal force," said his grieving captain, "but in the heat of the moment, his training and instinct took over and he discharged his weapon without thinking."

The officer's heart stopped. The weapon melted.

Miami, Florida: (Two Primary Killers)
- *One woman died trying to kill her husband.*

A woman, Natalie Foster (twenty-seven), who had recently taken out an insurance policy on her elderly husband, died in the process of trying to push him off the balcony of their apartment, thirty-six stories up. Instead, she fell over the railing herself, landing on the concrete below.

Witnesses corroborated her intended victim's story that, "She rushed at me and then just catapulted off the deck as if someone picked her up and threw her."

- *One man died trying to kill a police informant.*

A drug dealer, Shane Alexander, who was under surveillance by the Miami police department, died while attempting to deliver an overdose to a customer he'd pegged as an informant. Upon trying to inject the customer with heroin laced with a high level of fentanyl, the drug dealer immediately began convulsing and fell to the floor. The informant, who had seen Sarah speaking on *Oprah* earlier that day, told police he was pleased with the outcome.

"I saw Sarah on *Oprah*," he said. "I knew I had nothing to fear."

New Orleans, Louisiana: (Two Primary Killers)
- *Two men died trying to kill shoppers in a store.*

Two white supremacists were killed by God when they tried to fire assault rifles at shoppers in a crowded Walmart store, in a section of the city primarily occupied by people of colour. They immediately dropped dead, and their weapons melted.

"I never seen nothing like it," said one uninjured shopper. "God is finally having pity on us poor people. He makin' up for Hurricane Katrina."

Houston, Texas: (One Primary Killer)
- *One man died trying to murder his neighbour.*

An angry husband, who believed his wife had cheated on him with his neighbour, was incinerated when he attempted to burn down his rival's home, using gasoline and charcoal briquettes, while the neighbour was sleeping.

The intended victim smelled smoke and escaped, while the would-be murderer burned to death inside the home he was trying to ignite.

Firemen found the body under a pile of red-hot briquettes. "He must have piled them on himself," said the Houston fire chief. "I can't imagine why he wanted to die that way."

Brownsville, Texas: (One Primary Killer)
- *One man died trying to kill an illegal 'border jumper.'*

A rancher, Luiz Paulo (forty-nine), died while trying to shoot and kill a Mexican national who'd crossed the Rio Grande and ended up in his field. The Mexican man reported that as the rancher pointed his gun at him, a giant angel appeared and stood beside the angry rancher in the field. He claims the angel said to the rancher, "If you do this, you will die," but that the man didn't hear her or even note her presence.

Upon trying to fire his gun, the rancher fell to the ground clutching his chest, and the weapon melted. "It was like God sent that angel down to save me," the Mexican man told the police. "I got a wife and kids to feed. I was only trying to get into America to work."

Albuquerque, New Mexico: (One Primary killer)
- *One boy died trying to shoot his father.*

An eleven-year-old boy, Nathaniel Green, died while trying to shoot his father. Earlier, the boy had tried to protect his mother from a violent altercation that had left her with a black eye and the boy with a gash on his forehead and a broken nose.

Having been witness to, and victim of, his father's violent rages all of his life, the boy tried to exact revenge. He went into his father's den, procured the gun from where it sat unattended on a desk, took it outside, and pointed it at his father while the man was chopping wood. According to the mother, the boy said to the father, "Don't you never touch her again!" as he pointed the weapon. The man laughed at his angry son and threatened to throw the ax at him, causing the boy to pull the trigger. The boy immediately died, as did the father, who had left the weapon unsecured.

Samuel's gut wrenched and at the thought of this poor, cornered boy's desperation. He rubbed his eyes to stop the tears that were stinging them, and then reached into the drawer where the scotch should have been. His fingers came up empty. *Shit*, he thought, remembering how he and Lorena had finished that bottle the other night. He shut the drawer and sighed.

Suddenly, the pressure of the air around him changed, getting denser and thicker. His ears popped—and a familiar golden glow lit up his desk, the paper he held, and the Oval Office around him.

"Hello, Sarah," he said, blinking several times at her brightness as she materialized in front of him.

"Hello, Samuel," she greeted him in her golden, tinkling way.

Instantly, he felt less sad. The energy she conveyed through her presence was uplifting on a deep soul level, and it was almost—though not quite—enough to take away the ache caused by the story of the boy who'd died while trying to shoot his abusive father.

She picked up on his dampened spirits right away. "Samuel," she said, emitting her trademark rose scent. "You seem distressed."

"It's quite a roundup, this death list," he remarked morosely. "I guess losing a thousand or so Americans a day until people get the message is what we have to look forward to in the short term?"

"It seems like a lot, I know," she agreed gently, adding, "but don't lose heart, word is spreading fast."

"I have to admit," Samuel said, "I was relieved that Annie Bergen's killer died instead of her, but I was shocked to hear that Jacob Williams died as an enabler. For a Republican, I always thought he was an okay guy, but Angelica told me that you assured her that his death was solely due to his own actions . . . ?" He let his words dangle in the air as a question.

Sarah smile enigmatically. "Don't you remember the discussion we had about free will? About sowing seeds of goodness and building your own beanstalk? Senator Williams had choices, as do we all."

"But do you *really* think he expected that guy to fire on the governor?" asked Cummings.

"If God determined so, then yes," said Sarah, a warm rush of energy encircling Samuel like a hug. "God's opinion is all that matters, and God is never wrong."

"God's way of doing business is going to change a lot of things in the political arena," mused Cummings. "In the past, many politicians have used the old 'plausible deniability' defence to get away with things, such as inciting hatred—but it's not going to protect them now."

"No," agreed Sarah. "Such a defence is no protection from the wrath of God."

"I had no idea Jacob Williams was a populist," Cummings said. "It's sad, really. The few times I met him, I thought he was more balanced. He hid his fanaticism well. I can't reconcile that big smile with a man who supported fearmongering and conspiracy theories."

"And yet that's who he was and what he believed," Sarah said softly, "and he died for it."

"That's going to make a lot of people change their tune about democratic conspiracies," Cummings said. "His cronies will have to admit that all their theories are lies. And if they support radical groups like the one Junior Richards was in, they'll wind up dead, like Williams."

"God works in mysterious ways, Samuel," said Sarah. And then with a flash, she was gone.

The room felt empty without her. Cummings sighed, feeling his spirits sink once more. Her presence had buoyed him. Somehow, reading about all this death didn't seem so bad when Sarah was in front of him, putting it into perspective. He really didn't want to look at all this stuff alone, but he had to.

He sat down to review the rest of the list.

Detroit, Michigan: (Three Primary Killers)
- *Three men died attempting to hijack and crash a plane.*

Three Islamic extremists attempted to hijack a commercial airliner with the intent of crashing it into a theme park. Taking their cue from the events of September 11, 2001—when terrorists crashed hijacked airliners into New York City's World Trade Center and the U.S. Pentagon—they managed to smuggle boxcutters on board a Boeing 727 flying out of Detroit.

Security at Wayne County Airport said the men hid the blades in a box containing a three-dimensional, metal puzzle. Upon takeoff, they took a steward hostage, demanding access to the cockpit. The minute one of them tried to cut the man's throat, all three terrorists dropped dead, bleeding from holes in their necks.

Chicago, Illinois: (Three Primary Killers)
- *Three boys died trying to kill their parents.*

Three teenage siblings, brothers (names withheld), died trying to kill their parents with baseball bats. According to their parents, for several months the boys had been dabbling in drugs which were provided by older schoolmates, and the oldest was becoming quite addicted to meth.

Upon asking for a loan from his parents and being refused, the eldest became enraged. Knowing he and his brothers stood to inherit a significant amount of money from their lawyer mother and real estate agent father, he got his two younger siblings on board, and they concocted a murder plan.

They ambushed the couple one evening when the two were returning from a date night. As the eldest raised his bat to strike his father, he immediately dropped dead from a massive concussion. The two youngest raised their bats to strike their mother, and they dropped dead as well.

Kansas City, Kansas: (One Primary Killer)
- *One man died attempting to drive a vehicle into a crowd.*

A bus driver, Salvatore Ungaretti (fifty-five), died when he attempted to ram his bus into shoppers at an open air market. Somewhat depressed over the death of his twin sister from leukemia, Mr. Ungaretti had been self-medicating with extremely strong marijuana, known as 'shatter.'

The marijuana was so strong that repeated doses made him delusional, and he began to believe his sister was demanding that he sacrifice people on her behalf so she could return to life.

As soon as he aimed the bus at his intended victims, the rear axle seized, causing it to flip over a curb and into a parking lot. Mr. Ungaretti did not die on impact; He exited the bus through the door, which was topside after the crash, climbed down, and confessed his intentions to the people who rushed over to help him. Then dropped to his knees, saying, "Sorry, God," before falling over dead.

Wichita, Kansas: (One Primary Killer)
- *One boy died trying to kill his sister.*

A five-year-old boy (name withheld) died trying to shoot his older sister with his father's handgun. The sister, age nine, refused to share her chocolate bar with him and called him 'dumb.'

The boy, having just watched a cartoon in which the evil character shot the hero in the shoulder for calling him 'dumb,' initially tried to shoot his sister with his nerf gun. She, being older and stronger, took it away from him, sending him in search of another weapon.

He went into his parents' bedroom and saw his father's licensed handgun sitting on the dresser. He took it into the living room where his sister was watching television and told her that he was going to shoot her in the shoulder. Having never seen a real gun before, she did not understand the threat, and so she said, "Why don't you just kill me instead?"

The boy exclaimed, "Fine!" and immediately died when he pulled the trigger. His father also died because he left the gun loaded and unattended.

Denver, Colorado: (Four Primary Killers)
- *Four men died trying to kill a woman.*

Four college seniors tried to kill a female sophomore whom they had raped repeatedly at a frat party. Dead are Kevin Stevens (eighteen), Lowell Juch (eighteen), Chaz Delacort (twenty) and Marcus Flagg (nineteen).

According to the victim, she was lured into a dorm room, and they locked her in. When she said, "Hey, quit kidding around," Delacort, a star football player at the University of Denver, told the others to gag and otherwise restrain her. The victim says no one heard her muffled shrieks during the course of the attack because the music at the party was far too loud.

When done, her attackers panicked, afraid she would report them. Delacort said, "We have to get rid of her," and the others agreed. However, as soon as Delacort began tightening a noose around her neck, all four began gasping for breath and died.

When the woman was rescued, she told authorities that she felt the air in the room change when the men died. "I swear, God killed them on my behalf," she said.

San Francisco, California: (Three Primary Killers)
- *Three men died trying to kill a police officer.*

Three workers in a meth lab tried to kill a narcotics officer who had infiltrated their operation. Dead are Victor Hussein (thirty-six), Harley Baxter (thirty-three), and Jan Eidle (thiry-seven).

The officer had been contracted by the men to provide pseudoephedrine to their operation in the form of hijacked cold and sinus medication. The three would have remained unsuspicious of the agent's identity, except for his refusal to try the finished product.

"I told them a producer should never mess around with their own product, but they pegged me over that," said the officer.

The men put hydrochloric acid, a component of meth, into his cola, but as soon as he raised the tainted drink to his lips, the cup flew out of his hands, and the three men dropped to the floor dead, foaming at the mouth.

Los Angeles, California: (Three Primary Killers)
- *Two men died trying to shoot an intruder.*

Security guards at a gated Beverly Hills property tried to shoot an intruder, and they both died. The two men, employees of reclusive, aging movie star, Hedda Wilder, had standing orders, from their vulnerable and mostly bedridden employer, to shoot to kill intruders, police said.

When the intruder entered the property, and the alarm went off, one guard was off shift, asleep. The duty guard immediately roused him, and they gave chase. As they fired on the fleeing, would-be robber, both of them dropped dead, and their weapons self-destructed.

Neither man had heard the edict from God, as the old-fashioned Hedda Wilder would not allow Wi-Fi or cable television on her property. They were found by Hedda Wilder's gardener several hours later.

- *One man died trying to kill a woman.*

A sixty-year-old man, Edgar Summer, died because, in a fit of road rage, he tried to kill a seventy-year-old woman in a small economy car by ramming her with his half ton truck.

The woman, who was returning from her weekly bingo game, was (according to witnesses) driving slowly in the fast lane. The man, who was clearly impatient, beeped at the woman in the slow car, trying to get her to move into the slow lane. The woman, who was partially deaf, did not hear him.

According to witnesses, this appeared to enrage the man. "I think he thought she was ignoring him," said Lane Sanders, who was driving beside Mr. Summer in the right-hand lane when the incident happened.

According to Sanders, Summer tried to get into the right hand (slow) lane and nearly hit him. "I beeped and gave him the finger," said Sanders, "and then he gunned his truck. It looked to me like he was going to run the woman ahead of him off the road."

The minute his bumper touched hers, his left front wheel seized, and he flipped and crashed into the culvert on the other side of the road, dying on impact.

San Diego, California: (Two Primary Killers)
- One man and one woman died shooting at police officers.

Two bank robbers, Janice and Lee Browhurst (forty-two and forty-five), died when they fired on police as they were leaving the scene of an attempted robbery.

The robbers, a husband and wife team, remained in the First National Bank on Main Street after hours, hiding in a janitor's supply closet at the bottom of a small stairway. When the bank closed, they waited until the janitor left at 7:30 p.m. and then began the robbery.

As the husband decoded the safe, the wife rifled through the teller's drawers and accidentally tripped a silent alarm. When the police arrived, the pair raced for the back exit, and their waiting vehicle, but when they got there, they saw their driver had already been taken into custody. They drew their weapons, began shooting, and immediately died.

There was more, but Cummings couldn't take it. He looked up from this tale of tragedy, exhausted and hurting for the people of his nation. He and his team had done all they could to prevent these tragedies, but only time would tell if it was enough. But at least he was still alive. So far, he had not been tagged by God as an enabler. He would live to hug his wife another day.

He was about to shut off his computer, when he noticed a link on the left side of the page in the navigation bar that said 'Suicides.' He clicked on it to read:

Day One Suicide Preventions (Stateside)
Suicides prevented by God (eight)

"Oh boy, do I really want to read this?" Cummings asked himself out loud. But he knew he had to.

He noted immediately that Sarah's notes on the suicides were much more concise than the ones she had made for the attempted killings, and she didn't name anyone. He thought this was probably to prevent people from trolling the poor souls.

Burbank, California: (two)
- Homosexual, teenage lovers whose parents forbade the match tried to suffocate themselves by breathing exhaust from a running vehicle. God's intervention prevented them from carrying through with the suicide and forced them to confess to their parents. They are now being treated in a healing sanctuary in Encinitas that specializes in LGBTQ challenges.

Boise, Idaho: (one)
- A recent immigrant in an abusive marriage gave in to despair and homesickness and tried to drown herself in the Boise River. She was unable to do so and is now living in an immigrant-run shelter for women of her faith.

Peoria, Illinois (3)
- Three high school friends made a suicide pact after the little sister of one of them was abducted and then found several weeks later dead and sexually assaulted. The three erroneously believed that through a black magic ritual involving their suicides, they could be reborn as 'undead' and could hunt down and kill the murderer. They tried to throw themselves in front of a speeding truck but their legs refused to co-operate. They confessed to the principal of their school who contacted their parents. They were temporarily placed in a psychiatric facility that specializes in grief counselling.

Pahoa, Big Island, Hawaii (one)
- A woman whose lover left her for another woman became destitute and also drunk. Thinking that it would be fitting to offer herself to the volcano Goddess, she padded out in the middle of the night to an active lava flow and tried to throw herself on it to incinerate herself. She was surprised to find herself on a beach far from the lava the following morning.

Greensboro, West Virginia (one)
- A man who'd spent a lifetime working with physically and mentally challenged children began feeling the effects of his fight with cancer. He was drained from chemotherapy and no longer feeling positive. He tried to overdose on some of his medication, he began to shake violently, knocking the pills out of his hand. A voice within him said, "I cannot leave yet. The children still need me." As he pondered this, two of his 'graduates' came to his door with flowers, to tell him how much his work had meant to them.

At this, Cummings' heart broke. He thought of Flores' death, and wished God had intervened on that tragic day to prevent the promising young man from taking his own life, leaving such a big hole in the hearts of his family. He thought too of his son Geordie, and how much he loved him. He wished Geordie was with him so he could give him a huge hug and ensure that Geordie understood that God knew how much he'd suffered.

Chapter 12

State of the Union Address

"Good evening America," said President Samuel Cummings in his first ever emergency State of the Union address. "It has been twenty-four hours since our planet was visited by a being sent directly by God to intervene in our affairs. All across the world, the sounds of war have been silenced. Today is a great day for humanity."

It was 9:00 p.m., Sunday evening, in Washington D.C. It was also several days earlier than Cumming had expected to be giving this speech, but it was an appropriate time nonetheless. Given the death tallies that had been coming in fast and furious over the Sarah Says website, he'd pushed hard to gather the information he needed to impart to his people. He wanted everyone in America to have a crystal clear picture of what the edict from God really meant, in nuts and bolts terms. *Forewarned is forearmed*, he thought.

As he faced the cameras, on his right stood his vice president, Angelica Lopez, while on his left was Hana Shriver, the majority senate leader. Hana had readily agreed to stand with him on the podium.

"Yes," she said when he asked her to, "we definitely need to present a united front."

Cummings smiled at his two allies, and then resumed his speech. "Globally, more than 40,000 people have died at the hands of God in the last twenty-four hours, and several thousand of these were American citizens. Some of the dead were flat-out killers, some were desperate people who made mistakes that cost them their lives, but most—and this is what worries me—were 'enablers,' people who never stopped to think how their actions, deeds, and words might influence others, and so helped create conditions that led to someone attempting to kill another."

He paused for emphasis, glancing around the room at the swarm of reporters snapping his picture, filming, and otherwise recording him, and then said, "This concept of 'enabling' is one that everyone across this great land needs to clearly understand. It's not just people with guns in their hands who will die when they aim at another and pull the trigger—it is every single person who played a part in what makes a would-be killer decide to become a . . . well, a *killer*."

The cameras in front of him snapped madly at his words . . . and then the questions started coming. It was clear that the members of the press were not inclined to wait for the rest of the speech—they wanted answers *now*.

"What do you mean, Mr. President!?" shouted out NBC reporter, Taylor Wisniewski. "Are you saying that every parent who disciplined their child too harshly might die for, say, creating a hateful attitude in that person that made him or her want to kill others?"

"Not quite," said Cummings, "though perhaps, in some cases, this could be true. Think of the impulse to kill as a *final* link in a chain. The first link might be when an individual watches a movie or plays a video game where killing is normalized and rewarded. The next link could be an influential person who reinforces the belief that to take another's life is of no consequence—perhaps a gang leader. The next link could be the person who sells a gun to a would-be killer, perhaps knowing this individual is unhinged."

Wisniewski nodded his understanding and made a couple of comments into a recording device as Cummings continued, passionately saying, "Only God knows the links in the chain that culminate in killing—but *I* know that we can't simply blame parents. Most of them work hard to instill good values in their children and sincerely want them to evolve into compassionate adults."

There was another flurry of camera flashes at this, clearly meant to capture Cummings' genuinely pained expression. He didn't mind being on the cover of every American newspaper looking that way the next day, not if it meant people started thinking about their actions.

"Can you elaborate a bit more about this 'chain,' Mr. President!?" yelled out ABC reporter, Bethany Wilde.

"I'll try," said Cummings. "Here's an example. When I was a kid, I was taught to respect people, and special emphasis was placed on respecting women. Today, that attitude has shifted 180 degrees, to the point that certain musical artists sing about abducting and raping 'bitches,' and are applauded for it. In my admittedly old-school mind, that goes against everything we should be teaching our children. I don't think such trash should be marketed to easily influenced teenagers. It could become one link in the chain—the link that normalizes violent behaviour."

He paused and looked around before continuing, and then he said, "Worse yet are today's video games, which have significantly increased in violent content since Pac-Man was popular. What happens when kids play those games? Perhaps you remember 1999's Columbine shooting, when teen boys Eric Harris and Dylan Klebold killed twelve students, a teacher, and themselves? The boys' enthusiasm for violent video games was cited as a direct link to, and cause of, the shooting."

He frowned as he said this, and then Bethany Wilde shouted out, "Is it fair to say we live in a culture that glorifies bad boys!?" Cummings looked at her shrewdly and thought she had probably dated a few herself.

He responded, "Yes, something like that—but with higher stakes. A good girl dating a bad boy used to simply wind up pregnant. Now she winds up pregnant and *dead*, all because somebody heard a detestable song about how 'bitches' should be killed if they get 'knocked up.' Do you see where I'm going with this?"

"Yes, you're saying the song is a link," said Wisniewski.

"That's correct," replied Cummings.

"And you're also saying that if someone tries to kill someone else because they heard a song that influenced them to do so, possibly the person who wrote the song will die too, right?" Wisniewski prodded.

"Right again," said Cummings. "And not only the writer, but possibly the singer, the producer, and perhaps even the person who introduced the killer to the music."

"You said 'possibly' and 'might' . . . how do we know who will *actually* die!?" yelled out Bethany Wilde.

"We *don't*—only God can connect the dots," replied Cummings. "It's possible, for example, that the producer suggested changing the song's lyrics but was overruled and so produced the song under duress and remained morally opposed to it. God may spare him or her for trying to nip the darkness in the bud, so to speak, but take down the rest of the chain."

"Do we have to be afraid?" asked Wisniewski. "After all, any one of us could have done something to someone to loosen their hinges!"

"Afraid is a strong word," said Cummings, though admittedly he felt afraid himself. "The lesson here is, if you know in your heart that you are promoting hatred or violence with your words or actions, then you are risking your own life. God's intervention is about *responsibility*."

"What about our military!?" shouted out Bethany Wilde, trying to get the edge on Wisniewski. "You're the commander in chief of a massive force of trained killers. Won't you die if they do the jobs they have been instructed to do?"

"The short answer is yes," Cummings replied, "but all troops have been ordered to stand down. And beginning tomorrow, our military personnel will begin the process of returning home."

Wisniewski wanted to ask something else, but Angelica Lopez stepped forward and took the microphone. "Could we let the president speak, please?" she requested. "There will be time for questions later. Also, you'll find the answers to many of your questions on the Sarah Says website."

There was a murmur of assent in the room, and finally silence reigned.

"Thank you," Cummings said. "Now, getting back to the questions about the military. First, I would like to acknowledge the bravery of our military personnel. Until this day, every one of them has been willing to put their life on the line for the freedom of this country. I know they would do it again in a heartbeat if they were required to. I want it understood that our returning troops will be given all the tools and knowledge they need to integrate into mainstream life. Further, troops who don't find immediate employment upon being released from service will be paid regular wages and retain their health benefits for at least twelve months."

Cummings paused and looked around the room as if challenging the reporters to question him on this, but no one did. He continued, "My government has already created some preliminary plans for how to employ these skilled men and women, and it is my expectation that our valued service personnel will continue to serve the country in roles similar to their current military ones. For example, we will likely need some of our skilled forces personnel to protect our borders, deal with insurgents, and help bring criminal groups to justice if they try to take advantage of the 'do not kill' edict. To support this, some military bases will remain open, and equipment needed for surveillance and rapid deployment of forces will continue to be used. However, instead of arming our troops with guns, we will arm them with non-lethal weapons to ensure their personal safety."

Cummings noted some puzzled looks around the room as this information sank in. While it was one thing to intellectually understand that people were no longer going to be able to kill other people without dying themselves, it was quite another to ponder the specifics of that. Cummings could tell that some of the old hand reporters got the full picture... but younger ones, like Bethany Wilde, hadn't put it together yet.

Bethany looked like a nice Midwest girl, part of a breed that clung to an image of Americans as cowboys who could take down fleeing bandits while galloping across the desert on a horse. And now the horse was gone. As he watched Bethany put two and two together, he almost smiled.

"President Cummings!" she yelped. "Do you really think it's possible for law and order to reign without the use of lethal force?"

"Yes," Cummings replied benignly. "However, I expect the face of it to dramatically change."

She opened her mouth to ask another question, but Cummings saw Don Taylor, his bodyguard and security chief, shush her. He liked the eager reporter, though, and so when he continued his speech, he addressed her directly.

"To answer your question, Bethany," he said, looking straight at the flustered young woman, "the type of change I expect to see is—in one word—*reinvention*. We will continue to protect our nation, but we will deter would-be lawbreakers with such things as rubber bullets, tear gas, and water cannons instead of guns, and maybe we'll even use some new deterrents we haven't invented yet. Do I think we will need to use such things often? No, I do *not*—and the reason is, Bethany, that just as the good guys are disabled, so are the *bad* guys. Do you understand? They are as helpless as we are, if not *more* helpless." Then he smiled and said,

"I think life is going to get much more peaceful as the world gets used to God's edict—and you can quote me on that."

Cummings looked away from her and around the room again. "Other examples of reinvention I and my colleagues have been working on include a plan to convert decommissioned aircraft carriers into hospital ships to be stationed on our coasts and deployed around the world to help in the wake of natural disasters or during contagious disease outbreaks. Where people must be evacuated from danger zones, former troop carriers can be used to accompany these floating hospitals. Ultimately, we hope to mirror the exemplary work of the Doctors Without Borders organization, with whom we hope to partner, but on a larger, better funded scale.

"We also have plans underway to retrofit some of our nuclear submarines, with a goal to repurpose them so they can conduct deep ocean research. Further, we are looking at reassigning some military patrol boats to the Coast Guard to help in the fight against the drug trade and illegal immigration. And we hope to use members of the Army Corps of Engineers to help with major infrastructure upgrades across the country."

Wisniewski couldn't remain silent anymore. "The drug trade has killed millions, both directly and indirectly. How do you think God's edict will affect how the cartels do business?"

Cummings looked him squarely in the eye. "That's a good question, Taylor," he said, "but my answer remains the same as when we discussed the example of a hateful song influencing someone to kill. God is judge, jury, and executioner in every aspect of this edict we are under, including deaths that occur because of the drug trade. But I would expect to see some cartel business practices change. If you need more specific information on this, I suggest you direct your questions to Sarah over the Sarah Says website, and perhaps she'll bring it up in her next global presentation."

"But . . ." Wisniewski was not satisfied; However, he was immediately shushed by Don Taylor, for which Taylor received a nod of approval from Cummings.

Then Cummings continued with his State of the Union address. "Reinvention is about growth," he said. "As the old saying goes, 'when one door closes, another opens,' and so it is with our country and our people. Some of our best military pilots have indicated interest in reinventing themselves by joining America's reinvigorated space program. Some military aircrafts may be reinvented as evacuation aircrafts, to be used in disaster zones. We're discussing how to reinvent military radar and sonar systems to upgrade airports and commercial shipping controls, and how to repurpose military satellites to protect our borders or gather information on climate change."

"But what about the people? What jobs do you think our troops will do!?" shouted a reporter at the back of the scrum, a man Cummings did not recognize.

"It's not *just* our troops who will lose jobs as a result of demilitarization," Cummings said. "But to answer your question . . . we have a plan in development that will address options for disenfranchised troops and defence contractors. As I mentioned earlier, military personnel will receive support for up to a year, employees in the defence industry will receive six months' severance pay to a maximum of $50,000 per person."

There was a small flurry of activity as the assembled reporters recorded the numbers, and Cummings paused politely to let them finish.

Then, when attention was on him again, he said, "My government has high expectations that the majority of people will be employed again within three months because as we begin the work of dismantling and safely storing military equipment and nuclear weapons, tens of thousands of jobs will open up, many of them in the recycling business. Displaced military and defence industry personnel can certainly transfer their skills into these efforts. There will be at least a decade's worth of work, and we expect to be able to meet domestic needs for steel, aluminum, and metal well into the future."

Then Cummings looked at Hana Shriver, who stood stoically beside him. "Beside me is the face of change," he said, extending his arm to indicate her. "The world has been touched by God, and we all have to rise to that. My Republican colleague, Hana Shriver, has contributed to our planning efforts and added some fine ideas from her side of the senate floor. I want all Americans to know that everything that is done for this country in the wake of God's edict is being done on a bipartisan basis." Then he stepped away from the microphone to let Hana speak.

She stepped forward. "Thank you, Mr. President," she said, tilting the microphone a little toward herself to ensure she was heard. "I appreciate the chance to speak. I'll keep it brief. We all know that such change as we are experiencing at this moment is unprecedented. None of us have seen anything like this in our lifetimes. This is an opportunity to remake ourselves into the nation we have always wanted to be, and securing America's future is too important to let party politics get in the way. For this reason, I have agreed to work hand in hand with President Cummings' administration to ensure the best outcome for all Americans. Thank you."

With that, she stepped away from the microphone to stunned silence from the reporters. It didn't stay that way for long.

"Was there a payout to your party!?" yelled someone from the back of the room.

Shriver didn't return to the microphone; Instead, she simply shook her head from side to side, clearly indicating 'no.' There was a rumble of excited noise in the room as the reporters processed this information, and so Lopez, impatient and bristling a little, took charge.

"Calm down!" she yelled at the noisy reporters as she commandeered the microphone. "This is a State of the Union address, not a frat party!"

She had an air of authority that Cummings could only wish he possessed. At her words, the reporters immediately looked chastised, but until they were quiet, she continued frowning at them like an angry school teacher.

He stepped back up to the microphone and said, "Thank you, Vice President Lopez." Then he looked around the room as he further said, "There are many things that will be affected by God's new plans for us. Changes to the military industrial complex is only one aspect, and it is tied solely to God's 'do not kill' edict. But we also have to consider what some of God's other changes mean for us as a people and a nation."

"What do you mean?" asked Bethany Wilde, oblivious to how Don Taylor's security team was trying to stop her from talking until the speech was done.

Cummings smiled at her. "Well, Bethany," he said, "given the discussion we had earlier about the chain of links that create a killer, I expect to see significant changes to the entertainment industry. Pulling content that might encourage people to kill others will be a massive undertaking, involving everyone from studio executives to the librarians in hometown libraries. Unless people are willing to risk their lives for art, the wise course of action is to stop distributing all media that might influence people to kill."

He could see Bethany processing this, her brow furrowed, and again, he was struck by her youth. He was relatively certain she'd grown up with video games that involved hunting and shooting other humans, and he wondered what she thought of those endless hours in front of a screen now. *It seems harmless when you're doing it,* he thought, *but we know better now.*

Then he looked away from her and back at the rest of the assembled reporters, determined to speak before one of them lobbed another question at him.

"Other big shifts," he said, "include the economic impacts of physiological changes to the human body. Viagra and similar products have already lost a vast amount of their market shares, as have other consumer products based on enhancing sexuality in older people. And, of course, we expect a decline in the sales of personal weapons, such as handguns. While they are still viable deterrents for home protection, they are risky to own for obvious reasons. On the plus side, it is likely that new in-home personal protection systems and products will be developed to replace handguns."

"What kind of 'obvious reasons'!?" shouted the reporter at the back, who Cummings still did not recognize.

He saw one of Don Taylor's men head toward him, presumably to shut him up.

"Well, I would think you all know this by now," said Cummings, "but I'll spell it out. If you fire your personal weapon at someone with the intent to kill, you will die. If you fire with the intent to wound, but God determines the wound could be lethal, you will die. If you leave the handgun unattended and your child, friend, or spouse fires it with the intent to kill—or in a reckless way that could kill—you will die, as will the person who fired it. So it's really a risky business to hang on to such things, don't you think? It's kind of like having an attack dog that only attacks *you.*"

Cummings saw a member of the security team whisper something to the man at the back, as he added, "To stimulate the economy and offset the impact God's edict is going to have on some of our major economic drivers, I am announcing five major initiatives that will not only create jobs but will ensure the United States of America maintains and strengthens its leadership role globally for decades.

"First, we are going to create jobs in the water business. One of this country's major challenges is access to adequate clean drinking water, particularly in the southwestern part of our nation. Due to the downsizing of our military, we expect to have a larger budget for infrastructure initiatives in the future, and so my administration plans to work with states and municipalities to renew existing water systems, a major effort that will require billions of dollars of investment and will create many thousands of jobs for several decades.

"Second, we are going to develop a national electric train network that will unite our country, reduce reliance on air travel and offset the immense carbon footprint that our overreliance on internal combustion engines has created. We have some very forward-thinking engineers working on plans now, using the latest, greatest technologies. We want our system to be a shining example to the world, and we hope to leapfrog over the technologies currently in place in Europe and Asia.

"Third, we are going to become the world leader in climate change technologies and implementation. As I mentioned earlier, as part of this initiative, we expect to redeploy some of our military resources, including military satellites and some of our ships. We are also planning on creating a global climate change research centre in the present United States Army Research Laboratory in Adelphi, Maryland. We have solicited the help of world-renowned climate change activist Greta Thunberg, and she has tentatively agreed to become the face of our organization.

"Fourth, we are going to initiate a global 'Mission to Mars' initiative. We have developed a tentative plan to offer all countries of the world a stake in this mission. We expect to bring all nations together to work in tandem with the private sector. The first goal of this global, joint venture, will be to install a human habitable base on the moon within three years, complete with launch pad. The hope is that such a base will enable a Mars mission before the end of the decade.

"Finally, I plan for the United States to become a leader in 5G networks. Through greater use of the radio spectrum, 5G will allow far more communication devices access to mobile networks at the same time. One of the impediments this country has had to fully mobilizing a robust

5G network is that our military and intelligence communities have tied up many of the most desirable communication frequencies. With no prospect of military conflict in future, we can free up more bandwidth. With this in mind, I will be ordering a bandwidth auction within two months."

Again, the reporter at the back managed to be heard. "Mr. President!" he called out. "Do you truly believe man's need for dominance—our tribal natures as I've heard you call them—will disappear just because we can no longer kill one another? Won't the nature of war just *change*? If your 5G network is hijacked, your communications systems destroyed, your financial institutions crashed, isn't that an act of war?"

The reporter was immediately shushed by security again, but while the man was annoying, he was also right.

"Yes," Cummings responded, "it is. And you're also right about the tribal natures of humans. As a species, we're not going to change overnight—but we *will* change. In the meantime, rest assured that this country has its most highly skilled cybersecurity forces in place, just as we've always had. Further, as part of God's edict, cyberwarfare that could lead to human death is punishable in the same way as more direct killings."

"That seems pretty dicey," remarked the man. "Pointing and shooting at someone is cut and dried—you shoot, you die. But how can this 'eye for an eye' edict ever be measured when it comes to such things as hacking databases and crashing the stock market?"

Cummings looked levelly at him. "Try asking Sarah," he said—and just like that, the air in the room began to shimmer and change.

Cummings and his team knew what that meant; They'd experienced it already. However, the reporters before him had not, and so they looked amazed and uncertain. Their senses began to reel as a gentle humming filled the air, while the brightness in the room increased a hundredfold.

"What the hell?" asked Taylor Wisniewski, clearly shocked.

And then Sarah actually appeared, creating an immense, stunned silence in the room. At this point, about 80% of humans on the planet had seen her on social media or television—including the assembled group of reporters—but few had seen her in person.

The gloriousness of her presence caused Bethany Wilde to begin weeping aloud, and Cummings noted that some of the others in the room were covertly wiping their eyes as well.

"Hello," breathed Sarah, infusing the room with a mist of sunshine and roses.

Cummings noted how several of the reporters before him inadvertently clutched their stomachs, clearly experiencing the same tickle in their bellies that he did whenever Sarah emitted her golden, tinkling rays of love and joy.

"Hello, Sarah," welcomed Cummings. "I suspect you heard someone ask a question that a regular guy like me can't answer," he said with the appropriate amount of reverence. Her presence never failed to make him feel both more alive and more human than normal; Just being near her made him feel that anything was possible.

"Yes, I heard," said Sarah. Then she looked directly at the unknown reporter at the back of the room. "Abdul Amin, from Al Jazeera News, you ask illuminating questions," she said softly, "and I would see that you come away from here with the answers you seek. Allah is with you. Allah sees all. Do you understand?"

The man at the back looked stunned, but reverent as well. In his eyes was a glow of pure faith, released toward Sarah, a reflection of her glory.

"Abdul," said Sarah, "you will take the news of this to the people who need to hear it. You will make it known that there is no way around the eyes of Allah. I know you as a man of faith, and I know your news outlet to be more honest than many. You will tell those who have challenged you that God knows intent, and that Allah connects all the dots. You cannot hide from the eyes of God."

Abdul looked immensely relieved by her words. "I have never doubted Allah," he said with immense respect, "and I thank you for your attention to my concerns."

With that, Sarah released another waft of rose scent, perhaps tinged with jasmine, into the room, and as suddenly as she had arrived, she departed. When she was gone, the room stirred to life, and the other reporters looked at Abdul Amin with curiosity as they tried to determine if there was a story there for them.

Amin gave no clue; Instead, he remained stony-faced, not giving his secrets away.

As the reporters buzzed among themselves, confused and considering pouncing on the suddenly wary Abdul, Cummings seized control of the situation.

"Abdul, is there anything you want to share?" Cummings asked, secretly thinking it was funny how he sounded like an elementary school teacher trying to take away a child's gum.

"No, Mr. President," said Abdul. "I am as stunned as you that she knew about the story I have been researching. She has given me much-needed clarity about one of my main themes. And *no*," he said, looking at the reporters around him, who were clearly hungry to know what scent he was on, "I am *not* going to share my Pulitzer Prize winning topic with you!"

Cummings laughed. "Well, keep up the good work," he said. Then he looked around the room and said, "I only have a few more words I wish to leave you with. If America is going to realize its full potential—indeed, if the whole human race is going to do so—we must make sure we can survive over the long-term by reducing our footprint on the planet and our rate of resource consumption. Working with other countries around the world, my administration will administer a program to monitor global sustainability. We intend to establish accurate methodologies to measure consumption country by country and then, starting next year, we will begin work on an ongoing global program to reduce human impact on this planet, with an initial target of 1% resource consumption reduction per year."

At that, everyone clapped.

Cummings concluded with, "The next year will be a bumpy ride, but we are heading for a much better world, thanks to God."

Chapter 13

Financial Markets

On Monday morning after his State of the Union address, Cummings didn't awake until almost 7:30 a.m. Usually an extremely early riser, this was a remarkable sleep-in for him, proof of how drained the events of the last few days had left him.

As soon as he opened his eyes and noticed the time on the old style alarm clock beside his bed, he panicked. He was usually at his desk by 8:00 a.m., and now he was going to be late for an early meeting he had scheduled with Norman Feldman to discuss the closing of financial markets.

He rushed into the shower, hastily dressed, and then headed to the Oval Office, leaving Lorena peacefully sleeping.

He arrived at his desk at 8:30, just in time to hear his office phone ring. It was Feldman, punctual as always. "Good morning, Chief," Feldman said cheerily when Cummings said hello. "Did you sleep okay?"

"Yes, longer than usual," replied Cummings. "Last night's speech took it out of me. How about you?"

"I tell you, it was a relief to lay my head on a pillow," said Feldman.

Cummings knew exactly what Feldman meant. The world was preparing to adapt to a financial market that no longer relied on defence spending, and Cummings knew things would get worse before they got better.

The One-Week Market Shutdown

All financial markets were closed from Monday through Friday that week. During that time, central banks announced bank back stops (support for securities) and liquidity increases around the world, to support markets before the first ones reopened in Asia on the following Monday. The immediate concern was a run on bank deposits.

There was a level of panic initially, especially in countries where the defence industry accounted for a very high percentage of the overall national economy and export sales (such as Russia). To calm the public, the World Bank and the International Money Fund provided backstopping. For most countries, however, the disappearance of defence spending was greeted with relief. It meant that when the markets reopened, and there would be a significant and immediate improvement in their balance of trade, since they would no longer have to buy military equipment from other countries. Of course, they would have to deal with the issue of unemployed military personnel, but at least they would have lots of budgetary room to solve the problem.

Major defence contractors and other companies who anticipated being negatively impacted by God's intervention took the week to revise their corporate guidance systems and to make full disclosure in anticipation of markets reopening. Many filed for bankruptcy protection.

By the end of the week, the consensus among global analysts was that U.S. stock values were going to fall by about 8%, and that it would take about eighteen months for the economic stimulus package offered by Cummings' government to fully offset the impact. However, easing by the U.S. Federal Reserve would cause a rally in government bond prices—though credit spreads for adversely affected companies would widen, accelerating the threat of bankruptcy for some.

Globally, most stock and bond markets were expected to be affected relatively modestly because lower defence spending would strengthen the balance of payments, making the number of impacted industries small in scale. In 90% of countries, it was thought that equity market values would decline by only 2–3%.

Commodity prices were expected to dip due to the short term economic slowdown, with oil and steel being hit harder than other commodities due to decreased military fuel use and increased steel recycling. Gold prices, however, were anticipated to remain relatively stable.

Though the risk of war had evaporated, it was generally accepted that the positive impact on 'market psychology' would be offset by an increased risk of social unrest in some countries. Military dictatorships were likely to suffer most from falling currencies and rising debt, and this trend was likely to continue until political change was implemented. It was thought that currency prices would remain relatively stable for most countries, but that they would decline somewhat in the weapons exporting ones and increase correspondingly in the weapons importing ones.

As the week drew to a close, it became clear that Russia was going to have the most difficult time adjusting. The pressure of lower oil prices and the elimination of the defence industry were going to hit them hard, and financial experts predicted their economy and stock market might collapse. If the ruble sank, it would create a spike in inflation and debt, which would in turn add fuel to the growing social and political unrest in the Russian Federation.

North Korea was also extremely likely to become a mess. The country's strategy of gaining world recognition through military power had now been obliterated, and it had no underlying economy to fall back upon. A regime change was inevitable—and urgently needed.

Black Monday

The following Monday—Black Monday—when markets opened in Asia, there was less blood on the trading floors than expected. Equity markets were down an average of 5%, and there was significant offshore money flowing in. Chinese and Japanese currencies were up slightly against the dollar, and the general public seemed more curious than threatened by God's intervention. There was no significant run on bank deposits. Oil and steel prices dropped 10%.

When the Moscow Exchange opened for trading, stocks fell 30% in the first ten minutes, and trading was halted for the day due to a mismatch of orders. Ten-year government bonds dropped 15% at the open but recovered slightly after heavy intervention by the Russia Central Bank. The ruble fell 10% against the American dollar, leading the Russian government to impose capital controls to limit the flow of foreign capital in and out of their economy.

Russians flooded to their local banks to withdraw their funds, leading to a coordinated shutdown of the banking system. This in turn led to massive protests in major cities across the country. The army was called in to disperse crowds using non-lethal force. However, in the melee that followed, 460 people dropped dead trying to use excessive force with rudimentary weapons. Of these, 230 were military personnel, 150 were protesters, and eighty were police officers.

During the week preceding Black Monday, Russian President Misha Verenich had given three national speeches calling for calm and outlining how his government intended to stimulate the economy, but this had done little to quell people's fears. Russian citizens knew that their country's economy was founded on being a war machine, and that without this economic driver, they had very little gross national product to fall back on. The truth of the matter was that the situation was so bleak that it would be at least a decade before the ruble would rise above the rubble.

Foreign aid was required immediately to provide necessary food and medicine for an increasingly desperate nation. Verenich did not recognize this quickly enough and soon began to lose what little support he had. His closest allies—military leaders and corporate heads appointed by him— were dropping like flies. More than 80% of the military leaders and 20% of the corporate heads were now unemployed and seeking greener pastures.

Understanding that this was the end of the road for him, Verenich stepped down, leaving Prime Minister Sergei Grinkov in charge. Grinkov immediately announced that he would hold national elections in three months; However, with the power structure of the country in shreds, it was not clear who would contend for the presidency, what the political parties would look like, and what they would campaign for now that Russia had become a third-world country.

In London, and across all of Europe, as markets opened on Black Monday, it became evident that they would fall faster and further than Asian markets because of the Russian collapse. Several financial institutions with significant exposure to Russia had their share prices fall between 10 and 30 percentage points by the end of the day.

Overall, European and British equity markets ended the day down 8%. There was no unmanageable run on deposits in any of the countries, as British and European central banks had added liquidity to the markets ahead of the Black Monday opening. The euro, pound, and Swiss franc all rose slightly against the American dollar.

Markets in Central and South America also fared worse than Asian markets. The average drop was 9% across equity markets. Due to the drop in oil prices, Venezuela might have done much worse but for the fact that its oil industry was already severely depressed. In many of these countries, political uncertainty now that military force could not be used to protect weak or corrupt governments was the main factor in the downturn.

Currencies in Central and South America were not a major concern yet, though several countries experienced a threatening level of bank withdrawals. Their governments responded with imposed maximum withdrawal limits and capital controls. The world anxiously watched to see how the balance of power between governments and drug lords would change now that neither side could kill one another.

Canadian and Mexican stock markets fell 9%, as the peace dividend (public money that becomes available when defence spending is reduced) was greater for them than for the United States. Their currencies strengthened slightly against the greenback. There were no issues with runs on deposits.

The U.S. stock market dropped 16% initially but recovered to finish down 12% at the close. Easing by the Federal Reserve prevented interest rates from rising significantly, but the rate on the ten-year bond dropped fifteen basis points. Credit spreads on bonds of corporations most affected by the demise of the defence industry rose an average of 200 basis points (excluding those who had declared bankruptcy during the previous week). Borrowing costs for financial institutions with major exposure to the defence industry rose 150 basis points.

At the end of the week following Black Monday, Treasury Secretary Norman Feldman announced that he and the chairman of the Federal Reserve were monitoring the banking system closely and would step in immediately if any threat of contagion arose. He noted that the financial condition of the banks was much stronger than it had been in 2008 due to government imposed increases in reserve ratios and mandatory stress tests.

Aftershocks

Over the course of the next two weeks, equity markets in most countries oscillated in a +/- 5% range. Interest rates drifted slightly lower, but credit spreads widened for countries and companies in distress.

Russian equity markets were reopened and settled at -40%. The government had to devalue the ruble another 20% and assume direct control over the banking system. Capital controls were tightened and extended indefinitely. The World Bank and the International Monetary Fund promised $100 billion USD in financial support at the insistence of the United States and the Euro zone.

Meanwhile, inflation soared to 35%, showing no signs of stabilizing, and rationing of food and medical supplies began, causing social unrest. As the unrest continued to grow, the death toll in skirmishes between protesters and law enforcement personnel increased to more than 5,000 people. The government promised to continue paying soldiers if they stayed to help control the situation, but most went back to their hometowns to try to find food and shelter.

Disaster relief agencies refused to go into Russia until the situation stabilized. The 'caretaker' government appointed by Prime Minister Grinkov (composed of a coalition of his party and opposition party leaders) was seen as weak, and so civil unrest remained rampant. The election was scheduled for two months hence, and it was expected that some version of normalcy might return once a democratically elected president was in place. The United Nations agreed to provide scrutineers to help monitor the election.

North Korea was undoubtedly in an even worse state both economically and socially, although media remained mostly cut off from what was really happening on the ground. Satellite surveillance did not indicate any large public protests; However, the world knew this was only because most of the population had been brainwashed into revering their 'supreme leader' for decades. For a while at least, regime change seemed unlikely.

Unfortunately, most North Koreans lived barely at subsistence levels, though their leader, Park Jon-un, had denied this vehemently the few times he'd left his palace to meet with leaders of other nations—and he continued to stick to this party line after God's edict came down. Humanitarian aid was offered but rejected. Park Jon-un's message to the rest of the world was that in North Korea, it was business as usual, and that his business was nobody else's business.

In the demilitarized zone bordering South Korea, there was no evidence of troop reductions by the North. In fact, there were some indications that Park Jon-un was even continuing his nuclear weapons development program. The world watched anxiously, waiting for the cork to blow.

The market reset prompted the first steps toward regime changes in the Philippines, Venezuela, and Guatemala, but nowhere else. Despite God's best efforts, many powerful men were bound and determined to hold onto power. In the case of Catholic countries, many leaders still believed that a deathbed confession would save their souls, even though Sarah had told the world otherwise.

Sarah continued to keep track of global deaths from attempted killings. Excluding Russia, the daily count declined steadily as expected.

In the Oval Office, Cummings opened up the Sarah Says website and was relieved to see that the number of deaths in America had decreased by about 34%. It indicated that his people were getting the word and understanding the concept of 'thou shalt not kill.' Around the world, it seemed most other countries were also getting the message, although there were certainly a few pockets where hostilities remained high and the value of life remained low.

Chapter 14

The Cork Out of the Bottle

It was day twenty-three when North Korea started to hemorrhage. At 8:00 a.m. local time, three North Koreans on patrol in the demilitarization zone, and on the verge of starvation, made a run for South Korean territory. As they were trained to do, twelve of their colleagues in arms attempted to shoot them down. All twelve died instantly with their rifles melted in their hands. The unit commander and three levels of army brass above him also dropped dead—and so did the North Korean supreme leader, Park Jon-un.

President Cummings was sitting in the Oval Office with Vice President Lopez and Defence Secretary Blackstone, assessing a preliminary report about their efforts to reemploy disenfranchised troops, when they heard the news about North Korea.

After the NBC anchorman, Anthony Jessop, gave the high level details of the deaths, Cummings exclaimed in shock, "Good Lord . . . the North Korean army wasn't advised to avoid the use of lethal force! Park Jon-un must have had his head in a bucket! How did he not understand that this oversight might cause his own death? Sarah made sure he attended the meeting she held at the UN. He knew what would happen!"

"I guess he just didn't believe it," said Lopez, her eyebrows up in shock, clearly as surprised as Cummings.

Just then, Jessop introduced a special report, featuring NBC's White House correspondent, Taylor Wisniewski. Cummings, Lopez, and Blackstone stopped what they were doing to watch.

"It has been twenty-three days since God sent his emissary, Sarah of God, to intervene in the affairs of humankind," said Wisniewski, "and today is a day that will change the face of North Korea forever. Reporting from Sinuiju, North Korea, which is directly across the river from the Chinese city of Dandong, is NBC correspondent Johnathan Wang . . ."

When Wang came on the screen, he said, "Thank you, Taylor." Then he swept an arm behind him to show a city that was visible on the other side of a river. "Behind me," Wang said, "is the Chinese city of Dandong. Why is that interesting? Because I am standing on the outskirts of the North Korean city of Sinuiju. I have crossed the border illegally, and I am alive."

They were sobering words, and Cummings and his colleagues looked at each other in shock and amazement. "I never thought I'd live to see this day," said Cummings.

"Neither did I," said Blackstone. "Neither did I."

Wang continued, "Despite an official government announcement that the North Korean supreme leader, Park Jon-un, has simply taken ill and is recovering in his palace, word of his death has spread quickly. Photographic evidence was leaked to Chinese media by a high ranking North Korean government official, lending credibility to the story—but more telling is that the name Park Jon-un has been confirmed on Sarah's online list of North Korean casualties."

Lopez, ever the fact checker, immediately navigated to the website on her laptop. "Yup, there it is!" she exclaimed, pointing at her screen.

"In this notoriously private country," Wang said, "reactions to Park Jon-un's death are mixed. Younger North Koreans received the message with joy and hope, but many of their elders are instead in mourning."

With that, the camera zoomed in on an Asian man who was wearing a frayed, greying wifebeater shirt and a wicker hat that had seen better days. He was tending a small plot of land that hosted some scrappy, dry-looking crops, mostly corn. As the camera focused on him, he smiled toothlessly in a melancholy way, clearly self-conscious at the attention from the reporter. In contrast to his nervousness, however, a woman a few feet away from him sat in the dust, oblivious to the presence of Wang and his team, wailing inconsolably, aware of nothing but her own grief.

The camera panned back to Wang, who added, "As soon as word of the supreme leader's death spread, thousands of soldiers and civilians simply dropped what they were doing and fled into China and South Korea, taking advantage of the fact that they cannot be killed for doing so. In light of the flood of refugees, both South Korea and China have quickly moved to close their borders. They have also reached out to what remains of the North Korean administration with offers of food and medical supplies."

"The smart ones got out of the country fast," said Cummings.

"I'll say," agreed Lopez. "What do you think will happen next?"

Almost as soon the words left her mouth, the television began flickering in an unusual way, as if possessed—and suddenly Sarah was on the screen, emitting her trademark bright light into the Oval Office while the three of them looked on, somewhat stunned.

"Hello," said Sarah as her form became distinct, appearing three-dimensional on the television screen. Then she stepped out of the television, and her radiance filled the room. She spoke directly to the vice president in her usual wordless way, saying, "I heard your question, Angelica, and decided to answer in person, something I have been doing quite regularly with other administrations around the world. I enjoy the personal touch, don't you?"

"Hello, Sarah," said Cummings. "We're honoured to see you."

"Thank you," said Sarah, emitting her trademark rose scent, the multitude of faces comprising hers flashing with an unearthly smile. Then she said to Lopez, "With regard to your question . . . I have spoken directly with North Korean officials to ensure they understand the full message about God's intervention—and that they realize they are culpable for wrongdoing. Some extreme ideology shifts are already occurring."

"What a relief," Lopez remarked.

"I have also made certain they understand that redemption in the eyes of God is possible if they accept humanitarian aid for the good of the people, and I've encouraged connections between them and the presidents of China and South Korea. Finally, I asked them to announce my presence to their people."

"The way you had *us* do?" asked Lopez.

"Yes," said Sarah.

"But didn't you already spread the word of your presence to the North Korean people by hijacking the state-run television system?" asked Cummings.

"I did," Sarah replied, "but most North Koreans have been brainwashed into revering their leader, and so to hear about God's intervention from their head of state is more meaningful to them than hearing it from me could ever be. To many, Park Jon-un *was* God, which is why they mourn his death."

"It seems so strange for people to believe that a government leader is *God*," remarked the Catholic Lopez, a little taken aback at the thought.

"Yes," agreed Sarah. "But the oppressed believe what they are *told* to believe." Then, focusing her starlit eyes directly on Cummings, she said, "I am also here to say how wonderful it is that you are still alive. God is pleased with how you and your team have risen to your challenges. For the past three weeks, you have kept your people as informed as possible about the nature of God, and you've continued to work diligently to ensure their safety."

"Thank you," said Cummings humbly, inordinately pleased by the praise, "but I couldn't have done it without the support of my team."

***

For the next few days, Sarah stayed in constant communication with North Korean government and military officials, and within a week, the turmoil began to subside. Offers of international aid were finally accepted, and planes and supplies began arriving. Trainloads of goods came in daily from China and South Korea.

A rudimentary caretaker government was formed fourteen days after Park Jon-un's death, and elections were called for six months down the road. However, with no constitution, no political parties, and a public that had never even voted for a dogcatcher, it was apparent to most of the rest of the world that it would take years for elections to become truly meaningful in that country. Offers of political advice were extended, but North Korean officials were wary of accepting such delicate information from traditional rivals like the United States, South Korea, or even China.

At the end of the second month after God's intervention, North Korea reopened borders with China and South Korea to allow families to reunite for short term visits, but the country was still struggling with its political structure and plans for the future. In the end, Sarah offered to broker meetings between North Korean and Scandinavian officials.

She told the world about this offer to the country's interim leaders via televised broadcast, explaining, "Nordic countries are geographically far enough away that they do not pose any territorial threat to this emerging nation. They also offer a version of governance that may be more applicable than that of other countries. They have advanced social safety nets, along with vibrant elections, and they also effectively compete in free markets, which is a goal of North Korea's."

North Korea accepted the offer, and three months after Park Jon-un's death, the country sent its best and brightest officials to The Hague for a crash course on governance.

***

In the United States, the post-edict plans that had been so carefully crafted by Cummings and his team were in full swing and were going surprisingly well. Most of the military personnel who had arrived back from deployments were returning to their families and hometowns, and from all reports, were settling in quite nicely.

The plan to deploy the Army Corps of Engineers onto infrastructure projects across the nation had gotten legs as well, and two rudimentary bridge abutment projects were underway. As well, Angelica Lopez had recruited some top designers to work on schematics for the electric train system Cummings had promised the nation, and she seemed very excited about it.

None of Cummings' group were expecting another visit from Sarah, but when she showed up unannounced in the middle of a discussion about the electric train, they were awed and delighted.

"Hello," she breathed as her presence filled the room with lightness and possibility. "I've come ask if you would deploy some of your recommissioned military vehicles to help with the situation in North Korea."

"Satellite surveillance hasn't indicated any large public protests," offered Defence Secretary Blackstone. "I thought things were stabilizing."

Vice President Lopez, who was nothing if not quick on the draw, raised one eyebrow at Blackstone. "Have you forgotten the concentration camps, those abysmal pits of hell? I believe it's a tradition to have protesters thrown into them so they can be starved and beaten to death."

Sarah ignored the vice president's sarcasm, though she acknowledged that Lopez was on the right track by saying to Cummings, "And that's why the assistance of the United States is needed. North Korea has opened the concentration camps and released these people into mainstream society, which is taxing their limited resources. Ultimately, a slave labour system has been dismantled, and now there are hundreds of thousands of people needing aid and sustenance, and no slaves to grow the food. The situation is dire."

Cummings face paled as he thought of it. He'd read several books about these camps, especially the notorious Hoeryong camp, which alone detained upwards of 50,000 people. Books had been published both by escaped prisoners and former guards, and they all told the same story—that people were being starved, tortured, enslaved, and brutally killed on a daily basis. He could only imagine the chaos in North Korea as these poor beings, with their misshapen bodies and souls, were released into a world they no longer understood.

"Yes, of course the United States will help," he said passionately, wondering at how a country could deny the existence of concentration camps so big they could be seen by satellites.

"Good," said Sarah. "I knew I could count on American aid." Then she added, "And there's one more thing you should know . . ."

"What's that?" asked Cummings.

"North Korea did not dismantle it's nuclear weapons in the seven-day timeframe that was allotted to it."

Cummings' face paled. There had been no media reports of a nuclear meltdown—at least, not *yet*.

"You'll hear about it at the nuclear disarmament talk," she said to the group when she saw their shocked expressions. And then she was gone.

Cummings looked at Blackstone. "We're going to need a shitload of radiation suits when we go into North Korea with humanitarian aid," he said.

Chapter 15

Nuclear Disarmament Conference

Sarah scheduled the nuclear disarmament talks for the twenty-fifth day after God's intervention, within the thirty-day timeline as promised. The talks were held in Geneva. The five nations—the United States, Russia, China, France, and the United Kingdom—which had a right to have nuclear weapons under the Treaty on the Non-Proliferation of Nuclear Weapons (NPT), attended, as did North Korea, India, and Pakistan, who were not signees to the NPT but were known to have nuclear arsenals.

The prime minister of Israel was also asked by Sarah to attend, as was the supreme leader of Iran. Sarah knew Israel had nuclear weapons within its borders, and that Iran, which was hostile to Israel, was trying to accumulate weapons because they felt that without them, Israel had a military advantage.

Cummings was delighted at how Sarah teleported him and his team to Geneva. It was so much easier than flying; One minute, he was sitting in the Oval Office, the next he was in the impressive Palais des Nations—the Völkerbund (League of Nations) Palace—on the banks of Lake Geneva. The building had been the European headquarters of the United Nations since 1966, and while it was technically on Swiss soil, it was considered international territory.

The attendees—teams consisting of heads of state; department heads responsible for overseeing the disarmament process; technical experts (two from each country); and support staff (two from each country)—settled in the plush blue armchairs in the cavernous assembly hall in which they found themselves.

Sarah began by saying, "I would like to thank the government of Switzerland for hosting this meeting."

There was a murmur of acknowledgement around the room as the assembled group echoed her sentiments.

Cummings, who had Gordon Blackstone with him, took the opportunity to lean over and whisper to Blackstone, "Thanks for rounding up a team for us, Gordon."

Gordon had brought with him two nuclear weapons technical experts, Hans Friedrich and Lakshmi Khatri, and two administrative assistants, Dolly Peabody and Martin Jain.

Sarah resumed her introductory remarks. "Let me begin our meeting by reminding you of the message about nuclear disarmament that I gave world leaders almost one month ago, when I first arrived on Earth. At that time, when I announced God's intervention in human affairs, I told the world that countries or groups possessing or developing nuclear weapons, or processing weapons grade uranium and plutonium, must cease producing these things within seven days, or their production facilities would be destroyed by God."

Sarah paused, and as she whirled her ever-changing eyes around the room—alternately focusing on one world leader after another—they flickered wildly.

Then she said, "All countries present here today complied, except North Korea. Processing of weapons grade uranium and plutonium around the world ceased three weeks ago, except in in that country. Sadly, North Korean facilities making nuclear weapons and fuel were destroyed at the end of the seven-day grace period, which released a significant amount of radioactive material into the environment, killing hundreds of local people. Thousands more received potentially fatal doses of radiation, and unfortunately, the wave of contamination has spread into China and South Korea."

Cummings saw the Chinese president, Dong Yang, clenching his jaw, clearly frustrated at the situation, and wondered why the president of the 'sleeping dragon' had remained silent about this threat to his people.

"The reason the world has not yet been informed about this situation," continued Sarah, answering his silent question, "is that President Don Yang of China, and President Moon Myung-bak of South Korea, agreed to wait until this meeting had taken place before doing so. The hope is that by the end of this conference, we can discuss potential mitigation efforts for the situation, and when we announce the *problem* to the world, we can also announce the *solution*. In the meantime, while humanitarian aid is on its way . . ." she eyed Cummings and Blackstone as she said this, ". . . the interim North Korean government has been working closely with China and South Korea to provide medical assistance to those most severely affected by the disaster."

At this news, Blackstone looked over at Cummings nervously. "I feel like sending our aid workers over to North Korea, as Sarah asked us to do, will be like walking into a hornet's nest," he whispered into the president's ear.

"We'll be okay as long as we have enough radiation suits," Cummings whispered back. "Angelica already put in an order for 5,000 . . . but maybe we should double that."

Blackstone immediately pulled out his mobile device and typed a note to the vice president, asking her to do so.

"Thanks," Cummings whispered to him when he'd put his phone away.

Meanwhile, Sarah looked around the room again, making sure she had the assembled group's attention, before continuing, "Besides those of you at this meeting, God identified fourteen other 'nuclear powers' around the globe—in this case, nationalist and terrorist groups building 'dirty' bombs. As I'm sure you know, dirty bombs combine radioactive material with conventional explosives, and rather than being built for mass destruction, most are built for the purpose of creating panic as people flee from the threat of radiation. In every country where this was occurring, production facilities for weaponry have been disabled at God's command, and national authorities have taken those responsible for creating the weapons into custody. Stockpiles have been contained and cordoned off until all components of the weapons, and associated fuel, have been safely stored. The Swiss have led on all verification processes, and no other groups enriching uranium to make weapons have been identified."

"Well, thank God for that," Cummings whispered under his breath.

He hadn't intended for his colleague to hear his words, but he heard Blackstone mutter, "Amen" in response.

"The world knows the rules," Sarah continued. "As per my original message, within one year, all nuclear weapons and fuel on this planet must be fully disabled. Within three years, they must not only be dismantled, but all radioactive components must be placed in safe storage. If this does not occur, God will cause non-compliant weapons and fuel to melt in situ. Your lives are in danger if you don't comply. *Surely* you all understand?"

At her words, the room darkened slightly, and Cummings could feel the hair on his arms stand on end as if static electricity was permeating the air. He knew that the United States was on target with God's demands. They already had some of the best people in the nation working on getting their nuclear weapons stockpiles decommissioned and a new, ultra-safe storage facility was being planned by the Army Corps of Engineers, who would also be building it. Construction was slated to start in about a month.

Sarah continued, "I know most of you have spent the last twenty-five days planning for disabling your weapons as the first step to full disarmament and storage. You only have eleven months left for step one to be enacted, and my understanding is that most of you are well on your way to meeting this goal. So, for the purposes of this meeting, instead of focusing on this aspect of God's edict, our challenge will be to develop an agreed upon approach to completing full, global nuclear disarmament and waste storage within the three-year deadline as stipulated by God. World leaders, by a show of hands, indicate that you understand and agree," she said.

The hands of all the leaders went up. Sarah's many faces gave the impression of a smile. This was the answer she needed to hear.

"Good," she said, "To this end, I would like to get the technical teams assembled here today working on fleshing out a coordinated three-year plan for complete disarmament and storage, including a timeline for when to call in the verification teams. We need to agree on how to dismantle and safely store all nuclear weapons, and weapons grade fuel, within the stipulated deadline. World leaders, by a show of hands, indicate that you understand and agree."

All hands in the room went up, though Cummings noted that this time, it seemed that the Russian and North Korean leaders raised theirs rather reluctantly. However, there was no use fighting against God's edict, for to do so would go against the will of God . . . and would mean certain death for each of them, not to mention countless of their subjects.

"Good," said Sarah, a warm breeze wafting throughout the room as it carried her approval to each and every one of them. "My only other comment is that technical teams will have to define what 'fully dismantled and disabled' means for each of the various types of weapons. Is that clear?"

There was agreement noted throughout the room. The assembled group were all well aware that there were unique idiosyncrasies to every weapon, depending on its country of origin. The work of the Swiss team was going to be arduous and highly detailed. They would be expected to familiarize themselves with a variety of different blueprints and construction designs in order to oversee the safe deconstruction and storage of each weapon.

"Now," said Sarah, "we can get down to work." She looked around the room at the assembled leaders and their teams. "Presidents and leaders," she said, "the next section of this discussion will be highly specialized in nature and is better suited to your technical experts and their supervisors. For you, I have something else in mind. I would ask that you leave this assembly hall and gather in room A15. There, I would like you to hammer out a treaty regarding long-term care of the disassembled nuclear materials. Please review governance, responsibility, and first response should anybody try to steal or activate components of the stored items, and any other salient points you can think of."

At that, the assembled leaders mumbled assent and stood up, Cummings along with them.

"See you later," he said to Blackstone, and then he followed the other leaders into room A15, leaving behind the technical teams, and the Swiss verification team, to hammer out how they were actually going to dismantle and store the weapons.

Room A15 was smaller than the large assembly hall but nicely appointed. Cummings selected a plush blue seat and sat down. He looked around at the other heads of state, monitoring the expressions of each one. In general, most looked quite benign and agreeable. The two most threatening states—Russia and North Korea—were being represented by new leaders. Russia's Grinkov was a seasoned politician, but he had never had such a high level leadership role as the one he had today, and he looked uncomfortable at the responsibility resting on his shoulders. Former

President Misha Verenich had, for all intents and purposes, been a dictator, and until this moment, Grinkov's role had been largely to make his boss look good—under threat of death. But Cummings could tell that Grinkov wanted to play ball with the group; The man had an earnestness to him that was indicative of a sharp mind and a good heart.

Conversely, the representative from North Korea, Kyun Do Yoon, appeared sullen and put-upon, and Cummings could not help but wonder how heavily he had been influenced by Park Jon-un's brutal style of rule. If Kyun Do Yoon subscribed to the same philosophy as his predecessor, then he most certainly would find it difficult to let go of long-held hostility and mistrust.

The group sat down, and as soon as they did, Sarah appeared in a chair at the head of the table.

"Please get comfortable," she said in that airy, light way of hers. "We will stay in this room as long as it takes to hammer out a treaty. None of you have anything to gain by trying to stack the process in your favour, so I hope it will be a relatively short process."

Cummings hoped so too.

Then she said, "As I'm sure you're aware, I am meeting concurrently with your technical team, who are ironing out the mechanics of disabling and safely storing these weapons. We all have a lot of ground to cover, so let's begin."

She led the afternoon session by asking each leader to describe the technologies—as they understood them from the briefing notes their technical experts had supplied—in use in each country for storage of nuclear waste. Then she asked each of them to describe the long-term solutions they would like to see implemented, not only with waste from nuclear weapons, but from nuclear medicine and power generation as well.

"I'd really like to see a scientific global initiative to render nuclear waste harmless," Cummings said to nods of agreement around the room.

"I agree," said British prime minister, Charles Grafton. "The use of nuclear technology is not going away, but the technology needs to be safer."

"Nuclear power alleviates some of the challenges of traditional types of power generation," said Cummings, "but until we have better technology for dealing with waste, it's a dirty game."

With a nod to French president Marcel Brassard, who was seated to her left, Sarah said, "Japan and France have both displayed leadership in this area."

Brassard took his cue. "Yes, it is true," he said in English. "My country derives about 70% of our electricity from nuclear energy, though it is my government's policy to reduce this to 50% by 2035. And, with respect to what President Cummings said about safer technologies, about 17% of France's electricity is from recycled nuclear fuel. This is an area we should examine more closely. France is happy to share our experience with this."

"Then I would urge you all to not only plan for waste storage," said Sarah, "but to look at recycling programs and technologies to remediate nuclear waste."

"It is important that the public feels confident in what we are doing," said Cummings.

"Yes—we must ensure the verification processes are both thorough and transparent," agreed Grafton.

"And perhaps we need to include Japan in our discussions, even though they are not part of the NPT," suggested Cummings. "They have had experience with this."

With the exception of a dark frown from the North Korean leader, there were nods of assent around the room. The assembled group all remembered the Fukushima Daiichi nuclear disaster caused by the 2011 Tōhoku earthquake and tsunami and were aware of Japan's ongoing efforts to contain and mitigate the damage.

As the afternoon wore on, the best ideas were explored, and efforts were made to standardize them so a treaty could be drawn up and hopefully ratified.

Meanwhile, in the larger hall, the technical experts were working on the specifics of full disarmament and waste storage, taking into account not only the disposal of weapons grade uranium and plutonium but also waste generated by nuclear medicine and power plants. As she was doing with the meeting of the heads of state, Sarah was presiding over and guiding the conversation.

Later, the teams met over a shared luncheon at the Restaurant des Délégués on the highest (eighth) floor of the United Nations building so the technical group could update the leadership group on some of the proposed ideas they had generated during their workshop.

After lunch, and before each group returned to their respective meeting places, Sarah said, "Thank you, everybody, for your hard work today. We have made much greater progress than I expected."

There were pleased smiles from group members at the praise. Then Sarah added, "If all goes as well after lunch as it did this morning, I propose we issue a communique—signed off by all you leaders assembled here today—announcing that we have ratified an agreement about how to safely deal with the world's nuclear arsenals. World leaders, by a show of hands, indicate that you understand and agree."

Cummings noted that all the assembled leaders seemed pleased with the idea, including the North Korean leader. All raised their hands.

The afternoon was productive, and by 4:00 p.m., Cummings' group had come up with a robust, meaningful first draft of a treaty, which included a commitment to form an international task force to develop new technologies for dealing with radioactive waste. When the final in camera vote had been conducted on the treaty's contents, and it was ratified, even the North Korean leader looked pleased at the outcome.

"This has been a remarkable day," said Sarah to the assembled leaders. "As God intended, you put away your quarrels and have reached an agreement that serves the greater good. I propose we hold a press conference at 5:00 p.m. to announce what we have done here today."

There were relieved smiles around the room.

Later that night, as Cummings lay in bed beside his sleeping wife, he smiled broadly into the darkness. After today's meeting, he felt more positive about the future than he had for many, many years.

"Thanks be to God, and to you too, Sarah," he whispered before he shut his eyes and drifted off into a peaceful, dreamless sleep.

Chapter 16

Biological and Chemical Weapons Conference

The Tokyo conference on the elimination of biological and chemical weapons was held on the thirtieth day after God's intervention. Sarah scheduled it to be five days after the nuclear disarmament talks out so that heads of state would be free to attend if they so wished. She also made it clear to world leaders that, even if their governments did not actively pursue or support the production of biological and chemical weaponry, there could be factional groups in their countries that did, and so she insisted that all countries send representatives to this meeting.

Because Cummings was determined to be as hands-on as possible in all aspects of the disarmament of the United States of America, he elected to attend the meeting with the same team he'd gone to the nuclear disarmament conference with, including Blackstone. Most countries, however, were instead represented by government cabinet members; And as with the nuclear disarmament conference, attending parties each brought with them two technical experts and two support staff.

As she'd done at the Geneva nuclear disarmament conference, on the day of the meeting, Sarah teleported all attendees to the National Diet Building in Tokyo, the centre of all lawmaking in Japan. The National Diet is Japan's bicameral legislature, composed of a lower house and an upper house, both of which are directly elected under a parallel voting system. In addition to passing laws, the Diet is formally responsible for selecting the Prime Minister.

When they arrived at the historic building, which was completed in 1936, Cummings, Blackstone and their team marveled at the fact that it was constructed solely out of Japanese materials (with the exception of the stained glass, door locks, and a pneumatic tube system). Cummings was impressed with the architecture, especially with the mosaic floors created from more than ten different kinds of marble stones. The building also featured spectacular oil paintings of the four seasons.

"The Japanese always know how to do it right," said Cummings to Blackstone in admiration as he took a picture and texted it to Lorena, knowing how much she loved art.

Blackstone nodded curtly. A military man, he had a well-informed historical knowledge of World War II, and it was clear he was suspending judgement of all things Japanese until he'd reached a certain comfort level.

Soon Cummings, Blackstone, and their team entered the 460-seat House of Councilors hall and sat down in the middle tier (of three), where they were slightly elevated but not too far away from the action.

As they were getting comfortable, and the other attendees settled in around them, Cummings muttered, "I could use a cup of coffee," knowing that might be a challenge in this tea-drinking nation.

Blackstone smiled slightly. "I get you, Chief," he said. "It's 9:00 a.m. here, but it's almost bedtime in D.C. This could be a long meeting."

The room was almost full, and most people were already sitting when Sarah appeared out of thin air with a whooshing sound and a fluttering breeze. There was a collective gasp as she materialized.

Then, when all attention was upon her, she said in a booming voice, "Let us begin."

Then, apparently as a nod to the Japanese hosts, a flurry of cherry blossoms filled the air, causing a chorus of 'ooohs and ahhhhs' from the attendees.

As the last petal floated to the ground, Sarah said, "I would like to thank the government of Japan for hosting this meeting."

There was clapping around the room.

When it died down, she said, "Because the Japanese team is the lead on the verification processes for the dismantlement and safe storage of biological and chemical weapons, before we begin, I would like to ask the leader of the Japanese verification team to introduce himself. Akira Yamaguchi, please stand up."

Cummings saw a medium-height, middle-aged Japanese man, who was sitting near the front of the auditorium on the floor of the circular hall, stand up. He turned around and bowed to the assembled group, and then waved self-consciously at everyone and sat back down again. Cummings thought he looked like a very kind and intelligent man.

"I now declare this meeting of world leaders in session," Sarah said, a thunderous clap rocking the air to accompany her words. "Our challenge over the next two days will be to develop, and agree upon, how to best dispose of, or otherwise disable, the world's biological and chemical weapons within the three-year deadline stipulated by God."

There was a murmur in the room as the assembled groups spoke among themselves, processing her words. Cummings noted the administrative staff of every contingent busily typing notes on iPads, and even recording information in the old-fashioned way—with book and pen. He looked over at Dolly Peabody, and saw she was typing away on her laptop, while her cohort Martin Jain was scribbling into a book.

"Let me start by reminding you of God's edict," Sarah continued. "Upon my arrival on Earth, I shared with you God's decree that the production of biological and chemical weapons must cease within seven days, or production facilities would be destroyed by God."

There were nods of assent around the room. All government representatives were by now well aware of the edicts imposed by God, and most countries had already dutifully reported all their weapons and ceased their production.

Sarah continued, "God also decreed that all such weapons must be placed in safe storage in central repositories, within their countries of origin, within one year. Following completion of this step, these repositories will be monitored by international inspectors." She looked around the room with her ever-changing face and her deep, starlit eyes as if challenging the assembled people to contradict her. Predictably, no one did.

Finally she said, "Ultimately, God decreed that all such weapons must be safely disposed of within three years—or God will destroy them and kill all persons involved in the decision to keep them."

There was some uncomfortable shifting in seats as the assembled group pondered what this edict meant to their respective nations. Then the room went dark, and Cummings felt as if all the energy in the place had been sucked out, leaving a great void. He shivered and felt suddenly bereft.

"Only one country failed to cease production of biological and chemical weapons within the seven-day period as ordered by God," Sarah said, and Cummings knew what her next announcement would be. "North Korea chose to ignore the word of God, and did not move to shut down its biological and chemical weapons operations. Subsequently, all production facilities in that country were destroyed."

There were some worried looks around the room, most notably from the Chinese and South Korean contingents.

Cummings sighed silently to himself and whispered to Blackstone, "North Korea just keeps on producing this crap, even though it acceded to the Biological Weapons Convention in 1987. You name it, they have it all . . . anthrax, plague, yellow fever—and no doubt some things we haven't even thought of!"

"Yes," whispered Blackstone discreetly back, "and South Korea has lived in fear for years that it would use these agents against its food and water supplies."

"Well, I guess they don't have to worry anymore," said Cummings, shaking his head at the enormity of the threat that North Korea had traditionally posed to not only its nearest neighbours but the whole of the Western world as well. There were things about this rogue nation that he would *never* understand.

Blackstone, sensing his mood, elbowed him in the ribs. "Cheer up, Sir," he said. "By Western standards, their biotech infrastructure was rudimentary at best . . . they were never that much of a threat."

"Maybe not to us," said Cummings, "but if any of those toxins were released when God shut down the facilities, there is a medical disaster in that country that will require a global effort to fix. Between those affected by nuclear fallout, and those affected by biochemical agents, I can't help wondering whether God's intervention is making things worse for the people of North Korea!"

Blackstone simply shrugged. A man of action, he kept his opinions to himself unless they were needed as part of a plan. To him, there was nothing they could do for North Korea now . . . except, of course, to deploy aid.

God's Intervention

As was her way, Sarah responded to their private conversation as if she had been listening in. "Some of you may be wondering if there is need for humanitarian aid in North Korea, and the answer is yes. Not only have pollutants been released that are making their way into the neighbouring countries of China, Russia, and South Korea, but the detention camp doors have been opened, and there are hundreds of thousands of extremely impoverished people who need food, aid, and help with reintegration into mainstream North Korean society. North Korea is presenting a challenge to the world, and it is God's will that we work as one to help this country, and other countries that suffer from poverty and political unrest, to get on their feet."

At that, the lighting in the room flickered, and the rose scent Cummings knew to be her message of caring, wafted about more strongly than he had smelled it ever before.

Sarah continued, "However, because this meeting is specifically about dismantling the world's biological and chemical weapons, we must save that topic for another discussion. Right now, our goal is to globally dismantle biological and chemical weapons, whether in North Korea or elsewhere. To this end, I located 1,013 insurgency groups around the world who were working in secret on biological and chemical weapons, and who did not report their activities to the appropriate authorities within the seven-day window as God demanded. Please be aware that all of their production facilities were destroyed by God, and those responsible for making the weapons perished."

There were murmurs around the room as people absorbed the idea that there had been more than 1,000 largely unknown and unrecognized groups across the globe with access to such cunning and fatal weapons. The concern was palpable.

Then Cummings saw the president of Mozambique, Joaquim Mabote, raise his hand, wanting to speak. Sarah acknowledged him with a flash of her eyes and he stood up.

"Ms. Sarah," he said smoothly, "Good day to you."

"And to you," Sarah said coolly back, and Cummings thought he could smell creosote.

He looked over to see Blackstone wrinkling his nose; Clearly, he could smell it too. He wondered at the source. He could only think that it was Sarah's version of distaste.

Mabote said graciously, "Ms. Sarah, I would like to apologize to you for what you found in Mozambique," he said. "We are generally a peaceful nation—"

"No," interrupted Sarah, "there has been much strife in your country."

"Uh . . . but not recently," said Mobate, somewhat disconcerted at the way she cut him off.

"Not in the public eye," said Sarah.

Then her eyes flashed so brightly that Cummings had to cover his eyes to avoid the blinding flare of light. When Sarah spoke again, the timbre of her voice was such that Mobate, who had presented himself with a swagger, now cowered.

"Joaquim," Sarah said in a booming voice, "do not try to tell me that you were not aware of the weapons being developed in your country. You may fool your countrymen, but you cannot fool God. Because you are not the one who commissioned them, you are not dead. Please sit down."

Mobate looked seriously cowed and immediately complied.

When the showdown was over, and the rustle of surprised voices in the room had died down, Sarah spoke again. "While God's first milestone in the dismantlement of biological and chemical weapons was to identify the sources and stop production—which is now complete—the second milestone, as I mentioned, is to have such weapons moved to central locations to be safely stored. We will be discussing how to expediently do this as part of our meeting today. To aid in our planning, I have compiled a list of weapons on a country by country basis, including weapons created by insurgents. I have also sorted the weapons by the specific biological or chemical agents of which they are composed. This list has just been transmitted to the computers of your technical support staff."

As soon as the words were out of her mouth, Cummings heard Dolly Peabody's computer ping. He glanced over at it to see an open document, populated with the listings as Sarah had said, show up on the screen. Then he glanced up to see an open mouth on Dolly Peabody as she scrolled to the U.S.A. section of the document to discover that fifty-six of the insurgent groups were right in the United States, with seven of those in Washington D.C. and seventeen in New York City.

His eyes opened wide as he realized just how vulnerable the government of the United States was—indeed, how vulnerable *he* was. He was suddenly immensely grateful to God that nothing had happened to him, his family, or his people while he'd blindly believed that the country he was in charge of was well-monitored, when clearly it was not.

"Let us begin the discussion," said Sarah. "I have compiled a list of proposals for dismantlement timelines, country by country, as well as proposed security efforts. All of these ideas were submitted by various attendees here today. We will review them together and vote on them. From the accepted proposals, we will create a draft plan for neutralizing and safely storing all dangerous toxins and chemicals related to biological and chemical warfare. World leaders, by a show of hands, indicate that you understand and agree."

Cummings raised his own hand, and he saw a lot of other hands go up as well; However, bound as he was by his mortal senses, he had no idea whether *every* contingent in the room had agreed. Sarah did though.

Without further hesitation—and seemingly with no need to count at all—she said, "Good. We are all agreed. We will hammer out our draft agreement before lunch. Then, after a short recess, we will return to this room and start our phase two planning session—how to permanently destroy these biological and chemical agents within the three-year deadline decreed by God."

With that, they began. With so many attendees at the meeting, it was a labourious process and by noon, they had only reached agreement on four rudimentary points for the first document and were far from a completed first draft. However, they were at least making some progress, and Cummings could tell they were headed in the right direction. There was a group willingness that he was quite proud to be part of, and the general feeling in the room was optimistic.

In the end, the whole conference and the ratification of the two documents took two days longer than expected, but on the day of the formal signing ceremony, Cummings had never been prouder.

It was only when he was safely back in the United States that President Cummings got the cup of coffee he so dearly wanted. As he took the first sip, he thought, *This is the best thing I've ever tasted.*

Chapter 17

Cyberwarfare Conference

The cyberwarfare conference was held in Beijing on the same day as the biological and chemical weapons conference, and Cummings could not attend, as he simply could not be in two places at once the way Sarah could. He wryly thought how wonderful it would be if that were possible; He would be able to get *so* much more work done. He sent Angelica Lopez and Hana Shriver, the two of them presenting a united, non-partisan political front for the United States of America, in his stead.

The two women assembled their own team of technical experts and administrative staff, with Vice President Lopez ably selecting those with the most familiarity with national intelligence and security. Shriver requested her right-hand technical expert accompany them, Yusaf O'Hara, a man she'd worked with for several years who had studied computer security at the Massachusetts Institute of Technology and was widely regarded as a genius.

When Shriver asked Cummings about it, he readily agreed that she should bring with her whoever she saw fit, though he couldn't help commenting on the man's name. "It's unusual, isn't it?" he asked her when they met to discuss it, a bit worried that he sounded judgmental.

"Not that much more unusual than my *own* name," responded Shriver. "Hana is Japanese, while Shriver is German." Then she smiled at him and added, "If you must know, Yusaf is his grandfather's name—his mother's father. And as you can probably guess, his own father is from Irish stock."

Cummings chuckled, "America the melting pot, I guess," he said.

"All I know is that he's a computer genius, and he's the one who will bring the most to the table at this conference," she said.

As he hung up the phone, Cummings felt confident that the future of America's cybersecurity would be well in hand with Hana Shriver on the team.

As was her way, on the day of the conference, Sarah teleported Lopez, Shriver, and their group to Beijing. In a heartbeat, they found themselves outside the China National Convention Centre. A huge, glass building located beside the National Indoor Stadium at the Olympic Park, the convention centre was of great interest to the vice president and her companion because of its environmentally oriented design, which featured a gentle, concave roof (with the opposite curves to the neighbouring National Indoor Stadium building) that allowed it to collect rainwater to irrigate the surrounding landscape.

"It's a brilliant design," commented Lopez in admiration.

"Indeed," agreed Shriver, adding, "We need to work with this architect on our water problems in the Southwest."

The American contingent made their way inside the building and into the conference hall where they were to meet with security experts from all around the world, as well as senior bureaucrats responsible for national security.

"It's unbelievable how much threat there is to cybersecurity these days," remarked Shriver conversationally as they got settled.

"Why is it unbelievable?" asked Lopez, seizing upon what she saw as a teaching moment. "Unprecedented amounts of sensitive personal information are stored on networks, or in the cloud. It's the new battleground for criminals and terrorists."

"I guess you're right," said Shriver as she selected a seat. "If they can hack security on, say, a country's central bank, they can bring that country to its knees."

"Oh, it's much more than that," said Lopez, sitting down beside her and booting up the laptop she'd brought along. "Transportation control systems, from traffic lights to air traffic control software are key targets. Power grids are also attractive targets too."

She was about to elaborate, but suddenly the noise in the room stopped, and Lopez looked up to see Sarah slowly manifesting in the air as if she was a ghost.

The gentle sound of a Chinese guqin, a stringed instrument similar to a lute, permeated the atmosphere in an unearthly way as Sarah said, "I would like to thank the government of China for hosting this meeting."

Both Lopez and Shriver clapped, along with everyone else, in awe of both her entrance and her presence.

"As you know," Sarah continued, "God's edict, which I delivered thirty days ago, made it clear that cyberattacks of any form were to immediately cease, and anyone involved in designing, building, triggering, or commissioning them was at risk of death by God's hand, up to and including heads of state."

There were nods of assent, and murmurs around the room.

She continued, "There were twenty-four cyber-related deaths by God's hand—twelve in Russia, six in the United States, and six in Iran. While all *official* cyberwarfare programs ceased in an expedient manner as per God's edict, some private operators and terrorist organizations did *not*. At God's discretion, these people were killed. Half of the rogue developers were working on technologies to disrupt GPS navigation—leading to accidents and deaths—while the other half were developing cyberwarfare technologies designed to disrupt power transmission systems and nuclear plant safety systems. Any of these types of attacks could have disabled even such a great city as New York in as short a time as one week. With no gasoline, running water, or food, chaos would reign."

Sarah paused, letting the attendees absorb the information, and then, when the murmuring died down, she said, "For the purposes of our discussion today and to ensure that we are all on the same page as we move forward, I've sent a list to your computers of common cyber threats and vulnerabilities."

The computers of both Lopez and Shriver, along with Yusaf O'Hara's iPad, immediately dinged. Sarah's note read:

Common cyber threats:
- **Malware (malicious software):** Software that can be used to infiltrate, disrupt, steal, or damage data, including viruses, ransomware, trojans, and botnets.

- **Phishing:** Malicious emails or text messages that look legitimate and trick users into giving up sensitive information or their log-in credentials.
- **Man-in-the-middle attack:** Malicious entities that can impersonate an 'endpoint' and intercept information.
- **Denial-of-service attack:** When a server is overwhelmed with false data requests and becomes unable to perform.

Vulnerabilities:
- **Network security:** Protecting computer networks from attack or intrusion.
- **Application security:** Protecting software through updates and improvements.
- **Cloud security:** Protecting data in, and access to the 'cloud' (remote servers).
- **Information security:** Protecting sensitive information within a network.
- **Operational security:** Protecting physical systems through passwords and other verification policies.
- **Disaster recovery:** Restoration of secure operations after a cyberattack.

"Generally," said Sarah, addressing the group again, "the biggest threat posed by cyber interference has traditionally been to military applications. For example, GPS satellites used for weapons guidance and space-based surveillance have long been targets of cyberwarfare because taking out a nation's satellite capability forces it into old-school warfare—which is expensive and involves high casualties."

At that, Yusef O'Hara, who was sitting beside the vice president, put up his hand to speak.

"Hello, Mr. O'Hara," said Sarah.

"It is truly an honour, Sarah," said Yusef with a trembling voice. He had not been in Sarah's presence before, and he was beside himself with a combination of fear and awe as he looked into her startling, star-filled eyes. "Can you confirm that until this . . . uh . . . intervention by God . . . the Chinese and Russians were developing 'soft kill' counterspace capabilities?"

"I believe it's of no use to finger-point," said Sarah carefully, "though I can confirm that co-orbital satellites—meaning both ground-based and space-based—were poised to be targeted with electronic warfare."

"You mean warfare such as jamming and spoofing, microwave weapons, laser dazzling, and so on?" asked O'Hara.

Sarah's many faces nodded, and she added, "If a satellite is disabled, disrupted, damaged, or hijacked, it will provide false information, which is just as effective—if not more so—than physically destroying it."

At Sarah's mention of physically destroying satellites, Lopez suddenly remembered a public outcry a few years previous when India had tested an anti-satellite weapon—effectively becoming the first nation to weaponize space. *Too much like Star Wars,* she thought with a shudder, grateful that God was putting a stop to the madness.

Sarah, not quite finished addressing O'Hara, added, "And despite the fact that GPS spoofing goes *against* international norms, there are documented cases of Russia using it against NATO."

Lopez thought about the implications of that, and then immediately texted Cummings and Blackstone in Tokyo, saying, "The Russians have been up to what we suspected, jamming and spoofing. If they'd taken out our military satellites, we would have been left extremely vulnerable. We're so lucky God intervened."

Cummings texted back, "Remind me again, what are jamming and spoofing?"

With a sigh, Lopez passed her computer to O'Hara. "Can you answer him for me?" she asked.

Immediately, O'Hara typed, "To simplify, jamming a GPS signal causes the receiver to *die*, while spoofing causes the receiver to *lie*, giving false coordinates. It's a huge threat to public safety, especially in military applications."

"Thanks," Cummings typed back, "and tell Angelica I'm in agreement that we're so lucky God intervened."

Lopez elbowed Shriver, who was sitting, quiet and contemplative, beside her. She showed her the message exchange with Cummings.

Shriver read it quickly and then let out a long sigh. "Cyberattacks on satellites are effective and relatively cheap. I would imagine America has been targeted by not only Russia but Iran and North Korea for quite some time."

"That's what I thought you were thinking," said Lopez. "And so was I."

Then both women's attention was drawn toward Sarah again as a thunderclap filled the air, and she announced in a booming voice, "Today, we will work toward ratifying an agreement about the use of cyberweaponry. Delegates, by a show of hands, indicate that you understand and agree," she said.

Lopez was gratified to see that nearly every hand in the room went up.

As the afternoon progressed, plans devoted to firmly shutting down weapons development programs, and for creating a new Cyberwarfare Agency at the United Nations, were slowly shaped and ratified. All countries agreed to make cyberweaponry illegal and, in future, to work with the Cyberwarfare Agency to apprehend and incarcerate offenders.

As the day wore on, Lopez texted Cummings in Tokyo once more. "My heart is full," she said. "Everyone here wants to end war, and I feel like there is finally a glimmer of hope for this crazy world. Oh, and BTW, you're going to get teleported here to sign the treaty when it's done."

Cummings texted a smiley face back.

The conference took a total of three days. When it was done, the Chinese president held a formal, traditional tea ceremony, dedicating it to a brighter and more stable future for humankind. As Lopez told him would happen, Cummings was teleported in to sign the agreement, which he was happy to do.

Around the world, people's moods were becoming more positive and hopeful as the world's nations came together to work toward lasting peace.

Later, when she'd returned home from the conference, as Lopez laid down beside her husband, her beautiful twin girls, Audrey and Arianna, in the room next to them, she envisioned a bright future for her daughters, and a strong sense of relief settled on her. *Thanks to God's intervention, war will never return,* she thought gratefully.

Chapter 18

Glorification of War and Killing Conference

As with the cyberwarfare conference, the conference on the glorification of war and killing held in Brussels, Belgium took place on the thirtieth day after Sarah's arrival on Earth, and so Cummings could not attend. Instead, he sent a team led by his chief of staff, Bradley Northrup. Northrup had a strong interest in social issues, of which glorification of violence—and the impact it was having on American culture—was most certainly one, and Cummings trusted him completely to represent the interests of the United States at the meeting.

Sarah insisted that *all* nations send a contingent to this event and, as usual, she teleported the American group and all the other attendees to the venue—the SQUARE (Brussels Convention Centre)—on the day of the meeting.

It took Northrup a few minutes to regain his sense of 'feet on the ground' after the teleportation, as the experience left him dizzy. However, once he'd taken a couple of deep breaths, he was okay, and he began to marvel at the landmark, three-story, sixteen-meter tall glass cube in front of him. The cube formed the main entry to the premises, and it was glorious to look at. It's overall aesthetic was based on transparency and light, and it featured a terrace that had access to the Mont des Arts, an historic site in the center of Brussels.

Northrup had brought, as part of his team, several cabinet-level politicians with responsibility for education, arts, and mental health: Secretary of Education, Johanna Petrie; Secretary of State for Digital,

Culture, Media, and Sport, Miguel Arduino; and, Secretary of Health and Human Services, Elliot Fleming.

Sarah had asked each team to prepare a position paper in advance of the meeting, discussing four main topics. In conjunction with Cummings' inner circle (Lopez, Shriver, Blackstone, and Feldman)—and with advice from the group he'd brought with him to this meeting—Northrup had worked for several weeks on the American paper. He was now crystal clear on where his government stood on the following questions Sarah had presented, which were:

1. In light of God's ban on killing, should <u>new</u> production of violent media (movies, books, art, music, websites, electronic games) glorifying war and killing be completely banned, or should production continue with strictly enforced access restrictions (i.e. no one under the age of eighteen, no one incarcerated for violent crime, and so on)?
2. Should <u>historical</u> media (paintings, books, movies) glorifying war and killing continue to be available through museums, libraries, and the internet?
3. Will there be <u>legal or economic consequences</u> for your country if all existing media glorifying war and killing are banned?
4. Should decisions involving appropriate management (production, restriction, destruction) of media glorifying war and killing be a <u>domestic</u> responsibility or an <u>international</u> one?

For the purposes of the discussion, Sarah defined glorification as *'the action of describing or representing something as unjustifiably admirable, with the potential outcome of influencing a person (or persons) to kill another person.'*

Northrup sat down with Cummings and the rest of the group—the inner circle originally selected by Sarah to work with Cummings—to hash out the bones of the American position paper. For question one, the group was in complete agreement that, given Sarah's definition of glorification, all *new* creation of entertainment media glorifying violence should be completely banned, with the exception of simulations used for training purposes. Gordon Blackstone, the secretary of defence, rightly pointed out that, while the American military was no longer going to function as a killing machine (or 'international peacekeeper' as some referred to it), the U.S. would still need its domestic security enforced with non-lethal weapons, and simulated training was a requirement for expert marksmanship.

With regard to question two, the American team unanimously agreed that history should not be forgotten, and that *not* allowing people access to historical depictions of a former way of life was akin to a type of censorship that was not practical, nor fair. Northrup remembered Shriver's comment as they mulled the question over.

"Who are we to deny access to people's pasts?" she'd asked, adding, "Sometimes, knowing what you *don't* want is key to understanding what you *do* want."

Question three was trickier for the group. The entertainment industry was a significant economic driver in the United States, and to stifle it permanently from expounding on its favourite subject matter (violence, generally presented under the heading of 'art') was likely to cause some legal drama—though the team was prepared to advocate for such a ban if necessary, as per their decision when faced with the first question.

"Let's start by talking *only* about the movie business," said Northrup as the group sat down to brainstorm. "Movies and television cut most cleanly across all demographics, whereas violent music and video games are more age-specific, and tend to appeal to younger people."

"Agreed," said Cummings, frowning in concentration. Then he asked, "How many war movies do you think there are out there?"

"How many murder mysteries?" asked Angelica Lopez, shaking her head with the scope of it.

"You can't just isolate one director or producer who consistently promotes violence, and then ban his or her work," Shriver cut in, "at least not in the way you can target one rapper who sings about stuffing his dead mother in a trunk."

"Oh, that was *dark*," said Norman Feldman, looking up from his computer in surprise.

"So are some of those songs," Shriver shot back.

"Point taken," said Feldman.

As the conversation went on, it soon became clear that the idea of banning or destroying *all* movies featuring glorified aspects of war or killing would be prohibitively expensive, as the research required to root such productions out would be a bit like fishing in a haystack. Aside from movies or shows where the central theme was actually *about* war or killing, there were countless productions where murder scenes were simply a sub-plot to stories ranging from 'unlikely teenage romance' to 'superhero saves the world.' To ban every show with such a scene would cost a lot of money in man-hours, not to mention enrage Hollywood. Further, there was no way to tally—let alone destroy—all copies of any given movie; With mobile devices, anyone could have their own movie library in their pocket.

"It would also turn public opinion against our administration," pointed out Vice President Lopez. "I can already hear the cries of 'censorship!' and anticipate the lawsuits that would follow."

In the end, the group decided to compromise. "We need to work with Hollywood to develop standards about the level of violence that can be depicted in movies, as well as the amount of time per movie that can be allocated to fight scenes," said Northrup during one of their brainstorming sessions. "The key here is to ban 'glorification' as opposed to banning *all* scenes depicting violence."

"I agree, Norman," Cummings said. "But what about other artforms that glorify war and killing . . . or stuffing your dead mother in a trunk," he said, winking at Shriver.

"I think we should heavily—I mean *prohibitively* heavily—tax venues or streaming services that provide space for artists who incite hatred and intolerance of any kind," replied Northrup.

"That cuts them off at the knees," said Lopez, warming to the idea.

"Sounds like a rap song," remarked Feldman, causing smiles around the room.

Ultimately, the group endorsed Northrup's recommendations, accepting that this compromise was less than a full-on ban, but likely the best they could do.

"We can only hope that the attraction to such things will fade in time as Sarah has promised," said Cummings to nods of agreement around the room.

Question four, regarding policy management, was much easier for the group to reach consensus on. As blue-blooded Americans, they were all very much in favour of monitoring their own business. They all immediately agreed on that, and then called it a wrap. Northrup then presented the paper to the cabinet members who were attending the meeting with him today—Petrie, Arduino, and Fleming—and received endorsement from them all.

Now, as Northrup settled into his seat, he felt confident in the team's decisions. He turned to have a word with Arduino, who was on his right, when suddenly the lights in the room flickered gently and a warm rush of wind suddenly ruffled his, and everybody else's, hair. Like a starburst, Sarah appeared before them in a shower of sparkling light. There was stunned silence around the room at her entrance.

Then she said, "I would like to thank the government of Belgium for hosting this meeting."

The room erupted into clapping. When the noise died down, Sarah got down to business.

Her eyes flashed in their typical unearthly way as she said, "Welcome to the conference on the glorification of war and killing. We have much to discuss today. As you know, I asked you all to submit position papers to me before this meeting." Then she looked around the room with her starlit eyes and added, "I have summarized your positions and created a report, which you will find on your computers."

There was a round of pinging noises across the room as all laptops and mobile devices received a copy of Sarah's report. Northrup was surprised to feel a weight on his lap, which turned out to be a paper copy of the report. He glanced toward Sarah and was surprised to find her gaze focused directly on him.

"Some people are old-school, right, Bradley?" she asked with a golden tinkle of energy. Then the moment was gone, and she said to the group, "When we've finished reviewing the report, we'll hear from those who don't side with the majority."

The cover of the printout in Northrup's hands was blue, and it was entitled: *Position Paper Summaries: Glorification of War and Killing*. Northrup opened it to read:

Production Ban vs. Access Restrictions

80% of countries, representing 75% of the world's population, believe a total ban should be imposed on the production of all media glorifying war and/or killing.

Countries **not supporting** a full ban were generally those with a high economic stake in the entertainment industry. Arguments against a full ban ranged from protecting freedom of expression to the evils of censorship. The United States further noted that God did not mandate a ban on *all* depictions of war and killing, only on the *glorification* of it—that is, portraying it as somehow admirable. It was further noted that such violent acts as rape; the beating of humans or animals; torture; and other acts of violence have not been banned, and that perhaps they should be.

Countries **supporting** a ban on production argued that the human race is entering a new world order, and that we should only encourage the depiction of love and respect via the art and entertainment industry. They further put forward that, if consumers refuse to support violent artistic media, the market for such items will shrink and likely disappear, and subsequently, they advocated for social education programs encouraging people to stand against depictions of violence of all kinds with this end in mind.

A hand shot up across the room, and Northrup looked over to see a small, blond woman eagerly waving at Sarah.

"Yes, Esmée?" said Sarah.

"Hallo from the Netherlands, Sarah," said Esmée in Dutch-accented English. "Please tell me, has a direct link been made between violent entertainment and violent killings?" she asked.

Sarah had anticipated this question. Smoothly, she answered, "Not officially, but there is compelling evidence to demonstrate that consuming violent art amplifies aggression in both children and adults." Then she looked away from Esmée and around the room, her unearthly eyes flashing, and said, "I would like to share my views on this issue."

There was a sudden stillness in the room, and Northrup could feel the hair on his arm stand on end as Sarah said, "I represent the life force of 40 million *real* women—women who lived in every corner of the world, at every time since humans began walking this planet. All the women of whom I'm composed are now part of God, and they have knowledge of all of the wonders of the universe. I have been mother to 137 million children. I have experienced the joys of life on Earth, as well as the great agonies caused by war and killing. As part of God, I am witness to the true potential of civilizations that abandon war and killing. When war and killing ceases, spirituality and love *increases*—and not just toward one's own species but also toward the planet and all of its living creatures. The same is true in reverse," she added, looking at Esmée, "when war and killing are actively *pursued*, spirituality and love decline."

Then, scattering the glitter from her eyes like prisms of sunlight, she said, "Some civilizations in this universe have existed for billions of years in peace and harmony, though many first had to get over the developmental stage humans are at right now—so drunk on their own power that, without God's intervention, they will destroy themselves."

She paused, letting that sink in, before adding, "A million years from now, humans will no longer kill animals to nourish themselves. People will eat fruit and vegetables, seeds, nuts, legumes, rice and grains, as well as proteins produced directly by bacteria. They will also access electromagnetic energy directly from external sources through body wear that will help regulate body temperature and enhance kinetic capabilities. Computer chips will be integrated with the body to expand sensory awareness and augment the storage and processing power of the brain."

"And other intelligent creatures—such as dolphins and lesser primates—will evolve alongside humans and they will learn to communicate meaningfully, and to understand and love God. A *billion* years from now, humans will look and be much like me . . . but without the multiple personality disorder."

There was a ripple of laughter around the room at Sarah's joke.

When it subsided, she continued, "You owe this future to our children. The sooner you come together and eradicate all the vestiges of war and killing, the faster such things will disappear from your future. God offers humankind a life on Earth that will be similar to eternally being with God—the 'Heaven on Earth' you've heard so much about."

There was complete silence in the room as the assembled group pondered her words, and after a few moments, Sarah broke it by saying, "I would like to offer you a demonstration of the true agony of war. There is no glory in acts of atrocity, such as portrayed in the entertainment media. There is only pain and suffering. Even the *perpetrators* of the heinous crimes committed during times of war are haunted by memories of what they have done . . . that is, if they have any sense of God."

There was an uncomfortable shifting in seats around the room as the crowd tried to anticipate what she was about to do. Northrup remembered Cummings telling him once of Sarah sending a movie of some sort into his head showing him atrocities of the most vile kind. He was pretty sure she was about to use the same technique with the assembled group. He steeled himself. *If Samuel can go through it, I can too,* he thought, gritting his teeth.

Sarah said softly, "I will transmit to you real death experiences of the women whose souls are within me. You will experience the terror and pain. You will hear the explosions and the screams. You will smell the smoke and the blood. If you have a heart condition, please leave the room now."

Three people hastily got up and exited the room. For a moment, Northrup thought of joining them but he, and the rest of the American group, remained seated.

Then Sarah said quietly, but with a dark undertone to her words, "If you don't want to experience being burned at the stake in Salem, leave the room now. If you don't want to feel the horror of seeing your child cut in half by a high powered automatic rifle, leave the room now. If you don't want to experience the fear of having your five-year-old child aiming your husband's handgun at your head, leave the room now. If you don't want to be stuck on the top floor of the World Trade Center when a plane crashes into it, leave the room now. If you don't want to experience death with your loved ones in a concentration camp, leave the room now. If you don't want to be teaching a kindergarten class in Hiroshima when an atomic bomb hits it, leave the room now."

There were some pale, yet expectant, faces gazing up at her, some in rapture and some in fear.

She looked down at these people and said, "If you stay, but you want to stop receiving the images and feelings I am about to transmit to you, raise your hand and I will stop. I need you to understand that if you experience more than a couple of these horrific life events, you may become permanently emotionally damaged."

The people who remained in the room looked sincerely upset at the idea of experiencing the trauma Sarah described, and then Northrup saw a look of compassion flicker across her ever-shifting face as Sarah said quietly, "Now, do we really need to go through this process, or should we vote in favour of banning production of any media that glorifies war and killing?"

It turned out that nobody wanted to endure the pain of Sarah's collective real-life experiences. After a brief discussion, all countries agreed to banning new production of any media glorifying war and killing, and strictly controlling any media featuring violence of any kind. When this was ratified, Sarah asked them to turn to the next topic.

Historical Accounts

There was 95% agreement that historical media (paintings, books, movies) depicting war and killing should be preserved, primarily in libraries and museums, but also on reputable online sites. The small percentage of countries who voiced concern over preserving historical media were generally those whose histories were rife with shifting borders and repeated military occupations. Governments of such countries felt accounts produced by 'victors' in battles with them had a tendency to blur boundaries around winning and losing or who had the 'right' to what resource in any given situation.

Northrup was not surprised to learn that most countries in the world were in favour of preserving historical accounts. His own country certainly supported this and were, of course, among the 95% who did. However, he could understand the point of view of some of the small countries in the Middle East, such as Jordan and Israel, where the same small bits of land had been fought over for years, with every player in the game having a different tale of who did what to whom, and why.

Sarah gave voice to his thoughts by saying, "Generally, for any given war, there are at least two opposing versions of the 'truth.' However, that is not what we are discussing here today. Our discussion is about whether historical accounts *glorify* killing, and if so, whether they should be removed from public consumption."

A lively debate ensued, and after a thirty-minute discussion, the dissenters somewhat reluctantly agreed to ratify the point that historical accounts—even if inaccurate—should be preserved, provided they did not glorify killing.

By the time this debate was concluded, it was evening. The group were delighted to be dismissed, and Northrup and his team headed out to a pub to try some famous Belgian beer. Northrup was looking forward to continuing the discussion the next morning.

When morning arrived, refreshed, Northrup arrived at the SQUARE ready to take up where they'd left off.

Sarah wasted no time. "Turn to the third topic," she said as soon as everyone was settled. Northrup opened his program to read:

Economic Impact of Destroying Existing Productions

80% of countries signaled an intention to ban all books, movies, music, and video games glorifying war and killing. The remaining 20% of countries decided to continue allowing their use, subject to severe restriction.

For most countries, banning and/or destroying existing media was not expected to have a significant economic impact. However, countries with vibrant entertainment production industries were concerned about:

a) The cost of identifying, recalling, and destroying such media.
b) The cost of legal battles on a variety of grounds, including freedom of speech.

The United States argued that creating a code of conduct around the levels of acceptable violence (i.e. not glorified) would be one way to assuage the 'freedom of expression' argument, especially in the movie and gaming industries, which are largely visually based.

The music industry presented a separate set of problems. To stop the spread of violence through hate lyrics, the U.S. proposed implementing a 'hate tax' targeting venues, both physical and online, that continue to provide a forum for artists who do not voluntarily cease this type of violent 'art.'

There was applause at this, and Northrup was pleased to see that the suggestions his team had come up with were embraced as 'good thinking' by the majority of meeting attendees. Many jumped on the taxation idea as a way to suppress hate speech, while not putting an industry out of work.

"We will take this gentler approach," said Bollywood executive Sanjay Kahn, who was attending as a representative of India's film industry. "We will do what we can to discourage it, and let God mete out the consequences for those who choose not to comply."

"Then let it be so," said Sarah.

At that, Northrup and the rest of the group prepared to review the fourth and last topic.

Jurisdiction

All countries were in total agreement that monitoring the glorification of war and killing as portrayed in entertainment media should be a <u>domestic</u> responsibility, not a <u>global</u> one, although several countries suggested that some high level global protocols should be adopted. European Union leaders proposed that decisions for all member countries should be made in Brussels.

At that last sentence, Northrup fleetingly mused how glad he was that America was free to make its own decisions.

The group adjourned for lunch, and when they returned, Sarah said, "Welcome back, ladies and gentlemen. I have drafted a communique summarizing the results of our deliberations over the last one-and-a-half days, and it is on your computers."

Northrup had an iPad with him. He opened his to read:

COMMUNIQUE ON THE GLORIFICATION OF WAR AND KILLING

The Brussels conference on the glorification of war and killing as portrayed by the entertainment industry has concluded. I am pleased to announce that every nation on Earth has agreed that the production of new movies, books, music, or electronic games glorifying war and/or killing will be banned, following completion of such items currently in process.

There was unanimous agreement among nations that there will be no prohibition of historical movies, books, or paintings that depict war and/or killing, as long as they are not deemed to 'glorify' such activities.

For the purposes of this conference, 'glorification' was defined as *'the action of describing or representing something as unjustifiably admirable, with the potential outcome of influencing a person (or persons) to kill another person.'*

Defining 'glorification' for the purposes of <u>regulation</u> will be left to each nation, with the expectation that a global consensus will emerge over time.

Going forward, creative content depicting violence of any kind will be subject to severe restrictions, both in terms of its creation, and access to it.

The proposed communique was agreed to, and issued, that afternoon.

Northrup was quite excited about it, and he texted it to Cummings immediately. "You're going to be expected to sign it," he wrote. "At this point, all nations agreed in principle, but the official document has not yet been drafted for signature."

"Great job, Bradley," Cummings texted back. "And could you bring me back some Belgian chocolate? Lorena loves that stuff."

Northrup smiled. He had just enough time to get a box of chocolates for Lorena—and a six-pack of fine Belgian beer for himself—before Sarah teleported him and the rest of the contingent back home.

Chapter 19

Military Repatriation Begins / Denver Meetings

As the first month since Sarah's appearance on Earth ended, not only had several global conferences wrapped up, but the United States and Russia had agreed upon a timetable for withdrawing their troops and military equipment from third countries and international waters.

"This is remarkable," President Cummings confided to his defence secretary, Gordon Blackstone.

"Sir, I completely concur," agreed Blackstone, relief on his face. He, more than anyone in Cummings' inner circle, understood the toll of war—and the sacrifices made by the warriors.

The two men sat opposite one another on the facing couches in the Oval Office. Cummings was looking over the proposed withdrawal plan on his computer. All submarines and warships were scheduled to return to their home waters within one month, with the exception of troop carriers; These were expected back within two months, to give them time to 'round up the troops.' Overseas military air bases would be closed in six months, following a staged removal of aircraft and personnel.

"The international conference on conventional weapon disarmament will be held in Moscow, in two months' time," Cummings told Blackstone. "I expect you to attend with me."

"Of course, Sir," Blackstone said. "I fully intend to."

Then, gazing levelly at his colleague, Cummings said, "I never thought to ask you, Bradley, but do you have family members overseas? Or are you the only one in your family who has a military career?"

"I have a sister in Afghanistan," confided Blackstone quietly. "She's a Red Cross nurse."

Cummings nodded, his brow furrowed. He didn't need to hear or ask Blackstone more. He knew that the brave medical professionals overseas saw more than their share of trauma during the course of their work. Particularly devastating for them was dealing with the destruction left by land mines. He had heard horror stories about children who'd found them and mistakenly thought they were toys.

He looked at his computer screen, and then gestured Blackstone to come around and look at it with him. Blackstone arose and sat down beside his boss, and Cummings showed him what was on the screen.

"You'll be glad to know that, as of tomorrow, the international effort to disarm and remove all land and sea mines will be underway," he told his defence secretary. "Teams of bomb disposal experts, mostly our armed forces guys and some Russian military experts, will be out in over 300 locations, working hand in hand with former insurgents to locate and dismantle them all."

"I'm glad to hear it, Sir," said Blackstone. Then, with uncharacteristic fervor, he added, "Those things are a scourge on the Earth."

The following day, the Global Land Mine Removal Initiative (GLORI) began its work. Media coverage was intense, and in a very short time, the members of GLORI were global celebrities, as the world embraced the idea of former enemies cooperating to dismantle bombs once planted for the purpose of killing one another. Such a captivating idea was soon pounced on by the entertainment industry, and in short order, Netflix was running a new weekly documentary/reality show called *Bomb Busters*, which became an overnight hit. It was tangible evidence that the world had entered a new era.

But more pressing for Cummings was preparing for the influx of disenfranchised military personnel and equipment that were currently on their way home. To manage this, Cummings had appointed a change management expert to oversee both the repatriation of incoming troops and the repurposing of military assets. The man he'd hired was named Martin Grieves. Grieves, an MBA from Harvard, was also a one-time navy commander, which gave him valuable inside knowledge as to how the military worked.

Grieves' experience with change management was extensive. Upon leaving the military, he'd invested in a floundering microchip production company in Silicon Valley, and had single-handedly turned it around through corporate restructuring. Within one year, it became the highest-grossing company of its kind in America. Then, at the height of the company's success, he sold his shares (for an astronomical sum) to focus on change management contracting. Almost immediately, he was hired by the navy to restructure several service arms. He ably did so, combining related job streams in a way that proved hugely successful at saving several millions of dollars a year. His reputation quickly spread, leaving Cummings with no doubt who to turn to for oversight of the military repatriation.

The day after Cummings contacted him, Grieves, Blackstone, and Cummings met. Cummings liked the middle-aged, well-groomed Grieves on sight.

"So," Cummings said, "I hope you read our draft plan for repurposing our troops?"

"I certainly did," said Grieves, "and I have some ideas about how to implement it, as well as about how to streamline it."

"Tell us what you have in mind," Cummings suggested.

"Of course!" replied Grieves. "As you know, my change management company employs several hundred contractors, who we utilize depending on what services are needed and what our client's expectations are. I've selected twelve of my best, most relevant colleagues, and scheduled a meeting at my ranch in Colorado for a one-day strategizing session. I hope to come out of that with the seeds of an action plan, which we will take to the next level as soon as we can."

Cummings nodded. "Sounds good," he said.

"You are both welcome to attend the meeting if you like," Grieves offered to the two men.

"I don't think that will be necessary," replied Cummings. "We're both pretty busy at the moment, though I would like to link in for a video chat, if possible."

Grieves nodded his understanding. "That's a fine idea," he said. He was well aware of the challenges facing the president and his cabinet—and also how limited their time was.

Several days later, Cummings was online as Grieves welcomed his team to the planning session.

"Welcome, ladies and gentlemen," he told the assembled group. "As you know, my company has been contracted by the federal government to create a change management plan to help integrate returning American troops, and to repurpose military assets. We are working closely with President Cummings' inner circle—not to mention the president himself. In fact, he is online to welcome you."

At that, Grieves turned to a large computer monitor mounted on one wall and Cummings face flickered to life on the screen.

Grieves greeted the president. "Hello, Sir," he said. "Please let me introduce you to my top-notch group of planners." He extended his arm, palm-up, like a magician, to encompass the eight men and four women in the room.

"Hello," said Cummings from the monitor. "Thank you for being part of this team and for doing such important work."

The assembled group looked pleased at the acknowledgement.

Then, as Cummings observed the proceedings via video link, Grieves turned to his team and said, "I have been asked by President Cummings to do three things. First, to take the finest fighting force the world has ever seen and transform it—in less than twelve months—into a much smaller one, capable of deploying rapidly to protect borders, suppress insurgency, and apprehend criminal groups. Second, to repurpose military assets, including the troops that maintain and operate those assets, to other government departments, or to the private sector. And third, to retrain military personnel as necessary and repatriate them into 'regular' society." Then he looked around the room and asked, "Any questions?"

"Yes," said LaShonda James, a striking African-American martial arts expert and owner of an adult education advocacy and training centre.

"Yes, LaShonda?" Grieves said.

"Will we be negotiating compensation for these repatriated troops as well?"

"No," replied Grieves, "that will be handled by the feds. According to President Cummings," he said, looking at Cummings' face on the screen, "all military personnel will remain on full salary for up to one year as the government works with us to find them new employment opportunities. As well, their pension rights will be fully vested by the end of that period. Medical benefits will be extended a further twelve months for those needing coverage." He looked to Cummings for confirmation. "Is that correct, Sir?" he asked.

"Yes," Cummings said. "That is correct."

Then Grieves turned back to the assembled team, saying, "We are going to spend the next three days brainstorming, bearing in mind that some of what we are about to discuss is highly classified. Do you understand?"

There were nods of assent around the room.

"Good," said Grieves. "First, let me be clear that you're all here because of your particular areas of expertise. LaShonda, of course, is our resident expert on how to effectively retrain adults," he smiled at the woman, "but that is only *one* aspect of troop repatriation that we will need address in our action plan. There are many aspects to this huge corporate change. For example, the White House has asked us to look at the most efficient way to redeploy the Army Corps of Engineers onto infrastructure projects, to repurpose military bases, to recycle weapons . . . it's a huge list, and I hope you've all had the opportunity to review the ideas the White House has put forward."

There were murmurs of assent around the room.

"That's what I want to hear," said Grieves to his team. "Then today, let's pour all our energy into creating a functional action plan that we can run with. Today, we're all about creation—but *tomorrow* we need to be ready to start *implementing. Tomorrow*, you will all show up for work at the Kennedy Center Office Campus in southeast Denver—where the government has kindly rented us office space as well as equipment and personnel to assist us—and begin putting processes in place for streaming returning troops into best-fit situations the minute those men and women touch American soil. Capiche?"

A consulting engineer with infrastructure refurbishment experience, William Hanover, put up his hand.

"Yes, Bill?" asked Grieves.

"I read the White House plan, and the ideas are really quite good," he said. "I assume you want me to work on a plan for redeploying the Army Corps of Engineers?"

"Yes," said Grieves, "as well as some of the tradespeople."

Then LaShonda put up her hand. "What about that angel person, that woman . . . Sarah?" she asked. "Is she going to help us with this?"

"I can answer that," said Cummings from the video monitor. "Sarah will provide support as needed, and she is doing the same for all countries around the world. Of course, with Russia and the U.S.A., having the biggest militaries, we are getting more than our fair share of assistance."

At that moment, as if summoned, Sarah appeared, fluttering into the room with her typical golden radiance. "Good morning, team," she said, the faint sound of bells colouring her voice. "It is my pleasure to be able to work with you. I am at your disposal—anytime, anywhere."

The assembled group had not seen her in person before, and there was a collective gasp as twelve pairs of wide, startled eyes focused on her glorious presence.

Finally, LaShonda said into the silence, "You look a lot different than your picture . . ."

The comment broke the ice, and there was laughter around the room, including from Sarah, who emitted a burst of warm, jasmine-scented air. When the laughter died down, Martin Grieves assumed the floor again.

"It is truly an honour to meet you, Sarah," he said, "and on behalf of people around the world who are tired of war and its horrors, let me offer my most sincere thanks for this intervention."

Sarah's many faces, apparently delighted, speeded up their almost liquid flow across her face. "Thank you, Martin," she said in a gust of warm air. "But the thanks goes to God."

Martin Grieves bowed his head toward her, a gesture of reverence. "Yes," he said. Then he turned to his team and said, "Let's get to work. We need to hit the ground running with some concrete steps tomorrow morning."

The team knuckled down and between them came up with a high level series of actions and responsibilities that they could immediately start implementing the following day.

The next morning, at 8:00 a.m. sharp, they met in the Denver office on East Girard Avenue. Martin Grieves called them into the facility's well appointed boardroom for a quick meeting before they got to work.

"Good morning, everyone," Martin said. "As I mentioned yesterday, this action plan is going to be somewhat fluid, due to the short time we had to create it. However, I believe we have developed enough concrete steps for us to hit the ground running, and I trust you all to improvise as we move along. You all know the three goals, right? Resize, repurpose, and retrain—the three Rs. We got this, don't we?"

There was a cheer around the room from the enthusiastic team. Clearly, Martin Grieves was a leader who this group of professionals admired and respected.

Martin continued, "I think the best way to approach this is to break into three teams to get everything moving in parallel. Team one—the three of you with experience in military planning and logistics," he said, indicating a tall, balding Caucasian man, a beefy, short African-American man, and a young, overly handsome fellow with a strong military bearing, "will be working with me to develop plans for the new National Security Force. We're going to focus on resizing. Basically we need to create a fully functioning military-style unit that has teeth and claws, but no excess fat—and we need an executable plan for how we're going to do this within thirty days, because the minute returning troops are stateside, we need to start the staff selection process."

At that moment, Sarah shimmered, like a mirage, into three dimensions within the room, bringing with her an unearthly light and the smell of lilacs. "I have come to offer my assistance," she said in her voiceless, ethereal way. "I also bring greetings from President Cummings. And *these* . . ."

With that, a box of donuts appeared on the table in front of Grieves and the rest of the group. LaShonda James wasted no time in grabbing a pink one with sprinkles, and taking a huge bite.

"I'm on a carb lockdown as of tomorrow," she said. "I have a martial arts competition in two weeks. Gotta get my sugar fix while the getting is good!"

When the laughter at her comment had died down, and everyone had a donut of their choice, Sarah said, "I have a recommendation, Martin. Would you like to hear it?"

"Of course," said Grieves respectfully. "I am open to anything you wish to suggest, Sarah."

"I was thinking that, in order to attract the best candidates to the new National Security Force, perhaps a general notice regarding job opportunities should be issued *now* to all returning armed forces," she said. "My concern is that if these men and women don't understand the possibility of continuing to work in their chosen military careers, we could lose the best and brightest to the private sector. For example, I'm sure there are many military pilots who would be interested to know of the opportunities with the Space Service, and who would give their right arm, so to speak, to be on the team that is going to colonize Mars."

"I think that's a great idea, Sarah," said Grieves earnestly. He looked over at the fresh-faced, handsome young man—a Texas-born Navy Seal named Jed Hanover—and said, "Jed, could you get someone on that?"

"Absolutely," said Jed with a big 'Longhorn State' smile.

Rising from his chair, he immediately left the room, ostensibly to consult with some of the twenty support staff, provided by Cummings, who were just now settling into the office area outside the boardroom. These people were handpicked by the White House and would support Grieves and his staff with specialties ranging from communications to project management.

In short order, Jed found a communications person and got him working on some messaging.

When he returned to the meeting room, he asked, "Did I miss anything?" as he sat down and helped himself to another donut.

As Grieves said, "No, you didn't miss anything. We were just discussing the manner in which team one—the team you're on—is going to structure the new National Security Force. The key is, of course, 'reduce' . . . and I want you to handle the navy end of it."

Hanover just smiled and took another bite of his donut. As he licked sugar off his fingers, he replied, "Great. I already have some ideas for restructuring."

"Good," said Grieves. "So do I."

Then Grieves turned to the rest of the group and said, "Team two will work on 'repurposing'—specifically, repurposing military equipment and personnel. This might be as simple as recycling tanks and ships for steel, or as complicated as converting aircraft carriers to hospital ships. One favourite idea of the president's is using the Army Corps of Engineers to work on infrastructure projects across the country. It's one of the first items mentioned in the White House plan."

"There are a lot of crumbling, dangerous bridges around the country that the Army Corps could work on as well," came a dry voice from the back of the room.

The speaker was a thin, studious looking gentleman who was appropriately named Buck Bridges. Bridges was a man who had, in fact, lived up to his name. He was a structural engineer who owned one of the leading engineering companies in the country, and he had just accepted a thirty-year, $110 billion contract to build a floating bridge in Canada between Vancouver, British Columbia, and Vancouver Island (crossing two of the Gulf Islands), an engineering feat that had long been regarded as nearly impossible.

"Yes, Buck, that's for sure," said Grieves. "That's why you and your team are going to come up with a plan for that."

"Some sort of public/private partnership," mused Buck Bridges, mulling over the possibilities."

"Possibly," said Grieves, "or a three-way cost-sharing model between municipalities, state governments and the feds. There are a variety of options. Just figure out and prioritize the best ones, okay?"

"Of course, Martin," said Bridges to Grieves, blinking rapidly, making Grieves wonder if this incredibly intelligent man had already done so in his head.

Finally, Grieves looked at LaShonda James and said, "Retraining. That's you, LaShonda."

"Uh huh," she said. "I know."

"Team three will focus on retraining people and getting them out there into the regular workforce. I want a training and redeployment plan in place for all returning troops surplus to our new National Security Force, applicable the minute they are stateside."

"I already have some great ideas," said LaShonda James. "I suggest we offer nine-month work skills enhancement courses, starting with a basic course on job search skills, and then covering trades, entrepreneurship, business basics, and information technology."

"I like where you're going with this," said Grieves.

"Thanks, Martin," she replied. "I also thought we could partner with some job placement firms and snag some placements. If we back it with a national advertising campaign encouraging businesses to hire former forces personnel, I think we'll have no problem placing people."

"Great thinking, LaShonda," said Grieves, clearly pleased. Then he suddenly looked somber. "Maintaining the morale of these people as they adjust to their new lives will be essential," he said. "There may be some who feel resentful of the changes, and so we need to ensure their contributions are formally recognized. LaShonda, can your group work with the events people Cummings hired and arrange some sort of ceremony?" he asked her.

"Yes," she said with a smirk. "You know how I love a good party."

The group laughed. Even Sarah, who had been silently watching the proceedings, sent a ruffle of rose-scented air around the room.

Then she added a detail that, as yet, had not been brought forward. "All of your troops will be home by the end of this month," she said. "Initially, they will be housed in and around existing military bases, and housing needs will be coordinated by the military. However, there may be shortages and overcrowding, because military bases were never designed to have all troops home at one time."

Grieves furrowed his brow, pondering this problem. "I think the best solution is to work out some deals with local hotels," he said. "Some smaller towns might be grateful for the business. That would be a win-win. I'll get one of the project managers Cummings sent over on that right away."

Then he turned to Hanover and said, "I have one more job for you, Jed. Could you tell that comms person you were talking to earlier that before the end of the day tomorrow, I want every service person to understand that they are still in active service for eleven more months—unless they voluntarily take alternate employment. Also make clear to them that the Veterans Administration Department will provide medical facilities, clinics, and benefits as they have always done."

Hanover nodded and stood up. "I'll do so immediately, Sir," he said, and then he left the room.

Grieves turned back to the group. "All right, team," he said, "Let's get at it. I'm going to brief the president weekly, and I want good things to tell him!"

Chapter 20

Water Czar

President Cummings sat with the majority senate leader, Hana Shriver, in the Oval Office. Each of them sat on a plush, beige couch, facing one another, gazing at their computers. It was about 9:00 p.m., and the two of them had been reading resumes for the better part of four hours, trying to find just the right person to head up the newly created Clean Water Initiative.

"What do you think of Isaac Lee?" asked Shriver. "He's the Dean of Environmental Science at Berkeley."

"Too green," said Cummings with a sigh.

When it came to solving the issue of inadequate water supplies in the southwest of the country, the successful candidate needed extraordinary political acumen. While Cummings personally supported environmental initiatives, as president, he also had to think of budgets and other interests and find the sweet spot in between. Going with someone who leaned toward all green, all the time, would not only be expensive, but it would be sure to cause controversy.

"The successful candidate has to have no stake in outcomes," said Cummings thoughtfully, as they opened up the next resume, "and so far, all of the people we've looked at seem to have some sort of agenda. They aren't neutral enough."

"I can see your point," said Shriver, "but since we're down to the last three candidates, I wouldn't write Dr. Lee off that quickly."

"Point taken," said Cummings.

"How about this one? This man looks pretty good," said Shriver excitedly, pointing at her computer.

She was examining the resume of Herbert Baxter Sloan III, the recently retired Chair of the World Bank. Originally from the American Midwest, Sloan was a political moderate who'd also had extensive experience financing water purification projects around the world.

"This looks good," agreed Cummings, his interest piqued. "He's worked with both the public and private sectors, so he's likely to garner bipartisan support."

"We have a winner," said Shriver. "Should I call him in for a talk? Or do you want to call him first?

"You go ahead," said Cummings thoughtfully. "Call him for a preliminary chat and see if he's as good as he looks on paper. If he is, then call him in for an interview. I'll be free by 3:00 p.m. tomorrow. See if he can make that work. If necessary, we can interview him over a video link."

"Sounds good," said Shriver, rising from where she sat and stretching. "And now, I think I'm going home to bed."

The next day, Cummings had a busy morning. After a 'round robin' meeting (with Angelica Lopez, Norman Feldman, and Gordon Blackstone) to discuss the viability of Lopez's pet project, the electric train system, Cummings managed a quick bite to eat, followed by a check-in with Martin Grieves and his group. By then, it was nearly three o'clock and so, after a quick coffee with Lorena, he hustled back to the Oval Office to meet with Herbert Sloan.

Sloan had agreed to meet with the president and Hana Shriver in person, and when Cummings arrived at his office, he found his aide had already seated the man and brought him tea, and that Shriver and Sloan were in the middle of a heated discussion about the merits of building a clean water pipeline from the Great Lakes to provide water to the water-poor states.

"Herb Sloan," the man said, standing as Cummings entered the room. He stuck out his hand. "It's an honour, Mr. President."

Cummings smiled affably. "Please sit down, Mr. Sloan," he said.

"Call me Herb," said Sloan.

"Of course, Herb," said Cummings. "And you can call me Samuel."

The three of them quickly got down to talking. Cummings and Shriver were immediately impressed not only with Sloan's knowledge, but with his passion for the idea of ensuring sustainable water supplies in the United States. Within minutes, Cummings and Shriver knew they were looking at the right man for the job.

"Water aquifers throughout the region have been substantially drained in recent decades," said Cummings, "and despite multiple layers of government regulation, as usual, money talks—and only users who can afford to drill deep get access to water, leaving the rest to beg."

"I agree," said Sloan. "Water has become liquid gold."

"To solve the problems of water availability over the long-term, it's possible that aquifers may have to become public property," Cummings said.

"You're probably right," said Sloan. "Water utilization has improved somewhat in recent decades, but not at the pace required for long-term sustainability. And while waste water recycling is on the rise, the industry is moving much too slowly to meet the ongoing need for clean water."

"It's a sad truth, all right," said Cummings. "We could use some innovative programs to help us conserve water."

"We are having such intense rain events in some parts of the country that it's a shame that rainwater collection and usage are not widely accepted as a built-in feature in new homes or commercial buildings," replied Sloan.

"That is a great idea, Mr. Sloan," cut in Shriver. "Even if we just collected rainwater in cisterns for irrigation for the agriculture industry, it would make a huge difference. Did you know it takes over one gallon of water just to make one almond? And almonds are grown in the United States more than anywhere else on Earth—in fact, the United States dominates the global production of almonds!"

Sloan nodded sympathetically. "We use a lot of water, and security of our water is critical," he said. "If you give me this job, I assure you that I will develop recommendations for water preservation that are balanced with innovation. There are so many things we could do better!"

Cummings and Shriver looked at each other, pleased. "There certainly are," said Cummings.

Within an hour, a contract was inked. As Cummings shook Sloan's hand, he said, "This has to happen fast. We have only eleven months to get things flowing smoothly—no pun intended."

Sloan laughed anyway.

Within two days of accepting the job, Sloan had assembled a team of six people to assist him in creating and implementing America's Clean Water Initiative. The group agreed to meet in Chicago, and all of them were heartily surprised when Sarah stepped in to move them easily about the country, teleporting them efficiently on the day of the meeting to the Donald E. Stephens Convention Center, located in Rosemont, Illinois, a suburb of Chicago. There, hotel rooms and two meeting rooms awaited them, along with all relevant electronic equipment.

By 8:00 a.m., the new Water Initiative team were assembled in the larger of the meeting rooms, both of which were adjoining Sloan's suite. Some looked a little flustered; While they'd been told they would be 'transported' by Sarah to the meeting, several had not understood exactly what that meant. Teleportation, though painless, was unsettling.

"Good morning folks. Welcome to Chicago!" Sloan said to his team as they filed into the meeting room. "As you know, we are here at the request of the president of the United States, who has charged us with solving two problems. First, we are to find innovative ways to help municipalities across the country upgrade their fresh water infrastructure. And second, we are to solve the problem of chronic water shortages in the southwest part of our great country."

He looked about the room into the eyes of his team members, all of which were fixed on him.

He continued, "Fresh water is a complex business, mostly because its regulation and usage is covered in red tape from all levels of government—federal, state, *and* municipal. Add to that the self-interest of the private sector, and it's clear to see that, if we are to have sustainable water into the future, a concerted and coordinated national approach is required."

There were nods around the room.

"With regard to our first challenge," continued Sloan, "—that of upgrading municipal water systems—over the next eleven months, this team and I will build a company staffed by ex-military personnel that will compete for and win municipal water system upgrade projects across the country. Three of you will focus on this . . ." he said, looking over to a grey-haired, middle-aged man with strong military bearing, "under the leadership of General Robert Sutherland."

Sutherland nodded to the rest of the group by way of introduction.

And then Sloan said, "General Sutherland is the head of the U.S. Army Corps of Engineers. He has extensive experience with infrastructure and is a leader in this field. In fact, he's such a leader that he has already deployed some of his staff to meet with municipal water authorities to catalogue the state of existing infrastructure and prioritize those most in need of action."

Sutherland smiled at the praise.

Then Sloan looked over at two women, both in their midfiftiess, who were sitting side by side just to the left of Sutherland.

"The other two people on Sutherland's team are Mary Schaefer and Barb Friesen. Mary is an investment banker specializing in public/private water system projects," he said as Schaefer smiled and nodded politely to the group. "And prior to her recent retirement, Barb was president and CEO of an international consulting company that designed, built, and operated water treatment plants in seven different countries."

The two women smiled at the group, and there was polite applause.

When the noise died down, Sloan said, "So that's our infrastructure team. The rest of you will work with me to find a tenable way to eliminate the water shortage in the southwest part of our nation."

The remaining three people, all of whom were under forty, eyed each other briefly as Sloan pointed out, "You will note that this team is more youthful. That's because solving the water shortage problem is gonna take a *long* time—so we had to pick some low mileage models."

There was a small titter of laughter at the joke, but they all knew there was truth behind what he said; Whatever technology was developed and adopted was going to be a long-term project, taking decades and likely costing billions—if not trillions—of dollars.

A youngish man, probably in his midthirties, put up his hand to speak.

Sloan acknowledged him by saying, "Brandon Johnson—the eager beaver with his hand in the air—is Chair of the Colorado River Water Management Board and an acknowledged expert on the river and its dams. The American Southwest owes its existence to the water and power from the Colorado river system, but after protracted droughts in the region, reservoirs are so low that water rationing has begun in earnest, and power generation may soon be impossible. It appears that the only solution is to increase the flow of water into the Colorado River System. Brandon, did you stick your hand in the air so you could tell us about that?"

"Yes," said Johnson, "and I couldn't have said it better. But the solution is not as simple as that, because the amount of energy it takes to move water vast distances is really expensive. If, for example, you're talking about a pipeline from Duluth, Minnesota to Arizona, just imagine getting the water over the Continental Divide. The amount of energy it would take to move that water kind of boggles the mind. And it's an ongoing expense; It's not a one-time charge."

A short, dark-haired, lean woman sitting behind Johnson piped in. "Diverting surplus water from the Great Lakes to the American Southwest has been considered the ultimate solution to the problem for years," the woman said, "but the astronomical amount of money such a project requires makes the far larger, far closer water supply—the Pacific Ocean—more logistically feasible and affordable . . . at least if a commercially viable, large-scale desalinization method were to be devised."

"Thank you, Jennifer," said Sloan with a smile, "and you're right. It seems inescapable that this technology will play some role in solving this water problem." Then, to the rest of the group, he said, "Jennifer Black is an expert in desalination of sea water."

There were some greetings and acknowledgement of Jennifer, and then Sloan pointed to a casual-looking man with long, blond hair who, with his khaki shorts and Hawaiian shirt, looked more like a California surfer than an expert in anything, and said, "Only one person in the room hasn't been introduced. Craig Logan is a recognized global expert on water system integration. He was lead external advisor to the government of China in the design of the massive reconfiguration of water flows now being implemented in that country."

Logan smiled, delighted to be introduced, but looked surprised when Sloan added, "Despite that he looks like a hippy, he's our big picture guy."

The group burst out laughing.

"So," said Sloan, when the hilarity had died down, "you now all have an understanding of the scope of what we're going to do. Remember this . . . you are the thinkers, planners, and action heroes, and I am going to defer to your collective expertise. My talents, unfortunately, lie elsewhere. While you come up with solutions, I will be muddling my way through the minefield of resource jurisdiction. Are there any questions before we get to work?"

"Yes," said Robert Sutherland, of the Army Corps of Engineers. "What is the nature of the company you will form for working on water system upgrades?"

"Good question," said Sloan. "It will start as a limited partnership. The White House has proposed that the federal government hold 51% of the shares of the new company, and employees—including yourselves—hold the other 49%. The company will be privatized after five years."

"And can you tell me who will be organizing this company?" asked Sutherland. "Is that within the scope of this team?"

"No," replied Sloan. "A team headed by a man named Martin Grieves, a well-respected change management expert, is taking on that challenge. Their job is to 'resize, repurpose, and retrain' . . . meaning, they plan to reduce the military, repurpose assets, and retrain troops as appropriate. For you, and the rest of the Army Corps of Engineers, 'repurpose' is the key word."

Barb Friesen had the next question. "Existing private sector companies in the clean water business might not like government competition," she said. "What will we do to mitigate that?"

Sloan thought about it for a second and then replied, "Honestly, I don't think they will be overly threatened because the entire business is now a national priority, and the overall volume of work will increase rapidly. I would think they'd welcome another player in the arena."

Then he looked around the room. "Any more questions?" he asked. When no one spoke, he said, "I'm a guy who likes to have clearly defined boundaries, and it goes without saying that the multi-jurisdictional mess that governs water in this country makes me apeshit crazy."

There were some sniggers around the room at his choice of words.

Then he said, "I'm going to tell you my informed opinions about the situations we are facing. You may find some meat on these bones that might inform your planning processes, or you may have ideas of your own that make mine seem juvenile. But I've been in this business for forty years, and I have some opinions I want to share. First, in the case of rainwater, it is clear to me that a state should have full control over any water that falls on it from the sky, unless it makes a legal agreement with another state or legal entity to share that bounty.

"Second, a state should have full legal control over any water in aquifers within that state. If an aquifer is common to two or more states, a water management agreement should be negotiated. If an agreement can't be reached, then—and *only* then—should the federal government seize jurisdiction. Similarly, when it comes to water utilization and pricing, I think each state should retain full control."

Then he looked over at Brandon Johnson and said, "Finally, in the case of the Colorado River, it's clear that the federal government and other states or countries will likely become involved. An agreement will have to be signed, and I think it should be ratified by the original signatories to the Colorado River Water Supply Agreement."

"But what if the agreement is *not* ratified?" asked Brandon Johnson.

"Then the feds should jump in and seize jurisdiction," said Sloan. "I'm not for management from the top, but it *is* the ultimate authority."

"I guess so," Johnson agreed amiably.

"Oh, and here's my last thought before we get down to this," said Sloan. "If California builds desalination plants for its own use, so be it. But if the federal government helps finance such a project, it should stipulate that under the Colorado River Water Supply Agreement, a portion of the water be supplied to other states."

Sloan saw Jennifer Black nodding her agreement.

"Okay," said Sloan. "That's a wrap for the moment. Let's take a break for lunch. When we come back, we'll split up. Group one will get busy generating workable plans for the municipal water upgrade part of this initiative, while group two and I will spend some time with talking about the Great Lakes as a potential source of water for the Colorado River System. Also, before anyone asks, we have a lawyer on staff who will be advising us on how to best avoid inevitable court challenges."

As the group got up and began filing out of the room, he sighed and muttered, "Either you bring the water to LA or you bring LA to the water."

Only Sutherland, who was roughly the same age as Sloan, got the reference to the famous 1974 movie *Chinatown*, starring Jack Nicholson and Faye Dunaway, which was about land and water rights in Los Angeles. He replied, "Forget it Jake, it's Chinatown."

Sloan chuckled, and thought, *I'm going to use that line on President Cummings and see if I can get a laugh.*

After lunch, Sloan, Brandon Johnson, Jennifer Black, and Craig Logan met in the larger room, while the rest of the group took the smaller one. As the drought relief planning team settled into their seats, Sloan took a big sip from a vanilla latte he had picked up on his way back from a local sandwich shop.

"I hope your lunch was as good as mine," he said to the group when they were all seated.

Black smiled at him. "I didn't get a milk mustache from mine," she said.

Sloan laughed and wiped his top lip, before saying, "Okay team, let's start at the root of the problem. Beginning in the twenties, the western U.S. states began to divvy up the water supply from the Colorado River, which runs south for over 1,500 miles until it reaches the Gulf of California. Along the way, cities such as Phoenix, Denver, San Diego, and Los Angeles diverted water for drinking and to irrigate crops, so that by the time it reached its end point, over 70% had been siphoned off. I've always been fascinated by the idea of diverting water from the Great Lakes to help the Southwest recharge its reservoirs. I know this issue is controversial, but I believe it has some merit. I have not done detailed historical comparisons—or any projections regarding climate change on the Great Lakes watersheds—but I *do* know that between 2010 and 2020, when the Colorado River System reservoirs were disappearing, the Great Lakes rose to record levels. In fact, water levels in Lake Ontario, which is at the end of the Great Lakes chain, were so high they caused significant property damage in both Ontario and New York State."

"That *does* bode well for the idea of diverting so-called 'excess' water," drawled Logan, taking a sip of a green smoothie Sloan thought looked nauseating, "but it doesn't address the issue Brandon brought up about how to transport it."

"No," said Sloan, "we're not there yet. Think of this as a history lesson, okay?"

"You're the boss," said Logan, taking another sip of the slimy-looking green drink.

"The Saint Lawrence is the most heavily engineered waterway in the world, with dams and canals in place that strictly control the rate at which water is released from the Great Lakes," Sloan continued. "Water levels throughout the lakes are controlled by U.S. and Canadian federal agencies, through a binational partnership."

"Correct me if I'm wrong, but doesn't that lake system drain into the Gulf of Saint Lawrence and then into the Atlantic Ocean?" asked Black.

"Yes, that's correct," replied Sloan. "There are two primary control points. Outflow from Lake Superior, the first and largest of the lakes, is regulated by the International Lake Superior Board of Control, based in the twin cities of Sault Ste. Marie, Michigan and Ontario. Flows from Lake Ontario, the last and second smallest of the lakes, are controlled by the Moses-Saunders Dam as part of a system for balancing water—and flooding potential—between Lake Ontario and Montreal. This is crucial to Montreal; In spring, a one-inch drop in the level of the lake translates into a one-*foot* rise in the flood zones around that city. And in both cases, decisions on flow rates impact power generation as well as water levels."

"It seems to me that the most logical extraction point for transferring water to the Colorado River System would be Lake Michigan, since that's the only one of the lakes that is fully American," said Brandon Johnson thoughtfully, "and the most logical delivery points would be either Lake Powell or Lake Mead."

"Yes, that's one approach," Sloan said, "but a shorter, smaller water delivery line could feed into the Green River, upstream of both of those reservoirs. However, flow rates would have to be restricted, especially in the spring flood season—which is precisely when the Great Lakes regulators are most likely to approve maximum withdrawal rates from the lakes."

"Ah, the plot thickens," said Logan, who then slurped the dregs of his smoothie up loudly, causing Sloan to frown and roll his eyes.

"Yes, Craig," he said, "and it's almost as thick as that goo you're ingesting—but without the pond scum."

Johnson and Black burst out laughing.

"It's wheatgrass," said Logan defensively. "It's good for eliminating toxins."

"Uh huh," said Sloan dryly. "Now, getting back to the topic . . . I suggest we examine a high volume, direct water line from Lake Michigan to Lake Mead first, though the economics of a shorter line to Lake Powell should also be examined."

Black put up her hand. "I'm an ocean expert," she said, "and I don't know much about Lake Mead and Lake Powell. Can you elaborate?"

"Of course," said Sloan. "Lake Powell is on the Colorado River in Utah and Arizona, and it's the second largest man-made reservoir in the U.S., the first being Lake Mead. Due to high water withdrawals for human and agricultural consumption, and years of drought, Lake Mead has fallen below Lake Powell in terms of water volume, depth and surface area, which is why I think it warrants more immediate attention."

Brandon Johnson was clearly interested. "So, what does the water balance look like if we focus only on Lake Mead?" he asked.

"Well," Sloan said, "at the beginning of 2020, it became apparent that water rationing was in the future. That was when a record low of 130 feet below 'full' was noted on Lake Mead. Full-on level one rationing was triggered in 2023 and has been in place ever since. However . . . and this is a big if . . . if we could transfer just *four* inches of water from Lake Michigan in any given year, Lake Ontario would fall one foot and Lake Mead would rise *thirty feet*."

Craig Logan, now apparently fortified by the wheatgrass smoothie, offered his opinion. "I'm gonna assume you're aware of the *Great Lakes Compact*, right? It's an agreement between the eight states surrounding the lakes to safeguard the lakes' water supply. George W. Bush signed it in 2008. Its agenda is to prohibit large-scale water diversion beyond the Great Lakes basin. A similar, binational agreement is in place with the Canadian provinces of Ontario and Quebec. So first, you'd have to navigate an amendment to that thing."

"That's not impossible," said Sloan.

"But it's *unlikely*," Logan replied. "People are protective of those lakes."

"We have Sarah on our side, and she may be able to cut through red tape and protectionist hearts in ways we can't," retorted Sloan. "So, for the sake of argument, I suggest we start with the premise that we *will* be able to do so—at least for discussion purposes."

"I like it," said Johnson, "though I can't help thinking about cost of delivery. The driving distance from Racine, Wisconsin to Lake Mead is . . . what? I think it's about 1,800 miles."

"Yes," said Sloan, "and before you ask, I think a water delivery system that length would cost between $5 and $10 billion," Sloan said. "But, even if we make this idea fly, there are other tricky bits to consider—such as, how often will the Great Lakes regulators give permission for a foot of water to be withdrawn from Lake Ontario. Once a year? Once every two years? Also, how much is thirty feet of water in Lake Mead worth? And who will absorb the costs of transportation infrastructure?"

"The Colorado River System's water shortage is a drop in the bucket compared to the water resources of the Great Lakes," offered Logan thoughtfully. "However, the bureaucrats who would have to sign off on this deal would need to be able to offer some pretty sweet benefits to their constituents if it was gonna fly."

"Thanks for your observation, Craig," remarked Sloan. "Now, do you have any solutions?"

"Yes," said Logan, "I do. If we're really going to do this, I think we'll need to approach it from a national benefit perspective, the way they did in China. Of course, it was much easier to do that in China because the government owns everything anyway. Here—well, we're pretty individualistic over here. But I really do believe that a national approach would simplify the question of who's getting what economic benefits."

"We'd also have to be mindful of environmental impacts and Aboriginal rights," added Johnson.

"Of course," agreed Sloan. "Before one tablespoon of earth is moved, we'd make sure there were no errors in that regard. I have environmental and anthropological consultants on retainer. I'm well aware how such things can stop a project dead in the water."

"Ha," smirked Logan. "Dead in the water. Good one."

"You liked that, did you?" asked Sloan.

"Yes," replied Logan, "and here's another . . . you have a lot of water to navigate before you can even *ask* who will pay for it."

"Agreed," said Sloan with a sigh.

Jennifer Black joined the discussion at that point. "We don't have to put all our eggs in one basket," she said. "We can look at water diversion and desalinization *together* as a package. The United States only uses desalination to *supplement* water supplies—like in San Diego, where only 10% of usable water comes desalination. However, in the Middle East, some areas get up to 48% of their potable water that way. For our municipalities and states with abundant power, that's certainly an option."

"I don't know about that," drawled Logan, ever the devil's advocate. "A sheet of water one foot deep, covering one acre—an acre-foot—costs about $2,200 from San Diego's new facility. From the Colorado River allotment, it's only $1,200 . . . half the price."

"Desalination is not off the table," Sloan cut in, "but if power for desalination comes from thermal power plants, it just contributes to the problem."

"I agree," said Black, "but one of the beauties of desalination is there isn't political wrangling about it."

"I agree with you there, Jennifer," laughed Logan, "however, there are by-products of some processes that are just awful. Most facilities use hydrogen peroxide, chlorine, and hydrochloric acid to prepare the water for this process. Also, many facilities put the leftover brine back into the ocean, and that influx of salt decreases oxygen levels in the water, causing local marine life to suffocate."

Black looked deflated for a moment, then responded with, "But the big advantage of desalination is reliability of supply. If we fail to find new conventional water supplies to fill the Colorado River reservoirs, it's a good fallback plan."

"I agree, Jennifer," said Sloan. "I think we should first work on plans for water diversion, but we should also work on a backup desalination strategy, one that has effective ways to deal with the unpleasant environmental impacts."

Then Sloan drew the meeting discussion to a close by noting, "If new water supplies are not found, and drought conditions in the Southwest persist, water rationing will lead to a substantial escalation in the price of water—which will kill the agriculture industry. People will be forced to leave the region . . . which is not the outcome President Cummings has in mind!"

Chapter 21

Climate Change Czar

When Cummings had selected Herbert Sloan to be his water czar, he'd first rejected several applicants who he regarded as 'too green,' largely because of political concerns. However, the truth was that Cummings ran rather green himself, and he was intent on making the United States the undisputed leader in all aspects of environmental sustainability—sooner rather than later.

"Angelica, I need you in the Oval Office," he said over the phone to his vice president.

"Yes, Sir, right away," said Lopez, who was down the hall working with a team of engineers on a preliminary electric train design.

Minutes later, she entered the Oval Office and greeted Cummings with a smile.

"Sit down, Angelica," invited Cummings. "I need your input on something."

"Sure thing," she said. "What can I do for you?"

"Climate change," said Cummings. "I want to show the world that the United States of America is a leading global citizen in the process. I want this country to be an example to the world!"

"Well, I admire your enthusiasm," said Lopez with a smile. "What do you have in mind?"

"I'm thinking of a global climate change conference," he said. "The Paris Agreement on climate change was a remarkable achievement—and it's a disgrace America pulled out under the Trump administration. Thank God Joe Biden put us back in the game in 2021."

"I agree," said Lopez. "Although, to be fair to Trump, he wasn't the only one who didn't support the Paris Agreement. There was that NASA scientist—James Hansen—who was up in arms about it. He said very few firm commitments were made, other than an across the board tax on CO2 emissions."

"I know," said Cummings. "But it was still a good start. At least the world has some sense of direction now—and with God on our side, perhaps that will translate into a meaningful global effort to create lasting change."

"How so?" asked Lopez.

"Think about it, Angelica," he said. "The war machine has been silenced. There is a *lot* of pollution that goes with war. God is clearly steering us down the path humanity needs to take to save this poor, beat-up planet—despite the fact that some of us are still kicking and screaming about it."

"I agree," mused Lopez. "It does feel like we are on a path—that every crisis humanity has faced has led us to this point." She paused for a moment, reflecting, and then said, "Do you remember how, during the Covid-19 pandemic, people stopped commuting and pollution levels dropped dramatically?" Cummings nodded. "Well," she continued, "do you ever wonder if that was God's way of saying, 'Hey, if you won't voluntarily get out of your cars, then I guess I'll have to *make* you.'"

Cummings laughed. "I sure do," he said. Then he added, "Sadly, now that people aren't afraid of Covid anymore, they're getting back into those damn cars."

"I know," sighed Lopez. "I can't stand walking in Manhattan without a mask. Exhaust fumes and garbage. Not my thing."

"Not my thing either," said Cummings. "And that's why carbon dioxide stabilization needs to be front and centre in the political arena again. We had it well in sight, but we're regressing to our old, polluting ways. We need to become more sustainable, whatever it takes."

"I couldn't agree more," said Lopez. "That's why I'm so excited about the electric train project."

"That's good to hear, Angelica," said Cummings with a smile, "because today, I plan to announce two major steps the United States will be taking in the fight against climate change."

"Oh?" asked Lopez, raising one eyebrow.

"First," said Cummings, "I am appointing you to the position of Climate Change Czar."

"What? Me?" she asked in disbelief.

"Yes! I can't think of anyone better suited to the job. I have every confidence that you will make sure the U.S. moves aggressively forward in reducing carbon emissions—and also that you can work with Martin Grieves' team to find the most effective way to protect our coastlines from the threat of rising sea levels."

"Martin Grieves' team?" asked Lopez, slightly shocked. "What does he have to do with climate change initiatives? Isn't he the change management expert?"

"Yes," replied Cummings, "and as part of that, he's working to redeploy the Army Corps of Engineers. There may be resources there. I would encourage you to explore it. And this all dovetails nicely with the electric train project you're so interested in."

"Yes, it does," said Lopez thoughtfully. Then her face lit up with enthusiasm. "I am actually pretty flattered that you asked me to do this, Samuel," she said. "There are some pretty big names out there who are far more experienced and better suited to this job than me, so asking me to tackle this is quite an honour."

"There is no one I trust as much," said Cummings sincerely. "You will do a fine job."

The unexpected praise made Lopez suddenly bashful. "Thanks, Mr. President," she said, blushing a little. "And what is the second thing?"

"I'm going to move as quickly as I can on upping this country's climate change initiatives, Angelica," responded Cummings. "Within six months, I'm going to call a meeting of all the signatories of the Paris Agreement, and you're going to present America's brand-new Greenup/Cleanup Plan. In it, you're going to outline a two-part strategy. The first part will detail American environmental initiatives on our own soil. The second will make global recommendations with offers of aid from this country. With God's help, we're going to do our damnedest to fix this world."

Cummings could have sworn he saw his vice president's eyes glisten at this news. But all she said was, "That's a great idea, Samuel."

Later, as Lopez pondered the task Cummings had set before her, she felt awed at the idea that this might be the most important thing she'd ever do in her life. The balance of life on Earth was more fragile than people knew, and she was being entrusted with protecting this precious gift. Right then and there, she swore to the Catholic God she believed in that she would do her very best. As an environmental engineering undergrad, she'd had big dreams about ways to clean up the planet; Now, she was going to do just that. She immediately got on the phone and began assembling her crew.

It didn't take long for Lopez to put a team together. She had maintained lifelong friendships from her university days, and she knew immediately who the best people for the job would be. Seven days later, Vice President Lopez met the key players of her new Greenup/Cleanup initiative in a boardroom at the White House.

"Hello," she said excitedly as the people she'd recruited walked into the room.

The youngest of the women, her old college roommate Arabella Farnese, didn't say a word; She just gave Lopez a big hug and then took a seat.

Lopez and Farnese were roommates for four full years, and during that time, they became the best of friends. After university, however, their paths led them in quite different directions. Farnese now had a thriving environmental consulting business and worked closely with her brother Mario (environmental management) and his three business partners: Tom Sanders, Jerry Fung, and Alita Motto, who respectively specialized in microbiology, marine biology, and environmental geology.

Along with these four experts, Lopez had also recruited two of her old professors from her master's degree studies—Dr. Janet Filo, her environmental design prof, and Dr. Gerrard Paxton, her environmental law prof, and both of them greeted Lopez warmly when they entered the room.

But the person Lopez was most excited to have on board was Arabella's mother, Mia, a world-renowned expert on ecology and head of the prestigious Farnese Sustainability Foundation, a non-profit that worked tirelessly around the globe to promote sustainable development through environmental education. Dr. Mia Farnese had gracefully agreed to come out of retirement to work on the team, and as she entered the room, Lopez bowed her head reverentially.

"Hello, Angelica," said Dr. Farnese gracefully. "You are as beautiful as ever, my dear."

"Thank you," said Lopez excitedly, "and I'm so grateful you've agreed to work with me on this project!"

"It's my pleasure," said Dr. Farnese, taking a seat beside her daughter, Arabella.

"I can't believe you're the vice president of the *country*," said Arabella as her mother sat down.

"Yes, and I can't believe all the dirt you have on me," replied Angelica, smiling. "Please don't spill it, okay? You're dangerous."

"Spilling dirt would not be appropriate for a member of the Greenup/Cleanup team!" Arabella teased.

There was laughter around the room.

When it died down, Lopez got the meeting going. "These are unprecedented times," she said. "For centuries, humankind has wreaked havoc on Mother Nature—not to mention with one another—and we're paying the price. Now, with God's help, it's time to repair the damage—which is where *this* group comes in."

There were nods of understanding around the room as the team absorbed her words. She continued, "In just under five months, America will host a meeting in Miami to update the Paris Agreement. As I'm sure you all know, this agreement is part of the United Nations Framework Convention on Climate Change. It is a legally binding international treaty designed to reduce global emission of gases that contribute to climate warming, and it was signed on November 4, 2016 by 195 countries."

"Remind me what the temperature goals of the Paris Agreement are, please?" said Dr. Farnese.

"Absolutely," Lopez replied. "The original specified goal was to limit global temperature increase to well below two degrees Celsius in this century."

"Is it working?" Dr. Mia Farnese asked.

"It's a work in progress," replied Lopez cautiously. Then her resolve strengthened and she said, "However, we are here to develop a strategy that not only meets but *exceeds* these targets. We want zero emissions. Our lives depend on it."

"That's a tall order, Angelica," said Dr. Filo, her former environmental design teacher. "You know how the Republican senate likes to shoot down environmental initiatives."

"Not to worry, Dr. Filo," said Lopez. "This is a bipartisan effort. In fact, I've asked Hana Shriver, the majority senate leader, to sit in with this group to ensure we get support in the senate."

There were murmurs around the room as the idea of a bipartisan initiative sank in.

Lopez smiled at the surprise of the group, and added, "I have no illusions that support for our proposals will be unanimous. Nevertheless, I think we can all agree that the needs of the human race and our planet override party politics—and I'm sure a majority Republican senate can see the sense of that too."

"Will that angel person—that being who's on all the social media channels—help us reach our goals?" asked Arabella Farnese.

"You mean Sarah? Yes," replied Lopez.

At that moment, Hana Shriver knocked lightly on the door of the room and then slipped inside. "Sorry I'm late," she said. "I was briefing the president. Did I miss anything?"

"No," replied Lopez. "We were just getting started. We were talking about climate warming. Welcome."

"Thanks," said Shriver, taking a seat.

Lopez flicked on an overhead screen at the end of the room and a PowerPoint slide appeared on it, emblazoned with the words *Climate Change: The Facts*.

Then she said, "I'm sure you all know that carbon dioxide levels have risen astronomically over the last one hundred years, causing unprecedented climate warming on this planet. Emissions from internal combustion engines are the main culprit, but humankind's insatiable need for power—and the subsequent increased burning of oil, coal, gas, and wood—play a significant role as well. The situation is dire. The polar ice caps and glaciers are melting, making sea levels rise and weather patterns change, which has resulted in more violent storms and extreme weather around the globe."

Lopez paused for a moment, and Dr. Farnese cut in to say, "Political wrangling has not helped the situation, and quite frankly, some of our elected leaders don't believe climate change is a threat—though I don't know how they can deny such a thing in good conscience. Angelica, do you think the president has ever considered gauging the opinions of house representatives and senators via open vote—I mean with no guidance from the speaker or party whip—to find out what each member *really* believes? Given the state of the world, I think constituents need to know where the people they voted for stand on this."

"That's an interesting suggestion, Mia," replied Lopez, intrigued. "And I promise I will bring it up with him." Then the vice president pointed to the next slide. "There are three main issues for this group to address," she said.

The slide read:

1) Renewable energy.
2) Carbon fuel uses.
3) Global warming impacts.

"By 'renewable energy,'" Lopez said, "I mean bulk power generation, and its direct use by homes, businesses, and farms. By 'carbon fuel uses,' I mean not only the transportation sector but also bulk power generation. By 'global warming impacts,' I primarily mean protection of our coasts from rising sea levels and violent storms, though there are many other scenarios, including impending drought. The science is clear. The impacts of global warming are clear. We owe it to our children and their children to make this right."

"We owe it to all the children of the *world* to make it right," remarked Dr. Farnese. "This is not just an American problem."

"You are absolutely correct," said Lopez, "and it is President Cummings' goal that America take a *global* leadership role in this important battle."

"Hear, hear," said Dr. Paxton enthusiastically.

He started clapping, and the rest of the group joined in.

When the noise died down, Lopez said, "We're going to divide into three teams to brainstorm on these subject areas." With that, she handed out a list of names in three columns of three and said, "These are my suggested teams, organized by expertise. You will note there are only eight of us in the room but nine names on this sheet. That's because I have hired an environmental communications consultant named Jackson Withers to work with us. He is flying in from Oregon as we speak."

"A communications consultant?" asked Arabella's brother Mario in surprise.

"Yes. We're going to need one," said Lopez. "The American people don't know what to believe about climate warming anymore, and we need to change that. The Obama administration emphasized its importance, while the Trump one did not. The Biden administration got us back into the Paris Agreement, and Cummings has continued to build on that . . . but there are still a lot of misinformed people out there."

"That's an understatement," remarked Dr. Mia Farnese.

"I agree," said Lopez. Then she asked, "Are there any questions?"

There were not, so she said, "Okay, let's break for lunch. When we get back, let's discuss these three challenges in more detail, to get a broad overview. Tomorrow, we'll break into groups and start strategizing, setting our planning horizon for two generations down the road. It's our children's futures that are at stake, and we are going to stay the course until we win the battle!"

Once more, the group applauded, and then they dispersed for lunch. Lunch for Lopez was a bagel and cream cheese shared with her best friend Arabella on a bench in a local park, while a security agent lurked unobtrusively behind them. As they ate, they caught up on missed time together. Heavy job schedules and the responsibilities of their domestic lives, had kept them apart and out of touch. Much had changed for each of them, but one thing had not: Both were still passionate about environmental sustainability and had a lot to say on the matter.

"I worry about what kind of world Audrey and Arianna, my daughters, will live in when they grow up," said Lopez. "It's terrifying to think what will happen to this planet if we don't fix things right *now*."

"I worry about my kids too," said Farnese, "which is why I'm such a big renewable energy supporter—and it's also why I'm glad you put me on the team working on that."

"You've always been a forward thinker when it came to energy issues," Lopez said. "In fact, you were my first friend to buy a hybrid car!" She laughed and then added, "I'm really excited to see what kinds of ideas you come up with. A big issue with renewable energy is cost. Big oil continues to win the public purse."

"Oil *is* cheaper," said Farnese, "though large-scale electricity generation projects, such as wind and solar power, have become dramatically less expensive."

"Yes, but power output is variable—which, to a power system operator, translates to unreliable," Lopez sighed, biting into her bagel and chewing thoughtfully. "If power goes down for whatever reason, utilities have to have backup power. If they don't have the capacity to store power, they have to turn to another power source. Either way, it increases the cost of renewable energy."

"Yes," agreed Farnese. "That's a drawback, for sure."

Lopez took another bite of her bagel and watched a pigeon that was eyeballing her hopefully, looking for crumbs. She threw it a piece of bagel and then looked at her friend and said, "You know, Arabella, one idea that fascinates me is to use power dams on the Colorado River as giant batteries."

"What do you mean?" asked Farnese.

"Well," said Lopez, "for example, what if excess solar and wind power could be used to pump water into Lake Mead, and then when wind and solar supplies *drop,* this water could in turn be used to generate electricity."

"That's a pretty smart idea," said Farnese, wiping crumbs off her lip with a white paper napkin.

"Thanks," said Lopez. "It's not mine. I got the idea from Herbert Sloan, our water czar. He's examining ways to rejuvenate water levels in the Colorado River System, and he told me that pump storage proposals may soon look a lot more viable."

"Sounds like a smart guy," said Farnese.

"He is," replied Lopez. "I'll put you in touch with him to make sure your team and his are coordinating efforts."

"Sounds good," said Farnese, standing up and dusting crumbs off her fashionable black skirt.

Lopez stood as well. "I guess we better get back to work," she said.

The two of them began walking back to the White House.

As they walked, Farnese commented, "You know, another strike against public adoption of renewable power is that thermal power is so inexpensive."

"You're talking about natural gas?" asked Lopez.

"Yes," said Farnese. "Fracking for oil has created an oversupply of natural gas, making it so cheap that it's dominating the fossil fuel market."

"Well, if you go down that road, keep in mind that coal is a traditional favourite with most countries. Generally, it's locally sourced—and mining creates employment and other economic spin-offs. But from an environmental standpoint, it's by *far* the worst fuel to burn."

The two women reached the White House entrance, and they were quickly IDed and then allowed to enter.

Lopez smiled at the security guard, who reminded her of her father. "Thank you," she said as he waved them in. When they were inside, she said to Farnese, "Getting back to what we were discussing, I guess it's fair to say that most countries avoid using oil for power because the price of imported fuel is so volatile."

"Yes," said Farnese. Then she laughed and said, "If we were a communist country like China, we would just develop a thirty-year national energy plan and implement it. We could make reducing reliance on fossil fuel a top priority, and instead emphasize hydro-electric or nuclear power projects—along with wind and solar energy."

"But we are *not* China," said Lopez. "We have to be a little more circumspect in how we try to influence the future of our energy industry."

"We can develop a vision," insisted Farnese. "We can educate the public, provide incentives for the development of climate change friendly technologies—including nuclear power—and penalize carbon emissions. We can learn from the successes and failures of other democracies."

"I suppose you're right," said Lopez as she opened the door to the meeting room where the rest of the team awaited them, "but we will still have to watch our step, because whatever we do, there will be critics."

Because Arabella Farnese had quite a bit of experience with some of the finer aspects of renewable energy planning, as the group got to work, Lopez asked her to brief the team.

"Of course," Farnese said, "I'd be happy to." She addressed the group, saying, "I'd like to say a few words about privately-owned renewable energy installations on homes, farms, and commercial buildings. Homeowners, farmers, and real estate developers all have an interest in reducing utility and water bills, and sometimes, they generate their own power through such things as run off river, wind, and solar installations. When they generate surplus power, they sell it to utilities, and of course, they want to be fairly compensated for that. However, this gets into state and local regulatory jurisdiction, so all we can do is encourage projects that make sense *nationally*."

"That's good thinking, Arabella," said Lopez, "and just so you know, one of Herbert Sloan's groups is looking at rainwater collection on private land, which dovetails with this. We should have common recommendations on how to encourage such developments where they make sense."

Then Lopez segued into the topic of carbon fuel by saying, "Renewable energy overlaps with carbon fuel usage, our next topic, in the areas of power generation, and heating and cooling buildings. When we discuss carbon taxation—which will be part of our carbon fuel usage discussion—let's keep that in mind, okay?"

There were murmurs of assent around the room. Lopez began with, "Now, let's talk about carbon fuel, which generally means transportation. Personally, I'm very interested in transportation that doesn't rely on internal combustion engines that burn pollutants such as gasoline, ethanol, diesel, and compressed gas."

"Hear, hear," said Dr. Paxton once more. "Emission standards for vehicles in this country have not kept up with global performance levels, which I find shameful."

Mario Lopez cut in, saying, "Yes, but in recent years, the shift toward electric vehicles and hybrids, not to mention ride-sharing, is rapidly changing the transportation landscape."

"That may be true," returned Dr. Paxton, "but don't forget that during the Covid-19 pandemic, low oil prices *slowed* the move toward electric vehicles. Of course, auto manufacturers around the world were on life support anyway—but my point is that only the strongest companies will survive."

"I'm all for electric vehicles," Lopez cut in, "but if we shift too quickly to them, power utilities will wind up building thermal power plants like crazy to keep up with electricity demand. We don't want that any more than we want an ongoing proliferation of gas guzzling behemoths on our highways."

"We should support the move away from internal combustion engines and use some form of carbon pricing to incent efficiency," said Dr. Paxton.

"I agree," said Lopez.

"Well, that settles it," said Mario Farnese. "If we focus on incentives, it will encourage individuals, companies, and regulators to collectively make choices that will get us to a more sustainable energy future."

"Hear, hear!" Paxton hollered once more.

"That is a great direction to go in for the moment," Lopez said, "but tomorrow, let's examine a few other options as well. For now, though, it's getting late, and we should touch on our third topic before we end the day."

At that, Lopez brought up another PowerPoint slide, this one a depiction of a crumbling coastline with a house sliding into the sea.

"The protection of our coastlines is imperative. We need to mitigate the damage caused by increasingly strong storms, or we're going to have to start relocating masses of people," said Lopez.

There were some somber faces around the room. Two people in the group had beach cottages, and one—Alita Motto—had already had to replace the foundation when it became eroded by overly high tides.

"The last time the Earth had this much carbon dioxide in its atmosphere," continued Lopez, "sea levels were sixty feet higher than they are now. This fate awaits us, though likely not for hundreds, if not thousands, of years. Our scope of planning is only for what we need to do over the next two human generations. During that time, we are looking at about a three-foot increase in sea level, which sounds small—but trust me, that will give us lots to chew on."

"What kind of support will we have with this?" asked Mario Farnese.

"Thanks for bringing that up," Lopez said. "The White House has hired a change management expert named Martin Grieves to deal with disenfranchised troops as they return stateside. He's looking at ways to redeploy military resources to help with issues like protecting our coasts. As we move forward with our Greenup/Cleanup initiative, those of you working on coastline mitigation will be consulting with him to develop specific coastal reinforcement plans. We want to have repurposed troops working on that as soon as possible."

Suddenly, while the assembled group pondered the scope of their mission, an incandescent light filled the room, and the unexpected, shimmering form of Sarah appeared. Lopez saw Arabella Farnese's eyes widen in awe, while the mouth of her mother, Dr. Mia Farnese, curled up in the broadest smile. Other expressions varied from delight to shock.

"Wow," breathed out Dr. Filo. "You are an astounding being, and it is an honour to be in your presence.

"And the same to you," Sarah said as she shimmered into three dimensions.

"Angelica said you would be helping us in our efforts," Dr. Filo said. "We have a lot to do, and it actually seems a little overwhelming . . ." she added, her brow creased with worry.

"Ah, I understand," Sarah whispered, and suddenly an overwhelming smell of roses was released into the air.

The fragrance worked a sort of magic on the group, making them all simultaneously feel that anything was possible.

Then Sarah breathed into their minds the hopeful words, "You are working for God, and God is on your side."

"Hear, hear," said Dr. Paxton softly.

Chapter 22

High-Speed Electric Train

Cummings knew that Lopez had really high hopes of heading up the Efficient Electric Train (EEL) program, but he also knew that the right candidate for such an extensive, long-term project needed not only some high-profile project management experience under his or her belt, but they also needed to demonstrate competency with multibillion dollar major project budgets. He implicitly trusted his vice president to be competent, but the bottom line was that she just didn't have that kind of mega-infrastructure experience.

He broke it to her gently. "I'm sorry, Angelica," he said as they sat down together. "I know you really wanted to head up the EEL team, but I have someone else in mind. However, the consolation prize is that the fellow I've picked to head up the project will report to and consult with you under your environmental portfolio."

"It's fine, Samuel," Lopez said with a humble smile. "I really appreciate you considering me at all, and I'm just happy to be involved."

It was a win-win for her, and they both knew it; She could keep tabs on what was going on—electric trains were a subject she was passionate about—without actually getting her hands dirty.

The kick-off meeting for the EEL team was held at the White House, and forty-year-old billionaire Vance Waters was introduced as its chief executive officer. Waters had made his money in the delivery business. Following on the heels of the Amazon explosion that occurred during the Covid-19 pandemic, Waters had cornered a niche delivering only high value, low volume goods—luxury items such as art and antiques, and specialist industrial equipment—that required special handling or were considered too heavy for most delivery companies.

Waters had become wildly successful by developing state-of-the-art proprietary software that allowed his network of independent carriers to move goods faster and more safely than any competitor. Twenty years later, he had cornered the market in the auction business, once moving a twenty-car collection of vintage Lamborghini cars from China to a private collection in their Italian homeland. Eventually, his competitors took notice of both his success and his technological advantages, and knowing they could not compete with him, banded together as a conglomerate, approached him, and made him an offer he couldn't refuse for his company. Primed for a new challenge, he accepted readily, and then announced via an interview in *Fortune Magazine* that he was looking for a new challenge.

Cummings read the article and jumped on the chance to get Waters involved in the electric train project; Not only did Waters know all the strengths and weaknesses of all the U.S. transportation systems, but he had a crack team of software developers at his disposal who could easily be redeployed on the EEL project.

It was almost too easy to get the man on board. Cummings got Waters' number from Blackstone, who had dealt with him several times when getting sensitive military equipment shipped.

Then he simply called him up one day and said, "What do you think about developing an electric train system for the country, Mr. Waters?"

Waters laughed. "Mr. President," he said, "I thought you'd never ask."

Later, when the two men sat down for coffee in the White House, Waters confessed to Cummings that he had been thinking about a cross-country electric train system for several years and had even considered privately financing one for his delivery service.

"The only reason I didn't was because I somehow knew, deep in my heart, that the delivery business was a means to an end for me. I enjoyed the challenge of creating the business, and I loved the satisfaction of good customer service, but my heart wasn't in it anymore. And I was afraid that if I went ahead with a private venture—and then I made a major life change, as I have done—it would wind up being a waste of my money. But that doesn't mean I didn't start thinking and planning for one. I have some great ideas that I can't wait to share with your environmental czar!"

Cummings was more than satisfied to hear the man's words. He knew he could not have found a better candidate to head up the EEL project.

Within a week, Waters and a team of five key contacts met in San Diego in a suite of offices that not only had a clear view of the San Diego International Airport—and the clogged thoroughfares leading to it—but also of the San Diego Airport Train, which, while it did not provide service from San Diego Airport directly to the railway network (a flaw, in Waters' opinion), it at least provided options to arrive at the nearest station. From there, Amtrak Intercity and COASTER commuter trains connected passengers to downtown San Diego and also to coastal North County, including stops in Old Town, Sorrento Valley, Solana Beach, Carlsbad, Encinitas, and Oceanside.

As he waited for his handpicked team to arrive, Waters looked out the window, studying the antiquated transportation system spread out at his feet.

As his colleagues drifted into the room and got settled, he remarked, "We're going to need to link our new system with all of these existing subsystems—and hopefully, we can replace most of this old technology, in time." Then he turned to face his colleagues and said, "I think this group is more than up for the task."

As the last of his team members took her seat, Waters said, "Good morning, everyone, and thanks for coming. As you know, we're here at the request of the president of the United States. He's asked us to design and build a high-speed train network that will take America out of the transportation dark ages. It is the president's wish that America's new EEL system will demonstrate global leadership in fast, safe, environmentally sustainable ground transportation." Then he pointed to the window at the view of the airport he had been pondering earlier, adding, "I picked this office location to give us all a daily reminder of how inefficient things currently are, and to remind us of what we are trying to improve."

A silver decanter of coffee and some mugs and cream sat in the middle of the table and smelled inviting. Once coffee was poured for all of them, he began the introductions. First up was the team's legal beagle.

"This is Mary Wilson Lawrence," he said, indicating an attractive, well-groomed middle-aged woman to his left. "Mary will head up a team of seven lawyers who will fight any battles we come to in the area of legal and property rights. For those of you who have never met my dear friend Mary, let me just say that over her twenty-five-year career specializing in rights-of-way, she has worked throughout the transportation sector at all levels of government. She is unparalleled in her field, and we are lucky to have her."

The rest of the team clapped, while ash-blond, fifty-year-old Mary smiled and took a confident sip of her coffee.

Next, Waters proudly introduced his new director of technology. "I'm sure Dr. Yushi Takayama of MIT needs no introduction," he said. "Yushi is the leading American expert on magnetic levitation trains, and he has consulted on several such projects in both Japan and China. His services are very much in demand around the world, but he's informed me that that he'd rather be using his skills here in the United States than anywhere else."

Takayama, a short Asian man of indeterminate age, smiled and nodded his head politely. His intelligent eyes surveyed his compadres with a mixture of curiosity and respect. He had an air of self-containment about him indicative of a man who is concise and measured in everything he does.

"I have long dreamed of such a project here in America," he said quietly. "It is truly an honour to be asked to work on this."

Next, Waters looked over at an attractive, dark-haired woman of about thirty-five who was quietly sipping her coffee, her intense black eyes focused on the open laptop in front of her.

Waters extended his hand toward her and said, "This is Jennifer Rodrigues. She will be our communications director. She's worked on campaigns for some major corporate brands, including Roxy Cola. You probably remember how that formerly niche cola, with its organic branding, went mainstream almost overnight and now is giving Coca-Cola a run for its money? Well, that was Jennifer's doing. And with *that* kind of track record, I know we can trust her to build strong national and regional support for our project. As we proceed, I expect she will also be able to get a network of local champions to help with route selection."

Rodrigues smiled at the group. "Hello," she said companionably to her colleagues, "it's great to meet you all, and I'm very excited to be part of this project."

"It's a pleasure to meet you as well, Jennifer," said a tall, attractive African-American man who was sitting beside her, looking at her with obvious interest. "You've certainly accomplished a lot for such a young person. You impress me."

"Thank you, Sir," Rodrigues replied respectfully. She knew she was talking to Everett Lamont, Governor of Louisiana and past mayor of New Orleans.

Waters took a cue from the interaction. "Governor Lamont, welcome," he said.

"Thank you, Vance," said Lamont. "It's a pleasure to be here."

"It's great to have you," Waters said, beaming at the man. Then he said for the benefit of the rest of the team, "The governor will handle intergovernmental relations for EEL. While I'm sure a world of pain and frustration awaits him . . ."

There were sniggers around the room at Waters' dramatic pause.

". . . I can't think of anyone better versed in the differences between state and municipal regulations to work on this project with us."

Lamont smiled at the group. "Yes, that's me. I'm the pain and frustration king! I've been kicked in the butt at all levels of government . . . that's why I never sit down."

The group laughed, but Waters cut in with a more serious tone. "He's not joking," he said. "He is one of the best in the game when it comes to getting things done. When he says he never sits down, what he means is that he never stops *working*."

The governor made an 'aw, shucks' motion with his hand. It was easy to see that he was as humble as he was successful.

Finally, Waters introduced the last member of the team. "Rounding out our team is Simon Redmond," he said with a smile. "Simon will lead all EEL design and construction activities. He brings thirty years of experience in designing, building, and upgrading mass transit systems to the table. And just so you know, he's the genius responsible for the recent subway upgrades commissioned by the New York City Transit Authority in both Manhattan and Queens."

Redmond looked pleased at the introduction. "Thanks, Vance," he said with a smile. "I'm really happy to be involved with the project. The opportunity to work with the new maglev technology systems, such as those designed by Dr. Takayama, is extremely exciting for me, and I can't wait to get a look at some plans."

Takayama smiled an enigmatic smile at Redmond. Clearly, he couldn't wait to share those plans.

Then Waters looked around earnestly at the team and said, "Before we begin discussing concrete plans for the proposed EEL system, let me give you a little background on electric trains. Japan was the first nation to develop a high-speed electric train service, followed by Europe and much of Asia. Japan has traditionally been at the forefront of this technology—but today, China is by far the leader in terms of scale and scope. With more than 25,000 kilometres of high-speed electric train tracks, China's technology rivals anything Japan has to offer."

"That's impressive," said Rodrigues. "How fast do they go?"

"Traditional high-speed electric trains can travel up to 220 miles per hour. However, Japan and China are developing magnetic levitation systems that allow trains to hover above the ground and travel in excess of 300 miles per hour," Waters replied.

There were exhalations of admiration around the room as the assembled group processed just how fast that was.

"Still only half as fast as your average jet," mused Redmond, "but pretty amazing nonetheless."

"I agree," said Waters, "and the technology is already in use. There are six commercial maglev lines, located in South Korea, Japan, and China. They are incredibly efficient but also incredibly expensive, so this team will have to develop a pretty creative budget for our national train system—perhaps one that involves cost-sharing at the state and federal levels. I've hired an accounting firm to work with me on that . . . and of course, I'm hoping the governor will pull a few strings for me," he said, smiling at Governor Lamont.

"I'll do what I can," the governor said, smiling back.

Waters continued, "Up until now, high-speed train development has not been a national priority because population densities across the United States are lower than they are in Asia and Europe, which has hampered the economic viability. However, since the 'no killing' edict from God took effect, making much of the military obsolete, the national budget is suddenly big enough that we can actually make this happen!"

His enthusiasm was clear in his voice, and the assembled group suddenly felt as motivated and inspired as him. They began smiling in anticipation of the project they were about to embark on.

Redmond said thoughtfully, "The possibilities are certainly fascinating."

"Indeed!" exclaimed Waters enthusiastically. "Compared to automobiles and airplanes, electric trains reduce CO_2 emissions by a factor of up to ten. With the EEL in place, not only will the U.S. assume a leadership role in technological innovation, but it will become a world leader in the reduction of carbon emissions. I see this thing being used to move light cargo as *well* as people—which would take thousands of delivery vehicles off the roads."

"Excuse me for asking," said Mary Lawrence, "but what will be used to power this EEL? Will we have to create new sources of electricity?"

"That's not quite settled," admitted Waters, "but President Cummings has Vice President Lopez looking at it as part of her environmental portfolio. There have been some great ideas put forward to do with hydro generation, and even some 'out of the box' ideas about harnessing some of the power generated during extreme weather events. There are multiple options to consider, but I am certain that Angelica Lopez will come up with a plan that will not only create the power we need but will be environmentally sustainable as well."

"Isn't she from Texas?" asked Lawrence, her carefully styled hair swinging as she tilted her head to one side. "She's from the home of big oil. Are you sure she's the right woman for the job? What I'm asking is, how do we know where her loyalties lie?"

"She's as good as they come," said Waters, who considered himself to be a good judge of character. "I have had the opportunity to speak to her several times, and she is extremely knowledgeable about all things green, and unbiased in her opinions as well. I have *no* concerns in that regard. I am absolutely certain that she will champion this train."

"Well, you would know better than I," said Lawrence. "But I had to ask the question because we will face enormous opposition from the oil and gas industry . . . not to mention automobiles and aircraft manufacturers, and the companies that own the interstate and local rail networks."

"I'm aware of that," said Waters.

"Don't forget that we must navigate a legal and political system that fiercely protects individual and Indigenous property rights," added Governor Lamont.

"Oh, I most certainly did *not* forget that," Lawrence said. "It was next on my list. But getting back to my point . . . I guess that if the president trusts Vice President Lopez, then I will trust her as well. But if any particular loyalty to Texas big oil rears its head during the course of this project, I'll be the first to start shouting."

"That's fair," said Waters.

Suddenly, the soft-spoken Dr. Takayama spoke. "Mary," he said, "did you know that both California and Texas have been leaders among the handful of states dabbling with electric train projects? I know for a fact that Vice President Lopez has some insight on this technology already—and from all accounts, she has been very supportive of the Texas project. She even spoke in support of it when she and Cummings were on the campaign trail."

"Yes," said Waters, "Dr. Takayama is right. The maglev experiments in those states did feature in some of Lopez's speeches, but these initiatives are locally based—there has not been a coordinated national thrust until now. We are on the cusp of a new era, people . . . and I, for one, am very excited to be part of it."

There were smiles around the room at Waters' obvious excitement. As before, everyone was a little affected by it, and they began murmuring excitedly among themselves—and so, distracted as they were, when a dark shadow suddenly blocked out the sun and darkened the room, they were all quite shocked. As one, the group turned toward the window to see what had caused this sudden change, only to be greeted by a human-like form suspended in the air outside, a multitude of expressions crossing her face as she glowed in an ethereal way.

The group watched in awe (and a little fear) as the impressive, glowing form of Sarah melted easily through the window glass to stand before them in the meeting room.

Waters, normally a man with a million ideas and a clever tongue, was at a loss for words as he beheld Sarah.

She, however, was not. In a fluff of spring-scented air, she said, "I am Sarah, and I have come to help you."

The group remained awed and silent until, after a few moments of being tongue-tied, Waters managed to stutter, "You're the most amazing thing I have ever seen. I knew you would be something else, but . . . I . . . I . . . I have no words."

As was her way, Sarah sent her golden tinkle of energy coursing around the room, accompanied by the smell of roses. It was both relaxing and exciting, and those in the room drank it in like fine wine.

Finally, Governor Lamont managed to find his voice and humbly said, "It's an honour to see you, and to be in your presence. This is truly a remarkable day."

"You are doing good work," replied Sarah. "You are moving humankind forward into a world that is safe and much, much kinder. You will be assisted in every way. All you have to do is send a text or email to the Sarah Says website, and I will make myself available to you. Remember, God can open doors where human beings cannot."

With that, she simply evaporated, but on the table, she left behind a plate of chocolate truffles dusted with gold powder.

"Oh my God, oh my God, oh my God," muttered Rodrigues, acting for all the world as if she was coming out of a trance. "I can't believe she's *real*. She is *amazing*!"

Lamont said nothing—he just reached for a truffle and popped it in his mouth.

Waters managed to regain his composure enough to say, "Well, whatever doubts I might have had about getting this job done are gone now. We have God on our side. You can't get better support than that!"

"I'll say," replied Redmond thoughtfully.

"I've got to get home and tell my girlfriend what just happened," said Waters. "That was too amazing. I'm still shaking."

"I hear you," agreed Redmond.

Then Waters managed to gather his wits together by taking a deep breath and shaking his head a few times to get himself back in the game. He said, "I have just a few details about corporate structure I need to share with you all, and then let's break for the day."

There were nods around the room. He continued, "Mary and I are going to get the ball rolling by laying out the legislative framework for this job—and by that, I mean that we plan to create a federally-owned corporation through a special act of congress so we can acquire interstate land rights." Then he looked around the room, making sure he had everyone's attention, and said, "Over the next month, I want us to focus on three things. First, a corporate plan for the new EEL corporation—Mary, I'd like you to work on that as well," he said, looking over at her.

She nodded. "Of course," she said.

"Second, we need to work on a conceptual development plan to promote discussion and to solicit interest in the project—Governor, if you would," he said, eyeing Governor Lamont.

Lamont nodded. "Yes, that's right up my alley," he said.

"And third, a national branding and image building campaign needs to be established—which is your bailiwick, Jennifer," he said, looking at Rodrigues, who nodded and smiled.

"We want the EEL corporation to retain full control over this train system," continued Waters. "We will not only build the train and its infrastructure, but we will own it as well—although once its built, we may want to consider allowing private sector operators to use the network."

"That's a great idea," said Redmond. "It will generate revenue."

"Exactly," said Waters. Then he looked around the room, and his eyes shone once more with excitement. "Before I leave this job, I want to see the U.S. move ahead of China, not only in terms of technology and manufacturing capability but in miles of high-speed railbed. Oh . . . and the president and I want to see the new EEL corporation launched within six months—even faster, if possible. Are you up for it, team?"

There was a round of clapping in the room that warmed Waters' heart. When the noise died down, he was silent for a moment, savoring the experience.

And then his face lit up into a wide smile, and he said to Redmond, "Simon, I had a thought last night. Do you think we can incorporate social distancing options, such as pods, in the design of our passenger trains? It would give us a real leg up on the airlines."

Chapter 23

Colonization of Space

It was 10:30 p.m., and it was a lovely, warm evening. Cummings sat outside his White House living quarters on a private deck, sipping an ice cold beer and staring at the moon. *This is a time of great change,* he thought, *and I'm grateful to be alive to see God work miracles on this Earth.*

He heard Lorena coming toward him from behind, padding softly in her barefeet. He'd mistakenly thought she was sleeping and so had not greeted her when he got home.

"Hello, Samuel," she said softly, putting her hand on his shoulder.

"Hi, sweetheart," he said, covering her hand with his own.

"Are you staring off into space?" she teased.

He laughed. "It's what I'm best at," he replied with a chuckle. "I'm the guy who's going to see that America plays a leading role in colonizing both the moon and Mars, Lorena."

"Is that so?" she said. "You must be very proud."

"Very much so," he agreed, squeezing her hand. "In fact, I was just picking out a plot of land for our house on Mars. We'll have a green picket fence instead of a white one, to honour our Martian neighbours . . ."

She could not see his wry grin in the dark, but she knew it was there. Playfully, she cuffed his ear.

"You dreamer," she said.

"Oh, it's not a dream," he insisted, pulling her to sit on the chair beside him. "I am working on forming a global corporation that will spread humanity into the galaxy. It's amazing to think of people on Mars, but someday, it's going to happen."

"That's pretty ambitious," said Lorena. "How will you manage that?"

"I'm going to create a corporation that is owned and financed by all the governments of the world. I'm going to call it the Universal Space Exchange, USE for short."

"Well, not every country can afford to invest in a space program," said Lorena, gazing at the shining three-quarter moon that was lighting up their deck.

Cummings handed her a beer and said, "I know that. I'm going to work with Norman Feldman on a plan where investment is proportional to economy."

"Well, I guess that sounds good," said Lorena, sipping her beer, "but how would it actually work?"

"Using a ratio system, nations will share risks and rewards in proportion to their investment in USE."

"I get *that*," said Lorena. "What I mean is, how are you going to go about selling this plan to the rest of the world?"

"Ah, yes . . . that's more tricky," replied Cummings thoughtfully. "I think I'll propose that USE engage the private sector for transportation and development services, but that governments retain rights to land and other assets, perhaps under the central authority of the UN. We can't have bickering about this. I'd hate to think we take such short-sightedness into outer space with us. The world is in the mess it's in precisely because humanity has been bickering about land and resources for eons."

"You can say that again," said Lorena. Then she looked at her husband with deep concern, the moon lighting up her dark eyes. "Samuel," she said, "you have no idea how frightened I was for you when Sarah first came. I was afraid someone in the military would act on an order you'd given, and that I'd never see you again."

"God and Sarah spared me," he said, gripping her hand tightly. "That means I still have a purpose on this planet . . . and I intend to fulfill whatever role has been allotted to me. Right now, I think it's to colonize space, and I'm excited to be part of this push. Someday, maybe the human race will not only be advanced enough to communicate with the evolved beings Sarah has told us about, but maybe we'll be advanced enough to visit with them as well."

"I hope so," said Lorena. "It sounds so exciting."

"It *is* exciting," said Cummings, "and on multiple levels. It's not only about colonizing the moon and Mars—it's also about exploring the galaxy . . . and it will allow America to once again be a leader in the space race."

"It's not *really* a race," said Lorena, "especially if you are going to share the experience with all the countries in the world."

Cummings laughed, "Right you are, Wife," he replied. "To make this work, we have to pull a diverse group of cowboys together."

"Space cowboys?" she laughed, "Like the old Steve Miller song?"

Cummings couldn't help himself. The beer was going to his head, and so he started singing, with Lorena joining right in, "Some people call me the space cowboy, yeah, some call me the gangster of love, some people call me Maurice, 'cause I speak of the pompatus of love . . ."

It didn't sound too bad until Lorena tried to vocally insert the distinctive bass line into the song, and her voice cracked. Then they both wound up convulsing into heavy laughter.

For Cummings, who'd been working nonstop to govern his country to the highest of standards in this time of immense change, it was a huge stress release, and he laughed until there were tears in his eyes.

When the chortling had subsided, he managed to say, "Space exploration is actually quite a serious matter. Right now, it's like the Wild West out there, with more than a dozen countries—not to mention private sector companies—competing for dominance."

"I know," said Lorena. "I was just teasing. And I know how important it is for you to move this country forward in that arena."

"Thanks, hon," he said. "A shared goal like this is just the ticket to bring countries together. If the world doesn't work together on it, it will instead become yet another source of international tension. Working together—coming together—that's what God wants."

Lorena reached over and squeezed his hand. "Is that what Sarah told you?" she asked.

"Yes," he said. "Maybe not in as many words, but yes."

Then the two of them finished their beers in silence, gazing at the silvery moon as it drifted slowly by overhead, casting its unearthly glow upon them. When they were done, as one, they rose from their chairs and went inside to retire for the evening.

The next morning, Cummings was in the White House at 7:30 a.m., working on plans for the USE corporation. He had been thinking about how to manage this since Sarah had first arrived on Earth and had brainstormed with his team about how much money should be earmarked for it. The topic had further been on Sarah's agenda when she'd pulled all the world leaders together in New York for her initial global 'kickoff' meeting at the UN, where she'd laid out her timelines and plans for disarming the world.

As per the ground rules Sarah had laid out at that New York meeting, Cummings understood that the first step would be to set up a meeting of the twenty countries with the largest economies to determine not only how they would approach cost-sharing, but how they would merge diverse, proprietary technologies in a shared goal to colonize the moon and Mars.

Wanting to set his own country on a firm footing in the colonization process, he decided to get the ball rolling. From what he could see, the first priority was to determine whether all the countries of the world would even *agree* to work together to colonize space. *Well, there's only one way to find out,* he thought. He punched a buzzer on his desk to call his assistant, Janice Lang.

Janice walked into the room. "Hello, Mr. President," she said with a smile.

"Hi, Janice," he said. "Could you please book a meeting room in the George R. Brown Convention Center in Houston? It has to be big enough to host contingents of up to ten people from twenty countries."

"Of course," said Janice. "Prepare for 200 people. Is there anything else? Do you want me to book accommodation and catering as well?"

"Yes," he replied. "Accommodation and catering for three days. Thanks. Oh, and I plan to send out formal invitations by snail mail, classy ones with gold edging and the White House seal. Can you get me a few templates to review?"

She nodded and then turned smartly on her heel to do as requested, while he sat down at his desk to make a list of the twenty countries with the highest Gross Domestic Product (GDP). These were the United States, China, Japan, Germany, India, United Kingdom, France, Italy, Brazil, Canada, Russia, South Korea, Spain, Australia, Mexico, Indonesia,

Netherlands, Saudi Arabia, Turkey, and Switzerland. He was surprised that Saudi Arabia wasn't ranked higher, given its chokehold on oil.

Cummings had high hopes for the meeting. Most nations understood that colonization of a new, unpopulated planet should not be limited only to the rich, so he hoped his proposal would be well received. In this spirit of optimism, when his assistant returned, he had her schedule a second meeting for a month after the first—one which would be open to *all* world leaders.

Next, Cummings decided to work on a meaningful, robust agenda. Wanting to cover all salient points, he enlisted Lopez to help.

"Angelica," he said on the phone, "could you come in here?"

When she arrived, he told her, "Given your environmental portfolio and generally scientific nature, I'm counting on you to stimulate discussion on some of the harder topics, such as how power could be generated on the moon and Mars with no infrastructure and possibly very few natural resources."

"Thanks for your confidence in me," she said.

"I'm also going to book Clinton Marshall, NASA's administrator, to help with the agenda," he said, "as well as James Ruby. He's the chair of New Jersey Capital Credit, one of Wall Street's largest investment banks. I'm hoping we can all manage to meet tomorrow."

"Sounds good, Chief," said Lopez.

When Lopez had left his office, Cummings called Marshall and Ruby personally, and they graciously agreed to meet at the White House the following day.

The next morning, when they were all assembled, Ruby opened the discussion, saying, "Mr. President, we all know what you want to achieve through the USE concept—but unless we can bring all the key players to the table, it's doomed to fail."

Cummings heard Lopez—who he knew was 100% behind the idea of USE—mutter under her breath, "Well, aren't *you* just a little ray of sunshine."

Luckily, Ruby did not hear her. He continued, "Let me explain. While I completely understand that the colonization of Mars is a shared goal, and the expectation is that all nations on Earth can rally around it, I also believe that you, Mr. President, see USE as a vehicle for getting the U.S.

back into a leadership role in space exploration. Unless I'm reading it wrong, it's going against the very things you are purporting to champion. Are you sure that is what God wants?"

Cummings cleared his throat uncomfortably. Ruby was not wrong. He *was* feeling a little competitive, and he *did* want America to have an edge.

But before he could explain his motives, Lopez came to his defence, saying, "*Everyone* wants to be the hero who gets to Mars first. Is that such a crime?"

Ruby eyed her balefully. "It's not just about being *first*, Vice President Lopez," he said. "It's about claiming governance over resources in order to generate wealth. Governments have done it for millennia, and will do it again if they can . . . but first, they'll have to beat off the private sector players who have emerged in the last fifteen years, and who want to beat government at their own game. Governments rape and pillage, while the private sector wants to homestead, if you will, and make a fortune in the new 'wild frontier' without government interference. They won't settle for being United Nations cargo companies."

"I see," said Lopez. "In that case, I will put 'developing protocol for ownership' on the agenda."

"That's a start," said Ruby with a smile, "but there is so much more about this proposal that we should discuss. The Russians, for example, will protest the USE structure, as it will distract them from their own space program. And given the state of their economy, they might ultimately become a minority shareholder because their GDP has dropped significantly since God's intervention. I doubt they'll accept that. They have invested a great deal of money and resources into their space program. They're not going to want to start over as 'also rans.'"

Cummings had considered this very thing, but had high hopes that Russia's acting prime minister, Sergei Grinkov, would soon be elected president and would see the benefits of the deal Cummings was proposing. While Misha Verenich had been a power-inebriated dictator, Grinkov showed every sign of being a diplomat.

Ruby continued. "And let's not forget the Chinese! They will want to dominate space exploration in the way they currently dominate the world economy, and as a communist state, I doubt they will have any interest in a consortium involving private sector partners."

Frustrated, Cummings cut in. "Do you really think, after God's intervention, that such status quo still applies? The world has been through a dramatic change since Sarah arrived. I have a bit more faith than you that worldviews have changed!"

"Well, President Cummings," said Ruby thoughtfully, "I appreciate your optimism. It's possible the USE plan will get *some* support. Since Europe is currently a bit player in the space race, perhaps the European nations will be inclined to accept such a proposal. And the Japanese might line up with your plan—though the rest of Asia, most notably China, doesn't trust them. India will want into the tent, so to speak, and you can probably count on them to join a government consortium—but only if the voting structure gives them a loud voice at the table."

Cummings furrowed his brow, deep in thought. He didn't like what Ruby was saying, but he knew the words contained wisdom.

"Damn!" he uttered under his breath.

Ruby smiled bleakly, "That is the appropriate response, I'm afraid," he said. "If you ask me, you have a difficult negotiation ahead of you, and I'd put odds of unanimous acceptance at about 10%. We need to roll up our sleeves and come up with a proposal that better reflects the interests of *all* players—not just the United States."

Cummings sighed. Grudgingly he said, "I appreciate your candor, James. Let's split this discussion into a few key components and see if it makes things more clear."

"Agreed," replied Ruby, while Lopez and Marshall nodded.

"I guess the first thing we should talk about is that 'homesteading' thing you mentioned earlier," said Cummings. "The question is, who should own and control the resources of the moon and Mars?"

Lopez said, "I'm sure all heads of state would agree that it should be governments, rather than private sector interests, that control resources . . . but *which* governments? And what will the governance structure look like?"

"America, China, and Russia bring the most to the table in terms of existing space programs," mused Cummings, "and so, I think these three countries should be rewarded for their pioneering efforts. We need a framework that recognizes this, while proposing an equitable, inclusive investment scheme for the rest of the world."

"I agree," said Lopez.

"I like it too," said Ruby.

"Once we have a framework in place, the next thing we need to consider is whether a single, multi-national team should colonize the moon, and then Mars, or whether multiple teams should be unleashed to compete on some basis, in a free enterprise model."

"My gut tells me a *single* team should be operating until the actual colonization starts," said Marshall, speaking up for the first time. "It will be precarious to get established in these alien environments, not to mention to ensure that oxygen supply and appropriate resources for survival are available while a permanent settlement is built. Pooled resources will ensure safety for our people in the short term—but once a certain level of security and safety is in place, multiple teams might encourage quicker colonization."

"I was thinking the same thing," said Lopez. "Let's face it, this is going to be dangerous work and all materials, down to the rustiest of nails, will have to be imported from Earth. There will be some supreme trial and error when it comes to such things as, for example, ensuring airtightness of structures—which can mean the difference between life and death. I imagine we will send pre-fab buildings with our colonization teams—and I have no doubt that rigorous testing will be done before we send them—but trial and error are going to be part of this package, and more than one technology up there will be a benefit. That way, if one fails, perhaps another won't. It creates better odds for survival. We don't want to lose our brave pioneers!"

"I agree," said Marshall, looking at Lopez with thoughtful respect. "I couldn't have said it better myself."

"You're right, Angelica," agreed Cummings. "I think that's a good observation." Then Cummings paused, thinking hard, before saying, "The third thing we should address is how to attract both public and private sector investment simultaneously. Any ideas?"

"Well," said Ruby thoughtfully, "what if we were to hammer out an agreement with China and Russia to allow both private sector and state owned companies to compete against each other for the transportation systems? It would be messy, but no country can afford such development costs on its own."

"I like it," said Lopez with a smile. "That's excellent negotiating strategy. It will make them play ball or get off the team!"

"What do you think, Clint?" Cummings asked Marshall.

"I think you've laid out a practical way forward," Marshall said. "And I think Ruby is wrong about Russian resistance to this proposal. The Russian economy has been ravaged, first by the COVID-19 epidemic, and then by the loss of their military might due to the 'no killing' edict. It hit their economy *hard*. Their political landscape won't settle until after the pending election—and it will be much longer than that before they have the resources to refurbish their space program. The Chinese . . . well, that's another matter. In general, they don't play well with the other kids, and so all we can do is pitch our ideas to them and hope for the best."

"I hear you," Cummings said.

"In the meantime, I recommend we continue to build ongoing relations with private sector space pioneers, like Elon Musk," said Marshall. "To date, he and his ilk have had a natural preference for partnering with the U.S. rather than Russia or China, thank God—but perhaps it's time to cement that in a more meaningful way. If you can nail down the private sector and the Russians, then you will have a better chance of bringing the Chinese to the table."

"You're right," agreed Cummings, buzzing Janice, who came into the room immediately. "Hi Janice," he said, "I need you to line up the leaders of the most aggressive space travel companies for a meeting next week," he said.

"Certainly," she said. "Just the American ones? Or do you want me to do a global search?"

"Anyone you can get hold of. I'm not picky," said Cummings.

"Okay, I'll do that right away," she said as she left the room.

Cummings turned back to the others, "I'll get my counterparts in China and Russia to meet with me a week or two ahead of the USE conference to discuss their expectations. Maybe we can iron out the kinks early." Then he smiled brightly. "I have high hopes for this; I really do. God is on our side, and Sarah is here to help us. With a team like that, we are destined for success!"

Lopez gave him a wide smile. He could tell she was as excited as he was, and that she was probably dreaming of being one of the pioneers on the shuttle.

The meeting over, Ruby and Marshall stood.

"Thanks for coming, gentlemen," Cummings said as he shook their hands.

Then, as the men headed out with Lopez trailing behind, he phoned Lorena's cell phone.

"Hello?" she answered.

"Hi, honey," he said. "Are you up for another moon date tonight? It's full, you know."

"You bring the beer," she laughed, "and I'll bring my Martian costume."

Chapter 24

USE Private Sector Meetings

President Cummings was quite excited about meeting with three of the most prominent private sector leaders in the so-called 'space race.' His assistant, Janice Lang, had worked a miracle, and on very short notice, she'd managed to book noted American entrepreneur Elon Musk; Saudi Arabian investor and philanthropist, Sheikha Mariam Al-Amiri; and Chinese billionaire and spacecraft engineer, Jack Hou, to meet with the president the following day.

By coincidence, Al-Amiri was already in New York City for a conference, and she agreed to attend the meeting at the White House in person. That left only Jack Hou in a different time zone, and so Janice Lang set the meeting for 8:00 p.m. Eastern Time, which translated to 8:00 a.m. the following morning in China.

That evening, Cummings waited in the Oval Office with Blackstone, Lopez, and Feldman—who was busy trying to get Jack Hou linked in on the computer—for Mariam Al-Amiri, James Ruby, and Clinton Marshall to arrive. Al-Amiri was a polite ten minutes early, arriving in a cloud of perfume at ten minutes to eight, escorted into the Oval Office by one of the White House's female security staff.

Cummings could not help noticing that, though she wore the traditional black abaya, from under it peeked some attractive, stiletto heels and well-manicured toes. Cummings noted Lopez also appraising the woman's shoes. When her eyes widened slightly, Cummings knew that Al-Amiri's shoes were probably pretty expensive.

God's Intervention

Cummings had been uncertain what to expect from a Saudi woman. Though he knew Al-Amiri was astronomically wealthy, given what some saw as subjugation of women in the Arab countries, he wondered if she would seem slightly cowed. He was instead impressed with the grace and dignity she brought into the room, and the quiet strength she emanated.

"Welcome," he said to her, bowing slightly to indicate respect.

He'd brushed up on United Arab Emirates etiquette and knew that he was not to initiate a handshake with a woman. Al-Amiri smiled at his greeting and held out a sleeve-covered, well-manicured hand for him to shake. Upon this invitation, he shook and then placed his right hand on his heart as a token of respect as per Saudi custom.

"Thank you, President Cummings, for inviting me," Al-Amiri said regally as she took a seat on one of the couches in the Oval Office.

At that moment, Feldman managed to get Jack Hou on the phone. "Good morning," said Hou, his perfect English tinged with a British accent that was incongruous with his Chinese features—until Cummings remembered that Hou had a British mother who was linked to the monarchy, and that he'd received an Oxford education in computer science.

"Good *evening*," came back Feldman to the Chinese man on the screen before him. "It's 8:00 p.m. here."

"I know," said Hou. "You're living in the past over there. We're *way* ahead of you in China. We always have been."

Feldman laughed, while Cummings teased, "Not really, Jack. Don't forget that America got to the moon first."

"So you *say*," Hou replied with a smirk, "and yet, I find it strange that you never went *back* to the moon. Also, you've never properly explained those old videos where your flag is waving in zero gravity . . ."

Cummings laughed. "Sure, bring *that* up," he said. "Listen, Jack, the 1969 expedition was *not* a hoax. I swear to God!"

Hou laughed. "God may believe you, but *I* don't," he said.

Just then, Clinton Marshall and James Ruby arrived. "Sorry we're late," said Marshall. "I treated James to dinner so I could pick his brains about some NASA budget ideas."

"No problem," said Cummings, "we were just getting settled in."

Cummings made some quick introductions, just to be polite, but he needn't have bothered. Musk, Hou, and Al-Amiri were known across the globe, and while Marshall and Ruby had not met them in person, they were well aware of all they had accomplished—in particular, Elon Musk.

When the pleasantries came to an end, Cummings was eager to get the discussion going. "I'm grateful to you for coming," he said, "and I want to thank you for agreeing to meet with me and my team on such short notice."

"It's a great honour to be invited," said Al-Amiri graciously. "Thank you."

Cummings continued, "You may be aware that shortly after Sarah arrived on Earth, she proposed a global project to colonize the moon and Mars. On her behalf, I am putting together a corporation, the United Space Exchange, for this purpose, and that's why I've called this meeting. Sarah made it clear from the outset that the colonization of space should be a *global* initiative—a shared prize with the potential to unite the world in a common goal. I envision this corporation as a public-private partnership, and I would like you three to be part of this process. I could really use your expertise, and I hope you agree to it."

Out of the corner of his eye, Cummings saw Lopez watching him carefully. She understood better than anyone else in the room, except Feldman, that he was making a pitch to powerful, self-contained people to whom he could literally offer no incentives that they couldn't buy themselves—and how difficult it would be to convince them to be part of the USE initiative.

He continued, "It is the nature of men to create . . . but it's also the nature of men to *compete*. Healthy competition *feeds* creativity, while unhealthy competition blackens the soul—and can even feed the desire to kill. We all know that God has had enough of killing, which is why our ability to do so has been stripped away. We've been left with a mandate to refocus our competitive ways."

He saw Lopez smile at his words, and he was suddenly quite proud. The vice president was astute and not easy to fool; If she liked his speech, then it was a good one.

Bolstered by her smile, he finished with, "God wants us to unite our creative energies to move forward toward, in the words of *Star Trek*, 'space, the final frontier.'"

He paused then and looked significantly at Musk, Al-Amiri, and Hou.

"I'm calling on you three entrepreneurs and businesspeople to look at the situation from the point of view of a global endeavor with philanthropic overtones. If you were to consider investing your collectively impressive expertise and financial powers into USE, it would go a long way to stopping territorialism in space."

"Territorialism?" questioned Hou, his voice a little tinny through the computer speakers. "Don't you mean *colonialism*?"

"It's part of the same spectrum," Cummings replied, "but territorialism comes first."

"I see," said Hou, "and I'm impressed by your lofty speech. But here's the problem I have with that lofty speech. I am a practical man, and I've had enough involvement with the China National Space Administration to know that they are feeling *very* territorial right now. They want their piece of the pie—meaning colonies and squatter's rights—on both the moon and Mars. They want to lay claim to whatever resources they can extract profitably, without interference from your new corporation . . . and my country likes to win, President Cummings, just as America does."

"I understand," said Cummings.

Just then, James Ruby cut in. "Well, I know for certain that the only way we are going to get to Mars in *any* of our lifetimes is by crafting a deal that brings America, China, Russia, and interested private investors to the table," he said. "Governments have existing infrastructure, not to mention existing machines, for space travel . . . but the love of the chase that private investors bring is what will ultimately see this thing through. A massive project such as this carries a heavy financial burden—with no guaranteed return."

"Agreed," said Cummings. "The big question for governments is: is it cost effective to extract resources and ship them back to Earth?"

"Oh, and you don't think private sector investors aren't looking at the bottom line?" asked Hou.

"Of course they are," said Cummings amiably, "but I think other factors figure in as well. Perhaps those factors are personal. For example, as a teenager, Amazon's Jeff Bezos had a dream of building and developing hotels, amusement parks, and colonies for human beings who were in orbit, which is why he started his Blue Origin sub-orbital spaceflight services company."

"King of the midway," laughed Hou.

Cummings saw Lopez frown at his flippant remark. He could tell she didn't think he was funny.

"Whatever the motivation, there is no doubt that private sector investment is needed," Cummings said quickly, hoping Lopez wouldn't reply to Hou with a 'shoot-from-the-hip' comeback, "but we need to come to the table, design a playbook, and lay out the 'risk versus reward' parameters first. When that's in place, we will bring other nations and businesses on board."

"I see," said Hou snidely, "although it sounds strangely like a cartel strategy."

"Oh, come on, Jack," said Lopez impatiently, coming to Cummings' defence. "That's unfair and overly dramatic!"

"Is it?" he asked, in his upper-crust British accent. "Tell me, Mr. President, have you discussed your plans with the Russian or Chinese governments yet?"

"You know I have not," admitted Cummings, "but I intend to reach out to them as soon as possible. I just thought it important to engage the private sector first if possible, because they—*you*—have the advantage of not being bound by protocol. I admire your collective entrepreneurial spirit and . . . I won't lie, here . . . I'm banking on the massive financial infusion you will bring to the table if you sign on with USE."

"But," said Al-Amiri, "what is in it for us? We are already investing in our private projects. Elon has done so well with SpaceX, for example, and Jack has been pioneering an oxygen creation system based on reducing lunar regolith using hydrogen gas at high temperatures. As for me, given the country I live in, I have long been interested in climate-controlled, airtight structures, and so I have been investing in research and development in that area. My ultimate goal is to capture the market on building safe, reliable, airtight homes on the moon."

"I understand," said Cummings, "and I guess the primary benefit to you early adapters is a guaranteed greater market share in your respective fields of expertise. But isn't making your mark in history as benefactors— pillars of humanity's colonization of our solar system—just as enticing?"

"Ah," said Hou with a smirk, "so you're working the ego angle with us."

"Yes," said Cummings with no apology. "I am."

Hou's distinctive chuckle rang out of the computer, making the rest of the group inadvertently smile. "No beating around the bush then, Mr. President?" he asked.

"No," said Cummings, "I'm being open and frank with you, and I want you to be that way with me as well. Please feel free to disagree with anything I, or anybody on my team, says. This is all about brainstorming, not about selling you an investment idea."

His words were acknowledged by eye contact and nods around the room.

Then the president resumed. "The first thing that has to be determined before we invest billions of dollars into colonization is a governance model, particularly one that pertains to resources."

Lopez cleared her throat, looked at her boss, and said, "If all the nations of Earth come together to make this project *possible*, then shouldn't they also come together to agree on governance and resource ownership?"

Musk, who'd been silent up until now, suddenly laughed. "Are you kidding?" he asked. "Government red tape will not only kill any action up there, but it might actually kill *people*. Those who colonize the moon, Mars, or wherever humankind decides to set foot, should determine their own government—and their own *style* of government. Once that's in place, then *local* government should have the power to dictate the nature of resource development."

"Because . . . ?" prompted Lopez, her eyebrow in full arch.

"Because, Vice President Lopez, the brave pioneers we send up in those rocket ships will be the ones with 'boots on the ground,'" Musk replied. "They will need to find ways to survive in extremely hostile environments, through trial and error, and they will best know the *true* value—as opposed to the *monetary* value—of whatever resources are on the celestial bodies they colonize. For example, various metals are abundant on the moon, but unless those metals are worth their weight in rocket fuel, it probably isn't worth it to mine them. So let the people who *need* those resources *have* them."

"I see your point," said Lopez, her brow furrowing as she considered Musk's words.

"Good," Musk said, "because my next point is that you can't rule by committee. If the governments of Earth are in charge of the decision making in the colonies, it will not only stifle the creativity the president was talking about earlier but, in some cases, it could become a matter of life or death for the colonists. They should be allowed to mine, gather, or otherwise extract any materials that will enhance their lives and protect their well-being without government interference."

There was a murmur of discussion around the room as people pondered Musk's words.

When it died down, the refined, dignified Al-Amiri spoke up, saying, "Elon, I agree with your ideas about ownership and use of natural resources—but for slightly different reasons. In my opinion, the colonists will ultimately want to establish their independence someday, just as America did with Britain so long ago . . . and once they do, they will need their own resources so that they can barter with Earth for goods and services. To me, control of resources will give an emerging civilization much-needed economic power."

"That is a good point," Cummings acknowledged, looking at the woman with renewed respect.

"It is the story of Saudi Arabia," said Al-Amiri. "It is my history. Without our oil, we would have nothing at all."

Cummings was touched by the melancholy in her voice as she said this. She seemed very devoted to her country and her countrymen.

"I appreciate your perspective," he told her. "You are projecting into the future in a way I have not. I, for one, have not thought much further than getting a few astronauts and scientists set up to navigate the terrain and report back—but you've moved on a few generations, and you're absolutely right to do so. People will create lives, homes, and attachments to the land once they learn to live there. And they will want to be masters of their own domain, as we all do."

Al-Amiri acknowledged him with a slight smile, and he felt warmed by it.

Emboldened, he asked her, "So how do *you* envision a private sector role within the United Space Exchange model that I've proposed?"

"We would do what we do best," she said enigmatically.

Musk cut in. "Yes," he said. "My company can develop technologies and build things faster and cheaper than any government can. On the transportation side, we have rockets in operation that have already leapfrogged over anything any governments might have in stock, and we have even more truly amazing technology on the drafting table."

"I'm not surprised," said Cummings, "and if you consent to contribute some of that expertise to the USE initiative, I expect someday, you'll be richly rewarded."

"I'm *already* rich," said Musk, "and for me, money is just a means to an end. As Mr. Ruby said earlier, the thrill is in the chase, Mr. President." He smiled widely and Cummings was happy to know that the priorities of one of the smartest, richest men in the world were so very similar to his own.

"That's good to hear," Cummings said, "and I hope so much that we can work together. Tell me, do you think the idea of funneling both public and private money into the United Space Exchange, to fund space colonization, will work?"

"I *like* the idea," said Musk, "and I like the model you suggested in which all countries can participate proportionally based on investment contributions. However, if the U.S. provides half the funding, then it will also be in the position to provide half the colonists . . . and I'd caution you that there are some out there who will think that will give America an overly hefty say in governance. As much as Jack was kidding about being a cartel, he's not completely wrong. It *could* be perceived as opportunistic."

Cummings saw the truth in Musk's words. It was hard to swallow because he'd never had to look his own territorial nature before. So much of being the president of the United States was about statesmanship and overall maintenance of government programs that it had never occurred to him that he was as bad as everyone else. But then again, these were exciting times. He thought, *Whoever thought I'd live to see the day when the world would be arguing about who owns the moon?*

He sighed. "You're right," he said to Musk. "I guess part of me wants to be remembered as the president who forged an American presence on Mars. I wasn't thinking broadly enough. For that, I apologize."

Just then, Mitchell, who'd been silent almost since he'd entered the room, said, "Don't apologize, President Cummings. We need you to lead, and you have been handpicked by Sarah to do so. You've come up with an interesting, workable model for colonizing the moon and Mars, and you've lined up the players." Then he looked at Musk and Hou and said,

"New technology is the key to this whole endeavor, and you two are the guys who can provide that."

"It's true," said Hou, "the private sector has *way* better technology, though America has a long and storied space program. The same can be said for the Russians. Their rockets, as reliable as they are, look like hippos compared to what SpaceX and Blue Origin are building."

"Yes, the NASA space program needs significant upgrades to be competitive," Mitchell said, "which is why the USE concept is a game-changer."

Cummings caught Mitchell's eye. "When the military is fully repurposed," he said, "we plan to invest some of the dollars freed up from its dissolution into NASA. My hope is that NASA will function as an autonomous subsidiary of USE and contribute to the USE program."

"That sounds reasonable," said Mitchell.

Hou cut in. "President Cummings," he said, "what are your thoughts about production facilities on the moon for Mars rockets? It would be easier than launching rockets from Earth."

"I think that is a goal to work toward," said Cummings. "Why?"

"Are you envisioning a big workforce up there?" asked Hou.

"Yes. To start, I see people settling in for terms of two to three years at a time," Cummings replied. "First, they'll have to create safe living quarters, or course. I see the private sector taking a lead role in this."

"Perhaps we can bring back the idea of transportation," said Hou, "prisoner ships flying to the moon to deploy bad guys for slave labour—as the British did when they settled Australia."

There was a small silence in the room. Everyone knew what a dreadful thing the transportation ships had been.

"Uh—I don't think so," Cummings finally ventured cautiously, "and I do not even want to even *entertain* such notions. Instead, my hope is that construction jobs will be lucrative enough to attract skilled tradesmen who don't mind working in less than optimal conditions. I'm sure there will be money in it for workers. After all, investors will make good returns—especially if premiums are in place to offset the risk of working in space."

Cummings saw Hou's gears engaging as the man pondered the profit margin. Then Hou said, "Do you envision more than one transportation company working the route?"

"It's something I'd like to discuss," responded Cummings.

The group seized on the idea, and for the next two hours, they discussed not only this but topics ranging from mining techniques to homesteading. Ultimately, they agreed that transportation systems to the moon should be completely open to competition, but—since Mars rockets would be costly to design and construct, especially if produced on the moon—there should be a single source for them, at least in the short term.

"Any comments, folks?" Cummings said when they came up for air. He checked his watch, and noticed it was nearly midnight.

"Only one thing," said Ruby, "and that is that we need to get Russia and China in on this as soon as possible. If you can sell them on the idea of USE, they have a lot to offer. Russia has a stockpile of functional rockets—many large enough to be used as 'mules' to carry people and equipment to the moon—and if you give extra credit to them for bringing existing technology to the table, as you spoke of earlier, you may be able to sell them on it."

"Good thinking," said Cummings. "In fact, it might be advantageous to give Russia a bigger role in USE than their currently collapsed economy would justify. They are already cooperating with the Chinese on a joint project to get to the moon, and we need to sway them toward our team—especially if we can't get the Chinese to buy into the USE initiative."

"Mr. President," said Marshall, who was clearly a man who only spoke when he had something really important to say, "have you considered the possibility that if you construct your Mars rockets on the moon, multinational *manufacturers* could become the primary colonists?"

Jack Hou laughed. "That would be a bit of a governance concern, wouldn't it?" he chortled. "Corporations could end up controlling everything!"

"Good point, Clinton," said Cummings, "and that brings us full circle, doesn't it? There's no doubt Earth should govern in the short term . . . after all, it will take some time for people to decide if they can actually build lives worth living in these remote places. If they *do* elect to stay, then we need to build an option into our governance plan to allow them to develop their own constitution. If they *don't* stay, then governance simply becomes a matter of hammering out resource agreements with other nations."

There were murmurs of agreement around the room, as well as some subtle checking of watches. Most of the assembled group were feeling the hour; Only Jack Hou was fresh and feisty.

"What's the matter with you guys?" asked Hou when he saw a few stifled yawns around the room. "You look like the walking dead. It's barely lunch time here . . . I'm telling you, you're on the wrong side of the world."

Cummings saw Lopez wrinkle her nose slightly. He could tell she thought Hou was a windbag. He caught her eye, silently warning her to keep her cool. She did, but she didn't look happy about it.

"Well," Cummings said to Musk, Al-Amiri, and Hou, "it's getting pretty late, and we should wrap this up. I'm deeply grateful to you for coming today, and I would urge you to consider becoming part of USE. I know that my government, and governments all around the world, need *you* more than you need *us*—but there are advantages to dovetailing your programs with public ones, and I hope you find those advantages attractive enough to get on board with USE."

"Well, I support what you are doing, President Cummings," said Al-Amiri in her quiet, ladylike voice, "and I am interested in discussing what I can offer in terms of housing options for harsh, extraterrestrial conditions. I have some very interesting designs I would love for you to see."

"Thank you," Cummings told her. "That is music to my ears."

With that, the lady rose and made her goodbyes and departure, escorted by the same female security guard who had led her into the Oval Office earlier.

Musk rubbed his chin, lost in thought. Finally he said, "You know, President Cummings, the Europeans have a penchant for government enterprise. To me, this means that if you get *too* wedded to the private sector solution, you might not get the support you need from the rest of the world."

"That's a risk I'm prepared to take," said Cummings.

"Well, okay," said Musk. "Then I am prepared to step into USE in an advisory role—at least in the short term—and an investment capacity when I am more certain of direction and scope of USE."

"That's great," said Cummings with a wide smile. "You won't regret it."

"You know," said Musk, "Jeff Bezos might want to get on board with this thing. I'm surprised you didn't invite him to this meeting."

"I thought you guys hated each other," replied Cummings, "and while I know his Blue Origin company is working on getting to the moon, I invited you instead because you have been focused on Mars from day one."

Musk laughed. "We're frenemies, Jeff and I," he said, "but that doesn't mean we don't hang out once in a while. There are just not many people a person can talk to about rockets. We get on each other's nerves, but like you said, our competitive streaks have made us creative."

"Aha!" said Hou, who was munching on a sandwich, presumably his lunch. "I see where this is going. It will come down to two teams, with Jeff Bezos racing to get to the moon, while Elon races to get to Mars."

"All to dominate a couple of frozen space deserts," said Cummings.

"Sounds enticing," laughed Hou. "How could I miss investing in such an opportunity? Count me in, Mr. President."

Cummings was elated. He was three for three with his private sector investors—and if he was lucky, Jeff Bezos would get on board as well.

Chapter 25

Conventional Weapons Disarmament

The three-day Moscow conference on conventional weapons disarmament was held ninety days after Sarah's arrival on Earth. Primary and secondary heads of all nations were asked to attend, and countries with armed forces were expected to send their military leaders as well. All in all, including administrative and technical staff, over 1,000 people were there.

As usual, Sarah used her remarkable teleportation abilities to ensure all attendees arrived in Moscow fresh in thought and mind. The American group 'landed' two hours before the meeting, which gave everyone time to look around the historical city after they'd checked into their hotels . . . all except for Cummings and Lopez. Somehow, they disappeared in mid-teleportation, leaving Blackstone very concerned.

The American group had travelled without their standard security roster—after all, the experience of teleportation did not involve crowds of gawking people at an airport, so only two of their top men were needed— and so Blackstone was on high alert. He immediately engaged Don Taylor, the president's personal bodyguard.

"Don," he said, "I don't know where President Cummings has gone. He did not arrive here with the rest of the group."

Taylor, who'd seen Sarah's powers several times, managed to calm Blackstone significantly. "I can't imagine that 'travel by Sarah' would end in a kidnapping," he said to the agitated Blackstone. "Let's give it half an hour, and if he and Lopez don't show up by then, then we'll speak to the Russian authorities."

Taylor was right. Cummings and Lopez had not been kidnapped; Instead, they'd found themselves in the most unusual situation. Rather than being dropped feet first on the ground upon their arrival in Moscow, this time, when the swirling sensation of teleportation was over (Cummings likened the feeling to melding with the wind), they found themselves hovering in mid-air, gazing down at the famous Moscow Kremlin.

"What the hell?" Lopez asked, perplexed. "Why are we hanging around like a couple of birds? Do you think Sarah got the coordinates wrong or something? Why didn't she put us down?"

"I don't know," replied Cummings. "She's never parked me in the sky before. It's new territory for me."

"Well, all I can say is, thank God I'm not wearing a dress!" Lopez said vehemently.

Cummings laughed.

His reaction to being suspended in the air was different that Lopez's; While she seemed somewhat frustrated by the experience they were having, he felt a strange sense of familiarity, as if he'd floated like this many times before. In fact, it made him wonder, *Is this what it felt like before I arrived on Earth to become Samuel Cummings, mortal man?*

Just then, on a waft of jasmine-scented wind, Sarah materialized in front of them. "Hello," she breathed, creating little puffs of cloud around them. "I hope I didn't leave you two hanging around too long."

Cummings immediately recognized her question as a joke and chuckled, but Lopez had not yet got her sense of humour back and still clearly felt uncomfortable about their situation. She just looked perplexed.

"Sarah," she asked, kicking her feet in the air as if she could propel herself out of the situation, "what are we doing up here?"

"Why, admiring the view, of course," said Sarah.

"Won't someone see us?" asked Lopez, worried.

"No," Sarah replied, "we are not visible to others."

At that, Lopez smiled broadly with relief. Meanwhile, Cummings was admiring the famous Moscow Kremlin below them, an historical, fortified complex (citadel) in the centre of Moscow.

"It's an amazing thing, the Kremlin," he remarked in awe.

"Yes," agreed Sarah, "Did you know that as many as 400 kremlins existed in medieval Russia? Only about twenty of them remain fully intact now."

"And this is the most famous one, of course," said Lopez.

"Yes," agreed Sarah. "It is more than six centuries old. Let me take you to the observation platform of the Ivan the Great Bell Tower. It will give you a splendid panoramic view of Moscow. Follow me!"

With that, Sarah breezed her way forward, and Cummings and Lopez were left to discover how best to follow her. Cummings found that he could propel himself through the air if he made dog paddling motions with his arms, and while it felt like swimming through gelatin, it was effective. Lopez followed suit, and soon they were on their way, trailing behind Sarah like two little ducklings of the air.

When they arrived at the 266-foot-high bell tower, they were treated not only to a bird's-eye view of its twenty-two bells (the largest weighing sixty-four tons) but a panoramic view of the city of Moscow as well, as Sarah had promised.

"Wow, this is incredible," said Lopez, inhaling sharply at the sight.

Below them they could see the five palaces, four cathedrals, and enclosing Kremlin Wall with Kremlin towers, as well as the Grand Kremlin Palace that was formerly the Tsar's Moscow residence, now the official home of the president. Beyond that lay Moscow, Russia's capital and the largest city in the country. Encompassing 400 square miles, Moscow was home to more than 10 million people, one of the largest cities in the world. It stretched out before them in all its vastness, and they could not help but be impressed at the sight.

Cummings drank in the view for a few minutes, but eventually, his curiosity got the better of him and he had to ask, "Sarah . . . thanks for coming to get us, and thanks for this incredible experience . . . but where are Gordon Blackstone and the rest of the team?"

Sarah's tinkling energy bounced around the atmosphere, causing a delightful tickle in Cummings' tummy, as she replied, "He's at the hotel. He's having an impromptu meeting with his technical staff to ensure they're prepared for today's meeting."

"Why are Angelica and I not doing that too?" asked Cummings.

Sarah laughed. "Aren't you happy to be with *me*, looking at the Kremlin from the best vantage point you could possibly have?"

Cummings did not answer right away; A gentle breeze was slowly wafting them away from the Kremlin—courtesy of Sarah, who seemed to be able to control the wind—and he found himself momentarily disoriented. He turned his head, trying to get his bearings, and saw the Saint Basil's Cathedral in the distance, like a fairy tale with its onion domes magically sparkling in the sun like carnival spires as they had done since 1552.

All he could say was, "How beautiful!"

"Isn't it?" asked Sarah, almost jovially. "I knew you'd love it from this height."

"It is *amazing*," said Cummings as he floated along beside her, feeling more and more comfortable in the air, if a little chilly. Then he said, "Sarah, I appreciate that you have given Angelica and I such a special experience . . . but I must confess, I don't understand *why*."

"Ah, yes," Sarah replied enigmatically, "you need rational answers, don't you, my dear Samuel? And so I will give them to you. I have a special task for you at today's meeting. I need you to talk about *death*."

"Pardon me?" asked Cummings, shocked.

"Samuel," said Sarah gently, "the people at this meeting today are powerful men and women who, though they make life and death decisions daily, don't always fully comprehend the emotional impact of those decisions. You, Samuel, *do*. When you think of your son and the passing of his partner, I see the compassion in you. You lived through bereavement, Samuel. You understand loss . . . and so, you can speak to God's 'do not kill' edict in a way that others cannot."

"I see," Cummings said, not seeing at all. He didn't think his personal experience with loss was much different than that of anyone else.

Sarah, who could read his thoughts, astutely pointed out, "It's how you *processed* it, Samuel—without blame or judgement. Perhaps you take for granted the manner in which you dealt with Flores' death, but I don't. Your reaction was to comfort others . . . a reflection of the spirit of God that did not go unnoticed."

Cummings was a little bashful about her assessment. "I don't think I'm much different than other people . . ." he said.

She emitted a chuckle in the form of a rose scent before saying, "Well, *I* do, and because of this, I am asking you to update the meeting attendees with the global death statistics today—and to bring your compassionate nature to the table in the process. I want you to remind them of the *real* purpose of God's intervention."

A little unnerved at the idea that she wanted him to share his personal feelings about the death of his son-in-law with an auditorium full of government leaders—some of whom were hardened, warlike men who bordered on being sociopathic—Cummings responded somewhat nervously, "But I thought *you* were going to update people on those statistics."

"I was," said Sarah, "but I've decided your testimony will have more impact."

Cummings was about to protest further, but just then, he found himself looking straight down at the colourful onion domes of St. Basil's Cathedral, and the beauty of it made him silent. He suddenly remembered his father helping him with a Grade 3 school project about Russia. He'd been enamored with the pictures in the geography book, and to his eight-year-old imagination, the towers looked like colourful Easter eggs.

"Does the Easter Bunny live there?" he'd asked his father, not at all certain that the Easter Bunny was real but willing to continue to believe.

"No, son," his father had replied. "It was built by a man named Ivan the Terrible. The story goes that he poked out the eyes of the men who designed it so they could never make something as beautiful again."

His child-self had been shocked; It was the first time he'd ever realized that terrible people can sometimes do wonderful things.

Sarah's many faces whirled in a cacophony of expressions as she, Lopez, and Cummings looked down at the stunning building below them. And then suddenly, one face stopped for a moment, and a haunted-looking woman with an intelligent, noble expression locked her eyes onto Cummings'.

"I died there," said the woman. "The scaffold was high."

And then she was gone, and Sarah's faces began their hummingbird-like rotation again.

At his right shoulder, eyes wide, Lopez whispered, "Did you *see* that woman? Did you hear what she said?"

Cummings nodded. The experience brought home to both of them just how vast the compilation of souls within Sarah really was.

Then, in an instant, Sarah was gone, and the two of them found themselves standing on solid ground in front of the Moscow World Trade Centre, where the meeting was to be held. Cummings clutched at his stomach; She had deposited them so quickly that it felt like he'd left it somewhere in the air. When the sensation subsided, he noticed that his hand was inexplicably clenched. He looked down at it to find he was tightly holding a sheet of paper listing all the deaths that had occurred since God's 'do not kill' edict had taken effect.

Beside him, Lopez absently dusted her hands across her clothing as if feeling a need to clean herself. She simply said, "Wow. That was . . . I have *no* words. But I'm glad to be back in the presence of gravity."

"Agreed," said Cummings, stuffing the now folded paper into his jacket pocket.

Then the two of them began slowly making their way toward the entrance of the Moscow World Trade Centre.

They'd only gone a few feet when they suddenly found themselves surrounded by serious-looking, armed men.

"Stop!" one of them yelled authoritatively in a thick Russian accent. "Stop!"

"Do you speak English?" asked Cummings as calmly as he could, intimidated even though he knew these men would die if they tried to kill him. "I am President Samuel Cummings of the United States of America."

"*You* are President Cummings?" asked a burly man, his English slightly better than the one who had yelled 'stop.' "I am Dimitri Popovich of Federalnaya Sluzhba Bezopasnosti."

"You're *who*?" asked Lopez, and Cummings could see that her back was up.

"Dimitri Popovich from FSB. In your language, Federal Security Service," Popovich said. "You were reported missing. Now you are found. Secretary of Defence for America, Gordon Blackstone, asked us to find you."

"Well, you *found* us," said Lopez irritably. "Can you take us to Blackstone?"

"Most certainly," said Popovich, signaling for his men to stand down.

Without further ado, Popovich led them into a large, bustling concourse, ringed with signs all written in Russian—which made them glad that they had a guide despite being accosted in such a manner.

Soon they were at the massive auditorium where the meeting was being held, and Popovich led them right to Blackstone and the rest of the team, who were sitting about ten tiers up from the floor. Blackstone was clearly happy to see them.

"Where *were* you?" he asked.

"Sarah spirited us away for a private tour of the city," said Cummings. At that, Don Taylor looked meaningfully at Blackstone as if to say, 'I told you so.'

"Well, I'm glad she got you back in time for the meeting. I've saved you guys a couple of seats," Blackstone said, indicating two plush, fold-down chairs with desk-arms.

Cummings and Lopez gratefully sat.

Within a few minutes, the auditorium lights flickered on and off several times, indicating that people should quiet down and pay attention.

Then Prime Minister Grinkov, who'd stepped in to fill the hole left by the departure of President Verenich, approached the podium in the centre of the room and said, "Ladies and gentlemen, welcome to Russia—and to Moscow."

Miraculously, although he spoke in his native tongue, everyone heard the words in their own language, which was clearly the work of Sarah.

"As you know," Grinkov continued, "we are here today to work together to develop plans for the destruction of all conventional weapons of war. Over the next three days, we will create a plan for their collection and destruction that will hold up to global scrutiny. We will not only disarm this world, but we will do it in a way that is open and verifiable . . . because we must not only *be* above board, we must be *seen* to be above board."

There was polite applause around the room at his words.

He continued, "There are three types of weapons slated for destruction: weapons of war owned by armed forces; weapons of war owned by private individuals; and domestic weapons created for civilian use."

Beside Cummings, Lopez was furiously typing notes into her laptop.

"There will be a transcript sent around later," Cummings whispered to her.

"I know," she whispered back, "but I like to keep my own notes." Cummings silently admired her conscientiousness; It was what made her so effective at her job.

Grinkov went on, "Guns created to kill human beings directly oppose God's 'do not kill' edict, which is why all military grade weapons and ammunition must be destroyed, whether such weapons be owned by the state or private citizens."

There were murmurs of understanding around the room. All in attendance were well versed in the words Sarah had consistently repeated to them since her arrival on Earth; Nevertheless, destroying all guns still seemed unthinkable to some—especially to nations with long histories of war. That they should be expected to voluntarily surrender weapons they had clung desperately to for so long seemed, to them, like a personal violation.

Cummings thought of the weapons-stockpiling, right wing militia movement that had been slowly rising in his country, and the 'doomsday prophets' who periodically rose to prominence. It made him feel unsettled, and suddenly, he felt a need to speak.

He stood up and was acknowledged by Grinkov. "President Cummings?" the man asked. "Would you like to say something?"

Cummings noticed a small microphone clipped to his desk-arm.

He picked it up and attached it to his collar, and then said over the room's audio system, "People in my country do *not* like to be parted from their weapons, especially when guns and weaponry are tied to their identity," he said. "Our Second Amendment, the right to bear arms—created when we were firing muskets, not multi-round weapons—is trotted out anytime the issue of gun control comes up. Americans get pretty volatile when asked to account for their weapons. In my country, collection will be difficult without a massive public relations campaign."

"But don't they understand that they will *die* if they use their weapons?" protested Grinkov. "They are ineffective now!"

"I know," said Cummings, "but many people are so strongly dedicated to their need to be *right* that they are willing to take the chance."

"Americans are a fierce people," Grinkov remarked ruefully.

"Yes," agreed Cummings. "Stubborn, too."

"You have made a good point," said Grinkov. "We will add a community engagement component to the agenda as a way to address this."

"Thank you," said Cummings, sitting down.

Looking around the room, Grinkov caught the eyes of some notable warlords and coolly held their gazes as he resumed his talk. "Determining the best way to dispose of military grade weaponry, whether government owned or privately held, is our concern today. Private, licensed handguns are out of scope, as licensing is a domestic responsibility. A separate conference to address their collection and disposal will be held in the American city of Denver, Colorado. There are, however, *some* aspects of civilian disarmament that dovetail with our goals, particularly in the area of recycling, which we will discuss later." Then he asked, "Any questions?"

No one rose to speak, and so he cleared his throat and said, "At its most basic, a gun consists of a trigger, a firing pin, and a tube. The trigger causes the firing pin to ignite gunpowder in the bullet casing, and BOOM—the bullet goes flying down the barrel. More complex weapons require more complex delivery systems. For example, to launch a rocket, you need a rocket launcher, and to support a rocket launcher, you need a warship . . . and so on."

Without noticing, under his breath, Cummings began singing "If I Had a Rocket Launcher," a song by Canadian musician Bruce Cockburn, who'd been inspired to write it after witnessing the plight of Guatemalan refugees who'd fled a bloody dictatorship. Lopez immediately kicked him in the ankle. His microphone was still on, and his singing could be heard throughout the room. Cummings quickly stopped but not before a few chuckles broke out.

When the laughter died down, Grinkov continued, "It will take a long time to dismantle and recycle complex weapons and their delivery systems—possibly as long as it took to build them in the first place. Removing and destroying projectiles and bombs is the first relatively simple step, and while I've been told to plan for a five-year timeline, I hope we can accomplish this in as little as three."

There was a muted shout of, "Yeah!" from somewhere in the room, but Cummings could not see who'd yelled.

Grinkov didn't react; He just said, "The first priority, however, is to collect, dismantle, and recycle the approximately one billion guns in the world."

"I *say*," cut in an upper-crust British voice Cummings recognized as that of the British prime minster, Charles Grafton, "can you back up a little, Prime Minister Grinkov? Did you say one *billion* guns?"

"Yes," replied Grinkov.

"Who knew that military forces had so many guns!" exclaimed Grafton.

"Ah, but they *don't*," replied Grinkov. "Only 133 million are in the hands of military forces, and 23 million are used by law enforcement. The remaining 857 million guns are held by *private* citizens."

You could have heard a pin drop. Like everyone else in the room, Cummings was sobered by these statistics.

He leaned over toward Lopez and said, "It would seem the folks in Denver who are in charge of collecting domestic guns are going to have their work cut out for them."

"It literally blows me away," she said, "pun intended."

"And where did you get this statistic?" Grafton ask Grinkov. "It seems rather high!"

"It was provided to me by a global centre of excellence, the Small Arms Survey in Geneva," replied Grinkov. "The Survey generates statistics on arms for policy-makers."

Grafton looked annoyed. "Collecting such a vast amount of guns will be a massive undertaking, and it's not within the British budget at the moment. Didn't Sarah say all this weaponry was going to self-destruct anyway? Why are we putting all this effort into collecting and disposing of weapons if we don't have to?"

"I can't speak to that," Grinkov said thoughtfully, "beyond saying that it has been clear from the beginning that God wants us to help ourselves and be purposeful in doing so. Given the state of resource industries around the world, it would be wise to salvage whatever we can from our efforts—especially metal."

"Yes, I suppose so," conceded Grafton with a sniff. "It's true that mining is not what it used to be."

"That is one way of putting it," said Grinkov. "The other way of putting it is to say that humans have a long way to go when it comes to looking after what we have. We deplete resources faster than we create them—hence the global race toward strip-mining the moon and Mars."

At the back of the room, someone clapped, presumably the same person who'd shouted 'yeah' earlier. Cummings squinted to see who it was and recognized Blair Stewart, First Minister of Scotland. Suddenly, the enthusiasm made sense. Scotland had implemented a Zero Waste Plan in 2010, setting an example for the rest of the world, and the Scottish people were very proud of their thriftiness—embracing what had long been considered a stereotypical Scottish trait. Cummings shifted in his seat uncomfortably; The U.S.A. was certainly capable of following suit, but it had not.

Grinkov resumed. "I think it is now time for a break. After lunch, we will discuss weapon disposal by category. Most of you have submitted weapons inventories already, though some of you have requested extensions because the military repatriation process is turning up inventory deficiencies. This brings up the importance of outreach and public perception that President Cummings mentioned earlier. We need verifiable numbers to ensure the public trusts our processes. To this end, a United Nations team will monitor our progress and handle public relations."

At that, the group broke for lunch. Cummings and Lopez remained seated while the majority of people in their immediate vicinity filed out of the room.

Lopez sighed heavily and looked at her boss. "I feel sorry for Grinkov," she said. "God's ban on killing has caused Russian export revenues to decline, since they're heavily invested in weapons. I bet he's scared. How is Russia ever going to recover?"

"He'll figure it out," said Cummings. "Maybe Russia can get into the 'disarm, dismantle, and recycle' game and make some money."

"You think?" asked Lopez.

"Absolutely," replied Cummings. "This will be a highly competitive business, and the playing floor is level. There are enormous quantities of steel to recycle, and some people think it will take up to fifty years to get through it all, but I like to think it can be done within ten."

"That sounds ambitious," said Lopez. "As you said, there are enormous quantities. Just think of the size of your average aircraft carrier!"

"I'm a big believer in repurposing," Cummings told her, "and I think I'm going to bring some of my ideas about that to the table after lunch."

"Like using aircraft carriers as floating hospitals?"

"Yes," he smiled. Clearly some of the notes she so fastidiously kept included words out of his own mouth. "But I also think military satellites should be commercialized, transport planes should become commercial cargo planes, and nuclear submarines should become deep ocean research vessels."

As she hastily wrote *that* down, he smiled some more.

With only twenty minutes left in the break, Cummings and Lopez arose in search of lunch. They settled on muffins and coffee from a shop they found within the trade centre complex and took their lunches back to their seats with them, slipping in the door just before the afternoon session began.

"Welcome back," said the Russian leader. "Before we begin our discussion, I've been told that a very special guest will be joining us."

He did not need to explain further. Sarah materialized, ghostlike, behind Grinkov, to rapturous applause.

"Hello, world leaders," Sarah said in her voiceless voice as the din subsided. "I thank you all for coming today and for your willingness to work on disarmament with your fellow humans. It is God's will that humankind enter a new era of peace and harmony, and the first step is to *stand down* when it comes to arms."

Then her ever-changing eyes flashed and seemed to expand as the colour changed . . . blue . . . black . . . green . . . *golden*. To Cummings, it felt as if the air was being sucked out of his lungs as he watched Sarah suddenly grow in stature, density, and presence.

Then she looked right at him and said in a rich, evocative voice that reminded him of his long deceased grandmother, who he had loved well, "Collectively, the human race has been living in a culture of violence for *far* too long. What does it produce? Loss and grief on a profound level. No one wins when discord prevails."

With that, Cummings found himself standing up, as if summoned, and walking toward Sarah, who stood with Grinkov in the centre of the room. He could not have stopped himself if he'd tried.

When he arrived, his legs felt wobbly, and his heart felt as if it was going to burst from a combination of excitement and stress.

"President Cummings," said Sarah with a breath of jasmine-scented wind, which calmed him immensely, "could you please remind these people of why we are here today?"

"Absolutely, Sarah," Cummings found himself saying, his voice projecting calm that he did not feel. "I am here to talk about *death*."

There was a small gasp throughout the room. While all the people assembled knew the reason they had gathered, when Cummings actually *said* the word 'death,' a collective sense of revulsion grasped them—even while a significant number of them had been responsible for many deaths during their reigns.

"Sarah has provided me with the latest statistics on 'death by edict,'" Cummings said firmly to the crowd, though his heart wavered slightly within him. "Globally, deaths are declining, thank God. We're now down to under 250 per week, with gun-related deaths making up about 50% of that."

He stopped to clear his throat, examining the sea of faces looking coolly back at him.

Then he said, "Four heads of state have died since God's edict—from North Korea, South Sudan, Yemen, and Belarus—along with eighty-two military officers and 463 troops, all due to military initiatives taken with no regard for God's edict. Within law enforcement, 1,023 police officers died while trying to use lethal force. There have been 946 insurgent deaths, mostly in the Middle East—and I was surprised to learn that 13% of those insurgents died in my own country, the United States of America.

"In the world of crime, 612 people have died, with most deaths related to drug cartels in South America. A lesser number of deaths were tied to organized crime. Overall, there were 384 gang deaths, including twelve Hells Angels. The Hells Angels deaths were not categorized under organized crime because in each case, the would-be killers were recruits instructed to kill as part of an initiation ritual. Superior officers—enablers—died along with them. All other deaths have been due to impulsive acts of violence that immediately killed their would-be perpetrators."

Cummings looked around, eyeing the crowd, who seemed stony-faced and unmoved by the statistics.

Then he took a long, hard swallow and said, "There have also been 4,236 attempted suicides, all of which were prevented by God."

There was a sudden shift of energy in the room and some furrowed brows in the audience. By the glow on Sarah's face, he knew it was now time for him to tell his story.

"I lost a family member to suicide once," he began, paling slightly at the memory. "My son-in-law killed himself because he believed he had created a financial disaster for his family—but worse, he felt he had brought shame on us. When he took his own life, it shattered my world. I loved him. He was a good man."

He could hear the quiet buzz of whispered conversation around the room as people processed this deeply personal experience, and strangely, the buzzing voices lifted him as if on the wings of a hummingbird.

Bolstered, he continued, his voice stronger now. "All of us here today understand statesmanship, negotiation, and the art of war," he said firmly, "and until God stepped in, it was our purpose as leaders to negotiate for what we wanted, and when pushed to the wall, to *kill* for it. It was our prerogative to act in the interests of our country and to do what we thought was best."

He paused slightly before adding softly, "My son-in-law was no different. When pushed to the wall, he killed. He did what he thought was best." He swallowed hard at the memory. "I can't undo the past, all I can do is to go in good faith into the future. That is why we are here today. There have been too many backs against the wall . . . and too many families shattered because of it. We will end this desperate way of living. We will live in a way that sustains us. God has offered a second chance to humankind."

When he stopped speaking, the silence in the room was so great that all he could hear was the sound of his own beating heart. As the president of one of the greatest countries on Earth, he'd spoken countless times to masses of people . . . but he'd never spoken of such a personal matter before. He felt exposed.

Sarah reached into his mind and said, voiceless but poignant, "Samuel, you have done a great service today. You have built a bridge between cause and effect that will influence the decisions of these leaders for good."

He was humbled by her words.

Then Grinkov stepped toward him and put one hand on his shoulder. "Thank you, President Cummings," he said . . . and the room erupted into applause.

Cummings walked toward his seat self-consciously and returned to find Lopez wiping a tear from her eye.

"I didn't know about your son-in-law," she said. "I'm so sorry to hear."

He nodded his appreciation at her words and took his seat, while in front of them, Grinkov called for quiet.

"Ladies and gentlemen," Grinkov said loudly, "we have a lot of work to do. First, we will create a public relations plan to encourage the surrender of weapons. Second, we will draft a framework for global collection. Third, we will design a vetting system for contractors who will salvage metal and other components. Finally, we will finalize and ratify our plan. God willing, this world will be gun free within two years—and weapons free within ten!"

Chapter 26

Personal Guns and Personal Changes

President Cummings was standing at a podium in a conference room in the Denver Convention Center in Denver, Colorado, ready to address attendees at the Global Personal Gun Disposal Convention and to talk about how to get citizens around the world to voluntarily surrender their personal handguns.

Because the United States led the world in personal handgun ownership, he had been asked by Sarah to be the keynote speaker at the event, and so at the moment, he was fidgeting with his notes nervously, trying to key himself up for what lay ahead. He was not looking forward to speaking to a group of people who he suspected were going to be a hard sell.

"Good morning," he said as people settled into their seats. "If you have arrived at this meeting today via 'the Sarah Express,' and are not American, welcome to the United States of America."

There were some scattered chuckles at this comment, and then the room began to quiet down as the final stragglers took their seats.

When all chattering had ceased, Cummings looked around at the crowd, noting that there were less people than had been in Moscow at the conference on military weapons disarmament. This was because, unlike in the United States, many countries around the world had strict gun control laws, and so there weren't many personal handguns in their countries to surrender, voluntarily or not. In fact, many world leaders, justifiably felt that they should not have to have representation at the conference, but Sarah insisted there be at least two delegates from each country.

Echoing this sentiment, when Cummings and Lopez had met with Sarah earlier to discuss the agenda, Lopez had astutely asked, "Sarah, why are you insisting that all countries attend this conference? Some have been 'part of the solution' all along. Eritrea, for example, has completely banned firearms, and guns are severely restricted in many Asian countries, including China, India, Indonesia, and Malaysia."

"*Restricted*, yes. *Eradicated*, no," Sarah told the vice president. "The illegal gun trade knows no boundaries, Angelica."

Lopez absorbed the comment, and then sighed and said with a rueful smile, "Well, I guess a bustling gun trade goes along with a bustling drug trade, huh?"

"You're talking about the heroin and methamphetamine trade out of Asia, right?" questioned Cummings.

"Yes," said Sarah. "There are many illegal guns in this world, and we need to encourage all people, whether on the good or bad side of the law, to surrender their weapons. Guns have been the scourge of the Earth for far too long. America has the largest amount of guns per capita of any nation in the world, and subsequently, the most work to do . . . and that is why I'd really like you to kick off the conference, Samuel. As leader of the country with the most experience with gun-related killings, you can probably speak particularly eloquently as to why voluntary weapons surrender is desirable."

Cummings had expected her to ask him to do this—after all, the meeting was being held in his very own gun-loving country—but he was strangely embarrassed by the thought of standing in front of other global leaders to talk about America's gun problem. He was ashamed that little children had to go through security checks at their schools. He was mortified by how easy it was for people to get their hands on semiautomatic weapons. And he was sickened by the unchecked gun violence that had become so commonplace in his country . . . and the shattered families and communities that went with it.

Of course, he agreed to do it—there was no saying 'no' to Sarah—and now here he was, standing in a room full of expectant faces, ready to tear off the bandage and open the wound that was America's bloody history with guns.

He began his address. "I imagine you know why I am here at this meeting today," he said. "I'm here to extoll the benefits of voluntary surrender of personal handguns. I am here to try to convince you that encouraging personal disarmament should be a global effort, even while I understand that jurisdiction over personal firearms is unique to each country represented here today. It's no secret that the United States has more handguns than any other nation on Earth. In fact, at last count, we have 120 guns per 100 people . . . can you imagine? And while not *every* American owns a gun, some Americans own *many* guns—sadly, for reasons that are sometimes too evil to comprehend. I confess, I am grateful for God's edict. Not only is there finally an end to war, but there is also an end to the senseless bloodshed caused by irresponsible and illegal firearm ownership."

There was robust clapping at this comment; The phenomenon of mass shooting had touched nearly everyone in the room.

When the clapping died down, Cummings continued, "Over 175 nations allow their citizens to legally own firearms—but only three countries in the world constitutionally *guarantee* the right to own firearms. Those countries are Guatemala, Mexico, and . . . you guessed it, the United States of America. Sadly, America is the only one of these three that does not restrict gun ownership in any way. My country has the most liberal gun laws in the world—and this has led to mass shootings in schools, places of worship, grocery stores, entertainment venues . . . anywhere, really, that people gather."

At that, Chinese President Dong Yang stood up to speak.

Cummings acknowledged him with a nod. "Yes, Mr. President?" he said.

Dong Yang said, in excellent English, "In much of Asia, the need for citizens to be armed is not understood. As I'm sure you are aware, President Cummings, in direct contrast to America, my country has some of the most *restrictive* gun laws in the world. In China, we have control of our citizens, unlike in your nation. For this reason, we are opposed to a *global* initiative for personal disarmament. The move to disarm should be *local*."

"Thank you, President Dong," said Cummings, aware that he'd been attacked, if subtly, for his country's lax gun laws. He did not show annoyance, however. Instead, he said, "While I respect your point, I still strongly feel that we need to approach the problem from a global perspective. We need to ensure a singular, unified message is presented around the world to those who continue to think owning firearms is a good idea. Your participation would be invaluable in spreading this message, given the elevated position your country holds on the world economic stage."

Yang was pleased by Cummings' compliment, and he softened his stance. "You are speaking of public education, then? I can see how that may be a wise course of action," he conceded, and then he sat down, to Cummings' great relief.

Addressing the room again, Cummings said, "In terms of encouraging people to *voluntarily* surrender their guns, I know I have a mountain to climb here in America. To suggest that my citizens do so will inevitably bring out cries that their right to bear arms is being taken away . . . even though the value of owning such arms has *already* been taken away—by God. And I, for one, am happy about it."

There was a smattering of applause around the room, but it wasn't particularly fulsome this time. Some people didn't welcome God's edict in the way that Cummings did. He eyed the crowd and could tell at a glance which heads of state were having trouble accepting the new world order—and then he decided that he didn't care. He wasn't here to change minds about God's intervention; He was here to collect guns.

To his left, a tall, string bean of a man in a bowtie and nerdy glasses entered the room. Cummings had been waiting for him. He signaled for him to approach the podium, and the man did so, walking toward the president in an oddly jerky way as if his arms and legs were too gangly for him.

Cummings introduced him, saying, "Please welcome America's Secretary of Homeland Security, Terrance Wright. He will speak a little more in depth about the gun situation in the U.S., and then he will discuss what an effective gun collection initiative might look like."

There was applause.

Wright stepped up to the microphone and smiled nervously. "Thank you, Mr. President," he said respectfully, and then he addressed the audience. "Hello," he said, "and thank you for having me. Let me begin by saying that this government has no intention of limiting the right of any citizen to own a gun. The right to own a gun will endure . . . but truthfully, very few people *need* guns. The 'do not kill' edict has made them ineffective as weapons of aggression."

"But they can still be used to wound intruders!" shouted out a man's voice from the back of the room.

Cummings looked, but he could not see who had said it. He sounded angry, though.

Wright stayed cool. "Yes, I suppose so," he said, "but you can't deny how such an act would invite danger into the gun owner's *own* life."

"I may go down, but I'll take some asshole down with me!" shouted the man, who Cummings could now see. He appeared to be part of the Canadian contingent

"But you *won't* take some asshole down with you," insisted Wright. "In fact, there's a good chance will go 'down' alone. If you are a gun owner, sir, you will do yourself and your family a favour by surrendering your weapons voluntarily. The danger to yourself is far greater now than it has ever been."

Then he looked around the room at the rest of the crowd and said, "Don't get me wrong, guns still have their uses. Hunters, for example, need long guns for hunting. Farmers need guns to cull pests or put down sick animals. But *handguns* are another story. Such firearms in the wrong hands could be lethal to their owners—and this is why voluntary surrender is the clearest path to safety."

The burly, bearded man gazed back at Wright with a frown. He appeared to be thinking about it.

Wright went on, "I'm sure you are aware that preliminary planning is in place for gathering and disposing of military weaponry. While our goal today is to discuss how to manage privately owned *handguns*, private citizens often own military grade guns as well—at least in America—and so I expect overlap with the military weaponry collection efforts. It is my hope that we can take advantage of this. I see significant dovetailing in the areas of collection and recycling, and more importantly, I hope we can piggyback on the media campaign that is being created to continue to educate people about the 'do not kill' edict and the value of disarmament."

Wright's words created a buzz around the room. Audience members representing countries where weapons ownership was valued as a right were clearly worried that this was too much, too soon.

Within minutes, the somewhat agitated President of the Swiss Confederation, Andre Treichler, stood up to speak. "In my country," he said, "the Swiss Weapons Act requires not only an acquisition license for handguns but a *carrying* license as well. Nothing is left to chance. Strong regulation has served us well, and traditionally, there have been few deaths by gun in my country. In fact, while there is a shooting in the U.S.A nearly every day, in Switzerland we have less than fifty per year! The citizens of my country, while they understand they risk death if they shoot at another human, nevertheless feel that being armed is a *right*. I don't think I will be able to talk many Swiss into voluntarily surrendering their guns. It is part of our culture to be armed, just as it is part of the American culture."

Cummings sympathized with the man and was surprised to find common ground in terms of gun culture. He had not expected such passionate discourse from this militarily neutral country, but Treichler had made a compelling argument for private management, and Cummings could see he had Wright in a corner.

"I understand, but giving up a gun is not the same as giving up the right to *have* a gun," Wright countered.

He was correct, but Cummings could see he was not going to sway these people. The topic was rooted in emotion, not logic.

Soon, it was clear he had to rescue Wright, and so he stood beside the man and discreetly nudged him off the podium, saying, "Thanks, Secretary Wright. This has been valuable, and I appreciate your insight." Then he looked out at the crowd and said, "I know that my colleague and I have not moved you, and that you would prefer to handle handgun management in your own countries, in your own way. However, please bear in mind that *God* recommended the voluntary surrender of handguns—which is why it seems obvious to me that a united initiative would be beneficial to us all."

His plea was heartfelt, and reminding them of God's will had some impact. However, by the end of the conference, consensus on the issue had not been achieved. Cummings had not expected anything more. That night, he went to bed mulling the problem over. He didn't sleep well.

The following day, while drinking his first coffee of the morning at his desk in the Oval Office, he was still thinking about how to get people to surrender their firearms when Sarah unexpectedly appeared before him, wafting a gentle breeze across his cheeks as she materialized.

"Hello, Samuel," she breathed. Noting his sour expression, she said, "You look so disappointed . . . let me guess—people won't give you their guns?"

"Nope," he sighed, "even though they know they might die if they don't."

"Change never happens overnight," Sarah comforted him. "It's a process."

"What is *your* view on this, Sarah?" he asked her.

She laughed. "My view is that you will do the best you can to educate your citizens, and that is all you *can* do. Don't take their refusal personally, Samuel."

"I've been busting my hump trying to get things done, trying to please God, but I feel like I'm working in a vacuum," he said morosely. "It's really disheartening when I get all enthusiastic but can't get others on board. It feels like it's one step forward, two steps back—but at least, as far as I know, we're on target with meeting God's objectives."

"Of course you are," she said evenly. "Global disarmament is proceeding as hoped, though the issue of nuclear waste disposal is still hanging."

"I know!" Cummings said passionately. "There are some amazing new technologies for long-term safe storage, but most world leaders are hesitant to invest in them. But we have to do *something*. We need to disarm those warheads and safely store them. And safe storage is also required if we're going to use nuclear technology to generate the power America will need in the future."

"If you are considering more nuclear power facilities for America, perhaps you can work with Hana Shriver on a plan," suggested Sarah. "After all, I recall you saying that from now on, any decisions made for the good of the American people would be bipartisan . . ."

Forgetting his disappointment about the lack of consensus on handgun surrender, Cummings enthusiastically latched onto the idea of enhanced nuclear power generation, saying, "You're *right*—I'll get Hana to brainstorm with me on that. With *her* on board, any new bills we introduce won't get clogged up in the senate."

The thought of solving power generation problems for the future made him smile and stare absentmindedly into space.

Sarah laughed at his expression with a rush of rose-scented wind, and then said, "You're a dreamer, Samuel, and that is why God has a special place for you."

"Well, that's good to hear," Cummings replied. "I was worried that God would be disappointed in me. Not only could I not get consensus on how to handle collection of personal weapons, but I couldn't get my countrymen to agree on banning entertainment that glorifies war and killing. The entertainment lobby is too strong."

"Your people like a steady diet of violence and guns, it seems," remarked Sarah. "You also didn't get support for the idea of banning civilian ownership of military grade weapons."

Cummings sighed. Her words made him feel chastised.

Trying to bolster his spirits, she said, "As I mentioned earlier, Samuel, disarming the world and changing the way people think is a *process*. And you're not the only person who is discovering that change is an uphill battle. Religious leaders are struggling too. While there is progress in bringing religions closer together in their conceptualization of God, breaking the glass ceiling in houses of worship is not going quite as well. Redefining God will not change thousands of years of male-dominated religious practices overnight—yet change must come because if people flock to the new vision of God while organized religion does not, there will be repercussions," said Sarah.

"They will lose their flocks?" questioned Cummings.

"Or worse," replied Sarah. "There could be political and social repercussions so strong that it may require the intervention of your new National Security Force."

"Ah, yes," Cummings said. "Calling in the troops . . . it's the last bit of power I can wield that makes me feel manly."

"Oh? What do you mean?" asked Sarah.

"Oh, I think you know," Cummings told her, a hint of bitterness in his voice. "I'm not going to lie . . . I resent the physiological changes that came with God's edict, and I *deeply* resent that I can no longer make love to my wife. I miss the closeness Lorena and I used to have, and I think it's grossly unfair that God has removed this simple joy."

Sarah looked at him with compassion. "I understand," she said. "You are in your third month without testosterone, or sex, and it must be very hard to get used to. However, in order to reset the balance of power between men and women, the changes are a necessary step. Women have been dominated and controlled by men for millennia, and their true potential as a force for good has been thwarted. God wants their force for good to *thrive*. It might be what saves the human race from itself."

"Well, I miss being an old-fashioned man," said Cummings wistfully, "and I can't help but wonder what it will be like for the people coming up behind me to live with such a shortened reproductive timeline. Do you think it will make men obsolete? What if women don't want us as life partners after our 'juice' dries up, so to speak?"

"Then perhaps men should start thinking about what kind of life partners they *really* want," said Sarah. "Too often, men chose partners based on physical characteristics, when perhaps they should be thinking of less tangible qualities."

Cummings didn't reply. His jaw was resolutely set in an expression of frustration at the loss of this part of himself.

Understanding his pain, she focused her starlit pupils firmly on Cummings' eyes and said gently, "Tell, me Samuel, has it really been that hard to lose your sex drive and your manly hormones?"

Normally, the president wouldn't engage in this type of discussion with anybody but his wife, but he felt comfortable being honest with Sarah, and so he said matter-of-factly, "Physically, no. It doesn't hurt me not to have a sex drive. I don't mind only having to shave every four days, and I enjoy that I'm much more focused than I've ever been. However, *emotionally* . . . well, that's been much more difficult. I'm saddened that I can no longer make love with my wife—and she misses making love with *me*. Surely, being composed of women's souls, you can understand how it feels for Lorena! She had a healthy sex drive for a woman her age, and like mine, it's now disappeared. She complains that she's gaining weight, and wonders if I find her attractive. I *do*—and I want to reassure her of that—but I can't prove it to her intimately, which hurts us both."

When he finished explaining his feelings to her, for a moment, Cummings thought he saw an expression that looked like *longing* on Sarah's ever-changing visage.

Then, almost reluctantly, she said, "When God undertook this intervention, the first step in the process was to create me. As you know,

I come with the life experiences of 40 million women—and those experiences include many millions of interactions with other humans, sexual and otherwise."

"I know that, yes," said Cummings.

"Because you behold me as a woman, you expect me to understand how Lorena feels about losing her sex drive," she continued, "and I can only answer that, from an *individual* perspective, every one of my 40 million souls has loved and been loved in both physical and non-physical ways. However, I am *not* an individual; I am a collective soul, and as such, I am part of the larger purpose God has for humanity. While I remember what longing for intimacy feels like, I no longer feel *connected* to that emotional need. Instead, my greatest longing is to see God's plan for human evolution take root. In fact, in many ways, I *am* that plan."

Cummings considered her words for a moment. Because she was so unified and so personable, sometimes it was hard for him to completely comprehend that she was not a *singular* personality.

He took a moment to feel awed by her before saying, "Thank you for your candor."

"You're welcome," said Sarah. "Do you wish to ask anything else of me on this matter, or should we move toward less personal ground?"

Cummings sighed. He was still grieving for the man he'd been only a few short months ago. However, there was no going back, only forward.

And so, he changed the subject smoothly, saying, "Did you know that Gordon Blackstone has earmarked 20,000 military personnel for America's new National Security Force? He briefed me about it this morning and advised that he has also obtained military planes, ships, and other equipment—not to mention two satellites—for the NSF."

"That's certainly progress," said Sarah, "and your Army Corps of Engineers have already started some municipal water upgrade projects and are preparing plans for some coastal restoration projects."

"Yes," Cummings said. "I'm very pleased about that."

"May I suggest you speak to the Dutch prime minister about the coastal restoration?" suggested Sarah. "Given their extensive dike system, the Netherlands may have knowledge to offer."

"Brilliant," Cummings said. "We will have significant extra budget if we sell surplus transport planes, helicopters, satellites, radar, sonar, vehicles—and even military bases—to the private sector, and it is my hope we can use some of that money for coastal remediation."

"But not at the expense of your excellent ideas about repurposing!" said Sarah.

"No, certainly not," Cummings replied. "Some of my favourite ideas involve repurposing. In fact, there is already one aircraft carrier in the refurbishment process, being outfitted to be a floating hospital," he said proudly.

"I know," said Sarah, "America is leading the way by example. The effort to retrain and redeploy troops has tremendous public support. You have done your job well, Samuel."

"Well, I have to admit, it's been a challenge," said Cummings. "It's easy to redeploy such elite units as the Army Corps of Engineers and the Medical Corps, but half our forces are 'enlisted troops in boots,' young men and women with little more than high school educations. Most are on the payroll until year's end, and we plan to offer them training and further support such as health benefits after that . . . but finding meaningful employment for them is going to be tough. Other hard groups to place are pilots and military officers. COVID-19 ravaged non-essential air travel, so there is an oversupply of pilots. And *officers* . . . well, they specialize in commanding people but don't necessarily have transferrable skills. The joke is, 'an officer with nobody to command is like a border collie without a flock of sheep.'"

Sarah laughed, and then suggested, "Why don't you select promising pilots and officers to become part of the space colonization effort?"

Cummings nodded. "Yes, we should headhunt the best ones . . . and not just for placement in the space program—some should remain with the submarines, planes, and ships we're retaining for the National Security Force. And there may be opportunities for military pilots in the corporate world. There has been a run on corporate business jets since the Covid pandemic. If an entrepreneur acquired a squadron of jets for a decent price, he or she could start a very fast executive travel service—or a high end thrill ride business!"

Sarah laughed. "I admire your enthusiasm," she said, and then she fastened her unnatural gaze on his and said softly, "You must move quickly to procure the services of the proud, highly trained people you command.

Once they are taken off the payroll, loss of income and prestige could cause them great emotional harm."

"Yes, you're right, Sarah," he ventured cautiously. "Pride goeth before a fall—at least that's what the Bible says. I won't let these men and women fall. I will ask Martin to extend their health benefits, and I'll ensure they get excellent counselling."

Chapter 27

U.S. Economic Projects

It was 6:00 a.m. on a Saturday morning, and Cummings awoke earlier than he wanted to. He stumbled to the kitchen, rubbing his eyes, to get coffee. Usually Lorena was up before him, but today she was snoozing like a tired child.

He plugged in the kettle and ground some coffee for the French press they liked to prepare their coffee in. Then he yawned and stretched—and when he opened his eyes, he was startled to see Sarah standing in front of him, glowing restlessly, her energy flickering. She seemed concerned about something.

"You scared me," he said. He'd jumped slightly when he'd found her in his kitchen, and now there were coffee grounds all over the counter.

"Yes, I'm sorry about that," said Sarah. "But I needed to speak to you about a few things before you get too busy."

"It couldn't wait?" he asked, sweeping the spilled coffee into the sink.

"I suppose it *could*," said Sarah, almost off-handedly, "but I knew you'd be awake . . . and I thought we could have coffee together."

Cummings was surprised at this idea. "Do you even *drink* coffee?" he asked. "I thought you didn't need sustenance."

"Oh, I don't," said Sarah, "but it is my understanding that the act of 'having coffee' means more than simply drinking a hot beverage. I thought the drinking of coffee was really just an excuse to chat."

"Well, I can't argue with that," said Cummings. Then he asked uncertainly, "Soooo . . . Would you *like* a cup of coffee?"

"Oh, no, I never touch the stuff," said Sarah.

Confused by her answer and still cloudy with sleep, Cummings just shook his head and said, "Well, then . . . to what do I owe this pleasure?"

"I have to discuss some very important matters with you," she replied.

"So you've mentioned," he said, carefully pouring boiling water into the French press.

If she noted the slight sarcasm, she did not react to it.

"Let's start with climate change," she said, getting directly to the point. "It's the reason there is an ongoing drought in America's Southwest, and unless you come up with a way to fix that problem, America may be in for drastic changes. For example, you may have to move your farming greenbelt closer to the Great Lakes. The surrounding states and provinces won't go for exporting water, so perhaps the solution is to bring the farms north."

President Cummings yawned. It was way too early yet for him to think clearly, but he decided he would try his best.

"Moving farms is a tall order, Sarah," he said, "and thanks for bursting my bubble of optimism about the export idea." Then he took a long sip of his coffee and sighed with satisfaction.

Sarah watched his enjoyment with interest, and then suddenly, she emitted a flutter of energy that brought with it the aroma of something dark, like chocolate. Cummings intuitively understood that the many souls within her were remembering the sensation of coffee, and that she was conveying her emotions to him as best she could.

"You liked coffee once, I take it?" he asked her.

"About half of me did," she replied. "Many of me are Asian, and we were tea drinkers when we were alive on this planet."

"Ah," said Cummings. He put his cup on the counter and sat down on a tall-backed kitchen chair, feeling a little more focused. Then, fixing his eyes on her ever-shifting ones, he said, "Sarah, I'm aware that there have been high water levels from 2015 to now in the Great Lakes, but such periods don't last. Forecasts indicate there will be lower levels over time, and this will affect water levels in Lake Mead, the reservoir from which Arizona gets a big chunk of its water. So, before I do anything drastic—like offer subsidies to farmers to relocate—I'd first try building a pipeline."

"Yes, a pipeline during high water times could be used to divert excess water from Lake Michigan into Lake Powell or Lake Mead . . . but you will face opposition to the idea as I'm sure you know," said Sarah.

"I know," said Cummings, "but I'm certain that even if such a pipeline was only used sporadically—say, for three or four months every five to ten years—it would alleviate much of the problem in the Southwest."

"Except that the provinces and states that border the Great Lakes want to ensure they remain the largest fresh water reservoir on the planet," Sarah reminded him.

"They're not listening to the science," protested Cummings. "The International Joint Commission that regulates the water system sometimes *welcomes* water diversion, especially in the spring when flooding is a threat."

Just then, Lorena wandered into the kitchen, bleary eyed with sleep. She didn't remain that way long, though.

As soon as she saw Sarah, her eyes opened wide and she gasped, "Samuel! You should have warned me that we had a guest!"

Sarah laughed at Lorena. "I am hardly a guest," she said. "In fact, at the moment, I would consider myself more of an intruder. But I wanted to speak with your husband before he began his day, and so I invited myself for morning coffee with him. We are ironing out some ideas around water diversion from the Great Lakes."

"Well it's an honour to see you," said Lorena, reaching for the coffee pot and pouring herself a cup. "Samuel has mentioned a few of his ideas to me in passing, though we certainly haven't discussed them in any depth." She added some cream and asked, "What were you discussing?"

Cummings stood up to peck his wife on the cheek. "Good morning, darling," he said. "We were discussing how to use excess water and what kind of pushback we would get if we built a pipeline from Lake Michigan."

"Is this the idea about changing Lake Mead into a giant battery?" asked Lorena.

"Well, yes," said Cummings. "I'm surprised you remember that discussion." Then he looked at Sarah and said, "My idea was that during peak flow times, we could gather and store excess electrical energy to be used in *low* flow times to pump water back into the dam. This would in turn generate peak flows again and create more power."

"That is a *great* idea, Samuel," said Sarah, "but it doesn't help get water to thirsty people and crops in downriver states. For that, your pipeline idea is good."

"Yes," agreed Cummings, "though I think desalination plants will have to be part of the solution too, despite their unpopularity."

Lorena tiredly plunked herself down on one of the kitchen chairs and took a sip of her coffee. "And how does this tie in with the water infrastructure upgrades you've been talking about, Husband?" she asked.

"Well, it doesn't, really," said Cummings. "It's a separate project—so far, at least. However, such pipeline infrastructure could be useful in times of great need, I suppose."

"Desperate times might call for desperate measures—is that what you're saying?" asked Lorena.

"Yes, indeed," said Cummings. "And since you asked about the infrastructure initiatives, I can tell you that the project is well underway. In fact, the Army Corps of Engineers is already inventorying America's water systems to determine which are most in need of upgrading—under the capable direction of Herbert Sloan, of course."

"Well, that's good news," said Lorena. "Sloan seemed like a capable guy. Really smart."

"Yes," said Cummings. "He's got the whole thing well in hand. He's formed a company that is 51% owned by the federal government and 49% owned by its employees—all of whom have been pulled from the former armed forces—and he plans to bid on jobs."

"Aren't local governments a little proprietary about who does water work?" asked Lorena. "What if they shut Sloan's company out of the bidding? The federal government doesn't usually get involved in local water projects; I can't see that they'd want competition in that area."

"Well, you're right that we don't *normally* get involved, Lorena," Cummings replied, "but it's part of our economic stimulus program, so this time, it's warranted. And as for the bidding issue . . . well, I've been thinking that maybe in return for local authorities letting Sloan's new company bid on work, we could offer kickoff grants for projects that get started in the next two or three years."

"That is a great idea, Sammy," said Lorena, pecking him on the cheek. "You're on fire today . . . and it's only your first cup of coffee!"

Cummings laughed. "Thanks, hon," he said, raising his coffee cup in a 'cheers' salute.

He clinked his cup against hers, saw her playful smile, and suddenly realized how much he loved his wife—even though he could not *make* love to her anymore. *I am blessed that I found this woman,* he thought gratefully.

His sentimentality was interrupted by Sarah, who was ever on task. "Samuel," she said, "the bigger issue when it comes to water distribution is climate change. That is what is behind the drought in the first place."

"I know," Cummings said. "I've given it a lot of thought and decided that the key to creating meaningful programs and policy to deal with climate change—at least in *this* country—is to make it a bipartisan initiative. With Hana Shriver's help, I hope to develop a forty-year-plan, and perhaps create a constitutional amendment supporting it that will make it incumbent on successive governments to adhere to it."

"That's a tall order, Samuel," said Sarah, smiling in a way that made it clear she appreciated his moxie.

"Well, it has to be done. No meaningful change will happen if we keep redesigning the wheel every time there is a change of government."

"Never mind changes in government," cut in Lorena. "What about changes in the minds of people who still don't believe in climate change? And I don't mean *political* people . . . I mean members of the public. After all, these are the people who elect the politicians—and these are the people who do crazy things, like storm the capital."

"That's a good point, Lorena," said Cummings, "and I've been working with Johanna Petrie, the education secretary, on some initiatives that I think will help. I've asked her to develop a public education campaign outlining the four main truths about climate change, namely that CO_2 levels are rising, causing warmer temperatures; that human activity is contributing to this; that the unprecedented warmth is causing the ice caps to melt and sea level to rise; and, that warmer temperatures are changing weather patterns, causing more extreme weather. I'd like to see these truths become part of the curriculum in all schools, at all levels."

"It would be helpful if you could get the House and Senate to support those points before the Climate Change Conference in Shanghai next month," Sarah said.

"I intend to," replied Cummings. "I will do everything possible to make sure key members of both parties publicly acknowledge these principles—*and* their support of the Paris Agreement—even if it means berating members who voted against these undisputed scientific facts."

"Bravo!" said Lorena, clapping. "And how do you intend to hold people accountable?"

"I've been discussing some sort of carbon pricing mechanism, and I'm also looking at incentives to accelerate production and adoption of cleaner technologies. Luckily, emissions levels have been relatively low since the Covid pandemic, which gives me some wiggle room to set achievable short term carbon targets. But my long-term goal is zero emissions for America across all sectors, including industry, transportation, and energy use in buildings."

"Good for you," said Lorena, draining her coffee. "And now I'm going to take a shower and waste fifteen minutes' worth of hot water."

Cummings laughed at her flippant remark. "Don't you worry, honey!" he called as she left the kitchen. "I've got you covered!"

"No, *God* has me covered!" she called back over her shoulder as she disappeared down the hallway that led to their bedroom.

Sarah laughed, sending a rose-scented, rippling breeze around the room. "Your wife is funny," she said, "and she's also *right*."

"She *always* is," acknowledged Cummings with a sigh. "In fact, I wish she was wrong once in a while. It would make me feel better about all the mistakes *I* make!"

"Well, in my opinion, you are on the right track," said Sarah. "In fact, you have made more progress than I expected in some key areas."

Cummings perked up a little at this assessment. "Thanks," he said, "but while I think carbon pricing is the way to go, I know that if I introduce a carbon tax, it's going to make for some dicey politics. I've only just got to a place where most people accept that climate change is really happening—but, as Lorena pointed out, it's amazing how many deniers remain."

"Oh, I have *no* problem believing how many deniers are out there," said Sarah. "I am a supernatural being sent to do God's will on Earth, yet some people simply cannot comprehend my existence or accept that there is a God. To such people, both climate change *and* me are mere fairy tales."

As he stared at her radiance, Cummings wondered how anyone could ever doubt her. She was a blossom of energy, too big to be contained. When he was in her presence, he felt that all things were possible.

She interrupted his silent worship by asking, "How is the high-speed train project going?"

This brought him right back to Earth. He gathered his wits quickly and said, "I'm quite excited about that. We've made a start. Those states that are currently working on their own electric train routes have been contacted, and a pitch has been made to them to collaborate under a federal banner. There was resistance to the idea at first, but when they heard what kind of federal funding may be coming their way, they warmed up to the idea quickly."

"Has an approach to routing been developed?" asked Sarah.

"Yes, we're going coast to coast—across the country from New York to Los Angeles. At first, I was leaning toward coastal north-south routes, as populations are so high on the coasts, but then I decided if we built a mag lev line to *connect* the coasts, it would pressure the states into taking responsibility for providing technologically compatible feeder lines, which ultimately would ensure more consistent service."

"Brilliant!" said Sarah. "If you are going to unify the country and leap ahead of the rest of the world in high-speed rail infrastructure, it makes sense to build a cross-country line first."

"Yes," replied Cummings. "The project will come together faster, and ultimately, it will be more efficient as well."

Sarah smiled at Cummings. "Samuel," she said, "do you realize that the first time the U.S. built a national rail system, there weren't any cities at all on the west coast? It wasn't that long ago.

"I *know*," said Cummings. "It's hard to conceive of what America was like then. Now we have huge markets on both coasts, and the western frontier is no more . . . though I guess the *final* frontier still exists."

"Ah, yes . . . the space race," said Sarah. "Tell me, how are things going with that?"

Cummings sighed. "It's not quite as simple as I wish it was," he admitted. "In particular, I find China wants to go its own way. It sees little value in the type of global collaboration I have proposed."

Sarah's response surprised him. "There is a way forward with China, Samuel . . . but to grasp it, perhaps you need to start thinking more like a *woman*."

Cummings was not sure if she was teasing him, or why. He looked at her cautiously. "What do you mean?" he asked.

Her answer wafted through the room with a jasmine scent. "If you want to understand the Chinese leader, Samuel, just look in the mirror. Like you, Dong Yang is a proud man who is trying to figure out how to negotiate a deal that will see his country in the lead role. You are like two bulls about to butt heads."

Cummings was a little embarrassed that she had seen through his own motivations so cannily. He played dumb. "I don't get it," he said, a little sourly.

"Yes, you do," said Sarah sweetly. "While cows—*females*—gather in herds to graze cooperatively, bulls compete. It is much the same with the genders. Women tend to socialize and cooperate in ways that men do not," said Sarah. "I recommend you meet one on one with Dong Yang to collaborate and explore ways to bring your countries closer together."

"I suppose that *might* help," Cummings conceded cautiously.

"It will work," said Sarah. "And to ensure that it does, I suggest you bring with you your eleven-year-old granddaughter and Angelica Lopez—and I am suggesting to Dong Yang that he do the same."

Cummings was baffled at this request. "Why should I bring my granddaughter?"

"Because a family event is in order," said Sarah. "Bring your wife. Bring your daughter Laura, and your grandson Jayson as well, if you like. Meeting 'family to family' with Dong Yang will allow you to see the humanity in your adversary. If *all* the world recognized each other's similarities instead of focusing on each other's differences, God would not have had to intervene in human affairs!"

"Okay," Cummings said. "I get it. But I still don't understand what role Jessica is supposed to play in my meeting with the Chinese president," he said.

"Oh, I have something special in mind for your charming, intelligent granddaughter, Samuel," Sarah told him. "In fact, I would like to speak with both Jessica and Yang's daughter, Mingmei, in private before you and

Yang begin your talks. You see, I am putting these two girls in charge of a very special task."

"You want two eleven-year-old girls to lead a task force on colonizing space?" asked Cummings, confused.

"No!" laughed Sarah. "I want them to spread the word that God wants all the people of the world to be friends, and I want them to lead by example. Over social media, Jessica and Mingmei will become pen pals, and they will not only publicize their friendship, but they will demonstrate that though they come from completely different cultures, and speak different languages, they are similar at heart. Then, when they have a global following for their correspondence—in other words, when they have gone viral—they will use their platform to encourage a global 'pen pal' movement among their peers, the youth of the world. It is the children who will lead us, Samuel. They will develop the ties of love that will bless this planet."

"That is an astounding idea," said Cummings, pondering the logistics of it. "I guess the translation features on phones makes such outreach relatively simple."

"Yes," agreed Sarah, "and soon enough, they will learn each other's languages, which in time will teach people the world over to embrace other cultures without fear. It will do much to eliminate unwarranted mistrust."

"Remarkable!" said Cummings.

"In this, children can be our teachers," said Sarah. "These astute young people will also be able to speak in real terms about the effects of political decisions, and so I will also encourage Jessica and Mingmei to chat online with their counterparts around the world about political decisions made by their family members. In this way, those who make decisions will be held accountable. For example, if you, Samuel, impose a trade embargo on China, Jessica could ask Mingmei how that has affected Chinese families and learn the real truth."

Cummings blushed a little at the thought. Too often his job involved sanctioning other countries for various perceived infractions, but he rarely saw what impact such sanctions had. He could not deny that it would be powerful for him to hear from his beloved Jessica that one of her friends was suffering because of a decision he'd made.

In that uncanny way of hers, Sarah read his thoughts. "Yes, it changes the rules of the game, doesn't it?' she said.

He nodded.

Then she asked, "Are you wondering why I want Angelica to tag along?"

"Yes," he said.

"Because she is the highest ranking female in America's political structure," said Sarah, "and rank and associated honour is important to the Chinese. She is female, and she brings a voice of authority with her. She is a voice of 'sober second thought' for you, and she will keep you in line if you slip into competitive, bullish behaviour."

Cummings could not help but think of a few kicks under the table that she'd doled out when she'd noted him getting in hot water. "Yes, she is a voice of sober second thought," he admitted.

"Further, I want Angelica and her newly appointed Chinese counterpart, Chen Bao, to oversee the pen pal network Jessica and Mingmei will create," Sarah said.

Cummings was a little worried by this news; Angelica was key to the country's environmental initiatives, not to mention she was running the team managing the extremely busy 'Sarah Says' website.

"She has a lot on her plate right now," he protested. "She's heading up our environmental initiatives. I really want her to focus on that."

"She has big shoulders," said Sarah confidently. "She can assign the work to others; All she needs to do is *oversee* things."

"Fine," said Cummings reluctantly. He wasn't convinced Sarah was right but decided not to press the point.

"And finally," Sarah told him, her mysterious eyes flashing with something Cummings thought looked a lot like mirth, "I want you and the leader of China to meet at Shanghai Disneyland. I will teleport you there myself."

Cummings was not sure he'd heard her correctly. "What?" he asked. "Did I hear you correctly? You want us to meet at a *children's theme park?*"

Sarah smiled enigmatically, saying, "You two will form a much closer bond if you're with your grandchildren and are focused on building a better future for *them*. And then, after a fun-filled day with children you love, you and Dong Yang will sit down to a private dinner, and you will discuss your differences and how they have been impacted by God's intervention, over a few drinks."

"I thought we were going to talk about the space race," said Cummings.

"Oh, you *will*," said Sarah patiently, as if speaking to a child, "but there is *much* more the two of you should be considering. China is the economic powerhouse of the world; In other words, the 'sleeping dragon' that woke up. *You*, Samuel, need to have a crystal clear understanding of what China is if you want to work effectively with that country."

"I *know* what China is," said Cummings. "China is an emerging power. It is a force to be reckoned with. But it's also an archaic country with an outdated political system."

"Yes, I guess you could say that the one-party communist system of China is archaic . . . but China has 5,000 years of history to draw on and a dynastic culture with no rival. Feudal power systems still bubble beneath the surface. The Chinese, at heart, are warriors. Now, they've taken their warlike nature onto stages other than the battlefield. For example, China has made striking progress in green energy over the past decade, investing over $100 billion in renewable sources."

"That's impressive," said Cummings.

"It *is*," replied Sarah. "As well, it's invested heavily in its high tech, communication, and aviation industries as part of a conscious strategy to position itself as an economic power. And now I must ask you . . . do you see this as a challenge to America? Because, if you *don't*, you're a fool, and if you *do*, you must find a way to walk through the fire of competition so you can forge a lasting friendship with the Chinese. Kinship with them is for the good of the world. Do you understand, Samuel?"

She was right on all counts, and so all Cummings could do was say, "Thank you, Sarah, for your candid and helpful advice. I am really looking forward to some of those rides at Disneyland."

"That's the spirit," said Sarah with her trademark golden tinkle. "I knew you would be."

Cummings could only laugh, thinking of how rides in the 'magic kingdom' of Disneyland would pale in comparison to floating over the streets of Moscow with the incomparable St. Basil's Cathedral below him.

Chapter 28

A Family Meeting

It was the day before the Climate Change Conference in Shanghai, and Cummings was sitting with Lopez in the Oval Office, ironing out a few details.

"This is going to be a really different kind of conference," he remarked to his vice president.

"Yes," she said, with a sparkle in her eye, "and I'm not going to lie . . . I wish we would hold *all* our meetings in Disneyland from here on in."

Cummings laughed. "Well, it's not likely to happen," he said, "but I'll give it a chance after I see how this one goes." Then the two of them got down to work.

"How do you want to play this?" asked Lopez, eyeing the notes on her computer. "I don't think my role is overly large. I'm supposed to liaise with the newly appointed Chinese vice president, Chen Bao, and then she and I are supposed to work together to develop a 'pen pal' program for the girls to manage."

"Yes, that sounds about right," said Cummings. "I'm going to stick to the script Sarah provided me with, which is basically a statement on cooperation between our two countries, with a focus on the creation of sustainable power—and from that, I'll segue into how the youth of our respective nations should be inspiring us to end rapid climate change. Then we'll introduce Jessica and Mingmei to the reporters, and let them speak."

"Sounds good," said Angelica. "When Jessica and Mingmei are done, I'll step forward with Chen Bao and announce the pen pal initiative sparked by their instant friendship."

"I'm worried about letting the girls speak," said Cummings, every inch the concerned grandfather. "The press can be hateful."

"Don't be," said Lopez with a reassuring smile. "Sarah knows what she's doing."

The next day, as Sarah had promised, Cummings and his family—Lorena, daughter Laura, and grandchildren Jessica and Jayson—were whisked via teleportation to the Royal International Hotel Shanghai Disneyland, along with Vice President Lopez, her husband Andrew, her twin daughters, Audrey and Arianna, and assorted security and administrative staff.

Upon arrival in front of their hotel, Lorena—who was experiencing teleportation for the very first time—looked at Cummings with wide, somewhat disoriented eyes and said, "Samuel, I think that was the most incredible thing I've ever experienced!"

Cummings laughed at her awe. "I thought our honeymoon was the most incredible thing you ever experienced," he teased.

She smiled coyly. "Well it was until *now*," she joked.

The press conference was scheduled for 2:00 p.m., which gave the families lots of time to settle into their hotel rooms. Then, when they'd unpacked, it was time to introduce Jessica and Mingmei to each other. Sarah had asked Cummings to bring Jessica alone to meet her counterpart, leaving Laura and Lorena to tend to young Jayson. She asked the same of President Dong Yang and his granddaughter Mingmei, and so it was arranged that the four of them would meet in the lobby of the hotel.

Jessica was excited about the whole thing and so, after bidding her mother and grandmother goodbye, she eagerly got into the elevator with her grandfather and the two of them went downstairs. When they got to the main floor, Mingmei was waiting with Dong Yang on one of the plush brocade couches in the well-appointed lobby of the hotel. In her hands, she clutched a small stuffed toy, a delicately embroidered, red silk dragon with a white, furry ruff. She shyly extended it to Jessica as soon as she saw her.

"I am Mingmei," she said in slightly accented English.

"Is that for me?" asked Jessica, taking the toy. "Thank you. She's so *cute!*"

Mingmei blushed. "You're welcome," she said.

Jessica, who was wearing a small backpack, took it off then and said, "I have something for you as well." Reaching inside, she pulled out a little package and handed it to Mingmei.

Mingmei immediately opened the box. Inside were three varieties of flavoured lip gloss—strawberry, grape, and cherry blossom.

"That one made me think of you," said Jessica, pointing to the cherry blossom one.

"Thank you!" squealed Mingmei. "It's my favourite!"

It was clear after this exchange of gifts that the girls were going to be fast friends. Their grandfathers, seeing this, felt comfortable in taking them to a small internet café just down the street from the hotel for an informal lunch. There, Jessica and Mingmei dined on American style grilled cheese sandwiches and really got to know one another. There was no mistaking their joy in each another's company.

They were back in their rooms by 1:30, and at 2:00 p.m. sharp, both families assembled in front of the hotel, where a podium, speakers, and microphones had been set up. Security was omnipresent, but the general mood was not tense; After all, no one could shoot anyone anymore.

The two presidents were up first. Cummings ably conveyed in English to the press that today's event was to be the first of many meetings he would have with the Chinese president, as their two granddaughters were becoming close friends. Dong Yang did the same, in Chinese. They spoke briefly about respective sustainable resource management initiatives in each country, and the spirit of cooperation they wanted to cultivate.

And then Cummings ended by saying, "This is an historic day for both our nations, and I welcome China as a friend as we move forward into this new future that God has in store for us."

There was loud clapping from the assembled audience and press. Then the two men shook hands and stepped aside to let Jessica and Mingmei get up to speak.

The two girls were nervous at first. Behind the podium, Cummings saw Jessica discreetly reach for her mother's hand, but with a few whispered words, Laura encouraged her daughter to stand strong and be confident. There was a global media presence at the event, and Cummings recognized American NBC reporter Taylor Wisniewski right away. Hoping to spare his granddaughter any questions that were too pointed, he indicated to Wisniewski that he would allow the girls to take his question.

Wisniewski nodded his thanks and promptly asked, "Jessica, what is the most interesting thing about being in China with your grandfather?"

Jessica fielded the question like a pro. She replied, "I am excited that people have finally started asking us kids what kind of world *we* want to live in. Just about every day, I hear my grandfather making all kinds of plans for America, and I know he's doing good for our country, but the truth is he's *old* . . . and he won't be here to see what happens with his plans. So I think young people need to be heard because we're the ones who will be around to take up where the older people left off. That's why I'm so glad Sarah stepped in to help us be heard."

Cummings flinched at being referred to as 'old,' but when Lorena, who was standing beside him with her hand on his arm, smiled up at him with reassurance, he felt instantly better.

"Mingmei," asked Wisniewski, "what is the most interesting part about meeting Jessica and being part of this event today?"

Mingmei, who was every bit as smart as Jessica, answered, "I am very interested in environmental initiatives, and my heroine is Greta Thunberg. She is young like me, and she is not afraid to stand up to bullies and speak her mind. I hope that this meeting, and the attention Jessica and I have today, will bring awareness to protecting our environment and make this world stand up to people who pretend climate change doesn't exist just so they can continue making money."

Wisniewski seemed quite impressed by her answer. "Thank you, Mingmei," he said.

Then both girls giggled and Jessica added, "We're also very excited about going on some rides at Disneyland!"

Cummings was so proud of both girls. When he saw how well they handled the press, it almost brought him to tears. At first, when Sarah had proposed her plan, he had been nervous about exposing them to media 'vultures,' but at Sarah's request, he curbed his protective instincts. Naturally, they'd stolen the show.

That evening, Cummings and Dong sat down alone for a private Chinese feast featuring Shanghai's signature dish, xiao long bao (delicate pork-filled soup dumplings), as well as steamed crab, smoked fish slices,

Beggar's Chicken (a stuffed, marinated chicken sealed tight in lotus leaves and baked for up to six hours), and other delicacies.

"I am so proud of our girls," said Dong.

"Yes, they performed better than us!" laughed Cummings.

"I believe that Sarah is right when she says the children will lead us," observed Dong humbly.

"So do I," replied Cummings as he picked up a piece of the chicken with his chopsticks and put it in his mouth. After savoring it, he said enthusiastically, "Delicious!"

"Thank you," said the Chinese president. "Regional cooking in China varies from province to province, but it is very tasty no matter where you go."

"I have no doubt," replied Cummings, taking another piece and chewing thoughtfully.

"Does American cooking vary from state to state?" asked Dong Yang politely.

"Yes," replied Cummings, "though perhaps not as broadly as in China. But there are certainly state specialties. Louisiana, for example, has its Creole cooking, which was influenced by the French. The way I understand it, early seventeenth-century French settlers made use of traditional Indigenous herbs, a Spanish spice or two, and voilà—within a few years, Louisiana had legendary cuisine."

Dong Yang laughed. "Just like that!" he said.

"Well, maybe not quite that quickly," conceded Cummings with a grin.

Dong grinned back. "You are amusing, Samuel," he said. "I hope we can become friends."

"I do too," said Cummings, sitting back in his chair and wiping his mouth, convinced that if he took even one more bite, he would explode. Then he looked speculatively at the Chinese leader and asked, "Do you mind if I ask you a rather pointed question?"

"I have nothing to hide," said President Dong. "Ask away."

"Okay then," said Cummings, "given the communist stance on God—that there isn't one—how have you come to terms with the proof of God's existence?"

Dong laughed ruefully. "I admit that I am still grappling with that," he said. "It is clear God exists, and my people are demanding a return to the spirituality we denounced so long ago. My advisers tell me we should create some general houses of worship to accommodate public demand. They say our people insist that shared, communal worship will balance out the damage to our souls that has been created by a cultural commitment to the production of material goods."

Cummings, noting resignation in Dong's response, remarked, "This doesn't seem to surprise you."

"No," replied Dong. "Despite China's official communist stance since the 1949 War of Liberation—the Communist Revolution—worship and faith have quietly continued to take place. The faithful remain faithful. They've just been very quiet about it. And, in general, the state turns a blind eye."

"I see," said Cummings, thinking China's 'blind eye' did not seem to extend to the persecution of the Falun Gong practitioners in China—and the subsequent illegal organ harvesting. However, in the spirit of cultivating harmony, he decided not to bring it up.

"Communism has a social focus," mused Dong, "but apparently a government enforced social focus doesn't compare to one driven by God. Spirit is what drives individuals to willingly help other people, not government directives. In this matter, China has much to learn."

President Cummings had similar thoughts. "My country is largely Christian," said Cummings, "and Christ taught people to treat others as they wanted to be treated. That is the essence of the 'social focus' you speak of. However, despite paying lip service to this ideal, America guards its wealth jealously."

"Yes," said Dong with a sly smile, "and can I be so bold as to say that you are also the greediest nation on the planet?"

While Cummings did not like to hear such words from the lips of his rival, he had to admit it was true. "Yes," he said reluctantly, "you can be so bold. If undeveloped countries consumed at the same rate as the U.S., four complete planets the size of the Earth would be required. People who think that they have a right to such a life are quite mistaken."

"You are correct," said Dong. "5% of the world's population—Americans—consumes 24% of the world's energy. It is unsustainable."

"My country has forgotten the Golden Rule," Cummings said sadly, "but I recognize that our days of bullying others with military or economic might to get what we want are fading. The way forward is through cooperation and trust."

"Indeed," said Dong, adding, "in that, China has grown in the past decade. Through cultural exchange, we have come out of our shell as a nation."

"Yes, and you've grown to be a formidable economic power as well," agreed Cummings.

"This is true," Dong said, relaxing back into his chair and sipping on a small cup of fragrant green tea. "Strangely, however, as we open up to the world, the United States has seemed to withdraw in recent years. But now I sense that you want your country to return to the international stage. I welcome this change."

President Cummings replied, "You are absolutely correct, Mr. President. I *do* want the United States to step up internationally—but in a different way than in the past. I would like my country to take every opportunity to work with other nations to improve this planet. Human beings have overpopulated Earth and are overconsuming its resources. We need all nations to come together to create sustainable futures for Jessica, Mingmei, and all the future generations."

The Chinese president smiled at the thought of the two bright young girls. "I agree," he said.

"I also want to see hatred and intolerance reduced across the globe . . . but, unfortunately, *way* too many people—including in my own country—have those flaws." Then he let out a big sigh. "Sometimes, I admire the one-party system of China. With power at the federal level consolidated, meaningful change becomes much easier."

Dong laughed loudly. "Your political system is most definitely difficult to navigate," he said, "and often your massive corporations seem to compete with your own government! However, Samuel—may I call you Samuel?—I'm not sure a one-party system would make things easier. While having no opposition means I can move faster with decision making, when something backfires, all the blame is on my head."

"Ah, yes," mused Cummings. "With great power comes great responsibility, I guess."

Dong laughed. "The 'Peter Parker principle.' From *Spiderman*."

"Is that where the saying comes from?" asked Cummings.

"Yes," said Dong, and then he looked at Cummings very seriously. "China is not a very forgiving country, Samuel. If I mess up, consequences can be dire . . . in fact, until Sarah intervened, failure might have meant my *life*."

The words hung in the air for a moment, and then suddenly and discreetly, an army of waiters quietly swooped in to clear away the remains of their meal. The table top was sparkling within seconds, and then the head waiter, a gentleman in a fancy red brocade jacket, produced a bottle of brandy, Cognac from southwestern France. Without saying a word, the man poured the golden beverage into glasses and then silently stepped back, awaiting further instruction.

"Xiè xiè," said Cummings, taking a sip. His polite nod to the waiter dismissed the man.

"You have a good accent," remarked Dong at Cummings' attempt at Mandarin Chinese.

"Well, 'thank you' is the only word I know," said Cummings.

Dong laughed. "Bravo," he said.

Cummings took another sip of the brandy. "I admire your country very much," he said, savoring the delightful beverage. "You are winning the race, my friend. China's culture of hard work, and its massive population, guarantee that it will soon have the largest economy in the world, if it doesn't already. America can't keep pace."

"Yes," agreed Dong. "The 'Sleeping Dragon' sleeps no more. But you must be feeling an infusion of economic might from the dissolution of your military, no?"

"Yes," agreed Cummings. "The dissolution of our military industrial complex is a blessing in disguise. From a budget standpoint, it has created a disruption in our economy, particularly our exports, but in terms of spending, we can refocus our economy on infrastructure and other projects that alleviate the effects of climate change."

"This is good news, my friend," said Dong. "It is good that you can attend to such things without going further into debt."

"You're right about that," replied Cummings. "We're $30 trillion in debt already, and it pains me to think my generation is leaving such a legacy. I worry that our economy will collapse, and that the world will shift away from the U.S. dollar as reserve currency."

The Chinese leader responded directly to Cummings' concern. "China has no interest in moving to a new reserve currency," he said. "We hold more American dollars than any other nation, and not only would we like those dollars to retain their value, but we don't want to face the economic and social upheaval a change of reserve currency would cause."

"Well, that's a relief," said Cummings.

"There are a lot of things at play that you may not have considered," said Dong. "For example, in my view, economic tension between our two countries is not really between our respective governments but more between your multinational corporations and our state-owned ones."

"Yes," said Cummings. "That's a good point. My country faces similar tension with the European Union, which also has large, state-owned corporations."

"The primary allegiance of your multinational corporations is to their *business*—not their country," said Dong. "This is evident in the spate of data leaks you've experienced recently." Then he looked slyly at Cummings and added, "Your government should stop entrusting personal information to multinational corporations. You should invest in some state-owned, Chinese software companies. Our technology is much more secure."

President Cummings smiled wryly. "It would take a lot more brandy to get me to that point," he said with a small laugh. "However, you do have a point. As much as I like free enterprise, businesses abuse their power on a regular basis. I can barely watch television in my country due to the total dishonesty of advertisements."

"Lies in advertising? Who would have ever thought that could happen?" teased Dong.

"Very funny," laughed Cummings.

Dong seemed to be enjoying his drink. He relaxed into his chair with an easy smile on his face. "We are getting to know one another," he said, "and I think we have much in common."

"I agree," said Cummings, warming to the man. "In fact, there is something specific I want to discuss with you."

"By all means," said Dong.

Pleased to have a sympathetic ear, Cummings said, "For years, the southwest part of my country has suffered from prolonged drought. I am thinking of approving a major water diversion project as part of the solution. You are currently completing a massive water diversion project yourself. Can you give me any advice?"

The smile left Dong's face, and he almost cringed at the question. "*Retirement* comes to mind," he said uneasily. "There is no easy way to execute such a project. Even without climate change in the mix, moving massive volumes of water from one part of a country to another could have effects that are difficult to predict . . . and the citizens affected by your decisions will be against you. We had to relocate more than a million people while building our South-to-North Water Diversion Project in China—which I'm sure you know is the largest of its kind ever undertaken—and that decision will haunt me for the rest of my life."

Cummings stared morosely at his counterpart. "Unfortunately, I think I *have* to go ahead with this water diversion project," he said with a sigh. "I'm running out of options."

"I understand," said Dong. "Fresh water is destined to become an increasingly fractious issue between, and within, countries. Those who have it don't want to share it, and those who *don't* have it will stop at nothing to get it. So it is in China . . . and so it is in *your* country."

Cummings frowned and drained his glass. "I was hoping you could give me a magic pill or something."

"I'm afraid not," said Dong. "Just a magic headache."

Then Cummings said, "Please tell me it was less of a headache to implement high-speed train service because that's the other big project we're looking at. We want a cross-country mag lev line."

The Chinese president laughed. "Yes," he said, "a high-speed train network will be less of a headache . . . but it will still hurt a little."

Cummings furrowed his brows. "Damn," he said. "I thought I could get off scot-free." Then he looked at the Chinese leader and asked, "How do you feel about sharing some of what you've learned about mag lev technology with me?"

"I would be happy to do so, Samuel," said Dong. "In fact, I was hoping you would be willing to partner with China to create this cross-country line—though this time around, my people will want to provide more than just manual labour."

"I understand," said Cummings, thinking of the 20,000 or so Chinese workers whose backbreaking work created America's Transcontinental

Railroad. "However, I'm a little concerned about allowing state-owned Chinese companies to compete for design and construction projects. It might piss some people off."

"Not if we structure a deal that involves American manufacturing and technology," said Dong.

"That is definitely something to follow up on," Cummings replied thoughtfully, adding cautiously, ". . . and if we can partner successfully in that, perhaps we could also partner successfully in colonizing space. What do you think?"

The Chinese president had been expecting this question and so he didn't hesitate when he answered, "China is willing to consider partners in its space program, but I am not a fan of the global project idea. I think our countries should first approach Russia to discuss the possibility of working together on this, and if we agree to a partnership, *then* we should address how to involve other nations, not to mention how we will work with the private sector."

"That works for me" said President Cummings, slugging back the rest of his drink.

The bottle was now empty, and like some sort of Chinese ghost, the waiter in the red brocade coat appeared out of nowhere with another. He quickly refilled both men's glasses, and then disappeared again as if on a puff of wind.

Cummings took a long sip. "Years ago," he said, "when I was as buzzed on alcohol as I am now, I would find a beautiful woman, hope she was as drunk as I was, and bed her if she allowed it." Then, with exaggerated woe, he added, "Those days are gone now, my friend . . . and with the biological changes, I wonder how long it will be before I can no longer open a jar of dill pickles by myself!"

"That's not a problem for me, because we don't eat many dill pickles here in China," Dong laughed. Then he took on a more serious tone. "I know you are not really speaking of pickles, Samuel," he said, "and all I can say is that the loss of sexuality is difficult for *all* humans. It will change how men and women relate to each other over time, and I expect there will be a substantial increase in the relative power and influence of women. And maybe it's time for the world to change in this way."

"Our granddaughters will be some of the last humans to go through early puberty," Cummings mused, "and in some ways, I wish this wasn't so."

"Yes," agreed Dong. "I suspect it will give us a few more things to worry about."

At that, Cummings yawned. The meeting had come to a natural end, and it was time to turn in for the night. Tomorrow, both men would have a busy day at the theme park with their families.

Meanwhile, as the two men parted ways, in the bridal suite of the luxury hotel in which Cummings and his entourage were staying, two eleven-year-old girls were still wide awake and laughing uproariously. True to her word, while the two presidents had been enjoying dinner and conversation, Sarah had met with Jessica and Mingmei to ensure they understood her plans for them and to answer their every question.

The girls were thrilled to be in the hotel's luxury bridal suite and were over the moon at the chance to meet Sarah. Between them, they put Sarah through her paces.

Jessica began the interrogation. "Sarah," she said, "I know you are made up of 40 million souls, but when you are *you*, I mean one of you at a time, what do you *look* like?"

To answer, Sarah stopped her ever-shifting face in mid-rotation and presented to the girls a single identity, in this case, a Chinese woman of approximately thirty years of age. "This is *one* of me," she said to Jessica. "Right now, I am Ling. I died a thousand years ago, and this is what I looked like when I was alive. In my natural energetic home, often called Heaven, I *could* take this form—or I could take the form of any of the women whose energy resides within me. However, I usually exist without form. It is sort of like being invisible."

Mingmei jumped all over that response. "But you are so *pretty*," she said. "Why would you not want to show your face?"

Sarah's faces began their flickering rotation again as she responded, "There is no reason for souls to take on an appearance in Heaven," she said. "We are all pure, intelligent energy, at one with God and the universe, and so there is no reason to express individuality through physical form."

Jessica took her turn. "If you are pure energy, do you see or hear things the way Mingmei and I do?"

"No," replied Sarah, "not in the *way* that you do . . . but I do hear and see in a different, more heightened way."

Mingmei asked the next question. "Have you ever seen or heard God, Sarah?"

Sarah smiled, a flutter of tinkling jasmine scent. "Because I am part of God, whatever God sees, or hears, or thinks is what *I* see, or hear, or think. This will happen to every soul upon its earthly death, providing that soul returns to God."

"Do you remember who you were when you return to God?" asked Jessica.

"In a way," said Sarah. "Upon returning to God, we retain everything we personally saw or heard during our lives in a memory bank of sorts. Then, when we get to Heaven, we can access not only our own knowledge but knowledge gained by every other soul as well."

"Do you keep your senses in Heaven?" asked Mingmei.

"Yes and no," replied Sarah. "Because we don't reside in flesh bodies, we don't have eyes and ears . . . but in our energetic forms, our senses of sight and hearing are actually much more vivid than they were when we were mortal."

"How do people talk to each other in Heaven if they don't have mouths?" asked Jessica.

Sarah had to laugh at that question. She thought carefully about her answer before responding, and finally said, "I guess you could say that the compiled energy of all the souls in Heaven is like a collage of sorts . . . sort of like what *I* am, only on a much larger scale. I am composed of 40 million souls, and as a compilation, the energy inside me functions as one unit. We don't have to individually agree about things. We are *one*."

Jessica seemed satisfied with that answer, and quickly followed it with another question, "Were you . . . I mean, *all* of you . . . scared when you found yourself in Heaven with billions of invisible souls? I feel uncomfortable just going to a new school and meeting twenty-five people my own age who I can actually see and hear! I'm a little afraid of the idea of dying."

"No," Sarah said. "It is hard to explain, but all 40 million times that I arrived in Heaven, I felt nothing but warm, loving acceptance by God and every soul there. I felt at one with the universe."

"Well, that's good," said Jessica, wanting to believe her but clearly still a little scared of the idea of death.

Mingmei cut in. "I have my laptop," she said. "Let's look up 'Heaven.'"

She immediately fired it up, and in no time, the girls found themselves on the Tencent platform—the equivalent of YouTube in the United States. After looking up a few explanations of Heaven, and having Sarah debunk them, the rabbit hole of endless entertainment soon enveloped them, and before long, they were laughing at some Chinese sitcoms, giggling away together as if they'd known each other for years. The girls even passed up Sarah's offer to translate the shows into English for Jessica, because Mingmei was doing such a good job translating, and any mistakes she made just added to the giddy fun.

Soon they were hungry, and so they ordered snacks from room service. When Mingmei tucked into a bowl of noodles, Jessica marveled at her dexterity with chopsticks. She got her friend to show her how to use them, and though it took the better part of an hour, she managed to get most of her own noodles into her mouth. After that, they ordered hamburgers, which were much easier to eat—at least for Jessica.

It was a late night for the two girls, who didn't get to sleep until almost midnight, and so the next morning, when they were roused by Sarah, they were bleary eyed and a little cranky. They joined their families in a special dining room that had been booked for the two families, still yawning and rubbing their eyes.

"Good morning," said Cummings, greeting his tired granddaughter, "are you ready for a fun day at Disneyland?"

Instantly, she perked up. "Oh, I am so excited about that!" she said.

The day at Disneyland was joyous, and it was full of adventurous rides and junk food. Dong Yang brought his wife, Li Na, and this gentle, gracious soul easily hit it off with Lorena. Then, as the women rode herd on Jayson, the two presidents tried to keep up with Jessica and Mingmei, whose energy and courage knew no bounds.

As they watched their granddaughters screaming with joy on one of the rides, Cummings thought, *This is hope for the future of the world.* He smiled.

Chapter 29

A New Russian President

The trip to China was a success on many levels. Cummings couldn't believe how well not only he and Dong Yang had gotten on, but their families as well. It touched him deeply in a place in his heart he rarely accessed. He wondered sometimes why it was so hard to admit to having that hidden, softer side . . . but like most men of his generation, he accepted that false bravado was the armor that must be worn when facing the world. Secretly, though, he wondered . . . *Am I getting softer because my hormones have shifted due to God's intervention?*

"What do you think about this new, more sensitive me?" he'd asked Lorena, teasing a little but also prodding to see if she thought the hormonal changes had made him less masculine.

"I think all that matters is that you love and are loved in return," she'd replied sagely.

He'd had to be content with that because, soft or not, he had a country to run.

When his conversation with Lorena was over, he headed to the Oval Office to review some statistics with Bradley Northrup. As Sarah had requested, Northrup had set up a long-term study on the psychological effects of human physiological changes, and he was keeping tabs on all the other changes as well, from social to economic ones. Twice a week, Cummings went over these reports with his Chief of Staff, keeping his eye on what was or was not working for the country he governed.

Now, he sat on one of the Oval Office couches across from Northrup, and they both gazed intently at their computers. Northrup had just finished showing Cummings a spreadsheet on his computer summarizing and categorizing all deaths directly resulting from God's 'do not kill' edict, and Cummings was now examining a spreadsheet on his own computer analyzing halted suicide attempts.

"Deaths due to attempted killing are declining rapidly," Northrup said. "That's good news. It's shows that people are getting the message."

"It's even better news that attempted suicides are way down," said Cummings. "Quite frankly, I expected people to become . . . well, *depressed*, I guess . . . when the physiological changes took effect. I thought that suicide attempts might increase."

Northrup knew what Cummings was saying; He'd felt a little down about the changes himself. When he studied his image in the mirror, to his eyes, he looked somehow smaller, less robust. He wondered if others noticed too. It made him feel ashamed.

Cummings, unaware of Northrup's line of thought, continued, "On the other hand, social media makes being 'sexy' a competition. Some people can't stand the pressure, and so maybe they're relieved at the way things are going."

"Could be," said Northrup, keeping his thoughts to himself. "It's probably a relief for some that sexuality is out of the equation."

Just then, there was a quick knock on the door.

"Come in," said Cummings, and Angelica Lopez poked her head into the room.

"You wanted to meet us at nine o'clock, right?" asked Lopez.

"Yes, and you're right on time," said Cummings.

She gave him a big smile and entered the room with Norman Feldman, Gordon Blackstone, and Hana Shriver hot on her heels. Lopez was carrying a big carafe of coffee, and Feldman held a box of donuts.

"We came with goodies," she said as she began pouring coffee into paper cups handed to her by Hana Shriver.

"Thanks," said Cummings, gratefully accepting a coffee and donut from his vice president. He took a big bite of his Boston cream. "Yum," he said with great satisfaction. "Thanks, Angelica. I'm sure it was you who spearheaded this effort."

She laughed. "You know how I love donuts," she said.

After popping the last piece into his mouth and washing it down with a sip of coffee, Cummings began the meeting. "Thanks for coming," he said. "I thought we should touch base on how our programs are working to clean up any loopholes or overlaps we might find. Are you all okay with that?"

There were nods of understanding around the room.

"It's probably easiest to do a quick program by program update," he suggested, and then he looked at his defence secretary and said, "Gordon, why don't you start with an update on the military repatriation."

"Certainly, Chief," said Blackstone. "I've got lots of good news. Repatriation initiatives are working smoothly. Nearly 10% of our military personnel have signaled an intention to retire at the end of the year, and another 15% are excellent candidates for either working with Sloan's group on water projects, retraining to become part of the United Space Exchange, or redeploying into public or private enterprise—along with their equipment. We've also targeted 15% of repatriated troops to become part of the National Security Force."

"That's impressive," said Cummings.

"Thank you, Sir," replied Blackstone, "but the best news of all is fully 80% of repatriated personnel are enrolled in at least one of the nine-month training programs. It indicates that, rather than disgruntlement, returning military personnel seem to be embracing these changes."

"I'm so proud of our service men and women," said Cummings. "Anything else of note?"

"Not without getting into a level of detail not appropriate for this meeting," said Blackstone. "Suffice it to say, things are going well, perhaps even better than expected."

"Thanks, Gordon," said Cummings, before turning to Lopez. "Ms. Vice President," he said to her, "you're our environmental czar . . . tell us what's going on with your portfolio."

"Certainly, Samuel," she said with a smile. "The Greenup/Cleanup Plan is well underway. I have been so fortunate to have Mia Farnese on board to help with ecological analysis. She's really interested in sustainability and has focused on the idea of using excess solar and wind power to pump water into Lake Mead."

"Can you elaborate?" asked Feldman, who'd been busy on his computer until then.

"Yes, of course," said Lopez. "The idea is to use excess solar and wind power to pump water into Lake Mead so that when wind and solar supplies *drop,* this water can in turn be used to generate electricity. She's got a study underway to assess this plan for viability, and it seems like a really great option."

"I like it," said Feldman. "It makes economic sense."

"She's also doing feasibility studies on shoring up certain areas of the coastline on the Eastern seaboard," said Lopez. She looked at Cummings as she added, "I'm sure you're aware that one project in California is already underway, thanks to Grieves and a team made up of redeployed Army Corps members, who are doing the bulk of the structural work."

"I'm aware," Cummings said. "It's fantastic. Anything else?"

"Yes," said Lopez. "Herbert Sloan is going gangbusters on America's Clean Water Initiative. Right now, his group is busy inventorying water upgrade projects, and he's making contacts so his unit can bid on upcoming jobs. Everybody is eager to know how the federal government is going to participate financially, so you may want Norman to sit down with Herbert to work out a preliminary budget."

Cummings nodded and looked at his treasury secretary. "What do you say, Norman?" he asked.

"Not a problem," replied Feldman. "I'll schedule a meeting with him and get on it as soon as possible."

"Great," said Cummings, turning his attention back to Lopez. He asked, "And last but not least, any news with the mag lev line we want to develop?"

She frowned a little, a sign that it wasn't going quite as well as she hoped. "At your suggestion, I reached out to Chen Bao to see what kind of expertise we could get from China to help us with this project, and she's graciously arranged a comprehensive tour of China's new mag lev lines . . . but other than that, I have nothing new to report with stateside reception, except that the idea seems to be gaining traction."

"Well, that's a start," said the president, "and it's probably good that we go slow getting the train off the ground . . ."

Everyone laughed at the play on words, including Cummings.

Then he finished with, ". . . because the prickly issue of power generation is that it is no joke. We need to start looking at expanding nuclear power generation in this country, but that's not a popular idea." He looked over at Hana Shriver. "Tell me," he said, "have you had any success finding new technologies for dealing with nuclear waste?"

"Yes and no, Samuel," said the refined and ladylike majority senate leader. "I've looked at a couple of emerging technologies. One is called 'diamond nuclear voltaic.' It converts nuclear waste into electricity using microscopic diamonds. The diamonds have extremely good heat conductance, which means they move heat away from the radioactive isotopes so quickly the transaction generates electricity. According to preliminary reports, a battery powered by nuclear waste could keep a spaceship or hospital operate for 28,000 years without needing to be recharged or replaced—or so its developers claim."

"Wow!" said Lopez. "We probably have enough nuclear waste in the world to keep us all going for a million years!" she said. "It reminds me of how natural gas was considered 'waste' until someone found a use for it."

"I hope you're encouraging these innovators with the prospect of a government contract," said Cummings.

"Well yes, I am," replied Hana with a rueful smile. "Unfortunately, this technology would use only a fraction of the nuclear waste currently *stored*, let alone *generated*, on the planet. In our country alone, spent fuel from electricity generating nuclear reactors has left us with about 80,000 metric tonnes of used, spent fuel stored at more than seventy-five sites in thirty-five states around the country."

"What about defence waste?" asked Blackstone.

"There are also many hundreds of thousands of cubic meters of defence waste—accumulated since the earliest days of the Manhattan Project—and it's highly radioactive," said Shriver. "This waste is stored in large metal tanks at the Savannah River site in South Carolina, the Hanford site in Washington State, the Idaho National Laboratory in Idaho, and the Nuclear Fuel Services site in New York State. Unfortunately, the tanks in Hanford and Savannah River are way beyond their design lifetimes, so they're corroding and some have leaked."

"The radioactive fluid is being released to the environment?" asked Lopez in dismay.

"Yes," replied Shriver. "The rates are not high, but it's discouraging to think that that after decades of effort, we have not yet developed a successful plan for handling nuclear waste. Deep burial—encasing it in glass underground or possibly in sedimentary rocks beneath the ocean—still seems to be a necessary component of long-term planning unless we can find a safe way to launch it at the sun."

"How do we dispose of the waste from electricity generation?" asked Lopez.

"In some cases, the used fuel is kept in pools," returned Shriver, "but those pools have filled, and they weren't meant for extended storage. We should be trying to get that fuel into what are called dry casks: obelisks concrete and metal. Spent fuel from commercial power plants is less than from the defence industry, but the radioactivity is twenty to thirty times greater. It has to be dealt with."

"I'll say," said Lopez.

"I know 80,000 metric tonnes sounds like a lot," Shriver said, "but compared to the gigatonnes of carbon emitted by burning fossil fuels, its relatively small . . . and at the moment, it's well-contained."

Cummings looked grave as she concluded her report. "Well," he said, "that's a little discouraging. But keep working on it."

Shriver gave a curt nod. "I intend to," she replied.

Then Cummings looked around the room. "My turn," he told them. When all eyes were on him, he said, "Most of you know I was recently in China, and that I met with Chinese President Dong Yang. The meeting was held largely to see if we could get in agreement about environmental concerns, but of course, we talked about other things, including the space program as well."

"Yes," said Shriver with interest. "I saw coverage of your meeting on the news. I was impressed with the pen pal program your two granddaughters are spearheading. They show a lot of initiative for such young people."

"Yes, they do, Hana," said Cummings proudly, "and I have to admit, I'm pretty pleased about it. Of course, it was Sarah's doing."

"She knew they would find common ground," said Shriver.

"And they did, right away," said Cummings, "as I did with Dong Yang. We found we had much more to unite us than separate us as the saying goes . . ." Then his expression became a little more serious as he added, "Unfortunately, we still don't quite see eye to eye on the space program. He insists that if we want China to cooperate with the United Space Exchange, we must meet with Russia to discuss a three-way co-lead."

"Oh, interesting!" remarked Lopez. "They have some fine technology to share . . . but I'd like to know where the Russians stand on the space race, given their economic problems."

"So would I," said Cummings.

Blackstone interjected, "Did you discuss satellite technology as well?" Ever the military strategist, he was concerned about national security as the Chinese continued to make their mark in space.

"Not this trip," Cummings responded, "but don't worry—it's on my radar. Ultimately, I told Dong Yang that this was a reasonable suggestion, and I agreed to meet with Sergei Grinkov—who has just won the presidential election in Russia, by the way—to discuss the issue."

There was silence and some looks of surprise around the room.

Finally, Feldman spoke. "Well, that's great, Samuel," he said, "though a bit unexpected. What can he possibly have to offer until he gets his cabinet in place?"

"Well, that's just it, Norman," said Cummings. "It's up to me to *tell* him, isn't it? And in kind, it's up to me to help him get his country organized and back on its feet. Let's just call it a mutual exchange of services."

"Gotcha," said Feldman as he started to fiddle on his computer again. Then he added, "Sounds like Dong Yang is a pretty cagey guy."

"Not as cagey as you, Norman," said Cummings. "In fact, he's being pretty open. He offered to let an American delegation tour the Chinese high-speed rail facilities to give us a leg up as we move forward with the coast to coast mag lev line." Then he looked at Lopez. "It sounds like he followed through, right?"

"Yes, Chen Bao and I have set a date," she replied.

Cummings continued, "And when I mentioned my thoughts about water diversion from Lake Michigan, he offered to let us tour some Chinese water diversion projects."

"Water diversion?" asked Feldman. "Are you sure you want to go there?"

"It's no secret I'm looking at it with some seriousness," replied Cummings. "The southwest states are desperate for water."

"But the states and provinces bordering the Great Lakes don't want to share," said Feldman. "In fact, the international treaty governing Great Lakes water use specifically *bans* diversion, except for very limited local use."

"Perhaps the treaty can be renegotiated," said Cummings. "If a new deal is ratified that leaves total control of how much water is diverted in any given year—if any—to the Great Lakes Authority, perhaps it won't seem so sacrosanct."

"Maybe," said Feldman, "but even though the people between Lake Michigan and Lake Mead could use the construction jobs, and it makes economic sense to build one, they'll never do it because there is an ever-growing public resistance to new pipelines."

"At least the new pipeline would not be carrying oil or gas that could cause environmental damage," said Lopez.

"That might make the pipeline idea more attractive to *some*," agreed Cummings, "but I'm not sure it makes it attractive enough to sell to the masses."

"How do we clearly define the water shortage in the Southwest as a burning bridge to get this thing moving?" asked Lopez in frustration. "In terms of public relations, it might be worthwhile to ensure people understand how much of the fresh produce available in winter months comes from the Southwest."

"You're right, Angelica," said Cummings. "If people understand that their food is threatened, they might get on board."

And that's when Shriver cut in. "You know," she said thoughtfully, "one group we don't typically rely upon to 'get on board' is retirees. The populations of California and Arizona include quite a few 'snowbirds' who come south to escape winter in their home states and provinces. Because they are the most likely to become displaced if water rationing limits the number of people in the Southwest, I think they might make an interesting lobby group."

President Cummings was intrigued with the idea. "I see where you're going with this, Hana," he said. "Many snowbirds ran with powerful circles in their working days and are well connected. If we could mobilize them, it might sway public opinion. Why don't you chase this idea down with your team and some marketing experts?"

"I'd be happy to," replied Hana. "My in-laws are snowbirds, and my father-in-law was a Supreme Court Justice. He knows a lot of influential people. That's how I got the idea." At that, the ever-punctual Shriver checked her watch and arose. "I think it's time for your next meeting, Samuel," she said.

"Yes," said Cummings, "and thank you all for coming." Then, as the team began filing out of the room, Cummings called out to Lopez, "Angelica, I need you to stay, because . . ."

He didn't get to finish his statement. Barely were the words out of his mouth when there was a familiar rush of air, a flash of starburst light, and suddenly, Sarah stood before them in all her glory, emitting a rose scent as well as sparks of lights that twinkled to the floor like stars.

Lopez grinned broadly at her entrance. "Hello, Sarah," she said.

"Hello, Angelica," said Sarah. "I take it you will be joining Samuel in meeting with the new Russian president?"

"Yes, apparently so," said Angelica, looking at her boss. "He invited me to stay—and I'd like to congratulate President Grinkov on winning the election."

"The Russians made a wise choice," Sarah said gently.

"They made the *only* choice," remarked Lopez.

"Before you meet with him, I thought you might want to know what to expect from the man," Sarah ventured gently. "It was a close election with the reestablished Leninist party challenging him at every turn. People are harkening back to the old days—and a skewed perception of 'old ways'— just as they did when Donald Trump won the presidency. Ultimately, Grinkov won because of his progressive economic policies, but polarized ideologies have left Russia deeply divided. At the moment, the poor man is preoccupied with consolidating power. In short, he's in survival mode."

"What does Russia need most from us?" asked Cummings.

Sarah emitted a gentle breeze that filled the room with the smell of jasmine as she replied, "Their leader needs credibility and respect, while the country needs money and hope for the future."

And then with a light thump, suddenly Sergei Grinkov stood before them in the room.

"Mr. President," said Cummings to the somewhat disoriented Russian man, "welcome to America."

God's Intervention

Grinkov had a glazed look, and at first didn't seem to realize he'd been spoken to, but he recovered quickly. "President Cummings," he said in thickly accented English, "it is a pleasure to see you again."

"And you," said Cummings. Then, indicating Angelica Lopez, he said, "Let me introduce you to Vice President Lopez."

Grinkov, an old world gentleman, immediately took Lopez's hand in his own, and with a little bow, kissed it. Despite herself, Lopez beamed.

Cummings then indicated the plush Oval Office couches. "Please sit down," he said as a White House staff member quickly began clearing leftover coffee and donuts. Grinkov immediately stopped the staffer with a hand gently placed on her wrist. "Is that the famous 'donut' they eat in America?" he asked, pointing at a blue-tinged one, his eyes crinkling as he smiled in delight.

"Yes, that's a blueberry one," said Lopez, "and I think it has your name on it."

Grinkov released the staff member, who then quickly cleared the coffee debris—but left the donuts. She returned moments later with a fresh pot of coffee.

Grinkov examined the blueberry donut and said to Lopez, in puzzlement, "My name is on it?"

"It's a figure of speech," she explained.

He nodded in understanding and then unabashedly took a large bite. "So good," he said with a smile, savoring the doughy treat.

The staffer poured coffee for the three of them, and when she'd left, President Cummings said to his guest, "Let me offer my congratulations on your election victory."

"Many thanks," replied Grinkov. "It was a very close election, and I'm pleased that I won."

"I am also pleased," Cummings said cordially, "and I would like to personally assure you that the United States will be there to help you and the people of Russia energize your economy and retain a strong role in global affairs. God told us America needs to work more closely with *all* nations—and I intend to make sure the U.S. does exactly that."

The Russian leader responded cautiously, "Thank you, President Cummings, Sir," he said. "It would be most helpful to my country if we can find new ways to work together for mutual gain. But I don't want any handouts . . . although, I certainly enjoy a good trade profit."

"Fair enough," replied the Cummings, "and why don't you call me Samuel? I hate being called 'Sir.' It makes me feel old."

"Okay, Samuel. And you may call me Sergei," replied Grinkov with a smile that seemed a little shy.

Cummings continued, "I'm very pleased that you've agreed to meet with me today. These are interesting times we live in, times of great change . . . and it is my hope that the nature of the relationship between our countries will *also* change, from one of competitiveness to one of cooperation and trust. Do you feel the same, Sergei?"

"Yes indeed," replied Grinkov, taking a sip of his coffee. "Our two countries have worked together at the International Space Station for years, and we should be able to do this on Earth as well."

"Agreed," said Cummings, "and I'm glad you brought up the International Space Station because the exploration of space is exactly what I want to speak to you about most. I met recently with Chinese President Dong Yang, and we discussed efforts to colonize the moon and Mars. He told me he would only be interested in such a thing if we enlisted your country to partner with us in the initial stages."

"I am listening," said Grinkov warily.

"President Dong suggested a united front for the space colonization efforts—and given each of our country's respective knowledge and abilities, I agreed. I expect we can do a lot of joint business, beneficial to all three of our countries, if we collaborate. He proposed that before the global space colonization conference, scheduled for a month from now, we sit down for a pre-meeting. What do you say? We can meet in Russia if you would like."

"That would be most acceptable," replied Sergei. "Perhaps we could arrange a small trade delegation to join at the same time?" he suggested hopefully.

Remembering what Sarah had told him about the desperate state of affairs in Russia, Cummings replied with a gentle smile, "I find that most acceptable, Sergei." Then he paused tactfully before saying, "Another area where we both face major challenges is demilitarization, and retraining and redeployment of military personnel. I would be happy to have my team share with you the excellent planning they have done with regard to making this process smoother."

"That is a very generous offer," said Grinkov, "and I would be happy to accept. My presidency is new, and while I have done some preliminary planning around this, I had no idea whether I would be in office long enough to implement my plans, and so they are not fully formed. Now that I have won the election, I am eager to make some much needed changes, and military repatriation is high on my list."

"Sergei," said Cummings, "I am here to support you in your government's efforts to revolutionize Russia. You also have the support of Sarah. It is amazing how much good advice you can get from 40 million women when they speak with a single voice," he joked.

"Hey," said Lopez, "watch it!" She raised an eyebrow at Cummings as if to say, 'Don't cross the line'.

However, Sarah, who had remained silent as the two world leaders got to know each other, seemed to find the joke funny. A light rose scent permeated the air, and the energy around her seemed to flutter—her version of laughter.

Sergei cracked a smile. "I had not considered the value of 40 million brains that share information with a single voice," he said. "And she has God's ear as well!"

"Indeed she does," replied Cummings. "She's been a great source of wisdom when it comes to engaging the American people, and it's helped us move forward with hope and optimism."

At that, there was a light flutter of energy in the room. "Thank you, Samuel," said Sarah. "It's always nice to be appreciated."

Cummings laughed. "God created you for a reason," he said.

Replied Sarah, "God created all of us for a reason, Samuel."

Then Grinkov said, "I appreciate your willingness to share information about the projects you and your team are working on. Perhaps you will be able to help my country identify similar projects and move forward with some of them."

Thinking of the Russian rockets currently sitting idle that would add so much to the USE goals for space exploration, Cummings smiled and replied, "I'm sure we can work something out."

Raising his coffee cup in a toast, Grinkov looked Cummings in the eye and cheerfully said, "Huzzah!"

"Do you have some fine Russian vodka in that cup?" asked Cummings, wondering if the man had spiked his coffee before toasting.

"Oh no, I no longer drink," grinned Grinkov, "but I still like to toast!"

Cummings laughed and toasted him back.

Chapter 30

United Space Exchange

As they'd agreed to do, Cummings and Dong Yang met with Grinkov in Moscow two weeks later to discuss the specifics of a global program to colonize the moon and Mars, and to discuss what role the three counties would take in terms of leadership.

Cummings was a little nervous about the meeting. He had a good feeling about Grinkov, who seemed to be a surprisingly gentle man and a very deep thinker, but despite his newly developing friendship with Dong Yang, he wasn't certain that the Chinese man would play ball when it came to a shared space venture.

He was sitting in the Oval Office, pondering this and making contingency plans in his head should Dong Yang block his efforts, when he was unexpectedly graced by a visit from Sarah.

"Hello, Sarah," he said, feeling a flutter of joy in his heart as she materialized in a flow of light and flowery scents, the breeze of her wafting by his face like angel hair.

"Hello, Samuel," she replied in a rush of mist. "Are you looking forward to your meeting today? You are making history. This will be the first time three leaders of your respective countries have ever met to discuss such an ambitious joint venture."

"Yes," he said. "I'm interested to see how it goes. My hope is that we can work together to set the parameters for shared interests in the United Space Exchange so that when we present the idea of a global venture to the rest of the world at the meeting in Houston, the idea will be received well and easily ratified." Then he looked at her, questioning, and asked, "Would you like to hear my ideas?"

"Of course," she said, though both of them knew she was already familiar with all of his thoughts.

"Well," said Cummings, "the big picture is that I'd really like to see the top twenty global economic powers in the world agree to some sort of formula for jointly funding the colonization of the moon and Mars. But I don't know what that looks like yet."

"Ah yes," said Sarah, "and hopefully, you can iron that out with Dong Yang and Sergei Grinkov in advance."

"Yes," said Cummings. "But there are other factors too . . ."

"Such as the role of the private sector?" Sarah asked, intuiting his thoughts. "Elon Musk, Jeff Bezos, and Richard Branson have been quite active with their space programs of late, and Bezos had publicly stated an intention to set up heavy industry on the moon."

"I have been fully briefed on that," said Cummings. "He first started talking about that in 2019, when he said he was convinced that in less than one hundred years, heavy industry would all take place on the moon. He has always maintained that it would be easier to do such things in space because of solar energy potential, low gravity, and the raw materials that can be sourced there—which avoids the high cost of importing them from Earth. I think he might be right. It seems like the only way to ensure our planet can cope with the rising demand for energy and the stress that growing populations have put on Earth's environment."

"He is something of a visionary, this man, don't you think?" mused Sarah.

"He's definitely ahead of the curve," said Cummings. "He wants to use his Blue Origin company to smooth the way for millions of people to work in space, and he has even proposed that people live and work inside huge spinning habitats—a concept developed decades ago by a man he much admired, Princeton physicist Gerard Kitchen O'Neill."

"Ah yes, *another* visionary," said Sarah.

"That man was a genius," Cummings replied. "His award-winning book *The High Frontier: Human Colonies in Space* inspired a generation of space exploration advocates, and his work informs the Blue Origin company in their efforts to build the infrastructure for future space colonization."

Then the president furrowed his brow, remembering Dong Yang's words about private corporations having far too much control in America and unduly influencing government, and he added with some concern, "I think that as soon as I iron out the details of the United Space Exchange with China and Russia, I am going to meet with him. I don't like the idea of pioneers of free enterprise going out willy-nilly to stake claims on interplanetary bodies."

Sarah laughed at the vision he painted and said, "Take that spirit into the meeting with you, Samuel. You'll get Bezos on your side. He's your man for colonizing the moon, while Elon Musk is interested in colonizing Mars. Both are brilliant. Both will work with you if you find a way to make the idea of partnership attractive to them."

The next morning, Cummings, Lopez, and some of the key players in their space development program were teleported to Moscow by Sarah. As before, they arrived in front of the Moscow World Trade Centre—but this time, instead of being greeted by security, they were welcomed by a contingent of ten young women wearing traditional Russian sarafans, colourful, loose, long dresses belted over long linen shirts. One of the women was holding a round tray covered with an embroidered towel. On it sat a specially baked round bread loaf with a salt shaker on top of it.

She immediately stepped forward and presented it to Cummings, and before he had the chance to be *too* confused, Grinkov was standing beside him, saying, "If you are presented with a 'bread and salt' offering, you need to break off a piece of bread, dip it in the salt and eat it with a smile. You should not refuse, or the host will be greatly offended."

Cummings immediately did as Grinkov had instructed, asking, "What is this 'bread and salt'?"

"Bread is revered in Russia," Grinkov explained. "It symbolizes abundance and wealth, and salt offers protection from evil. In the Middle Ages, we Russians believed that if enemies shared bread and salt with each other, we would become close friends."

"In that case, I am honoured," said Cummings, helping himself to another piece and encouraging his entourage to do the same.

The loaf was very nearly gone when Dong Yang and his team suddenly appeared, courtesy of Sarah. Immediately, another young woman stepped forward with another loaf, and the process was repeated with the Chinese delegation. It was a charming custom, and Cummings was sure it would bode well for the negotiations that were soon to take place inside the Moscow World Trade Centre.

As Cummings had done, Dong Yang asked about the custom and was told its origins by Grinkov. He and his group had duly consumed the bread, and then when it was done, Grinkov clapped his hands together like a choirmaster, and the brightly clothed women all stepped back to reveal a security detail of about ten men, all neatly dressed in traditional, embroidered Russian peasant shirts.

"My men will guide you to the meeting room," said Grinkov, "and I have arranged for tea, coffee, and a more robust lunch while we meet."

Cummings was happy to hear this. The bread he'd just eaten reminded him that he'd skipped breakfast.

Cummings, Dong Yang, and the rest of the group followed the men into the Moscow World Trade Centre, and into the venue. Altogether, with the three presidents, their advisors and staff members, about thirty people settled into the well-appointed meeting room. As promised, there was food in the form of a buffet table laid out with fine cheeses, traditional Russian borscht (with more bread), and of course, the ubiquitous Russian caviar.

When everyone had helped themselves and were happily munching away, with a nod from Grinkov, Cummings began the discussion.

"First of all," he said, "let me say how great it is to be here today. I'm excited about the opportunity to work with both China and Russia in expanding the United Space Exchange to include other nations of the world, and possibly private sector partners as well."

There was polite head nodding as the two other presidents and their staff members acknowledged his words.

He went on, "The race to space is going to lead humankind in directions only few people ever imagined just decades years ago. I'm sure you're aware that in the not too distant past, our governments competed against each other in this missive . . . and that *these* days, we're not just competing with one another, but we're up against the private sector as well, which has made huge strides toward space accessibility."

"*I'm* certainly aware of that," said Dong Yang dryly, "and it makes me uncomfortable to think that some billionaire will lay claim to the moon so that he can make *more* billions!"

"You're not the only one who is not enthralled with that idea," replied Cummings. "Interplanetary bodies should be shared resources—which is why I suggested the idea of the United Space Exchange in the first place. Initially, my idea for USE was that it would be a global company funded in proportion to the size of each country's economy. In essence, each nation would be given a chance to invest in the project in return for future spaces for their nationals in the newly developed colonies."

"That is most equitable," said Grinkov, "though it sounds administratively difficult when you consider how often some countries change names and ideologies—including my *own* country. Think about it . . . it was not so long ago that Russia was known as the Union of Soviet Socialist Republics!"

"I remember," said Cummings, "and that is why—while I continue to believe in the involvement of all nations—I am rethinking this model. Ultimately, I don't want USE to be run like the United Nations, and sober second thought has shown me that nations with the most expertise in space programs need to have more say in how colonization occurs, or our brave pioneers are going to end up dead."

"This is wise," said Grinkov, "so, do you have a new proposal?"

"Yes," said Cummings. "I think we should maximize private sector involvement to reduce the risk borne by governments. It will improve the quality and speed at which the program is executed."

"You are suggesting we partner with Bezos, Musk, and their cronies?" asked Dong in disbelief.

"Yes," said Cummings. "I think it is the most effective way to move forward quickly."

"And what is in it for *them*? They will do whatever they want without government involvement, or so it seems," the Chinese president said. "It seems they don't really need us the way we need them."

"But they do need expedited permitting," said Cummings with a grin, "and they may benefit from knowledge sharing—after all, they aren't the only ones with excellent scientific personnel. Government has some very sharp minds as well."

"I don't know if that's enough for them," said Dong Yang petulantly.

Grinkov seemed more positive about the idea. The Russian President rubbed his chin, and said, "That is a most interesting idea. I do not object to the notion of working with the private sector, but I thought USE was meant to provide opportunity for countries that don't have their own space programs. Giving too much control to private sector investors might mean less opportunity for economically-challenged countries to get involved."

"I envision that these countries could still contribute to overall costs and risks," explained Cummings, "even if they cannot contribute to the technological aspects of the program."

"How do you mean?" asked Grinkov.

"Well, one way to do it is to divide it into percentages," said Cummings. "Perhaps countries outside the U.S., Russia, and China could, as a group, finance 25% of the USE annual capital and operating budgets."

Dong Yang nodded agreement. "Yes," he said, "and the countries with the most experience in space technology need to control the rest. I propose something like 25% control each by our three countries, with the remaining 25% from other countries. Also, China must be in a management capacity, and I assume your countries want the same."

His suddenly aggressive demands startled both Grinkov and Cummings, who looked at one another warily, surprised by how Dong Yang had started playing hardball all of a sudden.

Not wanting to go head to head with him, Cummings replied cautiously, "I was thinking similar thoughts . . . though I suspect we'll get pushback on those percentages. Some countries have more robust technology than we give them credit for—such as India—and they may not feel comfortable with such a small stake in the program. Perhaps we'll have to cross that 'percentage bridge' when we come to it."

"All right, then," said Dong. "Let us leave that idea alone for now and talk again about private sector involvement. You laid down a marker in favour of it, and now I will lay down a marker in favour of allowing *government*-owned businesses to bid on every aspect of this project too. State-controlled Chinese companies will expect no less."

"I have no problem with that," said Cummings, knowing that both China and Russia had powerful state-owned institutions, and their markets were less dominated by the private sector than American ones.

He was sure Grinkov would see support this, and he was right.

"This makes sense to me," said Grinkov. "But I have a question about outcomes. When we get to the stage where actual colonization occurs, will we send our respective teams to live in one shared colony, or many? Will there be Russiatown, Chinatown, and Americatown in these new places . . . or will it be a place of equality and shared knowledge as God no doubt wants it to be?"

Cummings chewed on this for a while before saying, somewhat reluctantly, "I think ultimately we should have multiple colonies on both the moon and Mars, though I'm not sure we should divide them by race and creed as you seem to be suggesting. I also think that these colonists should form their own governments—a local one on each celestial body and a higher one to oversee them both."

"Ah," said Grinkov. "While I agree that in the *distant* future, they will need their own governments, the idea is a bit premature. In the short term, the brave men and women who travel to these distant places will likely report to the countries that sent them—and it will probably be only to send back scientific data."

Then Dong Yang interrupted, saying darkly, "The world is at a crossroads, thanks to God's intervention. Wars and killing have stopped . . . but do you really think that after eons of struggle for ideological and territorial dominance, nations will go hand in hand into a new idyllic future?"

Cummings looked into Dong Yang's eyes and saw sadness under the bitterness. He hoped the man's bleak statement did not mirror his personal outlook but was afraid that it did.

He thought of how happy their two granddaughters had been together on that wonderful day in Shanghai Disneyland, and said by way of comfort, "You and I would like to see the world move to a more hopeful, less confrontational state—the sooner, the better—but neither of us can make this happen without God's help. All we can do is our own little part."

"Which is?" asked Dong Yang.

"Well, perhaps we can agree to a series of small steps to move our people forward until they reach the higher state of understanding that God wants for us all," suggested Cummings.

"What do you have in mind?" asked Dong.

"Well," replied Cummings, "our granddaughters started a small movement with their letter writing campaign. Perhaps we could initiate something similar. For example, when we meet to discuss the future of global institutions—such as the World Bank and the United Nations—why don't we invite a shadow council of bright, young twenty-year-olds from around the world to attend? They could speak up for the future of the planet and provide a fresh perspective."

"Yes, perhaps they can suggest a way to improve these antiquated institutions," said Grinkov with a wry smile.

There were titters around the room at that.

And then Dong pointed out, "If raising the awareness of human beings is the goal, then colonizing the moon and Mars will broaden *everyone's* perspective, regardless of how the project manifests. Why should we do more than that?"

"I agree it is a step toward becoming one with our species, and that it is in line with what Sarah tells us God wants. However, the old adage of 'God helps those who help themselves' applies . . . which brings us full circle to the issue at hand. How do we move forward with the colonization of space?"

There was a short silence between the three men, and a hush in the room. The feeling was like watching chess masters ponder a move.

Finally, Dong Yang broke the silence. "I agree with your ideas about involving the private sector," he said reluctantly, "even though I am not impressed by how private corporations are becoming more powerful than governments. However, I am not a fool, and I understand that they invest heavily in space technology and have gained an advantage over government-led initiatives. Given this, I would support a USE model that *incents* corporations to do what they're good at—but sees the technology they develop revert to public ownership after a specified period, perhaps twenty years."

"You mean the governments of the world would have the right to use the private sector technologies as they see fit after twenty years?" asked Grinkov in disbelief. "This will upset the patent system."

"Yes, but it sounds like a good compromise," said Cummings. "We just have to agree on how many years before technology becomes public domain."

"It is worth considering," said Dong Yang. "This way, corporations don't end up owning our souls."

Cummings did not reply. He looked a little perplexed and was clearly mulling something over.

Finally, he observed, "You know, if we applied this across *all* sectors, it would ease a lot of friction between our nations. And it could also be applied in the other direction as well."

"The other direction? What do you mean?" asked Grinkov.

"I mean that government technology could become public domain after the same period of time—tit for tat. The private sector might like that."

"Sharing knowledge," said Grinkov, almost in wonder. "Can we live in such a world? I like this idea."

Dong Yang didn't look so sure. "In general, I approve of this line of thinking," he said, "but only because weapons technology has been rendered largely obsolete. We would still need to be careful with sharing *some* technologies because despite the 'do not kill' edict, a nuclear bomb in the wrong hands can still cause environmental degradation and harm many people."

"You're right," agreed Cummings with a sigh. "As a race, we humans are not all on the same page yet."

"But we're getting there," said Grinkov with a winning smile.

"This concept of knowledge in the public domain is intriguing," Cummings said. "It might give us a bargaining chip with private sector companies such as SpaceX and Blue Origin."

"I agree," said the Chinese president.

Then he frowned, and Cummings' heart sank. He knew that Dong Yang was going to dig in his heels over something, and that his fears were going to be realized.

Dong spoke. "I have been thinking about governance of the colonies, and of Sergei's comment about 'Chinatown,' 'Russiatown,' and 'Americatown,'" he said. "This concerns me."

"Oh?" asked Cummings, wondering where this was going.

"I am of the opinion that it is best to define clear governance boundaries for an agreed upon period of time," Dong said. "Therefore, to protect China's interests, in the initial stages of colonization, my country will build its own colonies and govern them independently from Earth. I feel the scope of the United Space Exchange should be limited to developing transportation and constructing manufacturing and assembly facilities such as those required to build and launch Mars rockets from the moon."

405

Cummings was disappointed by this. While it cleared the way for America to demand the same privileges, it also put a wedge between the three nations in the room who were trying to build a framework for a shared, global institution.

He stifled a sigh as Dong added, "I must also insist that the voting structure in the United Space Exchange be weighted in favour of the U.S., China, and Russia. I suggest something like 35% for America, 35% for China, and 20% for Russia. The remaining 10% can be distributed between the EU, Japan, and India."

President Cummings suddenly felt like he'd been deftly outmaneuvered. He was uncertain which way to jump and did not want to risk offending the powerful Dong Yang—especially if his mind was already made up.

Ever the diplomat, he managed to calmly reply, "Well, I guess we will have to agree about how the manufacturing and launch facilities will be governed then . . . but I think our colonists will have a better chance of survival if they band together."

Then Sergei cut in, saying almost wistfully, "We are in a time in history where God has actually *intervened* in our affairs in order to promote harmony among all men and women . . . and so, while I understand governance of colonies from Earth will be necessary in the early years, I'm not sure I can support *protectionism*. It will lead to divisiveness, and this is not what God wants, my friends."

Dong Yang just looked at him balefully, and there was only one thing Cummings could say in an effort to reach the man.

"Do you remember saying, 'the children will lead us'?" he asked.

He could tell by his eyes that the Chinese man did.

"Think of our granddaughters," Cummings said earnestly. "What would they do?"

Chapter 31

Global Institutions

The meeting about how to update global institutions was only a week away, and on the heels of that, the global United Space Exchange meeting would be held in two weeks. Cummings was busy preparing for both meetings, but in the meantime, he was delighted to be invited by Martin Grieves to tour the first aircraft carrier. It was in the process of being retrofitted to become a floating a hospital, the USS Gerald R. Ford.

He asked Lorena if she wanted to join him on the tour. "We don't get to spend much time together these days," he told her over coffee on the morning of the tour. "You should come."

"Oh, I don't know," she teased. "I have a busy day of soap operas. I don't think I can give that up to see some silly old boat."

He fell for her joke and looked at her, puzzled. "You *hate* soap operas," he said.

She laughed. "I'm glad you remember. You've been pretty distracted lately."

"Guilty," he told her. "There is so much going on!"

"Honestly, Sammy," she said, giving him a peck on the cheek as she got up to put her coffee cup in the dishwasher, "you couldn't have asked me on a better day. All my plans fell through, and I'm all yours."

"All your plans?" asked Cummings.

"Don't you remember?" prompted his wife. "Laura and the kids were going to come to D.C. today, but she called and said they can't make it. Jessica has a soccer tournament that Laura forgot about."

Cummings was a little embarrassed that he hadn't remembered about his daughter and beloved grandchildren coming to visit, and Lorena understood without him having to say a word.

"Don't worry," she said, "I forgot too, until Laura called to cancel."

They both laughed.

"Thank God it's not just me losing my marbles," Cummings said, relieved.

"No, dear," replied Lorena, "We're losing our marbles together."

When Cummings was ready to leave for the tour of the ship, he waited patiently for his wife to finish dressing. When she came down the hall toward him, he was, as ever, struck by how beautiful he still found her to be. She was wearing an elegant, fuchsia-coloured dress that set off her eyes. He thought, *She is as lovely as the day I met her. I wish I could make love to her just one more time.* At the thought of the loss of their romantic past, he sighed.

Then he smiled at her and told her, "You get more beautiful with age, my dear."

She smiled back, and as if reading his mind, quipped, "You're just trying to get into my pants!"

He couldn't help himself. He let out a loud guffaw, and she joined in too. The futility of the situation made them laugh until they had tears in their eyes. When they came up for air, all Cummings could think was, *I'm incredibly glad I married a woman with a sense of humour.* And then they left to tour the Gerald R. Ford.

The Ford, the lead ship of her class of United States Navy aircraft carriers, was named after the 38th president of the United States. Commissioned in July 2017, it was the first of the Ford-class carriers. In its capacity as a war machine, it featured such things as improved hull design and weapons stowage, a new weapons elevator, more space on the flight deck, a new electromagnetic-powered aircraft-launch system, three times the electrical-generation capacity of any previous carrier, and it was powered by two nuclear reactors that could bring the more than 100,000-ton behemoth to speeds of over thirty miles per hour.

Now, these things were being repurposed in some striking ways. When President Cummings and Lorena climbed aboard, the first part of the ship they toured was the emerging hospital. One of the airplane hangars was being converted into a multi-patient hospital ward, and a new floor was being installed above it which would house a full diagnostic suite, including a computer tomography (CT) scanner, a mammography machine, and ultrasound equipment, among other things. A second hangar was being converted into a full operating theatre, complete with an anesthetic room and a scrub room. As with the first hangar, a second floor was being added above this hangar as well, for the intensive care unit, physiotherapy facilities, and morgue. The third bay would continue to house aircraft which would be repurposed from being fighting machines to being emergency aircraft that could take medical personnel to disaster zones when required. Two helicopter pads on the deck near the elevator to the active aircraft hangar remained as well.

Cummings was pleasantly surprised by how far along the project was. He'd only approved Martin Grieves' plans a few months ago. He remembered the discussion well.

He'd told Grieves, "Your plans look good, Martin. I'm impressed."

"Thank you, Sir," replied Grieves. "I'm quite pleased with this project. It's very forward-thinking, Sir."

Cummings smiled at the man, enjoying his military manners and crisp bearing, and asked, "How many of these 'mercy ships' do you think we'll need to cover the major risk areas of the world?"

"Well, Sir," Grieves had replied. "The highest risk areas are the ones prone to volcanic eruptions, earthquakes, tsunamis, hurricanes, and typhoons. In my opinion, the continental U.S. would be adequately covered if we had a ship stationed in Hawaii and another off the coast of Florida to provide emergency services during hurricane season."

"But we'd need a few more floaters around the globe if we plan to do humanitarian outreach, am I right?" asked Cummings.

"I'd say so, Sir," replied Grieves. "I'd advise coverage between Japan and Alaska. Malaysia is at risk for flooding and landslides, so a ship stationed in that area, perhaps off the Australian coast, would be wise. A ship in that area could also be deployed to India during monsoon season."

"Good thinking, Grieves," said Cummings, mulling it over. "Maybe one would be justified off the west coast of South America as well. They've seen their share of natural disasters down there. And perhaps one could be stationed on the west coast of Africa. That continent doesn't see many earthquakes or monsoons, but they need basic health care desperately. Famine and drought are commonplace."

"Yes," said Grieves. "That takes us up to six ships, Sir." Then he smiled and said, "But let's start with one."

Grieves had provided Cummings with a preliminary estimate to turn the Ford into a hospital ship. The price tag was $150 million over an eighteen-month schedule, which did not include the cost of dismantling and removing weapons. To Cummings, given the nearly $1 trillion he was no longer spending annually on America's war machine, it seemed like a bargain. He was certain he could get some of the former Army Corps of Engineers to work on the dismantling part, or perhaps some of the repatriated military who were seeking employment.

He said, "Make it happen, Martin. Make it happen as soon as you can."

"Yes, Sir," Grieves had replied.

Now he was touring the ship, and he was awed by what Grieves' team had already accomplished.

Grieves explained his plans. "The ship's crew will be reduced from 3,500 to 2,000," he said. "And my people are busy converting surplus crew quarters into private hospital rooms. When the retrofit is done, we will have 800 hospital beds."

Then he gestured to a plethora of activity occurring around them on the deck on which they stood. "This," he said with a sweep of his arm, "will be housing for medical staff."

Cummings was impressed with the seaworthy modular housing that was being assembled. While things were not yet complete, it was easy to see how amazing the living space would be when it was done. Martin's crew had added many thoughtful touches, including a community garden and a park for those who would be bringing children on board when they started their jobs as mobile medical personnel. Eventually, 1,200 medical doctors, nurses, technicians, orderlies, and their families would call the ship 'home.'

"What is the disaster response plan?" asked the president.

"My plan is that when a crisis occurs, 900 onboard medical personnel will be flown in shifts from the ship to an airport near the disaster zone—which is why one aircraft hangar is still active—while the other 300 will remain on board and prepare for intake upon arrival."

"That sounds good," Cummings said. "This is much better than I ever imagined."

"Thank you, Sir," replied Grieves, clearly pleased. "And now I have a favour to ask of your wife."

"You do?" asked Lorena, surprised.

"Yes," said Grieves with a big smile. "Will you do us the honour of rechristening the ship when construction is complete?"

Cummings could tell his wife was inordinately pleased by the offer. "Of course!" she exclaimed. "I'd be honoured."

When the tour was over, Cummings and Lorena had a rare opportunity for a private lunch at a nice restaurant. They even had a glass of wine, a fine Cabernet from California. When they got home, it was about two o'clock in the afternoon. Lorena had promised that she would meet with a group of childhood education experts at three o'clock to discuss funding an early education nutrition program—basically, a nationwide cooking program for six-year-olds—and Cummings had to finalize the speech he would be giving tomorrow at the United Nations in New York. Because the United States was the largest financial supporter of the UN, he had been tasked with giving the introductory remarks.

As they separated, Cummings said to his wife, "Knock 'em dead, honey."

"You too!" she called over her shoulder. "But not *too* dead, or you'll die too. Isn't that how the 'do not kill' thing works?"

"Are you saying you'd miss me if I died?" he quipped.

She just laughed.

He headed over to the Oval Office and began working on some of his ideas about improving global institutions—particularly the UN itself—in the wake of God's intervention. The biggest thing troubling him was the Security Council. What good was it now? There could be no more war, so in his opinion, its usefulness had expired. *It's an anachronism,* he thought. *It should go.* He decided to propose it the next day at the meeting.

When morning dawned, at the appointed time, Sarah transported him and his assistant, Janice—as well as all other world leaders and their assorted clerical staff—to the United Nations building in New York City. When Cummings arrived in front of the UN building, he looked at the familiar structure with a sense of kinship. He'd been on this neutral United

Nations ground so often that the building felt like a second home . . . but this was the first time he'd come here to discuss the nature of the UN itself.

He went inside and found the speaker's seat, and as the meeting room began to fill, Cummings thought of the momentous change he was helping shepherd into existence. *Never in my life did I imagine I would see this day*, he thought. Knowing he was part of positive change that would have lasting impacts on his nation—and on the *world*—made his heart pound with anticipation. Then, when everyone was settled and the lights flickered on and off a few times to bring them all to attention, he calmed himself with a deep breath and stepped up to the podium to do his job.

"Welcome to New York City," he began, "and to the United Nations, which since 1945 has worked toward building international peace and security, developing friendly relations among governments, and harmonizing the actions of nations. The UN was formed following World War II. After an exhausting four years, the world was tired of war, and so most nations of the world banded together to create this institution and imbue it with the lofty ambition of maintaining global peace.

"Over the years, the UN has indeed sponsored some successful peacekeeping missions around this troubled planet but with limited success because it's never had the power to actually prevent wars. Now, God has come to our rescue in that regard, and we don't *need* the UN to prevent wars anymore . . . and so, we have to ask the question: Do we need the UN at all?"

He heard some throats being cleared around the room. No one was ready to take a stand on this. The UN, something of a sacred cow, was not an outfit anyone felt comfortable criticizing, let alone revoking.

Cummings continued, "The UN has six principal components: the General Assembly; the Security Council; the Economic and Social Council; the Trusteeship Council; the International Court of Justice; and, the UN Secretariat. As well, the UN system also includes some specialized agencies, funds and programs, such as the World Bank Group, the World Health Organization, the World Food Program, UNESCO, and UNICEF. So I ask you again? Should we get rid of it?"

The silence in the room was deafening.

Cummings waited only a heartbeat before continuing. "I see the jury's out on this, so here's what I think . . . absolutely *not*. There is a lot that is *right* about the UN. Its objectives include maintaining international peace and security, protecting human rights, delivering humanitarian aid, promoting sustainable development, and upholding international law. And it represents almost all of the world's sovereign states."

He paused and looked at his peers, who were sitting at small chair-desks, staring intently at him.

"This is an excellent starting point for achieving God's vision, which is to learn how to become one with our own species," he said, "but in order for this institution to be effective going forward, the UN could use a little tweaking. In the new era we are entering, we will need a central organization with a global perspective on issues critical to human existence. We will *need* the UN—but for it to be effective, it needs an updated mandate. It needs teeth. It needs the power to settle inter-government disputes. It needs to become—and be recognized as—an international justice system. But to have such authority, it must have the support of every head of state."

His words caused a significant buzz around the room. Clearly, people were wondering about the consequences of ceding power to a central organization.

But Cummings was not put off message. "The first change I would suggest is this: Given that war is forever in the past, I think we should eliminate the Security Council. Why don't we replace it instead with a global judiciary body that has the power to settle international disputes? Doesn't that make more sense than a clique of so-called peacekeepers who are largely ineffective and are governed by 'permanent member' states who appointed themselves almost eighty years ago? Times have changed, my friends, and in my opinion, this model is no longer effective."

His words gave the people in the room something significant to chew on. The permanent members (P5) of the Security Council—China, France, the United States, the United Kingdom, and Russia—were awarded their status in the UN Charter of 1945. However, almost immediately, the organization was paralyzed by the Cold War between the U.S. and the Soviet Union. Then, when it became more globally active, its effectiveness was questioned because there were few consequences for violating council resolutions. Examples of this inefficacy include the Darfur Crisis in 2003, when government backed militia killed thousands of civilians despite

UN sanctions, and the 1995 Srebrenica massacre, where Serbian troops committed genocide against the Bosnians, killing 8,000 people in a UN safe area despite the protection of 400 armed Dutch peacekeepers.

Cummings could tell that his colleagues were mulling over what he'd said. Most knew the history as well as he did, and he was sure he would get support. He was right; Almost unanimously, the buzz in the room became a round of applause.

When the noise died down, Cummings said, "We need to discuss what we want and what will best serve the planet in this time of great change. We must decide which UN agencies are truly global in nature, dealing with issues fundamental to humankind's success as a species, and which are not. Those that seem self-serving should be eliminated and replaced with global agencies that should be centralized into what could ultimately be a de facto global government of sorts. I'm speaking of such organizations as the World Trade Organization and the World Court."

Then he looked around the room with a serious expression, trying to catch as many eyes as he could. "Make no mistake," he said, "the days of protectionism are over, whether you want them to be or not. There is one race, the *human* race, and it is time for us to act in accordance with that. With a show of hands, let me know if you support the idea of an enhanced UN, one with the capacity to keep individual sovereign nations in check."

There was some hesitation at first, but Cummings saw about two-thirds of the hands in the room went up. He was heartened by this, and he smiled. There was time to work on the doubters. He knew his plan made sense—he just had to continue selling it. And he intended to.

He was about to deliver his closing remarks when there was a sudden flash of light, and Sarah appeared in a cloud of mist beside him. Cummings welcomed her presence.

Unphased by her entrance, he simply turned to her and said, "As always, it is an honour to see you, Sarah."

"And you, Samuel," she said, focusing her starlit eyes intently on him for a few seconds before she captured the attention of the room with her hypnotic gaze and a light scent of roses. "Leaders, heads of state . . . *humans*," she said, "I am happy to see you here, asking yourselves questions about what would make this world a better place."

There were a slight rustle around the room, and someone in the back yelled out, "Hi, Sarah!"

Sarah smiled her enigmatic smile, clearly pleased, and others called out their 'hellos' as well, until a din of greetings rocked the room.

When the ruckus stopped, Sarah said, "You are happy, then? You are pleased to see humankind moving toward a life of more depth and working to create a planet that is not endangered? These are baby steps you are taking now . . . but a significant journey has begun."

"Yes!" came one strong voice, and then another, and another, the calls to Sarah growing more intense as people added their voices.

When the din died down, she said, "As President Cummings said, with some restructuring, the UN could become a meaningful global oversight organization as long as all nations of the world agree to collaborate with such an organization honestly and openly. It is a utopian ideal, but every nation will be better as a member."

From the back of the room were several shouts of, "Aye!"

And Cummings was pretty sure they came from Blair Stewart, First Minister of Scotland, or possibly the loud Canadian fellow who was part of Justin Trudeau's entourage.

Sarah smiled at Cummings and gestured for him to continue. "This is your moment, Samuel," she said softly.

Cummings stepped up to the podium. "Before I sit down," he said, "I would like to share my thoughts about the World Health Organization, one of the UN's most important agencies. The Covid-19 pandemic taught us just how quickly a highly infectious disease can travel the world—and it also taught us how important globally recognized health protocol is."

The men and women in that room gave Cummings their undivided attention. Covid, though greatly reduced, had never been completely eliminated because new variants kept popping up every few months like bad pennies.

"I firmly believe the World Health Organization should be a central repository for current health information from around the globe, and that its primary role should be to communicate this information as quickly as possible. As a non-partisan organization, the World Health Organization doesn't belong on the front lines of research. It needs to play a liaison role. I would like to see every nation's disease control and vaccine dissemination organizations plugged directly into the World Health Organization, which in turn can share what they know in an expedient manner so the whole world can be prepared when crisis occurs."

A high level of applause ensued, suggesting that the group agreed with the plan.

When the noise died down, Cummings added, "I have one last thought to leave you with. I recommend we hire an independent contractor to work with a UN team to develop a plan for a restructured organization. I further suggest that we reconvene in ninety days to agree on a new United Nations blueprint. All in favour, say 'aye.'"

There were resounding 'ayes' throughout the room. Cummings had no idea if it was unanimous, though it seemed so. However, he knew he could rely on Sarah to know if there were objectors.

He concluded with, "Thank you all for your attention and participation. I'd now like to turn the floor over to President Dong Yang of China, who asked for an opportunity to speak today."

When Dong Yang took the stand, he said, "Thank you, President Cummings. This is the third time in a month I have attended a meeting with you, and I continue to be amazed at how closely our values align. I agree with your proposals, and I support the idea of forming a team to develop a new blueprint for the UN. But I was thinking . . . since we have been getting along so well, why don't you just let *me* write that proposal?"

It was a well-placed joke; Both knew the team that would be selected would be chosen by free vote, just as both knew Switzerland would be on that team.

Cummings laughed and told his one-time competitor, "You can write the next proposal, Mr. President."

Dong smiled at Cummings and then turned to the audience. "I could never have foreseen that the elimination of war would help all our nations work as one," he said. "My country has relied on military might for five millennia. We are fighters, and we are proud. For us, honour is everything. If we think something will dishonour us, we do not share our weakness with others, for that would bring great shame—and for that, my great nation has paid a price."

He looked pensive; Cummings felt stirrings of compassion in his heart. Despite the fact that Dong could be a hard man, he felt affection for him, as well as for his lovely granddaughter, Mingmei.

Dong Yang went on, "China was slow to communicate the dire situation in Wuhan when Covid-19 first infected that city. Had we shared with the world what we knew about Covid more quickly, many lives could have been saved. Instead, our attempt to save face allowed the disease to spread more quickly and made many regard us as irresponsible at best and devious at worst. The backlash is that people of Chinese origin, whether Chinese nationals or not, have been subject to racist attacks across the globe in retaliation. But China has learned from that experience . . . and so have I. As the climate continues to change, and bacteria mutate and thrive, Covid will not be our last pandemic challenge—and that is why I am publicly declaring my willingness to cooperate with global agencies, particularly the World Health Organization. That is why I support a restructured United Nations."

Cummings found himself with tears in his eyes, clapping hard. *Thank you, friend,* he thought.

"I also firmly believe in building bridges across cultures," the Chinese president added, "starting as early as possible, with children. Many of you are aware of the pen pal campaign started by my and President Cummings' granddaughters. I was amazed and touched by the reaction to this simple event. A video of our two girls went viral on multiple platforms, and since then, the idea has blossomed in a way I could never have imagined. It seems our two eleven-year-old granddaughters touched a collective nerve. What a simple but effective way to build relationships and cultural understanding!"

Most of the people in attendance had heard about the friendship between Jessica and Mingmei, which had gotten a surprising amount of media coverage. It had been a front-page, feel-good story for several weeks.

Dong continued, "With this in mind, I would like to propose that the new, updated UN add to its mandate a youth program that will bring high school seniors to New York to represent their countries in learning how to work together to protect our species and our planet."

It was an unusual proposal to be offered up by the president of China, but the audience seemed to like the idea. The room erupted, people clapping heartily. The Chinese president gave a humble little bow to the rest of the world leaders, and then he went back to his seat.

It was time to break for lunch, and when the group reassembled for the afternoon session, the team who would work to develop the new UN blueprint was chosen. Ten people, one each from the U.S., China, the European Union, Russia, India, Egypt, South Africa, Malaysia, Brazil, and Switzerland would comprise the advisory group. Japan and Canada were selected as alternates.

When that was done, Sarah flickered her way into the centre of the room and hung, angel-like, suspended in space. All eyes fixated on her. How could they not? She glowed, translucent and fine, and she brought a lightness to the air that made people giddy.

She addressed the assembled leaders, saying, "God is pleased with how you are working together to ensure your species and your planet have a sustainable future. God, and the trillions of souls who are part of God, fulfill the same stewardship role for the universe that you are learning to fulfill for your planet. God has invested much into human beings, and your successful evolution is a high priority—and so I have been authorized to give you a few suggestions to help you survive the next several millennia."

There was some scrambling for recording devices, and she patiently waited until the room was still again before she spoke. When she did, her voice took on a deeper timbre, a depth that almost penetrated the skull.

She said, "The human population is approaching 8 billion, and this is threatening many species. Their habitat is being destroyed to support you all. Humans are physically larger, and they live longer than at any point in history. You eat more meat per year than ever before, and factory farming, complete with inhumane treatment of livestock, is the norm. Antibiotics to stop the spread of disease among animals raised in dirty, cramped quarters has led to reduced antibiotic effectiveness in the treatment of humans. The world's oceans are becoming severely overfished and polluted with everything from radioactive waste to plastics and other garbage. None of this is sustainable. You are aware of these issues but collectively fail to act.

"Your vision of a new United Nations is one of an organization that will provide an ongoing focus on these issues . . . but unless people change at a root level, that will solve nothing. *You* are the change agents. *You* are the ones who must learn to consume less. Technology can help. There are exciting new ways to grow proteins that look and taste like meat products but don't require killing billions of animals each year to produce them, not to mention destroying ecosystems on millions of acres of land. Also, God provided fruit, vegetables, grains, nuts, and seeds. Why do you insist on killing living *creatures* for your tables? There are many solutions to being more responsible consumers . . . but they have to be adopted by *all* people, one by one, if they are to become the norm.

"Here is my advice to you: Look to technology to help you reduce consumption. For example, clothing that regulates body temperature could reduce caloric need by up to 7%. And genetic engineering and/or societal preferences for breeding smaller people could become *choices*."

There was a small rustle of surprise at this thought. People knew genetic engineering was quietly going on, and that the rich could afford to experiment with creating perfect children—but not many had considered a practical application of this technology. It made many of them uncomfortable.

"Don't be dismayed," tinkled Sarah, reading the room. "Shorter basketball players will just use lower hoops."

No one laughed at her joke.

She waited in the uncomfortable silence, unperturbed, and then asked, "Have you ever considered how vulnerable city dwellers are when crisis occurs? Not only does disease, such as Covid-19, spread more rapidly in cities due to people's close proximity to one another, but supply chains are vulnerable. If they fail, city dwellers are . . . what is that expression? Up the creek?"

From the back of the room came a baritone voice, "Up shit creek without a paddle," it said gruffly.

This time, Cummings was sure it was the burly Canadian.

"Yes," said Sarah smoothly. "When the supply chain fails, there are no apples, there is no milk or bread . . . no one can store enough bulk items required to feed the hungry masses. And, of course, there is no toilet paper. Who will provide the toilet paper in times of need? The government? Maybe so. Maybe the government should regulate toilet paper."

There was nervous laughter at this. Everyone still remembered toilet paper running out when Covid-19 had emerged as a global pandemic.

"As we've heard countless times today, working together as a global community is the key," Sarah went on. And then she suddenly lit up the room as if with a thousand twinkling lights and said, "Do you love this brightness?"

There was a murmur of assent in the room. The light show she was putting on was spectacular.

Then she asked, "Do you like to come into a warm house on a cold winter's day? Do you like to brighten a dark room with a lamp when you want to read? Do you like to eat a tomato in the middle of December? Do you ever think who grew it, and how?"

People began looking at each other, confused.

She said, "You are entering a time of great change. Climate change is bringing severe storms, and with it, the threat of failing power grids. This is a threat you must plan for. Without electricity, computers, gas pumps, lights, air conditioners, elevators, and even your prized smart phones won't work. Food will spoil. Water supplies will last only as long as backup generators have power. Have you ever wondered how long after electricity dies will it be before chaos reigns? People used to kill each other for food and water. Prior to God's intervention, the half-life of an average city—the time it takes before half the people die fighting over resources—was three weeks. God's edict has lengthened this, but it is still a short time compared to how long it would take to make and install the power transformers and control systems necessary to power a city."

There were shocked faces at her bold and disturbing message.

She followed her words with, "When electricity is gone, civil disobedience will follow."

Sergei Grinkov, who was currently going through resource shortages in his country, and the associated civil disobedience, stood up. "Sarah," he said, in thickly accented English, "in developed countries, bulk power systems are interconnected, and their components are protected. In my country, some of this is failing right now, but even so, we have backup systems. We are not likely to face a long time of no power, I think."

"I understand, Sergei," said Sarah, "but while an Earthbound disaster may not completely destroy your grid, a massive solar flare could . . . and you all know that climate change is leading to increasingly severe storms that could cripple a city. There is also an ongoing risk to electricity sources from cyberattacks."

"Cyberattacks? But God's edict . . . ?" It came out as a question, and the Russian man looked terribly puzzled.

"God's edict means those involved in attempting to physically destroy critical power equipment or control systems will die, and the tools used in the attempt will be destroyed . . . but it doesn't mean hackers can't invade the business systems of electricity suppliers and bring supplies to a halt. Their ransom demands could be incredibly high."

It was a doomsday message, but it was also highly probable given climate change. Cummings shuddered at the thought. It was something to get his team working on.

Then Sarah closed by saying, "Multiple power generation systems around the country, and standardized backup power for farming, grocery stores, and gas stations will be useful in a crisis. And you should try to stop people from concentrating in megacities by offering incentives to make rural life more attractive. However, if people insist on being in urban environments, then food production programs in cities should be encouraged—which means smarter urban design."

Cummings thought of the gardens and the self-contained nuclear energy supply he'd seen earlier on the USS Gerald R. Ford, and he marveled at what good design choices Grieves had made for that small, floating city. *Today a ship, tomorrow a world*, he thought hopefully.

Chapter 32

Global Space Colonization

On the heels of the meeting regarding the future of global institutions—indeed, the future of the United Nations itself—came the meeting between the twenty countries with the largest economies in the world (G20) about the United Space Exchange and how to make it into a global corporation with representation from all countries.

Cummings had been looking forward to this meeting so he could expand on the ideas he, Sergei Grinkov, and Dong Yang had discussed at their pre-meeting. He'd bounced some of them off Angelica Lopez, and she'd been quite enthused.

Although, she'd cautioned, "In my opinion, positioning America, China, and Russia as leaders in this space race is brilliant—but you're going to have heavy competition from the private sector. Elon Musk, Jeff Bezos, and Richard Branson are big money boys who are already heavily competitive with one another. I hope they see the value in an alliance with government and don't see the United Space Exchange as just another competitor."

"Wise words, Angelica," Cummings told his vice president. "I was concerned about that very thing—how to ensure that the private sector is on board. I've added it to the agenda."

When the day of the meeting arrived, the G20 heads of state, along with advisors from their respective science and space programs, arrived at NASA's Johnson Space Center in Houston, via Sarah. The Johnson Space Center, home to America's astronaut corps, the International Space Station mission operations, the Orion Program, and a host of future space developments, seemed the most appropriate place to hold the meeting, given its fifty-plus years as a hub of science and technological knowledge.

When Cummings arrived, he took a seat at a small, raised table at which Grinkov and Dong were already seated. The three of them were co-chairing the meeting. He smiled briefly at each of them, and they returned the greeting with smiles of their own.

It was already almost 9:00 a.m., and so as soon as people had settled in their seats, President Cummings wasted no time in opening the conference. "Welcome to Houston, ladies and gentlemen," he greeted his colleagues warmly. "I hope your journey via 'the Sarah Express' was a good one."

There were chuckles around the room; Except for the fact that some of the people there would rather have remained snoozing, none could complain about the travel situation.

When the laughter died down, Cummings looked gravely about and said, "Friends and colleagues . . . Since my election as president of the United States of America, I have taken pride in leading my country, and I have governed in a manner that, at its heart, looks toward a positive future. However, though I've stood proud and strong when facing my fellow Americans, *inside* all I have been able to think is . . . *What kind of world am I leaving for my grandchildren?* I've been scared, you see, about the very real possibility of humankind blindly pursuing its own ends to the point where we make this planet—our fragile, beautiful Earth—uninhabitable."

He looked around, catching various eyes in the assembled group, all of which were gazing intently at him no doubt acknowledging to themselves that they felt the very same way.

He said, "Mere months ago, hope for us mortals arrived in the form of Sarah. Through her, God has eliminated war and killing . . . and we are now on the verge of a new era for humankind. Quite frankly, I never thought I would live to see this day."

There was a murmur of agreement at his words. *This is good,* thought Cummings, pleased.

Emboldened, he continued, "Sarah brought us truth about God. She told us, as holy men have tried to do for eons, that only by placing the needs of others above our own will we become at one with our species. The Golden Rule that so many of us learned at our mother's knee is our core mandate as intelligent beings. Is that so hard to understand?"

He looked around again and saw a variety of expressions. The leaders of some of the more warlike nations had poker faces; Most people in the room showed various degrees of concern, but some people looked, at least to Cummings' eyes, a little ashamed.

"We're here today," he went on, "because Sarah has made it clear that one way to unite people is to give them a shared goal or a shared great undertaking. Colonizing the moon and Mars could *be* this goal—are you ready for such an adventure?"

There was a murmur of positivity from the assembled group, and from the back of the room came a Scottish-sounding, "Aye!"

Cummings continued, "At the very least, it would be one positive step forward toward unifying our human species as Sarah has indicated we should strive toward . . . though, according to her, true unification may take as many as 10,000 years." Then his eyes flashed as he asked, "Are you ready for *that* adventure?"

"Yes!" came a cry to his left, followed by clapping in support.

As the clapping continued, Cummings raised a fist in solidarity and then stepped away from the microphone, signaling to Dong Yang that he should take over.

Dong ably took the reins, switching places at the podium with Cummings.

When the clapping subsided, he smiled at the eager faces around the room and said, "The United Space Exchange was created to ensure every nation in the world has an opportunity to participate in space colonization efforts. Under the umbrella of United Space Exchange programs, there is opportunity to pool knowledge and resources in an equitable way so that global representation on both the moon and Mars will not only become feasible but will be a shared project."

At the idea of an inclusive space program, there was optimistic murmuring around the room and a cry of, "We're listening!" from an unidentified male voice.

Dong acknowledged this with a nod of his well-groomed head, and then, indicating Grinkov and Cummings beside him, he said, "We three are of the opinion that all nations have something to offer in a shared colonization effort. America, China, and Russia have historically contributed the most technology, equipment, and money to the effort, but today, many other nations, and the private sector as well, are pursuing space goals. We can work as one to achieve this goal. Even nations that don't have the money or resources necessary to play a major role in space exploration can contribute skilled labour, or perhaps as-yet undiscovered great minds who can bring us to the next level."

At that, with a subtle nod of his head, Dong tossed speaking responsibilities to Grinkov, who rose as the Chinese man sat down.

He cleared his throat loudly and said in heavily accented English, "I am pleased to announce that Presidents Cummings, Dong, and I have a proposal for how to make the United Space Exchange space outreach program accessible to all. Please allow us to present it to you for consideration and discussion. There are facets of it that will require thought and negotiation, and we humbly ask for your opinion. Our hope is that we can work together for change. Our further hope is that by the end of this week, we will have an agreed-upon plan that we can bring to global United Nations meeting next week. There, we will invite all nations to be part of this initiative."

Grinkov then looked meaningfully at Cummings, indicating that it was his turn to speak.

Cummings switched places with the Russian man and said, "Thank you, Sergei." Then he looked around the room. "Before I present the general principles under which China, Russia, and the United States envision a single space colonization project moving ahead, let me assure you that the formation of the United Space Exchange is not intended to override existing space-related initiatives or partnerships, either with our three nations or between yourselves. This is a separate initiative that has a goal to ensure that all nations on Earth have a stake in colonization. It is not meant to usurp work already in progress."

There was clapping, a signal that the overall mandate of the United Space Exchange was appreciated.

Cummings said, "Thank you. I'm pleased that you share my enthusiasm for this project." Then he looked over at Dong, who was urgently signaling that he had something to say. "President Dong," Cummings said, "your floor."

Dong stood. "Friends and colleagues," he said, "I ask you this . . . does it not show what an unprecedented new era we are entering when my country and Russia are partnering with America in good faith? Too long we have been rivals and enemies. Too long we have let ill will rule the day. It ends now."

Then he sat down, and Grinkov rose to add, "The last one hundred years of war and fighting have come at a heavy price for humankind. We have the opportunity now to work on the challenges we *all* face and to build trust among nations. To start, I hope we can work together to make the colonization of space a single human initiative."

There was silence in the room as the significance of what the three presidents were proposing sank in . . . and then suddenly, every person in the room stood and gave them a resounding standing ovation. Cummings felt a rush of emotion in his chest. This was an exciting moment and he was deeply moved.

When the clapping died down, he rose to speak. He took a deep breath to steady the tremor in his voice. Then he cleared his throat and said, "Let me tell you a little bit more about the vision my colleagues and I have of how to use the United Space Exchange to kick-start the process of colonizing the moon and Mars."

Cummings looked at Grinkov, who was standing behind him, and Grinkov nodded and clicked a remote control in his hand. A video screen sprang to life behind the three leaders. On the screen a logo appeared—carefully crafted by Angelica Lopez with input from her Chinese and Russian counterparts—of a rocket ship with the UN symbol on its side.

"In our vision, ownership and control of the United Space Exchange would be proportional to investment, whether that investment be money, resources, technology, or manpower, creating a model that brings nations together to share in development costs and risk. You may note the UN symbol on the logo. I'll explain in more detail shortly. But first, let's start with rocket selection."

Grinkov clicked the remote, and the picture they were looking at changed to a three-panel image showing an American rocket in one panel, a Russian rocket in another, and a Chinese rocket in the third.

"Getting to the moon is much easier than getting to Mars, so we will focus our colonization efforts there in the short term. Before we start, however, we need reliable, multiple-use rockets to shuttle supplies, tools, and tradesmen back and forth." Cummings said. "We have choices from our countries," he indicated himself, Dong, Grinkov, "as well as from the private sector."

At this, Grinkov clicked the remote again, switching the image to show rockets created by Jeff Bezos, Elon Musk, and Richard Branson.

Grinkov then switched the image to one of the moon's surface, and Cummings continued. "It is expected that the moon will initially be a mining colony," he said. "Once we've created a habitable environment on the moon for humans to live in, we will further establish a robotics centre, with engineers populating it in shifts to monitor a fleet of mining robots which we hope will mine water from moon rocks."

He heard throats clearing, and he looked around the room at puzzled faces.

Smiling, he said, "I know what you're thinking . . . how can rocks have water in them? Let me explain: The rocks and regolith that make up the lunar surface are about 45% oxygen, and the solar wind—the constant stream of charged particles emitted by the sun—is mostly hydrogen. Where free oxygen and hydrogen exist, there is a high chance water will form. It's just a matter of technology, people. And once we have the technology to harness this, we not only have water, but we have the hydrogen and oxygen needed for rocket fuel."

His audience was intently focused on his words, so he continued. "And that's not all," he said. "Have any of you heard of Helium-3?"

Very few hands went up, so he explained, "Helium-3 is a critical element in fusion reactors. It's rare on Earth, but it is abundant on the moon; In fact, the moon is estimated to have enough Helium-3 to fill the electricity needs of Earth for 10,000 years."

There was loud murmuring at this; Everyone in the room knew that Earth's demand for electricity was growing exponentially.

Grinkov changed the slide again, this time to show a glowing Earth city, which seemed to be London.

The nighttime picture was quite stunning, and the multitude of city lights twinkled as Cummings said, "That is a remarkable resource, and it could change the face of the power industry."

Then the screen behind Cummings began cycling through a collage of landscapes and people from around the world as he said, "The United Space Exchange will encourage both private and public sector participation in all aspects of the colonization process, and all aspects will be put out to fair bid. The only goal of the United Space Exchange is to create long-term benefits to all people of the world."

There was enthusiastic clapping.

And then a lone, thickly accented Indian voice broke through the din. "Please, I have a question," it said.

Cummings recognized Aisha Singh, the Indian prime minister.

He acknowledged her, and she asked, "You've said you want to colonize both the moon *and* Mars, both of which offer vastly different sets of challenges. How do you plan to tie the two together?"

"I'm glad you asked that question," replied Cummings, "and the short answer is, given the smaller gravitational force on the moon, we have a long-term vision of it becoming a rocket launching pad for interplanetary space travel. And if the natural resources I talked of earlier are effectively harnessed, it could become a refueling hub as well. We may even be able to locate fueling stations offshore of the moon, so big rockets don't even need to land there."

"Do you really think getting human beings onto Mars is feasible?" Singh asked, her brow furrowed. "At its closest, Mars is 35 million miles away . . . and when the Earth and Mars are in opposite orbits, that number is 250 million miles! Even when they are close together, that's a lot of fuel to carry."

"Yes, it's a hell of a distance," said Cummings, "but of course, the goal would be to produce rocket fuel from local resources once Martian colonization is achieved, so return fuel doesn't have to be packed, and overall payload is less."

"Well, until there is refueling capability on both the moon and Mars, it is likely travel will occur only on a biannual cycle when the planets are closer together," sniffed Singh.

"I agree," said Cummings, "but new technology is being developed all the time. We should not underestimate the ingenuity of future generations of human beings."

Singh cocked her head and looked at him, assessing his words. She did not comment, and so Cummings looked around at the raptly staring audience, all of which were thinking of the possibilities.

"Until we begin planning and jump in with both feet, we're not going to know what is possible," he told them. "However, as I mentioned, the first hurdle is to settle on a rocket system that meets our needs. After that, we will develop an equitable system for seat and cargo allocation... which brings me back to the structure of the United Space Exchange."

At that, he gestured to Dong to speak.

"Thank you, President Cummings," Dong said. Then he addressed the room. "Presidents Cummings, Grinkov and I propose that a voting system recognizing the main contributors to the United Space Exchange—in this case, our three countries—be adopted. We have developed a plan designating the U.S., China, and Russia as 'primary sponsors' for the colonization project, which would give our countries significant voting rights. We're looking at a percentage system which would give 35% of voting rights each to America and China, and 20% to Russia. After that, the next five largest supporters of the United Space Exchange would each share 10% of the votes."

There was a rumble of dissent around the room and Aisha Singh led the charge, criticizing the plan by attacking President Cummings directly.

She looked at him and said angrily, "How is this different, Samuel, than what you so soundly criticized last week at the global institutions meeting? You said that the permanent five members of the Security Council appointed *themselves*, and that they control the others. And now you are proposing to do the same!"

Cummings felt himself redden. It was no secret that India would soon become the fourth nation to conduct independent human spaceflight, and that under Singh's leadership, the Indian Space Research Organization intended to start a space station program, followed by crewed lunar landings and interplanetary missions.

"There is room for negotiation, Prime Minister Singh," he said with a sigh. "The top five second-tier partners would be *India*," he looked significantly at her as he said her country's name, "Japan, the United Kingdom, Germany, and France as their space programs are significantly developed. And to level the playing field, we can build a mechanism into our planning to ensure other countries can lobby primary sponsors for seats. Also, please note that the United Space Exchange's goal is only to get the colonization process *started*. Within a few decades, it will not be required any longer and will be dissolved—though perhaps it will be resurrected someday to kick-start colonization of the moons of Jupiter and Saturn."

Singh politely nodded her understanding, though it was clear she felt the program was not a good bet for her own country unless India was offered a more significant role.

"Qu'en est-il de l'Agence Spatiale Européenne!? And what about the European Space Agency!?" yelled out the French president, Marcel Brassard.

"The European Space Agency is not a single nation, and so it is not included in this list," replied Cummings.

Cummings saw Singh roll her eyes. Clearly, she still did not trust his motives.

And so he said specifically to her, "The primary sponsors are firmly committed to making the moon and Mars open to all nations, and all countries of the world will be invited to become non-voting members."

However, his words had no impact. She just glared balefully at him.

Several seats to his left, Cummings saw Angelica Lopez trying to catch his eye.

She mouthed, "She doesn't buy it."

He just shrugged, and then he sat down and let Dong Yang take the speaker's reins.

Dong said, "As my colleague, President Cummings, stated, this is a proposal only, so let us move on. Two things I'd like to touch on are the bid process and intellectual property rights." He paused dramatically, looked around the room, and continued, "To allow both public and private sector companies equal access, all bidding will be managed by an independent third party selected by the UN. And to get around concerns over intellectual property rights, we propose a free trade mechanism wherein successful bidders agree to an 'open architecture' approach, meaning that after fifteen years, their technology will be made freely available to others."

There was disgruntled murmuring at this. People did not like to share their secrets, and sensing dissent, Dong swiftly moved on before it could catch fire.

"There is one final subject to discuss," he said hastily, "and that is governance. My colleagues and I favour the idea of the moon and Mars developing their own governing bodies over time—however, in the short term, they will be governed from Earth through a renovated United Nations. We propose that the UN will also establish the ground rules for colonization and resource extraction on the moon and Mars as well. Are there any objections to this?"

There were no immediate comments.

And so, Dong quickly ceded the floor to Cummings, who said, "Well then, if there are no objections, then let's end this meeting with a show of hands. All who think this is a good model in principle, please say 'aye' and raise your hands."

A surprising amount of hands went up and a rumble of 'ayes' shook the room. A knot in Cummings' stomach that had been formed by Aisha Singh's disapproval began to dissolve.

"Excellent," he said. "I will arrange for the minutes of this meeting to be circulated, as well as a call for comments and suggestions that will make this global initiative *fly*, so to speak."

There was laughter at his comment, and the group began to shuffle out.

"Remember!" he called to the departing backs. "My goal is to have signoff before the UN meeting next week!"

As the G20 members left, Lopez hastily made her way over to her boss.

As he picked his notes up from off the table, she said, "I know it seemed like no one was ready to commit, but you made a great pitch."

"Thanks," Cummings said a little morosely. "It's too bad Aisha Singh is so mistrustful of the structure we've proposed."

"Well," Lopez said thoughtfully, "India has invested a lot in their space program, and I guess she feels disrespected that her potential contribution is regarded as some sort of pittance."

"But it's the only way I can think of to structure things equitably," protested Cummings, ruffled. "Not to recognize that America, Russia, and China will be investing the most time, money, and manpower in this effort is to disrespect our *own* contributions."

"I know," said Lopez carefully, "but from her point of view, I guess it seems a bit biased."

Cummings met her eyes, and then said with a sigh, "Oh well, I guess except for Aisha Singh, we got a reasonable amount of support—and next week at the global meeting in New York, we'll get a clearer picture of what's going to work."

"Or you'll get a kick in the ass," quipped Lopez.

Cummings laughed as his vice president took her leave.

The next day, Cummings met briefly with Lopez to ensure that the G20 meeting minutes were circulated; that voting on the United Space Exchange structure was tabulated; and that a call-out for suggestions to improve the plan was circulated to all G20 members. He couldn't help fretting about getting consensus on the planning documents. He desperately wanted signoff from all G20 members in time for the New York meeting.

He needn't have worried; Lopez was a miracle worker.

"Here you go," she said as she passed him a sheaf of papers two days after the meeting. "The feedback from the G20 in Houston was largely positive, though the second-tier group felt they should have more say, more power, and more opportunity to invest."

"Do you agree with them?" Cummings asked her, remembering her defence of Aisha Singh after the G20 meeting.

"Well," she said, taking a deep breath, "you're not going to like this, but yes—I think you should give them more stake in it. In my opinion, there is room for others at the top of the heap."

She was right; He didn't like the answer. He conferenced Dong and Grinkov to discuss it.

"I don't like it," said Dong when he heard the demands of the second-tier group.

But Grinkov thought differently. "I am willing to give up 5% of my stake," said Grinkov. "My country is preoccupied with rebuilding. I can move over to let keener countries feel more included . . . and in the process, I will save my country some money, which I can invest in improving our economy."

Cummings sighed. "I'm with you, Sergei," he said. "I will give up 5%."

Reluctantly, Dong got on board as well. "It is agreed," he said. "30% voting rights each for China and America, 15% for Russia, and 5% each for Japan, India, the United Kingdom, Germany, and France."

"Yes," said Cummings. "It's a fairer model. And perhaps the United Space Exchange can buy back shares from countries that want to decrease ownership and sell them to countries that want to become voting members."

"Good," said Grinkov. "Huzzah!"

"And now the final piece of the puzzle is governance," said Cummings. "We've established that a revamped UN will govern newly established space colonies, and it makes sense that it also sets the ground rules for resource development in the short term as well."

"But revenues should accrue to those bearing costs and risks," said Dong firmly.

There was silence between the three men for a moment.

And then Grinkov smiled softly and said to Dong, "Is it not God's will that we walk a path where our actions benefit others? Is this a mission to make money? Or to make peace?"

Cummings felt his face sting with sudden shame. He realized he'd been so lost in planning that he'd forgotten God's instructions.

"Sergei, you're right," he said. "I think we have some revising to do."

At that, the three men set to work. They worked well into the night and then forwarded their completed proposal, which specified that 30% of all profits be used for humanitarian aid, to Angelica Lopez.

Then, Cummings filled the rest of his week with meetings. Herbert Sloan told him America's Clean Water Initiative was going well, and that he'd begun testing rainwater collection systems. And Martin Grieves reported positive things about the Ford retrofit and military repatriation efforts. These positive reports heartened him as he anxiously waited to hear whether the G20 nations would accept his revised proposal.

It was literally twelve hours before the New York meeting of all nations on Earth that he got his answer; Unanimous signoff was finally achieved. The president of the United States celebrated by falling into bed, exhausted.

On the morning of the UN meeting, Cummings rose late. He barely had time to brush his teeth and gulp down a coffee before Sarah stood before him in all her radiance, ready to transport him.

"I'm sorry I'm late," he said, so startled when she appeared in his kitchen that he splashed coffee on his clean, white shirt.

Sarah simply fluttered energetically in response. "You are talking to a being who can control time," she said. "Go and change your shirt, finish your coffee, and make sure you've eaten something. I'll get you there in plenty of time."

Grateful, he did as she said, and when he was calmer, more relaxed, and had a piece of toast in his belly, Sarah deposited him in front of the UN as promised.

As at the G20 meeting, he was jointly chairing this meeting with Dong and Grinkov. He quickly made his way to his seat between them, and after exchanging quick greetings, began his introductory remarks.

"Good day," he said to the assembled national heads of state. "I invite all nations to join us in the first global initiative to colonize space!"

Then, as they'd done a week before, the three men presented their proposal. He felt optimistic about a positive response, given the unanimous signoff by the G20 nations.

And so he was quite shocked when the Australian prime minister, Ben Morrison, said bitterly, "I see almost no chance of getting a seat on a Mars mission in the next fifty years. So why should my country participate? The large countries that control the United Space Exchange will make the large money. It sounds like another case of the rich getting richer and the poor getting fleeced."

"Prime Minister Morrison," said Cummings as coolly as he could, "Australia is one of the largest mining countries on Earth, and the moon will be a mining colony. There is great opportunity for Australia's participation. Your country could align with Canada to become a centre of expertise for extraterrestrial mining. Or with your skill at dealing with water shortages, you could partner with South Africa to become preferred water project partners."

Morrison did not answer, but he appeared to be considering Cummings' words.

Then Cummings addressed the rest of the room, saying, "The goal of the United Space Exchange is to provide global access to colonization—but there will be independent missions to the moon as well, and in the same way towns have been built near industry since human civilization began, independent populated colonies may spring up to support them." Then, looking directly at Morrison, he added, "In fact, there may be Australians hopping around all *over* the moon."

Laughter broke out at the idea of Australians hopping on the moon.

It had just died down when suddenly Sarah appeared in a waft of rose-scented air and a flurry of mist that dissolved as her form took shape.

Her gracious voice rang throughout the room like chimes as she said, "Hello, world leaders."

People couldn't help clapping at her arrival. Her presence always inspired awe.

When the noise died down, she said, "It is so good to see you all, and let me applaud you on the good work you are doing."

Something about the way she delivered the words caused a sense of possibility to permeate the room.

"I only have one thing to add," she said. "As with any great venture, there will be those who feel left out. This needs to be approached with compromise and care." Then, looking directly at Cummings, she said, "Samuel, perhaps you could address this?"

He stood, knowing the solution—and also knowing she'd telepathically transferred it to him. Feeling confident and calm, he said, "We could allocate a specific amount of seats on each flight—perhaps 5%—and through a lottery system which could be determined by population instead of economic strength. Qualification criteria would have to remain standardized, of course . . . but this allows global participation. We will also ensure that some of the revenues from mining royalties are shared with all nations through UN-sponsored humanitarian aid program."

The clapping in the room indicated that he'd hit the nail on the head. It was a perfect solution.

"Thank you, Sarah," he whispered.

She simply glowed in her special way, and then disappeared.

The proposal that 5% of seats be allocated to non-owners of the United Space Exchange, combined with the decision to donate to humanitarian aid, pushed the whole deal over the top. Ultimately, 85% of the world's nations—representing 95% of the global population—voted in support of the United Space Exchange concept and structure, with unanimous agreement that a revised UN should be the governing body for colonies until they were able to govern themselves.

Chapter 33

Climate Change Conference

Cummings awoke to the sound of chimes. Exhausted by the events of the past week, he tried to ignore it, but it wouldn't go away. He groaned and reached for Lorena, but she wasn't there; In fact, his hand found nothing but air . . . no sheets, no blankets, no pillow either. Distressed, his eyes popped open, and he was alarmed to find himself floating weightless in the air in the dawn light, over the ocean, in his striped pajamas.

"What the . . . *heck* . . ." he gasped in surprise. "Sarah? Is this your doing?"

"Of course it is, Samuel," said Sarah pleasantly from within the air around him. "I thought you might like to watch the sunrise with me."

"Well of course I'm *honoured* to do that . . . but I need to get back to the White House. I have tons to do today. The blueprint for the revised UN is being presented, and we're going to vote on it. And then there's the climate change meeting coming up . . ."

"Shhhh . . ." said Sarah. "Look to your left. The sun is about to rise."

Cummings was in no position to argue, and so he simply did as she asked, and he was greeted by the spectacular sight of the sun sliding up over the ocean, raising its pink, orange, and gloriously yellow head over the edge of the world. Despite his annoyance, he was moved by the sight.

"That's incredible," he said in awe. "It's like a painting by God."

"It is," agreed Sarah, "and God wishes more people would take the time to enjoy this great work, Samuel."

"Well, I guess all great artists want their work to be appreciated," he offered, knowing he sounded a little lame.

"Yes, but that's not the point," said Sarah. "The point is that you humans rush through your lives so blindly that you miss the pure joy God has created for you. It's part of the reason you're so warlike. You feel absence more than you feel presence, and so there is always *lack*. Lack causes unabated desired, and so you constantly want what others have . . . yet if you would only pause and reflect once in a while, you would see that all you have ever needed was provided when God created you."

"But that's not true!" protested Cummings. "Some animals can walk seconds after they're born and know instinctively how to forage, while we need clothing, nurturing, holding . . ."

"Yes, you are more dependent on others of your kind than your average furred beast," agreed Sarah, "but once you are past that stage, you are completely capable of happiness without outside accoutrements. Happiness is something in your *spirit*, and it is something you must feed, just as you feed your body."

"I appreciate that," said Cummings cautiously as he started to enjoy the process of floating. "But why are you telling me this?"

"Because you are worried," said Sarah, "and you needn't be. I will help you, as I will help all the world, to work toward the goals you have set. You will get a positive reaction on the revised UN proposal that will be unveiled today; You will be able to move ahead with a sense of optimism; And this new organization will be able to finally make meaningful progress in the battle against climate change . . . but right now, you will feed your soul by enjoying this sunrise with me."

Cummings looked again at the sunrise. It was brighter now, shades of purple and gold exploding over the ocean with sparkling, coloured light. He saw the plume of a whale in the distance and heard the squawking of gulls as they, too, admired the morning glory . . . And as he watched the world awaken, he felt a calmness in his soul that had been missing for the past month or so, and he realized that he was tired, *so* tired of shouldering the great responsibility that had been heaped on him since God's intervention. He sighed heavily, letting the burden drop as he relaxed into the surprisingly warm breeze that carried his body. Feeling lighter, he drank in the colour, sounds, and freshness of the morning, savoring the experience with a unique rapture.

Soon the sun was fully over the horizon, big, bright, and shining. Cummings continued to look at it for as long as he could, but eventually, it became too bright, and so he shut his eyes... and was suddenly awakened by Lorena's hand on his shoulder.

"Do you want some coffee?" she asked, extending a fragrant cup. "I know you have a lot on your plate today, so I thought I'd bring you coffee in bed. Now I'm going to make scrambled eggs while you shower."

"Thanks," he said as he sat up and stretched.

He got out of bed and sauntered into the bathroom, wondering if the sunrise he'd experienced had been real or a dream. He supposed it didn't matter. Sarah had made her point; *Slow down and smell the coffee*, he thought. And he did just that, taking a long sniff before sipping the fine French roast Lorena had made him. His responsibilities would remain constant, but this moment, he realized, would not come his way again. Later, when he sat in the Oval Office preparing for the climate change meeting, he remembered the smell of that coffee, and it made him smile and think fondly of his wife and of the beauty of a sunrise.

When he got into the Oval Office and fired up his computer, there was good news to greet him. The UN restructuring team—made up of representatives from the U.S., China, the European Union, Russia, India, Egypt, South Africa, Malaysia, Brazil, and Switzerland—had developed their proposal for an updated United Nations and had posted it online on a secure site for comment.

Cummings logged on and found the document with no problem. He read:

Proposed Revised UN Structure

Name: Earth Council

Purpose: To bring all countries of the Earth together before God to promote cooperation among nations in all matters related to human fellowship, human endeavor, and human physical and spiritual wellness, and in all matters related to sustainable use of the resources of the planet.

Structure: The Members of Earth Council ('Members') will be the Heads of State of each country. The Members will elect an Operations Committee to organize the biannual meetings of the Council. The Members will also appoint the Boards of Directors and Chief Executive

Officers of all of the Council's subsidiary organizations. The Members will approve the mandates, business plans, and annual budgets for each subsidiary organization and for the Council. (*Note: Compensation for Chief Executive Officers will be performance based*).

Subsidiary Organizations: All existing UN subsidiary organizations have been reviewed to determine their relevance on a 'go forward' basis. It is recommended that six of the fourteen large organizations be eliminated and two others be combined into one to cover marine and air navigation. The World Meteorological Organization should be subsumed under a new World Environment Organization. It is also recommended that the World Court and The World Trade Organization be brought into the Earth Council.

Funding: Funding of Council costs will be borne by Member countries in proportion to their gross domestic product. Most of Earth Council's costs will be in subsidiary organizations, and each of them will have a different funding formula. Some have the opportunity to implement 'user pay' services for a significant portion of their costs (e.g. the World Court, the World Trade Organization, the IMF, and the World Bank). World Health Organization and World Food and Agriculture Organization transfer payments will be allocated on the basis of population, while other expenses of subsidiary operations will be allocated on the basis of GDP.

Voting: The vote of each Member Country will carry the same weight as that country's percentage of the organization's funding. Every Member Country's vote will be counted on every issue, and no country or group of countries will be able to veto anything. (*Note: There will be no concept equivalent to the UN Security Council which allocates higher percentages to specific players*). Major issues will require a two-thirds majority to pass.

Approval of this initial charter requires a 75% majority. As preliminary estimates indicate that the U.S. and China will provide approximately 16% and 15% of the total funding responsibility of Earth Council, their votes will likely add up to 31% on any issue.

The ten countries who participated in the preparation of this proposal have a combined voting weight of 67%.

Cummings read the document with interest. He was particularly pleased to read about the idea of the UN's World Meteorological Organization becoming part of the proposed World Environment Organization. *This could really make a difference,* he thought.

A meeting to discuss the proposal was scheduled for 10:00 a.m., which was only fifteen minutes away. Instead of meeting in person, it had been agreed that this meeting was to be held via Zoom, as some world leaders had expressed reticence at the idea of attending yet another meeting in person. Most were gearing up for the climate change meeting that was just two days away, and they wanted to be physically present for that, so it was decided that discussion and voting on the proposal could be done online.

Cummings got up to pour himself a cup of coffee just as his assistant, Janice, poked her head into the room.

"Today's the big meeting to vote on the UN restructuring, Sir," she said. "Do you want me to help you set up your Zoom meeting?"

"Yes, please, Janice," said Cummings, adding, "I've invited Angelica Lopez, Bradley Northrup, Norman Feldman, Gordon Blackstone, and Hana Shriver to join me as well. I imagine they will be here soon, but if you could rattle their chains, so to speak, that would be great."

"No problem," said Janice. "I'll do that as soon as I've got you set up."

She immediately got to work making sure the Bluetooth link between Cummings' computer and the overhead monitor was working, and then she opened the meeting, which was not yet online.

She said, "There! It's all set. As soon as the moderator lets you in, it's go time."

"Thanks, Janice," said Cummings as she disappeared out the door of the Oval Office.

About ten minutes later, she poked her head in again to say, "Your team is on their way, Sir."

"Thanks again," he told her.

She left just as Lopez entered the room, followed closely by Feldman.

"Hello," Cummings said to them. "Have a seat."

They were settling into their seats as Blackstone, Shriver, and Northrup arrived.

"The old gang rides again," said Shriver with a smile as she looked at her colleagues.

"Yes, indeed," Cummings replied.

Then he clicked on the meeting link to find that for the first time ever, a global meeting was chaired by Sarah herself, who miraculously managed to make the Zoom connection feel and function as if they were all in the same room together. Soon they were in communication with leaders from around the world.

"Leaders of the Earth," she said, her many-faced form flickering over their screens like water. "This is a big day for Planet Earth. Today, you are looking at creating a de facto world government, which until now has been a very divisive topic. We are going to discuss and vote on the efficacy of a one-world Earth Council, a body that would have more authority than its predecessor, the United Nations."

"Hear, hear!" yelled several of the meeting participants.

"Under the authority of the Earth Council," continued Sarah, "the law of the world community will be placed above that of individual nations, and there will be a supreme law against war. As well, the Earth Council will have the authority to regulate friction between the peoples of the world through whatever means necessary. The mandate of the Earth Council is to enable all citizens of the world to grow and expand physically, mentally, emotionally, and spiritually. The Earth Council will function on the premise that all people are members of a common society with common objectives of world peace, economic advancement, respect for human rights, and environmental preservation."

A chorus of whistles and cheers erupted through Cummings' tiny computer speakers, and through the magic of Sarah, it trickled out in a wave and filled the room with sound as loud as if they were in an auditorium.

"That is *truly* remarkable," said Shriver, reacting to the people's enthusiasm. "I can't believe how pumped everyone is about this initiative!"

"I know," Cummings replied. "All I can say is that with God—and Sarah—all things are possible."

"Apparently so," remarked Shriver, still awed by what was happening.

"You have all had a chance to review the proposal," Sarah continued, "and now is the time for discussion and debate. Please address your concerns via text to the panel who put the proposal together. You will find them in your contacts lists under the name 'Earth Council Working Group.'"

There were many questions, and Cummings and his team read them as they rolled up the side of the overhead monitor. What was heartening, however, was that most of them were about proposed mandates, business plans, and budgets for the Earth Council's subsidiary organizations instead of about the Earth Council itself. It was clear that the idea of the global governance and oversight was not only accepted but welcomed by a world that was tired of constant war. Ultimately, by day's end, many suggestions had made it into the revised plan, including a mechanism to ensure that minority voting countries (33%) could vote in two directors on each board of every Earth Council organization.

It was an historic moment when agreement was reached, and when the discussions about various points ended, and the document was amended to address them, there was a call for an electronic, anonymous vote. And just like that, the UN became the Earth Council—an upgraded, global governance body.

Cummings and his team were elated.

"I expected so much more resistance," said Blackstone, rubbing his chin. "Warfare is so culturally ingrained in this world that I never thought we'd see the end of it!" Then he laughed suddenly and said, "Well, I guess this military man is out of a job!"

"Oh, I'm sure we'll find something else for you to do," joked Cummings. "How about you start by getting me a coffee?"

"I don't know how to make coffee, Sir," Blackstone deadpanned back. "Out in the trenches, we drink mud."

"Touché!" laughed Cummings. "What I really meant to say is that you are a valued member of this team, no matter what capacity you are in. And I'm sure the new National Security Force will be run with the precision and attention to detail that you have brought to your military career."

"Thank you, Sir," said Blackstone. "You can count on me."

On that note, the team broke for the day, and Cummings returned to his presidential quarters to find Lorena already asleep. Checking his watch, he realized that it was already nearly 10:00 p.m., and so he crawled into bed beside her, doing his best not to wake her as he gave her a soft kiss on the cheek. He was asleep himself within ten minutes.

The next morning, Cummings woke before his alarm went off and hopped out of bed with a spring in his step.

"Whoa there, cowboy," said Lorena sleepily as she opened her eyes to a bright, sunny day. "What's the rush?"

"I have to prep for the Climate Change Conference," said Cummings. "I need to familiarize myself with the Earth Council's new World Environment Organization. This organization could be key to saving this planet of ours, Lorena."

Lorena just looked at him, not quite comprehending his words through her sleep-fuddled brain. "The Climate Change Conference . . ." she began to ask sleepily . . . but then suddenly, she was wide awake—and inordinately pleased. She asked, "Are you going to this meeting in person?"

"Yes, why?" Cummings said as he tied his tie.

She sat up. "Don't think you're going to Miami without *me*," she said. "I'm not missing that trip."

Cummings was a little puzzled by her insistence on going, though both of them liked Miami well enough.

However, he laughed at her enthusiasm and replied, "I wouldn't think of it!"

On the morning of the meeting, Sarah transported them to Miami, depositing them gently outside a complex of buildings that included the Miami Conference Center, a theatre, a convention centre, an auditorium, and a lecture hall. As soon as the two of them had regained their equilibrium after the teleportation, Lorena looked at her husband and smiled like a cat who'd eaten a canary.

"What?" asked Cummings.

"It's too bad you have a meeting," she said, pointing to the nearby James L. Knight Center, "because in just three short hours, I'll be listening to Andrea Bocelli from a third row seat. I wish you could be there with me, honey."

"Oh, aren't *you* the clever one," laughed Cummings. "No wonder you were so eager to come with me. Well, you enjoy the show. But thank me when I strike a home run on climate change today, will you? Fixing the disaster we're living in is the only way to ensure you live to see another opera star strut his stuff."

Lorena kissed him. "*You're* the star," she said, "and I have every confidence that your meeting will go well."

They parted ways, and in short order, Cummings was ensconced in his seat facing the other global leaders, this time in person. As the meeting was being held in America, he had been tapped once again to chair.

"Well," he said to the now familiar faces of his colleagues, "it seems that we just can't get enough of each other."

There were some chuckles around the room because all of them were feeling the same way. They'd been to so many meetings together in the past few months that they were getting quite comfortable with one another; So comfortable, in fact, that Cummings noted some of them were wearing casual clothing instead of traditional business outfits. He smiled to himself; Nothing engendered good relations more than familiarity and a sense of comfort.

"Welcome to Miami, ladies and gentlemen," he began. "Today is the day we're going to make meaningful strides toward alleviating climate change before it renders the Earth uninhabitable. In 2016, 175 countries—including my own, the United States of America—signed the Paris Climate Agreement. Today, 191 members of the Earth Council's Framework Convention on Climate Change—a former UN initiative—are parties to the agreement."

Cummings' simple introduction received a standing ovation from the 600 delegates. For once, it seemed the whole world was standing together on something. It warmed Cummings' heart to see this.

"The Paris Agreement set targets for greenhouse gas emissions," he continued, "which, while seen as aggressive by many, are acknowledged by others as only baby steps. Predictably, when it was signed, the agreement was lauded by world leaders; However, environmentalists and analysts were quick to point out that it had no teeth, as none of the recommendations contained in the agreement were binding." He looked around the room solemnly. "Why do you think this is?" he asked.

Cummings did not wait for response. He simply said, "I'll tell you why . . . it's because the truth about change is that people don't want to do it—not if it costs them jobs or requires them to give up the only way of life they know. And what is that way of life? Certainly in the developed world, including my own country, it's one of excess consumption. Think of what we take for granted . . . hot water on demand, multiple cars per household, entertainment at our fingertips, food so plentiful that a significant number of us are obese. We don't want to give this stuff up, do we?"

He looked around the room. He was aware that he had everyone's attention. "The hard, sad truth," he said, "is that if every car manufacturer and every gas pump shut down tomorrow, we'd all scream bloody murder. We'd rally with cries of 'Don't take away our jobs, rights, transportation' and so on until we were blue in the face. We want someone *else* to make sacrifices. Certainly it shouldn't be us, right? So, the reason the Climate Accord has no teeth is because social pressure has made politicians weak. We've relaxed emissions targets because people don't *want* to change. And we're getting flak for that, just as we got flak for implementing changes in the first place. As politicians, we're damned if we do and damned if we don't, am I right?"

He could hear muted noises of agreement from the assembled group.

"Then Covid-19 hit the world," he said, pausing to look around the room. "Now don't get me wrong with what I have to say about the pandemic. I don't wish deadly illness on anyone . . . but you can't deny the *positive* impact the pandemic had. Oil consumption evaporated almost overnight, and many countries responded to this with societal and economic changes. Even now, with Covid downgraded from pandemic to 'problem to be managed,' we still see the impact. For example, teleworking is becoming the norm for many companies, which not only cuts down on commuter pollution but on the astronomical costs of office heating and maintenance. How odd that a pandemic has been a *gift*. And this is nothing compared to the reduction in oil consumption and associated greenhouse gas emissions that have been occurring since the elimination of war. And the good news is that about 90% of this reduction will be *permanent*."

Another standing ovation thundered around the room, so loud Cummings thought he might soon be deafened.

He waited until it completely petered out before he continued. "I'm sure you agree with me that this is great news," he said. "However, it does not mean the battle is over. While the rate of carbon dioxide increase in the atmosphere has slowed—and may even stabilize in the short term—it is still at a level that could eventually lead to a sixty-foot rise in sea level . . . about twenty meters, for you metric thinkers. Think about what that means; Almost all of Florida will be submerged. This building we're sitting in today will likely be completely underwater. Luckily, this process will probably take hundreds, if not thousands of years. Most of us will be long gone before beachfront property becomes available in the Midwestern U.S."

A spattering of laughter greeted this comment, and Cummings paused dramatically to let it fill the room and die out before continuing.

Then he said, "Despite my joke, it's nothing to laugh about. This is a huge threat to our planet. Even if carbon dioxide levels remain stable, we are going to see a rise in our oceans of at least three feet, or about one meter, over the next forty to fifty years. In my country, we're preparing. We've been making plans to reinforce our coastlines and protect coastal communities. We are redeploying many of our former military members to work on this project, and we expect the cost of this to exceed $1 trillion."

"In addition," Cummings continued, "weather events are getting worse, and they are going to continue to get more violent and more frequent as time goes on. Sadly for America, the U.S. will be at the epicenter of many of the worst ones. Our experts predict that parts of our country hit by flooding, wind damage, and tornadoes will sustain damage that will cost hundreds of billions of dollars to repair. Conversely, other parts of the country will be thrown into drought conditions—which is currently happening in the southwestern United States. Food production is suffering, and it's a real possibility that not just people, but whole *farms* will have to be relocated."

He paused, gazed solemnly around the room, and then said, "In recent times, the world has seen how disruptive it is when hundreds of thousands of people are forced to seek asylum in other nations, such as what happened when Syrian refugees were forced to flee their homes. Think about this: With rising sea levels and more violent storms, the creation of 'climate refugees' is a real possibility, and the movement of mass amounts of people who are fleeing unbearable conditions will pose a much *greater* problem than the relatively small amounts of people who've historically fled war zones."

There was a rumble of concern around the room as the assembled group pondered just where climate refugees would go in a world that was getting increasingly erratic in its climate patterns, not to mention increasingly hostile to refugees.

"I know you're wondering where all these people will go," Cummings said, reading their thoughts. "I wonder the same thing. And I guess the answer is that it will depend on what they can afford. The rich will be proactive. They will follow climate news and transport themselves to wherever things are stable. The poor will be *reactive*. They will run when they have to, and they will be forced take risky avenues of travel. People smuggling will take on a whole new visage, and it won't be good. But—despite the risks—migrate they will . . . After all, who wants to live in a community that's burning up or ravaged by floods? We all want to live so-called 'normal' lives somewhere, don't we? But what if there is no normal ever again? What do we do? Do we simply hang our heads in shame and apologize to our grandchildren? What do we say? Do we tell them, 'Hey, I'm sorry we really messed up the planet—but I'm sure you'll make the best of it?'"

He gazed fiercely around the room, and then raised both fists in the air and shook them. "That is not what responsible people do!" he cried. "And it is not what the United States is going to do! Starting now, the United States of America is taking a leadership role in reducing the American carbon footprint on this planet. Not only is my country going to implement carbon pricing and incentivize renewable power generation, but we are going to encourage off-grid power and water solutions. We are going to *be* the change we want to see, and we are going to make a difference. The words 'sustainable development' are going to have real meaning in the United States—perhaps for the first time in a century—and I urge every nation of the Earth to stand with me!"

At his words, another standing ovation shook the room. Cummings reveled in the support, feeling confident in both his words and his promises.

When the noise died down, he swept his arm in a half-circle to indicate communion with his fellow world leaders and said, "I look to all of you to begin the process of measuring and monitoring the carbon footprints of every nation on Earth so that we can find meaningful ways to reduce carbon emissions. Sarah has taught us that God wants us to put the needs of others ahead of our own. By reducing our carbon imprint, we are putting the needs of our children and *their* children ahead of our own. Do you agree? Are you with me on this?"

A mighty roar of assent shook the room. "Yes!" cried the people.

Cummings felt carried away. Instead of simply chairing a meeting on climate change, it seemed he was leading a movement. He couldn't help but think of the words Sarah had spoken to him shortly after he'd met her.

She'd said, "Samuel, you can't second-guess yourself or wonder about your choices anymore. The only way is *forward*."

He finally understood what she meant.

Chapter 34

Women's Changing Roles

"Where the heck are my silver hoop earrings!?" called out a flustered Lorena to her husband from their bedroom.

It was nine o'clock on a Saturday morning, and Cummings had allowed himself a rare day off, which was why he was home watching his distressed wife hunt for lost jewelry. She was a nervous wreck; Sarah had asked her to be the honorary chair of the conference regarding the changing roles of women in society, and it was Lorena's first time on the hot seat. She was leaving tomorrow for Cairo, Egypt, and she was more than a little nervous about taking on such a prominent role.

"I haven't seen them," Cummings replied to her, rather unhelpfully. "Do you think you left them on the nightstand like you usually do?"

"Not *those* silver hoops," she replied mournfully. "I want the *small* ones. They're my good luck earrings."

And then she began rushing around, turning small dishes over to root through any loose change she happened to find in them.

Cummings, with his typical male need to solve things, said, "You probably left them in the bathroom somewhere. Don't you dump all your jewelry in the makeup drawer?"

At this, she stopped searching and gave him a calculating look. "I'm not sure if you're making fun of me or not," she said, "but you might be right."

Then she turned and marched into the bathroom.

A few moments later, Cummings heard, "Aha! Thank God!"

He smiled to himself, relieved. He hated it when she was agitated. And he liked it when he was right about things.

"Thanks, honey," she said, returning from the bathroom to peck him on the cheek. "I'm going to need as much luck as I can get. There are going to be some incredible people at this meeting, and I feel like I'm in over my head."

"What do you mean?" asked Cummings.

"I mean that I've been asked to speak because I'm the president's wife, while some of the other speakers have accomplishments to their names that I can only dream of," she replied, a little ruefully.

"Are you telling me it's not enough for you to be the wife of the president of the most powerful country on Earth?" Cummings teased.

"I'm not sure 'most powerful' applies to this country anymore," said Lorena. "With no more war, there's no more 'most powerful.' But to answer your question . . . I feel like I'm basking in reflected glory."

"Oh, honey," said Cummings, taking her hand in his and looking into her eyes, "you have been a wonderful wife, mother, teacher, friend, and confidante. You have nothing to feel ashamed of in your life's journey. It sounds corny, but I mean it when I say I'd be nothing without you. Don't ever compare yourself negatively to others. You have no idea what your sphere of influence is."

He saw tears prick her eyes. "Oh Samuel," she said, "you're such a softie." Then she hugged him tightly, and he could tell she was glad for the reassurance.

The conference Lorena was attending was to be held at the leading convention centre in Egypt, the Cairo International Conference Centre, which covered an area of around thirty hectares and featured four halls covering more than 160,000 square feet.

The presentations didn't actually start until Monday morning, but Lorena had been invited to attend a Sunday 'meet and greet' with the eight guest speakers as well as 250 of the more prominent guests. The social event had been arranged by Sarah, and refreshments were variations on tea and pastries from thirty different countries, including green tea from China, baklava from Turkey, chai tea from India, beaver tails from Canada, and much, much more. Lorena wanted to try as much as she could, but in the end, she only managed to eat about five separate items—most with chocolate in them—before she'd had enough. Luckily, the servings were small, so she didn't feel sick.

This particular conference was the first one since God's intervention to which not a single politician had been invited. Instead, Sarah had handpicked both the delegates and the speakers for reasons of her own.

"This conference is close to my heart," Sarah said soulfully to Lorena when asking her if she would give the introductory remarks. "The women who will attend, and the women I've chosen to speak at the event, reflect the 40 million female souls of which I am composed. They are modern day sisters of the females within me who are now part of God."

"Why did you specifically select 4,000 delegates to attend this thing, instead of some other number?" asked Lorena.

Sarah explained, "I'm composed of 40 million women's souls—and I am honouring each of them by selecting a percentage of that number to reflect a spark of their energy."

"That's a pretty small percentage," remarked Lorena, trying to do the math.

"Yes," Sarah laughed. "It's only .01% to be exact. But the women who will attend the conference represent all major cultural groups; all ages and economic status; all gender identifications and sexual preferences; and every type of partnership, short of male-male ones. Like me, this will be a vast confluence of female spirit, soul, and energy."

The eight speakers Sarah had selected were women of note from around the globe who'd carved positions for themselves from the fabric of a male-dominated world, sometimes against incredible odds. They were:

1. Nobel Peace Prize laureate Malala Yousafzai, the Pakistani activist for female education who was shot in the head by the Taliban when she was only thirteen years old.
2. Noura Al-Matroushi, the first female astronaut in the United Arab Emirates.
3. New Yorker Ai-jen Poo, whose worker-led movement won better conditions, and legal representation, for abused domestic workers.
4. Frenchwoman Christine Lagarde, the first female managing director of the International Monetary Fund.

5. Indian Trisha Shetty, lawyer and founder of SheSays, an organization that fights against killing women over dowry disputes, or burning them alive for perceived indiscretions.
6. Jang Hye-yeong, a South Korean member of parliament who drafted a bill banning favouritism based on sex, race, age, or sexual orientation, in direct opposition to the Korean patriarchy.
7. Dr. Endah Trista Agustiana, Indonesia's first gender studies expert, whose dissertation, "Living in Crisis: Women's Experiences of Violent Conflict in Poso, Central Sulawesi, Indonesia" led to a global gender specialist career.
8. Award-winning Canadian Samantha Nutt, a physician with over sixteen years of experience in war zones who founded War Child Canada and War Child U.S.A., and authored the best-selling book *Damned Nations: Greed, Guns, Armies, and Aid.*

When Sunday morning arrived, Lorena was much calmer; In fact, she was positively glowing with excitement at the thought of what she was going to experience. A dutiful husband, Cummings waited until his wife had been spirited away to Cairo before he went to work in the Oval Office. After waving goodbye to him, Lorena almost instantly found herself standing in front of the Cairo International Conference Centre. She quickly checked her outfit to ensure that her skirt hadn't ridden up during the teleportation, and then she looked about, noted where the door was, and marched bravely forward toward her moment in the sun.

Inside the Cairo International Conference Centre, the tea party was already in full swing. Lorena looked about for familiar faces and was immediately spotted by Cammy R. Abernathy, the dean of the University of Florida's College of Engineering, who came over and welcomed her immediately.

"So great to see you, Lorena," said Dr. Abernathy. "And I really appreciate your work on getting young women interested in engineering."

It was easy for Lorena after that. Naturally social, she enjoyed the flurry of activity that her presence as the wife of President Samuel Cummings engendered. And soon she was enjoying tea, treats, and the company of some remarkable women. Later, alone in her hotel room, she texted her husband.

"You would have loved the beaver tails," she wrote. "Canada knows how to fry up dough better than any other country."

"They learned it from the Indigenous people," her husband texted back. "The story is that when the first settlers saw the Aboriginals cooking the tails of beavers over an open fire, they figured they could cook bread by stretching sticky dough over one or two sticks in the shape of a beaver's tail."

"Somehow those beaver tails don't sound like they have chocolate crumbles and powdered sugar on them," Lorena texted back.

"LOL, nope, I don't think so! Goodnight . . . and good luck tomorrow," replied her husband.

The next morning, Lorena made it to the conference hall with lots of time to spare. An usher greeted her respectfully and guided her to her seat of honour. She nervously sat down, arranging her notes in front of her so that she would be prepared to open this big convention with the messages Sarah had requested she pass on to the delegates.

She read and reread her notes, making marks in the margins to ensure she had highlighted the important points . . . And then suddenly, it was 9:00 a.m., and a flickering on and off of the lights several times indicated that everyone should sit down and prepare to listen. Before she knew it, the hall was silent, and a spotlight was upon her.

She stood and cleared her throat. "Good morning," she said.

A multitude of murmurs of 'good morning' came back from all around the great room in which she stood. She suddenly became aware that thousands of eyes, filling up two massive rooms at the convention centre, were watching her keenly—but though she felt great fear at this, she persevered in her duty; After all, she'd given Sarah her word.

"Sarah has asked me to give opening remarks," she said, trying to keep an anxious squeak out of her voice, "and I'm more than a little nervous."

There was sympathetic laughter at the comment.

Bolstered by the empathy, Lorena smiled. Then she said, more firmly now, "God's intervention on planet Earth heralds a new direction for humankind. It is a less warlike, kinder direction, a direction where people are more respectful and tolerant of one another. It means huge changes for women. The things so many of us have been fighting for, for so long, will finally be realized—things like equal economic opportunities, educational equity, and an end to gender-based violence. We have made great strides in the fight for equality, but all these years later, we are stuck with the realization that we've never really achieved these lofty goals. Now, with God's intervention, all genders, all nationalities . . . all *people*, will finally have the same opportunities."

The room exploded with clapping, making Lorena feel proud.

When the noise died down, she continued, "Sarah has asked me to discuss some things with you, a refresher, if you will, of what God's intervention means specifically for women. First, let's talk about reproduction. In my country, about 750,000 American teens get pregnant every year, resulting in about 400,000 teen moms. This is not necessarily a bad thing, but often it is not something the young mother, or her family, want to deal with, because for every successful 'teen mom' story, there is a tale of woe and poverty. This tale of woe is what God is addressing by delaying human puberty until the age of eighteen. For young women, the delay in menses ensures they are physically and emotionally mature enough to bear children before becoming pregnant, and for young men, it means there will be less impulsive sexual behaviour—and more opportunity to learn about what the consequences of unplanned pregnancy really mean."

She looked around the room and felt fortunate that the spotlight in her eyes was blinding; Had she been able to see all the women watching her, she might have lost her nerve. As it was, the light-blindness caused her to imagine she was alone, and that calmed her a little.

She continued. "Another part of God's edict is that no woman can become pregnant unless she *wants* to have a child. I will let Sarah speak to how this will work for women who wish to become pregnant."

At that, a flash of light illuminated the auditorium, and Sarah materialized above the crowd, glorious with light and colour. There was a communal gasp as she became fully formed, and immediately, all eyes turned toward her, reverence glowing on many faces.

"Hello, women of Earth," said Sarah. "You have no idea how it heartens me to see you in all your beauty. It delights my heart to be here with you today."

There were calls of 'hello' from the crowd, and some sobbing sounds from different spots around the room. Sarah's presence had a way of calling forward deep emotion from people, and even Lorena, who'd met Sarah several times, found a lump forming in her throat and had to wipe her eyes.

A light, jasmine-scented wind wafted around the room, causing several people to sigh, dimming the hubbub.

When it was quiet, Sarah said softly, "Isn't human conception wonderful? Isn't it a miracle how a tiny human is created? What is *not* wonderful is that sometimes it happens to people who don't want it to happen . . . or it *doesn't* for people who do. To address this, God has tied women's emotional states to their ability to carry a child to term. If a sexual act results in conception, and the woman has misgivings about the wisdom of carrying a child to term, a hormone imbalance will occur and the implantation into her womb of the fertilized egg—which usually occurs within six to ten days—will be disrupted. This simple biological change will give women absolute, final control over the process of human reproduction."

Lorena could hear people's gasps of surprise, and she had no doubt that the idea of no longer feeling the shame associated with morning-after pills and abortion was impacting the assembled women. The changes Sarah had outlined were truly freeing.

"Of course," Sarah continued gently, "this is not a guarantee that people won't have underlying fertility problems and need medical assistance to get pregnant; Rather, it is a safeguard against taking a path to parenthood that one is not ready, or willing, to take." Then she flashed brightly and disappeared, leaving nothing but a gentle mist in her wake.

Lorena was surprised by Sarah's sudden departure and felt unsure what to say next. There were mics in the aisles for people to get up and speak, but she didn't want to encourage questions at the moment since there were four guest speakers and a panel discussion on each of the two days of the conference.

Instead, she pushed ahead, saying, "On a similar topic, Sarah asked me to say a few words about the other physiological changes human beings have experienced due to God's intervention—most notably the end to the human sex drive at the age of forty. God has put us women into premature menopause, something not all of us are happy about . . . though I'm sure we can all agree that we're pleased about an end to night sweats and hot flashes!"

There were murmurs of agreement around the room; While losing their libidos early was not a welcome thought for some of the assembled women, no one over the age of thirty-five enjoyed the slow buildup of symptoms that heralded the coming of 'the change'—and most welcomed the thought of having it all over with by age forty instead of dragging out into their fifties and beyond.

"Women's libidos—our libidos—are precious to us, and yet recognition that we have them is still considered taboo in some cultures," Lorena went on. "Socially speaking, in most of the western world, sexual freedom for women has been a right of sorts since the sixties when 'free love' and 'the pill' came along. Before that, fear of unwanted pregnancy—and 'good girl' expectations fostered by the church—kept women sexually repressed."

Noises of agreement indicated that the audience was with her . . . which is when she dropped her bomb. "But have we women ever really been 'equal' to men in terms of sexuality?" she asked rhetorically, adding, "It never really worked out that way for most of us, did it?"

The noisy crowd suddenly quieted down.

"Sure," she said, "sexual freedom meant we were no longer judged harshly by others for 'taking our pleasure' as the saying goes . . . but we judged *ourselves*, didn't we? What did we get from this experiment with social justice? What did we get from acting like men? Unplanned children? STDs? Broken hearts? All of the above?"

She knew she'd struck a nerve when the crowd went silent. You could have heard a pin drop.

"You know what I mean," she said, "we've all been there. And for many of us, so-called sexual liberation wasn't liberating at all. It was humiliating, degrading and heartbreaking. We learned not to value ourselves and taught others not to value us as well. And that's why I think losing our sex drive at forty is not really such a bad thing. It puts a limit on the wonderful gift of our fertility and sexual youth. It increases its value in our own eyes *and* in the eyes of others . . ." and then she paused for effect and added, ". . . plus, as I said before, it allows us to say 'goodbye and good riddance' to a long, slow menopause! Win-win!"

There was a round of chuckling at that.

When it died down, Lorena said, "So, we have a good idea about how the shift in our hormonal cycles, and the end of our sexual lives, will affect us *women*—but here's the million dollar question ... how will diminished testosterone at age forty affect *men*? How will it affect *families*?"

She paused, eyeing her audience.

Someone near the front called out, "Amen!"

And she smiled. "Amen is right," she said. "Sarah says that when men no longer have any interest in pursuing new sexual partners, they will value their long-term partners more. She says the purpose of an intimate union is supposed to be mutual respect and commitment—though, to be fair, there are many men who *are* committed to their wives and children ... but we all know at least one classic 'cheat and dump' guy, don't we? We all know at least one guy who left his wife for a younger, more compliant model, right? And that's going to *stop*!"

She heard a faint voice toward the mid-section of the room call out, "What, now I can't be a trophy wife? That was my retirement plan!"

There was a round of catcalls and hoots.

Lorena giggled along the frivolity. "No," she said, "I guess 'trophy wife' will not be on anyone's resume."

Then, when she'd finished laughing, and the chortling in the room had died away, she suddenly became somber, her voice taking on a darker, warning tone as she said, "But there's a difference between a trophy *wife* and a *trophy*, isn't there? We can joke about being a trophy wife—after all, it's a mutual agreement, and they get something out of the union, even if it's just material goods. It's harder, however, to laugh when a man, through money or power, simply takes a trophy, isn't it?"

There was an uncomfortable shifting in seats. The women she was speaking to knew exactly where she was going next.

"Sexual predation, trafficking and tourism ... exploitation of children, rape as a spoil of war ... the list goes on. Such activity, which is generally the province of men, is poison to our collective souls. It is truly evil, and it detracts from the life force. But now, with God's edict, much of it will stop. This is a gift, and we must look at it as such. We ..." she indicated the assembled crowd with a sweep of her arm, "are the lucky ones. I, for one, have not experienced such injury in my life ... and so I willingly sacrifice my sexual life if it spares just one person from hurt, defilement, injury, and pain."

As she said the words, she thought of her beloved granddaughter, Jessica, who was at a prime age to be scouted by sexual predators. She shuddered and then said hotly, "Because of God's edict, there will be no more wealthy, old men abusing children in this way!"

The crowd erupted in cheering. Many of the assembled audience were frontline human welfare workers—physicians, counsellors, psychiatrists, and social workers—who dealt with the fallout from sexual and other forms of abuse every day. They were beyond pleased at the idea of a reduction in such depravity.

Lorena continued, "I realize," she said, "and certainly God realizes, that twenty-two years is a short window of time to enjoy our sexuality, but won't it make such experiences more meaningful if we know it is only a gift for a little while? And how much more joyful will sexual activity be for women if we can be secure in the knowledge that we will only become pregnant if we want to?"

Just then, Lorena heard a mic squeal, and realized that a dark shadow in one of the aisles wanted to speak. She could not make out the woman's face, but she could see she was wearing a hijab.

"Madame Speaker," came a tenuous voice.

"Yes?" asked Lorena, squinting to see the woman.

"In my country, this ability to choose when to have babies may be a terrible thing," she said in heavily accented English. "Where I come from, men already blame women for things such as infertility or the sex of the baby. Now that they know it is the woman's choice whether to have a child or not, when a man wants a baby, he will beat the woman until he sees her pray to Allah for a child. Then, if Allah doesn't bring a baby, he will beat her some more. Men can no longer kill women, but they can still torture, imprison, and enslave us. So, how does it benefit us to have control over childbearing when we cannot control the actions of men?"

Lorena had not considered that basic human rights were not available to all women, and there was an uncomfortable silence in the room as she and her audience thought about how Sharia law, as enforced by extreme Islam, was affecting the lives of the women who lived under it.

Then, like an angel on high, Sarah materialized again, a ghostly fog that slowly took shape to dangle above the crowd.

"Shalom, little one," she said to the agonized woman who trembled on the floor beneath her. "I hear you, and God hears you too. For thousands of years, women like you—many of whose souls reside within me—have lived under tribal rule, which often includes brutal male dominance. However, killing infidels is no longer possible, and it can no longer be a rallying cry for your male leaders . . . and so, what is left for these men if they are to continue to feel a sense of purpose?"

There was a hiccup of a sob from the distressed woman. "I don't know," she said, "but I am afraid it involves enslaving women."

"No," said Sarah calmly. "The old ways must give way to the new. Raping and pillaging will not hold up under God's new world order, and neither will terrorizing the weak—and your country and its leaders must change or sink. Soon, your people will be offered choices they've never before dreamed of as part of a global shift in human values. This is my message to you, and when you return to your country, I ask that you spread my message of release from bondage to your countrywomen to give them hope."

The woman was overcome by Sarah's words. She began shaking so badly that those around her had to help her to sit.

Then Sarah glowed brightly, drawing all eyes to her. She appeared to flutter in the air, almost like she was vibrating at a supersonic speed, and when she suddenly stopped, she said, "This woman, our sister in Islam, comes from a culture where men think of women as property—an extreme version of gender relations, to be sure. It's easy to regard such misguided men as ignorant, and to gloat at their rage at being denied their will, but think of this . . . for the first time in history, women have total control over reproduction, which many men find threatening. I would ask that all of you use your power wisely."

Then with a puff of air, Sarah was gone.

The room was absolutely silent except for the distraught woman's muffled sniffles, which compelled Lorena to say, "Please let me express my compassion for your situation."

She did not expect a response, and she did not get one.

She took a deep breath, regained her composure, and went on, "The physiological changes that have been imposed on humankind are already affecting social dynamics and human relations around the world. The eight experts who will speak to you all over the next two days, all of whom specialize in women's and humanitarian issues, will look at some of these dynamics more closely. Collectively, we will examine how humankind's new physiology is impacting social change and family structure. Following each presentation, there will be opportunity to ask questions. It will be facilitated by a team of moderators—who you've probably mistaken for ushers."

At that, the lights went up and a group of about fifty uniformed women, stationed near microphones in the aisles, waved at the attendees.

When the lights went down again, Lorena continued, "For the final two hours of each day, after our speakers have concluded, there will be interactive roundtable discussions. Twelve gender relations experts—all handpicked by Sarah—will host. Comments and questions will be welcome." Then she smiled at the crowd and concluded with, "Once again, thank you all for coming."

There was much clapping, and then the conference began. The first speaker was Pakistani citizen and activist Malala Yousafzai. Malala spoke of how, as testosterone in men declined, women and girls in Pakistan were already benefiting from reduced aggression. She felt that, with God's edict in effect, men would ultimately develop more compassion for their mothers, sisters, aunts, and daughters, and this would lead to better educational opportunities for women and girls, something Malala was passionate about.

Noura Al-Matroushi, the UAE astronaut, was next. She spoke of the struggles she'd faced as a female engineer in primarily male environments, and she said that she welcomed the cessation of menses after the age of forty, as it was a constant struggle to deal with her monthly cycle within the context of her job.

At this, murmurs of assent rumbled around the room. No one enjoyed their monthly cycles, with incessant bleeding and accompanying painful cramps. For some, life became unbearable at that time of the month—yet they had to go to work, discipline children, prepare food, and just carry on, all the while pretending nothing was wrong.

"I once read a book that said a woman only bleeds a tablespoon a month!" shouted out a woman somewhere near the front of the room.

"It was obviously written by a man!" yelled out someone else.

At that, everyone burst into laughter.

The third speaker, Ai-jen Poo, talked about the systemic abuse that immigrant nannies, housekeepers, and elderly caregivers routinely faced when they came to the U.S., including human trafficking and sexual assault. She remarked that she'd already seen a change in how men over forty were treating these primarily female workers—with less aggression and more compassion—but said she wasn't sure if it was because of men's hormonal changes or because of the domestic workers' union she'd founded.

The day ended with a talk by Christine Legarde, who said the physiological changes imposed by God were bringing gender equality to the workplace. She told the assembled group that research had shown that when women's employment equaled men's, economies were more resilient, and economic growth was higher. Further research had shown that adding just one more woman to a firm's senior management or corporate board—while keeping the size of the board unchanged—was associated with an eight to thirteen basis points higher return on assets.

When the session wrapped up for the day, Lorena went to her hotel room and called her husband.

"How did it go?" Cummings asked.

"I can't believe how interesting this is," she told him. "When the guest speakers finished their presentations, there was a roundtable discussion about men's traditional roles in heterosexual marriages and how that would change now that humans had shortened sexual lives. There were twelve people in the group, each from a different culture. Did you know that in traditional Swahili culture, women and men lead segregated lives? They interact, but tasks related to food and guests are dealt with by women while men deal with problems and work."

"That's old-school," said Cummings, thinking of how his grandmother used to wait on his grandfather who, as a farmer, did all the outside, laborious chores.

"Yes," said Lorena, "and according to the Kenyan woman who told us this, she liked it that way. She was worried that the hormonal changes would make men effeminate, and that they'd try to infiltrate the women's area."

"Oh?" said Cummings.

"I don't feel that way," said Lorena. "You're welcome to pick up any kitchen chores you want."

Cummings just laughed. Then he asked, "What was the takeaway for the day, then?"

"Well," said Lorena, "I guess the general sense of the discussion was that now that men and women can't run around on each other, unless the marriage is crummy, partners are likely to continue to want to live in their families until 'death do us part.'"

"No surprise there," remarked Cummings.

"No," she said thoughtfully, "but then again, you and I already *know* sex is not the main thing, right?"

At that, Cummings sighed. "I miss you, Lorena," he said.

"And I miss you, too, my love," she replied, knowing what he was really saying was that he was mourning their lost intimate life.

Then they said their goodnights and hung up.

The next morning, the conference resumed. The first speaker of the day was Indian lawyer Trisha Shetty. She welcomed the gender equality that came with the cessation of sexuality, seeing it as relief in the uphill battle for rights that the women in her country faced. Also, as president of the Paris Peace Forum Steering Committee, she expressed her belief that less testosterone meant less aggression, which would contribute to more robust social welfare around the world.

The second speaker, Jang Hye-yeong, talked about South Korean patriarchal culture and how she felt that women in heavily male-dominanted cultures like her own would face pushback from men when they tried to exercise their newly found control over their reproductive cycles. She said it would likely push women to construct family units that did not involve men, such as multigenerational, female-dominated situations where grandmothers or aunties cared for children.

Endah Trista Agustiana of Indonesia, a gender expert and human rights activist, spoke next about her experience growing up poor. She told the audience that poverty, geographical isolation, minority status, early marriage and pregnancy are just some of the reasons why, in many parts of the world, young women and girls forgo education and end up victimized. She welcomed the twenty-two-year reproductive cycle and saw it as a way to stop predation of older men on younger, vulnerable, impoverished girls such as she had once been.

Samantha Nutt, the last speaker, was the one who moved Lorena the most. As soon as she began talking about children growing up in war zones, Lorena's eyes began to water, and she was more grateful than ever that God had put an end to killing and war. Canadian physician and philanthropist Nutt, with more than sixteen years of experience in war zones—primarily with war-affected women and children—was certain that the physiological changes God had imposed would ultimately better the species. She said she welcomed a less aggressive world.

As with the day before, when the speakers were done, a roundtable discussion was held. Today's topic was whether the classic man/woman partnership would remain the primary way in which children would be brought into the world.

Later, when Lorena recounted the discussion to Cummings, she said, "There was one Dutch lady who said she and her female partner planned to visit a sperm bank, where they could select a sperm donor based on his personal success and genetic history. She insisted that the biological changes were going to make men obsolete, and that we should start freezing more sperm right away . . . but then she got taken down by a Filipino lady who said, and I quote, 'Each to their own, but I believe that when love between a man and a woman is expressed in the creation of a child, it is a special thing. I don't think men are going to become obsolete any time soon.' And Sam? I want you to know that I agreed with her."

"Well, thank God for that," Cummings told his wife. "I like to think I'm good for *something*."

"Of course you are, silly," Lorena giggled. "You're the best grandpa ever!"

"I think Jessica and Jayson agree with you," Cummings told her, "especially since I took them for ice cream yesterday."

"Without me?" yelped Lorena.

"Sorry, honey . . . you're too busy hanging out with the girls," teased Cummings.

"I miss you," Lorena said, "and I'll be home tomorrow. But first I have to go to a morning wrap-up session. Sarah's going to discuss the data you have Northrup tracking on how the biological changes are affecting the cultural landscape."

"Oh yes," Cummings replied, "he's already compiled some interesting stats."

"Awesome," said Lorena. "Oh, and I should warn you that there will be a follow-up conference in Singapore next year."

"Oh, I'm not missing that one," said Cummings. "Maybe I'll take in a show while you go to work."

"Haha!" said Lorena. "I think you should . . . how about Andrea Bocelli? I hear he's excellent!"

Cummings roared with laughter as he hung up.

When Lorena returned home from the women's conference, she felt as if she was floating on air. It had been a profound experience for her to be in the company of so many accomplished women, and it really got her thinking about her own life, and the choices she'd made. At one time, she had been a promising business student and had graduated with honours from the business program at the University of California, Berkeley. She'd considered going on to do her master's degree, but instead she'd met a promising young economics major named Samuel Cummings—and her path had dramatically changed. Now, though she didn't regret her marriage, she *did* regret not testing herself academically and professionally.

"I want to go back to school, Samuel," she announced about a week after she returned from the conference. "It's high time I got my master's degree in business."

Cummings' mouth dropped open, but he quickly shut it, swallowed hard, and said, "I think that's amazing, honey."

He knew better than to give voice to his thoughts, which were, *Why on Earth would she want to start something like that when we're so close to retirement?*

"You know what I learned at that conference?" asked Lorena of her befuddled husband. Then, without waiting for a response, she said, "I learned there are hardly any women at the top levels of business and government! Christine Lagarde said that she'd like to see all countries publish an annual global scorecard about this, and I told her I'd bring it up with you."

"I appreciate that," Cummings said with interest as he knotted his tie. He was preparing for the World Religious Forum and had to leave in an hour.

Lorena started rooting through a bag of conference materials she'd brought back with her until she triumphantly pulled a pamphlet out. "Here's a handout I got along with some information about Sheryl Sandberg, the CEO of Facebook. She has an organization called Lean In, which promotes no gender bias in business. These stats were in the package."

Cummings took the paper his wife handed him. It read:

The average level of female participation at the CEO level is 18% weighted by revenues. For the largest multinational corporations, the rate is only 4%. The statistics for executive level positions is 26% weighted by revenues but only 8% for the largest companies."

Government positions were only examined at the national level and were divided into three categories: Heads of State, Members of Congress or equivalent, and Leader of one of the country's ten largest bureaucracies. Only 7% of Heads of State were female (2% when weighted by population). At the Congressional level, 15% of Members were women (11% weighted by population). Bureaucrats fared better with 18% being women (15% weighted by population).

"Yikes," he said, "there's no doubt about the male bias . . . but I'm not sure what you want me to do about it. Do you want me to get Northrup to commission a study, Lorena?"

"Samuel Cummings," she said coldly, "I think you underestimate me."

"What do you mean?" he asked.

"I mean," she said, "that you are looking at a woman who graduated at the top of her class with a business degree, and who means to pursue an MBA. I am perfectly qualified to track the data and write a critical review of how God's intervention is affecting social change."

The penny dropped for Cummings. "Oh," he said.

"Men have had it easy for a long time," Lorena said. "They band together, give each other a leg up, and when it comes to plum jobs, generally maintain an 'old boys' network that amounts to nothing less than nepotism."

"I agree *somewhat*, Lorena," said Cummings, "but here in America, don't you think women get a pretty fair shake?"

"Compared to what?" asked Lorena. "Think about sports scholarships. They are few and far between for women, but many young men get into schools that would *never* accept them on their academic credentials because they're aggressive on a football field."

"Are you suggesting women compete head to head with men for sports scholarships?" asked Cummings.

"No," said his wife. "I'm hoping financial advantages for young men, such as sports scholarships, will disappear. But that old boys club is hard to crack."

"Who are you calling an 'old boy'?" teased Cummings.

"Don't deny it, old boy," laughed Lorena, moving in for an embrace.

As he hugged her, he whispered in her ear, "You'd make a good president, you know."

"I know," she whispered back.

Chapter 35

World Religious Forum

Zion Square is located at the four-way intersection of Jaffa Road, Ben Yehuda Street, Herbert Samuel Street, and Yoel Moshe Salomon Street, right in the heart of downtown Jerusalem. Cummings landed in the square courtesy Sarah, and upon finding himself smack-dab in the middle of one of the oldest and holiest cities in the world, he immediately felt a rush of awe. One could not come to such a place and ignore the history, godliness, and endless battles that had been waged in, on, around, and for this prized place. Sacred to all three major Abrahamic religions—Judaism, Christianity, and Islam—the city could not be owned, despite the fact that both Israel and Palestine claimed it as their capital. It was, and always had been, a city that belonged only to God.

Zion Square, usually busy day and night with tourists, elderly immigrants, overseas students, local youth, street performers, and religious activists, was today roped off to the public and fixed with seating, first aid tents, sheltered sections, and several outdoor, bistro-like cafés. It was also organized into secular and non-secular halves, with world leaders—such as Cummings and his crew—sitting on one side of a wide, centre aisle, while high-ranking clerics and their support personnel sat on the other.

Along with his advisory circle of Angelica Lopez, Gordon Blackstone, Norman Feldman, Bradley Northrup, and Hana Shriver, Cummings was here to attend the World Religious Forum, the last of the world forums Sarah had set for planet Earth. He was excited to be witness to the coming together of religious and political leaders from around the world to discuss the true nature of God with Sarah. Beside him, Angelica Lopez suppressed a shiver. As a Catholic, Cummings knew her spiritual senses were on high alert.

Flanked by Lopez and Northrup, Cummings quickly made his way to his seat, which was clearly marked with an American flag. Taking up the rear were Blackstone, Feldman, and Shriver. The six of them sat down together in two rows of three. They were fortunate enough to be seated in the first two rows, just to the right of centre stage. Beside them on the left was an aisle, and to their immediate right sat the German contingent. Behind them were four representatives from Uganda.

There was excitement in the air. This was the first and only conference that Sarah was running herself. She'd taken no leadership roles in any of the other conferences, maintaining that it was humankind's job to fix their own messes; However, when it came to explaining God, that was a different matter. Only Sarah could speak with authority about God, and so today, it was most definitely her show, and hers alone.

Cummings looked around, taking in the crowd. State and religious leaders from vastly different cultures and faiths, many adorned in traditional ceremonial garb in a dazzling array of colours, surrounded him. Some of the religious leaders clutched satchels, briefcases, and intricately adorned boxes, a further source of fascination for Cummings. He knew some had brought sacrosanct religious treasures with them in the hope that somehow Sarah could bless them, and he marveled at the fact that he might very well be mere feet away from the Dead Sea Scrolls (the oldest biblical texts in existence, discovered in 1946 in the West Bank) or the seventh century Codex Parisino-Petropolitanus (one of the oldest manuscripts of the Qur'an).

Sarah was not yet visible, though Cummings had no doubt she was present in one form or another. In her absence, there was room for those in attendance to talk to one another and to connect. Cummings imagined she had planned this; If there was one thing he'd learned for certain about this godly being in the past few months, it was that she encouraged communication and understanding.

Strangely, when Sarah finally arrived, she didn't do so in any grand manner; Instead, she simply floated into view over the horizon, the sun at her back, her face in shadow, while the assembled leaders who'd come to hear her words obliviously chatted and fussed, getting settled as they waited for the big event. One or two may have looked at the sky, wondering about the one, single, dark cloud that seemed to be moving closer, but ultimately, no one paid any mind until she was practically right on top of them, big, regal, and imposing. Only then did all eyes look up and all necks crane to see her better as she hovered above them, silent, her long, flowing robes glittering and bubbling in the light, like water in a fast flowing stream.

A hush came over the crowd as she slowly descended to land gracefully on the stage, right in front of Cummings and his team, her trademark rose scent permeating the air. She stood silent in all her glory, towering over the humans who were on the stage with her—the pope, the Dalai Lama, the Grand Imam and about twenty other prominent men and women of faith.

Beside him, Cummings heard Lopez whisper to herself, "Wow . . ."

He didn't know if she was reacting to the spectacle in general or to that amazing dress.

"Welcome, ladies and gentlemen," Sarah said.

Cries of, "Hello, Sarah!" and "Shalom!" and "Namaste!" and other greetings of welcome and faith rang throughout the square.

Sarah smiled brilliantly, her face radiant and flickering. "How do you like your new world so far?" she asked. "How do you like this Earth now that it is without war, without killing?"

The roar of voices raised in response answered her question only too well.

"I'm pleased and happy for the human race. With war gone, you can now focus on yourselves. You can become better, kinder. You can learn to love and accept, instead of to hate and judge. You can open yourselves to absorbing the good among your fellow humans. How do you feel about that?"

Multiple shouts of approval raced through the crowd, and Cummings felt himself caught up in the emotion of it all, his heart beating strongly at her words. Sarah was gloriously charismatic—more glamorous and compelling than any movie star—and Cummings could not help but respond to her remarkable energy. Beside him, he heard Lopez cheering as loudly as he was. He felt immensely joyful, and he wished Lorena was with him so he could squeeze her hand.

"Let's talk about who you really are," Sarah said. "Let's talk about the marvelous, intelligent life forms that you humans are. You are young as far as civilizations go, but you have so much potential. And that is why God has stepped in to set you on the right path. But don't feel bad about being course corrected; God has had to intervene on many planets in order to steer intelligent species away from the brink of destruction. God does what needs to be done to ensure the life force thrives."

Then she looked around intently, her gaze vast and unreadable.

To Cummings, it felt like she was staring directly into everyone's souls as she said, "We're here to talk about bringing humankind together so you can become at one with your species—not mankind, not womankind, not straight or gay, not white, black, red, yellow or any other designation . . . one race—the human race. One people united in love. To do this, intolerance of all kinds must end, and you must learn to see each other's light instead of each other's darkness. This is the goal. This is what you must strive for."

Cummings' heart stirred, and he involuntarily put his hand on his chest. "Yes," he whispered under his breath, enchanted by her words along with everyone else.

"Since I have been here on Earth, it is clear that this healing has started," Sarah continued. "Since the 'no killing' edict took effect, former enemy states have begun working together on shared missions; Political groups have started cooperating with one another; Disarmament is well underway; And climate change mitigation plans with actual teeth are being finally developed. Soon, I expect all nations to come together under one global governance structure, eliminating conflicts that have plagued your race for millennia. And finally, when harmony is achieved among you, then—and only then—your species will be able to focus upon becoming at one with Earth and all its life forms."

There was cheering at this. The promise of a peaceful, loving world was one people of faith had been holding onto for thousands of years.

"However, this will not happen overnight," cautioned Sarah. "It is a process, part of your evolution, which will take many thousands of years. But your life force will continue to grow throughout this evolution, until humankind ultimately contributes much more than it does now to the universal life force that is God. It is your destiny."

At this, she smiled with a radiance that was instantly reflected onto the faces of the people in front of her, causing a palpable glow to light up the dusk descending on Zion Square.

"Do you think you can do it?" she asked. "Do you think you humans can become whole, at one with yourselves, and eventually, with your planet?"

She didn't wait for an answer; Instead, she raised her arms gracefully above her head in a circle. The sun, glowing gold behind her, made them look like a ring of fire.

She said, "As peace and unconditional love spread, you will find that placing the needs of others above your own desires will bring you great and lasting joy. You will stop competing to accumulate larger shares of Earth's resources. You will find delight in one another."

Behind him, Cummings could hear someone weeping, but he was too transfixed by Sarah to turn and see who it was.

She went on, "Let me explain what lies in store for you. When you are at one with yourselves and your planet, you will become aware of the health and well-being of *all* life-forms—which will grow your life force enormously. You will also be able to communicate with other people without regard to physical or linguistic separation, establishing intimate friendships through energetic self-projection. You will not have to travel to experience foreign lands; Instead, in your new, heightened state of awareness, you will be able to sit in a kitchen in Denver while connecting with a Sherpa climbing Mount Everest—and you will not only enjoy the magnificent view, but you will feel the cold and exertion of the climb."

Beside him, Lopez whispered, "I guess we won't need the internet, or air miles, anymore."

Despite himself, Cummings chuckled.

"In the long-term, when you reach this state of evolution," continued Sarah, "the human life force may even become strong enough to allow you to physically—not just energetically—teleport from location to location. There are some advanced beings in the universe who have achieved this—and of course, you've experienced it already via what some of you call 'the Sarah Express.'"

There was stillness around Zion Square as Sarah delivered these words. It was enticing to think about moving through the ether at will, though difficult to grasp for some.

"In the short term, however," she said, "there are several other stages humanity must go through before it becomes fully unified. First will come some important technological adaptations. As humankind works toward a new, more sustainable world, the introduction of bodywear that absorbs energy from the sun, or any other electromagnetic sources, will be a true revolutionary breakthrough."

There was some puzzled murmuring in the crowd.

A voice from the back called out, "Why would we need that!? We've been dressing ourselves since we were toddlers. We know how to dress for different temperatures!"

"Ah, yes," said Sarah, "but climate change can't be stopped overnight. It's going to get worse before it gets better—and the solution to being climate-adapted is *not* to burn more fuel in heating or air-conditioning buildings; The solution is to personally adapt through temperature-regulating bodywear. This remarkable innovation will reduce energy use in homes and buildings, ultimately shrinking the global carbon footprint."

"Will we even need buildings once we have this amazing bodywear?" asked one man on the cleric side of the square.

"Yes, buildings won't ever go out of style," said Sarah. "But you will no longer need to use so much energy to heat and cool them because your bodywear will personalize temperature for you no matter where you are or whether you are inside or outside. Such temperature regulation will further reduce your carbon footprint because your caloric needs will decline, curbing the 'big agriculture.'"

"Uh, Sarah?" called out a rather robust man from the non-cleric side. "When you speak of 'caloric need,' are you implying that we will evolve to eat only for sustenance, losing our taste for fine food and wine?" He looked appalled at the idea, and Cummings noted he was sitting with the Dutch contingent.

Having just shared a nice Dutch Gouda cheese and a bottle of Merlot with Lorena the night before, he found his comment apropos. *He has a point,* he thought. *Caloric need and the pleasure of eating are not the same thing.*

Sarah smiled at the man. "Maybe a little," she said. "However, many of the foods you currently enjoy are likely to fade away anyway because as humankind evolves, you will cease exploiting animals for food. Harvesting other sentient beings for food goes against the creation of life force; Instead, you will sustain yourselves with grains, seeds, nuts, fruits, vegetables, and bacterial protein cultures."

The man looked crestfallen. "But won't we become small and weak?" he asked.

"You will become smaller," said Sarah, "but this is not a bad thing. You will become like the wiry, short guy in your gym class who was always the quickest on the basketball court. You will become physiologically more efficient in movement and calorie expenditure. Further, your bodywear will feature a lightweight, mechanical exoskeleton, which will make you stronger and more mobile than humankind has ever been before. Ultimately, it will become very easy for all humans to meet basic survival needs."

Cummings heard people clearing their throats and murmuring to their colleagues as they pondered this.

A gentle breeze wafted through the room as Sarah asked, "Are there questions?"

The Palestinian leader, Izzat Farsoun, stood up. "Sarah, are you saying that all of this will come to pass—these future marvels you describe—if we feed the life force by being kinder to each other?"

"Yes," replied Sarah. "The warm feeling you get from helping others is the feeling of the life force within you growing—growth that will last a lifetime. And by feeding the life force through benevolent acts, you ensure humanity's continued survival."

Then Farsoun said, "Sarah, the Christian religion believes God created the universe in seven days. My wife, a devout Christian, believes this explicitly and argues with me when I tell her about your messages. Her arguing makes me very unhappy."

The crowd laughed loudly at this.

He continued, "In our faith, we are mismatched. I am Islamic, and I am pleased to find your words are supported by the Qur'an. You say all elements required to develop the universe existed 14 billion years ago and have expanded through space and time ever since. Similarly, at 51:47 the

Qur'an says that, '. . . the heavens, We have built them with power. And verily, We are expanding it.' Since knowledge of the universe's expansion was only recently discovered, this has caused great debate among Muslim scholars. However, I don't care about *their* debates—only the one in my home. So tell me, please . . . are you asking humans to abandon the notion that God created the universe?"

"I don't ask humans to abandon anything," replied Sarah gently. "All I do is inform you of the truth, which is this: The universe was created by a singular event, and the laws of nature have driven its evolution ever since. God was there when the early universe formed, and God patiently waited for stars and planets to appear. Once conditions were right for the formation of primitive life, God provided the life force that eventually led to intelligent life on billions of planets."

"But scientists imply that evolution has nothing to do with God—a great divide," the man noted.

"Human scientists have barely scratched the surface of understanding the origins of life," replied Sarah. "Your technology is unable to detect fundamental elements like dark matter and dark energy, let alone the life force itself. But I can tell you this, the interaction of matter and energy, as per the laws of physics and chemistry, provided the preconditions for life. Then, upon receiving life force from God, primitive life forms evolved, becoming more complex over time as per the laws of nature and conditions on their planets."

"You specifically say *human* scientists don't understand," the Palestinian man questioned. "Are you implying that other beings do?"

"Yes," replied Sarah. "Other beings—your neighbours in the universe, if you will—have a much better understanding of the interactions between energy, matter, and the life force. But don't worry. Upon your death, if you become part of God, you will find out these things."

"Is there no way to show us proof of some sort?" he persisted.

Sarah just smiled. "The science is complex, and humans currently have no frame of reference to understand the full truth," she told him kindly as if speaking to a child. "All I can tell you is that I have been sent by God, and that my message is true. I would also counsel people of faith to accept the work of scientists when it comes to how the physical universe behaves, and I would counsel scientists to accept my word that God exists apart from the physical universe. Science and God need not conflict."

The man looked disappointed. "Thank you," he said and sat down.

Then Cummings saw the pope, who was on the stage with Sarah, rise. A frail, elderly man, he was assisted to his feet by aides dressed in long, white robes.

"Greetings, Pope Julius," Sarah said warmly, and Cummings felt loving energy charge the air as she welcomed the holy Christian man.

The pope made the sign of the benediction and smiled beatifically at Sarah. "Greetings, most holy of beings," he began.

Sarah laughed, "We are all holy beings, and I am no holier than you," she said.

The pope, who was known to have a quick wit and a good sense of humour, replied, "I'll take that bet. The odds are 40 million to one."

There was ripple of laughter at his remark.

When it died down, he asked, "I would like more detail about how humans came into existence. Specifically, my question is this: When God breathed life force into matter—which you say is the truth about how life happened—was that not an act of creation?"

"In a way," replied Sarah, "but while God provided the initial life force, once life took hold, evolution occurred. Then, as it progressed, God harvested and reseeded the growing life force."

"But if it is all so . . . well, *impersonal* . . . then how did humans come to seek God as they do?" asked the pope. "In my faith, as I'm sure you know, we believe God planted that need inside each of us. Is this the truth?"

"Yes," replied Sarah, "it is. Once humans evolved to the point where they were intelligent enough to need moral guidance, God sparked the development of spirituality, fueling the potential for exponential growth of the life force."

"I understand," said the pope, "but I still find it hard to believe that God did not have a bigger hand in creating the world. This is a primary tenet of my faith, and I find it difficult to accept what you are saying."

"You are studying works by early human scholars," replied Sarah. "To explain the world and its creatures, the only plausible answer for them was to propose that God created everything as a magician would—and that is simply not the case."

"Would it be fair to say that God is like a farmer who plants and then harvests an ever-growing life force to increase power?" the pope asked.

Sarah smiled. "It is true that God is always harvesting life force, but it is not simply to increase power—at least not in the way you are implying," she replied. "The life force is the sum total of all love and joy ever expressed or felt, and through God, it allows us to transcend the physical world. It is the only intelligent form of energy. When we join with the life force as part of God, we will survive the explosion of the sun, the destruction of the Earth, and even the end of the universe—and we will rise again in a different universe."

She finished her words with a ripple of air that mussed up a few people's hair, including Cummings' own. The pope looked perplexed, and Cummings was sure the man was trying to meld her words with his current belief system. He sat down, rubbing his chin, deep in thought.

A quiet, Asian man in orange robes, who was seated beside the pope on the stage, slowly stood up. It was the Dalai Lama.

"Greetings, Sarah," he said in a gentle, peaceful voice. "I have a question for you if I may."

"Of course," replied Sarah.

"Buddhists believe the world has simply existed forever, that it continues to recreate itself, and that it is in a constant state of Samsara—the continued repetition of birth and death. Clearly, this is not in line with what you've said about 'the singularity' as you call the idea of the 'Big Bang.' However, for more than 2,500 years, Buddhists *have* expressed the idea that humanity and nature are interdependent, their energies constantly flowing together, which *is* in line with your revelations. That is why Buddhists are vegetarian. To eat meat would be to disrupt this flow. My question is this—how do you expect the 'one God, one way' faithful to discard their ideas when they have rejected such beliefs for so long?"

"Ah, yes," said Sarah. "How, indeed, do you get anyone to change ingrained beliefs? Well, Your Holiness, all I can tell you is that God sent me as compelling evidence."

"Yes," replied the Dalai Llama, "you are compelling evidence indeed... but some people just do not want to see."

"It takes time and much reflection," Sarah said, "something Buddhists are good at."

"Yes," replied the Dalai Lama, and as the man sat down, Cummings saw he was smiling like a child, his eyes alight with peace and joy.

Next, a distinguished man in flowing white robes with a pillbox style hat on his head stood up—a Muslim imam. He was quite perturbed.

"Sarah!" he called out. "Are you telling us that people cannot join God in the afterlife if they do not change their beliefs about how the universe was formed?"

"Not at all," replied Sarah. "There is only one requirement for joining God after death, and that is to place the needs of others above your own, as this generates positive life force for God. Think about this . . . There were more than 500 million human souls who left this world and joined God before organized religion even existed. They helped their fellow humans escape from wild animals, or showed them how to start fires, or tended to their wounds . . . In short, they demonstrated love and care for others. And all this occurred before humans had the remotest idea about how the bright lights in the night sky came to be."

The man seemed about to ask something else, but just then, the Australian prime minister, Ben Morrison, jumped to his feet, clearly agitated, to interrupt.

"What about reincarnation? Are you saying it has no merit at all? Billions of people around the world—Buddhists, Hindus, what have you—believe it to be the truth. It certainly makes more sense to me than streets of gold and angels with harps. Are you saying it's all bullshit?"

Sarah, knowing he wasn't the only one wondering this, answered, "At death, those who lived by the Golden Rule go to join God. There is no reincarnation as commonly conceptualized, except, perhaps, when it comes to children or other innocent beings. Upon death, the life force of innocents is infused into newborns and returned to Earth—with no memory of former lives."

"Soooo . . . do the bad guys go to hell, then?" Morrison questioned.

"There *is* no hell," Sarah explained patiently. "Those who lived lives of hatred, intolerance, and greed cease to exist, and upon death, their life force is split apart to be redistributed to lower organisms."

"Are you saying you have to pass some sort of entrance exam to get into Heaven?" Morrison mocked. "And then what? You disappear into the sky, floating on the breeze with the seagulls?"

"Ah, Ben," said Sarah, emitting a calming lavender scent as she laughed at his scorn. "There is no exam. If you've lived a life of compassion and care, you become one with God, even while everything that was uniquely you continues."

Morrison spread his arms wide, palms up, in a 'What the hell are you talking about?' gesture. "Say what?" he asked.

There was a ripple of laughter around Zion Square. The Australian prime minister was both charismatic and funny . . . Although, he wasn't joking about being confused. Cummings caught his eye, and Morrison just shook his head at him, as if to say, 'I have no idea what she's on about.'

The German chancellor, Berdine Schmidt, stood up next to ask a question. She looked pained as if straining her intellect to wring meaning out of Sarah's words.

In clipped, accented English, she asked, "Dying and having your soul join God must be an overwhelming experience, no? What does God look like? What do you do as part of God?"

"Guten Tag, Berdine," said Sarah, sending a gentle breeze to waft through the crowd. "First of all, yes . . . it is overwhelming to leave your body and join God—but those who make the transition are immediately immersed in absolute, unconditional love, and so it is not the least bit frightening. However, physical descriptions of the afterlife are impossible to provide. God, and those of us with God, exist as pure energy, outside of space and time as you know them—though we retain our own identities and are free to pursue our own interests."

"If this is true," said the German woman, "since you are part of God already, you must still be in Heaven—even though you are here."

"That is a valid observation," agreed Sarah, "and yes; Technically, all 40 million of the souls of which I am comprised are in astral from and so are still with God. However, we have agreed to manifest on Earth as a unit so we can help humankind heal from the damage you have inflicted upon yourselves."

Schmidt appeared ready to sit down, to the extent that she bent her knees and tucked her skirt under herself, but then she had a second thought and quickly raised her hand. "I am very confused about what you do as part of God. You are here, so I can see what, uh . . . 40 million of you are doing right now—but what do the other souls do?"

Sarah laughed, jasmine mingling with something richer, like pine. Cummings inhaled deeply and was reminded of something personal and wonderful, his grandfather's cottage in northern Canada, and the first time his grandfather took him canoeing.

He relaxed into the feeling as Sarah replied, "To better answer that question, I will allow three of the 40 million women within me to take turns describing their version of life as part of God to you."

At that, a clap of something that sounded very much like thunder boomed over the crowd, and Sarah—large, angelic and seemingly omnipotent—disappeared in a cloud of sparkling dust to be instantaneously replaced by an attractive, young Caucasian woman in dark-framed spectacles, jeans, and a black turtleneck sweater.

The newcomer looked shy and a little bewildered. She brushed her hands over her body, examining it like it didn't belong to her, then looked around at the crowd. She blinked a few times as if to clear her vision, and hesitantly took hold of a microphone on the podium in front of her.

"Hello," she said, "I'm Rachel Hawthorn." Then she pulled the mic away from her mouth as if it was alive and examined it cautiously before carefully putting it in front of her mouth once more. "You'll have to excuse me," she said nervously, "I have not heard the sound of my own voice, or been in human form, since 1993, when I died of cancer."

There was some murmuring as people absorbed her words, and then a few shouts of "Hello, Rachel!" rang out.

Hawthorn continued, a bit more authoritatively. "I was born, and I died, in Vancouver, British Columbia, Canada. At the time of my death, I was enrolled in a master's program in sociology at the University of British Columbia. My thesis was on technological change, specifically how the advent of the internet, cell phones, and social media were impacting people. Everyone was touting these new innovations as amazing, but I noted how people were actually communicating less—even while talking more. My markers for real communication included facial expression, tone of voice, and body language. I predicted that, in time, this lack of communication would contribute to a breakdown in social mores like manners and cultural customs, and that this would have a negative impact on communities. As it turns out, I was right. The breakdown in human values, across all cultures, has played a significant role in the events that have led up to God's intervention."

Cummings was impressed by young Rachel; She was clearly an intelligent woman who could have offered a lot to the world had she lived long enough. He thought it was a shame she had died before she reached her obvious potential.

"You've asked what it's like to live with God," Rachel continued, "and I can only answer from my own experience because it's different for everyone. When we are in physical bodies, we are individuated, and we pride ourselves on that. After death, we are much more connected, and every soul continually interacts with other souls, sort of like the *Star Trek* premise of the Vulcan mind-meld. We share our experiences and are bathed in each other's life force . . . yet we also retain the individuality we had on Earth. For example, as a sociologist, I have always been interested in how other people function, and this aspect of my personality remains with me in Heaven. There, I am drawn to newly-arrived human souls, many of whom need comfort and reassurance as they adjust to their new soul freedom. I guide them into the life force and encourage them to let go of their attachment to the physical plane. For some, this release is exhilarating. For others, it is quite disorienting. For me, dying and finding myself free from the heaviness of being human was something of a relief. My body was sick, and it was no hardship to leave it."

At that, Rachel gave a nervous smile, and then suddenly disappeared in a swirl of stardust, to be instantly replaced by a small, slightly heavyset, dark-haired woman of about sixty years of age who was wearing a coarse, shabby grey dress and a black apron.

The woman, seemingly surprised to find herself in front of an audience, looked around nervously and twisted her hands into her apron. Then she approached the microphone uncertainly. She was almost too short to reach it, and so she stood on her tiptoes, took it out of its clip, and then moved to stand to one side of the podium where the audience could see her better.

"Hola," she said with a wide smile that radiated friendship and warmth despite her widely spaced, heavily stained teeth. "I am Gabriela Torres. I was born in a small village south of Madrid, and I died in 1492, the year the explorer Christopher Columbus—sponsored by our new King Ferdinand and his queen, Isabella—sailed for the Americas. One of my sons sailed on the Pinta and made it to the new world along with Columbus. I never saw my boy in his earthly body again because I left my human form before Fernando returned home to me. But we are both with God now, at one with each other and all others." At this, as if to honour her dead son, she crossed herself in his memory.

"You want to know what life with God is like," she said, "and it is hard for me to tell you. When we connect with another soul, we experience everything that soul did during its physical life—sounds, tastes, smells... even feelings. We are not equipped in our human forms to do this. Only after death do we truly understand other people. As for what I do now that I am in spirit form, what Rachel said—that individual talents pass forward—is true. In my human form, I lived in a village where honouring ancestors was a big part of my culture. I continue to do this. I am drawn to souls who died long before me, and then I honour them by connecting them to their ancestors or descendants—which leads to endless encounters of pure joy."

At that, she beamed. Then she put the microphone back into the stand, stepped away from the podium, and like Rachel before her, instantly twirled away into stardust to be replaced by a woman of about forty years of age with short, blond hair; a muscular body; hard, crisp facial features; and a severe set to her mouth.

This new woman strode confidently to the mic and said firmly, "I am Katrina Volshensnky. I died accidentally in a car accident in 1967. I was the first female astrophysicist in the Soviet Union."

Some of the more technologically-minded audience members clapped. In some circles, she was well-known.

"I have always been fascinated by science," Volshensnky went on, ignoring the applause, "and this continues for me. I seek out advanced life forms, intelligent species whose physical lives took place on other planets, and I study them. Such beings are ahead of humanity both spiritually and technologically, and so what I learn is sometimes difficult to conceptualize. As these beings evolved, their command over energy and matter grew to the point where their consumption of physical food dramatically decreased or was sometimes completely eliminated—sort of like the fabled 'breatharians,' or Indian swamis who survive on 'prana,' which means 'life force' in Sanskrit. Such was their command over energy and matter, that they were able to teleport their small frames freely about their home worlds and to communicate telepathically. In time, this is in store for the human race as well."

In the back row of the religious leader's section, a man in colourful green and orange garments, with a headdress of the same colour, stood up. He was tall, almost seven feet, Cummings estimated, but he was easy in his big body, graceful even. Volshensnky acknowledged him.

"My name is Bakary Kouassi. I am from the Ivory Coast. Can you tell me about the most advanced civilization you have ever encountered?"

At that, Volshensnky's straight mouth curved up into a slight grin. She said, "I am happy to tell you that. I met a soul who, until the end of its planet, lived as one with it. This soul has been with God for more than one billion Earth years, and prior to the destruction of its home world, its species lived in peace for three billion Earth years." Then she sighed and stared dreamily into the sky before looking back at Kouassi. "I have never experienced such intense love from any other soul," she said, "and since that experience, I have been changed. There is so much to learn . . . and so much love to experience. For me, the afterlife is about learning and living in constant wonder."

Then, in a swirl of stardust, she too was gone, replaced once more by Sarah in all her glory, who hovered over the crowd, mighty, pure, and untouchable. Light fell from her in droplets, only to disappear in the air before it touched the heads of the leaders below, who looked up at her in awe.

Then, in a booming voice and a rush of wind, she said, "With God, we spend our time connecting with others, weaving tightly the cloth of interconnectedness that is the overall life force of God. God does not need to monitor the activities of our souls because we are as one, though occasionally, a group of souls is commandeered to perform specific tasks in the material universe."

"Such as when God created you?" called out Cummings from where he sat.

"Yes," replied Sarah. "I was created to communicate the message of God's intervention on Earth and to assist this planet through its changes. I have powers, such as the ability to be in multiple times and places concurrently, because I contain the life force of so many souls. However, the power to impose the 'do not kill' edict, and to change human biology, is much greater than my abilities. That is directly from God."

And that's when Ben Morrison sprang to his feet once more. "Sarah!" he yelped. "You say God is a compilation of souls and energy and not a willful old man behind a cloud who smites us when angry. Yet you've just said God willfully implemented the 'do not kill' edict. So what would you have us believe? That God has independent thought and will, or not?"

"That is a valid question, Ben," answered Sarah, "and it ties to the concept of being 'at one' with other souls. God is a collective but is energetically and spiritually as one. Therefore, God can act as a unit to implement change. I guess you could say that God is similar to me but to an infinite degree of power."

Morrison pondered this for a moment, and then asked, "Fine, I will try to accept that. But let me ask you this: What good is prayer and devotion if God is not equipped to hear or respond?"

Sarah tinkled, a golden sound, and emitted her trademark rose scent once more. "Prayer and devotion remain important tools if they teach people to place others' needs above their own. But if such rituals actively separate people from one another, then they are not useful and should cease."

"Well then," Morrison said petulantly, "in your version of 'what's what,' what role does Satan have in the universe?"

Sarah laughed. "Oh, Ben," she said. "Satan is a Christian myth. Satan does not exist—and neither does hell. The concept of the devil is a metaphor for the animalistic tendencies, such as hatred, intolerance, and greed, present in human beings. Blaming a mythical devil is much easier than taking personal responsibility for one's own flaws, don't you think?"

"So . . . there's no eternal damnation if you screw others around?" asked Morrison bluntly.

"Your life force will not grow, and you run the risk of being permanently extinguished if you go down that path," said Sarah, "but no. There is no eternal damnation. However, only by placing the needs of others ahead of your own will you feed the life force and become one with God, in joy, after death."

Morrison sat down, his face a mass of conflicting emotions. Several rows behind Cummings, Dong Yang stood. Cummings recognized his voice and turned to smile at him. He was rewarded with a slight wave.

"Hello, Sarah," Dong said, bowing slightly. "I am interested to know which, if any, of the existing religious structures best reflect what God believes religion should be."

"None of them . . . and all of them," replied Sarah enigmatically. "All contain a lot of misinformation—but some form of the Golden Rule exists in each as well. As I've said, religion is not a factor when it comes to who makes it into Heaven. True spiritual growth is determined by individual actions."

"So people who practice specific religions are no more likely to go to Heaven than agnostics and atheists?" he asked anxiously.

"No," replied Sarah, "religious inclination doesn't make a difference unless it is tied to an overall emphasis on helping others."

Dong sat down, and beside Sarah, the pope rose unsteadily to his feet once more. He looked pained, nervous even.

"Your Holiness," Sarah acknowledged him.

"Your Grace," he responded, genuflecting. Then, rather shakily, he asked, "Sarah, it pains me to ask this most basic of questions, as my faith is founded on the belief in the holy trinity, but . . . was Jesus not the son of God?"

"Ah, Julius," she said sweetly, exuding the rose scent along with a warm, gentle breeze. "We are all children of God to greater or lesser degrees—but from birth, Jesus was selected to be an emissary of God, sent to spread word of the love that awaits humankind if they obey the Golden Rule."

"An emissary like you?" asked the pope, fearful that he was about to hear blasphemy.

"No, Jesus was much different than I am," said Sarah. "Jesus is a singular being while I am a conglomeration of soul energy, though Jesus contains substantially more life force in his one, fully developed soul than normal humans do. However, while the souls of which I am composed are weaker individually than his, in combination, I have the capacity to do things he could not do without God's direct assistance. The same applies to other spiritual icons sent by God to teach humanity how to generate life force through love—such as Mohammed, Buddha, and many more. God created me as a multi-soul being to allow me to communicate directly and simultaneously with all human beings. In the past, individual prophets appearing in different locations at different points in history have inadvertently created multiple versions of the true nature of God. There is only one truth!"

The pope looked stricken.

"What is it, Julius?" asked Sarah.

"I love Jesus," the man said simply. "I love Him with all my heart."

"And so you should," said Sarah gently. "Jesus is a true son of God. His care is always for others and rarely for himself. However, it was his early followers who decreed him to literally be the one and only son of God. If he was here with us today, he would tell you exactly what I am telling you: You are all children of God, with the capacity to become as perfect as Him."

The pope had to be content with that. He sat down.

The dark-robed leader of the Greek Orthodox Church stood up to call out, "Sarah! You've said so many things that are difficult to process. You've said, for example, that our holy scriptures hold little weight, and that religious institutions are not the way to God . . . but you've also said that clerics like me still have a role to play in helping people find their way to God—though apparently, we're not very good at it! I'm so confused that I'm starting to think I should have listened to my father and become a doctor!"

There was a roar of laughter throughout the square at this, and even Sarah chuckled breezily.

She said, "You have chosen a respectable, valuable calling . . . but your teaching manuals are out of date. However, you now have new guidance from God, and the message you should share with your respective congregations is that the path to eternal life is straightforward and can be attained by anybody."

"It sounds so simple when *you* say it," deadpanned the man to snickers from the appreciative crowd.

"It *is* simple," insisted Sarah. "Forget all the rituals and dogma. Forget interfaith competition. Follow the Golden Rule. Teach your people to treat others as they would be treated themselves."

The man sat back down, content with the answer, while beside him, a well-groomed man in a smart business suit got to his feet. He looked rich, healthy . . . and American. Cummings recognized him as Jonah Stalwart, the leader of America's largest non-denominational, modern fundamentalist church. For many Christians in America, he was a rock star of sorts. He'd purchased an old stadium in Houston for his church services because his congregation had exploded, partly due to his charismatic sermons, and partly due to the spectacular Sunday services, complete with a Christian rock band and accompanying light show.

Stalwart placed one hand on his hip, a gesture Cummings took to be arrogant, and said, "Sarah, my religion believes that one day, all people will be raised from death. However, while Christians will be raised to everlasting glory, those who do not trust in Christ will be raised to judgment. Your description of God and Heaven makes no mention of such a process. Please clarify this for me."

"Gladly," replied Sarah. "Life and death are ongoing and so is the process of recycling the life force. There is no resurrection. At death, intelligent life will either join God or be recycled."

"How does God define 'intelligent life'?" asked Stalwart. "You've said there are beings in the universe who are so much more advanced than humans that it makes us primitive, little better than chimps. So how does God determine where that curve stops? Chimps love and nurture their young just as we do . . . They even use rudimentary tools! Why do humans make the grade, yet chimpanzees don't?"

"For God's purposes, intelligence is defined by the ability to think about things abstractly and to plan ahead, rather than responding to external stimuli and behaving instinctively. The ability to conceive of God would be an example of something an intelligent being would do," Sarah replied, and Cummings thought he could detect a note of amusement in her tone.

Stalwart mulled that over for a moment, and then asked, "Are there planets on which two or more species qualify as 'intelligent' and each sends life force back to God?"

"Yes," replied Sarah, "but only on the most advanced planets. However, a million years from now, another species on Earth may qualify."

"Which one?" asked Stalwart.

Sarah only smiled and said, "You'll find out in a million years, Jonah, if you are with God."

"Well, that'll be the day, won't it," muttered Stalwart as he sat down.

Cummings was certain it was the first time the preacher had ever been at a loss for words.

Chapter 36

The Church of Humanity

When the religious forum was over, there was a lot for the world's spiritual leaders to think about. Sarah's description of the true nature of God and the universe had made many of them uncomfortable. To believe Sarah meant to question the very foundations of their respective faiths, and while they were in agreement that the 'Gospel of Sarah' should be recognized as the truth, they were not prepared to remove historical texts from circulation, let alone rewrite them.

"Why would we?" asked the pope. "The truths in the Bible are as valid now as they ever were. Only the semantics are different."

There was also mixed reaction to the debunking of the creation story. Religious leaders who believed in non-Christian versions of creation, such as Indigenous North Americans and Australian Aborigines, felt comfortable integrating Sarah's version of events into their belief systems. Those with polytheistic faiths struggled to find common ground and had trouble letting go of thousands of years of doctrine. Many Christian leaders were aghast at the idea that God did not create the universe and everything in it.

However the pope, a man of compromise, held firmly to his opinion that "A spark is enough of an act of creation for me to continue to thank God for my life. Perhaps it's not the same as the biblical accounts of Adam and Eve, but I don't think the two theories are mutually exclusive."

One by one, the world's faith leaders tried to come to terms with the various components of Sarah's message, and most gradually began to understand and accept her message and started thinking about how to share it with their congregations and devotees.

However, a week later, when Sarah linked with the leaders holographically in their homes, it was clear there was still one major sticking point—at least when it came to some of the more male-dominated faiths.

"Since the beginning of some of the more well-known, organized faiths," Sarah said, "women have systemically been excluded from influential roles. This exclusion must end."

The usual suspects just looked at her in disbelief as she fluttered three-dimensionally above them.

"But women *do* play a big role in the Catholic faith!" sputtered the pope "They are theologians, abbesses, missionaries, martyrs, religious sisters, Doctors of the Church—even saints, like the Blessed Virgin Mary!"

Not to be outdone, the Grand Imam chimed in, "Men and women are equal in the sight of Allah, and both must be fully respected and honoured," he said. "Women are allowed to lead prayer; They are just not allowed to lead *men* in prayer."

"And why not?" asked Sarah. "We are all here to serve God, and gender is not a factor."

The pope looked pained. "Jesus did not ordain any women," he protested, "and he personally selected all his apostles—none of which were women."

"But Julius," said Sarah calmly, "the Gospels of Matthew, Mark, Luke, and John are more than 2,000 years old, and were written well after Jesus walked the Earth."

"Well, it's not like you were there either," sniffed the pope.

"Oh, but I *was*," Sarah said. "The 40 million women's souls inside me have collectively been witness to the birth of every religion on this planet, and have participated in them all as well. Interestingly, those women sometimes recount much different stories than men have done."

"You speak of my faith as if it's nothing but stories," said the pope, offended. "In that vein—since many prophets have visited this Earth since the death of our Saviour, the Lord Jesus Christ—tell me why not one of them has relayed the same story as you? Had they done so, it most certainly would have changed the nature of the church, not to mention women's roles in worship!"

"What Pope Julius says is true," came a gentle, Indian-accented voice that belonged to an orange-robed swami. "At no time during Hinduism's

5,000 year long history has a revelation come to any of our saints about God's true nature either. Had such a message come, I know we Hindus would have explored its truths."

"Indeed," said Sarah with a waft of rose-scented air, "but isn't it true that sometimes, you already do?"

The swami smiled coyly. "It's true that some swamis are capable of transcending the physical body," he admitted. Then he paused, squinting a little as if adjusting his vision, and added, "and this includes women, you know. There are many women saints in India, some living still. Amma, our hugging saint, travels the world promoting selfless service, inter-religious harmony, environmental protection, desegregation of science and spirituality, and the importance of women's empowerment for the cultivation of compassion, patience, and selflessness. She has many devotees, in all countries."

The pope looked appalled. "I believe her to be more of a teacher than a saint," he said, rather ungraciously.

Sarah didn't let him get away with it. "Think of the Apostle Paul," she said, "didn't he say, 'There is neither Jew nor Greek, servant nor free, male nor female, since we are all in Christ'? There is no doubt that Amma is doing God's work, Julius."

The pope cleared his throat, chastened. "Yes," he said, "I know, and I apologize. I just find all of this to be a bit much."

"I understand this is difficult for you to accept," replied Sarah. "However, you are simply learning the truth before your earthly death, which gives you opportunity to share it with others. Spread the joy. Offer comfort and guidance to your followers and teach them that love, tolerance, and support for all of humanity is the way to join God in the afterlife that you call Heaven. Lead by example."

"I have *always* led by example," the pope insisted, "the example set by Jesus, my Lord and Saviour." At this, he crossed himself.

"Ah, yes," said Sarah, her gentle voice like the fluttering wings of a dove. "And you have done much good in the world. However, it is time for a belief system where actions speak louder than words. Surely you, of all religious leaders, understand this? The organization you've given your life to has been cut open, and its blackened heart exposed. Many of your priests are less than stellar examples of what it means to be compassionate, Julius."

"I am aware of this," said the pope tartly. "And I have prayed to the Virgin Mary, the spiritual mother of humanity, for guidance." Then suddenly, his eyes lit up. "Sarah," he said, "by any chance, is one of the 40 million souls within you that of the Blessed Mother?"

A breath of springtime air massaged the faces of the audience, despite the fact that they were each in their own kitchens, bedrooms, living rooms, and studies. "Yes," whispered Sarah.

"I would so love to see her . . . and to hear her story," the pope said wistfully.

"Then you shall," said Sarah . . . and suddenly, she disappeared.

An expectant silence replaced her. In their homes, the religious leaders' senses all went on high alert as they waited for something to happen, though they knew not what. Suddenly, a small, blue tornado funnel spun at lightning speed into each of their realms, causing a few to cower as curtains flapped and dogs and cats fled the room. The vortex grew larger and wilder, twirling crazily—and then with a loud pop, it dissipated, leaving behind a diminutive, dark-haired, middle-aged woman with fine features and expressive black eyes, to hover in hologram shape where Sarah's form used to be.

"Hello," she said evenly in Aramaic which, with Sarah's help, was instantly understandable to those watching. "I am Mary, the mother of Jesus."

She radiated pure love; No one could help but feel it.

"I am very nervous," she confided. "Sarah has asked me to tell you my story, and I am afraid that what I will say might be painful to hear for those who revere me. To Christians and Muslims alike, I am the 'Blessed Virgin Mary'—or 'Maryam' as I am called in the Islamic faith."

The Grand Imam began weeping loudly, so in awe of Mary's presence was he. In Islam, Maryam held the highest position of all women, with two of the longer chapters of the Qur'an dedicated to her and her family.

"My story is no different than that of many women of my time," Mary began. "I was born in Nazareth, a small village about twelve miles southwest of the Sea of Galilee. Until I was fifteen years of age, I was a simple Jewish girl who lived with my parents, Joachim and Anne—albeit alongside the armies of the Holy Roman Empire, who were not always kind to Jews. At fifteen, I was considered of marriageable age, and I became betrothed to a good, reliable man, a carpenter named Joseph. We began courting, but as is customary in our faith, we never touched each other before marriage. However, about four weeks after we agreed to marry, we each had a dream that I would become pregnant with a son. We laughed about it and hoped it would become true once we were married."

At that, the weeping Grand Imam cried out, in words he had clearly memorized long ago, "The Qur'an says, 'She was a virgin and had not been touched by a man. One day, Mary saw a vision of a well-built man. The man told her that he was sent by God to give her a boy who will be an example and a mercy for mankind.'"

"Yes," Mary agreed, gently, "this indeed happened. While my mother was planning my wedding, I went into seclusion in the countryside east of Nazareth to purify myself and spiritually prepare. I was deep in meditation, sitting under a fig tree in the shade, when a voice startled me out of my trance. I opened my eyes to find Joseph standing in front of me, clothed in a white tunic of a style I had not seen before. Although I was still partially in a deep, meditative state, I knew that I was viewing an apparition, as Joseph was hard at work in Nazareth. I fully believed the spirit of Joseph when he said, 'It is God's will that we have a male child to carry the message of God's will throughout the land.'

"When I returned from my seclusion, we were promptly wed, and I became pregnant as was God's will. When Jesus was born, we were both overjoyed, though the timing was not ideal. As you know, we were travelling from Nazareth to Bethlehem and had to take shelter in a stable. However, we brought Jesus back to Nazareth when our business in Bethlehem was done and I was well enough to travel.

"Jesus was a remarkable child. At three years old, he wanted to know all he could about God, and by the time he was eight, he could argue theology with the local rabbis. I can't count the times Joseph hauled him home from the temple. My husband thought he was being disrespectful of his elders, but secretly, we were both proud of his intelligence. He told us he was here on Earth to help people get into Heaven . . . It seemed he might be right."

Then Mary's face darkened as she remembered her son's early life. "Nazareth was not big enough for Jesus," she said quietly. "Both Joseph and I knew it. However, when he disappeared from our home at just twelve years old, we were still taken by surprise. I was so worried, and the longer he was gone, the more heartbroken I became. However, I had to go on because I had other children to care for."

She paused, thinking of her life so long ago, a small smile playing on her lips, her eyes wistful. "Yes," she said, "we had a boisterous household of three boys and two girls, which helped me accept that my oldest son was probably lost to me forever . . . and then eighteen years later, when he was thirty, he suddenly returned. He apologized for leaving without saying anything, and he told me that he'd travelled down the Silk Road with traders, studying all he could about God, from people of all faiths, along the way. He said, 'Now I am ready, Mother, to share the love that God gave me.' Then he began his ministry . . . and the world knows the rest."

Mary paused, and her words stuck in her throat as a shadow of grief crossed her face. "I thought my life would end when I witnessed his torture and death," she concluded. "No mother should ever have to go through such sorrow and horror."

She remained silent for a moment, and then brightened as she added, "Several years after his death, I joined Jesus in Heaven. To feel his presence again was a moment of indescribable love and joy. I finally understood everything he had tried to teach the world during his short life—and now, more than 2,000 years after my own death, I, too, have been resurrected in the service of God."

The Episcopalian leader cleared his throat self-consciously, hoping for an opportunity to speak.

"Yes?" asked Mary.

"Most revered mother," he said, and Mary smiled, "there are many accounts of miracles attributed to you. Do you answer prayers?"

"I am aware that many people on Earth call upon me for help in their daily lives," she replied. "Their cries touch my heart, and I wish for them to be helped. However, they thank me erroneously if they overcome their trials . . . for it is not me who causes them to recover."

Mary paused, assessing her audience, her warm, dark eyes emitting the compassion for which she was legendary. It was clear she was a kind and godly soul . . . but her first-hand account of her life did not sit well with those who placed a premium on the thought of her forever being the virginal mother of Christ.

Sensing this, she said, "I don't imagine this is the story some of you expected to hear; Nevertheless, the greater truth I am sharing with you is that who I am, or whether or not there was an immaculate conception, doesn't *matter*. What matters is that my son Jesus left a legacy of love, despite the fact that people have endlessly torn apart his message to further themselves. He strived to create a compassionate world . . . and he wants you do the same."

And then, as suddenly as she had appeared, Mary disappeared, leaving her words hanging in the air like fog over the ocean. Except for a long exhale from the pope, there was complete silence across the e-meeting space, as if a spell had been cast. Only the return of Sarah, who slowly misted into view, broke it.

"Mary is the epitome of what it means to be a woman and a mother in both the Christian and Muslim traditions," Sarah said after she had fully materialized. "Do you not agree?"

There were choruses of "Blessed among women" and "Holy Mother" and the like.

"She is revered," Sarah continued quietly, "and yet, this reverence has not translated into spiritual equality for women in the eyes of the world. This must be corrected, which is why I've created a streaming network dedicated to spreading the new gospel. I've named it Godvision."

"Godvision?" asked a thin, academic-looking Asian man. "I don't think this network will be available in China."

"Yes, it will," Sarah said. "In fact, it's available all over the planet right now. Google it, and you will see."

"What do you offer on this network?" asked the Grand Imam who, now that Mary was gone, was no longer weeping.

"Any programming that furthers my message of the true nature of God," Sarah replied. "Let me show you."

With that, she projected into each cleric's home a vision of a woman in drab, rough clothing, who was sweeping a dirt floor in an adobe style building. She was speaking to someone as if being interviewed, while chickens strutted by at her feet.

"Oh, yes," said the woman. "Jesus was close with John when they were boys. He was a lovely lad, very smart. When he disappeared at twelve or thirteen, he caused his mother no end of heartache . . . but he came back as a leader, a good man. Many thought him brazen to challenge how things were done, but others were grateful he was calling out the Romans on their brutality. He was a remarkable person, a gifted soul." Then she paused in her sweeping and said sadly, "It was terrible what those Romans did to him."

Sarah paused the broadcast to speak. "This program," she said, "is called *What Do You Know*. It profiles key religious figures from the point of view of their female friends and family members—mothers, sisters, aunties, wives, lovers, and so on. I call these women forth from inside myself, just as I did with Mary a few moments ago, and ask them to comment from a female point of view on major events in religious texts . . . and then I conclude their interviews by asking them, first, whether the religious figure we are discussing is now with God; and second, if they will confirm that the true nature of God is as I have been telling the world."

A puzzled-looking, dark-skinned man in colourful, yellow African print clothing called out, "I am Bakary Kouassi, from the Ivory Coast! I practice Akan and believe Nyame, the supreme being, created all things. I do not know, who is this woman with the chickens you are showing us?"

"Welcome, Bakary," said Sarah. "She is Mary's cousin Elizabeth, and her son John, who is known as John the Baptist, was Jesus' cousin and boyhood friend."

Sarah then restarted the interview with Elizabeth, who said with a smile, "Life after death is exactly how you say it is. When the body dies, the soul is freed to join with God and know all there is to know. It's a beautiful thing."

Then the interview with Elizabeth faded away, and once more, Sarah's imposing, holographic form hovered over the clerics.

"I would urge you to use Godvision as a teaching tool in your places of worship," she said to them. "If you embrace it now, then it will not lure your flock away. If you don't, then your congregations will eventually find it and make their own decisions about what is true."

She was right, of course, but it didn't make the pill easier to swallow.

Finally, the Chinese man asked, "What other things will you show on your network?"

"For those who need irrefutable facts when it comes to God, there will be scholarly programming. One show called *It's Gospel* is styled as a weekly debate between male and female religious scholars. The teams will be asked to analyze cases of people who lost their lives by attempting to kill somebody, and then try to determine whether or not that person was banned from Heaven."

"Entertaining," remarked the pope, "but so far, none of your programming seems to make significant strides toward elevating women's roles in religion, which you've said is a goal."

"Ah, Julius, you are so perceptive," laughed Sarah, the scent of jasmine permeating the individual rooms of her audience, causing everyone to feel the peace she offered. "Later this week, I will debut a quiz show where low-level female clerics quiz leaders from the top ten faiths—including *you*, Julius—about how they plan to incorporate my gospel into their practices, as well as increase the role of women in senior leadership."

"What?" gasped the pope. He appeared highly offended.

"Please, Julius," said Sarah as if speaking to a child. "The Catholic Church has had over 2,000 years to create a faith that is real and true, yet you continue to cling to outdated ways and harmful beliefs. You don't allow women to hold positions of power, you expect chastity from your priests—which has gone against their natures to the point of rampant sexual abuse—and you practice archaic rituals that people don't understand. It's time for a change. You can't deny it."

The pope's lips flapped, but no words came out. He had nothing to add because what she'd said was true. His face turned red, and he cast his eyes downward.

"I realize," said Sarah to the whole group, "that changing tradition is not easy. I realize that some of you will either flat out refuse to do it or will drag your heels. But change will come, with or without you."

At that, she brought another Godvision program forth, a news program. The feature story was about a demonstration that took place on a Christian university campus in Colorado. The group watched as young men and women milled about a leafy green campus, raising placards reading, "I Believe the Gospel According to Sarah" and shouting, "Sarah, Sarah, one, two, three . . . She's the one that I believe!"

"Upon hearing about the true nature of God," Sarah said, pausing the stream, "the female students called for a campus-wide assembly and discussion. The faculty, which is mostly male, tried to deny them, but a grassroots movement took place, and the assembly occurred anyway—outside, as you can see, since they were not allowed access to an auditorium. This rebellion was supported not only by female students but by males as well. In fact, the only people who didn't support it were the faculty members who, of course, have much invested in male-dominated religious education."

"Social unrest of this nature should not be tolerated!" yelped the pope.

"But if it's more than just social unrest? Could it not be called 'much-needed change'?" asked Sarah gently.

At that, imagery from universities and college campuses around the world—faith-based and secular alike—began invading the rooms of Sarah's audience, picture upon picture floating above their heads like dreams, and it soon became very clear that this 'grassroots' movement that was openly embracing Sarah's gospel was as unstoppable as a tidal wave. Not only that, but leaders were emerging. One young woman, a fiery redhead from Ireland, was particularly compelling. Sarah showed the group a few minutes of her in action as she rallied not only fellow students but people of all stripes, at a public square in Dublin.

"This new gospel is the truth!" she exclaimed in her Irish brogue. "And I aim to step into the light and start a place of worship where all are welcome. In this new and equal house of worship, anyone who can effectively communicate light, goodness, and love can lead, no matter their gender, sexual orientation, skin colour, or life choices. All that is required is that goodness shines from within, and that they possess a true desire to serve humankind. We will elevate! We will become free from spiritual oppression! We will understand that our *bodies* are not who we are—but that it is our *spirits* that matter. We are one race—the *human* race—and we are all children of God. We will go forward with a mission to treat one another with love and respect."

The crowd roared their approval and began chanting, "Sarah, Sarah, she's the one . . . out of darkness, into the sun!"

The religious leaders watched in fascination and awe.

"This," Sarah said to them softly, "is where it begins. You are witnessing the beginning of the Church of Humanity."

CHAPTER 37

Worthiness in the Eyes of God

Cummings sat at his desk in the Oval Office, looking intently out the window at the carefully manicured White House grounds as dusk came down. He'd put in a very full day. He'd spoken with Herbert Sloan about America's Water Initiative and was, as always, impressed with the capability and integrity of the man. Under Sloan's leadership, he had no doubt the drought in America's Southwest would soon be alleviated. He'd also spent several hours with Martin Grieves, checking on the status of military redeployment and was more than satisfied with what had been accomplished on such short notice. He felt that things were really coming along in his country . . . and yet, he was not at peace.

As the sun sent out its last colourful rays, announcing its retirement for the day, he sat still as a mouse in the darkening room, pondering the changes that had come to his world, his planet, and his life in such a short time. Sarah and her messages were compelling to him—though sometimes overwhelming. He implicitly believed her version of the true nature of God and the universe . . . but—as he'd felt from almost the first moment he'd laid eyes on Sarah—he still had a nagging sense that he was falling short on what it meant to be a spiritual engine for God.

I'm nothing but a drop in the ocean, he thought a little morosely. *If I do my bit and everyone else does their bit, humankind will someday heal. So why do I feel like I've failed?*

Later that evening, he talked it over with Lorena.

"You know, Lorena," he said, "ever since Sarah arrived on Earth, I've been running from meeting to meeting and crisis to crisis, trying to fix the world. I know I've made a difference nationwide, and on the global stage—but that's my *job*. It's my responsibility to do what needs to be done, and I take it very seriously. So, as president, I've made a great difference, but sometimes I wonder . . . what difference has Samuel Cummings, *human being*, made?"

Lorena was shocked that he felt this way. "Honey, you've taken on enough responsibility to prove the worth of a legion of men," she said gently. "You don't need to do more. You've capably led your country through a time of crisis and change—at great risk to yourself, I may add. All it would have taken was for one soldier to fire his gun at another in the line of duty and as an 'enabler,' you would have died in the chain reaction! Your goodness as a human being should not be in question!"

"Thanks, Lorena," he said. "I'm glad you think so, but despite everything I've accomplished, I feel like I haven't put my money where my mouth is. I'm a powerful politician, paid by the people to make decisions and allocate resources on their behalf . . . but when was the last time I stuck my neck out on a personal level? It's been so long that I don't actually remember!"

Lorena had no idea what he was on about. "I don't know why you feel that way," she said. "What more do you think you should be doing? Handing out blankets to the homeless?"

He looked at her, his gaze direct. "Yes," he said, "something like that."

That stopped her cold. "Well," she said after a minute, "that was actually a joke, but if handing out blankets to the homeless will make you feel better, I'm right behind you."

He kissed her cheek. She responded by taking his hand and squeezing it.

Then he said, "You know, all my life, I've had the luxury of putting myself first. My mom treated me like a little king, and then I met you, and you've treated me like a *big* king. I'm a spoiled man."

"Well, obviously," she said.

"You've let me get away with a lot over the years, Lorena," he told her.

"I know," she replied. "But when we were young, you were so busy trying to get your business off the ground that I just picked up the slack. And now that you're president . . . well, I have a role as First Lady, and I enjoy it. We're a team, Samuel. You seem to think I've given up so much that I should be sad or something, but I live a life I love. To me, doing things for my family is no big deal."

"It *is* a big deal," insisted Cummings. "In terms of things that come from the heart, you've done much, much more in your life than I have. Throughout our marriage, you're the one who did the meaningful things, like setting up the Christmas tree, and getting the kids to soccer practice . . ."

"And it was a royal pain in the ass," she agreed good-naturedly. "But you don't owe me anything."

"That's not the point," he said with a laugh. "What I'm trying to say is that those day to day things, done over a lifetime—like helping the kids with their homework without getting frustrated—are what generate the life force for God. This is what Sarah's been telling the world. It's not the grandiose gestures of a president that count, it's consistent, willing sharing of energy over time. And Lorena? I think I may have missed the boat on that. God knows I've done those grandiose things . . . but I've failed at consistent, loving actions."

"Darling, you have not failed at anything," said Lorena compassionately. "You've always been there for me and the kids."

"Have I?" he smiled ruefully. "You and I both know that's not true. The way I remember it, I was away a lot of the time, building my business while my talented and beautiful wife gave up her own career to raise our kids."

"Well, it's not like you *made* me do it," she said by way of comfort. "I offered. We didn't want strangers looking after them."

"But I didn't have to throw myself into my work quite as hard as I did," he admitted, digging into a little dark spot in his heart. "In fact, sometimes I worked late just so I could get away from the responsibilities of family life. I was frightened of what I'd got myself into with you and the kids. Working hard and building a business seemed easier—and much safer than being vulnerable to the three of you."

"Oh, Sam," Lorena said. "You're not the first husband, and certainly not the last, to practice the fine art of avoidance. Luckily for you, I could see right through your little game . . . and I understood you needed time away from the family chaos. It's nothing to be ashamed of. You were always there when it counted." Then she poked him in the ribs, trying to cheer him up. "Come on, Sam," she said. "I am not quite the saint you make me out to be. Kids are annoying little jerks. There were lots of times when I yelled at them and wished I could ditch them."

"But you *didn't*," he pointed out. "You tended to their boo-boos, helped them with piano lessons, and even taught them to ride bicycles. And where was I?"

"Earning the wages to buy pianos and bicycles," she replied. "*Someone* had to keep them in diapers." Then, wanting to boost her husband's spirits, Lorena said, "Let's have some coffee." And she switched on the coffee machine. As it burbled to life, she said, "You're just overwhelmed, Sam. You've been working non-stop since Sarah arrived."

"Maybe you're right," said Cummings with a sigh. But he knew his angst ran deeper than that.

They sipped their drinks in silence until Cummings, knowing his wife was concerned, tried to lighten the mood by changing the subject to something positive.

"Hey, do you remember the pen pal program for middle schoolers that Angelica was working on?" he asked Lorena.

"Yes," she replied, heartened to see that her husband was coming out of his bad mood. "That was a great idea."

"Yes, it was, and it's really taking off," he said. "The pilot program has forty-two member countries on board, and it's been such a hit that students of all ages from around the world are clamoring to try it—even kids in higher grades."

"How *wonderful*," said Lorena enthusiastically. Then she asked, "Are Angelica's girls part of the program? They're around Jessica's age, aren't they?"

"Yes, she told me they're writing to twin boys in Thailand," Cummings replied.

At the mention of Thailand, Lorena's brow furrowed. "Is that safe?" she asked.

Cummings knew immediately that she was thinking about the possibility of sexual predators hacking into the correspondence system.

"Don't worry," he said. "The first thing Angelica did was get some major tech companies on board. They jumped at the chance to offer their security services free of charge, simply for the good press. You can't buy advertising like that."

"That's definitely a 'feel good' win . . ." offered Lorena; Then she saw her husband's expression get somewhat dour, and she asked cautiously, ". . . *isn't* it?"

"Yes," said Cummings—but he didn't sound too enthusiastic.

Lorena eyed him shrewdly. "Aren't you happy about Angelica's success?" she demanded.

"Of *course* I'm happy," he replied. "It's just that—"

He never finished his sentence because she cut him off. With her hands on her hips, she said firmly, "Samuel Cummings! Don't tell me you're *jealous*!"

He flushed, appalled at having this pointed out to him so succinctly.

"You wish you were doing what she's doing because you're sick of making decisions where you don't see the end result," Lorena continued, getting right to the heart of the matter.

"Yes, but . . ." Cummings tried, not enjoying the grilling she was giving him.

Lorena huffed, annoyed. "Sam," she said, "how many times do I have to tell you that you are worth your weight in gold? And I don't mean in your capacity as president; I mean as a man. You have *more* than proved that, to both me *and* to the world. You need to let this go."

Cummings knew she would not say such things if she did not believe them, but her words of care didn't help him shake his angst. However, not wanting to upset her further, he decided to stop complaining. He would have to iron out this uncomfortable feeling on his own.

"Thank you for your confidence in me, my love," he said to his wife, "and you're right. I'm going to let it go."

"Good," she said firmly, though he heard underlying concern in her voice.

He stood. "Well," he said as he drained his coffee cup, "I'm off to work. I've a full day ahead of me."

Then he gave her a quick peck on the cheek and headed out the door toward the Oval Office to begin another day of trying to heal a broken country.

He arrived at his desk and was quickly briefed on the morning's events by Janice. First up was the issue of reproductive rights. Now that these had landed solely in the laps of women, the Republican right, bolstered by their evangelical Christian supporters, were starting to accept that there was no need to fight with the Democrats about abortion anymore. To celebrate, state-level Democrats had begun organizing pro-family 'birthday parties.' While on their soapboxes, they made sure the public understood that their forty-year-old, pro-choice stance had been about supporting women—something they were quick to point out that Sarah endorsed—rather than undermining the rights of the fetus. They received very little criticism for this; In fact, in some instances, their Republican opponents joined them on the podium.

Four decades of ongoing battle are fading into the background now, Cummings thought, pleased. He dashed off some presidential messages of support in an effort to keep things moving on the right track.

Cummings was further pleased when Northrup arrived in his office and provided him with the latest gun surrender statistics. The compliance rate had jumped to 72%, much higher than he could ever have anticipated.

"There are always fringe groups who don't want to play ball," Northrup told him, "but even the National Rifle Association is starting to soften its stance on Second Amendment rights. After all, what's the point of owning guns if you can't use them to shoot others?"

Cummings stifled a chuckle at the comment.

But, as the end of his busy day approached, and he pondered going home to Lorena—and possibly continuing the morning's rather uncomfortable discussion—he felt his confidence waning again. He wondered if it had to do with his lowered testosterone levels, or if this was an existential crisis that had been a long time coming. *Or maybe it's because there's only sixteen months left in my presidential term,* he thought. The idea of hitting the campaign trail in the midst of the country's restructuring was daunting, and he didn't want to think about it.

When Lopez had sensibly brought it up at their last meeting, he'd put her off, saying, "Uniting the world starts on the home front, Angelica, and I am not going to backslide into divisive politics now."

"Okay," she'd replied, clearly worried by his unwillingness to get the campaigning started. "Just let me know when you're ready."

That was a very acquiescent answer from the normally fiery Lopez, and Cummings knew she could tell something was bothering him; However, she was not the type to ask what it was. In some ways, he wished she would;

She was a smart woman and could possibly offer some perspective. She was much better at intuitive understanding than he was.

Intuitive understanding . . . Suddenly, he remembered something, a long ago event from his youth. He'd been about nineteen, in the thick of his party days, when he'd learned about intuitive understanding. One night, when stumbling home from a bar with his friends, they'd passed an elderly woman, alone and seemingly frightened, waiting for a bus in a sketchy part of town. Normally, he would have continued on, lost in the intoxication of youth; That night, however, he was intuitively struck by her perceived need, and so he turned around to ask if she was all right.

The woman, in her late seventies, told him in halting English that her German husband had suffered a massive heart attack and been rushed to hospital for emergency heart surgery. She had disembarked from the cruise they were on, and needed to find both a hotel and the local hospital. She was lost and desperate, as well as frantic with worry and fear. Telling his friends to carry on, he stayed with her. They took a bus to the hospital district, where he found her a clean, inexpensive hotel and arranged for the concierge to help her locate her husband in the morning.

Finally, when he bid the woman goodnight, in tears she hugged him and said, "You are an angel!"

And in all his nineteen years, Samuel Cummings had never felt better about himself than he did at that moment. *That's what is haunting me now,* he realized. *Human connection feeds a person's soul.* It was a revelation to finally understand that the presidential pedestal upon which he stood had actually been impeding his ability to connect with others—and now, for the good of his soul, he needed to figure out how to fix that.

He decided to take a short walk around the grounds to mull over how to incorporate more hands-on experiences with helping others into his life. It was dusk, and the air was cooling outside, so he put on his overcoat.

Then he buzzed his bodyguard, Don Taylor, to say, "I'm going to take a short stroll outside, Don."

Taylor, who'd been standing just outside the Oval Office, came into the room immediately. "I'll get my coat and accompany you, Sir," he said.

"There's no need," said Cummings. "I just want a bit of air—and some privacy. I won't go far."

Taylor looked uncomfortable at being dismissed in this way, but he could hardly go against Cummings' request; After all, the president had no real need for protection now that people could no longer kill one another.

Reading Taylor's discomfort, Cummings said, "Don't worry, I'll be fine. I'm just going out on the lawn, and it's not even dark yet. You can keep an eye on me from the window if you want."

"Very well," said Taylor stiffly.

Cummings chuckled internally at his vigilance, then stepped outside through a side exit and walked out onto the lush, green lawn of the White House. Inhaling deeply, he luxuriated in the scent of mown grass. It made him think of his father's lawn, and of the five dollars he got each week when he mowed it, by hand, with a push mower. Every time he finished the job, he was so hot and sweaty . . . but that five dollars was gold to him. It was the price of popcorn and a movie—*Star Wars*, mostly.

Enjoying the cool of the evening and the soft grass beneath his feet, he decided to sit down. He spread his overcoat down onto the grass and then plunked down heavily. It had been a warmish day, and the ground beneath him was just starting to lose its heat. It felt good to touch it. In the darkening night air, birds called to one another, making him feel like he was on a planet all his own, even while in the middle of bustling Washington, D.C.

Letting the day's emotional baggage drain from him, he thought gratefully of his wife, and how she had tried so hard to bolster his flagging spirits earlier. He hoped what she'd told him was true—that he'd generated more life force than he suspected during his time on Earth—but he knew that despite all he'd achieved, he needed something more personal in his life to touch his heart and remind him that he was tied to God. *I want to feel the way I did when I helped that German woman,* he thought.

The grass was temptingly lush. He lay back on it and began running his fingers through its short, fluffy coolness, savoring the memory of her grateful hug, and how close to God that had made him feel . . . and that's when he sensed someone near him. He immediately tried to push himself to his elbows but stopped when he felt something cold and round pressed against his temple.

"You're pretty much a sitting duck, aren't you?" a man's voice asked. "Why on Earth didn't you bring Don Taylor with you?"

Cummings immediately recognized the voice as Norman Feldman's. In the dusky light, he couldn't see his face well, but he had no doubt it was him.

"Norman?" he asked in astonishment. "Is that you?"

There was no answer, just raspy breathing as if Feldman was very upset.

"Do you have a gun against my head?" he asked. "Are you planning to kill me?"

"As if I could!" exclaimed Feldman in an anguished voice.

Cummings' heart was pounding hard. Intellectually, he knew he would not die if Feldman pulled the trigger, yet adrenaline still coursed through his body. For the sake of self-preservation, he remained still, frozen—though ready to spring if the opportunity presented itself.

"Well," Cummings managed to say coolly, "I'm not sure what you hope to accomplish by shooting me. We both know that if you pull that trigger, you are going to be the one to die. At least that's how I understand it."

"I know," said Feldman with a heavy sigh. "I'm not a fool, Samuel."

Cummings was mystified. "Norman, what's going on? Can we talk about it?"

"There's nothing *to* talk about," growled Feldman, not removing the gun. "God's stupid intervention means I can't commit suicide—which is *bullshit*. But there's a loophole . . . if I pull this trigger, God will take me out as a would-be killer. It's a win-win in my book."

Cummings was shocked. "Why the hell do you want to die?" he asked. "Aren't you happy?"

Feldman laughed bitterly. "Happy?" he asked angrily. "How can I be happy? Everything I've worked for all my life is gone, thanks to this stupid intervention. I bet the farm on what I thought was a sure thing—and BAM! Along came the intervention. It changed the world, and I lost big time."

"Wait a minute, Norman," Cummings said as calmly as he could. "What is going on?"

"I'll *tell* you what's going on," he said angrily. "Before Sarah came along and changed everything, I invested in a digital spyware company whose product was specific to Chinese government platforms. I was going to keep you apprised on China's economic moves. I was going to be the best friend you ever had. But after God's intervention, the stocks rock-bottomed . . . and, well, I guess Dong Yang is your best friend now." He laughed again, but it sounded more like he was choking. "I was going to make a killing when their stock soared, and I borrowed against that. I never thought it would all come crashing down."

Not quite following, Cummings asked, "You're saying you lost money because Dong Yang and I have a cooperative relationship?"

"There's no one to spy on now, is there, Sam?" asked Feldman bitterly. "We're on the road to a world government—which kind of makes spying obsolete. I invested in a technology that was outdated before it even got going. And even when I saw the writing on the wall, and the alliances you were working toward, I hung on, believing that change would be a long time coming and that this software had a chance. But I was wrong. And it cost me big time."

Hearing the desperation in his voice, Cummings said soothingly, "Norman, you don't have to do this. You are my friend and trusted advisor, and your loss would be felt deeply by me and everyone you know. Please reconsider. You will bounce back from this, I swear."

"How!?" cried Feldman. "I have nothing left! I'm pretty sure I'd be better off dead!"

It was the 'I'm pretty sure' part of Feldman's words that made Cummings do what he did next. Reading it as uncertainty, he put his hand around the barrel of the gun, covering Feldman's hand in the process. Feldman flinched and tried to hold steady, but Cummings tightened his grip and slowly forced the loaded weapon away from his head. Then he maneuvered himself into a sitting position until he could see Feldman's eyes glinting brightly in the moonlight, just inches away from his own.

"God, Norman," he said with a relieved exhale, "I thought you meant it."

"So did I," Feldman replied, stifling a sob.

"I'd noticed you've been argumentative lately," Cummings said, "but I had no idea you were in trouble."

"I'm so ashamed," cried Feldman. "I meant to do something big for myself, something to guarantee a good future . . . but I screwed it up. Just like I screw *everything* up!"

Cummings immediately thought of his son-in-law; Flores had felt exactly the same way—defeated—before he'd ended his life. But his death had not solved anything; It had just caused pain and heartache for those left behind.

"You took a risk, and it didn't pan out," he said soothingly. "That's all."

"That's easy for you to say," said Feldman, angry now. "Everything you touch turns to gold. You're the fucking president, for Christ's sake!" His grip on the gun tightened, and in kind, Cummings tightened his own grip over Feldman's.

"Take it easy, Norman," he said. "It's just money."

"It's money that was supposed to go to some investors who will break my damn kneecaps if I don't pony up!" yelped Feldman. "I told you, Samuel, I'm better off dead! They're coming for me, and they'll keep at me until they get what I owe them. They've already called my mother and my brother. They know where my family lives!"

At that, he unexpectedly tried to wrench his gun hand out from under Cummings', but Cummings was ready for him. Hanging on tightly to Feldman's arm, he quickly jerked backwards and rolled to his side, causing Feldman's wrist to bend over at an unnatural angle.

"Ow!" shrieked Feldman—but he dropped the gun. "Give me the fucking gun!" he cried as Cummings tossed it as far away from them both as he could. "It won't hurt when I shoot you! If you have any respect for me at all, let me die!"

"I will *not*," said Cummings coldly. "You are my friend, and I am going to help you."

"How?" asked Feldman tearfully. "No one can help me now! I've lost my career, my house, my car . . . everything!"

Cummings pondered this for a moment, but there was no question about what he had to do.

"Norman," he said, "I'm your friend, and I will help you get on your feet, whatever it takes."

As soon as the words left his mouth, he felt powerful, warm energy course through him in a rush, making him feel as if his whole body had expanded. It was the same feeling he'd felt when he'd stepped out of his comfort zone to help the German woman. It was the feeling of creating goodness for God.

"No one can help me now," Feldman said sullenly, "not unless they have a shitload of money to lend me."

"Well, we'll have to discuss what 'a shitload' means," said Cummings firmly, "but we will find a way to set things right. I have money, I have a house you can borrow, and I have a company that's always looking for economic specialists. Let me help you."

Feldman was silent, pondering Cummings' selfless offer. Finally he asked, "Why? Why would you do this for me? You don't even like me!"

"Why would you say that, Norman?" asked Cummings.

"Don't give me *that*," said Feldman crustily. "You know I'm the devil's advocate in all the meetings."

"Yes, but you're good at your job, and I rely on you," Cummings replied evenly. "That's all that matters to me."

Silence reigned as each man tried to take the measure of the other. Finally, Cummings put an arm around the shivering man's shoulders.

"It's going to be okay," he said, the words shining out of his soul like a light. He knew, at that moment, that he'd never doubt the power of his own life force again.

Cummings stood and pulled Feldman to his feet after him. "How about a drink?" he asked.

Feldman seemed unnerved at the offer, and so Cummings grabbed his elbow and began steering him back toward the White House. Depressed, defeated, and lost in his walk of shame, Feldman didn't notice when Cummings discreetly stooped to pick up the discarded gun as they passed it. He slipped it into his pocket. He would hand it off to Blackstone for disposal as soon as he next saw the man.

They entered the White House through the same door Cummings had come out of—and nearly bumped into Don Taylor, who was on full alert, and preparing to exit on the other side. When Taylor saw Cummings and Feldman together, he stopped short and looked puzzled.

"You're okay," he said. It was more of a statement than a question.

"Yes, Don, I'm fine," Cummings said smoothly.

Taylor eyed Feldman. "I thought I saw you tussling with some guy out there, and I ran to get my body armor in case I had to take him down."

"It was just Norman," Cummings said disarmingly. "He saw me and came to chat, and then next thing I knew we started wrestling on the lawn like rowdy kids. Childish, really . . . I haven't done such a thing since high school—and then I was usually fueled by too much beer!"

Cummings forced a smile, while Feldman stood beside him and tried not to appear as nervous and miserable as he really was. Taylor eyed Cummings doubtfully. Every protective instinct he had for his boss was on full alert; However, because Feldman was part of the president's inner circle, he had no reason to doubt the story.

"Okay," he finally relented, still bristling. "My job is to ensure your safety, and clearly you are safe." Then he eyed Feldman suspiciously and added, "But if you ever need my help, you know how to activate the security call button on your jacket."

Feldman paled at the words; The two of them had rolled all over Cummings' jacket and could have set off that call button at any time.

"Thanks, Don," Cummings said graciously, "but no harm, no foul. And now my friend and I have some business to take care of."

With that, Cummings marched Feldman down the hall to the Oval Office.

After settling the shaking Feldman down on one of the couches, Cummings found his whisky in the drawer where he always hid it and then poured two stiff shots. He handed one to Feldman and quickly downed the other. Feldman did the same.

Then, bringing the bottle with him, Cummings sat down across from Feldman. He looked him in the eye.

"Here's what's going to happen, Norman," he said. "You and I are each going to have another drink, and then I am going to put you in a cab and send you over to my place in Georgetown for the night. Tomorrow, you're going to come in early and tell me in great detail about this mess you are in. And then, one step at a time, we are going to get you out of it."

Feldman nodded, relieved to let someone else take charge. "Thank you," he said. "I just can't believe I let it *get* to this. I kept putting off dealing with these guys because I thought the stocks would bounce back. Also, I was arrogant enough to think they'd leave me alone because I was part of your cabinet. But they don't care about that. They've let me know quite clearly that they can get to me. First, they called my mother and told her I was in MedStar Georgetown University Hospital, on a respirator, dying of Covid, and told her to come right away. Luckily, she called me to confirm before leaving her house. So she's okay . . . but that's when I got scared."

"That's pretty invasive, all right," said Cummings. "But we'll find a way to get them off your back."

"It's my own fault. I should have just admitted I couldn't pay them. Maybe they would have offered me a deal. But instead, I kept ducking them. I guess I was in shock. I feel like such a fool. I just had to reach for that damn brass ring, the big gamble. And I lost it all."

"You lost some money," said Cummings, "and clearly you underestimated your business partners. But try to think of this as a fresh start, a less materialistic one. Remember, the reason you're here is to be kind to others, not to die with the most toys. It's time to reevaluate things. This is a second chance for you, my friend."

Feldman looked intently at his boss, hopeful for the first time that night. "Now go get some sleep," Cummings told him. "Things will look better in the morning."

After making sure Feldman was escorted to a waiting cab, Cummings returned to the Oval Office to sit by himself and think for a few minutes. In a strange way, he was honoured Feldman had chosen him—a compassionate witness—as the 'target' of his suicide attempt. It indicated a level of intimacy he'd been unaware he inspired in the man. It was also oddly fitting, given what had happened to his own son-in-law.

"You have a sense of humour, don't you, God?" he asked aloud, smiling wryly at the ceiling.

Then Cummings began to think about what it really meant to point a gun at someone and shoot, whether the intent was to kill oneself—as Feldman's had been—or to kill others, as he and Blackstone had together instructed legions of military people to do before God's intervention had put an end to it. Having so recently had a gun pointed at his own head, he had a clearer understanding now of how that might feel, for both killer and victim. It made him shiver with discomfort.

It's ironic, he thought, *how much I crave the feeling of having done good in the world, yet have been the architect of so much death. How do the men and women who pull those triggers live with themselves after watching the light of life leave the eyes of their victims?*

There was only one person he knew who could answer that question. He spontaneously decided to give his military leader a call.

"Hello?" answered Gordon Blackstone, picking up his phone on the first ring. If he was surprised to see the president's number show up on his call display, he didn't let on.

"Hello, Gordon," said Cummings as lightly as he could. "How are you this fine evening?"

"Not bad, thanks," said Blackstone. Then he asked, "To what do I owe this pleasure?"

"Well," said Cummings, a little self-consciously, "I just wanted to tell you what a great job you've done as head of America's military, and I want you to know you're valued, even though our world—and your job—has changed so much since God's intervention."

Blackstone was silent for a moment, clearly surprised by the unexpected praise. Finally, he said, "Well, thank you."

Cummings' found himself suddenly tongue-tied. He hadn't rehearsed a speech, or planned any reason—real or not—for calling the man at home, and he didn't know how to broach what was on his mind.

When he remained silent for a heartbeat too long, Blackstone politely asked, "Sir? Are you okay?"

"Yes, I'm fine," Cummings said, "but I guess, now that Sarah's time on Earth is coming to an end, I'm reminiscing about things . . . mostly about what you and I were responsible for before the 'do not kill' edict came down. Quite honestly, it troubles me, Gordon. It troubles me more than I like to think about."

He felt vulnerable saying the words.

He was relieved when Blackstone calmly responded, "I understand, Sir."

"Call me Sam," said Cummings.

"Okay . . . uh . . . Sam," replied Blackstone.

"How do you cope with it?" asked Cummings.

"Well, I just tell myself that we were doing what we had to do under a set of rules that applied at the time. It may not have been moral in God's eyes, but it was the way of the world at that time. Kill or be killed. The law of the jungle."

Cummings sighed softly. "It's been a long time coming, Gordon, but I've just had a bird's-eye view of my own complicity in the deaths of so many people. I wasn't even the one pulling the trigger. I can't imagine what it feels like to be that person."

In an equally soft voice, Blackstone said, "Well, I can, Sam. And while I'm not proud of taking any other person's life, I *am* proud of fulfilling the oath I took when I enlisted to protect our constitution. I've taken it seriously all my life, and I still do."

"You're a better person than I am, Gordon," said Cummings. "All I've done is sign orders for others to do the dirty work—and I feel like shit about it."

"I understand," replied Blackstone, "and all I can say is that you have to face your remorse and guilt and move on. That's what veterans do so they can cope with their lives. But some never get over it. It's no secret that veteran's hospitals are busy places."

Suddenly Cummings had an idea. "You know," he said, "we've done a good job getting jobs for returning troops, but we're dealing with people who've experienced things others can't even dream of, people who need redemption—like you and me. I think we need a program focused on helping these people heal. We need to create jobs that will help them grow their life force."

"I'm listening," said Blackstone.

"Tell me," Cummings said excitedly, "how would you feel about spearheading a new effort for ex-military personnel, something that supplements what the VA is currently doing, as well as the programs we have already implemented?"

"Like what?" asked Blackstone.

"Something where hands-on helping figures in," Cummings said, thinking of the warmth that spread through him when he offered Feldman a helping hand. "We should create jobs that involve building personal relationships . . . something like . . . oh, how about 'goodwill ambassadors' who coach immigrants on the ins and outs of living here, like opening bank accounts, getting driver's licenses, registering for college . . . things like that."

"Not bad," said Blackstone thoughtfully. "And I know our schools could always use more teacher's aides. How about 'public education aide' as a potential job?"

"Yes!" exclaimed Cummings. "That's a great idea. I hadn't even thought about how shorthanded our schools are. Brilliant."

And that's when he heard a little, high-pitched voice say sleepily to his single, bachelor colleague, "You been on the phone a long time. I want a story."

Puzzled, Cummings assumed Blackstone's sister must be visiting with her brood—which would explain the man's interest in propping up an understaffed educational system with ex-military personnel.

"I didn't know you had company," said Cummings. "Have I caught you at a bad time?"

"Oh," said Blackstone, an unexpected smile in his voice, "that's not company. Now that I'm not travelling as much for work, I thought it was high time I bit the bullet and signed up for the foster parent program."

Cummings suddenly remembered that Blackstone had told him how he wanted to be a father someday.

Blackstone continued, "There are a lot of kids out there who need loving homes . . . and now two of them are mine."

"Well . . . that's *great!*" exclaimed Cummings.

"Yes, it is," replied Blackstone. "They've been with me for four months now, and I'm going to apply to adopt them. They were apprehended from drug addict parents and lived with an elderly aunt for the last three years. But she had a stroke, which is how they wound up in foster care. She fully approves of me adopting them as long as she can see them."

Cummings heard a giggle and a squeal from one of them, and it made his heart ring with joy. "How old are they?" he asked.

"The boy is six, and the girl is four," said Blackstone.

"Daddy, pick me up!" he heard a tiny voice squeak in the background. "Pleeeeeeeeeeez . . . now! Now! Now!" This was followed by a thump.

"Just a minute," said Blackstone. Cummings heard him ask, "Are you okay, sweetie?"

When he returned to the phone, Cummings, marveling at the idea of the stoic Blackstone being the parent of two small children, asked, "What are their names?"

Blackstone paused before he answered, then said with a note of reverence. "The boy's name is Jackson . . . and the girl is called Sarah."

Chapter 38

Sarah's Manifesto

A lot of things changed for Cummings after that moment with Feldman on the White House lawn. A sense of calm pervaded his everyday doings, something that had not been there for many, many years. *I have proved to myself that I carry great love, and that I am worthy of the place of power I occupy,* he realized when he tried to determine what had shifted in his soul.

He was grateful to Sarah for stirring up these emotions; After all, if she had never come to Earth to tend to the *real* needs of humankind—as opposed to 'needs' for status, possessions, and other inconsequential things—he would never have understood just what kind of personal power he carried. Knowing this, he wore the mantle of president much more comfortably. He even gave his campaign team the go-ahead to start stumping, much to Lopez's relief.

One thing was troubling him, though. When Sarah had arrived on Earth, she'd told the world she would stay for only one year. By Cummings' calculations, that year was almost at an end. She would be leaving soon, and it would be up to him and the other world leaders to somehow carry on, ensuring that the good works that had been started on Planet Earth continued so that humankind could grow toward its destiny as Sarah had insisted it must.

He inadvertently ground his jaw at the thought of her departure. It was comforting to have her oversight; It was like having a capable older sister who always had his back, no matter how obtuse he was. However, he knew that he had to stand on his own now if he was to build upon the changes her presence had wrought.

By Cummings' calculation, when the day of Sarah's message of farewell finally came, it had been 360 days since she'd arrived on Earth. That particular morning started like any other—he showered, shaved, put on a suit, had coffee with Lorena—and yet despite these little rites of normalcy, he felt distracted and anxious.

"Are you all right, honey?" Lorena asked, cutting into his thoughts as she paused her usual morning chat—a stream of words that today sounded more like a monologue to him than a conversation.

"What?" he asked as he realized she was addressing him. He felt on the spot because she clearly knew he hadn't been listening.

"You seem preoccupied," she said a little tartly.

"I'm fine," he replied guiltily.

"Sure you are," she said. "I just told you I was going to throw myself in front of a bus, and you didn't even bat an eyelash."

"That's because you didn't mean it," he backpedaled quickly. Then, trying to deflect her accusation, he added, "Besides, we both know suicide doesn't work."

She wouldn't be thrown off the scent. "That's not the point. The point is that you're not paying attention, and I want to know why," she demanded.

He sighed. "Okay," he said. "I'm sorry. It's just that I feel like I'm waiting for a hammer to drop. It's almost over with Sarah, and I don't know what the world will be like without her."

"Relax," said Lorena comfortingly. "This is a changed world. We will go on. Humans always have."

"I suppose so," Cummings said. "As always, you're the voice of reason. Thanks." Then he stood up and kissed the top of her head. "I have to get to the office now, but do you want to meet me later for lunch?" he asked.

"Only if you like grilled cheese sandwiches," Lorena replied, "because that's what I'm making."

"You don't want to go out?" he asked.

"Nope. I want grilled cheese and tomato soup. And I make it better than any restaurant."

"I know you do," Cummings replied with a smile, "so make one for me. I'll see you at noon."

When he got to the Oval Office, Janice quickly filled him in on the relevant events of the morning. There was nothing pressing for him to deal with; The groundwork he'd laid over the last year—with Sarah's guidance, of course—was impeccable. It was rare for a crisis to rear its head these days.

He opened his computer to review the programming he and Blackstone had developed for helping veterans grow their life forces. The two of them had dived head-first into planning, and a pilot project would be ready to launch in a matter of days. They had thirty willing veterans lined up for the pilot. Fifteen would be sent to work in refugee crisis centres, acting as coaches for new immigrants, while another fifteen would be sent to assist in inner city schools, which were notoriously short staffed. Blackstone had personally drafted a list of expectations and a code of conduct for the participants, and upon sign-off, each would take part in a week-long orientation program before starting their new jobs, where they would be paid about the same as they had earned in the military.

Cummings was enjoying his grilled cheese sandwich with Lorena in their kitchen when the awaited farewell message from Sarah finally arrived, heralded by nothing more than an unusual tinkling of bells sounding from his laptop. He knew immediately that it was her, and with Lorena sitting across the table from him eyeing him anxiously, he reluctantly opened the machine to read:

I am Sarah. I am of God. And I must leave you soon.

"Oh, shit," he mumbled.

"What's wrong?" asked Lorena, putting her sandwich down.

"It seems too soon . . ." he replied glumly. "I'm not sure I'm ready for it." Then he said, "Turn on the TV. She's probably on it."

She was. She had taken over every television network, every streaming channel, every radio station, every email account, and every personal mobile device of every person on the planet. Her words were for the world, and she wanted everyone to pay attention to them.

Through the TV screen, she glowed in an unearthly way, shimmering and swirling like sparkles in a child's toy. When her words came out of the television speakers, it sounded to Cummings as if she was in the room with him, talking directly into his ear in her reassuring, authoritative voice. She was impossible to ignore.

During the past year, humanity has taken baby steps toward changing its destiny, and for this I salute you. However, countries, cultures and religions will not find the common ground they seek for a very long time, and so I will not completely abandon you to your own devices. Instead, God has decided I should return to Earth for one week every five years to help humankind travel the road toward its destiny. God wants you to find your way to eternal life and to enrich it with the universal life force when you do.

Despite your progress, humankind has much work to do, and so to aid you in your journey, I will impart a few truths to you before I leave. This is my advice:

First, curtail your greed. If you approach every task asking, 'What's in it for me?' your ability to put others' needs ahead of your own will be limited, and you may not accrue enough life force to return home to God.

Second, be sensitive to your fellow humans, or you will miss opportunities to help them grow. Helping others is key to expanding your life force. Cultivate empathy at all times.

Third, respect others. Every person on the planet has skills and abilities deserving of your respect. If you do not respond to the light that shines in others, you will not put their interests first, stunting your ability to grow your life force.

Fourth, hatred and intolerance, even if not acted upon, ensures banishment from God. You must generate good energy in thought and deed, or you detract from the life force. Question yourself. It is your own responsibility to change.

Fifth, the more you interact with people from other cultures, the more you will understand what you have in common with them. More unites than divides humankind. Reach out to those who are different from you. Celebrate diversity in all its forms, and your life force will blossom.

Sixth, unite with others to support the world community. There is power in numbers. Participate in actions designed to bring attention to, and protect, your fragile home planet and the beings who call it 'home.' Join groups that are trying to improve the world, such as organizations supporting the homeless, refugees, animals, and the environment. Stay focused on doing good works to ensure your place with God.

Seventh, share your wealth. There is nothing wrong with being wealthy as long as you earned your fortune ethically. The wealthy are uniquely able to generate life force through charitable deeds. Use your resources to help your fellow humans move smoothly forward on the journey toward oneness.

Be good to each other!

Cummings looked at his wife with shining eyes. "This message really gives me hope for the future," he said, a catch in his voice.

"Me too," she replied, putting her hand on his arm and squeezing a little.

But Sarah was not finished yet. She continued:

I would like to offer humankind some advice on actions you can take to ensure the future of your planet and the harmony that is your destiny.

First of all, for your species to become as one, you must move beyond the tribalism you currently practice and embrace your higher natures. A good first step would be to govern your planet from a global perspective, letting the fear and prejudice of 'us and them' go.

Tribes are no longer key to survival. The world has moved on. There is a saying that describes how 'free will' weakens when tribes form. It is this: 'If you give me one boy, I will show you a delightful young lad. If you give me two boys, I will have only half a boy. If you give me three boys, I will have no boy at all.'

It means that when a tribal mindset takes over, people become like sheep. Then, as part of a flock, they collectively become capable of horrendous acts they would never condone as individuals. Hitler and the rise of the Third Reich is a prime example—however, human history is littered with countless atrocities resulting from 'us' versus 'them.'

You are one family, the human family. Unite under a shared banner. Choose leaders who will unify instead of divide. Embrace your oneness . . . and bring your world to wholeness.

When this portion of Sarah's broadcast was over, Cummings said, "Most world leaders give lip service to the idea of greater international cooperation, but it would be a hard sell to convince them to give up governing their own affairs."

"Well, I don't think Sarah could have been any clearer about global governance being the way forward. The European Union is a step in that direction," said Lorena.

"Yes," replied Cummings, "though some member governments feel the move to a common currency has curtailed their ability to act independently. That's why the United Kingdom opted out in 2020."

Lorena was about to respond, when suddenly, Sarah appeared again, glowing iridescently on both the television and the computer. The intensity of her gaze was such that Cummings felt as if she was staring right into his soul. Inadvertently, he put his hand to his heart.

In love and light, I leave you now. All I have shared with you about the true nature of God, as well as what you need to do to ensure a smooth passage from this life into the next, can be found in perpetuity on the Sarah Says website by typing 'Sarah's Final Message' into the search bar. If you seek more knowledge about how to ensure your future in the afterlife, send a message via the same site. I am able to monitor all electronic communication from my true home with God, and I will reply.

You will not see me again for five years, but rest assured that I will see you. *I will watch as you change the course of your destiny, and when I return in five years, I will celebrate your successes with you with a global festival of joy. Your new Earth Council will prepare for this. Support them in this initiative—and join me in celebration when I next visit the Earth! Until then, be kind to each other . . . and God bless you all..*

Five days later, Sarah's final day on Earth arrived—all too quickly, from Cummings' perspective. Sarah made good use of the five days between her goodbye message and her departure by meeting with all world leaders one on one to bid them farewell and provide final instruction on how best to move forward into the non-violent future she'd helped create.

Cummings was in his office, signing off on the final papers required to launch the 'Life Force for Vets' program he'd created with Blackstone when she came to him. As she had on the day they'd met, she appeared in the Oval Office, fluttering into view like a butterfly—gentle, soft, and heartachingly beautiful. When he saw her, his heart beat so hard it felt as if it was going to jump into his throat. Her magnificence made him feel small and humbled, like a Grade 6 boy who has just had the best-looking girl in the school notice him for the first time.

"Hello," she said as she morphed into being.

"Hello," he replied, a little mournfully. "Or should I say, goodbye?"

"Both," she told him, "that is why I am here. I will miss you, Samuel Cummings."

"Well, if you're going to miss me, then perhaps you should stay," he said.

She laughed in her tinkling way, sending a breeze around the room. "You know I can't do that," she replied. "However, before I go, I wanted to ensure that you know how wonderful it is that you rose to the challenges placed before you in such an admirable way. You should be proud. You have created much more life force for God than you know."

"Thank you," he replied awkwardly. "Likewise, I'm sure. You are leaving the world so much better than you found it, Sarah. We all owe you—and God—our eternal gratitude. How can we thank you?"

She shimmered in the air before him, glowing angelically, her many faces fluttering across her visage like a hummingbird's wings. "You already have," she replied. "I feel confident that you will continue to lead your country, and the world, in uniting the human race, and I delight in the bond of friendship you and Dong Yang have created. It is a shining example of what it means to put aside differences for the good of all. For me, that is thanks enough."

"But how do I keep this momentum going?" Cummings asked, annoyed that the question sounded needier than he'd meant for it to.

"Just keep listening to the children of the world," replied Sarah with a tinkle of rose-scented air. "Your granddaughter Jessica, in particular, has much to teach you."

"No doubt . . . she's a bossy girl," joked Cummings. "She takes after my wife, I'm afraid."

"Surely that's not *bad*?" teased Sarah.

"No, of course not," Cummings said. "Lorena's counsel is the next best thing to the wisdom of 40 million enlightened women speaking with one voice."

Sarah laughed, sending a gentle rush of air coursing around the room, causing the lights to flicker. "What a delightful compliment," she breathed, her voice like the wind, "though even my exquisite compilation of wisdom and enlightenment was not enough to unify Earth's religions. As we speak, the old men at the top are up to their same old tricks, interpreting everything I've taught them as proof that only *their* religion is in line with God's expectations. As they have done for ages untold, they are missing the point."

Cummings laughed. "What about the Church of Humanity?" he asked.

"Oh, it's percolating in the background," said Sarah. "But it may not take hold as quickly as I wish it would."

"Well, with the young people leading the charge, I think things will look a lot different in five years when you come back," said Cummings.

"I think so too," said Sarah. "I just hope there is not too much bickering about the true nature of God's will before that happens."

Cummings laughed. "Oh, there will be," laughed Cummings, adding, "It's a damn good thing God banned killing."

"Isn't it, though?" asked Sarah with an angelic sigh.

And then, with a puff of stardust, she was gone.

Chapter 39

Sarah Returns

Sarah had always maintained that she would return to Earth in five years, but when she joined Samuel Cummings in the Oval Office, appearing in a glow of light, her trademark rose-scented air gusting around him, he realized that in a secret part of his heart, he hadn't dared to hope it was true.

"You're here!" he exclaimed with joy as she morphed into three glorious dimensions. "I can't believe it!"

"Oh ye of little faith," teased Sarah, her biblical reference pointed squarely at Cummings' Anglican upbringing. "I am of God; Did you actually doubt me?"

"I deserve that," he said, laughing, "but please, don't think I have no faith. In my heart, I knew you'd come."

Sarah emitted a pleased flutter of energy, causing the lights to flicker and the air to feel suddenly fresher. Then she said, "It is good to see you, Samuel."

"And you, Sarah. I've been looking forward to this meeting. So much has happened since you left!"

"Well, there is plenty of time for you to tell me about it," she said, "but right now, all I want to hear about is how *your* world is."

Inordinately pleased that she cared to know about his circumstances, Cummings replied, "Things are going well, Sarah—though I'm nearly six years older than I was when I last saw you, and I'm starting to feel it. I'm halfway through my second term as president now, and I'm looking forward to taking it easy when I step down."

"I was so happy for you when you won a second term," said Sarah. "Your fellow Americans made the right choice—and you have served your country well."

"Well, I've certainly *tried* to," he said with a shrug, shy as a schoolboy at the compliment. "I had a lot of help, though."

"Yes," said Sarah. "I know your team has supported you every step of the way—as has your wife, the First Lady." Then she asked, "How is Lorena?"

"Lorena is amazing as always," replied Cummings. "After you left, she really embraced her MBA studies. As part of her master's certification, she piloted a program critically reviewing how God's intervention is affecting social change and projected how it would ultimately affect international business. She got the idea after the women's conference in Cairo."

"You must be so proud of her," remarked Sarah.

"Yes," said Cummings, "she's brilliant. And she's also an excellent grandmother. She and Jessica are as thick as thieves. Jessica is about to enter university. She's going to study business like Lorena."

"Such ambition! How is young Jessica?" asked Sarah.

"She's very bright, keen on her studies, and hopes to someday work with a non-profit that funds business ideas for women in third-world countries. She is still close friends with Mingmei and has been to China three times to visit her. And Dong Yang and I still have excellent relations as well—so I have to say, your insistence that President Dong and I cultivate closer ties is paying off in spades."

"Is the pen pal program Jessica and Mingmei started still as popular as it was when I left?" asked Sarah.

"Oh, it's even *more* popular," replied Cummings. "It's now operating in nearly every country in the world, in a whole span of age ranges. Some schools are making it part of the curriculum, especially in the language arts programs. Kids are growing up multilingual because of this program—and there has not been a single incidence of cyber-hacking or predation."

"Encouraging love and acceptance in the young is a wonderful way to unite the world," remarked Sarah with a smile.

"Yes, indeed," said Cummings. Then he asked, "And what about you? Did you miss us?"

"It's lovely to be back on Earth," replied Sarah, "and I missed having a physical form. However, I never missed my human friends in the way that you are suggesting. I am everywhere because I am part of God, and so I was not separated from you . . . though you most certainly were separated from me."

"Well," said Cummings, pondering her words, "given the true nature of God, I understand . . . though sometimes, I wish I could actually feel what it's like to be with God the way you are."

"You do?" asked Sarah. "Let me show you."

At that, she the fragrant scent of jasmine tickled Cummings' nose, and the lights in the room dimmed slightly. Then something almost electrical flickered through Cummings' body, which tickled more than hurt. He laughed. His spirit felt light. He had no words to describe what he was feeling except to say it was unbridled joy, and it filled him so completely he thought he might float away like a helium balloon. He laughed again, drunk with sensation. Then, just when it felt like his heart might literally burst with happiness, Sarah eased off.

As the sensation whooshed out of him, Cummings felt deflated, heavy with the sense of gravity.

When he recovered, he said, "Let me guess . . . Does it feel something like that?"

"Yes," said Sarah. "Joy and wonder so big it cannot be contained." Then she wafted her rose scent into the room once more and said, "I'm sure you know I'm here to check up on this planet, to ensure that the world is moving toward its destiny and that the work that has been done is bearing fruit. I can imagine there is much for you to tell me about your country's progress, Samuel."

"Yes, of course," he said. "And most of it is good news. Angelica put a presentation together to summarize it. Would you like to see it?"

"That would be wonderful," replied Sarah.

"Do you mind if I call in my advisory council first?" asked Cummings. "I promised they could be a part of this."

"Yes, of course, I'd be delighted to see them!" Sarah exclaimed with pleasure.

Cummings quickly notified Janice to round up Angelica Lopez, Gordon Blackstone, Norman Feldman, Bradley Northrop, and Hana

Shriver. Within minutes, the five of them entered the room. All looked at Sarah with reverence as they reacquainted themselves with her gloriousness.

Finally, Lopez spoke for all of them. "You look amazing as always," she said with a big smile.

"As do you," replied Sarah graciously.

"But I'm only human," Lopez said. "I have more wrinkles than I did five years ago—probably because I have teenagers now. You, however, look more radiant than I remember."

"That is an effect of living with God," said Sarah with a flutter of energy that coursed across her swirling faces like a glimmer of light. "God is the source of all energy. I am renewed every day."

"Recharged?" ventured Northrop. "Like an electric car?"

"More like a nuclear-powered car, I'd say," quipped Blackstone.

Sarah laughed.

Picking a remote control up from off his desk, Cummings activated the Oval Office's overhead screen. It opened to a map of the world, with America highlighted in dark green.

When he had everyone's attention, he said, "First, let's look at domestic stuff. Now that war is no longer on the table . . . well, all I can say is that my country is in better shape than it's been in for a very long time."

Then he clicked to the next slide, which read: *Hi, Sarah! Welcome back! We missed you! Love, Angelica.*

He reddened. "I guess I should have vetted this first," he said, looking accusingly at his smug, grinning vice president.

"I'm glad you didn't," said Sarah as Cummings hastily clicked the remote again.

He reddened even more when the next slide announced boldly:

DOMESTIC ACHIEVEMENTS

- *Samuel Cummings won a second presidency term with the widest margin of victory in American history.*

"Well done," said Sarah.

"Angelica, you're . . . sneaky," said Cummings, who couldn't help chuckling a little at his vice president's prank. Then he said, "My success, as always, has a lot to do with my very capable vice president."

There were other bullets. The next one read:

- *Democrats took control of both the House and the Senate, at least in part because the election caused the Republican Party to split in two. A newly formed Green Party, headed by Hana Shriver, captured two seats in the House and one in the Senate.*

"Good for you, Hana!" Sarah said.

"I'm living the dream," said Shriver with a big smile. "The Republican Party was not really a good fit for me ideologically. I really feel like I'm headed in the right direction with this."

"I'm sure you are," replied Sarah brightly.

- *Less than 1% of former military personnel is currently unemployed. That figure has been consistent for the past six years.*

"So all of your efforts to repatriate the troops have been successful!" exclaimed Sarah happily.

"Yes," said Cummings. "That transition was so much smoother than I expected it to be."

- *Upon conversion of the USS Gerald R. Ford into the world's first aircraft carrier / hospital ship, a deal with Russia and China to create a global fleet of six hospital ships was reached. America added two more carriers, China added two, and Russia added one. The Ford was launched as part of the inauguration ceremonies for President Cummings' second term. The other five ships were launched as conversions were completed.*
- *A massive, nationwide overhaul of municipal water systems is still underway, using services provided by the former Army Corps of Engineers. All systems over one hundred years old will be replaced within ten years. The federal government has recouped more than half the stimulus money provided for the water system upgrades, as the privatization of the Corps was oversubscribed (demand for shares exceeded supply).*

"Bravo," said Sarah admiringly.

"Thank you," said Cummings, "though I couldn't have done it without the support of this team, not to mention Martin Grieves and Herbert Sloan. The next two points are all Sloan's doing."

- *The water supply line from Lake Michigan to Lake Mead is nearing completion, with start-up planned in twenty-four months. Water curtailments were in place for most of the project development period, leading to a 30% reduction in agricultural water usage in the Southwest. Based upon current water levels, and average rainfall for the past five years, Lake Mead's water level will be above the 'automatic water curtailment' level this year.*
- *The program to protect the U.S. coastlines from a three-foot rise in sea level will be complete in five years. The projected budget of $500 billion is mostly being allocated to constructing sea walls and levies, but it also includes funding for a 20% increase in natural wetlands and a 10% increase in coral reefs. However, despite our best efforts, storm damage over time is expected to cause beaches to continue to shrink at a rate of 1% per year.*

"That last bit kind of sucks," remarked Lopez.

"Yes," agreed Cummings, "but at least we're trying to mitigate it."

- *Coal fired electricity generation is now prohibited in the U.S., and renewable energy power generation at the bulk power level has been incentivized. Twenty states have adopted building codes requiring solar panels on all new residential and commercial buildings. Ten of these states also require rooftop rain collection systems on new homes for lawn and garden watering needs.*

"Great idea about the water collection," said Sarah.

"Yes," agreed Cummings. "I'd really like to expand that as a nationwide regulation."

- *Funding is available to replace aging nuclear power plants on their existing sites. Four sites have received the necessary permitting for modernization, and construction has commenced on two. Funding is*

- *also available for the construction of new plants on new sites, but only one project is currently being considered.*
- *Two years ago, a carbon tax was imposed on retail sales of gasoline, heating oil and natural gas, and a carbon trading system was imposed on industry. Only two companies in the U.S. are still making internal combustion vehicles, and their fleets must now meet standards for emissions and fuel efficiency equivalent to those in Europe. As of today, all electric vehicle sales have surpassed those of traditional internal combustion vehicles.*

"And now here's the best one," said Lopez excitedly. "I finally get my train! This has been a real labour of love for me."

- *The interstate east/west electric train trunk line is projected to be complete within twenty-four months. The system is using magnetic levitation technology, with top speeds expected to reach 250 miles per hour. It will feature direct service between New York City and Los Angeles. There will be four switching terminals along the route, similar to airline hubs. Passengers can disembark in Indianapolis, Kansas City, Denver, and Las Vegas. From Indianapolis, they can connect to a mag lev feeder line north to Chicago and on to Minneapolis, or travel elsewhere by conventional means. From Kansas City, they can take a mag lev feeder line to Dallas and on to Houston, or travel elsewhere by conventional means. From Denver and Las Vegas, they can travel to other destinations by conventional means.*

"I'm so excited about this," said Lopez. "The engineers I've been working with are just genius! It will be such a comfortable ride. Each car will have fourteen small 'bubble' compartments and a washroom at the end of the car. The bubbles will have between two and six reclining seats, for a maximum of seventy passengers per car. Each seat will have an entertainment system similar to those on newer airplanes. The bubbles have independent air supply systems, to curtail viruses. Food and drink will be delivered after being ordered and paid for through an electronic console, like at McDonalds."

"Fantastic," said Sarah. "This is great planning and engineering."

"Thank you," smiled Lopez proudly.

Cummings clicked to the next slide, where the list continued.

GLOBAL ACHIEVEMENTS

- *Disarmament efforts were completed on time, and the world is now free of weapons of mass destruction. Except for a few private guns still in the hands of some Americans, there are very few guns of any kind anywhere in the world. The voluntary buy-back program implemented by the federal government generated massive response. Interestingly, many of the surrendered guns were family weapons turned in by young people when their parents passed away. Most gun manufacturers are now out of business.*
- *The first mission back to the moon was a joint trip by American, Chinese, and Russian astronauts, completed two years ago. Using a SpaceX rocket, astronauts landed on the moon and installed the first reusable moon shelter. The mission lasted three weeks and was a complete success. The world watched the whole mission in real time on streaming networks. There have now been a total of fifteen missions, and three colonies are largely in place. In the next twelve months, construction of an assembly plant and launch facilities for the mission to Mars will begin. It is expected to take approximately five years to complete.*

"I am impressed that space goals are being reached so quickly," said Sarah.

"Well, a lot of it has to do with the relationships I developed with Dong Yang and Sergei Grinkov, thanks to you," said Cummings as he clicked to the next slide, which read:

SOCIAL CHANGES

"This next one kind of touches my heart," said Cummings. "My granddaughter is just about seventeen, and this is going to be such a big change for her."

- *The delay of puberty to age eighteen is fully in effect. Male and female athletic performance is now very similar throughout the high school years. College scholarship programs for athletes have diminished in scale, and offers are generally the same for both genders. This has generated inclusivity for people who gender identify in non-traditional ways. Exclusive high school recruiting of male athletes for professional sports teams has come to an end.*

"How does Jessica feel about being on the verge of the hormonal change?" asked Sarah.

"I think she's excited," Cummings said, "though I'm a little nervous. She's going to make a significant jump from child to adult soon—but at least puberty won't take her by surprise, like it did the rest of us."

"Agreed," said Lopez. "No one is ever ready for that."

The final points of the presentation were:

- *There has been no change in the percentage of heterosexuals marrying for the purpose of creating families, though the average age of such couples has increased by two and a half years. Teen marriages in those under eighteen have declined, although some women choose to marry, and/or have children, as soon as they become fertile at the age of eighteen.*
- *Divorce rates have declined dramatically, and data indicates that couples are choosing to stay together once the sexual drive ends at age forty. Preliminary reports show that 'May-December' romances appear to be declining, though long-term monitoring may show different results.*

"It seems people are becoming more content in their family situations than ever before," said Sarah.

"Yes," said Cummings. "So far. Time will tell, I guess."

"Most of what you've shown me indicates that the world is changing for the better, just as I'd hoped," Sarah said.

"Unfortunately, not everything is positive," said Cummings. "There's a remaining bee in my bonnet . . . multinational corporations."

He clicked to the next slide, which listed in bold letters twenty of the largest companies in the world.

"These guys are so rich and powerful that they are like governments unto themselves," he said, "and this is causing problems. They're motivated solely by profit, and they just do what they want. Mostly, they set up shop in countries that have low wage rates, or weak environmental laws, and make unholy messes without a care in the world. It sickens me."

"It's next to impossible to rein in their activities through legislation," added Lopez, "and it's a sad reminder of how weak and outdated our political structures are."

"Yes," said Cummings, "while poorer countries are pleased to get a boost to their economies when corporations set up shop, the downside is that it's creating ecological nightmares in some places, and the companies are not being held accountable. It's also making stateside constituents howl about wage equity and losing jobs."

"Maybe it's time America quit living beyond its means," remarked Lopez dryly.

"You got that right," muttered Feldman, who was still in the process of clawing his way out of gigantic personal debt.

"But our lifestyles are expensive, not so much because we're all greedy, but because we live in a society in which we need a damn car just to get to the grocery store," said Blackstone, frowning. "We are literally our own worst enemies."

"And that's why there are so many blogs and YouTube channels advocating for simpler, alternative lifestyles, such as the 'off the grid' communities," said Cummings, clicking to the next slide, which showed a picture of a cloud.

"Is that a *cloud*?" asked Blackstone

"Is it Sarah's home?" quipped Feldman, trying to be funny.

"It's not Sarah's home . . . and it is indeed a cloud," replied Lopez. "I was trying to get Samuel talking about the impact of technology on domestic manufacturing and thought a picture of a cloud said it all."

"It does," said Cummings, "though the cloud Angelica wants me to speak about is the one composed of servers around the globe hooked together so massive amounts of information can be manipulated and stored. That, and advanced robotics, are making domestic manufacturing jobs disappear—and pissing many people off. There's pressure on me to protect America's livelihoods, but I have no control over where corporations want to set up shop. They go overseas because it's cheaper, and who can blame them? It makes good business sense."

Lopez cut in. "But even when they stay in America and set up domestic facilities, we don't have much control over their business practices because we don't have the legislative framework to keep them in check. Our constitution is more than 200 years old; It wasn't meant to deal with the business pressures we face today."

"Yes," agreed Cummings. "Case in point, the Second Amendment was written when it took more than half a minute to load a single shot musket. The men who wrote it could never have conceived of an automatic weapon. Similarly, they could never have seen the advent of global corporations, and the power such entities would one day wield."

"Agreed," said Lopez. Then, with an outraged sniff, she added, "Ever since some lawyer convinced a judge that there's 'corporate personhood,' corporations have invoked the Fourteenth Amendment when challenged. The federal government can't deprive them of life, liberty, or property, without due process of law. It's outrageous!"

"I'd like to change the constitution to give corporations their own status," said Cummings as he clicked off the overhead, and the screen automatically rolled upward and put itself away, "but we have an adversarial Senate. In the democratic West, that gives corporations a lot of power. All they have to do is buy off a senator or two."

"If only democratic governments could compete on a level playing field with the corporate world," mused Shriver.

"Yes," said Lopez excitedly, "we need a global institution to set standards for equity and sustainability. Then investors would shun those that aren't on board with humanity's new direction."

"Agreed," said Shriver. "We also need to make people aware of the true cost of all the junk they buy. How many of those useless toys in kids' meals get immediately thrown away? If people knew the environmental cost of those toys, they might make different decisions about what they purchase."

"Let's ban it," said Lopez hotly, "and while we're at it, let's also ban planned obsolescence in appliances."

"And enforce truth in advertising," said Feldman. "It's not French perfume if it's made in China."

Everyone laughed; Even Sarah sent a delightful golden tinkle around the room.

Then she said, "The Earth Council has the potential to provide the type of oversight and global leadership you're discussing, but only if it has strong leaders with proven track records at its helm. Samuel, perhaps when you step down as president, you might seek a leadership role there. I think you and Dong Yang both have a lot to offer."

"You're kidding, right?" asked Cummings. He'd never really thought further than turning over the reins of the presidency to a new, incoming leader, and then stepping down to relax and spend time with his grandkids.

"You still have a lot left to give the world, Samuel," coaxed Sarah. "You're not done yet."

He remained silent for a moment, absorbing her words as he thought about how far he had come, both as a president and as a man. He realized that, except for the moment of joy Sarah had briefly shared with him earlier in the day, he'd never felt happier than when he was serving his fellow humans in word and deed. Retire? It was not really something he'd be good at.

"Well," he said, finally. "That's a long way from the retirement plan I had in mind, but it's not a bad idea. I'll think about it."

But there was nothing to think about. It was a perfect fit for him, and he knew it. He was all in.

Chapter 40

Unity Festival

On the morning after Sarah's return to Earth, Cummings awoke with a keen sense of anticipation. He jumped out of bed and quickly showered, humming loudly to himself the whole time. Wrapping a towel around his waist, he came out of the bathroom to find Lorena awake and rubbing her eyes.

"Let me get you a coffee," he told his wife, who nodded sleepily.

He went into the kitchen and poured two cups of steaming coffee, adding cream to Lorena's. He'd been trying to take his coffee black since noticing the beginning of a belly paunch, but it didn't come easy. He was sure the extra weight was creeping on due to his loss of testosterone. *Damn hormones,* he thought.

He brought Lorena her drink.

"Thanks, honey," she said as she took the cup and gratefully sipped. Then, noting his cheeriness, she said, "You're just full of beans this morning. You must be excited about going to Sydney."

"Yes," said Cummings. "It's going to be an amazing week."

He was looking forward to the Earth Council convention that was to be held in Sydney, Australia in the next few days . . . but more, he was excited that two years of meticulous planning would come to fruition during the trip: On Sarah's last day on Earth, the world would partake in the first ever Unity Festival, an epic celebration of all that humankind had achieved over the past five years, which would be held in and around the Sydney Opera House. He and a team of twenty Earth Council employees and civilian volunteers had been planning the event for the past two years.

"It's kind of like celebrating five years of sobriety, isn't it?" joked Lorena. "No one has given in to the urge to murder anyone else for five whole years—all thanks to our higher power!"

Cummings laughed but cautioned, "It's a lot more than that. Humanity has pulled itself out of a pretty deep hole, Lorena. We could easily have wiped ourselves off the face of the Earth if Sarah hadn't come here and set us on the right path."

"I know, I know," replied his wife as she stretched her arms high into the air and yawned. Then she said, "So, I guess we're packing for Australia today?"

"Yes," replied Cummings with a big smile. "Bring your bikini!"

Lorena grinned. "You naughty boy!" she exclaimed.

"Well, I used to be," he said wistfully.

She got out of bed and gave him a hug. "At least we got two great kids out of the deal," she said. "We can't really complain."

"We got some great grandkids too," he replied.

As Lorena padded into the bathroom for a shower, Cummings dressed. Then he headed into the living room with his laptop. He had some final touches to add to the Unity Festival planning, most notably finding the right artist to open the festival. He wanted something powerful and haunting for the first act, something that showed respect for traditions that the modern world had so callously tossed aside—and he also wanted something that would both honour and impress Sarah.

Lorena liked to tease him about his devotion to Sarah. Whenever she found him hard at work on concert details, she'd ask, "Are you still working on that tribute to your 40 million girlfriends?"

Smiling, he'd reply, "How did you know about them?"

"The scent of roses on your collar gave you away," she'd tell him with a lewd wink, at which point they would both start laughing.

When she came into the living room, fresh from her shower, he decided to ask her opinion about whether he should leave well enough alone with the opening artist or if there was room for improvement.

"I've been puzzling over the opening act for the Unity Festival," he told her. "Initially, I had that Czech opera singer, Agava Novak, in the opening spot . . ."

"Oh, she's fantastic," said Lorena enthusiastically, "and she's established all those children's orphanages in Czechoslovakia!"

"Yes," agreed Cummings, "but somehow that doesn't feel right . . ."

"Hmmm . . . I know what you mean," Lorena said, pondering. Then she said brightly, "Well, since the show is in Australia, doesn't it make sense to start with a didgeridoo player?"

During the selection process, Cummings had considered a variety acts that incorporated the didgeridoo into their show, and several groups where it was a side instrument were on the roster, including an Australian roots band where the singer also played the didgeridoo, and a traditional Australian dance band which was supported by didgeridoo, congas, and other percussion. But he had not considered a solo didgeridoo artist . . . and as soon as Lorena suggested it, he knew it was the right choice for opening the show.

"You're brilliant," he said, giving her a kiss. "I sure hope I can find the right player on such short notice. I'll email Ben Morrison and ask for a recommendation."

It was Monday—Sarah had arrived the day before—and he and Lorena were flying to Australia on Wednesday, giving him two days to prepare for the Earth Council seminar he'd be attending on Thursday and Friday at the Sydney Conference and Training Centre. On Saturday morning, when the conference was over, he and Lorena planned to tour the Opera House so he could get a sense of what final touches might be required before the first ever Unity Festival was launched the following day. Cummings was excited to see the venue. Designed by Danish architect Jørn Utzon in 1957—and completed in 1972—the unique complex became a UNESCO World Heritage Site in 2007.

As he waited for Morrison to respond to his email question about the didgeridoo player, he thought about all the planning he'd done over the last two years leading up to this moment. Ever since Sarah had suggested the idea of a world celebration before she'd left Earth, he'd imagined what such a festival would look like . . . and over the last two years, he'd brought those visions to life.

Planning the Unity Festival

One of the first challenges he'd faced was booking the multi-venue Sydney Opera House on Bennelong Point and the surrounding grounds on the banks of the Sydney Harbour. He'd had to get special permission from the Australian government—but after a quick chat with Ben Morrison, the way was cleared.

Selecting talent had also been a growth process. He and his team spent the better part of a year agonizing over what artists they should hire. They wanted performers who not only reflected the precious unity that was emerging on Earth but also represented as many of the world's diverse cultures and ethnicities as possible. Ultimately, they chose a total of fifty acts, some that would play inside the Sydney Opera House and others that would perform on the grounds. The Sydney Symphony Orchestra—the home orchestra of the opera house—was in line to play, as was the Vienna Boys' Choir, a British punk rocker who sang about finding peace, a popular Jamaican reggae group, some traditional Congolese rumba performers, an American gospel singer, and a Chinese Taoist ensemble. Overall, he was highly satisfied that the choices they'd made reflected the principles he stood behind.

Publicity and broadcasting were tricky to organize. On the day of the Unity Festival, he expected Sarah would work her magic by hijacking people's phones and computers so that every citizen on Earth could watch the show. However, Cummings wanted excitement and anticipation to build beforehand—after all, never before in human history had the planet been without war somewhere on the globe, and there was much to celebrate.

He pulled together a top notch communications team to keep global media informed about every stage of the Unity Festival's planning process but was concerned that he was not reaching some of the technologically challenged areas of the world . . . and then something happened that not only trebled his broadcast power but put him in the spotlight at the festival himself—albeit reluctantly.

About a year into the Unity Festival's two-year planning process, he and Lorena were watching a documentary about the burgeoning Church of Humanity. The film showed footage of a boisterous, joyful assembly of people sitting on a sunny hillside in front of a clear, turquoise body of water. Most looked like throwbacks to the 1969 Woodstock Festival at

Yasgur's Farm in Bethel, New York—shaggy young people, between the ages of twenty and forty. All of them had love in their eyes.

"The people you see are all members of the Church of Humanity," noted the documentary's narrator, "and they have assembled on the shores of the Sea of Galilee at the request of an emerging church leader."

It was clearly some sort of festival. The crowd was resting on blankets on sandy soil dotted with hardy grasses, while a band played music on a stage near the water. When the band ended, a young, red-headed woman of about thirty years of age jumped nimbly onto the stage and grabbed a microphone.

In a distinctive Irish brogue, she called out, "Bread and fish! The feeding of the multitudes was performed by Jesus near this very place. And Jesus didn't discriminate when it came to who he fed. You got bread and fish no matter what your faith!"

Cummings recognized her as the young Irish woman Sarah had once shown him rallying people in Dublin. He remembered her as being quite charismatic—and clearly his assessment had not been wrong. The people in front of her were hanging onto her every word.

"Hello, people of faith!" she called out to them.

"Hello!" they roared back.

"Are we here to do the work of God?" she called out.

"We are!" the crowd answered.

"As long as you do unto others as you would have them do unto you, does it matter what race, creed, or faith you belong to?"

"No!" the people called in return.

"Good. I'm glad we got that settled," she said with a smile. "And now, I would like to speak of the true nature of God as taught to us by Sarah when she last visited our fragile planet."

"Well, I'll be," Cummings had said to his wife.

"Do you know that woman?" Lorena asked.

"I do," he replied.

The documentary narrator on the television began speaking once more.

"This young woman's name is Caitriona Ó'Flannagáin," he said, "and she has become the face of the Church of Humanity. It's not an organized church in the same vein as the ones we attended with our parents when we were kids. Instead, it's more of a grassroots spiritual movement, based on the true nature of God that Sarah told us about when she was here . . ."

The TV showed Ó'Flannagáin on the stage again, calling out to the crowd. "Sarah said if we treat others as we want to be treated and work together to build the life force for the good of all, we will no longer pose a threat to each other or to our planet!" she cried.

There was a roar of approval from the crowd, and a few pockets of people began chanting, "Sarah said! Sarah said!"

Ó'Flannagáin continued, "Sarah also said that God wants humans to be at one with their species. She said we must think in terms of growing our life force *collectively*. What do you think? Are we able to create unity?"

This time, the whole crowd roared, "Sarah said! Sarah said!"

Astounded at the crowd's emotional response to Ó'Flannagáin's prompts, Lorena turned to her husband, saying, "This girl is a force to be reckoned with. She's the voice of the future."

"Yes," Cummings replied. "She has a real presence, and she knows how to rally people. Of course, it doesn't hurt that she has Humanity Now at her disposal."

'Humanity Now,' a multimedia empire funded by generous philanthropists, was the Church of Humanity's congregational home. It served up twenty-four-hour multimedia programming, dedicated to developing humankind's spiritual growth, via its own cloud and digital streaming services. It also managed the Godvision network Sarah had established.

"You know," Lorena then said, "in my opinion, the Church of Humanity and the Earth Council are on similar paths—the church unites people in spirit, while the council unites them ideologically. Maybe you could work together with them, Sam."

"Well, they might help me with the concert because that's clearly up their alley," said Cummings, "but I'm not sure they really care about whether the Earth moves toward a global governance model or not."

"I don't see why they wouldn't—after all, they're all about unity," said Lorena. "I'm sure many of their members would agree that such things as the environment, disease control, trade, and finance should be managed globally."

Cummings thought about that for a moment, and finally said, "Maybe you're right. I think I need to meet that girl."

A week days later, he did. He flew into Dublin on one of the two Air Force One jets and then hired a car to take him to the Liberties section, near the historic brewery founded by entrepreneur and philanthropist Arthur Guinness in 1759.

He saw Ó'Flannagáin as soon as he stepped out of the car. She was leaning against the front door of a compact, grey building, sipping coffee out of a cardboard cup and gesturing wildly to a group of rough-looking teenagers as she told them the benefits of treating others as they would like to be treated.

"I know what you lot are up to," she said firmly to the biggest one, who eyed her threateningly, "because I used to be that way meself. But stop acting the maggot, ya gobshite, or I'll tell your mother at church. I know who you are, Robby O'Leary."

Her pegging his identity shocked the boy. He tried not to let on, though. "Stop yer yappin'," he said in as menacing a tone as he could, while his friends giggled at Ó'Flannagáin's threat to rat him out to his mom.

She stood her ground, unbowed. Then, with the biggest, brightest smile Cummings had ever seen—and with the tiniest touch of menace—she said, "God's watching you, young fella."

Cummings could see the boy's wheels turning as he considered this. Whether he was scared of God or scared that Caitriona could give as good as she got was unclear; Whatever it was, he and his friends abruptly turned tail and ran off.

"God love ya," Ó'Flannagáin called after them, "and you can find out all about lovin' yer fellow humans on one of Humanity Now's many fine programs!"

She cackled as one of them gave her the finger and then, when the group of young hoodlums was well gone, she acknowledged Cummings' presence.

"President Cummings, is it?" she asked pleasantly.

"Yes," he replied.

"Glad you could make it," she said, turning her hundred watt smile onto him. "Come on in."

She opened the door of the building and ushered him into a small office, where a young man and woman were busy working on computers.

"This is Liam," she said, indicating the boy, "and this is Fidelma. They're working on church programming. We do all our services online, you know—and a lot of outreach too."

"I know," said Cummings. "The things you've accomplished are impressive."

"Thanks," she said with a bright smile. "Most of our programs are recorded and edited right in this building. We have a sound stage in the basement for filmin' and such, and a team of editors upstairs who put the gloss on our shows, podcasts, movies . . . We even have a group that designs video games about how to grow the life force."

"That is . . . amazing," said Cummings, taking in the small, no-frills environment and wondering how so much could be accomplished by so few.

As if reading his mind, Ó'Flannagáin said, "It's not magic, President Cummings. It's computers. They're marvelous little beasts. We've got three floors of people here and a team of home-based performers and editors around the globe, all networked through our very own cloud. We're spreading the message in the most entertaining ways we can think of. We want the whole world on board, ya know."

Then she smiled, and Cummings felt pure goodness emanating from her. *No wonder people follow this girl,* he thought. He'd never experienced anything like it.

"So," said Ó'Flannagáin, offering him a chair in a relatively private corner, behind a stack of boxes, "I understand you want to use our services to promote the work of the Earth Council?"

"Well, yes," said Cummings, taken off guard by her candid approach.

She laughed at his discomfort. "Relax," she said. "It's no secret that the two things that have caused the most war during the course of human history are religion and ideology. Sarah talked to me about that before she left. I took it to mean she thought Earth should move toward a world government—though I'm sure you know that government's not my bailiwick." Then she paused and looked Cummings in the eye. "Wouldn't a world government stop a lot of bickering, though?"

Cummings couldn't help but laugh. "Yes," he said, "it sure would."

Ó'Flannagáin smiled disarmingly. "My purpose on this Earth is to unite people," she told him, "and I have been blessed that from an early age I understood that. I have also been blessed to live in a time when the tools to do this are at my disposal. I will help you, President Cummings, because Sarah assured me that you believe in unity as strongly as I do. So tell me what it is that you need."

Grateful for her open-mindedness, Cummings outlined his plans. "The Unity Festival will celebrate how much progress we've made toward becoming at one with our species and our planet," he said. "It will showcase performance art from around the world that inspires and celebrates commitment to growing the life force and protecting the Earth."

"Go on," said Ó'Flannagáin, clearly interested.

"It is my expectation," continued Cummings, "that Sarah will hijack everyone's cell phones and computers so that every person on the planet can witness this event . . . but I was hoping we could get some promotion on Humanity Now beforehand, and that you could broadcast the whole concert on demand on one of your streaming networks. What do you think?"

Ó'Flannagáin smiled. "Yes," she said, "I think it's a fine idea—and we're happy to do it, too. And I can do you one better. I can offer you volunteers on the ground for your festival. Church of Humanity members are easily mobilized and always willing to contribute to the good of humankind."

Cummings felt a combination of relief and gratitude. "Thank you, Caitriona," he said. "You're more than generous."

"Not at all," she replied. "I offer our services because I believe in Sarah's message. She said unity must occur on *all* levels if humans are to reach their full potential—mental, physical, spiritual, intellectual . . . ideological too."

Cummings couldn't believe her generous spirit. "If I can ever return the favour, I will," he said.

"Oh, wonderful!" she exclaimed. "I *do* need a favour."

Cummings hadn't expected that. "Oh?" he asked.

"Well," Ó'Flannagáin replied, "I have a friend, a young composer from Korea, named Baek Hyeon. He's written a piece of music called 'Call to Unity.'"

"That's wonderful," said Cummings, "but what does this have to do with me?"

"A little birdie told me that you—the president of the most powerful nation on Earth—and your Chinese counterpart, strongly support the idea of global governance . . . and are perhaps thinking a shared leadership bid."

Flabbergasted, Cummings asked, "How did you know that? That's not public knowledge!"

"How do you think?" laughed Ó'Flannagáin.

"Sarah?" guessed Cummings.

Ó'Flannagáin laughed even harder. "No," she said. "Your wife!"

"Lorena?" He was shocked.

"Yes," she said. "She called here looking for you. She said you hadn't picked up, and you probably had your phone on airplane mode. She wants you to call her. Anyway, we got to talking about the Sea of Galilee concert the two of you watched on the telly, and before I knew it, we'd been yakking for the better part of an hour. Lovely woman, your Lorena."

Cummings swallowed hard. He was at once annoyed that Lorena had been so careless with closely guarded information and concerned about why she'd been so eager to reach him in the first place.

"Well, it's true," he admitted reluctantly. "The president of China and I have discussed the possibility of running on a shared ticket for leadership of the Earth Council—when my presidential term is over, of course."

"Well, that's an amazing thing, and I wish you the luck of the Irish," she said. "After all, you and I are both Irish Gaelic, am I right?"

Cummings nodded. "Yes," he said. "My great-grandfather hopped off the boat in 1891. Bless you for knowing . . . Now tell me how my career goals have anything to do with your friend's musical composition."

"Well," said Ó'Flannagáin, "the London Symphony Orchestra is interested in performing the piece . . . but it has a spoken word component, and it needs two males to speak the parts. I was thinking that if you and Dong Yang performed it as part of the Unity Festival, it would make a real statement . . . and it might earn you a kettle full of public support."

Cummings paled. "I'm not a performer—I'm a politician," he said. "I think those things are mutually exclusive."

"Of course they're not!" laughed Ó'Flannagáin, slapping him on the knee. "What is politics if not performance art? Besides, don't you think it's a great way to get support for your leadership bid? Let's face it, my generation is the future—and if you want us to see you as more than just a grey, old head who until God's intervention was part of problem, you need to make yourself relevant. What better way than by *showing* your unity, President Cummings? Be one with the celebration!"

Cummings was not at all comfortable with the idea, but he knew she was right; Performing in this way was an opportunity for him to not only promote the Earth Council as a governance body but to promote himself and Dong Yang as leaders.

He took a deep breath. "I don't know why I'm saying yes to this," he said, "but yes."

"You're a smart man," Ó'Flannagáin replied with a gleeful bark of laughter. "I think you'll do a bang-up job, too. You'll duet with a trumpet, while President Dong will work with the French horn. I've already heard the piece—in fact, I spoke your part at a rehearsal. It's wonderful!"

Later, back at his hotel, he called Lorena and told her what had happened.

After she stopped cackling with glee, she said, "You've always been the best shower singer in the household. You got this, Sam! I can't wait for the show!"

"Thanks for your vote of confidence," he said. "Now why on Earth did you tell Caitriona that I was considering a leadership bid at the Earth Council? I just got re-elected, and the last thing I want is for American citizens to think I am going to abandon my responsibilities to my country."

"Oh, I'm sorry, Sam," she said, "it just slipped out. She's so easy to talk to."

"Yes, she is," he said. "But I wish you'd been more careful. Anyway, she said you wanted me to call you as soon as possible. What's up?"

At that, Lorena let out a little shriek—excitement, Cummings presumed. "You're not going to believe this," she said, "but Geordie is trying to adopt a child from Southeast Asia. According to him, he's been greenlighted through the first two stages of the adoption process, and things are looking good. I'm so excited, Sam! We're going to be grandparents again!"

For the first time in a long time, Cummings couldn't speak. His throat went as dry as chalk when he thought of his loving, kind son, whose sense of hope had disappeared for several years when he'd lost his partner to suicide. Geordie had come out of his slump eventually, but since then, he'd been pining for something to give his life greater meaning—and Cummings knew this was exactly what he needed.

With a frog in his throat, and a tear in his eye, he managed to say, "Oh, that's wonderful news!"

"Isn't it?" his wife said, followed by, "Hurry home, okay?"

"I'll see you soon," he replied.

He flew out of Dublin the next morning, returning home to a celebratory dinner, which the whole family attended. He was happy to see Jessica and Jayson, pleased that Laura and her partner Leon were able to join them . . . and when he saw the light in his son's eyes, all he could do was hug him tight.

Later, he retired to his study with a glass of wine, and when the time was right—it was fourteen hours ahead in China—he called Dong Yang.

"Greetings, my friend," said Dong. "I hear we are going to be rock stars."

"I take it Caitriona talked to you?" asked Cummings.

"Yes," his friend said, surprising Cummings when he added, "This will be so much fun!"

"Are you crazy?" asked Cummings. "We'll be performing with an *orchestra*!"

It was terrifying to think of this. He was used to speaking of political things in front of mass audiences . . . but performing an art piece was *so* much more personal.

"I know! I can't wait!" the Chinese president said, dashing all Cummings' hopes of an evening of commiseration.

Cummings sighed. The only thing to do was to book the services of a vocal coach.

A few weeks later, he found one, and she came to the White House once a week for the better part of the following year to help Cummings with his enunciation. Four months before the event, Dong and he had once-a-month online rehearsals with the orchestra, and finally, about a month before Sarah was scheduled to return to Earth, he flew to London to rehearse in person with the LSO in the Barbican Centre, their London 'home.'

When he walked into the building, Dong Yang was already up on the stage.

As soon as the conductor saw Cummings, he called out, "Come in, come in . . . there's a microphone ready for you!"

Cummings swallowed nervously when he found himself in front of the mic. He looked over at Dong, who was smiling broadly. *Maybe it won't be so bad,* Cummings thought, allowing himself to relax. The rehearsal went well after that.

The Day of the Festival

And now, after two years of effort and planning, it was time for the show he'd worked so hard on to unfold in front of the world. Tomorrow, he and Lorena would fly to Sydney and land in the glorious Australian heat. He could hardly wait.

The flight to Australia was long but uneventful. They left Washington D.C. early and arrived in Sydney about twenty hours later. They had time for a bite to eat, and then they crawled into bed, hoping to shake their jet lag. As the events of the day faded into sleep, Cummings could not help thinking how much easier it was to be teleported around the globe by Sarah.

When morning arrived, Cummings showered, dressed, bid Lorena goodbye, and then taxied to the conference centre. He entered the massive complex to find a standard conference 'meet and greet' in progress, complete with refreshments. He took his usual black coffee but nixed the muffins. He'd eaten oatmeal before he left, trusting Lorena's advice that it would 'stick to his ribs' and stop him from eating junk food later.

The meeting started at 9:00 a.m. with a round of budget reports. He gave a short presentation on the financial scope of the Unity Festival. There were no questions. Most everyone in the room agreed he'd done an amazing organizational job. The group adjourned at four o'clock, and he returned to the hotel to join Lorena for dinner at a steakhouse nearby. After dinner, he tried to prep for the next day's meeting, but it was too hard to concentrate. All he could think about was the Unity Festival and the moment that he would have to get up on the stage with the London Symphony Orchestra.

When he arrived at the conference centre the following day, after a general call to business followed by a discussion about the moon colonization project, as two of the Earth Council members initiated a discussion about the future of nuclear power, a gentle breeze and the smell of roses began wafting around the room. Cummings' heart started thumping as Sarah slowly took shape in front of his eyes. Her presence never failed to move him.

"Hello, Earth Council," she said when she'd fully materialized. "I am so happy to see all of you!"

Calls of "Hello Sarah!" started emanating from various sections of the room.

"I am here to tell you how very impressed I am with how, in the five years since I left Earth, the global community has worked so hard to make this world a better place. With the exception of only a few nations, you are all finally on the same page with regard to most world issues. I applaud you!"

Her words and presence brought the house down with thunderous clapping and cheering.

When it subsided, she said, "I want to show you something. As politicians, you are aware of how things have changed on a political scale . . . but as a divine being, I am aware of how people's hearts are changing."

With that, she projected a three-dimensional vision into the air. First, she showed two young men rigging up a water system in a drought-ridden village in Zambia and then refusing payment. Next, she showed a group of Bosnian women who returned every day to a veteran's hospital to help the nurses care for men with PTSD. In all, she showed about ten such scenes, each more poignant than the last, keeping the group entranced for the better part of the afternoon.

Finally, she said, "People around the globe are helping others, just as God meant it to be. I'm here to tell you that the effect can be felt in the life force, throughout the universe. You are changing your destiny, one person at a time. I am so proud of you all."

Then Sarah finished the same way she'd started—with a gentle breeze and the scent of roses as she faded slowly from view, leaving Cummings and the others with hearts full of joy.

That feeling of joy carried into the next day. On Saturday morning, Cummings awoke early, eager to tour the opera house and to oversee the final preparations for the Unity Festival which would occur the following day. Their taxi arrived at 9:30 a.m., so he and Lorena had a quick, light breakfast and then left. Upon arrival at the Sydney Opera House, Cummings could not believe how amazing the building was. But as he marveled, he suddenly realized he'd been so busy with travel and meetings that he had not yet booked a didgeridoo player to open the show.

"Oh no," he muttered as they toured the 1,500 seat Joan Sutherland Theatre, home of the Australian Ballet.

Lorena looked at him in alarm. He cast his eyes downward as he silently cursed Ben Morrison for not getting back to him about the didgeridoo player, but mostly he was angry at himself for letting this little detail slide.

When the tour was over, and they stepped outside, Lorena put her hand on his arm. "What on Earth has got you so wound up?" she asked.

He was about to reply, when suddenly, he heard a long, low tone coming from somewhere to his left, deep and resonant. He couldn't believe it. He looked around, trying to spot the source of the noise.

It was Lorena who saw it. "Look, Sam," she said, "that man is playing a didgeridoo!"

The man, clearly of Australian Aborigine heritage, was sitting under a shady tree, the long, wooden instrument at his mouth. He was poorly dressed yet gave the impression of regality. Certainly, he was king of the didgeridoo.

Cummings immediately knew this was the man who was going to open the Unity Festival for him. He began walking toward him, Lorena hot on his heels. When he reached him, he stood and listened for a good five minutes.

The man finally stopped, looked him straight in the eye, and said, "I was calling you. I thought you would never come."

That was not something Cummings had expected to hear. "You were calling me?" he asked, confused.

"Oh, yes," said the man. "You need me to open your show. I was told this by an angel. She said her name was Sarah."

At that, Cummings burst out laughing. *Thank you, Sarah*, he thought quietly to himself.

To the man he said, "Let me buy you a coffee."

Cummings' coffee with the didgeridoo player proved to be fruitful. The man, from Arnhem Land in the Northern Territory, was a relative of renowned didgeridoo artist Djalu Guruwiwi.

"Call me Darryl," he said.

Darryl told Cummings that the didgeridoo, so-named by white settlers who tried to imitate its sound, was mostly played only in the northern part Australia.

"There are more than 200 Aboriginal groups," he said with a wide smile, "and not all traditionally used the didgeridoo . . . but now it is the symbol of Australia."

Cummings liked the man, and was grateful to Sarah for sending him his way. After setting him up with the staff member in charge of booking the acts, they parted ways.

That night, Cummings could barely sleep, and when morning finally arrived, he woke early, jumped into the shower, and began rehearsing the part he'd be performing that day with the LSO.

When he came out of the bathroom, Lorena said softly, "You're going to be amazing, Samuel."

In the hotel lobby, they were met by a long haired, friendly Church of Humanity volunteer.

"President and First Lady Cummings? This way please," he said as he helped them into the back of a black Range Rover and then climbed into the front.

He easily navigated Sydney traffic, and before they knew it, they were at the opera house, where Caitriona Ó'Flannagáin awaited them. She seemed most pleased to meet Lorena and shook her hand enthusiastically.

"You are truly a remarkable young woman," Lorena told her in admiration.

Ó'Flannagáin laughed. "I try," she said, "but sometimes I make a right bags of things, just like everyone else."

Cummings appreciated her humility, but so far, he hadn't seen her make a 'right bags' of anything.

Finally, at high noon, it was time to open the show. The Outdoor Forecourt in front of the opera house was packed. The 'Monumental Steps' leading to the opera house was full of thousands of people.

The opera singer who Cummings had initially tagged to open the show walked onto the stage.

"Hello," she said, "I am Agava Novak. I have been asked to introduce our first performer, and to acknowledge that we are standing on the traditional lands of the Aboriginal people of Australia, who lived peacefully for millennia on a continent isolated from the rest of the world. So, for each Aboriginal person and each living being, let's sound the didgeridoo and pay homage to those who are sharing their homeland with us today. Thank you!"

At that, Darryl came onto the stage with his elaborately decorated didgeridoo. Naked from the waist up, his torso was painted with traditional markings, and he wore a bright red loincloth over his hips. He said nothing; He just put the instrument to his lips and began to play, allowing its low-pitched drone to do the speaking. When the drone had transported his audience into a receptive trance, he began making a variety of animal sounds: a kangaroo hopping, a dog growling, a kookaburra calling out in birdsong that sounded like laughter.

Cummings, transported in spirit to the Australian forest, found himself trying to spot creatures who eluded him, leaving only their echoing sounds to taunt him. It was a magical experience, and when Darryl finally stopped—to wild applause from the crowd—it took him a moment to get his bearings . . . but he felt like something inside him had changed. In his mind's eye, the forest lingered whenever he closed his eyes.

The London Symphony Orchestra was scheduled to play at 6:00 p.m., and "Call to Unity" would be their third song. Cummings tried to remain calm, but he was fretting. All of a sudden, it was 5:40 p.m., and the orchestra began mounting the stage. Then, all too soon, it was six o'clock, and they started their first piece, Brahms' "Academic Festival Overture, Opus 80," which was met with appreciative applause. Next, they played the theme from *Star Wars*. The audience went crazy for this, humming, singing, and dancing along with the familiar song.

Then, before he knew it, the conductor was saying, "Ladies and gentlemen, I give you 'Call to Unity' . . . and joining us in this performance are Presidents Dong Yang of China and Samuel Cummings of the United States."

There was great applause at the introduction. Under Cummings' direction for the past six years, the United States had been restored to its global leadership role on the world stage. Similarly, with Dong Yang's guidance, China had been lauded for softening many of the harsh Communist policies that had plagued the Chinese people for decades.

Cummings had never been more nervous than when he mounted that stage. He surveyed the people who'd gathered to celebrate humankind's progress on this momentous day and was overwhelmed by the immensity of it all. Then, as he marveled, the orchestra began. He took a couple of deep breaths, trying to still his furiously galloping heart.

At first, the song was instrumental, but soon enough, it was Dong's turn to speak his part. He didn't miss his cue.

In poetic parlance, he carried on a conversation with a mournful sounding French horn, concluding with, "United, into the future we'll go . . . sharing council and knowledge, connected in goals . . ."

The French horn answered him with a rich, high-pitched melody—and then all too soon, the trumpet spoke, signaling to Cummings that it was his turn.

He stood a little taller as he prepared to relay the stanzas he had rehearsed and was happy to find that they came to his tongue easily.

"One people united, at one with our kind . . . our life force abundant and not in decline . . ."

As his words tailed off, Cummings put his hand on his heart, feeling relief that his performance had gone as planned. The audience began cheering, whether for him or for unity, he did not know. Then, just as the orchestra broke into Beethoven's "Ode to Joy," a collective gasp from the crowd made him look up to see an immense apparition of loveliness, both terrifying and breathtaking, hovering above them all.

It was Sarah.

The orchestra squeaked to a stop, a few violin noises echoing across the stage as the music ceased.

"Hello, everybody," Sarah boomed into the ether, her voice like thunder, her rose scent permeating the air in a subtle, sparkling mist.

Some in the audience were so overwhelmed by her presence that they began sobbing.

"Don't be upset," Sarah said soothingly. "I've come to tell you how wonderful it is to see how humankind is healing. Where once there was division, I see cohesion. Where once there was mistrust, I see understanding. I am so proud. Your beautiful souls have lit up the universe. May you continue to shine."

Suddenly, there was a yelp from the stage, and all eyes turned to see a bald man with a crucifix drawn on top of his head run up and grab the mic so recently vacated by Cummings. Judging by the uniform, it was one of the security detail, who had apparently been biding his time, just waiting for the right moment to do this.

The man yelled angrily to the audience, "You sheep! You will burn in hell! Do not believe these lies! God created the Earth and every living creature in seven days! Nothing else is true! Repent, or you will be damned!"

There was a stunned silence, and then, like an angel, Ó'Flannagáin appeared from the stage wings.

She turned toward the man and asked him calmly, "But Sir, what would you have us repent from?"

"From your false beliefs!" he screeched, clearly agitated.

"Our beliefs are simply that placing the needs of others above one's own are all that is needed to get to Heaven. Why should we repent from that?" she asked.

"You believe in other crazy things," he stammered, his voice high-pitched and trembling as he looked up at Sarah, who still hovered angelically over the crowd. Then, despite what his eyes were taking in, he yelled out, "Sarah is nothing but a hoax, just like the Covid pandemic! She is one of Satan's lies. I tell you, God created Heaven and Earth in seven days—and he did not create aliens, or a 14 billion-year-old universe!"

Caitriona just smiled at him. "Sir," she said politely, "you, and everyone else, are entitled to your beliefs. There is one rule only that is sacrosanct: Do unto others as you would have them do unto you." Then she faced the crowd and yelled, "What do we have to say to this man!?"

The crowd responded with a rousing cry of "We love you!"

With that, the man's mouth dropped open, and he trembled and fell to his knees, his anger lifted from his shoulders by the unity of the people surrounding him. When Caitriona Ó'Flannagáin knelt beside him and put a comforting arm around him, he began to weep.

Cummings happened to look up at Sarah just at that moment to see a wondrous, gentle smile, full of unspeakable love, play across her ever-changing face . . . and then, as the conductor urged the orchestra to finish playing "Ode to Joy," she quietly dissipated, leaving nothing but sparkling, rose-scented mist in the air.

"Goodbye, Sarah," Cummings whispered to himself. "I'll see you in another five years."

Epilogue

Earth Council

The winter snows had not yet set in, and it was relatively warm for November on the day President Cummings officially stepped down from his duties as U.S. president. He stood in front of the American people, who had assembled on Capitol Hill to bid him farewell, his heart pounding in anticipation of the words he would soon say, his eyes a little wet. It was a bittersweet moment. His two terms in office had defined him, both as a politician and a man, and during his tenancy, he'd guided the citizens of his country through challenges never before known to humankind—yet now, when it was time to say goodbye, it seemed like those eight years had gone by in a flash.

He stepped onto the podium. The crowd cheered as soon as they saw him, which buoyed his spirits considerably. He was touched at their loyalty, pleased that they saw him as the steady helmsman who'd steered them safely into a new future.

When the cacophony died down, he began. "Friends and countrymen," he said, "it is with great sadness that I bid you goodbye. It has been an honour and a privilege to serve you these past eight years, and I thank you for your support and your faith in me. Together we have weathered a storm of change, all of us holding onto the light that will take us into a new dawn."

The cheering erupted again, so loud he thought his ears might burst. He smiled at the crowd's enthusiasm. He felt like he was greeting old friends instead of saying goodbye to them.

When the noise died down, he continued, "I consider myself to be the most fortunate president America has ever had. Due to God's intervention, I was able to implement programs to benefit this country that could never have been conceived of just a few short years ago. With no disrespect to the noble servicemen and women of our armed forces, I'm grateful that we no longer need to prepare for war. Preparing for peace is so much better. We have a new high-speed rail line in the works. We have the promise of even distribution of water in this great country. We have solutions for our eroding shorelines. We are fixing our outdated infrastructure. All this is possible because war is no more."

A great cheer arose, and chants of "War no more! War no more!" sprang up in pockets of people throughout the crowd.

Cummings was touched. "Yes!" he shouted gleefully into the microphone. "War no more!" And then he laughed, and the crowd laughed along with him.

"One thing I know for sure," said Cummings, "is that I am grateful. I'm grateful for having had the opportunity to lead this great nation, grateful for God's intervention, grateful for my family, and grateful for the legacy I leave." And then he paused and smiled broadly. "I'm also grateful," he said, "to introduce the president elect. This person is the only reason I can smile as I step down from this job I love so much."

He turned around to scan the small group of people standing behind him until he spotted his target. Grabbing her arm, he pulled Angelica Lopez to stand beside him.

"You all know *this* woman," he said. "She has ably served for the last eight years as my right-hand woman, and I am pleased that you saw it in you to elect her as your new president."

Lopez blushed. She didn't move.

Cummings gently elbowed her. "Angelica," he said, "take a bow!"

That woke her up. She did as he suggested, bowing formally, one hand in front of her waist and one behind her back as if she was attending an old-school dance.

The crowd began roaring, "President Lopez! President Lopez!" and leaping up and down.

Cummings saw the tips of her ears turn red with bashfulness.

"Say something," he said, nudging her.

"Okay, okay," she replied, grabbing the microphone. Squaring her shoulders, she took a deep breath and shouted, "Thank you!" over the din, which died down enough for her to tell the enthusiastic crowd, "I am grateful for your faith in me and for your votes. I will take this job as seriously as my predecessor did, and I promise to build upon the good works that he started. I am honoured to have this opportunity to serve the American people, and I promise to work toward unity, both within this country and within the global community!"

The response from the crowd was deafening. Angelica Lopez—well liked, well respected, and considered a trailblazer due to her electric train project—was a hero to some. And now, she was the first woman president of the United States of America. It was a watermark moment in American history, and Cummings could not have been more proud of his colleague and friend. He beamed at her.

"Congratulations, Angelica," he said softly. "No one deserves this more than you."

She smiled at him. "Thanks, Samuel . . . and thanks for being a great mentor." Then she hugged him, taking him by surprise.

He laughed. It felt good.

It was only a few short months after this emotional goodbye that the voting results for presidency of the Earth Council were revealed. The meeting was held in mid-January in the former UN building in New York. Cummings attended with Angelica, who was representing the United States as its new president.

They met Dong Yang at the entrance to the building.

"Nǐ hǎo," Cummings said to his friend, who had just stepped down as the head of the Chinese Communist Party.

"Hello, Samuel," returned Dong Yang, "and hello to you, President Lopez."

Angelica beamed at being addressed by her new title.

Then the Chinese president gave Cummings a questioning look. "Are you ready for this?" he asked.

"Yes," replied Cummings, beaming broadly. "It's going to be a good day. I can feel it."

They would not learn the results of the voting until one o'clock, and so the three of them patiently sat through a morning session of budget approvals and formal reports from Earth Council agencies. Finally, the council secretary stood up.

"And now, the news you've all been waiting for," he said in a monotone voice that gave nothing away. "The Council has chosen its leadership for a five-year term."

Cummings felt his heart thumping like a drum as he waited to hear the election results. He was optimistic that he and Dong Yang would win but knew they had stiff competition from Berdine Schmidt, who was well regarded in the international community.

The council secretary cleared his throat. "The winner—or should I say the *winners*—of the presidency of the Earth Council are Samuel Cummings of the United States of America and Dong Yang of China. Would incumbent leaders Cummings and Dong please stand?"

Beside him, Dong Yang elbowed him in exultation. "We won!" he exclaimed.

"We won!" Cummings responded excitedly in return, awed at the incredible opportunity to shape the world that had been laid out before the two of them.

Around the room, cries of "Congratulations!" broke out, though representatives of a few of the more autocratic states did not appear as enthusiastic about the election results as others.

However, Cummings didn't let a few dour faces destroy the moment; He just soaked it all in.

Later, Cummings did not remember much of the afternoon session. He knew he'd given a speech, but he couldn't recall what he'd said.

"I winged it, Lorena," he told his wife. "Mostly, I think I just I thanked everyone for their support."

"That's not what the news says," Lorena told him, drawing his attention to the television. "They say you gave the best speech of your career!"

Cummings looked at himself on TV. Usually self-critical, today, when he saw his own image, he found himself watching a confident, capable leader.

"Today marks the beginning of real change for humankind, a great step toward us finally coming together as one people," said Cummings. "Too long have we been divided by inconsequential things. When did we decide the colour of someone's skin determined their character? When did we decide a person's chosen faith was wrong, and ours was right? When did we ever think it was okay to shed blood over such things? Such madness has been with us for millennia. Let us all thank God that it has stopped."

Then he rested his eyes on the Chinese leader beside him. "Today," he said, "my co-leader and I pledge to freely give our service to humankind, for the betterment of all."

The applause was deafening.

When it was Dong Yang's turn to speak, he simply said, "I thank you for your support. As one people, together we will shine!"

Both leaders were well aware that they were setting a precedent never before seen on Earth—co-leadership of the world, in a spirit of cooperation and mutual respect, by two former political adversaries who had come together for the common good.

It was stardust and dreams. It was the smell of roses.

THE END